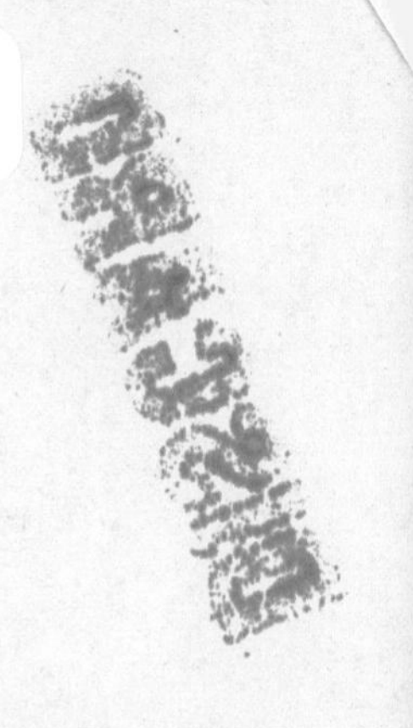

RANDOM
HOUSE
LARGE
PRINT

The Flight Portfolio

The Flight Portfolio

Julie Orringer

RANDOM HOUSE
LARGE PRINT

This is a work of fiction. All incidents and dialogue, and all characters with the exception of some well-known historical and public figures, are products of the author's imagination and are not to be construed as real. Where real-life historical figures and public figures appear, the situations, incidents, and dialogues concerning those persons are entirely fictional and are not intended to depict actual events or to change the entirely fictional nature of the work. In all other respects, any resemblance to persons living or dead is entirely coincidental.

Published in the United States of America by Random House Large Print in association with Alfred A. Knopf, a division of Penguin Random House LLC, New York.

Owing to limitations of space, all acknowledgements for permission to reprint previously published material may be found at the end of the volume.

Cover photograph by Gary Yeowell/Getty Images
Cover design by Abby Weintraub

The Library of Congress has established a Cataloging-in-Publication record for this title.

ISBN: 978-1-9848-9220-1

www.penguinrandomhouse.com/large-print-format-books

FIRST LARGE PRINT EDITION

Printed in the United States of America

10 9 8 7 6 5 4 3 2 1

This Large Print edition published in accord with the standards of the N.A.V.H.

For Ryan, Jacob, and Lil

Have you ever seen my face
In the middle of the street, a face with no body?
There is no one who knows him,
And his call sinks into the abyss.

—Marc Chagall

ONE

despise what is not courage

1

Gordes

There was, as it turned out, no train to the village where the Chagalls lived: one of many complications he'd failed to anticipate. He had to pay a boy with a motorbike to run him up from the station at Cavaillon, ten miles at a brainshaking pace along a narrow rutted road. On either side rose ochre hills striated with grapevines and lavender and olive trees; overhead, a blinding white-veined sky. The smell was of the boy's leather jacket and of charred potatoes, exhalate of his clever homemade fuel. At the foot of the village the boy parked in a shadow, accepted Varian's francs, and tore off into the distance before Varian could arrange a ride back.

The streets of Gordes, carved into a sunstruck limestone hill above the Luberon Valley, offered little in the way of shade. He would have given anything to be back in Marseille with a glass of Aperol before him, watching sailors and girls, gangsters and spice vendors, parading the Canebière. The Chagalls had only agreed to see him on the basis that he not bring up the prospect of their emigration. But what other subject was there? The Nazis had taken Paris months ago, they were burning books in the streets of Alsace, they could send any refugee over the border at will. At least the Chagalls **had** agreed; that was something. But as he reached the house, an ancient Catholic girls' school on the rue de la Fontaine Basse, he found himself fighting the urge to flee. His credentials, if anyone examined them, amounted to a fanatic's knowledge of European history, a desire to get out from behind his desk in New York, and a deep frustration with his isolationist nation. And yet this was his job; he'd volunteered for it. What was more, he believed he could do it. He raised his hand and knocked.

An eye appeared in the brass circlet of the peephole, and a girl in a striped apron opened the door. She listened, strangling her index finger with one dark curl, as he stated his name and mission. Then she ushered him down a corridor and out into a courtyard, where a stone path led to a triangle of shade. There, at a bare wooden table, Chagall and his wife sat at lunch: the painter in his smock, his hair swept back from his forehead in silver waves; Bella in a close-fitting black dress too hot for the day.

"Ah, Monsieur Fry," Chagall said, rising to meet him. The painter's eyes were large and uncommonly sharp, his expression one of bemusement. "You've come after all. I thought you might. You won't forget our agreement, will you?"

"All I want is your company for an hour."

"You're lying, of course. But you lie charmingly."

They sat together at the table, Bella on Varian's left, the painter to his right—he, Varian Fry, sitting down with the Chagalls, with **Chagall,** author of those color-saturated visions, those buoyant bridal couples and intelligent-eyed goats he'd seen in hushed rooms at the Museum of Modern Art. Bella filled a plate with brown hard-crusted miche, soft cheese, sardines crackling with salt; she handed it across the table, assessing Varian in silence.

"Had you been here a few days ago, we would have had tomatoes," Chagall said. "A farmer brings them up to the market on Thursdays. I'm sorry we don't have more to offer. The bread's a little hard on the tooth, I'm afraid, but c'est la guerre!"

"This is lavish," Varian said. "You're too kind."

"Not at all. We like to share what we have." He gestured around him at the bare yellow stones, the rough benches, the shock of gold-green hillside visible through an archway in the wall. "As you see, we're living a quiet and retired life in our little dacha. No one will bother us here at Gordes."

"You have a studio," Varian said. "You're still producing work. That's what makes you dangerous."

"Our daughter says the same," Bella said. "She's been saying it for months. But you understand,

Monsieur Fry—my husband's reputation will protect him. Vichy wouldn't dare touch us."

"With respect, Madame Chagall, I don't believe that for a moment. Vichy is subject to the Nazis' whims. And we all know what they're capable of. I've seen it myself. I was in Berlin in '35—sent by the magazine I worked for. My last night in town there was a riot on the Kurfurstendamm. The things I saw—men pulled from their shops and beaten in the streets—an old man stabbed through the hand at a café table—boys dragging a woman by her hair—"

"These things happened in Germany," Chagall said, his tone harder now. "They won't happen here. Not to us."

"Let me speak to my friend at the consulate," Varian said. "Ask him to start a file for you, at least. If you do decide to leave, it might take months."

Chagall shook his head. "My apologies, Monsieur Fry. I'm sorry you had to come all this way in vain. But perhaps you'd like to have a look at the studio before you go—if you've finished, that is."

Varian couldn't speak; he could scarcely believe that a person of Chagall's intelligence, a person of his experience, could fail to see what he himself saw clearly. Chagall rose and crossed the courtyard to a set of ten-foot-high blue doors, and Varian got to his feet. He nodded his thanks to Bella, then followed Chagall across the broken paving stones. Beyond the blue doors was a long, high-ceilinged room with a wall of windows: the former refectory of the girls' school. Canvases lay about everywhere, and for long minutes Varian walked among them in silence. As well as he knew the painter's work, he had never seen it like this: in its pupal state, damp and mutable, smelling of turpentine, raw wood, wet clay. From the canvases rose ghostlike images: a grave-eyed Madonna hovering above a shadowed town, serenaded by cows and angels; crucified Christ wrapped in a prayer shawl, his head encircled by grieving sages; a woman kneeling beside a river, pressing a baby to her chest; clusters of red and white flowers rising like flames.

"It's no small matter to cross an ocean," Chagall said. "More can be lost than canvas and paint. An artist must bear witness, Monsieur Fry. He cannot turn away, even if he wishes to."

"An artist can't bear witness if he's dead."

The painter removed his hat and set it on his knee. "The Emergency Rescue Committee mustn't concern itself further with our welfare," he said. "Save your resources for those who truly need help. Max Ernst, for example—he's rumored to be in a concentration camp at Gurs. Or Jacques Lipchitz, my friend from Montparnasse. Who knows where he's fled to now? Or Lev Zilberman, who painted those massive murals in Berlin."

"Yes, I know Zilberman's work. Alfred Barr fought to get him on our list."

"You're not entirely on the wrong path, then. Help

Ernst, help Zilberman. Not me." And he turned away from Varian, toward his canvases, toward the brushes and knives, the wooden boxes cluttered with crushed tubes of paint. "I'll mention your name among our circles," he said. "I know plenty who are eager to leave."

———

Varian stumbled along the road toward Cavaillon, down the hill he'd seen through the courtyard arch. It would take him two hours to reach the station at this rate; another two on the train after that, and then he'd be back in Marseille, having made no progress at all. And what would he report to his colleagues in New York—to Paul Hagen, who directed the Emergency Rescue Committee, or to Frank Kingdon, its chair? That summer, when he and Paul and Ingrid Warburg and Alfred Barr and the others had compiled their list—two hundred artists, writers, and intellectuals who'd been blacklisted by the Gestapo and had no way out of France—they hadn't imagined that their clients might resist being helped, nor that they'd consider themselves beyond Vichy's reach. There were so many things they hadn't considered; his life in France had become a process of discovering them, often to his embarrassment. It was a miracle he'd managed to get anyone out at all. There had been only twelve so far, a minuscule fraction of his list.

What he ought to do, he thought as he kicked stones along the rutted road, was to write his wife that night to say he was coming home. He'd confess—and what a relief it would be—that his work wasn't going as planned. How had he imagined it would take a month, **one month,** to find and extract two hundred endangered artists? He'd envisioned himself riding a rented bicycle through the countryside, rounding up refugees by the dozen, as if they'd be waiting in the lemon orchards with traveling papers in hand. He'd imagined that the consulate would contort itself miraculously to help him. But then the chaos of this place, the innumerable bureaucratic barriers, the cretins in the U.S. Visa Office, the resistance of the artists themselves. What a mistake he'd made, crawling out from behind his desk at the publishing house. How could he have presumed to take the lives of men like Chagall and Ernst into his hands when he had no idea how to manage them—no idea, even, of how to convince them they were in danger? Eileen wanted him home; she feared for his life. Her letter from last week had made that clear. Well, home he'd go. He'd write her at once; he'd write her as soon as he reached the Splendide.

2

La Dorade

He arrived at his hotel to find the usual line of refugees waiting at the entrance, in the shadow of the petaled glass awning. Those who had visited before called out in recognition or waved papers in his direction, and those he'd never seen crowded close to speak to him or touch his sleeve, as though he were the goddamned pope. He told them, as gently as possible, that they'd better go home for the evening. Then he went inside to ask for his mail at the desk, hoping for some word from Eileen. But there was nothing from the States at all, no blue airmail envelope, no telegram. Only a telephone message, scrawled on a slip of yellow lined paper: **La Dorade 19:00. Vincit labor ignorantiam.**

If we could pin down the moments when our lives bifurcate into **before** and **after**—if we could pause the progression of milliseconds, catch ourselves at the point before we slip over the precipice—if we could choose to remain suspended in time-amber, our lives intact, our hearts unbroken, our foreheads unlined, our nights full of undisturbed sleep—would we slip, or would we choose the amber? Would he have chosen at that moment to live forever in a time before that message, intact but unchanged? Would he have chosen to turn around and walk out of the Splendide, out of his life in France?

Vincit labor ignorantiam. A refrain from the **Hound and Horn,** his literary quarterly at Harvard, conceived over drinks one night in the Gore Hall bedroom of his friend and sometime bedfellow, Lincoln Kirstein. **Work conquers ignorance.** Meant ironically, of course, because that night they'd said to hell with work in favor of Kirstein's scotch. Now he touched the words of the Latin motto with his thumb, the hotel clerk's penciling soft and smudged against the yellow slip. Could Kirstein be here in France? He'd heard nothing from him in months. Last spring, an après-ballet party at Kirstein's midtown apartment had devolved into an argument about whether or not the States should enter the war; Varian had left before he could get himself in trouble.

He could imagine nothing at that moment that would cause him to hesitate. He thought only that it would be interesting to see his old co-conspirator, former co-editor of the **Hound and Horn.** He could conceive of no one else who could have left him that message. And so he went upstairs, changed his shirt and tie, combed his hair, and brushed his hat, trying to guess what news Kirstein might bring, or what service he might ask Varian to render. At the door of the hotel room he took a shot of whiskey, then regretted it at once; his gut burned always, chronically, and drink made it worse. But he owned this burn, would own it all his life. Fortified, he went out into the fine-grained fog of an August evening in Marseille, ready to meet whatever awaited him at the Dorade.

The walk from his hotel took him down the boulevard d'Athènes and across the aorta of Marseille, the Canebière, where diners lounged at café tables and jazz angled from the open restaurant windows despite the post-occupation ban. The street smelled of diesel fuel and cardamom and wet gutters, of tobacco and women's perfume. From the base of the Canebière, the Vieux Port exhaled a constant fragrance of seaweed and salt. At this hour the port was still faintly illuminated by a horizon line of brilliant yellow, the last liquid dregs of a sunset that had insisted its corals and saffrons through the fog. But in the streets, darkness had already fallen; the alleys of the port district snaked into ill-lit caverns on either side of the boulevard. He'd visited this quarter of small undistinguished shops his third day in town, in search of a cobbler to repair the valise he'd torn on the flight from New York. On the way, he'd become distracted in an antiquarian bookstore, where a slim volume of Heraclitus had corrected a lapse of memory: οὐδέν, not ἴδιος, in the old quote about everything changing, nothing remaining still. He'd wanted to put the line into a letter to Eileen and didn't like the thought of getting it wrong. The bookstore was shuttered now, its awning furled for night.

The Dorade, de facto headquarters of Marseille's black market, stood on a corner of the rue Fortia, crowded by crustacean sellers on either side of its canopied entryway. Charles Vinciléoni, the proprietor, often held court at a table in the back, as if daring the police to interrupt him. As far as Varian could tell, they did so only to congratulate him on the quality of his liquor. Vinciléoni always seemed to be conducting a louche version of academic office hours; his silver-shot hair and his small ovoid glasses gave him a professorial air. And he affected a style of dress that might almost have been called Oxonian: tweed jackets with patches at the elbows, faintly scuffed shoes that could only have come from a Savile Row cobbler, pants of a looser cut than the French favored. As Varian entered, Vinciléoni marked his arrival with a nod. Varian had made himself a regular at the Dorade in the hope of opening avenues of escape for his clients, but he'd never had the nerve to approach Vinciléoni himself: one of many small failures. He took a table for two and ordered whiskey and water, scanning the line of tilt-hatted men who leaned against the zinc bar. No familiar face came into view through the cigarette smoke. He'd made his way to the final millimeter of his drink before a man approached his table. Varian raised his eyes.

Not Kirstein.

Grant.

There are moments when the filament of time bends, loops, blurs. The present becomes permeable; the past leaps forward and insists itself upon us without warning. The orderly progression of our days reveals itself to be a lie, and the sensemaking brain flounders. What was he supposed to call this impossibility that insisted itself before him as reality? A hallucination? Déjà vu, that cheap cinematic trick of the mind? Waiters passed with trays of bouillabaisse and mussels; glasses clinked at the bar, and a cocktail shaker played its Cuban rhythm. He got to his feet and removed his hat. He, Varian, who prided himself on always knowing what to say, how to act: wordless, frozen.

Grant offered his hand and Varian took it. Twelve years since he'd disappeared from Harvard, from Cambridge, from Varian's life. And now here he was at the Dorade, pulling out a chair and lowering himself into it with loose-limbed ease. There was the familiar crescent-shaped scar above the left eyebrow. The familiar eyes, their color more haze than hazel. His skin, pale amber. The only signs of time: a certain leanness to his cheek, a harder cast to his gaze. That and the sharper lines of his clothes, a gentleman's tailoring.

"I'm dreaming," Varian managed to say at last.

Grant lowered his eyes. "Sorry for all the cloak-and-dagger. I wasn't sure you'd see me if I gave my name."

The sound of his voice: the soft terminal **r,** the elongated Philadelphian vowels, the low, intimate tone. Varian put his thumb and forefinger to the bridge of his nose. A metallic taste bloomed in his mouth. The hum of the room seemed to contract around him, and he blinked again. Grant was still there.

"You'll forgive me if I don't quite believe this," he said.

Grant flagged a waiter. "What'll you have?"

Varian paused for a moment, then said, "Uncle Scorch, of course." The signature drink of their **Hound and Horn** revels: the cheapest whiskey in the house.

Grant ordered for both of them and sat back in his chair. He took out his cigarette case, but it was empty. "Can I trouble you for one?" he said.

"I've given them up. You should too."

"I've got worse habits," Grant said, with his low, familiar laugh.

"How on earth did you find me?"

"It seems we've been hanging around the same

quarters here in Marseille. Hugh Fullerton at the consulate mentioned you in the most unflattering terms. Apparently your work is inconvenient to the American diplomatic mission in France."

"Right. Better to sacrifice the liberal democrats of Europe than offend the fascists."

Grant smiled. A complicated moment of reconnection passed between them, a jolt of electricity through a completed circuit. "My mission's not so different from yours," he said. "I thought perhaps we could be of use to each other."

"Of use!" Varian said, as if in a dream. **Of use.** And where had Grant been for the past decade, when it might have been of use to know he wasn't dead?

"I know how it sounds," Grant said. "That's not exactly what I mean."

"Then what do you mean?" Varian said. "What's your 'mission'? What am I supposed to do for you?"

Grant let out a long breath, a smoker's sigh without a smoke. "Long story," he said. "Perhaps it's not wise to get into it here."

"Let's start with the official version, then. The one you'd give a gendarme if he asked."

Grant rearranged his long limbs and sighed again. "Okay," he said. "I'm here on an academic sabbatical, finishing a book on the subject of nineteenth-century French verse. Staying at a colleague's house in La Pomme."

"Literary research, while a war's on? Original, if not convincing."

"And what about you?" Grant said, meeting his eye again. "What's your official version? You and your journalist wife, handing out American aid to refugees?"

"You knew I married Eileen."

"I saw the announcement in the **Times.**" Grant turned his gaze toward the bar, twisting the silver cufflink at his wrist.

"Eileen's not here in France," Varian said. "Right now she's at her dad's place in Vermont, working on a book until she has to go back and start the semester at Brearley. That's her job now. She teaches the English canon to straight-backed young ladies. But she's been driving down to Westchester on weekends to look for a house for us there. A place big enough for a family."

"You've got kids, then?"

"Not yet. What about you?"

Grant gave him a level look, as if in reproach.

"I don't suppose I should ask if you're married," Varian said.

"That's not exactly what they call it."

"And what about your work? Sabbatical from where?"

Grant pulled a card from a silver case, and Varian learned, with some surprise, that he was an assistant professor of literature at Columbia. So he'd finished school after all. More than finished. He'd done well enough to pursue the doctorate and secure a position uptown. And he'd been living in New York for—how long? They might have run into each other on the subway, at the grocer's, in the park. The thought was enough to make the table seem to tilt, the bar lights swing on their cords.

"You're a lucky man," Varian managed to say. "There's no sabbatical at the Foreign Policy Association."

"What's that? A government outfit?"

"Publisher. International affairs."

"And you're what? An editor?"

"Director of an imprint," Varian said, with some pride. "Headline Books."

Grant nodded, tilting the glass with its inch of amber drink. "You know, I used to pick up **The Living Age** now and then, those years when you were editor in chief. I read your pieces for the **Times,** too. I must have read everything you wrote about the rise of the Third Reich." He shook his head. "So much incisive thought about our political moment. And all you cared about in college was what had happened a hundred or a thousand or two thousand years ago. You must have done your homework since then."

"The history **was** the homework," Varian said, struggling to keep his tone even. So Grant had been reading him all that time. And wasn't that what he'd secretly hoped when he'd written those pieces for **The Living Age** and **The New Republic** and the **Times**? That Grant might come across his name in print, might read a sentence he'd written, and feel—what? Envy? Regret?

"It can't have been **all** the homework," Grant said.

"I went to Germany in '35," Varian said. "Four months, June to September. You wouldn't believe some of the things I saw. My editors didn't at first. But the Nazis aren't shy about their methods. They practically advertised the worst of them."

"Nothing surprises me now," Grant said. "Here we sit, drinking in fallen France."

"You've already seen, I'm sure, how bullheaded our own consulate can be. Try to get a visa for a European artist, particularly if he's ever written for a communist paper or run afoul of his fascist government. It's like trying to invade the Krak des Chevaliers."

Grant scrutinized Varian for a long moment, a look Varian knew from years before—as if his gaze could penetrate the surface, the carefully hung scrim of Varian's manner, his speech and movement, the armor of his tailored suit. Then, as now, Varian felt it was what he deserved: both the implicit admiration, and the suggestion that Grant had glimpsed a thread of fraudulence. He was right, of course. Varian had never performed relief work of any kind, he knew nothing of contralegal immigration, he had few useful contacts here in France. He'd entered the field at the direst of moments, intending to take on as his clients the most elite of Europe's cultural elite. Now he was in over his head, half-drowning; Grant had seen it at once. Nonsensically, the thought flushed him with indignation: Who was Grant to show up after all this time and accuse him of ignorance, of incompetence? Did Grant think he knew better?

"What is it you want?" he said. "Why are you here, really?"

Grant fingered his cufflink, a miniature silver nautilus rendered in detail so exact it seemed the animal itself had abandoned it on his wrist. "I must ask you a favor," he said. "It's for a friend of mine—the colleague I mentioned. The one with the house in La Pomme. I need you to see him in person. He can't come here to town—or he'd rather not, to be more accurate." He took a pen from his breast pocket and picked up the Columbia business card from where it lay on the table, just under Varian's middle and index fingers. He wrote a few words on the back, then handed the card back to Varian. And there was the familiar handwriting, that mess of upright loops and points, like a child's rendering of grass.

"What's this?" Varian said.

"His address. I'd like you to speak to him, see if you might be able to help. I wanted him to come with me tonight, but he refused. He's afraid of running into the police."

Varian turned the card over in his fingers. It occurred to him that he could leave it in the glass ashtray before him, that he could get up from this table and walk the length of the Dorade and exit through the doors flanked by the crustacean sellers, that he could go home to the Hôtel Splendide, climb the stairs, walk the long hall to his room, and close the door. Lock it behind him. Lie down on the bed, take a sleeping pill. If Grant called the next day, he could refuse to speak to him; if Grant showed up at the Splendide, he could refuse to see him. It was what he should do: Rise from his chair. Wish Grant luck. Tell him he was sorry, but that he couldn't spare time or resources for anyone but his own clients. And then do just what he'd planned to do earlier that day: Write to Eileen. Tell her the truth. Get out of France as soon as possible.

He ran his thumb over Grant's writing, scarcely knowing what he was doing. The scotch he'd drunk had risen to his brain, and turned there now like a storm.

"I'm afraid I," he said, and faltered. "I'm afraid my—"

Grant's gaze narrowed, his eyes on Varian's. Again there was the feeling of uncomfortable scrutiny, of being seen clearly for the first time in—God, how long? He wished he had a cloak to pull over himself, some way to protect himself.

A long moment passed in silence. Then Grant said, "Do you remember the day you made me buy a hat?"

"A hat, Skiff?" And there was the old nickname, buried in his mind for years.

"You remember. It must have been about ten below, mid-February. We were walking along Brattle Street past the shops, I was bareheaded and cold, and you made me go in and try on that extravagant Borsalino. I hardly recognized myself. It wasn't just the hat, of course. It was my position at the **Hound and Horn,** our friends at Gore Hall, all of it. And do you remember what you said?"

"I have no memory of any of this," Varian said, which was a lie; he remembered every detail—the terrible weather, the shop, the hat, and twenty-year-old Grant, that lucid-eyed, smooth-skinned boy, who stood before the glass and marveled.

"You quoted Seneca at me," Grant said. **"Vivamus, moriendum est."**

" 'Let us live, since we must die'? That's rather pretentious, even for a sophomore classicist."

"You're the one who said it, Tom."

And there was his own alter-name, the one Varian had tried and failed to pin on himself in seventh grade, when he'd most hated his given name. He'd told Grant the story a lifetime ago. How like him, Varian thought, to show up out of nowhere after an eon, still in possession of Varian's inmost self. And what now? Was he supposed to pack it all away, pretend it hadn't happened, this contortionist's backbend of time? **Tom.** Good God. Without thinking, almost without sensation, he produced a black diary from his pocket and opened it on the table. Drink-induced tinnitus, a kind of auditory hallucination, drowned the warning klaxon in his head.

"All right," he said. "When?"

"How about Wednesday morning at ten?"

He was doing nothing more than arranging a time to meet Grant's friend; he was promising nothing. He might still change his mind. He inscribed the appointment in his datebook. Grant wrote it in his own, then pulled out a slim pocketwatch.

"I've got to go," he said. "Lost track of time. I'm late to meet my friend."

"Of course," Varian said, coolly. "Don't let me keep you."

Grant raised an eyebrow. "What's that look for?"

"After twelve years, Skiff, you might have cleared more than an hour."

"I'm sorry," Grant said. "I wasn't sure you'd speak to me."

"Perhaps I shouldn't have," Varian said, but it was beyond his will to incite an argument; the reality of Grant's absence was still rewriting itself, still transmuting itself into the unbelievable fact of his presence. And now Grant was leaving. He stood and shook Varian's hand like the old college friend he was, and went as quietly as he'd come.

A few minutes later Varian found himself back on the street in the chill August fog. He leaned against the damp brick wall of the building and let it all come over him: **Elliott Schiffman Grant.** Skiff

Grant. To whom could he report this incredible news? Eileen? He thought of cabling Kirstein, but couldn't imagine the words. GUESS WHO CRAWLED OUT OF MARSEILLE FOG STOP. He knew what Kirstein would say: leave it alone. It was what he needed to hear. He spoke Grant's name aloud now into the fog of the Vieux Port as if testing its solidity, as if speculating that the meeting had been nothing more than a flight of his own imagination. But there was the business card in his pocket, the address inscribed on its reverse; and here, in his head, the fine hot buzz of Uncle Scorch, a drink he hadn't drunk in twelve years. As he turned to go, he saw a glint of silver on the sidewalk: Grant's cufflink, the perfect nautilus shell. With a thrill that felt like theft, he bent and took it into his hand.

———

The way home was dark, the night wet enough to make him regret his linen jacket. He worked the cufflink in his pocket, thumbing the sectioned whorl of the nautilus and the loose T-bar. Elliott Grant. Skiff. He found his mind returning to an October evening in the tiny room at Gore Hall where Grant had invited them all over for drinks. They sat on the floor, four or five of them, drinking Grant's port and smoking the loose cigarettes Kirstein assembled in the firelight. It was meant to be a housewarming; Grant had fled his previous quarters, which had been overrun by mice, and he'd invited each of them to bring something to throw into the fire for luck. Their managing editor, Nat Marlow, had brought the business card of the establishment where he'd been relieved of his virginity; Edwin Tewkes, poetry editor, had brought a single rose-colored silk stocking. Varian himself had brought a pocket copy of a Latin dictionary so riddled with errors it seemed to have been intended as a prank by one generation of classics students upon another. And Kirstein brought a copy of the Ezra Pound poem from which their magazine drew its name:

THE WHITE STAG

I ha' seen them 'mid the clouds on the heather.
Lo! They pause not for love nor for sorrow,
Yet their eyes are as the eyes of a maid to her lover,
When the white hart breaks his cover
And the white wind breaks the morn.

"Tis the white stag, Fame, we're a-hunting,
Bid the world's hounds come to horn!"

They threw those talismans on the fire and finished the port, then went down to the sitting room on the ground floor, where Grant played Broadway standards on the piano while the others shouted approximate lyrics. Grant couldn't seem to keep himself from catching Varian's eye, as if to be sure Varian had noticed that all of this was his doing, that these men were caught up in an energy he had created and that he controlled.

As Varian walked home with Kirstein that night, Kirstein asked what he thought of promoting Grant from editorial assistant to cultural critic. His tastes were refreshingly irreverent, Kirstein said, his knowledge broad and deep. He was a good writer too: that week he'd read an essay aloud in the American literature class he shared with Kirstein, in which he'd been witty and penetrating on the subject of Hawthorne's influence on Melville. And he might be even better suited to writing about music—he had an impressive collection of classical recordings, modern stuff like Schoenberg and Stravinsky, accumulated by his father on his travels through Europe. Did Varian know that Grant's father had been an internationally renowned botanist who'd died in the Amazon on a sample-gathering expedition?

Varian walked in silence, swinging a slender hawthorn twig he'd picked up outside Grant's place. Cambridge was rife with fences good for running a stick along; now he made a harsh music against a stretch of white pickets. The fact was, he already knew a good deal more about Grant than Kirstein did. The records, wherever they'd come from, certainly hadn't come from Grant's father, who wasn't a botanist either.

Varian said, “I think you’ve taken a shine to our friend Grant.”

Kirstein laughed, almost exultantly. “Jealous?”

“How is he on Whitman? Penetrating?”

“Oh, now, Varian.”

“It’s your call. If you want him, sign him up.”

“You’re co-editor. You’ve got a say.”

Varian had paused a long time before assenting. And later, in the privacy of his room, he’d been subject to a great many complicated thoughts about Grant. Among his feelings was a blunt envy that came from Grant’s having achieved, without apparent effort, the sheen of intelligent artistic cosmopolitanism Varian had struggled to affect since boarding school. Varian’s father, a stockbroker, was not unsuccessful at his work, but had never managed to vault his family out of the middle class; their home in suburban New Jersey was a politely unexceptional version of all the others on their street. The things that had set Varian apart in boyhood—the fact, for example, that his mother was so often sick (no one said **crazy,** of course), and that his aunt lived with them to take care of her—were unexotic, even shameful. If he was different from his classmates, it was only because they seemed slow in comparison to himself. He wasn’t interested in baseball or bikes or boxing, and they weren’t interested in chess or books. At Hotchkiss he’d resisted the brutal rituals of inclusion: the paddlings of younger boys by older ones, the night wakings, the trials by burning or stuffing or starving. His protest had felt heroic at the time, but he knew it hadn't set him apart in a way that might be read as anything but petulant or sissified. And so, in his early days at Harvard, he'd struggled to create a persona that would win him the admiration of other boys. He thought in detail about his clothes and hair and shoes, hoping to project an inarguable urbanity; at a low-lit café on Mount Auburn Street he held forth nightly about the books he read and the lectures he attended, turning the stocked cabinets of his mind inside out for inspection. He collected like-minded young men and threw parties for them and their friends. But it was all a pasteboard construction, and he knew—and it chagrined him—that the effort was visible.

Grant, on the other hand, wore his difference like a bespoke suit. Every detail of his being—the foreign cigarettes he smoked, the leather satchel like an artifact of war, the European phonograph records, the ignominious closet-sized dormitory room with its genuine-looking antique Persian rug, even the vaguely anomalous color of his skin—seemed to suggest, entirely without exertion on Grant's part, that the owner of such things possessed a certain alchemical magic capable of transforming the old and the ordinary into the wondrous and unique. Step into my circle, he seemed to say, and you too will be transformed. It was a quality Varian had observed in certain boys at Hotchkiss whose popularity transcended the usual snobbery about pedigree and class. One boy by the name of Prasad was the son of wealthy Bengali Brahmins, but obviously considered himself the peer, or indeed the superior, of the school's old New Yorkers and Boston Brahmins. He had a perfect English accent, an agile analytical mind, and the ability to recite poetry in six languages. Varian had spent his last term at boarding school nursing an attraction to Prasad so fierce he feared it would declare itself in some mortifying public way. He'd felt a jolt of the same attraction the first time he'd met Grant, and the feeling had only intensified. But whereas Prasad had seemed merely intelligent and unusual, Grant seemed dangerously unpredictable, as if beneath his outward costume was a creature of another shape, limbs ghosting beneath the surface like the folded wings of a chrysalid. Impossible to tell if this cloaked being was benign or malign or something between, or what its motives might be. And the more he'd learned about Grant—about his parentage, his past, the bending of truth that had landed him at Harvard—the less he felt he knew.

To have him appear again now, here in Marseille, as if reconstituted from the fog itself, seemed to Varian as appropriate as it was astonishing. Marseille, more than any place he'd ever been, was the province of unexpected convergences, of hidden things brought to light, of things that bore one name in public and another in private. Of anyone he'd gone to school with, Grant was the last he would have expected to encounter here; you could even say he was the one Varian would have least wanted to see. At the same time he was the one whose presence seemed most natural. Varian felt for the business card in his pocket and drew it out, pausing beneath a streetlamp. **Les Cyprès, La Pomme,** written in Grant's near-illegible script. Again he felt the pull of those letters, the suggestion of the hand that held the pen. He carried the card home in his damp palm, and didn't realize until he'd reached his room that he'd forgotten to ask at the desk for a message from Eileen.

3

The Splendide

By the time he left his bed the next morning, squinting against the cataract of sun coming through the window, he'd convinced himself that he would write Grant to cancel their meeting. Wednesday morning was twenty-four hours away; in that time, anything might happen to impede his going out to La Pomme. He dressed, careful not to exercise unusual care in his sartorial choices; there was no reason to think he'd see Grant today, and even if he did, what could it possibly matter if his tie illuminated a certain green fleck in his eye, or if his tweed lent him an air of authority? He ordered breakfast: the standard dry toast with watery marmalade, the burnt-chicory brew that passed for coffee. As he waited for it to be delivered, he sat at the desk, took out an airmail blank, and uncapped his pen. But instead of writing to Eileen, he found himself staring at the silver nautilus cufflink where it lay in a square of light on the desktop. He took it into his hand now, the small hard weight of it, and turned it over in his fingers. He knew nothing about the nautilus except that it was a mollusk, and that it moved forward into new chambers as it aged, walling off the past behind it. Where had he gleaned that fact? Some long-ago biology class at Hotchkiss? There was some special math behind the progressive size of those chambers, a biological mystery mirrored elsewhere in nature. To know that this silver shell had rested against Grant's sleeve—to be holding that object in his hand—seemed mystery enough.

The usual unsmiling boy in his too-large jacket delivered Varian's tray. Not even a generous tip could change the boy's expression; his polite bow and his curt bonjour were impenetrable. Alone again in the temporary silence of his room, Varian drank his chicory coffee and ate his dry toast, forcing his mind toward the urgent work of the day. Their supply of francs was running out; they had to find a way to exchange a lot of dollars without tipping off the Préfecture de Police. And it had to happen soon: more refugees showed up daily, hungry and ill clad and unhoused. Then there was his costly new project: five high-risk clients' exit over the border into Spain, to take place in a few weeks if the U.S. visas came through. The clients—Heinrich and Nelly Mann, brother and sister-in-law of Thomas; Golo Mann, Thomas's son; and the writer Franz Werfel and his thrice-married wife, Alma—had been living for weeks in a state of barely contained panic at the prospect of deportation by the Gestapo, Golo hiding out at the U.S. vice consul's villa, the elder Manns and the Werfels in an ancient hotel in an out-of-the-way quartier. Werfel's mood, in particular, had been growing darker by the day. That weekend he'd joked, looking out the window of their fifth-story hotel room, that if the Gestapo showed up, he could always defenestrate. Varian didn't take any of it lightly. A rash of suicides had moved through the refugee population in late June, and there were new reports of self-inflicted deaths—some false, some true—nearly every day. The thought of it now was enough to push Grant from his mind, and then Lena was knocking at the door.

"**O mój Boże,** Monsieur Fry," she said, edging past him into the room. "This heat!"

His secretary lived at the Hôtel des Postes, not ten minutes' walk down the Canebière, but she always arrived looking as if she'd just crossed a desert in the harmattan, a plume of cigarette smoke chasing her down the hall, her turquoise earrings asway, her hair in need of emergency rearranging at the dressing table. She was Polish, passportless, Jewish, multilingual; she spoke all her languages with wild abandon, and often in combination. She'd entered France on foot some months before and drifted down toward Marseille during the **pagaille.** She'd meant to become Varian's client, but when she'd seen what a disaster he was making of things—and having grasped that her own case was unlikely to reach the standards of the Emergency Rescue Committee—she'd volunteered as secretary.

It hadn't taken her long to set things right. There was now a filing system for the clients' paperwork, a set of interview forms, a precious address book kept hidden beneath a loose corner of carpet in case of a police raid, a pinboard for refugees' messages. She'd insisted that Varian engage a professional bookkeeper, so he had recruited a man named Oppenheimer, a former political economist who now made his living by hiding illegal expenses inside legal ones. Lena herself knew nothing of the illegal side of their practice—nothing of the fake Czech passports Varian had been handing out; nothing of Leon Ball, the former American cowboy who'd been conducting Varian's paperless refugees over the border into Spain; nothing of the back-channel negotiations about escape boats, all of which had thus far ended in failure. The less anyone else knew, he figured, the safer they all were.

After Lena had rearranged her hair and made her apologies, she sat down at the dressing table and uncovered the ancient Contin they'd bought from an antiques dealer on the rue Paradis. The typewriter stuck at every third stroke and stank of rancid oil; the type it produced skewed upward, and left more than a little to the reader's conjecture. But it was a typewriter. More than any other object they possessed, it seemed to lend their operation a note of legitimacy.

"And so," Lena said, as she slipped a sheet of onionskin between the rollers, "how are the Chagalls?"

"Both well. Not leaving France anytime soon."

"Nicht wahr!"

"I'd rather not discuss it at the moment. Let's start with something else."

She raised her chin at him, her turquoise earrings glinting. "Shall we not send a letter to the consulate?"

"Not yet," Varian said.

She arched an eyebrow ceilingward, then opened a client folder. The tilt of her chin communicated that she would return to the subject of the Chagalls before long. She wanted to save them in particular, wanted to have a hand in it; she considered nothing to be impossible. To any form of demurral, to any note of alarm, she had one response: **Il ne faut pas exagérer.** Now she extracted the first set of client interview notes and began to transcribe Varian's hasty scratch into type, while he stood over her shoulder and corrected her.

Albert Hirschman materialized ten minutes later, carrying a small metal thermos and a bag of the North African pastries to which he'd become addicted. Varian couldn't tolerate anything sweet in the morning, but it pleased him to watch Albert—perfectly blond, perfectly slim, always dressed as though he meant to conduct a lunchtime romance—tear open the bag and lay out three gold eggs of sugared dough on a square of waxed paper. For Lena there was always a sesame-covered **chebakia.** It was impossible to predict how long the Moroccan bakery could keep producing its pastries, wartime shortages being what they were, but Varian suspected that Hirschman would find ways to get what couldn't be had. A Berliner, a Social Democrat, and, at twenty-five, a doctor of economic philosophy, he'd been running from the German authorities for the past eight years, had been trailed by Nazi soldiers across the Austrian border, starved in a Paris garret while pursuing his studies at the Sorbonne, fought for the Republicans in the Guerra Civil and been wounded twice; but here he was, undaunted, immaculate, always plotting his next move. Even his approach to romance was strategic: the most recent of his many conquests, a platinum-haired secretary at the Préfecture de Police, had access to the commissaire's files and had already delivered a few gems.

"And what do you have for me today?" Varian asked, as Hirschman finished the last of his golden eggs.

"Something better than pastry," Hirschman said. But there was no time to elaborate; at that moment the first of the potential clients came through the door. As usual they'd been arriving at the Splendide since dawn. They queued along the outside wall of the hotel until eight o'clock, when the manager finally consented to admit them. Of the three thousand American dollars Varian had brought with him to France, a hundred—no small sum—had gone to this manager in exchange for his not calling the police every day as soon as the line formed. Once they were admitted, the refugees climbed the stairs and lined up outside Varian's door, all the way to the window that overlooked the back alley. Last week there had been ten refugees a day; this week, more than fifty. They waited all day, until midnight if they had to.

The first person through the door that morning was a young woman in a white batiste dress, her skin scrubbed to a high polish, her hair arranged in a corona of honey-colored braids. Her dress looked freshly pressed, her shoes clean and new-looking enough to suggest that they weren't her only pair. She carried a neat and unfrivolous bag, big enough to hold a sheaf of papers. With a schoolgirl's easy lope, she crossed the room and seated herself in the spindly chair before Varian's desk. Even before she spoke, Varian knew she must be an American.

"Miriam Davenport," she said, in a Boston accent that rounded her **r**'s into **ah**'s. "Smith College, class of '36. Recently of the Sorbonne."

"And how can I help you, Miss Davenport of the Sorbonne? We're generally not in the business of providing aid to Bostonians."

She gave a trumpetlike laugh. "Actually, I haven't been a Bostonian for some time. But I suppose you can't take the city out of the girl."

"I won't hold it against you," Varian said, and smiled.

"I'm not here on my own behalf," Miss Davenport said, lowering her voice and leaning across the desk. "Walter Mehring sent me, or rather I volunteered to come in his stead, since he's terrified to leave his hotel room. I met him at Toulouse when I came down in June. His case is rather urgent."

"**The** Walter Mehring, German poet?"

"Yes, that one."

"If that's true—if you've really got Walter Mehring stashed away at some hotel nearby—then you've already made my day."

"I've got a few others, too. Konrad Heiden, Hitler's unofficial biographer. And Hertha Pauli, actress and writer—she's tight with Mehring, if you get my meaning."

Varian turned to Hirschman. "Albert, meet Miss Davenport. Miss Davenport, Mr. Hirschman. He'll take down all the necessary information, and we'll get started on the paperwork at once." And to Miriam: "You're wise to speak quietly about Mehring. He's got to be among the Nazis' top ten. He's near the top of my own list, to be sure."

"You have a list?"

"Oh, yes. But not a long one. Our funds are quite limited."

Her eyes widened. "You'll be able to help him, won't you?"

"We'll try."

"And Heiden?"

"He's on the list, too."

"Oh, thank goodness," she said. "They'll be glad to hear it. There's been little in the way of hope these last few weeks."

"Well, we can't offer much of it, but at least we can get the process underway. I'll see my friend at the consulate about their visas. Sometimes it takes a while. In the meantime, do you think they'd consider moving to the Splendide? I'd rather have them closer by."

"Good luck," Miriam said. "Mehring will barely look out from beneath his bed."

"Tell him he'll be safer here. Tell him to come today, if he can. Sit down with Mr. Hirschman for a minute and let him get all the details. But don't let him ask you to dinner. He's a terrible roué."

"I wouldn't," Miss Davenport said; she flashed an engagement ring set with tiny diamonds and rubies.

"All's well, then," Varian said. "We'll do what we can for your friends."

She settled in to talk to Hirschman, and Varian opened the door to the next supplicant: a lean, haggard-looking man in beret and turtleneck, his handlebar mustache drooping, a battered sketchbook under his arm. His name was unfamiliar to Varian, his German nearly incomprehensible. He fell into the spindly chair as if he'd reached it from the farthest corner of the world. For a long moment he closed his eyes, and Varian was afraid he'd fallen asleep.

"And where are you from, Mr. Rubasky?"

The artist gave a rusty cough and opened his eyes. "Warsaw."

"Forgive me, but I don't know your work. Have you exhibited recently?"

The man's eyebrows came together. "Exhibited?"

"Are you—or were you—affiliated with a university? Represented by a gallery?"

"What is this? An audition? An inquisition?"

"The Emergency Rescue Committee has limited funds," Varian began. "Our mission—"

Rubasky's eyes narrowed. "Professor of painting," he said, slowly. "I was a professor. At the Academy of Fine Arts in Kraków. My work was exhibited in twenty countries. If not for the war, if not for my religion, I would have had a retrospective at the Prado this fall. And now I must argue my case in front of you, Mr. Fry, a mere boy!"

From over his left shoulder, Varian heard a quiet throat-clearing. It was Miss Davenport, eyes large and serious, hands clasped under her chin.

"Monsieur Rubasky?" she said. "Agnon Rubasky?"

The painter raised his head.

"Perhaps you should open your sketchbook for Monsieur Fry."

At the sound of another American accent, Rubasky

raised a skeptical eyebrow. But he agreed to do what she'd asked. He opened the book and laid it on his knee, flipping through the pages, and Varian caught glimpses of dense charcoalwork, human figures in frenzied motion, lines that suggested a cataclysm, a deluge. "Here, a study for a painting of an interior," he said, of a densely hatched sketch of what looked to be a burning staircase in a collapsing synagogue. "And here, portrait of my wife and son." Beside a series of scratches that might have been a rutted road, a desperate gesture in charcoal bent over a smaller scumbled shape, offering something—a black knot of bread, or a bowl of water. Varian drew a long breath.

"Monsieur Rubasky's work was exhibited at the Salon des Indépendants in Paris eight months ago," Miriam said. "He's revered by my professors at the Sorbonne. You see, don't you, how his compositions borrow from the cubists but contain echoes of Caravaggio?" She pointed to the shading of the sketched woman, the swift dense flock of marks that gave her volume. "He's a student of the symbolist Malczewski, but most critics seem to think he shares more with the surrealists. Writers like Richardin and Zabrest compare his work to that of Tanguy—and not, may I say, unfavorably."

Varian looked from the painter to Miss Davenport, then back to the painter again.

On Rubasky's face, a look of dawning relief. "Mademoiselle . . . ?"

"Davenport," said Miss Davenport.

"Mademoiselle Davenport, you are the hand of fate."

"Not at all, Mr. Rubasky, your work would have spoken for itself."

But Varian was not at all sure of that; his training was in classics and history, not in European art, and while he trusted himself as a critic of literature, he knew he would have failed utterly to see the influences of Caravaggio and Tanguy, much less of Malczewski, in the charcoal sketches in front of him.

"If Mr. Rubasky's name is not on your list, it should be," Miss Davenport said.

"Mr. Rubasky, forgive my ignorance," Varian said. "I'll urge my committee to take your case."

The painter gave a grunt, smoothing his brushy mustache with one finger.

"Please see Mr. Hirschman, there," Varian said. "He'll take down all your information, and we'll cable your name to New York tonight.

"Danke schön, Herr Fry. **Sie sind wirklich freundlich."**

"At your service, Mr. Rubasky."

The painter got up to speak to Hirschman, taking Miriam's place; Miriam nodded her thanks to Varian and, having finished her business, edged toward the door. But Varian found himself calling her name, and she turned.

"Miss Davenport," he said. "Would you perhaps be interested in a job?"

Sixty-three refugees. That was the number they interviewed before five o'clock that day, one after the next, more than half of them utterly hopeless—no papers, not a penny, nothing to render them of interest to the Emergency Rescue Committee in New York. Miriam, who had stayed for two more hours, left to arrange matters with Mehring and Pauli and Heiden; Oppy, the bookkeeper, had dropped in with a packet of sandwiches and a pile of bank forms for Varian to sign, but Varian hadn't had a moment to stop and eat. By five, having had nothing but the dry toast at breakfast, he thought he might melt into a senseless jelly on the floor. His vision swarming with paisleys, his throat tight with dehydration, he got up to revive himself with cold water from the bathroom tap.

As he leaned over the sink and looked at himself in the glass—the indoor pallor of his skin, the hammocks of exhaustion beneath his eyes—it came to him that he hadn't yet canceled his meeting with Grant. He sat down at the edge of the bathtub and put his head between his knees. What had led him to agree to that meeting, what had possessed him? Alcohol, panic, sheer surprise? He saw Grant's cool, composed face again, the scar above the eyebrow, the long fingers devoid of their wished-for cigarette. God. Already the heat was gathering in his chest, already he felt he had to see Grant again, whatever the consequences. Stop it, he told himself. Stop it at once. He stood up from the bathtub edge so precipitously he nearly fainted again, and had to put a hand on the doorframe to steady himself. When he managed to open the door, Hirschman was waiting behind it.

"Excuse me," Hirschman said. "We'd better draft our cable."

Varian glanced at his watch. "Oh, God. I lost track of time."

The wire to New York had to be dispatched by six. Hirschman had already cleared the room of refugees, and Lena sat at her desk with her steno pad at the ready.

"All right," Varian said, and took a seat again in his spindly chair. "Lena, Albert. Let's have the names."

Lena and Hirschman called out, one by one, the names of the refugees they'd interviewed that morning, and Varian wrote them on a large newsprint pad. Each day they sent nearly two dozen names to the office on Forty-First Street; he'd been strictly discouraged from sending more, short-staffed as they were at the New York headquarters. For each one of those names, someone would have to open a visa inquiry, a process that involved trips to three different federal government offices and the pains-taking completion of a stack of forms in triplicate. Mehring's and Heiden's names must go on the day's cable; so must Rubasky's. Varian circled those three in red. Then there were all the others—none of them on Varian's list, all of them artists or writers or political refugees of some achievement and reputation, all of them in danger of arrest and deportation.

Hirschman looked down despairingly into his sheaf of papers. "Perhaps we should be using a numerical rating," he said. He drew a handkerchief across his brow, pushing a ridge of hair high onto his forehead.

"Numerical!" Lena said. "How to rate sculptor against philosopher, or composer against Social Democrat?"

"Anyone who's been in a concentration camp must go into the cable."

Lena glanced through the forms. "But you've had eleven former inmates today. And not all of them we could call artists."

"This is a moral disaster, nothing less," Hirschman said.

Varian cleared his throat. "Look," he said. "Every afternoon for the past three weeks we've had to make this decision. We'll do it again today. If we don't, the list doesn't go at all."

"Absolument," Lena said. "**On ne faut pas exagérer.** Forgive me, Mr. Fry."

"It's no use trying to express any refugee's situation

in quantitative terms," Varian said. "And though I hate to put it this way, New York didn't say the aid was to go to those who'd suffered the most."

"The office must allow us to send more names," Lena said. "That is all."

"Truly, Lena, they don't have the money or the staff."

"Money, staff, they can get! Write to your wife. She will tell Paul Hagen what must be done."

"But what would happen," Hirschman said, "if the New York office **did** allow us fifty? A hundred? How would we get them all out?"

Varian looked at him in silence. This was the essential problem, insoluble now. Even if he could manage to get every refugee a passport, stamped with all the necessary visas, all of them with coordinating dates, all valid—the refugees still had to find a way across the border without being arrested and deported, and then through Spain and Portugal and across the ocean. All of it took luck, money, connections, time. And what did he have? What the Spanish called **ganitas.** Desire.

"Lena, pick ten names," Varian said. "Albert, you pick another ten. We'll send those with the three I mentioned. And then we'll strategize."

Varian and Hirschman always went to the telegraph office together; they each carried a separate copy of the list, in case one of them was arrested en route. While Varian cabled, Hirschman waited outside. And then, as they always did, they stopped in at the tiny café-bar across the street, a dark place called La Coquille de Noix, and installed themselves at a back table where they could talk unmolested. Two glasses of excellent Irish whiskey appeared from some hidden stash; the owner of the bar, as Varian happened to know, was an avid supporter not only of de Gaulle, but also of the black market.

"What have you got for me, Albert?" Varian said, once the waiter had left them.

Hirschman reached into his leather bag and produced a folded newspaper, which he handed to Varian as if to share current events. Inside, Varian found a sheaf of small pink and green folders printed with official seals. He looked at them from within the newspaper's V, fanned them with his thumb, squinted to make out the details. Polish and Lithuanian passports, more than a dozen of them, already filled with clients' information, lacking only photographs.

"And more where those came from," Hirschman said.

Varian folded the newspaper again, and with a single swift gesture, Hirschman made the packet disappear into his leather bag.

"How on earth, Albert?"

Hirschman shrugged, as if still surprised by his own success. "I asked myself who might be most sympathetic to our clients' plight. First I tried the Lithuanian consulate, then the Polish one. I merely explained our situation to a few officials. Showed a facsimile of your letter from Mrs. Roosevelt. Mentioned a few names. Chagall's. Mann's. The Poles were only too glad to help, as you can imagine—anything to hoodwink the Germans—and the Lithuanians were easy enough to persuade, once I told them a little about our clients."

"Do they understand the possible consequences?"

"They seemed, as I said, only too glad."

Varian shook his head. "Albert, you're a genius, do you know that? We couldn't have gotten on much longer with those fake Czech passports."

"It was easy enough, really. And that's not all I've got for you."

Varian raised an eyebrow, and Hirschman reached again into the leather bag. What he extracted this time was a book of matches from the Dorade: a gold-foil D on a black background, a diminutive gold-foil fish at its center. Varian thumbed the cover open. Inside, someone had written a name: **Moreau.** And an address on the rue Grignan.

"Who's Moreau?"

"Someone who's got an office he wants to unload. A proper office. Not a hotel room. A place to do our work."

"What are you talking about?"

"You know we can't do business out of the Splendide anymore. We're practically sitting in each other's laps already, and now you've brought on Miss Davenport. And we both know your bribes can't hold that concierge forever. Our people are too visible, waiting out in the street."

"We can't pay rent on an office. Every dime's got to go to the refugees. Ask Oppy. We're already shaving it too thin."

"Moreau's a leather merchant," Hirschman said. "He's got another four months on his contract, but he wants to leave town as soon as he can. He says he'll cut us some manner of deal."

"What sort of deal?"

"A generous deal. Talk to him."

Varian turned the matchbook over in his fingers. "When?"

"Tomorrow at four."

"Albert, I don't know what to say."

Hirschman smiled, lifted his glass, drained it. "Say **merci.** And give me the evening off. I've got a date with Betty from the Préfecture, and I'd better not be late."

"By all means," Varian said. "And thank you. Truly."

Hirschman rose and gave Varian a salute in farewell, leaving him to contemplate his last sip of whiskey and the gold-stamped matchbook. An office! 60 rue Grignan. Not ten minutes' walk from where he sat. A real place of business. Something more than a temporary space to park his makeshift organization. He would see it tomorrow afternoon.

Perhaps he could convince Miss Davenport to accompany him; he sensed she had powers of persuasion and judgment that exceeded his own. He'd send her a message at once, as soon as he got back to the Splendide—as soon as he'd written to Grant to cancel their meeting, he reminded himself now.

He got up and threw some francs on the table, then went out into the lengthening shadows of the evening. The sun still hung on at the edge of the port; slanting bars of light followed him through the streets. At the Splendide, there was another message waiting for him at the desk. Not a telephone message this time: a handwritten note. Grant's writing. And along with the note, a paper bag full of ripe figs. He must have just dropped them off minutes ago; when Varian reached into the bag he found they were warm, as if they'd baked all day in a market stall in the sun.

Remembered you liked these, the note said. **See you tomorrow 10AM.**

"For God's sake," he said aloud. He took the paper bag to his room, closed and locked the door behind him like a fugitive, and ate the figs one after the other. They were pink and sweet and thready, their taste somewhere between pastry and strawberry, their crisp round seeds like firecrackers between his teeth. He ate them until they were gone, and wished for more.

4

Les Cyprès

The next day was bright and hard-edged, the wind from the Vieux Port smelling of ozone, as if from a storm out at sea. A black bird and its shadow jittered along the sidewalk ahead of Varian as he made his way toward the tram stop. Now and then the bird paused and cocked its head as if to listen for his footsteps, then walked onward, past the sidewalk detritus of cigarette butts and pistachio shells and discarded tram tickets. To be in Marseille, not Paris, still carried a certain novelty, a whiff of the unknown. If Paris reeked of sex, opera, art, and decadent poverty, Marseille reeked of underground crime, opportunism, trafficked cocaine, rowdy tavern song. Paris was a woman, a fallen woman in the arms of her Nazi captors; but Marseille was a man, a schemer in a secondhand coat, ready to sell his soul or whatever else came quickly to hand. If it hadn't been for the war and the ERC, would Varian ever have crossed the borders of this town? Yet he felt oddly at home here, as if he'd returned to his grandfather's Brooklyn, to the streets where growth and decay lived side by side, and where a quick word could earn you a dollar or a clout to the ear.

He caught the #14 tram, paid his twenty centimes, and took a seat by a window, leaning his head against the sun-warmed pane, trying to turn his attention toward anything but Elliott Grant: that sidewalk market with its curving rows of stalls like uneven teeth; the shadowy alleys where children raced along on scooters made from lemon crates; the graffiti scrawled in red on the sides of buildings, punningly substituting **Putain** for **Pétain.** Gradually the four- and five-story buildings gave way to smaller ones, then to freestanding houses with cramped gardens, and finally to views of the sage-green countryside with its olive trees and almond orchards, its soaring scarf-strewn blue sky. At La Blancarde a crowd of schoolboys pushed onto the tram, their teacher lecturing them upon the geologic features of the landscape: There to the east, we see the Massif de Marseilleveyre, culmination of the Calanques, steep cliffs of limestone formed when the sea receded; a sample of that rock, boys, reveals infinitesimal marine fossils perfectly preserved.

At La Pomme he found himself straining to see if Grant was among the few young men waiting on the platform. He wasn't, of course. Grant was late, he was always late, by ten minutes exactly, no matter how urgent the appointment. And Varian was always on time. He couldn't help it. His father had taught him that the man who arrived first at a meeting possessed control. Thus far it had proved true, in all cases except those concerning Grant.

Ten minutes later he appeared from behind the station restaurant—Skiff Grant, still extant, rematerialized—with a book in his hand, as if he'd expected to read while waiting. Varian descended the stairs, and then Grant was before him, freshly shaven, in an open-collared shirt and a light wool suit correct for the season, smelling faintly of pastries and of the region's famous milled soap. There was a certain rudeness in his substantiality, an insult that arose from the fact of his continued existence during all the years when he'd been a ghost to Varian. They had, for God's sake, inhabited the same city, had breathed the same exhaust-scented air and ridden the same trains beneath the streets of New York; he had been as real as this all that time.

"And how was the ride?" Grant asked now.

"Full of schoolboys."

"Oh, yes, the **lycées** send them out to see the countryside. It's something, isn't it, that view across the valley? And the Massif de Marseilleveyre—you can see halfway across the ocean from up there. You ought to go sometime."

"You've hiked it?"

"Yes, Gregor and I."

"Ah, Gregor—your colleague?"

"That's right," Grant said, and fell silent, swinging the book in his hand as he walked. They continued that way until they reached a turning at an iron gate.

"Here we are," Grant said. "Les Cyprès. And there are the **cyprès.**" Along the private drive that led to the house, tall, slender evergreens pointed skyward toward a nest of cloud. As they walked the lane, a profusion of birds rose from the trees like sparks from fire; at the end was a little castle. The Medieval Pile, as Grant called it, was not medieval at all. It dated merely from the seventeenth century. The material was native limestone, the design borrowed from the original villas that had clung to this hillside in imperial times, and the conveniences, such as they were, were convenient only in relation to what had existed then. The taps dispensed cold water, the heating was all by fireplace. Though electrical power had come to La Pomme years before, his colleague preferred gaslight. The gas lamps only worked, Grant said, thanks to the ministrations of an ancient caretaker who lived in a neighboring cottage. They leaked and guttered and blackened their glass housings, which had to be cleaned daily if you wanted to read at night.

The Pile's chief luxury was solitude—that and the view, a scoop of valley that rushed across sage-hazed scrublands toward the Marseilleveyre. And here was a tiny orchard of persimmon trees, imported from

China on the professor's whim. The trees, still in full leaf, were decked with small vermilion fruit. As they walked through the orchard, Grant reached up and picked a few, explaining that they couldn't be eaten till they were soft and black. Then they reached the threshold, and he turned to Varian.

"Don't let Gregor scare you," he said. "He's tender underneath."

"Why would he scare me?"

"He's rather—unfiltered, I suppose you'd say. Do you remember our German philosophy professor, Brauer? With the beard and the too-short jackets, whose specialty was Schopenhauer and the insatiability of the will?"

Varian nodded. A trapdoor of memory: Grant beside him in lecture, their legs pressed together from ankle to knee, the heat of Grant's body obliterating Varian's attention to Professor Brauer's words, rendering him mute and stammering when Brauer turned to him and asked, "But what **proof** is there, how can we be certain beyond a doubt, that the world we inhabit exists?" At the time there had been only one certainty, as far as Varian was concerned: the molten line of contact between his leg and Grant's. He had been silent then, as now.

Grant opened the door and ushered him into an echoing darkness. A wind seemed to blow through the upper levels of the house, a ghost's voice susurrating along unseen passages. Around the interior of the atrium, a stone stairway traced a hexagonal path; the stone gave off a scent like the bottom of a ravine, earthy and wet and cold. The chandelier overhead was stuffed with wax candles, none of them lit. The only light came from the deep slash windows, one at each turning of the stairs. Varian would have expected the bare stone walls to be hung with the kind of portraits whose eyes followed you when you walked.

"Gregor's in the solarium," Grant said.

"Solarium! Is there one?"

"The place is a little vampiric, isn't it?" Grant sent a fleeting smile over his shoulder as he led Varian into a corridor, one that ran toward the back of the house. They entered a high-ceilinged sitting room with a wall of uncurtained windows; a cushioned seat ran the length of that wall, strewn at intervals with books and pillows. On the floor lay a rug of deep marine blue, and the furniture was upholstered in kilim. In the far corner, in an armchair beside a carved mahogany table, sat a tall, broad-shouldered man with shadowed eyes and a shock of thick black hair. At the sight of Varian he removed his glasses and stood. He didn't offer his hand; instead he gave a short gentlemanly bow and indicated the coffee service on the low table before him.

"Won't you sit, Mr. Fry?" he said, in a German-accented basso. He ran a hand through his unruly hair as if to arrange it. He was younger than Varian had imagined, under fifty, to be sure; his shoulders, beneath the fall of his well-cut white shirt, seemed barely to contain a tense power, as if of folded wings.

Varian took the companion armchair, and Grant arranged himself in the window seat, kicking off his shoes and exchanging them for a pair of blue Moroccan slippers. At his right hand lay a stack of volumes of nineteenth-century verse, and beside them a leatherbound notebook. Varian understood that this was his pet place in the room, his accustomed seat. And did it bother him, could it really bother him, that Elliott Grant felt so comfortable here in his colleague's home? Grant had chosen to live the past twelve years of his life in places that bore no reference to Varian. He had had his reasons for it, and those reasons hadn't changed.

Professor Katznelson leaned forward to pour the coffee, or whatever it might have been; the liquid in Varian's cup had an amber tinge and smelled faintly of charcoal. Katznelson apologized for the lack of sugar, saying he'd already spent his ration.

"I don't take it anyway," Varian said.

Katznelson turned to Grant and said a few rapid words in German; it wasn't the first time a German speaker assumed he wouldn't understand. **You did say he took it unadorned,** was what he'd said. But he'd used the word **ungeschmückt,** which could also mean **naked.** Grant nodded and turned his attention to his coffee cup, stirring it with a tiny spoon.

"Your friend tells me you're in the business of rescues," Katznelson said, in English now. "As it happens, I am in need of one."

"Why don't you tell me the whole story," Varian said. "From the beginning."

Katznelson raised his eyes to Varian's, narrowing them slightly, as if in distrust. "It will not be very interesting to you, I imagine."

"You've got nothing to fear from me. Mr. Grant has vetted me thoroughly. And he's known me a long time."

"So I understand," Katznelson said. He curled his fingers around the ends of his armrests and took a breath. "I will tell my story, then. Mr. Grant will interrupt if there is something I've forgotten." He shifted in his seat, crossing his legs at the knee; his cuff retracted to reveal a diamond-patterned sock. "As you know, my field of study is European political history. I've been a member of the faculty at Columbia for some six years now, but I returned to Europe this summer on personal business."

"After the occupation?" Varian said.

"Yes, after. The business was urgent."

"It would have to be."

"I failed to comprehend the danger, I'm afraid. I am not a naturalized American citizen, but I thought my American papers would protect me. I've since found out they will not. I am stateless, you see, a former German. I would have done well to take Professor Grant's advice and remain in the

States. He did offer to come in my stead." He and Grant exchanged a weighted look, as if this were a subject they'd discussed many times; then he drew a long breath. "Even if I were not a Jew, my academic work would displease the Nazis. I knew it when I lived in Berlin, I have known it for years. My specific subject is the rise of socialism in European nations. American scholars are quite interested in this work just now. Nazis, too, but for different reasons. They would like to see me made an example of to German scholars."

"I see," Varian said. "But you must have known that before you came back. Why would you do that, Professor? If you don't mind the question."

Another look passed between Katznelson and Grant. "As I said, I had personal matters to arrange," Katznelson said.

"You understand, I've got to know if you've had your hand in anything illegal. Not to put it too bluntly. And not that I'd fault you for it, under the current political circumstances."

"Nothing like that," Grant said, quickly. Varian tried to meet his eye, to read his tone, but Grant had lowered his gaze to his cup again.

"I have not yet concluded my business here," Katznelson said. "But I've come to understand that I must leave the country as soon as I can. Three former colleagues of mine were apprehended in Nîmes last week. I'm sure the authorities know my whereabouts."

"Yes, that's likely," Varian said.

"What is your counsel, then, Mr. Fry? Do you think you can help?"

"This is precisely what we do, Professor. We've gotten our clients passports and visas under circumstances more precarious than yours. I've got a colleague who's been conducting my people into Spain, and if he can't get you through by rail, he knows how to get you over the mountains."

"And how many of your clients have been apprehended? How many have been imprisoned for breaking the law?"

"None so far."

"I insist upon having a valid U.S. visa," Katznelson said. "I'll not risk being stranded somewhere en route."

"With your position at the university, you'll have a fighting chance. My friend Harry Bingham at the consulate will know more."

"Professor Grant has already been to the consulate," Katznelson said curtly, uncrossing his legs and resting his long arms on his knees. His hands, laced between them, looked like the hands of a man accustomed to hard work, not like those of an academic; Varian had a sudden vision of those sinewed fingers working at Grant's collar, his cuffs. "He spoke to Fullerton, the consul," Katznelson went on. "He says it's out of the question. As a young man, I was editor of the **People's Collective.** A communist newspaper in Berlin. How the consulate obtained this information is unknown to me. Nonetheless, it is a barrier. And then there's the matter of my religion. I've spent enough time in America by now to know its prejudices."

"There are challenges," Varian said. "The political climate makes it hard. There's a lot of mistrust, as you know. But your case is far from hopeless."

"You see, Gregor, that's just what I told you," Grant said.

"I'll need to ask a few more questions," Varian said. "Tomorrow I'll pay a visit to the consulate. Our friend Bingham doesn't care much what Hugh Fullerton thinks. He follows his own agenda, which is, generally speaking, friendly to ours. It may take a while, but I think we can get you your visa."

A cloud seemed to have descended over Katznelson; his powerful shoulders curled inward. He spoke again to Grant in German: **In the meantime we'll keep looking for him.**

We'll talk about it later, Grant said in reply, also in German, and without a glance at Varian; he knew Varian spoke the language as fluently as he did himself.

"Let's begin, then," Varian said, and took a small notebook from his pocket. He licked the tip of his pencil and began to question Katznelson, reminding himself that Katznelson was, in the end, just a client; that his association with Grant, whatever its nature, mattered not at all; that Varian's only concern was to get his clients off the continent. They talked for half an hour, Varian taking notes, Grant occasionally finishing a sentence when Katznelson hesitated, interposing some elaboration or minor correction, or supplying a place-name or an address, as if every detail of Katznelson's life was known to him. Once, as Grant leaned forward to ask a question, he touched Katznelson briefly upon the ankle, one slender fingertip on that diamond-patterned sock. Varian forced his attention back to the interview itself; Katznelson was giving a detail about his wife—he had a wife!—who had remained behind in Berlin. Her elderly parents lived with her, he said, and she would not think of abandoning them to join him in New York.

When he had finished the interview, Varian tucked his notebook away and explained that he had to get back to town for another meeting. Katznelson stood to shake Varian's hand, casting a long blue shadow over the marine-colored rug. He asked Varian to be in contact as soon as he had any news at all. Then Grant walked Varian back through the dark gaslit corridors of the house, back through that strange echoing entryway with its hexagonal staircase and its high narrow windows, and opened the door onto the dust-hazed afternoon.

"Thanks for coming all this way," Grant said. "I could never have persuaded Gregor to come see you in town."

Gregor. In the soft roll of those consonants, a history, a present.

"Of course," Varian said.

"Oh, Tom, I nearly forgot," Grant said, and disappeared into the house. A moment later he reemerged with two orange persimmons. "These are for you," he said, and slipped their cool smooth weight into Varian's hands, a gesture so intimate it was a long moment before Varian could speak.

"I never thanked you," Varian said. "For the figs, I mean. Yesterday."

"Yes," Grant said, his dark eyebrows drawn together. "I saw them in the marketplace in town, and . . ." He shrugged.

"Well, thank you," Varian said. "They were—still warm when I got them. I ate them all in one sitting. I exercised no restraint." He smiled, but found it impossible to raise his eyes to Grant's.

Grant shook his head. "Same old Varian. Go on, now. You'd better catch your train."

"Right," Varian said, but he made no move to leave. Grant gave him the swiftest smile, and in an instant they were back at school, in the doorway of Grant's room late at night, and he was doing just this—what Grant had pointed out, affectionately, that he did. **Lingering.** Now here again, on the threshold of this villa, twelve years later in the South of France. For God's sake. Had he lost his mind? Without another word, he turned on his heel and marched down the drive, toward the station, knowing Grant was watching him walk away.

5

Rue Grignan

From the Canebière it took him not five minutes to reach the address on the matchbook. 60 rue Grignan: a biscuit-colored nineteenth-century building with a men's clothier on the street level, three floors of offices above, white shutters splayed in the southern light. Above the main doorway was an iron railing worked into the shape of two ancient oil lamps, between them an oval encircling an intertwined R and J. Marseille was full of these little architectural mysteries, coded keys to the city's secret life.

On the doorstep stood Miriam Davenport, having come to give her professional opinion. And she was not alone. Another woman stood beside her, athletic-looking, smoking a slender cigarette, her hair a blond halo, her skin burnished bronze. She worked the edge of the curb with the toe of her high green snakeskin sandal; she seemed almost to be cultivating a grudge against it. In a close-fitting afternoon dress of viridescent silk, the sun illuminating her corona of chaff-colored curls, she looked like nothing so much as a young Apollo in drag. And where had he seen her before, in what movie or magazine?

Miriam introduced her friend as Mary Jayne, and Varian shook her hand, still wondering. Mary Jayne had a fierce handshake, an adventurer's, not at all what he would have expected from someone in those shoes, smoking that kind of cigarette. And then he knew where he'd last seen her: in the society pages, thanks to the **Times**'s foreign social correspondent, cavorting on a beach in Monaco at a season when everyone back home was muffled up in furs and woolens. Mary Jayne Gold: a mildly famous Chicago socialite who had spent much of the past three years flying her Percival Vega Gull from one spangled playground to another. At the start of the war, the rumor went, she'd donated the plane to the French air force, and no one knew whether the Axis or the Allies had it now.

"Mary Jayne's here to help us inspect the office," Miriam said, linking her arm with her friend's.

"What can have induced you?" Varian asked Mary Jayne. "It's not much of a way to spend an afternoon." In fact, he found her presence a mild annoyance; he and Miriam had business to conduct, and they didn't need an accessory debutante, not even one with a handshake like that.

"Miss Davenport induced me," said Mary Jayne. "You'd be surprised what she can get me to do."

Miriam replied with her trumpetlike laugh. "Actually, Varian, I wanted you to meet Mary Jayne. She's a bit of a legend. And I thought she might help us."

"I **am** a legend. Don't say that lightly."

"I never would, Emjay."

"And maybe I **can** be of help, Mr. Fry." She pushed an Apollonian curl behind her ear and tapped her ash onto the pavement.

"How, exactly?"

"I'm good at convincing people, if they need convincing. And I can pay them, too, if there's paying to be done."

"There may be that," Varian conceded.

"Anyway, I'm here, so you'd better have me," she said, and Varian found it impossible to argue. They rang the bell and waited. A moment later the door opened to reveal a blond gamine in a pink-stained pinafore, the heiress (apparent) of the concierge, one guilty raspberry still held between her fingers. She stared openly at Mary Jayne and Miriam, then pointed them all across the terra-cotta-tiled entryway to a winding stair.

On the second floor stood their host, Monsieur Moreau—mustachioed, compact, a pair of dark-rimmed specs winging the apex of his nose. He ushered them up the stairs and through a pair of tall red doors, into a high-ceilinged room cluttered with wooden packing crates of pocketbooks and belts, briefcases and valises. Beneath the dusky scent of leather was the smell of black-market coffee trafficked from Cameroon. They sat down in a corner near a tidy desk, where logbooks were spread on a leather blotter and the coffee service sat nearby on a trim blue table. Moreau was clearly proud of his coffee service and the contents of the pot; he poured off three tiny cups and handed them around.

"I trust Monsieur Hirschman has explained to you my situation," he began in hesitant English. "I prepare to emigrate to South America, near my trade partners. My papers have arrived"—and he gave Varian a wink—"both **vrai** and **faux.** A friend will sell my goods and wire the money to Lisbon. From there I go to Argentina—or at least, this is how I plan. I depart next Tuesday. But we have still four months' lease. And Monsieur Hirschman tells me you seek an office."

"Well, I wouldn't say I was seeking one, exactly. But Hirschman disagrees."

"**Il joue l'entremetteur,** as we say."

"He's a good matchmaker, if the price is right."

"We have already paid to the end of the lease. Nothing more is necessary to pay. Afterward, you will arrange with the owner. You will find him to be a reasonable man."

Mary Jayne Gold squinted at Moreau. "Are you saying you'll just **give** him the place for four months, free?"

Moreau shrugged. "If he pays me, how can I carry so many thousand francs out of France? I have paid already, it is done. And Monsieur Hirschman has explained your work. In such work, funds are short. Take what I offer, Monsieur Fry. It is not much."

Miriam sent Varian a look, clearly meant to ask whether Moreau was to be trusted. Was it worth wondering whose agent he might be, or why, apart from sheer generosity, he was offering his fully paid **bureau** to the Emergency Rescue Committee? The inhabitants of Marseille were famously pragmatic, its businesspeople shrewd. But there sat Moreau with his hands folded over his knee, his expression one of tranquil satisfaction: the look of a man who's given a gift he knows to be both necessary and apt.

"Let me show you something," Moreau said. "You might find it of interest. It is, I think, a piece of art." He went to the filing cabinet and removed a cardboard dossier, then sat down again and unwound the red string from its circular clasp. He extracted a set of crisp documents: a Vichy identity card, stamped with the official Commissariat de Police stamp and French exit visa; and transit papers stamped with Spanish, Portuguese, and Argentine entry visas. "Now you tell me, Monsieur Fry," he said, grinning with pleasure as he pushed the papers toward Varian. "Which is real, and which is false?"

Varian glanced from Miriam to Mary Jayne, then at the documents, their sharply creased corners, their neat stamps. "You'd be wise not to wave these around, Monsieur Moreau, in front of people you've just met."

"Monsieur Fry! I trust you absolutely. Monsieur Hirschman explained all."

Varian hoped Hirschman hadn't explained quite **all;** he wondered how many drinks he'd had with Moreau at the Dorade. Now Miriam and Mary Jayne were looking at the documents too, and then at Varian, for a verdict.

"Alors?" said Moreau. **"Vrai ou faux?"**

Trying to keep his expression impassive, Varian squinted at the documents, scrutinizing the forms and their seals. The papers were thick, official-feeling, rich with cotton; the lettering on the stamps was perfect, nothing to suggest the irregular movement of a pen or brush in a human hand. There was none of the blurring of forgery; nothing he recognized from the refugees' growing catalogue of clumsy fake papers. Finally he pushed the documents back toward Moreau. "None of them are false," he said. "Or all of them. If you've got a forger, he's an awfully good one."

Moreau collected the papers again. "All false," he said, with obvious delight. "Even the Commissariat stamp."

"Bravo!" said Miriam. "Brilliant. Where did you get them?"

"There is a man called Freier, an artist of cartoons, from Vienna. He is **elusif,** as you might imagine. He moves about. But if you can find him, he will charge a fair price. What one needs, he can produce."

"I know Freier's work," Miriam said. "He lived in Paris for a while, published his cartoons in the left-ist papers there. I heard he was arrested and sent to Vernet. Are you saying he's here in town, Monsieur Moreau? Did he do this work recently?"

"Yes, mademoiselle, just this week."

Miriam glanced at Varian.

"Our work is all aboveboard, Miss Davenport," Varian said, "as I ought to have made clear. We can't go breaking the law while we're guests of France."

"Of course not," Miriam said. "Unless you actually want to get your clients out."

Moreau laughed. "Miss Davenport is your associate, Monsieur Fry?"

Varian glanced at Miriam. "I've only just hired her. Let's say she's still on probation."

"You must take her advice," Moreau said. "She is wise already in these matters."

Miriam laughed with pleasure. Mary Jayne sent her friend a look of unguarded appreciation, then leaned forward across the desk, tapping Moreau's leather blotter with her manicured finger. On her wrist was a narrow bracelet of diamond baguettes punctuated by sapphires, a piece that meant to communicate, without vulgarity or equivocation, the superfluity of the wearer's wealth.

"I know some people who can help you between

here and Lisbon, Monsieur Moreau," she said. "Consider it my thanks for your being so generous about the **bureau.**"

"Ah, Miss Gold, I would be most grateful."

"There's a certain Madame Simplon, a friend of mine who used to run a salon in Paris. She has a house at Montpellier. I'll send her a note. And once you reach Madrid, you must see my old friend Guillermo Rosecrans at this address." She pulled a small green leather address book from her bag, copied out an address onto a blank page, and handed the page to Moreau.

He bowed again in gratitude. "And you are certain the **bureau** will suit?"

"Perfectly," Varian said.

"Ah, **bon**!" said Moreau. He reached for the coffeepot and poured off another round of Cameroonian brew, and as they drank, they talked about the details: when Varian and his associates might move in, whom to see about the utilities, how to manage the recalcitrant concierge. They agreed upon a date, Wednesday of the following week, when the ERC might commence business on the rue Grignan, and then they stood, bowed, expressed their mutual delight with the agreement, and wished each other luck. Varian followed Miriam and Mary Jayne down the stairs, where, in the foyer of the building, they found the bare-legged daughter of the concierge playing jacks in a rhombus of sun. As they passed, she looked up and caught her red ball between the V of two fingers, as if she might smoke it or scissor it in half.

"Mesdames et monsieur," she said, "good day and God protect you." And then she bounced the ball and made a handful of jacks vanish into thin air.

"God protect **you,** mademoiselle," Miriam said, with a bow so low she might have been making reverence to an empress. The girl gave Miriam a nod of acknowledgment—**you may rise**—and gestured toward the courtyard door.

Miriam walked out laughing into the midday light. "The situation will do fine, Varian, if your refugees can get past that little gatekeeper."

"She's formidable, but perhaps she's just what we need."

"Well, then," Mary Jayne said, threading her arm through Miriam's. "Now that's done, let's have ourselves a drink."

"Oh, no," Miriam said. "I have to get back to the Splendide. Mehring will be expecting me. He's still in a state of shock from the move. And then there's work to be done. I've got a job now, Emjay."

"Oh, bother," Mary Jayne said. "Jobs!"

"But I've made us a dinner date at nine," Miriam went on, as if Varian weren't there. "A couple of Legionnaires. I hope you don't mind."

"Legionnaires! You didn't mention that earlier."

"I've only just thought to tell you."

"Splendid," said Mary Jayne. "I'll conduct myself to a bar in the meantime." To Varian she said, "I hope we'll meet again soon. It's been a pleasure."

"I still think, Miss Gold, that it must have been a terrific bore."

"Not at all!" She shook hands again with Varian, kissed Miriam twice, and went off toward the Canebière, her green snakeskin heels clicking against the cobbles.

"Well," Varian said. "Mary Jayne Gold!"

"Isn't she something? I adore her."

"She's something, all right. But you'll kindly let me know in future when you're planning to bring a friend along on official business."

"Mary Jayne **is** official business," Miriam said, stopping to fix Varian in her hard gaze. "I didn't bring her along just for fun."

"She strikes me as something of a dilettante."

"She's not," Miriam said, bluntly. "She's quite passionate about your cause, and means to help. I've told her all about it."

"And that's another thing," Varian said. "When it comes to our cause, you might exercise a little more discretion. Assume we're being watched at all times. The less you discuss our work around town, the better."

Miriam walked onward, carrying the coronet of her braids with a proud uptilt, refusing to meet Varian's eye. When they stopped on the curb of the

Canebière to let the traffic pass, she inclined her head as if in thought. Finally she spoke, with measured deliberation.

"If you employ me, Mr. Fry," she said, "you'll have to trust me. As a woman abroad—in charge of my own fate for years now, let me add—I know something about exercising discretion. Also a little something about calculated risk."

At the Splendide, refugees waited in an unbroken line from the bottom of the stairs all the way to Varian's room. But Hirschman and Lena were alone in 307, Hirschman perched on the dressing table and fiddling with the inner workings of the Contin, Lena standing before him, twisting her hands in anxiety. Apparently one of Lena's turquoise drop earrings had fallen into the depths of the machine; while Hirschman fished around for it, all activity of the Emergency Rescue Committee had ceased. Lena gave Varian a single anxious glance, and he had a moment's curiosity about what she and Hirschman might have been doing to cause her earring to fall into the typewriter. When Hirschman surfaced with the blue droplet, Lena clapped her hands with unfiltered joy.

"**Mon héros!**" she cried. "**Ich bin so dankbar!**" And then to Varian and Miriam: "**Hélas,** we have wasted so much time!"

"You and Miriam call the next clients," Varian said. "I'd like to confer with Mr. Hirschman."

Lena nodded, and Varian beckoned Hirschman into the bathroom and turned on all the taps.

"What is it?" Hirschman said, squinting to read Varian's expression.

"I've just seen the work of the most astonishing forger," Varian said. "He makes a Préfecture stamp that's indistinguishable from the real thing."

"Where?"

"Moreau's. The man made him a full set of documents. He pulled them all out, right there in front of Miss Davenport and another friend, unfortunately. But it was perfect work. We've got to have him. Can you track him down? Moreau says he's elusive. I couldn't grill him for details under the circumstances, but perhaps you could pay him a visit this evening. I want his work for a new client of ours."

"What client?"

"A special one. Friend of a friend. A Columbia University professor, German-born, who came back to Europe last summer and got stranded."

"Why would anyone be so foolish?"

Varian shook his head. "He refuses to say. But now he's got to get out, or he'll be deported for certain. And I'm not sure I'll be able to get real papers and visas for him before the axe falls."

"I see. And do we know anything more about the talented forger?"

"Bill Freier. Viennese, lived in Paris for a time. Imprisoned in Vernet, and somehow got out. Miriam knows his work. Maybe he needs to get out of France, too."

Hirschman made a series of notes. "If he can be found, I'll find him."

"Moreau's office will do nicely, by the way. And for the moment, he's giving it to us gratis. You're a smooth operator, Albert."

Hirschman blushed with pleasure. "I'm delighted, really."

"Not half as much as I am."

"I've got news too," Hirschman said. "About the money." He smoothed his hair with one hand, a gesture of quiet pride, then began to explain: Last night, after his drink with Betty, they'd run into a friend of hers, a Corsican black marketeer called Malandri. One of the good guys, this Malandri—hated the Nazis, had been using his underworld connections to get refugees out. When Hirschman mentioned their money problem, Malandri told Hirschman he must go directly to Vinciléoni, proprietor of the Dorade. He'd done so at once, and Vinciléoni had told him he needed Kourillo.

Varian frowned. "What's Kourillo?"

"Not what, who. A certain White Russian émigré, formerly an aristocrat, who made his living in Paris for a time at the American Express office. Learned a few tricks there, it would seem. Vinciléoni finds him quite useful."

"For what purpose?"

"He helps people get scads of money out of France."

"Oh? Say more."

"Kourillo's clients are émigrés too. Rich ones. So rich, some of them, they can't get all their money out legally. So he's always looking to set up a foreign exchange. Particularly with parties in the States."

"Forgive me, Albert, I'm not entirely following."

"Vinciléoni proposed a mutually beneficial system. Kourillo tells us how much his client wants to export. We direct the ERC to wire that amount into a U.S. bank account in his client's name. Then, once we have proof of the transfer, Kourillo turns his client's francs over to us."

Varian laughed aloud. "The ERC wires the money first? What's to keep Kourillo's client from disappearing with his francs, once the money's safe in the American account?"

"Vinciléoni has dangerous friends. And he gets a cut of the deal. If one of Kourillo's clients misbehaves, it's the end of him."

"Kourillo takes a piece of the profits too, of course."

"Yes. And I'll take the third."

"You, Albert?"

Hirschman smiled again. "I had to say I would. Kourillo and Vinciléoni would never have trusted me otherwise. But my cut goes back to the ERC, of course."

Varian shook his head. "Sounds like a racket, all of it."

"Maybe. But at the moment, it's what we've got. And we need to turn our dollars into francs. They're useless otherwise."

Varian wanted to believe it could work; they were badly in need of a solution. But he didn't have any way to judge the risk, no way to know whether he might be setting them all up for a long stint in French prison. "How about a test run?" he said. "Start small. See if we can trust this Kourillo. If it works, we'll try again with more."

Hirschman nodded. "When shall I put it in motion?"

"At once," Varian said.

Hôtel Splendide
Marseille, France

9 September 1940

Dear Eileen, dear Eileen.

The poor desk clerk must be so tired of my pestering. Is there a letter, a cable, anything at all for Varian Fry from New York City? Some indication that my messages have been reaching Manhattan? Are you there still, Eileen Fry, thousands of miles away on Irving Place, in our little apartment with a poet's view of half a tree and six garbage cans?

I must ask, dear E, how you would feel about my staying here a while longer. It would mean we couldn't start a lease on a new house before the first of the year (though the properties you mentioned in your last letter all sound fine, particularly that old stone house with garden in Woodcliff Lake). I've got a few new projects I can't abandon. And though I long to tell the ERC to find someone to replace me, I'd have to spend time training whoever came. At the moment I can't foresee returning to New York before late October or early November. I feel I **must** stay, at least until I can be sure that what I've created will go forward.

Though the American Consulate would rather I be gone, I assure you I'm not making too great a nuisance of myself here in France. Soon I'll cease even to try the patience of the Hôtel Splendide, as next week our operation moves to a proper office on the rue Grignan. We'll be known as the Centre Américain de Secours, and we'll all have room to stretch without fear of braining one another. (Though I'll retain my room here at the Splendide to sleep in, insofar as I ever sleep—so please use this address for correspondence.)

And now I must tell you a funny thing: Do

you remember my old friend Grant from the **Hound and Horn,** that long-legged fellow we used to call Skiff? The one—you must remember—who declined to come with us that night when we went sailing in Ardmore's boat, up in Maine on Blue Hill Bay? You called him a wet blanket and I daresay you were right—though I was awfully glad when he turned up a few days ago here in Marseille. Now Skiff's become a professor of English at Columbia and is on sabbatical at a colleague's home, though I believe he and the colleague will soon be departing for points west.

And finally, speaking of the **Hound and Horn,** one of my refugee clients showed up this afternoon clutching a copy. And what did I find inside (apart from traces of my own **sanguinem, sudorem, et lacrimas**)? That lovely bit from Cummings, the one I stole for a Valentine's card for you:—Let's then / despise what is not courage my / darling (for only Nobody knows / where truth grows why / birds fly and / especially who the moon is

V.

6

Montredon

Posting a letter to Eileen always felt a little like heaving a bottled message into the sea. No idea if or when it would reach her. And it if did, how would he want her to reply? Did he want, as he claimed, for her to grant him license to stay in Marseille until he'd discharged his duties? Or did he want her to call him back to New York, to tell him that they must take the stone house with garden at once? In the course of her daily life—the classes she taught at Brearley, the literary salons she attended, her work for the New York office of the Emergency Rescue Committee, her various rendezvous with friends—how often did she even think of him? For years before they'd met, she'd conducted a fully formed life in Boston. She was eight years older than he was, a deputy editor at **The Atlantic Monthly;** his initial role in her life had been that of an intellectual apprentice, a literary acolyte. **My protégé,** she'd called him, and not always in jest. Of course, things had quickly become more complicated between them; Eileen could be fiercely self-critical, vulnerable to any slight to her intelligence, jealous of Varian's friends. But they'd been together now for more than a decade. When Varian had embarked on this mission to Marseille, intending to be gone a month, it had hardly occurred to him to consider the state of their marriage. They both saw the opportunity as a grand adventure, possible only because the Foreign Policy Association had been willing to grant Varian a leave. Had Eileen's fall semester not been about to start, she might have joined him. She would likely, he realized, have been running the show here, and doing a better job of it. But now that his stay had stretched into its sixth week, he could only wonder what she thought and how she felt. Her letters came seemingly at random, and had thus far contained only light-toned news of her work back home and expressions of concern for his safety. He would cable her tonight, he told himself. Not for any reason in particular, certainly not for any reason concerning Grant. Only to be a little wasteful for the sake of romance.

He caught the streetcar on the Canebière and rode it west, then south; he was going to visit Harry Bingham at the visa division of the American Consulate, in a white villa in the cliffside suburb of

Montredon. The division was located at an inconvenient distance from the center of town, up a linden-lined drive that was hell to climb in any weather and nearly always cross-blown by a seaward wind that pulled one's clothes sideways, made a wild nest of one's hair, and stung one's eyes with salt and dust and whatever else happened to be flying through the atmosphere that day. It took nearly an hour to get there; per usual, he arrived at the doors of the visa division in a state of disarray, resenting the consulate in general, the visa division in particular, and whomever he might encounter first beyond its stout oak doors. Today it was the tall American guard whose incongruously excellent French must have given false hope to the applicants. Varian gave his name and told the guard he had an appointment to see Bingham. The guard thumbed him into the usual waiting room, where Varian stood at the window and watched the palm trees flip their headdresses toward the bay.

He had a vivid memory of his first meeting with Bingham—not here in Marseille, but years ago, at Harvard. One afternoon, as he'd been riding home on his bicycle in the rain, he'd veered onto Bow Street, slipped on the uneven cobbles, and skidded onto his side. Bruised and stunned, he lay facing a fleet of oncoming cars. A young man in glasses and a Burberry coat flung his books to the wet curb and rushed to Varian, stopping traffic with an upraised hand. He hauled Varian to his feet, brushed him off, straightened his jacket, and restored his fallen bag to his shoulder.

"Okay now?" he'd asked, curtly.

"Okay," Varian said, his insides knotted; but something about the young man's uplifted face, his angled chin, made Varian feel he had to take hold of himself and be okay. The man looked like the dashing sea captain in a book Varian had loved as a child, **The Adventures of the Tramontana:** a picture of a storm-canted ship on the cover, young Captain Daunt straining against the wheel.

"Who do I have to thank?" Varian asked, and coughed. "Whom?"

The young man offered his name card, then touched his cap and went off down Bow Street. Varian glanced at the card. Hiram Bingham IV. Son of the famous Yale professor who'd discovered Machu Picchu. Varian wanted to call after him, wanted to ask what it felt like to have been born with an identity intact, into a family whose scions might expect to live lives of grand adventure.

Now here was Hiram Bingham IV again at Varian's service, appearing at the door of his office, ushering Varian inside. Harry still wore the same small round glasses, still had the same sharp-cut jaw, the same uptilted expression; he managed always to give his interlocutor the impression of absolute unbroken attention. His office must have once been an extravagant library: the polished oak shelves, nearly empty now, had obviously been intended for a large leatherbound collection of French classics, and the bow window behind the desk deluged the room with reading light. Varian took his usual seat. Bingham settled himself behind the desk in a high-backed chair, flanked by the American flag on one side and the consular banner on the other.

"You're looking well, Varian. Like you got some sun."

"You too, Harry. And how's Golo?" Thomas Mann's son, who'd been liberated from the concentration camp at Les Milles, had by now been hiding out at Bingham's villa for a month.

"Better. Eager to get off the continent. And what's the news from your side?"

Varian lowered his voice. Bingham had assured him that the office wasn't bugged—he checked it himself every morning—but one couldn't be overcautious. "Another group got away without a hitch," he said. "My friend Leon Ball has a route over the foothills and around the Spanish checkpoint."

"Yes, I've heard. But don't you think we'd better try to get the Manns through on the train?"

"Of course. But if we can't, there's a back door."

"And what about the passport situation?"

"We've got a couple of new connections, thanks to Hirschman."

"That's good news. I know those fake Czech passports couldn't have held out long."

"And the American visas for the Werfels?"

"All in place now," Bingham said. "Not that they were easy to come by. Fullerton is no help whatsoever. And he's none too fond of you, either. You'll have to keep your operation quiet if you don't want to get any farther on his bad side."

"Listen, Harry. He didn't happen to mention a German visa applicant by the name of Katznelson, did he?"

Bingham's eyebrows came together. "I don't think so. Why?"

"A friend of mine came here earlier—last week, I believe—inquiring on his behalf. I spoke to the client himself yesterday. It's an interesting case."

"Haven't heard of it. What's the story?"

Varian explained, and Bingham laced his hands, tilting his chin toward the flag. "How badly does Columbia want this fellow back?"

"I don't know. He's rather well regarded in his field."

"Fullerton's a friend of Nick Butler, president at Columbia. I don't know why Nick would tolerate Fullerton at his dinner table, but he does, with some regularity, if Hugh is to be believed—anyway, his name came up a time or two among Hugh's social boasts. If Butler put a little pressure on him, Fullerton might grant the visa."

"There's another complication, I'm afraid. Katznelson used to edit a communist rag in Berlin. Long time ago, student days."

"Bad luck for him. But not insurmountable."

"All right, Harry. Thanks. I'll cable Butler this afternoon."

"Good. What else does the client need? Funds?"

"He's got plenty of his own, it would seem. A French exit visa might be nice, if I could get one without worrying that I'll be tipping off Vichy to his whereabouts."

"There's an inspector at the Préfecture, Robinet—maybe I mentioned him to you before. I had a drink with him last night. He's the man you want. French patriot of the old school, horrified by Pétain. He'll put you in touch with the right person in the visa office. As for the Spanish visas, the consulate may or may not be granting them today. And the border guard may or may not honor them once your man gets there."

"Yes. And then we'd have to rely on the mountain route."

"Well, at the moment, the border's rather permeable. If you can get an answer from Butler with some speed, and if the Préfecture cooperates, you might be able to get your professor out within the next few weeks."

Varian nodded. "You don't think—could we make it happen in time to append him to the Werfels and the Manns?"

"Send them all through Cerbère together? Why not? That way you'd be there if anything went wrong."

The plan had always been for Varian to accompany

the sensitive group; he had to go to Lisbon anyway, to send uncensored mail and cultivate a few contacts there. It hadn't occurred to him until that moment that he might be able to get Katznelson out among those clients, that he himself might accompany Katznelson and Grant on the train. The thought of being able to bring that piece of news to Grant gave him an unreasonable thrill.

"And what about the Chagalls?" Bingham asked now. "Did you see them at Gordes?"

"God, yes," he said. How had it not been foremost on his mind? "They won't hear of my making an official appeal on their behalf. But perhaps, if you can do it under the radar, you could make a few inquiries. Or if you're inclined, drop them a note. They could use some convincing. Maybe a gentle scare. They're under the impression that Chagall's reputation will get them through anything."

Bingham sighed. "How many others are thinking the same thing? You can't blame them, of course. Not that long ago, France was to them what America is to all these others." He gestured toward the window, through which they could see a segment of the queue of refugees as it made its way down the linden-lined drive. "I'll do my worst," he said. "And in the meantime, let's hope they come to their senses."

———

Varian dispatched the cable to Butler that afternoon: PROFESSOR G KATZNELSON IN VISA TROUBLE IN FRANCE STOP. CABLE FULLERTON AMERICAN CONSULATE MARSEILLE EVIDENCE OF KATZNELSON'S EMPLOYMENT. CONFIRM COLUMBIA FULL SPONSORSHIP STOP. THANKS FRY EMERGENCY RESCUE COMMITTEE MARSEILLE. Then he walked at speed back to the hotel and went upstairs—not to his own room, where Lena and Hirschman were interviewing clients, but to another down the hall, the one that now housed the poet Walter Mehring.

His knock at the door brought not Mehring but Miriam, businesslike and high-spirited, in librarianesque gray slacks and a correct little sweater that might have been prudish if not for the keyhole at its neckline. She stood with one foot against the doorframe, clipboard in hand, having just taken down a list of Mehring's immediate needs. Mehring himself lay in bed in his pajamas, his hair an electrified cloud. Around him lay a tumult of items: intimate articles of men's clothing, chewed-looking notebooks, a pearl-backed hairbrush missing half its bristles, the remains of breakfast on a Splendide tray, and, divided neatly into its various sections, the European edition of **The New York Times.** He held the front page in his hands, regarding it with dismay.

"Oh, Mr. Fry, here you are," he said, and rustled the paper at Varian. "Look at this. **Nazis Demand**

Fifty-Eight Percent of Agricultural Yield of France. Fifty-eight! Already there's nothing to eat in this country. And then there's this." He turned a few pages. "The U.S. can't seem to locate a hundred and thirty bombers it loaned to France before the Armistice. They've been searching for them since June. You can be sure the French aren't giving them up, wherever they are."

"Mr. Mehring," Varian said. "You're looking well this morning. Sleeping better now, I hope?"

Mehring seemed really to see Varian for the first time; he laid his section of the paper down and scrutinized him from head to toe. Then he glanced toward the door of his hotel room, beyond which the voices of refugees made an anxious percussive music.

"I thought I heard Nazi officers in the corridor last night," he said. "Am I losing my mind?"

"Not at all. There are a few officers here—just down the hall, I believe."

Mehring turned a shade paler and looked at Miriam. "You didn't mention that, Miss Davenport. You said it was safe here."

Miriam shrugged. "There were Nazis at the Royale, too, but I never mentioned that to you either. What would have been the point?"

"To keep me properly afraid! Fear is my food. It keeps me alive."

"And too much of it can make you sick."

"Ah, well said, Miss Davenport. Now, won't you

sit down, Mr. Fry, and talk to me a little about my escape plans? I'm eager to get out, as you may imagine." As Varian pulled a desk chair to the bedside, Mehring tore open a pack of Reines and selected a half-crushed smoke.

"Your escape is going to be something of a challenge," Varian said, lacing his fingers over his knee. "I understand you'd like to travel under an assumed name, and that you have a false Czech passport already."

"Yes. Do you think it'll do?"

"Hard to say. I think we've used too many of those Czech passports lately."

"But they've worked, have they not?"

"Yes, but you never know whether they'll work the next time. We have some new Polish passports now, real ones. It wouldn't take me more than a few weeks to get the necessary stamps, perhaps less time if we can find a certain forger who's been doing brilliant work for refugees around town."

"I don't have a few weeks, not with German officers walking the hotel corridors. I must leave at once."

"I don't advise it, Walter. Not when we can send you out more safely if we wait a little longer. Why don't you let Miss Davenport pay a visit to our friend Bingham at the consulate? He'll do what he can to help."

"And what do you suggest I do in the meantime?"

"Gather your strength. Don't read the paper too

much. Write, if you can." He paused, looked at Mehring. "Can you, under these circumstances?"

"With Gestapo officers walking the halls? I'm not sure. A handle of gin might help."

Without a moment's hesitation, Varian picked up the phone and ordered Mehring a bottle of the best gin, charging it to his own room.

"You're too kind, Mr. Fry."

"The Committee is at your service," Varian said. And he nodded to Mehring and Miriam, got to his feet, and slipped out.

The client list was a real thing, not a memorized phantom. It was typed in triplicate on near-transparent paper, the carbons safe in a filing cabinet on the Upper West Side of Manhattan. On his way to Marseille, Varian had carried his own copy in the lining of his valise—not in the lid, where anyone might think to look, but in the suitcase bottom, beneath layers of crisply folded clothes, between the fabric lining and the reinforced leather of the exterior. The list. Those names, assembled in late-night sessions over port and cigarettes at Ingrid Warburg's apartment behind the Museum of Modern Art: they came from letters, from memos, from cocktail-napkin jottings, from phone conversations, from idle rumors, from the badger-holes of memory. Alfred Barr, who had thrown famous parties at Harvard and who had basically invented the Museum of Modern Art, which he now directed, hand-delivered the names of contemporary artists in trouble: Duchamp, Lam, Chagall, Lipchitz, Zilberman, Ernst, Masson. Thomas Mann, writing from California, sent lists of German poets and writers: Mehring, Hertha Pauli, Lion Feuchtwanger, Friedrich Wolf. Jules Romains and Jacques Maritain sent volumes of French literary names. Jan Masaryk, the exiled Czech foreign minister and a personal hero of Varian's, insisted that Franz Werfel make the top of the list, but then the **New York Post** had reported Werfel dead, shot by the Gestapo in Paris. The list was a lacework, many of its artists and writers untraceable. The arguments over its two-hundred-something names had been deafening and vitriolic; the outcome, everyone knew, was a matter of life and death. As he walked home from those sessions, the disputed names ringing in his head, Varian had to remind himself that these were not merely political ciphers, nor scrawled signatures, nor ghostly photographic images; they were human beings, real men and women whose genius placed them at risk, who were in peril, in concentration camps, in hiding, or, worse, living in plain view, ignorant of the threat to their own lives.

Now, when he returned to Room 307, he found himself face-to-face with Werfel himself, who was not, in fact, dead, not having been shot in Paris; on the day the article appeared, Werfel had been sheltering at Lourdes, where he'd landed after a convoluted flight through Biarritz, Bayonne, Hendaye, and St. Jean-de-Luz. He sat now in Varian's spindly chair at the desk, tapping one foot on the carpet. He was compact, wire-haired, clear-eyed, vaguely old-fashioned-looking in his high-collared jacket; grave and calm, he sat holding the hand of his wife, the composer Alma Mahler Gropius Werfel, who perched at the edge of the ottoman in a spotless white suit. They were obviously waiting for Varian, and the look about Werfel's eyes was fierce.

"Well, Franz!" Varian said. "And Mrs. Werfel. A pleasure to see you, though I wasn't expecting you." Varian glanced at Hirschman for information, but Hirschman only widened his eyes and shrugged.

"Is there somewhere we might speak in private, Mr. Fry?"

Varian smiled, glancing around the room. "I'm afraid there's not much privacy to be had around here."

"I must insist," Werfel said, putting a hand to his chest. "I must discuss with you a personal matter. One that concerns our . . . er . . . day in the country." That was the term he used for their imminent escape attempt, always pronounced, to Varian's continual chagrin, with a clipped emphasis and at heightened volume; no one overhearing them could have failed to understand it as anything but code for an illegal emigration.

"Well, it's nearly lunchtime," Varian said. "If you

don't mind my ordering something for us from the room service menu—though, you know, the fare is rather limited here—I can have it delivered and clear the room for a little while."

"Yes, that will suit us," Werfel said.

Varian performed the feat he'd promised, releasing Lena and Hirschman from their duties for an hour. Then he telephoned the café, and the usual grim boy in his too-big jacket delivered a pyramid of sandwiches on day-old baguette, accompanied by a carafe of white Languedoc. Varian distributed the fare and invited Werfel once again to tell him why he was there.

Werfel drained his glass of wine and began to explain. He and Alma had just been conferring with the Manns; they had sat together a long while. In the course of their discussion, Mann had mentioned—and Werfel hoped he'd misunderstood!—that the other clients who had recently crossed the border had traveled not by train but on foot, over treacherous mountain terrain, in the company of an uncertain type, a sort of demi-cowboy named Ball. Was this what Monsieur Fry intended for the Werfels and the Manns? Did not Monsieur Fry understand that he, Werfel, was unfit for an adventure of that sort—that he'd experienced cardiac troubles lately, shortness of breath, disequilibrium? And was Mrs. Werfel, eleven years older than her husband and unaccustomed to strenuous exercise, meant to undertake the same journey?

"With luck, you won't have to take that route," Varian said.

"So we're to rely on luck?"

Alma straightened the lapels of her jacket and inclined her head toward Varian. "Franz exaggerates my fragility, perhaps. But we must consider his own."

"Alma, you insult me," Werfel said.

"Not at all. I protect you."

"And in doing so, you insult me."

"**Lass uns nicht streiten,** Franz." She gave him a stern look, then turned its equivalent on Varian. "My husband must have a doctor along for the journey, Herr Fry. Otherwise, his fate is in your hands."

"We can't bring doctors along," Varian said. "We have to assume that Mr. Werfel's undertaking the trip will be safer for him than staying in France."

"But what good is it to escape if I perish on a mountain path?" Werfel said. "My heart is very weak. I might well write, like Proust, 'Dear Friend, I have nearly died three times since morning.'"

Varian wished Lena were present to say **Il ne faut pas exagérer.** "The path leads over a foothill," Varian said. "Not a strenuous trek. I wouldn't advise you to go if I thought it would cost you your life."

"You are not a doctor, Monsieur Fry."

"You're right, Franz, of course. Well, then, we'll have to have your health certified in advance by someone who knows more about these things than

I do. In any case, we can't leave just yet. Your papers aren't quite in order."

"And when can we expect them to be?" Alma said, still holding Varian's gaze. He could see, or could extrapolate, how she'd managed to fascinate the geniuses who had lived and died for her. Before Werfel she'd been married to the architect Gropius, with whom she had deceived her first husband, the composer; hence her name, a miniature history of her life as a fertile but fickle creative muse.

"We're awaiting only your French exit visas. I expect them imminently. Our friend Harry Bingham at the consulate has put me in touch with a sympathetic person at the Préfecture, someone who might facilitate our contact with the visa office. I'll meet with him tomorrow afternoon. And if that fails, we know of a good forger."

"Excellent," Mrs. Mahler-Werfel said, smoothing her immaculate white skirt. She hadn't touched the sandwiches; Varian had never actually seen her eat. "And in the meantime, we must have Franz's heart examined. That will reassure us all."

"Indeed," Werfel said. "Though no doctor can turn aside the hand of Atropos."

"I'll try to round one up who can," Varian said, and smiled.

And that seemed to satisfy the Werfels, at least for the moment. Alma stood, tucked a slim white calfskin purse beneath her arm, and allowed Werfel to escort her to the door. Watching them cross the room, Alma on her sculpted heels and Werfel unsteady in scuffed brogans, Varian couldn't help wondering whether by leading them toward the border he was ushering them to their doom. But they were doomed here in France, he told himself, just as doomed as the refugees who'd already lost their lives in the camps or along the road. And then he went downstairs to announce that he was open for business again, but the hotel lobby was eerily empty; he learned in short order from the concierge that while Monsieur Fry was having his lunch, all the refugees had been rounded up and hauled off to the Préfecture.

A **rafle.** That was what they called it. It happened periodically and without warning: the Sûreté Nationale would show up at the Splendide and transport everyone to the Evêché, current seat of police power, where their imperfect papers would be scrutinized and they would be threatened with deportation. Then the police would squeeze them for information about the Emergency Rescue Committee and about what exactly Varian the American was doing in Marseille. The refugees had little information that could have been of use to the police. The purpose of these raids, as far as

Varian could tell, was to demonstrate that the police were aware of Varian's doings; also to keep tabs, for Vichy's benefit, on the Nazis' persons of interest. Bingham had told him how it worked: the Marseille police had to give the little gift of information periodically to Vichy, who passed it along to the Nazis, who used it to maintain their lists; they all existed in a strange equilibrium, the French apparently having not yet decided whether they ought to round up all these inconvenient types and hand them over to the occupiers directly, or let them trickle over the border and cease to be a French problem.

The Evêché, called that because it had once been the bishop's palace, was a Baroque confection, overbaked and over-iced; it welcomed visitors through an arched stone entryway crowned with the legend HÔTEL DE POLICE on a lozenge-shaped shield, surmounted by coquilles and flanked by lush fronds of Provençal greenery rendered in bas-relief. The **portail** seemed to suggest a police force characterized by its tenderness and clemency. But at the reception desk he learned that Bingham's friend Robinet was out and could not receive him until tomorrow; without the least hint of tenderness, the officer at the desk suggested that Varian clear out until then. When Varian refused, the officer made a series of grudging telephone calls, then marched him to a walnut-paneled waiting room. Half an hour later, a wizened functionary called Varian's name. He was, he learned, to have an audience with Captain Villand, secretary-general of the Préfecture of the Bouches du Rhône. The functionary led him to a door carved with fleurs-de-lis, where he was received by Villand, a round pink-skinned person in military dress, his Midi French muffled by a winglike white mustache.

"Please explain, Monsieur Fry," began Villand, sitting down at his inlaid mahogany desk. His tone was inquisitive, not unkind, but the look in his eyes was unyielding. "Why it is that so many paperless refugees have been observed to gather outside the doors of your hotel on the boulevard d'Athènes, and what service it is exactly that you're rendering?"

"I represent an American refugee aid organization," Varian said, though of course Villand must have known that by now; on the desk lay a fat dossier labeled with Varian's name. "We provide money, contacts, and visa help. We've got friends at the American consulate."

"The consulate disavows your actions," Villand said, lacing his fingers. "We take note of that sort of thing and draw our own conclusions."

Varian smiled. "I suppose it depends on who you talk to at the consulate."

Captain Villand opened his desk drawer and took out a narrow cigar. He made a show of trimming it with a miniature clipper, then reached for a gleaming brass pineapple whose fronds flipped backward on a hinge to reveal a lighter. Villand seemed to enjoy Varian's observation of his smoking; though he made no move to offer Varian a cigar, there was something intimate in his actions, as though they were relaxing at his club rather than sitting in adversarial positions on either side of his massive desk. "Monsieur Fry," Villand said. "The eye of the French law observes your activities at all times. If I were to receive intelligence that your organization was engaged in contralegal activities, I would have to order you immediately expelled from France. Frankly, I would find that distasteful."

"Fortunately for both of us, there's no reason to expel me."

"And yet," Villand said, drawing and releasing a bolus of smoke, "those who appeal to you for aid always happen to be the refugees whose papers have expired, or who've been imprisoned in concentration camps, or who have been turned back at the border for trying to cross illegally."

"I consider all cases," Varian said. "I have no control over who comes to me."

The captain harrumphed, tapping the ash from his cigar. "We always control the company we keep."

"I'm not keeping company. I'm providing aid to refugees. And if you don't mind my asking respectfully, Captain Villand, I'd greatly appreciate your not hauling them down here for questioning. If there's anything you want to know, I invite you to ask me."

"I'll thank you to let me do my job as I see fit, Monsieur Fry."

"I don't see how it's necessary to frighten nursing mothers and babies, or two-bit painters who've heard that I'm dispensing aid to artists."

"That's sufficient," the captain said, rising from his chair. "You are dismissed from my presence, Monsieur Fry. Consider yourself cautioned."

"And what about my refugees?"

"They've already been released. They were useless, just as you said."

Varian got up before the secretary-general could say more. He quick-stepped across the waiting room, down an echoing hall, and out through the massive front doors. As he walked back to the Splendide, he thought with some pleasure of the brilliant forgery he'd seen at Moreau's shop: all those beautiful visas, and especially the official stamp of the Préfecture of the Bouches du Rhône. He wished he knew the whereabouts of Bill Freier that very moment. He felt a new and urgent desire to defy France in general, and Captain Villand in particular.

At the front desk, the clerk handed him an international cable. He ran upstairs to his room, sat on the bed, and tore open the pale blue envelope.

CAN YOU ESTIMATE PROBABLE DATE YOUR RETURN MY PRIVATE INFORMATION ONLY I MISS YOU COME SOON REPLY IRVING PLACE LOVE EILEEN

He lay back against the narrow pillow, one hand on his chest. How to reply? **Impossible to estimate date of return. Escape operation imminent. Grant quartered with lover nearby. I am exhausted. Confused. Overwhelmed. But still yours faithfully, VARIAN.**

7

On the Vieux Port

The moment his operation moved to the rue Grignan, his room had become an oasis of quiet. The clamor of European languages, the tap and bang of the Contin, the heat of bodies pressed too close together, the tremor of desperation in the air: all had vanished, or had at least become displaced, leaving him the bed with its smooth white skirt, the spindly chair and desk, the block of sun falling through the window, the arpeggios of girls' voices from the school below. In a luxury of solitude he prepared for his afternoon meeting, glad not to have to justify his casual dress, nor his mounting anxiety, nor the decision to ignore pressing responsibilities in order to meet a friend on the Vieux Port. At the thought of it—the thought of Grant traveling that moment by tram, heading in his direction, toward a point at which their paths would intersect—a familiar heat-lightning of shame flashed over him. But this wasn't an errand of pleasure, he reminded himself; this was part of his mission, his work. And as he adjusted his collar in the mirror, smoothed his hair with a damp comb, and resettled his glasses on his nose, he told himself there was nothing to be ashamed of, nothing to apologize for. Even Eileen would have agreed, knowing what she did about Grant, that this was a blameless way to spend an afternoon. He retied his shoelaces and stepped into the corridor. No one was waiting there. The coast, at least in this private corner of Marseille, was clear.

Out on the street he walked with his newspaper under his arm, his mind pinned on a particular conundrum. He had always thought, given enough time, that he could crack any code, unravel any knot, unmaze any maze, master any beast, however venomous or wily. Since childhood he'd lived in an adversarial dance with his own mind, filling it with whatever seemed impossible, daring it to prove him wrong. He'd entered and inhabited the Latin grammar, eaten its conjugations and declensions for breakfast, lunch, and dinner. Having consumed Latin, he turned to Greek, its alphabet a further goad (the tongue-parted teeth of **theta,** diminutive **o-micron** and its elder sister **o-mega,** the pointed fork of **psi** and the birdscratch **xi,** and all the others, who became like old lovers), and then he met and mastered Hebrew, learning, as he did, to appreciate the stark poetry of the Old Testament, its bold declaratives and absolutes, its numerical mysteries and nested meanings. On to German and French, and the derivatives thereof. And then there were the mazements of literature, particularly the modernists, whose efforts to make sense of chaos through language gave rise to other variants of chaos. Most recent evidence: Joyce's new novel, **Finnegans Wake,** wherein, like a fluttering banner, his own name appeared (**To funk is only peternatural its daring feers divine. Bebold! Like Varian's balaying all behind me**). For every problem there was a solution, either within his extant knowledge or within his ability to seek it out. He knew he'd taken on his current mission in France not just for humanitarian reasons, though those were foremost, but also for the thrill of its difficulty.

What troubled him as he walked along the north side of the Vieux Port, toward a boatslip near the rue Henri Tasso, was a problem of a personal nature, the same one that had dogged him since his Harvard days. How was it, he wondered, that a certain human being—for example, a pianist's son from Philadelphia, remarkable perhaps for his own particular talents and intelligences but still, as far as Varian knew, an ordinary human being, one who breathed the same air everyone else breathed, who ate and slept and woke and pissed and shat just like the rest of humankind—how could this person evoke in Varian a series of feelings so uncontrollable as to seem a threat to his sanity? It had been true back then, twelve years ago, when what he'd loved most was to be behind the wheel of his long yellow Packard, in the company of some bright pretty boys and genteelly iconoclastic girls, well supplied with gin, en route to some amusement or other; and it was true of him now at thirty-two, true of the man he'd grown into, whose current mission was to rescue the intellectual treasure of Europe. Under the present circumstances, and considering the weight of responsibility he bore, how could he find himself thrilled like a plucked string at the prospect of meeting Grant at the Vieux Port? Why had it given him so much pleasure to receive Grant's invitation? What could it matter? Why should he care? But he did care; he cared so much he could feel it like a fist beneath his breastbone, crowding the air from his lungs.

It wasn't just the still-fresh shock of Grant's reemergence, not just the pleasure of being able to read the next chapter of a book that had seemed lost overboard years ago. It was something deeper, something permanent, a malady that called itself by Grant's name, as if particles of Grant had passed into Varian's blood and established a colony in his brain. After they'd met in college, it wasn't long before every action Varian undertook seemed to refer to Grant, every decision to matter insofar as it might affect Grant's regard for him. Knowing Grant was vain about his height, for example, Varian fervently wished to stop growing before he became taller than Grant. (He had.) He remembered choosing a striped tie one evening, not a solid blue, because Grant had said in passing that he favored stripes, then the next evening choosing the blue tie over the striped because he was angry at Grant and hadn't wanted to wear what he liked. And hadn't Grant behaved the same way? Hadn't it mattered to him urgently what Varian thought? He knew it had, though the idea was difficult to keep in mind; what Varian felt for Grant seemed to close him in, to make him blind to everything and everyone else, even to Grant himself.

And now that Grant had reappeared, here in France in the midst of a war, Varian's existence had fallen again into the same pattern, the same concern over the smallest things. Take, for example, the care he'd given to his reading that morning at breakfast, not because, he was ashamed to admit, he could yet make heads or tails of Joyce's new novel, but simply for the thrill it gave him to remember the conversations he and Grant had had about **Ulysses** long ago, and to anticipate how they might talk about this longer and stranger work. The coincidence delighted him: for more than a decade, Joyce, in his Paris studio, had worked away at the honeycomb of this novel like a mad bee, packing its stacked hexagons with ideas, feeding them a nectar of words and images distilled from all of literature, flavored with his private pathology, and rendered in a mash of Western tongues; in May of last year the thing had come to light, and now he and Grant had reintersected here in Marseille, as if taught each other's location by the secret language of the text. This was insanity, of course. He wasn't so far gone as to be unable to see it.

The Vieux Port was a knitwork of sailboat masts, their angled guy ropes crosshatching the brilliant steel blue of the water. You could walk almost from one side of the water to the other on the decks of boats. All manner of light craft swayed and kicked on the tide, rendered useless as toys by the new transit rules. Of course, at the Dorade or the other bars where black-marketeer captains made their deals, there were whispered promises of escape by sea; it hadn't taken long for Varian to learn the value of those promises. Not long after he'd arrived, he'd booked places for the Werfels and Manns aboard an escape boat, the project of a loudmouthed labor leader named Bohn. He'd been sent by the American Federation of Labor to get its European counterparts out of France; Varian had met him on his first day in Marseille. Bohn, it seemed, had found a trawler and a captain willing to spirit refugees away by sea. Varian had lined up passengers and papers; an expected break in official vigilance, thanks to a national holiday, promised a chance for the boat to sail. But word must have gotten out: by the time his clients arrived at the dock, the boat had been impounded by the French authorities, its captain hauled off to the Préfecture. Varian was sure

Bohn was to blame. He possessed no **sotto voce,** and talked about his work constantly, in private and in public. Varian was lucky he himself hadn't been arrested. Altogether it was an informative disappointment. But the port exerted its magnetic pull, the ocean lapped seductively at the shore; you could touch it and know that America was just on the other side. He half-fancied that Grant had called him to this boatslip to introduce him to someone who might spirit his clients away in the night, in the hold of a silent vessel.

But when Grant came into view, leaning against a dock post in what might have been the same sailing attire he'd worn all those years ago in Maine, there was no black-haired blackguard at his side, no ostensible captain; he was alone, holding a bottle of white Bandol. He raised a hand in greeting.

"Thought you might like to get out on the water," he said.

Varian laughed. "Wine and a sail, as if all were well in the world."

"Not much of a sail. Like sailing in a bathtub."

But just then the sun penetrated a bank of broken cloud in the west, shooting planes of bright nacrescent light across the waves, and Varian had to shield his eyes against the dazzle of it. The city could shock you that way—could, for a moment, pull its blemishes aside like a veil to reveal a blinding vision of beauty. Millions of metallic scales shuddered across the surface of the port. And then the moment passed: the sun reentered its cloudbank and the light was pale flat September light again, and they were stepping down into a narrow boat, Grant collecting the lines as he made his way toward the stern.

Varian had learned to sail at Hotchkiss, on the inevitable chop of Wonoskopomuc Lake, where he and a group of tangle-haired boys had been taught to pilot twenty-two-foot racing vessels. It was a point of pride for him to know what to do in a boat; it had made him popular in Maine. When he and Grant had sailed before, he had always been the one to hold the lines. Now, as if to nullify that small point of superiority on Varian's part, here was Grant motioning him to the leeward side of the boat—a Monotype National, not so different from the ones Varian had raced at school—then taking a place beside him, raising mainsail and jib, and steering them out into the port, where there was barely room to tack. Grant turned their bow into the wind and let the sails luff for a moment; the wind was high enough to make a chuddering racket in the canvas. When he spoke, Varian had to lean in and ask him to repeat.

"They can't record a conversation on the water" was what he'd said. "Not like in a hotel room, or a bar."

Varian doubted it was true; a recording device might be hidden on a boat just as easily as in a hotel room. And sound traveled across the water, scattering unpredictably over the surface. But he hardly cared what had gotten them out there, the two of them alone, without sharp-eyed Katznelson or anyone else at all. Grant trimmed the jib and mainsail and sent the boat on a slow tack toward the south corner of the harbor. It was obvious he knew what he was doing; he sailed with a sleek economy of movement that bespoke total control. Almost without thinking, Varian uncleated the mainsail and gave it a little more wind. Grant raised an eyebrow, but let him do it. The boat tipped up a few degrees, and Varian felt for the first time in many months the chest-expanding thrill of being on the rail of a sailing craft, skimming a dark plane of water. The smell of it was a tonic, that particular tang of salt and wet wood and sailcloth. Speed gave an illusory feeling of escape. Grant eased them into a less-trafficked pocket of the port, almost in the shadow of the steel transporter bridge that spanned the outlet to the sea. The thing looked like a playground toy for a child giant, a mammoth glider suspended on a gargantuan metal scaffold. It had long ago ceased to serve its initial purpose of moving goods from one side of the port to the other, and now acted as a prospect from which the Nazis could monitor all traffic entering or leaving the port. From this distance it looked devoid of life, but Varian knew it contained a constant detail of watchers, **tireurs d'élite** they were called, rumored to be able to see beneath the water's surface to a distance of three fathoms, and armed with snipers' rifles. But it was there in its shadow that Grant stalled the boat, dropped anchor, and began to tell Varian what it was, after all, he and Katznelson were doing in France.

Grant really had come here on sabbatical, meaning to hole up at the Medieval Pile while he finished his book. Back home, a publisher's deadline loomed. He'd arrived in April. It had seemed foolery to come even then, and various parties had tried at length to talk him out of it. But he'd visited the Medieval Pile before, and loved it; he felt it was the only place he could get the work done, and he wanted access to certain manuscripts that could only be found in French libraries. Then, a month into his stay, Katznelson had cabled from New York in a panic: his only son had disappeared. Tobias, twenty years old, had been living with his mother in Berlin; he'd been studying physics at the university, but had been forced to drop out when Jews were barred from colleges. Since that time, more than a year earlier, he'd been tutoring the children of illustrious Jewish Berliners. He seemed content enough with the work, and willing to continue his own studies privately, until one morning his mother had come in to bring him his coffee and had found his bed and closet empty. He'd left a note saying that he planned to join his father in New York. He regretted that he couldn't bring his mother along, but her health was delicate and he knew she wouldn't leave her sisters and her ailing parents. There had been a quarrel with his mother some time earlier:

it seemed that even after he'd been forced to leave school, Tobias had been involved in research at the Kaiser-Wilhelm-Institut for Chemistry, under the secret tutelage of Max Planck, the Nobel laureate in physics. Tobias's mother had begged him to cease his work at the institute, fearing for her son's life, but the boy had refused. Finally he'd fled Berlin and Germany altogether. They speculated that he was making his way to the family summer house outside Marseille, and from there that he'd try to assemble forged paperwork, raise money for a ticket, and gain passage to the States. His parents feared, of course, that he'd end up in a French concentration camp. Despite the danger to himself, Gregor Katznelson had come to France at once to look for his son. At the time, France was not yet occupied, and Katznelson had thought he would be safe as long as he stayed within its borders. But then the Nazis had marched in, and Katznelson was trapped. For the past three months, he and Grant had been scouring the countryside for any sign of the boy; none had emerged. All the while, friends of Katznelson's were being sent to concentration camps; others had killed themselves in despair. Grant became afraid not only for the boy's life, but for Katznelson's. He convinced him that he must return to the States. But of course Katznelson's papers were a disaster, his route back to New York barred. And the boy was still lost. All seemed hopeless.

"And then I heard you were in Marseille," Grant

said. One long-fingered hand was wrapped around the halyard; his eyes were turned toward the sky, cloud reflecting cloud. He lowered his gaze to his own hand on the rope. "Varian the American, saving the unsavables. Imagine how I felt, hearing that name passed among refugees in a bar."

Could he imagine how Grant must have felt? How accurate had he ever been at guessing Grant's feelings? He kept silent, and let Grant continue.

"So I dropped you that note, not knowing how you'd reply. Or whether you'd reply at all."

Varian looked out toward the transport bridge, its giant industrial lacework thrown across the movie screen of the sky. Against the flat gray-blue, silhouettes of birds pulled a glittering raft of cloud.

"Did you really think I wouldn't answer you?" he said.

Grant concerned himself with knotting and unknotting the loose end of the anchor line, and Varian instantly regretted having asked the question. For twelve years, in fact, Grant had kept his silence. And Varian had not called on him, though a few quick inquiries might have revealed his hiding place in Morningside Heights.

"Here's another question," Varian said. "Why didn't you mention Katznelson's son in the first place? Why didn't Katznelson ask me himself? You know we're casting a wide net across the South of France, looking for dozens, hundreds of people. Someone might know where this boy is."

Grant breathed for a moment into his curled hand, contemplatively, as if deciding whether or not to answer. "Let's just say," he began, and fell silent a moment. "Let's just say this is all a little more complicated than it looks. Toby Katznelson isn't just any science whiz. He's been at university since age fourteen. By eighteen he was considered an authority on Planck's quantum theory. A Pencils," he said, meeting Varian's eye again; he was referring to a type of single-minded mathematical savant they'd identified during their Harvard career. "The Nazis' intelligence men are on Toby's trail. They believe Planck's theories have military applications. The Ministry of Defense wants Toby's work for themselves, and they want him back in Germany to develop it. They don't believe anyone else can do what he can do."

"How do you know all this?"

"Gregor tells me everything."

Varian managed a half-smile. "A Pencils," he said, and for a moment they might have been twenty years old again themselves, sailing the Charles instead of the Port de Marseille. The air had become taut between them, snapped into a sharp transmitter of movement and respiration. "But let me come back to my question," he said. "Toby's case is sensitive, I understand. But Katznelson wants his son back in the States. Why wouldn't he just ask me to look for him?"

Grant cast his sharp gaze again across the surface

of the water. "Katznelson is not, let us say, the most trusting person. He didn't want me to contact you in the first place. He knows the consulate doesn't support your work. And he knows you're a novice here, relatively speaking. I'm not sure he believes you can really be of help. And the fewer people who know how sensitive Toby's situation is, the better. That's how he put it to me, anyway."

Varian experienced an inward flare of indignation, though what Grant had said was obviously true; why, in fact, should Katznelson, who had everything to lose, place his trust in Varian?

"But I told him you could do it," Grant said. "I told him I knew what you were capable of. And once he met you, he gave me leave to talk to you about all this. That's why I wanted to see you."

Varian nodded in silence. **What you were capable of:** how many things that could mean! The wind shouldered into the sail and pushed their stern toward the south wall of the port, and the shadow of the transport bridge darkened the deck, then lifted.

"And now what?" Varian said. "Does he want me to look for Tobias, to get him out?"

"Gregor wants to get out, himself. And that's what I want, too—to know that he's safe." Grant averted his eyes; the tone of his voice made things clear enough to Varian. "And if you can get **him** out, then he wants you to try to do the same for his son. Though Toby's case, you understand, is far more sensitive than Gregor's. The minute they find him—Vichy police, the Nazis, anyone—they'll throw him into a camp and ship him back to the dark heart of Germany. And if he doesn't give them what they want, they'll kill him."

"I see. And what's your role in all this, Grant? Are you going to cross the border with Katznelson? Then follow him home to New York?"

"Yes, I'll go with him. But only as far as Lisbon, only to trace the route. To see how it can be accomplished with Tobias. Then I'll come back here to Marseille until Toby's found, or until it's clear that he can't be."

Grant in Marseille alone, for an unspecified time: the news engaged an alarm in Varian, a self-protective impulse. "You've got no idea what you're dealing with, Skiff," he said. "A thing like this could land **you** in a camp, or worse."

"I don't care. I want to help Gregor find his son. And I need your help, Varian. I can't do it on my own."

"My clients are artists and writers, not physicists. They aren't wanted by the Nazi Ministry of Defense. If I go down this road, I'll put my own people at risk. I can't get involved, Grant. It's not my line. I've got a mandate from my committee, and work to do for people whose whereabouts are known. People in imminent danger of arrest. The Manns and the Werfels, Walter Mehring, Konrad Heiden—all of them waiting to shuffle over the border as we speak."

"Understand what this means to me, Tom," Grant said. "Katznelson isn't"—and he paused, turning his gaze toward the sky—"he's not just a colleague. I can't stand by and let him lose his son."

Varian watched Grant closely. At his jaw, twin strands of muscle twitched; now his eyes rested on Varian's with a slight waver, remnant of the retinitis that had afflicted him in childhood. Not just a colleague; what, then? A person worth the sacrifice of one's own safety, apparently. A person worth the risk of one's own life.

"Here's how it stands," Grant said. "I'm going to try to find the boy, with or without your help. But on my own I'm really lost, and the kid probably will be too."

"Oh, Skiff, for God's sake," Varian said.

But he was already in. He knew it and Grant knew it too. He raised his eyes to meet Grant's. And he would always remember the look Grant turned on him then: relief, trepidation, triumph. Neither of them knew what they were doing; neither was experienced as a saver of lives. For as long as they'd known each other, they'd lived inside the written word—often in the observation and recording of untidy human experience, but always, or nearly always, with the comfortable medium of pen and paper standing between them and the blood and mud and grief. But here was the real thing. The stakes were as dire as they could get. There was no choice, not if they were to live with themselves after.

No one knew that better than Varian. And indeed, Varian thought, what was there that Grant could have asked that he would have refused?

As if to seal a pact, Grant reached into the hold for the Bandol, opened the bottle, and took a drink; then he handed it to Varian. The wine was sharp as a whetted knife on the tongue. They drank it as the shadow of the bridge marched up the port and entered the sun-blind city.

8

St. Cyprien

Certain people, his father had told him, were assets; others were liabilities. A shrewd businessman quickly learned to tell the difference. His father had delivered this kernel from his oak-paneled study in Ridgewood, the night before Varian left for Harvard. It was Arthur Fry's habit to impart wisdom on the eve of some great change: Varian's departure for boarding school, his entry into high school, his graduation. The wisdom could not be dispensed unless Arthur was sipping from a cut-crystal glass of Balvenie with ice. He wasn't a smoker, had always dismissed the habit as injurious to the constitution and offensive to the senses, but he praised the virtues of the occasional and judiciously chosen drink. For him, Balvenie on the rocks was a religion in miniature, and involved a series of incontrovertible strictures. The Balvenie must be aired for some minutes before it could be poured. It must be taken with large blocks of ice to minimize dilution by melting. It must be imbibed slowly, from an unfaceted vessel small enough to rest securely in the hand, one that, held to the light, would reveal the leonine shadings of the drink. Crystal, not glass, for its clarity. The ritual of Balvenie, performed on the eve of momentous change, always brought forth drops of wisdom from Arthur Fry. Varian was in the habit of dismissing them out of hand. He'd been trained in the Socratic method, and had learned to reject unexamined thought. But the Balvenie Fryisms came back later with doglike persistence, resisting oblivion. They had scarcely let him alone for a moment here in Marseille, where his own lack of wisdom had provided a gaping aperture.

Some people were assets; some were liabilities. Which was which, and could Varian trust himself to know the difference? Take Miriam Davenport, for example, who sat now at her desk in the new office, laughing at top volume, as rich in casual confidence as she was devoid of self-consciousness. Before her sat another young woman who had arrived at the office claiming talent and reputation as a painter in Prague, but without a scrap of work to show for it; her portfolio, she claimed, had been stolen on the train. Miriam had sent her down to the Vieux Port with some oil pastels and a block of drawing paper, and she had just returned with six works whose choices of line and color conveyed unquestionable brilliance to Miriam's eye. She was now preparing client intake forms for the otherwise paperless young woman, whose case Varian would now be forced to argue to the ERC. But it would have been even harder to argue with Miriam, who, three weeks in his employ, had become the **regina de facto** of the rue Grignan. The daughter of the concierge must have felt sorely displaced, watching her enter and exit the building, trailed by her various subjects. And she was always trailed by someone; like certain honey-scented wildflowers, she attracted bees. He hadn't known, when he'd hired her, that she would insist on his hiring Gussie Rosenberg, an eighteen-year-old German refugee who'd fled on his own to France and then followed Miriam south; Gussie, now their messenger and errand boy, equipped with his own bicycle, required housing and clothing and feeding, and had last week been arrested for no reason at all, costing Varian thousands of francs in lawyers' fees. And then there was Mary Jayne, who had already donated five thousand dollars to the ERC but now expected to be employed as an interviewer of refugees. In a cloud of Chanel No. 5 and a series of jewel-colored afternoon dresses—unwitting insults to the refugees in their overwashed and threadbare clothes—she occupied her own desk in the corner, talking and jotting notes and assessing the urgency of various cases.

Before her now sat the novelist Lion Feuchtwanger,

thumbing the pages of a silver-edged journal she'd given him as a gift. If he was going to be stuck in France a bit longer, she said, waiting for his U.S. visa to materialize, he might as well spend his days writing. "Record everything you can," she said. "They're going to need to hear all of it in the States."

Feuchtwanger smoothed his hair with one hand and resettled his wire-framed glasses, new ones, bought with ERC funds; the old ones had been crushed beneath a concentration camp guard's boot at St. Nicolas. He had regained weight and taken on some color during a stay at Harry Bingham's villa, where he spent his afternoons with Golo Mann in the vice-consular swimming pool.

"You want me to make a mockery of myself, Miss Gold," Feuchtwanger said, teasingly. "You want me to record for history my escape from St. Nicolas, dressed in women's clothing. You want me to write about being whisked away in Mr. Bingham's red Cadillac and hidden at his house like a secret lover!"

"No one else could do it better," Mary Jayne said. "And someone has to do it, because it's too rich a tale not to tell."

"But we don't know yet how the tale ends, do we?"

"All the better!" Mary Jayne said. "Write the ending you want. Then we'll cause it to materialize, like magic. It's our job."

Asset, Varian thought, as he edged around crates of abandoned leather goods and into the cubicle that served as his office. Certainly an asset. But then, as he sat down at his desk and looked out at the marbled sky through his sliver of window, he remembered where it was he'd first heard of Mary Jayne and that Percival Vega Gull. Not in the social pages; long before, at a party one evening in Maine, a few months into his engagement to Eileen. Half a mile off the road to Surry, a family called Parrish had a grand vacation house on a bluff overlooking Morgan Bay. The place had been home to late-afternoon entertainments that featured lobsters and champagne, high-stakes cards, live jazz, and, in a marble-tiled bathroom off the central hall, a little mirrored snuffbox of cocaine. The women wore white linen dresses, the men sailing clothes. The wines were French, the cigars Cuban, the literary and geographic references transatlantic, the circle of friends small enough to create a fantasy world in which these pleasures were commonplace. The younger generation of Parrishes, children and grandchildren of the bluebloods of Blue Hill, scandalized the community with their intrigues and foibles, but were essential to its commerce. The year-round residents could live for a twelvemonth on what they earned during a summer in the service of these Betseys and Vivians and Oswalds. Mary Jayne's name had drifted across the lawn one evening as Varian and Eileen were engaged in a half-drunk game of croquet. The talk, he remembered now—and where in the brain were these details stored, these endless fragments of conversation, shadowy glimpses of women's bodies, vague scents of ocean and pine and gin?—concerned the monoplane, and how Mary Jayne, who had been the boarding-school classmate of one of the Betseys or Vivians, had flown to Monaco for a weekend to confront the unfaithful husband of another boarding-school friend. Apparently the mission had been a success. Mary Jayne, meeting the man at a casino table, had punched him in the jaw and landed him on the floor, out cold. Eileen and her friends, retelling the story, had whooped in admiration: here was an ardent and impulsive woman whose loyalty consisted of action, who showed no fear in the face of injustice. But now, in Marseille, would those qualities be assets or liabilities to his mission? Impossible to tell.

His father, he felt, would insist that he trust his instincts. If Varian argued that his instincts were hazy, his father would call it evidence of a weak character. Certainly, here on the rue Grignan, he felt a new confidence in the work they were doing; he couldn't name the force that had created it, and he refused to strike it up to a desire to prove himself to Grant. But in the past few days he'd been up all hours, writing letters to influential persons in Washington, drafting coded missives to New York, begging money from donors in the States, rushing back and forth from the rue Grignan to the Préfecture in search of visa stamps, poring over the finances with Oppy, meeting with the Manns and the Werfels, exerting the gentlest of pressure on Harry Bingham. And certain essential factors were beginning to come together. The Manns' and Werfels' U.S. visas had materialized at last. The francs had materialized too, thanks to Hirschman's plot with Vinciléoni. Even Bill Freier, the cartoonist whose pen had produced Moreau's perfect forgeries, had at last materialized, drawn to the Centre Américain through a network of rumors. On Varian's desk at that very moment sat a stack of safe-transit passes, the forms stolen from the Préfecture by Hirschman's girlfriend; on those crisp white forms, Freier had forged stamps and signatures indistinguishable from the real thing. He'd also inked the missing visas onto the Manns' and Werfels' passports.

But the real coup, the one he held closest to his heart, had been the reply from Nick Butler at Columbia. Within two days' time the consulate had received a cable not from Butler's office but from Butler himself, assuring Fullerton that Katznelson had Columbia's full support. Cables followed from the dean of graduate studies and from Katznelson's department chair. Not twenty-four hours later, Fullerton had responded with a note to Katznelson, assuring him that a visa was forthcoming. Harry Bingham had sent a facsimile of the note to Varian, who'd informed Katznelson that he should prepare to travel with the Manns and Werfels the following Monday. Freier could provide any missing visas; the rest would be up to chance.

The journey was to start with a three-hour train

ride to Cerbère, and then, after a track change, a sprint across the border to Portbou. Then onward through Spain, to Barcelona and Madrid, and finally to Lisbon, where Varian could write uncensored letters to the New York office and to Eileen. A letter from Eileen, a real letter, had finally reached him at the Splendide: **Dear V, believe me: I understand the urgency of your work. I admire what you're doing, wildly so. But you mustn't delay your return. Not only because I miss you—and I do!—but because you underestimate the danger you are in. The war closes in upon you daily. You would say you know the risks better than I do, Europe and its political convulsions being your area of expertise. But your desire to be of help, I believe, may cause you to ignore plain facts. You know that to be true, dear V.**

She was right, of course; there were certain facts, inconvenient ones, that he chose to ignore. But here was one that couldn't be ignored: He had spent the past month weaving webs, drawing lines of connection between himself and his employees and the forces in power, legal and illegal. He had made himself irreplaceable. When he wrote to the New York office, he meant to make an argument to that effect.

He had taken out a notebook and begun to draft a letter to Kingdon when his office door flew open; in came Miriam in a state of panic, pale and trembling, her hand rigid on the doorframe.

"It's Walter," she said. "He's been arrested at the border."

"You can't mean **Mehring,**" Varian said. "Mehring's at the hotel."

"Not anymore. He made a break for it early this morning. The police caught up with him at the station café in Perpignan. It was the fake Czech passport that did it. And now he's being taken to St. Cyprien." She meant the concentration camp there, where a typhoid epidemic had killed a hundred and eighty that summer.

"You're kidding me."

"I wish I were! Or that I'd known he might run. He was too scared to leave his hotel!" Her voice had begun to tremble; he could see in her eyes that she believed this was somehow all her fault.

"There's nothing you could have done, Miriam."

"But now what? St. Cyprien! That place is a cesspool."

"I'll call Bingham at once. He'll help us get a lawyer."

"All right," Miriam said, her eyes bright and wet.

Varian looked at her a long moment, wondering if he dared say what had just come to his mind.

"Miriam," he said, finally. "You're not—you and Mehring—"

The color flew back to her face, and her eyes widened. "**Lord** no! Mehring's in love with Hertha Pauli. And anyway—" She gave a fleet smile and flashed her engagement band, with its tiny diamonds and rubies. "I'm faithful to Rolf. But I adore Mehring. And I can't bear to think of him locked up in that place."

"All right," Varian said. "Just wondering. I'll get on the phone to Bingham right away."

"Wonder not. I'm a straight shooter." She mustered another half-smile, then went out to the front room to tell Mary Jayne what had happened. And Varian picked up the phone to call Bingham, succeeding only in reaching a musical-voiced secretary with a Michigan accent, who told him to wait while she went to see what was what.

Varian waited, trying to push from his mind the thought that he meant to lead his own group of escapees to the border via Mehring's route in a few days' time. Werfel would never survive in a place like St. Cyprien. And Mann, who was nearly seventy—he could almost see him now, cuffed and bent, being marched by a rifle-toting guard through the camp's toothed gate. Varian had never considered this a game, had always grasped what the consequences might be if he steered his clients wrong. But now it was real: Walter Mehring himself had gone in a matter of hours from the relative safety of his white-sheeted bed at the Splendide to a pestilent barracks behind a chain-link fence.

Exhaustion came over him then like the crushing dullness after cocaine, and he put his head down against the cool smooth plane of the blotter. He wanted not to be in charge of any of this, wished himself home in his own white sheets in Manhattan, Eileen in the other room with the **Times,** the drape of her linen skirt just visible through the bedroom door as she read in the chair by the window.

Mehring's situation, he told Hirschman that night over drinks at the Coquille de Noix, was an important reminder: anything could go wrong at any time, and it was foolish to think otherwise. Everyone's papers had to be in order; forgeries could only be of the highest caliber. They couldn't take any risks. And no more fake Czech passports, under any circumstances.

Hirschman sat over his glass of whiskey, stirring it with a narrow paper straw. "Can this lawyer get him out? What does Bingham say?"

Varian shook his head. "Bingham says it'll depend on factors beyond our control."

"Why would he try it—Mehring, I mean—after you told him those Czech papers were dangerous? Why couldn't he sit for a few days? A Polish or Lithuanian passport could have gotten him across."

"There was no stopping him, once he'd heard those officers in the corridor."

Hirschman turned his drink on its coaster. "I

suppose there's no telling what they'll do if they're scared enough. Bolting with a fake passport is hardly the worst of it."

Varian knew what he meant: some of them killed themselves. And did Mehring himself possess cyanide capsules? Would he use them at St. Cyprien if circumstances got bad enough? How long would it take him, susceptible to panic as he was, to reach a state of despair? Varian raised his own glass of whiskey and emptied it at speed. It filled him with a burning like self-punishment.

"Bingham's lawyer will come by the office tomorrow morning. The case seems promising, he says, at least superficially. But I may have to go to St. Cyprien and speak to the commandant. Or perhaps you'll go in my place, since the Manns and the Werfels . . ."

"Of course," Hirschman said. "And, Varian—"

"Yes?"

"Don't let this interrupt our plans. Let's hope the Manns and Werfels don't get word of it. Their papers are in place. You could keep them back another week or two, worrying about their getting arrested and thrown in St. Cyprien, but the situation's not the same. I'm not saying there's no risk—there's always risk—but the longer they wait, the greater the danger."

"Of course you're right," Varian said. He hadn't even known how seriously he was considering keeping the Manns and Werfels back, but once

Hirschman mentioned it, he realized that he'd been writing excuses in his mind already, inventing reasons to delay. His own health. An intimation of bad weather. But Hirschman **was** right: he had to follow the advice he'd been giving his refugees all along. When all the papers were in place—as soon as they were—it was time to take a chance. And for the Werfels and Manns, and for Katznelson, that time had come. They'd make their attempt on Monday.

9

Westbound Train

He climbed the broad stairs to the Gare St. Charles in the predawn blue, his nerves lit with adrenaline, suitcase in his hand. Above him the station lifted its columns and pediment into a bruise-colored sky, a French Parthenon on a French Acropolis. But this was far from holy ground: the Romans had staged battles here, famous conflicts he'd studied in school and remembered now as though he'd witnessed them. As he reached the top of the stairs and looked down, he could almost see the **cohors militaria** striking in wedge formation downhillward toward the enemy at the port, a dentition of swords glinting in the Mediterranean light. He wished he had a sword in hand that morning. His tired suitcase, with its scattering of stickers, seemed ersatz, like a stage prop.

Inside the station, his refugees waited beneath a

red-and-gold advertisement for Lyons Tea, Qualité de Luxe: a ship with white sails taut with wind, like a promise of escape. The Manns—steel-eyed Heinrich with his close-trimmed goatee; round, pale-blond Nelly, twenty years his junior; and Golo, their nephew, tall, lank, knit-browed—all looked journey-ready, their few things standing neatly beside them, their clothes sharply pressed, their shoes reflective with polish. Golo, who had spent five leisurely weeks at Harry Bingham's villa, sported a toast-colored tan and held his cigarette with languid ease. But Heinrich thumbed his collar as if the starch made him itch, and Nelly Mann kept pushing stray hairpins back into her coif, her hands trembling visibly. Then there were the Werfels: Franz in a wrinkled suit, his lips an anoxic blue, and Alma in her astrakhan coat and pearl choker, placid as ice. Behind them stood a flotilla of trunks, hatboxes, banded satchels, and leather hardcases, too numerous to count at a glance.

"Golo, Heinrich, Mrs. Mann!" Varian said, shaking their hands. "And Franz, and Mrs. Werfel. Good Lord." He glanced at the fleet of luggage. "Did I mention the necessity of packing light?"

Alma Mahler-Werfel nodded, unperturbed. "You see, Monsieur Fry, I transport my former husband's priceless scores, and the only manuscript copy of Bruckner's Third, and all of Franz's current work. A certain cultural capital, if you will. I've reduced already. Nothing more can be abandoned."

"Of course," Varian said, though he could hardly be blamed for wishing they weren't transporting a museum. He secured a porter, who began to tag the suitcases with tickets. A whistle blew two sharp blasts; in ten minutes they would have to board. Where were Katznelson and Grant? He had told them clearly where they were to meet. What if Katznelson had had a change of heart? What if he'd been arrested in the night?

But then there was Grant himself, striding up the platform with his sleek suitcase in hand, a linen coat draped over his arm, and at his side was Katznelson with his own slim case. Grant's eyes went directly to Varian's, and Varian's mind slid into the memory of riding the rail of that sailboat on the Vieux Port, Grant straining against the ropes, driving the boat into the sharp chop of the sea. But Grant and Katznelson looked perfectly matched, both tall and dark-haired, their chins upraised, their shoulders squared against whatever was to come. Impeccably shaved and dressed and brushed, they gave the impression of heading off into some urgent adventure where their talents and taste would be necessary, their intelligence equal to whatever awaited. Varian introduced them to the assembled group, employing what he hoped was a tone of cool dispassion. Katznelson, it turned out, had known the Manns in Munich, and had met Golo at his father's house. And Werfel knew and praised Katznelson's work, which caused Grant to blush with obvious pleasure. Katznelson seemed to take note of Grant's blush; he drew almost imperceptibly closer, his knuckles grazing the leather of Grant's suitcase.

Last to come was Leon Ball, who'd been conducting Varian's clients over the border for some weeks now. Dressed in his usual traveling garb—olive-green jersey, black pants, black beret, black military-issue boots—he looked like a soldier, though as far as Varian knew, he'd only ever served in an ambulance corps. Ball was the scion of a cattle-ranching family in Montana, and had left home at nineteen to study international business at the Sorbonne. Now, at thirty, he owned a lard factory outside of Paris and a two-hundred-acre pig farm in Nemours. When the Germans had marched into the city, he'd left his factory in his foreman's hands and followed the exodus south, animated by a vague idea that he might do something to subvert the occupation. And when he'd reached Marseille, he discovered what it was. Refugees, he learned, were fumbling their escapes, failing to speak intelligible French to the customs officers, getting arrested for saying the wrong things, or getting disastrously lost on the Pyrenean paths. Ball had spent months in those mountains not long after he'd arrived in France, and knew every path that existed. One day he'd shown up at the Splendide, having heard about Varian's operation from Harry Bingham, and proposed a collaboration.

Varian liked Leon Ball, this caterpillar-browed, square-shouldered young man whose wealth meant nothing to him, who swore like a cowboy but had picked up five Alsatian dialects, who wanted nothing more than to get himself to the border and over it, burdened with clients, as many times as he could manage. Ball had the perfect confidence of a person whose life had found its ideal use. He strode up to Varian now and pumped his hand.

"Looking ready, Fry," he said. "And here are all the rest. Everyone set?"

Nervous glances all around; from the elder Mann, a nod of assent. Varian checked their travel documents and distributed the rail tickets. As soon as the whistle blew, they boarded the train.

There were nine of them, divided between two compartments. Katznelson and Grant followed Varian into the first; behind them came Nelly and Heinrich and Golo. Leon Ball led the Werfels into the neighboring compartment. Varian took a seat by the window, across from Grant, and Grant met his eye again as he slid a few books into the leather pocket beneath the window. On the platform, with the aid of a porter, Alma Werfel's flotilla of luggage invaded the baggage car piece by piece. Minutes passed. Katznelson inclined his head toward Grant's and whispered something. Nelly Mann checked the outline of her lips in a compact mirror. Golo ate a yellow apple. At last the final whistle blew; the train gave a jolt, and they were off.

They trundled through the industrial backways of the town, past the rusting warehouses and crumbling brick workshops, the ironsmithies and loading yards, all of it cold and blue in the predawn light. Inside the first-class car they were in a different world, every surface smooth and polished, every noise muffled by velvet drapes. The smell was of seat leather and of pipe tobacco. As they rumbled through the warehouse district, Varian's mind fell into an ancient memory of riding the train to New York with Arthur Fry, one morning when he was about nine—something had been wrong with his mother that day, and his aunt had to accompany her to the doctor. Sitting beside his father, Varian had rested his forehead against the window glass and watched the dense summer leaves of the suburbs pass in a verdant blur. He'd asked his father for a story, though his hopes were low: Arthur already had his **Times** open to the section that mesmerized him, the financial page. What Varian really wanted, what he was gunning for, was another installment of the Tale of the Night Prowler, the one Arthur had been telling lately at bedtime, about a rangy long-limbed long-furred wolfish bear, a creature of deep appetite, who climbed the gutterpipes of houses, entered bedroom windows, and devoured nine-year-old boys. What Varian remembered now, what had stayed with him all this time, was the moment when Arthur had laid down his **Times,** bent to his son's ear, and intoned in his breath-laced baritone, **On a wet and treacherous night.** For that moment, and for some time afterward, Varian had understood himself to be his father's chosen, situated at the bright core of his attention. He'd experienced a deep sense of **mattering,** a sensation rare in the face of his mother's capricious illness and his father's constant and all-consuming work. Where else had he had that feeling, who else's attention had placed him at the center of the known world? Only one person's. And here he was, sitting across from Varian again, though he might as well have been behind impenetrable glass.

Varian watched Grant open a tiny box of mint pastilles and offer one to Katznelson; a few minutes later, Katznelson bent toward Grant to show him a line in a book. Grant laughed, and a cord in Varian's chest seemed to tighten to the point of intolerability. He wished himself on the other side of the partition with Leon Ball and the Werfels. But he felt incapable of moving: Grant was a magnet, and Varian's blood oriented toward him by some law of nature. With effort, he directed his gaze out the window at the passing landscape. They had moved by now into the wide salt marshlands of the Camargue, south of Arles. Green and yellow grasses bent in the gulf wind, their seedheads heavy with birds, and flat whalelike clouds breached the broad blue plane of the sky.

At Nîmes, a brace of gendarmes strode through the car to check papers. The policemen, clad in brown and wearing the tricolor badge of Vichy, leaned into the compartment and demanded the travelers' identification cards and visas. A rustling of papers ensued; the gendarmes squinted over the documents for an unnervingly long time, particularly Katznelson's, then returned them without comment. To Varian's relief, they hadn't picked out Freier's careful forgeries.

As they passed along the coastal railway route, Grant leaned toward the window and blinked into the glare. He seemed to be committing to memory the railway stations they passed, the jagged topography, the cast of platinum light from the Gulf of Lion, as if imagining how he might cover this territory with Tobias. At Sète, hometown of Paul Valéry, he gazed out at the Venice-like waterways with their profusion of boats, possible routes of escape; at Narbonne he watched the bicyclists stream over the river bridges.

At the tunnel between Collioure and Port-Vendres, when the compartment lights failed to come on, Varian heard Grant conferring quietly in German with Katznelson. Tobias's name passed between them, and, from Grant, a note of reassurance: **Ich könnte diesen Weg mit ihm reisen.** But the challenges all lay ahead, Varian knew; the true test of this route would come when they reached Cerbère.

On the other side of the tunnel were the Pyrenees, a fleet of frigates for a race of giants. The train made its way through the steep hills along the coast, along the broad bilevel viaduct modeled on the ancient Roman exemplars at Marseille, and there was a general rustling, a stowing of things, an arranging of clothes, a smoothing of hair. As they pulled into Cerbère, the top level of the viaduct widened enough to accommodate the station house and switching yard. To get to Portbou they would have to change trains, then pass through another tunnel, under the peak that cast its shadow on the town. But first everyone would have to file into the station and surrender their tickets to the stationmaster. To be admitted onto the border-crossing train, they would have to pass document clearance.

Varian's party was buoyant, almost effervescent, as they disembarked. The awareness that they'd reached the border of France had come over them like a tonic. Golo smoked a celebratory cigar, ignoring Alma's protest. The elder Mann spoke animatedly to his wife, and Nelly Mann, released from her anxiety for the first time all day, linked her arm through his and laughed. They all made their way down the platform toward the document control hall, Varian's back aching from the too-upright seats, his gut full of silvery fire. At his side Grant strode along, cool and correct; he looked as though he'd arrived in Cerbère merely for a stay at the old hotel and a swim at the palm-shadowed beach. But there was Katznelson keeping pace beside him, holding his slim suitcase and consulting his watch: a reminder, a corrective.

In the customs area, passengers had formed four long lines. Officers checked papers at one end, and militant-looking gendarmes strolled the queues, scanning faces and packages. Beyond them Varian could see the Portbou train on the platform, the last one out that night.

"What do you think we ought to do?" he asked Leon Ball, eyeing the lines.

Ball straightened his black beret, contemplating. "If we wait, we'll never get on that train," he said. "We can't risk our people having to put up in town overnight. The town's crawling with police."

"What do you suggest, then?"

"Give me the passports. I know the guy in charge, he's not a bad egg. If he's in the right mood, maybe he'll give us a wave-through."

Varian considered this. "What if he doesn't like the state of our people's papers? What if he confiscates them?"

"He won't. Not this guy."

Varian glanced toward Grant, who'd been following the conversation in silence; he seemed to be waiting now to see what Varian would do.

"All right," Varian said. "Let's do it."

"That's the spirit," Ball said. He explained the problem to the travelers in a few words, and they all handed over their papers. Then he stalked off to the stationmaster's office, where the commissioner could be seen drinking from a glinting flask.

"Now it's over," Werfel said, in German. "Now it's to the camps with all of us."

"Nonsense," said Heinrich Mann. "Delays are to be expected." But his wife wasn't comforted; her hand shook as she lit a narrow cigarette, and then she dropped her smoke and cursed.

Varian suspected he was doing a poor job of hiding his own anxiety. He'd hoped they would arrive to find a sleepy border station, its gendarmes few and easily bought off. Beyond the station windows they could see the slopes of the Pyrenees, and along one hillside the pale thread of a footpath. How many had gone that way recently, and how many had reached Spain? Among their assembled company, who would be willing to try? Who would be fit enough to make it? He tried to catch Grant's eye again, but Grant had inclined his head toward Katznelson and was now engaged in some urgent exchange. Again Varian felt a bolt of silver heat through his gut, and his skin seemed to contract painfully around his skull.

A few minutes later Ball reemerged from the stationmaster's office, his forehead bisected by a grim crease. He displayed his empty hands as if he'd just performed an act of prestidigitation; the beautiful passports had vanished.

"Well, that's that," he said. "We're staying the night."

"What can you mean?" Katznelson said sharply. "What happened?"

"The commissioner says he'd like to hold your papers overnight. Make yourselves comfortable in town, he said. Go down to the hotel, have dinner, get some sleep. Then come back in the morning and try again." Ball lowered his voice. "He's not a bad guy, this commissioner. He says border control's turning everyone back today. Vichy's got a team of inspectors at the station now. But he expects they'll be gone by tomorrow noon."

The travelers looked at each other anxiously.

"What if they're not?" Heinrich Mann asked.

"We'll have to take the man's word for it. We don't really have a choice."

Mann turned a look on Varian. Was Ball a man to be trusted? Could they be sure he wasn't in collusion with the commissaire? He had taken their passports and made them disappear; paperless, they were trapped. But Varian, disinclined to trust anyone, did in fact trust Leon Ball. It wasn't just that he hailed from Montana, which struck Varian as an honest state; he'd held vulnerable lives in his hands before and had delivered them to safety, at no benefit to himself. As a volunteer in the French ambulance corps, he'd gotten dozens of English soldiers out of France while he could, before the Germans had taken the Atlantic coast. And a few weeks ago he'd conducted one of Varian's most sensitive clients, the Nobel laureate Otto Meyerhof, over the border into Spain. He had no interest but to help, no motives beyond the refugees' motives. Varian thought of Miriam, her crowned head held high, lecturing him on calculated risk. Here was one he knew he had to take.

"We'll go down to the hotel," Varian said. "We'll eat and get some sleep. It'll be a long day tomorrow, whatever happens."

Except for a few essential pieces, the luggage remained behind. Down the hill they all went, to a salt-scrubbed white hotel on the beach; it wasn't the grandest place in town, but the owners knew of Varian's mission from the refugees who had come that way before, and were sympathetic. The hotel, built as a summer-season playground, had a drafty outdoor restaurant overlooking the strand.

As he dressed for dinner, Varian couldn't help but listen to the rise and fall of voices in the room next door: Grant and Katznelson engaged in an argument. He couldn't make out the words, but the tone was clear enough. Katznelson's basso, tightened with anxiety, climbed into a higher register, and Grant, who seemed to begin by conciliating, fell into an insistent protest. He imagined Katznelson angrily questioning Varian's competence, and Grant defending him; he resisted the urge to put his ear to the wall. Whatever was occurring was their business alone. Hoping that he wouldn't have to listen when they made up, he hurried through his preparations and left the room.

Downstairs, at a long table on the veranda, he found Ball and the Werfels scrutinizing the menu, Golo Mann already nursing a martini. As Varian sat down beside him, Golo reported that his uncle and his wife would take dinner in their room.

"And who could blame them?" Werfel said, dolefully. "A trip like this could make anyone sick."

A moment later, as if to confirm that assessment, Grant came out onto the veranda alone. He took the seat beside Varian, explaining that Gregor had a headache and had already gone to bed.

"A shame," Alma said. "I meant to ask about his son."

In an effort at nonchalance, Grant extracted his cigarette case and took his time selecting a cigarette. "Katznelson's son," he said. "Do you know him?"

"For a time, he was pursuing the daughter of a friend of mine," Alma said. "But then he disappeared."

Grant raised his eyes to her. "You've heard from this girl?"

"Sara? No. She's in the States already. But her father's here in France. A German painter of some repute. Lev Zilberman. Do you know his work, Mr. Fry? It's quite remarkable. You ought to help him if you can."

"Chagall said the same thing," Varian said, and

lowered his voice. "You don't know where he is now, do you?"

"I'm afraid not. Franz and I lost touch with him after we fled Paris."

"And what about the boy?"

"That's what I wanted to ask Professor Katznelson. I know he's been looking for him for some time now."

"Yes, so I've heard," Varian said. He didn't want any of them to speak another word about Tobias Katznelson, not there at that outdoor table, where anyone might hear. "So many are lost. It's the hardest part of my work, not knowing where to look."

"These are terrible days," Alma said, turning her glass of Banyuls in a strand of light. "Everything has changed. I visited this place once before, Mr. Fry. My former husband and I spent a summer here. And now Gustav is dead, and the world is at war again." She raised her chin and blinked bravely, her mouth pursed against trembling.

Werfel cleared his throat, as if to remind his wife that he was still there. "There's no use crying over it, **mein süsser Engel,**" he said. "What's gone is gone."

They drank their drinks and ate calamari, avoiding the subject of what they would find over the border in Spain if they were lucky enough to get there. Varian had seen it all on the way to Marseille: the decimated buildings, roofs blown open to the sun, windows shattered; blackened fields with their smell of burnt maize; bombed bridges collapsed into mud-colored rivers; children walking near-naked in the streets, begging for bread. Life had failed to resume its ordinary shape after the Guerra Civil, and now the rest of Europe was at war. It seemed an unlikely place to escape to; it seemed, as Varian had experienced it, a place to flee with haste. He could only hope their transit to Portugal would go swiftly. The thought of it killed his appetite, and he crumpled his napkin and tried to follow the refugees' conversation: light complaint about the day's journey, speculation as to the next day's weather, commentary on the wine and food, which was, despite rationing, excellent. Grant kept refilling Varian's glass when it got low, and after a while he felt the strings of his paralytic anxiety loosening. He allowed himself to become aware, sometimes for moments on end, that Grant sat at his side without Katznelson—close enough to bend to Varian's ear when he had some private commentary, close enough to give off a subtle but insistent heat. Grant's proximity had not yet taken the shape of the ordinary; Varian doubted it ever could. But he was aware of following an old script as they waited everyone out at the end of dinner, drinking another drink and then another as the others finished their desserts, made their adieux, and drifted off to bed. At last, inertia delivered them unimpeachably to their goal: the two of them presiding over a landscape of crumbs and empty glasses, finally alone.

"And so," Grant said, leaning back in his chair. "Here we are, **mein süsser Engel.**"

"Why is it you never called me that, back in our day?"

"You didn't exactly deserve the name."

"Now, that's not true, Skiff. I was sweet."

"Mostly on yourself, if I recall. Particularly while addressing a group of your admirers. Remember how you used to hold forth to everyone at the Pendragon?"

"If I was so full of hot air, why did you sit and listen?"

"Yes, why did I?" Grant said, and, unbearably, laid his hand over Varian's wrist. "I can scarcely remember, myself."

An intolerable flush rose to Varian's neck. "In any case," he said, removing his hand from the table, "you lent me credibility. The others stayed because you did."

"On the contrary, you lent **me** credibility. You treated me as though I belonged in those rooms."

"Which you did, of course."

"Not according to some." He extinguished his cigarette. "You remember Hank Worthington, the guy who owned the place? Now there was a salty old snob."

"An exalted barkeep," Varian said. "Anyway, he didn't seem to mind hosting a barful of fairies."

"Only because he was one himself."

"Perhaps he was part Negro too."

"I think not," Grant said. "In any case, I wouldn't want to claim him as a brother." They laughed, but uncomfortably, since this was venturing close to the question of whether Grant, in fact, claimed himself; in the Pendragon days he did not. Varian had to wonder how he characterized himself now. Did Columbia University know that it employed a Negro professor? What about Katznelson? To what race did he understand Grant to belong? The question hadn't occurred to Varian when he'd visited the Medieval Pile; he had, in fact, ceased to think about Grant's race long ago. Grant was simply Grant; his personal characteristics were somehow incidental—to Varian, anyway, if not to Grant himself.

It wasn't something they'd ever easily discussed, in any case, and they were not to discuss it now. An impatient waiter hovered, eager to usher them out of the restaurant. Grant and Varian stood and wandered toward the front of the hotel, where a circlet of white settees corralled a trembling palm. Grant made no move to sit, nor to climb the stairs to his room. He passed a hand over his eyes as if to clear them of liquor fog.

"And so to bed," said Varian. But he made no move in that direction either.

For a long moment they stood at the center of the hotel lobby, eyes averted. Grant felt for his cigarettes as though he hadn't smoked the last one half an hour ago.

"Perhaps I'll sit down here for a while and look at the day's papers," Grant said finally, indicating the white settees. "I couldn't read a word on the train."

"Goodnight, then," Varian said brusquely. "See you in the morning." And he turned and went upstairs, so as not to be accused of lingering.

The night offered little in the way of sleep. Even if the bed had been soft and the sound of waves against shore muted, even if a cold wind hadn't thrown the shutter against the wall again and again, he could scarcely have closed his eyes: too much uncertainty, too much residual tension after a long tense day. It was hardly a comfort to hear Katznelson snoring on the other side of the wall, nor to hear, finally, the door of that room open and close, and the water clanking through the pipes as Grant prepared for bed.

How many years had it been, he wondered, since the word **Pendragon** had flashed across his cortex? He blushed now at the thought of those evening lectures, Varian declaiming to a group of like-dressed and like-minded young men, a collection that often included Grant. Though they both lived at Gore Hall that year, the Pendragon felt more like home; the place had the reputation of being kind to their kind, whereas on school property one had always to be careful. It was preferable to conduct one's private business in a place where one didn't have to worry about who was watching. And in those days, Varian wanted to be watched. Grant, unlike Lincoln Kirstein, who always preferred to be the center of attention, didn't mind letting Varian occupy the spotlight; on the contrary, if all eyes were on Varian, then Grant himself would attract little notice.

If there had ever been a time when Varian hadn't known Grant's secret, it had been so brief as to seem negligible. He'd known Grant was half-Negro in the same way he'd known that Grant's sexual tendencies ran along the lines of Varian's own. Perhaps the same faculty he'd honed in scanning for the latter also delivered information of the former; it was nothing you'd have known right away. Like a quarter of their classmates, Grant was Jewish. His dark hair and lion-colored skin might easily be attributed to that fact. His eyes were that surprising color, an earthy gray that reflected light. He was what he was; he was what he presented himself to be.

Except, of course, that he wasn't. Over their time together, the details had emerged: His family was from Philadelphia, his mother from a prominent Jewish family that believed in the education of its daughters. Celia Schiffman, while taking her degree at Barnard, had wandered down to the Tenderloin District and to Marshall's Hotel, where the best black musicians congregated and played. That was where she'd met Grant's father. About the elder

Grant the younger rarely spoke, but Varian knew he'd been a pianist, and a formidable one. He'd been classically trained, but his passion was for ragtime; that was what he played in those late-night sessions at Marshall's. He and Celia were married at City Hall, against her family's strenuous objection, and Grant had been born a year and a half later. The Schiffmans, particularly proud among the proud Jews of Philadelphia, let slip to their friends that their daughter had married a **goy,** but never that the **goy** was a **schvartze;** perhaps they prayed he'd vanish from Celia's life before the truth could emerge. And in fact, some time before Grant's second birthday, Clayton Grant had gone to Europe with a vaudeville outfit and had chosen to remain.

Celia moved home to her parents' house in Philadelphia, and Grant had been raised there. No one spoke of his father. As a child, Grant had only the vaguest idea that Clayton was a Negro, and that he was never to bring it up. He knew, too, that his father had been a musician, and that he'd gone away to Europe and hadn't returned. When Grant hit elementary school, he started telling people that his father had been killed in the war, a lie his mother slapped out of him when it reached her ears. The sacrifice of the war dead was not something to be taken lightly. But it might as well have been true; years passed, and no word came from Europe. Grant seemed to revert entirely to Celia's possession. She raised him as though he had no race but her own, and no one at Grant's mostly Jewish elementary school thought to question his whiteness. His looks were an unremarkable variation on a familiar theme.

Had his grandparents' relation to Grant been different—had they met their returning daughter with fury or smug vindication instead of sympathy and dismay, and treated her offspring as a stranger instead of as a child of their own blood—he might have wondered more actively about his father's people. But they treated him as their own, and he had a happy childhood under his grandparents' roof. Instead of quashing his early musical talent because of its connection to his father, they nurtured it, engaging a certain young Mr. Weatherstone who had studied at the Royal Academy in London and had a talent for teaching young prodigies. They sent him to a prestigious Philadelphia preparatory school, one of the few that welcomed Jews, and they secured for him all the things—the dancing lessons and fine clothes and pine-shaded summer camps and gadgety toys—that came to other privileged young Jewish Philadelphians as a matter of course. They taught him, through persistent love, to see himself as inherently valuable.

If Celia sometimes resented in her son a cast of eye or tilt of mouth that resembled his father's, if she sometimes found it impossible to fix young Grant's collar and tie his tie without being struck by the paralyzing memory of doing the same for Clayton, she didn't let him know it, or not often. In receipt of her undivided attention, Grant was a happy child who returned happiness to his family. While Varian had spent his childhood either quitting or getting kicked out of schools, Grant had spent his becoming class president, winning statewide piano performance awards, and earning citizenship medals. No one had a more thoroughly decorated Boy Scout sash. And no one, Varian was certain, would have borne the burden of his merits with more demurrals, more natural grace.

It had been a surprise to almost everyone—to Grant's teachers, his mother, his grandparents, and his friends, if not to Mr. Weatherstone, who had continued as his piano teacher and musical mentor through Grant's junior high and high school years—when, early in his senior year, Grant had decided not to pursue a degree in music, and chose instead to seek admission to Harvard. He would not be persuaded to reconsider. He'd seen a flaw in his own ability, he told his family, one that would keep him from becoming a solo performer; any other musical fate wasn't to be borne. He couldn't tell them, of course, that the flaw was located elsewhere than in his talent and preparation. Not in a million years could he reveal that he'd repaid his grandparents' generosity and his mother's sacrifices by falling in love with his mentor.

It began, as Grant had told Varian all those years ago, with a kind of dawning physical awareness—a sense of Mr. Weatherstone, who had been a presence in Grant's life long enough to render him as invisible as the furniture, coming slowly into focus; he smelled, Grant discovered, of sandalwood and mint; his hands on the keys were not just agile, but slender and strong. Grant had read enough of English literature to know that falling in love with one's piano teacher was a terrible cliché; he was no better than an incidental character in an Austen novel. But that was what he'd done. For months he existed in a state of horrified, trembling anticipation—of what, he could scarcely imagine. Then one afternoon there was a declaration, followed by a conflagration. It seemed Grant had not been alone in a sense of dawning physical awareness.

He recalled to Varian the feeling of leaving Mr. Weatherstone's apartment after that first encounter, feeling as though a terrible distance had opened up between his former and present lives. He watched a new self, Impostor Grant, perfectly imitating what the old self had done. **Now he's walking his bike to the gate. Now he's unlatching the gate. Now he turns the bike toward his house, where his grandmother will be making Friday-night dinner. Now he straddles the bike.** At home, Grant felt he might as well have been wearing a sign announcing what had happened. How could his family fail to notice? But to them, Impostor Grant was simply Grant, and life, unbelievably, went on.

At first it seemed to Grant that his ardor was specific to Charles Weatherstone. He could no sooner imagine touching another man than he could a woman. But Mr. Weatherstone, somewhat melancholically, assured Grant that it wasn't the case, that Mr. Weatherstone was simply a convenient conduit for a tendency Grant would soon find to be general. And it was true. Grant may have been in love with his mentor, but he was also, he soon discovered, a man who loved men. And that was where his self-acceptance ended. When he ran from music, he was running from that problem; when he sent away for the Harvard application, wrote his essays, and sat for the entrance exam, it was in flight from who he'd discovered—in fact, had always known—himself to be.

As the application forms revealed, the admissions board was interested in each aspiring Harvardian's parentage. It was part of what they called "character," by which measure, Grant understood, they hoped to control the composition of their entering classes. There were plenty of Jewish guys he knew who'd gone to Harvard; his religion cost him little worry. But there was no chance he'd tell the truth about his father's race, or what had become of him. Certainly there were Negro students at Harvard, but they were a kind of brilliant pinfeather in Harvard's cap, a tiny ornamentation that established the university's enlightened state. Harvard educated these students the way a U.S. president might cultivate a highly public relationship with the leader of a small foreign nation whose country he'd once invaded and ravaged. Negro students were rare. Grant, who did not consider himself Negro and couldn't see any reason to bear the attendant disadvantages, didn't want to take the risk of being one too many. Instead he neatly fabricated a father, a William Grant who'd been educated not at Oxford or Cambridge (he feared the admissions committee might too easily check his lie there) but at the Sorbonne. William Grant had been, according to young Elliott, a gifted paleobotanist, French on his mother's side and English on his father's, who had met Elliott's mother during a postdoctoral fellowship at Columbia. Dr. Grant, or Papa, as young Grant referred to him in the application, had died of influenza on a research trip to Peru. With a kind of burning rectitude—his father **had** abandoned him after all, and now he'd found a way to use that abandonment to his advantage, in a sense—Grant signed the application, affirming that all the information within it was true and correct.

Harvard College could scarcely have responded to the catalogue of young Grant's achievements, and to the wildly enthusiastic letters of his high school teachers, with anything but the ardent wish that he join the incoming class of 1931. And so he packed his bags, certain that when he left Philadelphia he would leave behind that unnatural and troubling desire, the one that must remain unnamed and that had taken his musical career—indeed, all his pleasure in music, from the simple feeling of his fingers on the moiréed ivory, to the delight he felt in mastering a difficult sonata, and, perhaps most problematically, his idea of what he might be in the world when he grew up—thoroughly and painfully away from him.

But not long after his arrival, he learned that Harvard was fertile ground for men like him, that there were secret clubs, parties, covert and overt relationships, liaisons between faculty and students, hidden corners of campus, of town, of Boston at large, where one might encounter, at a certain time of night, like-minded Harvard men. Some of these had fallen into the habit at boarding school and were loath to give it up; others, like Grant, found themselves inductees into a society they hadn't known existed. Still others, like Kirstein, had always understood themselves to be members of a third sex, their natures immutable as the stars. It was a society with its own rules, its own passkeys; it had its own dark history. Everyone knew about, though no one really discussed, the time, not so many years ago, when the university had convened a secret court to seek out and punish students, tutors, faculty, and even unaffiliated men in the community who had "gotten gay" with each other at parties, gone about the dormitories dressed in women's clothing, and turned up at certain Boston gathering places for men who favored men: the Lighted

Lamp, the Golden Rooster, the Green Shutters, and, most notoriously, Café Dreyfus, gold-curlicued and velvet-curtained, in a luxurious hotel on Beacon Hill. Some of the men had been expelled. Two had committed suicide. After the deaths, an article had appeared in the **Boston American** that described the court's interrogations in a darkened room, a curtain stuffed into the crack of the door so no one outside could hear what was taking place within. Tattered copies of the article existed in the possession of the society's members, and men passed them around as a reminder. But the fact that so little had been written about that event—and the fact that the university seemed to have submarined all records of it—suggested that the episode was a shame to Harvard itself, unlikely to recur. It would have been untrue to say that men who preferred men were at their ease at Harvard, that they didn't fear being discovered and punished. But they considered themselves inevitable, and their sense was that the school could do nothing but agree, however much it might officially loathe them. It was at one of those parties, laced with acts of the kind that the secret court had condemned as "faggotty" and "queer," that Grant had run across Varian—literally run across him, as Varian and a few others lay unclad on a raft of mattresses while other young men trod barefoot on their bodies. Not long after that came the evenings at the Pendragon, and the editorial meetings of the **Hound and Horn,** and everything that had followed, including, eventually, the sudden absence of Grant from Varian's life.

Varian had grieved and recovered. And now Grant slept in a hotel room not twenty feet away, at his lover's side, also apparently recovered. Had they emerged from a shared nightmare, or was this a new one? What would happen if they both made it back to Marseille? Here in France, so many things had fallen into the territory of the uncertain. The outline of his life, once as firm as if inked, had become obscured. Ostensibly he was a writer, an editor, a husband; but he wasn't writing, he'd abandoned his editorial position, and he was half a world away from Eileen. He was a rescue worker who didn't know how to rescue, a detective who didn't know what to look for or where. He was a maker of lists, which meant by definition that he was an excluder; he was the dreaded Fate, Atropos, holding the abhorred shears. He was a man, God help him, just a man, with a bad gut and a red-wine headache; he was a man who had stayed up all night in a bed in Cerbère, under the shadow of the Pyrenees. And there he lay awake into the dawn, listening to the lap and luff of the sea on the ash-blue shore.

They met in the lobby at nine that morning and walked up the hill to the train station, trading complaints about the hotel mattresses and the gruff elevator operator, of whom Golo Mann did a frowning, finger-wagging imitation. Among them only Grant seemed well rested; the red-wine hangover had spared him, if the clarity of his eyes and the lightness of his step were any indication. There was no trace of rancor, as far as Varian could see, between Grant and Katznelson. On the way to the station they walked with their shoulders nearly touching, and when Grant made a joke in German, Katznelson laughed.

At the station café, the travelers drank wartime coffee and read the newspaper. **Le Monde** reported that Herschel Grynszpan, the young Jewish man who'd shot a German diplomat in Paris two years earlier, had been sentenced to twenty years in prison. Varian had raised funds in New York for the boy's legal defense; the news of his sentencing seemed a bad omen. The refugees waited in silence as Leon Ball disappeared into the stationmaster's office. When he emerged ten minutes later, he was holding their passports, though his expression was as grim as it had been the day before.

"It's a no-go," he said. "The higher-ups from Vichy are still here. They're watching our guy's every move. No chance he can wave you through today, though he says he wants to." He distributed the passports to the refugees.

"I knew it," Werfel said, his head in his hands. "This was all a mistake, a terrible mistake."

"But what does it mean?" Heinrich Mann

demanded. "We can't stay now. The commissaire had our passports overnight. Vichy knows we're here. If we don't go now, we're simply asking to be arrested."

"But we can't go, don't you see?" Werfel said.

"At least not by train," said Golo. "But there are other ways."

Ball handed some francs around the table. "Everyone have another coffee on me. I'm going to have a word with our fearless leader." He rose, and Varian followed him out of the station café and into the street, where a passing shower had slicked the cobblestones and brought up a smell of damp clay.

"Cigarette?" Ball asked.

Varian shook his head. "I've quit."

"Take one anyway. It'll buck you up."

He did, and Ball lit it.

"It's a blasted shame," Ball said. "Those Vichy officers hanging around."

"What does the commissaire think we should do?"

"He says we've got to try today. End of story."

They both glanced up at the hill above the town, a bent knee of the Pyrenees; sand-colored hiking paths threaded the olives and oaks. The sun was bright and hot in a cloudless sky. Somewhere over the ridge of the hill lay the French border post; farther along, the Spanish one.

"Someone's got to go through on the train, with all that luggage," Varian said.

"You'll do that," Ball said. "I'll take them over the hill."

"What about Werfel's heart? And Mann—he doesn't complain, but he's nearly seventy, and not in the best of health."

"I know. But the commissaire says there's no telling what'll happen if you stick around. I don't know if he means some kind of roundup's about to happen, or if this is a case of better-safe-than-sorry. But there it is."

"There's nothing safe about it, that's for sure."

"I'm game for whatever you decide, Varian."

"Give me a minute. I'm going to sit out here and think."

"Sure. You know where to find me."

Ball went back inside, and Varian sat down on a curbside bench where some pigeons were examining the curled tip of a croissant. There were people in the world, he knew—his own wife, for example—whose decisions that day were no more dire than those pigeons' choice to peck or not to peck. No, that wasn't fair: his wife was teaching English literature to young girls. That mattered. Of course it did. But the girls would not live or die, not today, anyhow, because Eileen took one perspective or another on **Henry IV.** It seemed profoundly unfair. But then he was the one who'd chosen to go to France, he was the one who'd insisted. And now he had as his audience none other than Elliott Grant, the last person in the world in front of whom he wanted to look like a fool. What was he supposed to do? How to fake it convincingly?

The way he'd done it in the past: take a cue from others. Ball thought they should go. Varian could walk in and pretend the decision was his own, that he believed it to be the right one. That was all he could do, in fact. No bolt from the sky was going to save him, no godly hand was going to lift him out of this. He got to his feet and went in.

At the restaurant table the group sat at attention, having finished their coffee. They all looked anxious, though Grant's expression was of a slightly different cast: having intuited the weight of the decision Varian faced, his anxiety contained a shade of concern for Varian himself. It was enough to give Varian courage to do what he had to do.

He sat down at the table and told the refugees that he thought it best for them to try to go over the mountain that afternoon. He couldn't promise that their situation would improve if they waited another day; all the information he had, incomplete though it was, suggested that waiting might make matters worse. Ball would lead them, and Varian, with his U.S. passport and all its genuine visas, would ride the train through the Pyrenees tunnel, taking all the luggage with him. They would meet on the other side, at the Portbou railway station.

A stunned silence followed. Werfel, consulting

his pocketwatch, observed that today was Friday the thirteenth. Wasn't it courting disaster to leave at such an inauspicious moment? And Katznelson leaned toward Grant and began to make a quiet case in German against Varian's motives, suggesting that he and Ball were in collusion with the gendarmerie and were plotting to turn them all in at the border for a reward.

"I beg your pardon, Professor," Varian said, also in German. "Please trust that I have your best interests in mind."

Katznelson lowered his eyes and tucked his chin into his collar, wordless.

"We have absolute faith in Mr. Fry," Heinrich Mann said, a reproof, a prayer.

And so it was decided: they would go. There was nothing to do but gather their things and start. Half an hour later they walked together to the edge of town, where the buildings gave out and the hill commenced; behind a cemetery wall they found the path the commissaire had pointed out. The Werfels were traveling under their own names, on fake passports, and the Manns under false names with real American papers. Varian collected all evidence of the Manns' real names—an embossed address book, a sheaf of postcards, a library card—and promised to return it on the other side. Finally he took Heinrich Mann's hat, opened his penknife, and effaced the initials on the hatband. Then he transferred to Grant's care a few cartons of cigarettes for bribes.

Grant, taking the knapsack that contained them, let his hand rest for a moment against Varian's.

A hot rush of blood ascended through Varian's head. "Take care," he said.

"See you on the other side," Grant said, and then the travelers began to climb.

10

The Open Gate

Hotel Métropole
Lisbon

25 September 1940

Dearest Eileen,

Lisbon! Finally I can write to you without fear of the censors. But where on earth to begin? Perhaps by thanking you for your patience. I'm sorry I've made you wait so long for news. It's no easier to wait for yours here, when the mail is so capricious. How often do you write? What fraction of your letters makes it to Marseille? The last word was your letter of Sept. 15, which I treasure. Maybe another awaits me back at the Splendide.

You may well ask what I'm doing in Lisbon. In part I came simply to be able to write to you (and to Washington, of course, and the ERC) censor-free. But also I've just accompanied a group of clients on an escape: Heinrich Mann, his wife, their nephew Golo, Franz and Alma Werfel, my old friend Grant and his colleague Katznelson. We left Marseille by train, and when the commissaire stopped us at Cerbère I had to send them all over the hill on foot. I was sure Werfel or Mann would collapse en route. It was about eighty-five degrees and not a cloud. Imagine it: wishing them godspeed on a hill-side, not knowing whether or where I would see them again. I had to wait till afternoon to take the train to Portbou. Brought all the luggage with me, twenty-one pieces And half of it full of women's clothing. The customs officer didn't look twice at my mountain of bags, but what might he have thought if he'd opened them?

The train ride took forty-five minutes. Fortunately, I hadn't much time to sit and worry. Mann and his wife were traveling under false names with American papers; I had their Czech ones with the real names, and thought I'd better burn them in the train bathroom in case I was searched. What a mess I made. Absolutely blackened the sink. If we hadn't been in the tunnel at the time, Frenchmen and Spaniards would have seen the smoke for miles.

At Portbou I asked the station police if they'd seen anyone who fit our clients' description.

They hadn't. I nearly drove myself crazy with worry until I remembered a young porter I'd met on my way to France in August. The boy had confessed that he was a Republican. I knew he'd help me if he could. I found him at the baggage drop and gave him a load of cigarettes. He embraced me like a brother, then told me to go up to the border post on the road into town and ask there. So up the hill I went, to a bombed-out shell of a guardhouse where the patrol was sitting outside playing gin. The guard-in-chief made me sit and wait while he telephoned someone, and for a while I thought I was going to be hauled off to jail. But then the guy came back grinning: my friends were down the hill at the railroad station. They'd just passed through customs.

How I ran down that hill! And what a relief to see them all, looking none the worse for the trip. They told me everything: how they'd trudged up for hours, half-carrying Heinrich Mann between them; how, when they'd met a French border patrol just as they reached the crest of the hill, they thought it was the concentration camp for all of them. But the guard just told them they'd better take a detour around the French exit post and go straight to the Spanish entry point a little farther on. That was where they met our gin-playing friends. One guard recognized Golo Mann right away:

"Are you not the son of Thomas Mann, the famous writer?" Golo was surprised into telling the truth, and again they thought the jig was up. But the Spanish guard bowed and said he was honored to meet the son of so great a man, and sent his fondest regards to Golo's father. Then he picked up the phone and called down to the station for a car. Not to haul them to the police station, but to spare them the trouble of walking.

Imagine how we all felt that night. The Manns and Werfels and Katznelson had made it out of France. That was more than half the battle. And for my own part, I'd seen firsthand how the border crossings worked: how much depended on caprices of fate, and what factors were under our control. We drank ourselves blind, then went down to Barcelona the next day to see if we could get our clients on a plane to Lisbon. There were only two seats, and we decided Mann and his wife must take them. The rest of us went on to Madrid, where there was another plane with two open seats. So the Werfels were up and away.

I stopped in at the British Embassy, hoping to get the military attaché to promise me an escape boat. Nothing doing. But he gave me some vital information which I shall not repeat here. Then I got a few seats on the next plane to Lisbon, and thus Grant and Katznelson and I made our way here. I'd planned to stay out the week, but at the hotel I received an emergency telegram from Marseille: a few clients are in danger. I am obliged to return as soon as I can. Tomorrow at nine I fly for Barcelona and will take the train from there.

After this experience, I must reiterate what I said in my letter of Sept. 9: I can't see leaving anytime soon. The more I consider, in fact, the more it seems to me that I must stay. No one knows the political landscape like I do, at least no one who could safely come. And much of the work I've already done is the building of trust; that can't just be passed along to someone new. For my own part, Eileen, I could scarcely go about life back home knowing what's going on here. No one who saw it could stand for it, and now I've seen it.

But you mustn't worry for my safety or my health. I'm fine, better than fine. The day before yesterday I was swimming in the Mediterranean off Portbou with Golo Mann, entirely in the nude, while the others had their siesta. Fine young man, Golo. Under different circumstances you might have been jealous.

And you, too, I trust, are also well; your students love you, and your friends keep you busy. Your bed must be full of boyfriends by now, and I can't blame you, as long as you kick them out before I get back.

Have you perhaps by now settled upon one of the houses you described in your earlier letter? Whichever it is, I promise I'll love it. I'll get home to you, and to it, as soon as I can. For now, dear E, imagine how grateful I am to have a wife who understands the necessity and urgency of my work here, as I sincerely hope you still do.

With love, as ever—
your V

He blotted the letter and capped the pen. Grant, reading over his shoulder, made a noise of quiet bemusement.

"I hardly merit a mention," he said.

Varian turned in his chair. "I wrote your name twice, didn't I?"

"Perhaps I'm not as fine a man as young Golo."

Grant sat before him on the bed; they had agreed to meet for a drink on Varian's balcony while Katznelson visited a colleague at the university. Grant in Lisbon: from some secret linguistic reserve, he'd produced a knowledge of Portuguese that had allowed him to shop for a sky-blue cravat in the manner of the local dandies; in his pocket, a silver cigarette case filled with a set of Cuban cigarillos and a diminutive silver cutter. What could Varian have written to Eileen about Elliott Grant, the apparition who refused to disappear? Varian had nothing to hide, as regarded his own behavior; not that he and Eileen were in the habit of hiding anything. Eileen detested ignorance above all else, and most of all her own ignorance in personal affairs. When they'd agreed, early on, that a cosmopolitan marriage allowed for an occasional adventure on the side, they'd also agreed to be perfectly honest. It was no secret to Eileen that he'd had liaisons with men; she tolerated them as a peculiarity of his character. But how was he to be honest with her about Grant, when Grant's presence was still a matter of consternation and confusion? To be honest simply about the confusion seemed weak. To do otherwise would be to lie. But was a sin of omission better than one of commission? Both could be lethal.

"Don't look that way, Varian," Grant said.

"What way?"

"Like you've just taken a bite of glass."

"For God's sake, can't we just have a drink or something?"

Grant's eyebrows rose. "Of course. Let's have a drink."

Varian followed Grant out onto the balcony and poured them each a glass. Without thinking, he drained half his wine at the first sip.

"Thirsty?" Grant said.

"Don't you think I deserve it?"

"Try to savor the lovely wine. There's no rush."

"All right. I'll try to savor the lovely wine. But

let's talk about something else, shall we? What do you think Admiral Torr told me at the British Embassy?"

"What?"

"There are fifteen Nazi armored divisions at the border. Apparently the Führer is trying to decide whether to move into Spain or to go east into the unoccupied zone."

"Ah." Grant tapped ash from his cigarillo into a lozenge-shaped bowl. "So the Manns and Werfels were lucky to get out when they did. And Gregor. But we've got to get to Tobias as soon as we can."

"Yes. Who knows how long we'll be able to use the Cerbère route? And in the meantime, we're at the mercy of a thousand caprices."

"If Tobias is game to walk a steep mile or two, we should be all right over the mountain. I'll remember the path. I made notes."

"You'd better memorize them and burn them before you come back to Marseille."

"All right."

Varian took another long drink. If it hadn't been for Katznelson, he thought—if Grant had merely come to Marseille to work on his book—would they have ended up in bed by now? Would they, at this very moment, be tangled on the hotel floor, or pushing each other against the wall in the bathroom, the shower drumming their bare skin, their thrown-off clothes entwined on the marble tile?

"On my way back through Madrid," Varian

forced himself to say, “I hope to meet the British ambassador. H.E., as Admiral Torr calls him.”

“Well, send my regards to His Excellency.”

“I’ll do more than that. I’ll tell him about Tobias, if you’ll let me. And I hope you will. You’d better use all the advantages you’ve got. The boy could be anywhere. You need a web of contacts to catch your fly. And so far we’ve got nothing.”

“Not true,” Grant said. “There’s what Alma Werfel said.”

“About what?”

“Zilberman. Maybe he knows something. If his daughter really was, as she says, being pursued by young Tobias.”

“That’s right. But we don’t know where Zilberman is, either.”

“Then you’d better get looking as soon as you get home,” Grant said. “Particularly if the Führer plans to take the rest of the country. And I’ll see what I can learn from here. I suspect our people aren’t the only refugees in town. And perhaps Tobias has already found his own way out, and is hiding somewhere nearby.”

“Careful asking around, though, Grant. You never know who’s listening.”

“I’ll be careful,” he said, and a silence settled between them, a space that seemed to fill with electric charge. Someone had better say something else, Varian thought; but he said nothing, and Grant said nothing, and the space filled and filled. It took scarcely a movement, scarcely a tremor, for his thumb to contact Grant's sleeve, there on the table, as Grant reached forward to tap his ash. Grant saw it and failed to remove his arm. They sat that way a long moment, Varian's thumb against Grant's sleeve; they had entered a kind of standoff. Then they both laughed, and Grant refilled Varian's glass.

"What about you, Tom?" he said. "Do you really have to turn around and rush back to Marseille?"

"You saw the wire," Varian said. It was in his pocket, the cable he'd received from Lena shortly after he'd arrived at the Métropole. BABY PASSED CRISIS BETTER NOW BUT OTHER CHILDREN QUARANTINED DOING OUR BEST LENA. Varian had puzzled over it for a good quarter of an hour: **other children quarantined.** Clients arrested, or dragged off to camps, did she mean? How many of them? And what in fact had happened to Walter Mehring, code-named Baby? Had he made it out of the camp? Gotten back to Marseille? Wouldn't Vichy just come for him again? In any case, the urgency was clear. He'd already bought his ticket for the next morning. And he knew—more than he'd ever known in the past, more than he'd known before he'd sat down to write that letter to Eileen—that he was going back to stay for as long as it took; that in Marseille he could be of greater use to humankind than he'd ever been in his life. The fact that he'd brought the Manns and Werfels out of France only proved it was possible to do the same again with others. And then there was Grant. Of course he hadn't said more to Eileen. She was wise to Varian and always had been. For a decade they'd enjoyed perfect honesty because there'd been nothing significant to hide. Their foibles—his encounter with a brace of college boys at a party downtown, her late nights after work with a fellow who taught history at Brearley—meant nothing at all, and they both knew it. Worthless cards were easy to lay on the table. But this. If he so much as wrote another line, she would know more than Varian himself. And what was the point, anyway? Who was to say Grant would come back to Marseille at all? He might learn, in the next few days, that Tobias Katznelson had already escaped to Lisbon. Then he would disappear as quickly as he'd appeared. Even here on the balcony, as a haze of smoke rendered him indistinct, he seemed in danger of dissipating into the gathering fog from the Rio Tejo.

Grant's eyes rested on Varian's as they considered the last inch of wine in the bottle; tacitly they agreed that it must be finished. That gaze: Varian remembered times when he wished he could turn it off like a light, conceal what it revealed. Having drained their glasses of wine, they stepped into the room, where blue shadows had fallen across the deeper blue expanse of the bed. Without speaking, without touching, they skirted that abyss and went out into the Lisbon night.

TWO

Implicatus

11

Borders and Barriers

The train back to Marseille retraced the path it had followed a few days earlier: across the plains, through a corner of Provence, past the ragged outskirts of town, and into the city, where mean-looking buildings gave way to taller and grander ones until the train reached the Gare St. Charles. On the platform, the sharp-edged mistral shot through the fabric of Varian's jacket. The Romans had called it **ventus magestralis,** and marveled that a wind that blew with such brutal force and speed, sometimes for days on end, wrecking boats and flattening crops, could come out of a crisp, high, cloudless blue sky.

As he made his way down the broad bank of steps from the station toward the boulevard d'Athènes, it was a homelike relief to see the awning of the Splendide, and then, moments later, to see Lena and Hirschman and Miriam making their way from the

Canebière to meet him. Hirschman clapped him on the back and congratulated him on their clients' escape; Miriam greeted him with a kiss on both cheeks, the fragrance of her hair bringing a memory of his mother in a striped hat on the beach at Wellfleet. Lena demanded to know if he'd brought her the white cakes of soap she'd requested, refusing even to shake hands until he'd shown her the evidence. Then they all went up to his hotel room, with its sounds of the girls' school coming through the window, its familiar green curtains, its spindly-legged furniture. None of them wanted to talk business. After a sleepless night on the train, Varian was happy just to hear the cadences of Lena's French-Polish-English, to hear Miriam's trumpetlike laugh, to see the intelligent glint in Hirschman's eye. But he wanted to know first of all what had happened to the Feuchtwangers, who had left for the border a few days earlier.

"Monsieur Ball met them in Cerbère," Lena said. "From there they went through on the train. All is splendid. They reached Lisbon this morning. Mr. Ball telegrammed as soon as they arrived."

Varian exhaled. "And what about Mehring?"

"The clever lawyer got him out of St. Cyprien," Hirschman said.

"Oh, thank God! Where is he now?"

"Here at the Splendide," Miriam said. "Just down the hall. But not entirely out of danger. Bingham only barely managed to keep him out of jail. His residence permit had expired, and the police showed up yesterday morning to deport him. So he called me, and I called Bingham, and we came down here and shamed the police for trying to arrest a sick man."

"Sick?" He looked at Miriam, then at Hirschman. "What's wrong with him?"

"He's perfectly fine," Hirschman said. "The lawyer was the one who suggested that ruse. Miriam was to say that he was too weak and frail to go down to the Evêché and get his permit renewed."

"And it's working?"

"So far," Miriam said. "We need to produce a doctor's note, but then, apparently, they'll leave him alone for a while."

"That can be done. But what about 'other children quarantined'? Your telegram, Lena, was marvelously cryptic."

"I meant Madame and Monsieur Breitscheid, and Monsieur Hilferding," Lena said. "All have been arrested and placed under the house at Arles."

"Do you mean, Lena, placed under house arrest?"

"That is precisely what I have said, Monsieur Fry!"

Breitscheid and Hilferding: the leading lights of European social democracy. If there was a future for the continent after the war, they were the ones who would make it. Their names had been among the first to be added to his list, despite the fact that they weren't artists; they were so deeply endangered, and so vital to the cause of freedom, that they were considered to be everyone's responsibility. Breitscheid and Hilferding were, meanwhile, heedless of their own safety. More than once, Varian had found them at a café along the Canebière, berating various Hitlerian sympathizers and critiquing Vichy policy in broad, clear tones. They knew no conversational mode except for that of public address; no words of caution on his part had yet been able to curb them. And now they'd been arrested.

"I'll go see Bingham," Varian said. "He'll know how to manage this."

"In fact you are scheduled to visit the consulate today," Lena said. "Not to see Monsieur Bingham, however. To meet with Monsieur Fullerton. A message arrived at our office yesterday demanding it."

"Fullerton? Why? He can't have anything good to say to me."

"It seems there has been some **dérangement** about your actions here in Marseille," Lena said. "Some communication from Washington."

"What actions?" Varian said, anxiety coiling in his gut.

"Apparently you are accused of breaking French law. The consul requires an explanation. That is the **effet** of the message."

"There's nothing to explain. My actions are unimpeachable."

"The consulate must be under severe pressure," Hirschman said. "The situation worsens by the day. Have you not seen the news about Gibraltar?"

"What news?"

"The French bombed it yesterday for hours on end. Decimated the British installations there, and a great British warship besides—to get back at the Brits, I suppose, for their attack on Dakar. And the bombers were American-made."

"Weren't the Nazis supposed to have disarmed the French?"

"Ah, yes. That was the official line. Apparently they've just induced the French to use their armaments to the Nazis' aims. You must know that your State Department fears the same fate for the French fleet. They won't look favorably upon an American's flouting of French law, not at this sensitive moment."

"De toute façon," Lena said, "Fullerton wants you at once."

Hugh Fullerton, Varian knew, was overcautious and circumspect, a slave to orders from the consul-general. He got to his feet and crossed to the window, where he stood looking down into the now-empty schoolyard. Gibraltar bombed, the Brits' installations decimated: it was the State Department's nightmare exactly, the conversion of Allied assets to Axis control. A litter of leaves blew across the paving stones and tumbled against the courtyard wall. "Fullerton's going to demand that I leave," he said. "I know that much."

"Well, you'll have to tell him that's impossible," Miriam said. "You'll have to tell him you're your clients' only hope."

"And not just the clients," Lena said. "Without you, Monsieur Fry, we go to the concentration camp, Monsieur Hirschman and myself. Vichy will not hesitate. Only your presence protects us."

"What time's this meeting?"

"Immédiatement," Lena said.

"Not even a moment to catch my breath."

"**N'exagérez pas,** Monsieur Fry: you've already taken your coffee."

"Oh, all right, Lena," Varian said, and lifted his hat from its hook.

Hugh Fullerton, narrow-shouldered and puritanical in his small bow tie and navy jacket, was garrisoned behind a gray steel desk that looked to have been crafted from the hull of a dreadnought. On its deck lay a slew of correspondence attesting to one set of facts: Varian Fry's insistence upon carrying out illegal activities in France, and the State Department's refusal to support him. The jewel among these papers was a recent cable from Cordell Hull, secretary of state.

INTELLIGENCE SUGGESTS VARIAN FRY IN REGULAR BREACH OF FRENCH LAW. IN LIGHT OF THE FORMER MUST REQUEST HIS RETURN STATESIDE IMMEDIATELY.

Fullerton smoothed the cable against the desk. "Mr. Hull had an understanding with you," he said. "You were not to compromise, under any circumstances, our diplomatic mission in France. The French fleet hangs in the balance. If we lose our ties to France entirely, think how many American lives may be lost."

"The American diplomatic mission to France is a bald farce, Hugh, and you know it," Varian said. "France is in bed with a fascist nation now, in case you hadn't heard. The States' collaboration with Vichy is a violation of our nation's founding principles."

"Keep your voice down, Mr. Fry."

"I'm not afraid to speak the truth," Varian said. "Cordell Hull had better get his allies and enemies straight."

"And you'd better do the same. You're losing allies by the minute."

"And making others all the time. Ones who actually care about the fate of refugees, unlike your boss. You've helped us in the past, Hugh—I do appreciate your getting that visa for Katznelson, and for letting Bingham do what he can. But I'm telling you, if we play by Vichy's rules, we're letting people die. Sending them to French concentration camps, or inviting the Gestapo to deport them."

"The United States government isn't in the business of derring-do. We're trying to stay out of a war.

If we lose our relationship with France, we'll lose a great deal more than a few artists' lives."

"I'd like to know what Cordell Hull thought I was going to do here in France. The State Department knew I wasn't coming over to pass out toothbrushes and tinned beans."

"Whatever they thought when they issued your passport—and I'll confess, I don't know what that could have been—there's no mistaking what they think now. Here it is, in sum." He took up another cable from the clutter. "This has gone out to all the consular offices in France, in reference to you."

> THIS GOVERNMENT DOES NOT REPEAT DOES NOT COUNTENANCE ANY ACTIVITIES BY AMERICAN CITIZENS DESIRING TO EVADE THE LAWS OF THE GOVERNMENTS WITH WHICH THIS COUNTRY MAINTAINS FRIENDLY RELATIONS.

"Does not repeat does not?" Varian said. "Why only two iterations? Why not a third, to make perfectly clear that the U.S. is happy to kowtow to Nazis as long as we can stay out of the war?"

Fullerton's bow tie quivered, a neat barometer of his anger. "You will address me in a tone of respect, Mr. Fry."

"Hugh, you're not my elder. Quit acting like it."

"Bear in mind, please, I can turn you over to Vichy's mercy anytime."

"But then they'd have to prove I've been in breach

of French law. And I can assure you there's no evidence to support that claim."

"Really? I hope you've been doing a better job of hiding your activities from them than you have from us. We know about Bill Freier. And we know what Leon Ball's been doing for your operation. The consul himself ran into Ball at the border—he was leading that physicist across, Meyerhof, was it?—and Ball asked him to vouch for Meyerhof at the checkpoint. He did it, but even he could see that Meyerhof was carrying false papers. We know about that too."

"You understand my mission, Hugh. You know what I'm bound to do here—morally speaking, I mean. I understand why Washington wants me out. I understand that the situation's worse each day. But I made a decision, coming here, and I've made a few more since I've seen what's going on here. I can't abandon this ship."

"What am I supposed to tell Hull? That you'd rather just ignore his cable?"

"Tell him you've passed along the message, and that I heard it loud and clear. Tell him I've agreed to go, but that I can't just pack up this instant. Tell him I've contacted the ERC about sending a replacement, and that once he gets here I'll have to train the man. Promise that in the meantime you'll force me to keep a low profile."

"Just how much time are you looking to buy?"

"I don't know. How much do you think I can get?"

"If it were up to me, none."

"Okay, Hugh. But practically speaking, if I'm to be ejected sooner or later, I do have to make some plans. I have to let my organization know, at least."

"I think we can get you another few weeks. Eleanor Roosevelt stands by you, even though the State Department doesn't. But the situation's delicate. Worse than delicate. I don't have to tell you my job's on the line here, too."

"I'll cable Cordell Hull myself. I'll let him know I got his message."

"No, you won't. I'll cable him. Now, let me get to it. And for God's sake, no more forgeries or fake papers. I'll be watching you."

"Goodbye, then, Hugh," Varian said. "And thanks. You've been kinder than you'd have to be. I appreciate it."

"Don't press your luck," Fullerton said, and dismissed him with a flick of his hand.

At 60 rue Grignan, the little gatekeeper—Clotilde, she was called—gave him a censorious look as he entered; a skipping rope hung over her arm like a noose. "No bonbons all week," she said as he passed, with a glance at the sky, as if bonbons were a meteorological phenomenon that had failed to materialize. She unlooped the rope and began to skip, the rope ticking out a brisk accusation against the pavement.

"Pardon me, my dear, I've been out of town," Varian said.

"Out of town! Bah."

"My colleagues will vouch for me."

She skipped with increasing fury. "I'm sure."

"My pockets are empty. I don't even have a coin to give you."

She stopped abruptly and turned a look on him so bitter and mature he felt he'd been caught in some clumsy romantic prevarication. Without another word, he went out again and crossed the street to the chocolatier, perused the depleted ranks of sweets behind the glass, and spent two precious ration tickets on four buttercreams that smelled as if they had been made with actual butter. He didn't know why he felt it necessary to tithe the child, only that, strangely canny as she was, he believed she might someday either protect or betray him. She received the gift mutely. She didn't deign to eat the buttercreams in his presence; instead she dropped the small gold box into the pocket of her dress, hooked the skipping rope onto her wrist like a fashionable bag, and slipped out through the door to go about her mysterious errands.

Having shut the courtyard door behind her, Varian climbed the stairs to the office, planning to report upon his meeting to his colleagues. No refugees waited outside the office door, and no sound of conversation or of work reached him through the glass. All right, then; he would relish a few moments of isolation. But the door opened at his touch, and he entered to find Hirschman and Lena standing silently at a window, a single shivering telegram held between them.

"What is it?" Varian said, looking from one stricken face to the other.

"Walter Benjamin is dead," Hirschman said.

"Oh, God, no. How?"

"By his own hand, at Portbou."

Varian dropped into a chair and closed his eyes. Walter Benjamin, the German Jewish philosopher, critic, scholar; Benjamin, whose work had burned with a quiet and persistent fire in Varian's mind since he'd first encountered it in college; Benjamin, whose name had crowned his list, and who was rumored to be writing a new book. "Who's that from?" he asked, indicating the telegram.

"A German refugee, Lisa Fittko," Hirschman said. "She and her husband have been doing what Ball's been doing, more or less. She was the one who led Benjamin's group over the border. They made it all the way to the station at Portbou, but they were stopped at customs. The officer said they could spend the night in town but would be sent back the next day."

"And?"

"They checked into a hotel in town. And Benjamin took morphine that night."

The thought was intolerable. A few hours earlier, less than a single day, Walter Benjamin's mind had existed intact; then, sometime in the night, he'd opened a bottle of pills, put one on his tongue, and another, and had swallowed, and repeated the process until he knew he'd had enough. Then the drug had gone to work, shutting down the intricate machinery of the body, breaking its fine linkages, silencing its humming wires, dimming the electric light of the brain until it went dark. That beautiful brain ceasing to send its beacon out into the night.

"And all he would have had to do is get sent back," Varian said. "Just get sent back and try again in a few days. Jesus."

"He was carrying a manuscript," Hirschman said. "Likely he didn't want to bring it back over the border."

"A manuscript? Not his new manuscript! Who has it now?"

"Lisa doesn't know," Hirschman said. "No one knows, apparently."

"But how can that be? Who collected Benjamin's body? Where are his things?"

Lena twisted her fingers. "They cannot locate his suitcase, Lisa says."

He brought his hand down on the desk. "For God's sake! Call this Lisa Fittko at once. Call Azéma, the mayor of Banyuls. Get someone to Portbou, to the prefecture or wherever the Spanish authorities are holding his stuff."

"Ne vous dérangez pas," Lena said. "I will telephone."

"It's not your fault, Varian," Hirschman said. "He wasn't our client."

"Ours or somebody else's, what does it matter? Anyway, he should have been ours. He's on our list. And now he's dead by his own hand!" Varian got to his feet and went to the window, where, in the street, two workmen were unloading the skeleton of an awning from the bed of a truck. They lifted it between them like an awkward boat on a portage; the wind wrestled them for it, threatening to send it through the window of the haberdashery. "The State Department washes its hands of me," Varian said. "Did you know that? They've delivered an ultimatum of sorts to the consulate. Now Fullerton wants to throw me out on my ear."

Lena gave him a frown of concern. "On your **ear**?"

"It's an expression, Lena. Anyway, they can make any threat they want. I'm a free man, whether they like it or not." It wasn't exactly true, of course, but the forces that bound him weren't the laws of any country.

Hirschman smiled gravely. "You must protect yourself," he said.

"From what? From my own government? Let them try to send me back. Then we'll see who needs protecting." But what was he threatening, exactly? Did he intend to take on Washington single-handed? Wasn't that, in effect, what he was doing in Marseille? The U.S. didn't want the refugees he was sending. But he wasn't going to sit by and watch the European cultural pantheon burn. Benjamin was dead. Others would follow, unless he did his work—perhaps even if he did. Let Cordell Hull deliver his official sanction. Let Fullerton wash his hands of him. Let Eileen implore him to come home. He didn't care what anyone said; he was staying.

12

La Fémina

Though Walter Benjamin had had nothing to do with the Centre Américain, though he hadn't been a client, though he hadn't died at the hands of French or Spanish police, or lost his life trying to traverse a mountain pass, his death acted as a deterrent. For a few days at first, then for more than a week, the influx of clients slackened. There were moments of quiet in the office, moments when Varian might look up from his work to see Mary Jayne gazing through the window, her eyes trained on the clouds as if to catch a glimpse of her surrendered Vega Gull. He might find Hirschman sifting through client folders for some new avenue to pursue, or Miriam examining a portfolio with a painter, not to determine the artist's merit, but simply because she'd seen something in the work that she wanted to revisit. One quiet morning, Gussie

Rosenberg arrived with a cable in hand from Paul Hagen in New York. Varian's first thought was that the Emergency Rescue Committee was notifying him that they'd found a new director for the Centre Américain, and that this person would arrive imminently. Instead the cable contained a newspaper headline: <<FLIGHT OVER PYRENEES DESCRIBED BY FEUCHTWANGER. DRAMATIC STORY BARED.>>—FRONT PAGE MONDAY TIMES. HAGEN.

Without a word to the staff, he ran to the foreign-press newsstand near the rue Fort Notre Dame and waited for the **Times** to arrive. As soon as the delivery van pulled up, as soon as the driver could heft the first bundle of papers to the curb, he tore a paper from the stack. And there it was, in black and white: **Flight over Pyrenees Described by Feuchtwanger.**

"Hey!" the newsboy shouted. "Hey! Aren't you going to pay?"

Varian stuffed a coin into the newsboy's jar, then took the paper down to the quai de Rive Neuve and sat at the edge of a pier. There he read the whole story: how Feuchtwanger had escaped from the concentration camp at St. Nicolas, how he'd hidden in Marseille and where, how he'd gotten out of France, and how the Manns and Werfels were currently en route to the States, having escaped via similar channels. Feuchtwanger described how some American friends had aided his escape, withholding names but giving enough detail that anyone in Marseille could recognize Varian or Mary Jayne or Harry Bingham. He went on to talk about how he'd gotten his false passport with its cleverly forged Spanish and Portuguese visas, praising the work of a talented cartoon artist. Then he gave a painstaking account of crossing the Pyrenees along a smuggler's pass, guided by an American émigré who hailed from Montana, and aided by a German refugee who'd helped dozens of refugees herself, though she'd failed to save Walter Benjamin from suicide. If he neglected to name Leon Ball or Lisa Fittko explicitly, the omissions couldn't have provided more than the slightest hindrance to the French or Spanish police.

Varian folded the paper, tucked it under his arm, and walked the six blocks to the office, half-expecting to find the Sûreté Nationale waiting for him already. The fact that they weren't there yet was little reassurance; surely it was just a matter of time. In the front room he assembled Lena and Hirschman and Miriam and Mary Jayne and told them the story. There could be no mistake about it: Feuchtwanger had blown the Centre Américain's last shreds of cover. The consulate's patience would now come to an abrupt end. He, Varian, was likely to be expelled from France in short order, and it might be weeks before the ERC could send a replacement. The others would have to do what they could to protect themselves, and to carry on operations in the meantime. They should expect the first ripples of this process to reach the office that day.

Lena dashed away tears with the back of her hand. "Monsieur Fry," she said, "you have proved me wrong. I argued often to Albert that you were **absolument fidèle** to the law of France, that you would not allow us to break it. But I am proud," she said. "Proud to know you are braver than you appear."

"Apparently I'm a lot more of a fool than anyone thought, too."

"It's hardly your fault that Feuchtwanger spoke to the press," Miriam said.

At her side, Mary Jayne looked stricken, shoulders curled, eyes round with shock. "It's my fault," she said, quietly. "Feuchtwanger was my client. I should have cautioned him. Instead I talked about his escape as if it were a grand adventure. Told him to record every detail for posterity." Her hands shaking, she drew a long cigarette from her case and lit it.

"For **posterity,**" Miriam said. "You didn't tell him to give an interview to the **Times** the minute he hit New York!"

"I practically did. I remember exactly what I said. I said, Oh, Lion, what stories you'll have to tell when you get to the other side!"

"I was there too, Mary Jayne," Varian said, quietly. "I heard everything you said. I didn't find any of it inappropriate."

"Here is what we know," Hirschman said, laying his hand over Mary Jayne's. "It's done, and we can't undo it. The consulate never believed that the ERC was entirely aboveboard, in any case. Fullerton made that clear enough last week."

"C'est vrai," Lena said, in stern agreement. "And they do not extinguish us yet! **On ne faut pas paniquer.** We must return to work at once!" She went back to her own desk and opened a client folder, and the others soon followed, though a stunned silence persisted through the morning.

And in fact it wasn't long before the first summons arrived from Fullerton, delivered by a crimson-cheeked bicycle messenger who looked as though he'd been plucked from an ecclesiastic ceiling mural. Under different circumstances Varian might have relished the sight of him. Now he could only take the folded communiqué from his hand and read it with dread. FRY: YOU ARE TO APPEAR AT CONSULATE AT ONCE TO DISCUSS REVELATIONS IN THIS MORNING'S PRESS. Varian tipped the boy more generously than he deserved, wrote a polite note to Fullerton declining his invitation, and sent the boy on his way. Half an hour later the same seraph returned, out of breath and carrying a more insistent note. Varian gave him the gift of a perfect apple, then neatly squashed and defenestrated the rectangle of official consulate note stock. The boy stared in alarm at the open window.

"You've done your job, young man," Varian said. "Nothing to worry about."

The messenger angel gave Varian a dread-laced glance, then went on his way. But he was back an hour later with a yet more insistent note, which Varian sent sailing after the last.

"You make a dangerous joke, monsieur," the boy ventured to say.

"Don't worry about me," Varian said. And all afternoon he continued to defenestrate notes as quickly as they arrived, while messenger and staff grew more and more desperate for his safety. It was hardly a surprise when a Sûreté officer rapped his stick against the office door and pushed inside. Varian got to his feet, smoothed his hair with one hand, and refolded his peacock-colored pocket square. The policeman read out Varian's name from one of the crushed notes.

"Yes, sir," Varian said. "That's me."

"I must cite you for littering upon a public street," the policeman said, and drew out his official pad to write a ticket. "In the future, you are to dispose of your office correspondence in a manner that shows respect for our city's hygiene, Monsieur Fry."

"Absolutely," Varian said. "Please accept my apologies."

"The Préfecture will accept your prompt payment of the fine," the policeman said, and, turning on his heel, removed himself from the office. Varian adjusted his glasses on the bridge of his nose and read the citation aloud. He was hereby found to be in breach of Marseille public decency regulation number 45 section 2, and was required to pay seven hundred and fifty francs.

"Could have been worse," Miriam said. "I thought he was here to arrest you."

"Me too," Varian said.

"Maybe the police have bigger fish to fry."

It appeared that the consulate did too. No further communiqués arrived from Hugh Fullerton. But later that afternoon, a call from Harry Bingham brought bad news: Spain had closed its borders. Vichy officials, he told Varian, had been conducting secret meetings all week with Franco's staff in Madrid; the content of these meetings was unknown, but the immediate effect was that Spain had ceased to allow anyone to pass through its checkpoints, refugees and travelers alike.

"Do you think the **Times** story had anything to do with it?"

"Hard to say," Bingham said.

"How long do you think it'll last? I've got seven clients set to leave this week. Three were supposed to go down on the train to Cerbère tomorrow morning."

"You'll have to tell them to wait, I'm afraid."

"God. What'll I say? Their visas expire in two days' time. It took months to get them, Harry. Months."

"I know. I'll do what I can on this end."

"All right. Thanks." He put down the phone and sank his head into his hands. The visas, he knew, were only part of the problem. Leon Ball and the Fittkos had been exposed; if they weren't arrested that very afternoon, they would at least have to go into hiding for a time. When they emerged, they'd have to reconfigure their escape routes. Bill Freier, meanwhile, would surely be arrested. Either they would have to find a new forger, or all the stamps and visas would have to be real.

There was no time to consider these complications. The soon-to-depart refugees had to be located, the bad news delivered, the imminent departures stalled. New visa applications had to be submitted at once. He got up to put on his hat, dreading the calls he would have to pay. But before he could leave the office, Gussie put another telegram into his hand.

"More bad news?" Varian said.

"I don't know, Monsieur Fry. I didn't look."

"All right, Gussie. Whatever it is, I won't hold it against you." He slit the telegram open, unfolded the paper, and learned that Grant was scheduled to return to Marseille that evening. TRAIN ARRIVING 20:30H. MEET FOR DINNER LA FÉMINA RUE DU MUSÉE. G.

He stood in silence, staring at the neat narrow capitals of the message. The air had left his lungs.

"Is it trouble?" Gussie said.

"Hard to say," Varian said, and put on his hat.

Grant's train was expected at half past eight. At seven forty-five Varian returned, exhausted and dispirited, to the Splendide. At the front desk there was no word from the office, and no further word from Grant; but there was a cable from Eileen, stamped *PRESSANT.* He tucked it into his pocket and ran up the stairs.

When he opened the door to his room, he found Mehring installed at the spindly-legged desk, reading **Les fleurs du mal** and smoking the last of a pack of cheap Reines. Mehring's fake illness chained him to the hotel, but he couldn't bear the monotony of his own four walls; Varian's room, if nearly identical, at least provided a change. The window offered a better view and southern light. And Mehring didn't like to write in the room where he slept. Varian found the smell of his cigarettes near-unbearable, but he was hardly going to protest anything that might keep Mehring from making another premature run for the border.

"Good evening, Walter," he said. "How's the dire illness?"

"Worse and worse," Mehring said, with cheer.

Varian tore open the cable from Eileen, read it, and tossed it on the table. "My wife joins the general opinion," he said. "They all say I should go home at once."

Mehring picked up the cable and read it aloud.

" 'PAUL INSISTS'—and who is Paul? Hagen is it, your comrade at the ERC? He insists 'YOU ARE IN DANGER IF YOU STAY STOP.' Indeed, we can't argue with that, can we? 'YOU PLACE YOUR STAFF UNDER CONSTANT RISK OF ARREST STOP.' Your wife does not mince words, does she, Mr. Fry? 'IN PROCESS OF SELECTING SUCCESSOR STOP.' Successor! As though you might be replaced, like a rotten tooth, with a clever simulacrum. 'CABLE YOUR RETURN DATE IMMEDIATELY.' And yet I don't see you packing your bags." Mehring extinguished his final cigarette in the ashtray. "I don't think you plan to leave at all, in fact."

"You're right," Varian said. "Though maybe I'm a fool to stay."

"Sometimes a fool is precisely what's needed," Mehring said, and turned back to his Baudelaire.

Varian stripped off his soaked shirt and dust-cuffed trousers. At the bathroom sink he filled a cup of water and prepared a lather of shaving soap. "In any case," he said, "no one's going anywhere at the moment. The Spanish border's closed. No one knows when it'll reopen. You may as well make yourself comfortable, Walter."

"I am as comfortable as I can be, Mr. Fry, with Nazis as bedfellows. Last night, Gestapo officers spent the night in the room **directly next door** to mine. I could hear them saying their prayers in Boche."

"Nazis don't pray," Varian said. He applied the

lather, then cut neat swaths with his blade, relishing the scrape of steel against his skin.

"These did," said Mehring.

"Well, I can assure you no one was listening besides you."

"That's little comfort, I'm afraid."

"Tell me, Walter," he said, following an impulse. "When you lived in Berlin, did you happen to know a family by the name of Katznelson? The father a professor of German literature? The boy, Tobias, a student of physics?"

Mehring smiled. "Oh, yes, I saw Katznelson often."

"You did? Gregor Katznelson, do you mean?"

"Yes, precisely. We both favored a café on Charlottenstrasse, near the university. Sometimes he brought his son. Always with a serious look, that boy. Always working on something in his little notebooks. But he liked to play with a kind of spinning top on a string, how do you call it in English?" He mimed a yo-yo. "Katznelson was usually in a hurry, though when he stopped to talk, I liked to hear what he had to say. His thoughts did not follow the usual channels."

The quality, obviously, that had appealed to Grant. "The boy's gone missing somewhere in Europe," Varian said.

"I see," Mehring said. "You'd like me to inquire among my Berlinese friends."

"If you can do it with utmost secrecy. We're not the only ones looking for him."

Mehring glanced up at Varian. "Who else is looking?"

"Wehrmacht intelligence."

"He's a communist, perhaps?"

"I don't know his politics. It's his smarts, apparently, that make him dangerous."

"I see," Mehring said. "Well. I'm entirely at the mercy of my friends' desire to visit me. But when they do, I will learn what I can."

Varian finished shaving, then pulled trousers and a freshly laundered shirt from the closet. Pinstripes, a white collar, crisp cuffs: sanity lay in these details. From a cluster of blooms in a pewter cup on the dresser, he extracted a pair of carnations. "What do you think, Walter? Red or white?"

"I have no opinion on the matter, dear Mr. Fry."

He put the red carnation into his buttonhole. "I hate to rush off and leave you to your cell," he said.

Mehring flattened and folded his empty cigarette box: crackle of paper, scent of toasted fig. "I shall look forward to your return," he said. And then, contemplatively: "Has the ERC already found a successor for you, do you think? I would hate to lose your company."

"My guess is no. You'd have to be crazy to want this job."

"Well. I hope you are correct, my friend. And where are you going tonight, may I ask? Dressed so impeccably—to the nines, according to the charming English phrase?"

"To carry on some selfish business of my own."

"Good for you, Mr. Fry. Good for you." Mehring clapped him on the shoulder. "And now I'd better get back to my own cell. Miss Pauli promised to visit this evening."

"Splendid, Walter. I hope you'll do more than talk writing."

"I share your hope," Mehring said. "Fervently." He went to the door and nodded to Varian; then they undertook the ritual they'd developed to ensure Mehring's safe passage back to his room, or at least the illusion of it. Varian listened at the door, then looked out. Having ascertained that the corridor was empty, he walked the length of it to be sure there was no one waiting just around the corner. At the center of the hallway, he listened for the elevator. When he was certain that the coast was clear, he gave a signal; then Mehring ducked his sleek head and ran.

La Fémina, the famous Moroccan restaurant, stood in the middle of a gold-lit block on the curving rue du Musée. Varian received an elaborate greeting from the maître d', Youssef A., who was privy to the comings and goings of a great many people of note; he had already helped Varian locate nearly a dozen clients. With a wink, he conducted Varian to one of the tiered platforms along the walls, seating him at a corner table that overlooked the service floor and offered a view of the assembled guests. Moments later he returned with an olive-adorned martini, and Varian drank as he watched the flow of traffic through the room, the diners entering and leaving, the waiters with their steaming trays of couscous, the busboys with their precipitous stacks of plates. A claw clenched his gut from the inside, giving an occasional twist: hunger laced with anxiety, desire cut with foreboding. Did he want Grant to walk through the door of this restaurant? Was that what he ached for? Or did he prefer him to have been delayed indefinitely in Lisbon or Barcelona, subsumed into the grand confusion of Europe? His delight in not knowing the answer—yes, **delight,** the feeling he remembered from boyhood rides on roller coasters, the thrill and fear of clicking to the top, not knowing whether the descent would bring incredible speed or a clattering, crushing death—should have been a warning, he told himself; it should have been enough to get him up from this table and out through the front door. Instead it was pure pleasure, a fine distraction from the terrible day he'd had. The feeling spread through his chest, infused with the scents of cardamom and saffron, set free to float on a sliver-thin layer of gin. He closed his eyes and took a long breath, and when he opened them again, Youssef A. was leading Grant through the honeycomb of tables.

Grant looked exhausted, even disheveled, insofar

as that was possible given the general luxuriousness and correctness of his clothes. He stood before Varian for a long moment as if confused; he seemed unsure whether he was meant to take the chair across from him or not, or what he was supposed do with his suitcase. Varian realized he was waiting to be greeted, and got to his feet. But what was he to do? Crush Grant against him there at La Fémina? Shake his hand as though they had last met the day before? He laid a hand on Grant's shoulder, and Grant, to his relief, returned the gesture; apparently it had been the right one. Then Grant sank into his seat like a sail cut from the mast.

"A drink, monsieur?" Youssef A. asked. "Honey wine?"

"No wine," Grant said. "Water."

"At once," said Youssef A., and disappeared.

"Don't you want a drink?" Varian said, resisting the compulsion to touch Grant again.

Grant ran a hand across his reddened eyes, a boy's gesture. "You'll have to pardon me, Tom. I'm not likely to be good company tonight. I've been traveling for the past twenty-four hours. I should have gone home to bed."

But he hadn't gone home to bed. He'd come here to meet Varian. "So the border's still permeable in this direction, at least to an American with visa and passport," Varian said. "And bribe money, perhaps."

"Yes, rather too much bribe money. And a

rather—a rather brutal search of my person, I guess you'd call it. I don't know what they thought I might be smuggling into the country, but whatever it was, it must have been awfully important."

"God, Skiff. Are you all right?"

"I'm here, aren't I?"

"Yes, but—are you sure you want to stay?"

"Now that I'm here, I'll stay."

"We can go anywhere you want. This room's a little loud."

"That's an advantage, isn't it? A cover. Couldn't we use a cover?"

Varian's heart clamored in his chest. "Yes. But you'll still have to keep your voice down if you've got anything delicate to say."

"Isn't it all delicate? Your situation in particular. I must admit I'm a little surprised to see you here. I wasn't sure I'd find you in France at all. I've heard consular officials slandering you all across the Iberian Peninsula. Apparently you've got some enemies in the State Department. And now Feuchtwanger's blown your cover."

"Oh, yes. But to hell with all that, Skiff—how are you?"

"Fine," he said, then touched his side and winced. "A little bruised, maybe. A little out of spirits. I just sent my colleague across the ocean, you know."

"You don't have to call him your colleague," Varian said.

Grant gave a pained laugh. "All right. Sorry." He

touched another rib, winced again, resettled himself in his chair. "I'm rather frustrated, actually. No one I spoke to in Portugal or Spain offered any help whatsoever. Not even the Unitarians. They say they can't touch a case like Tobias's, not with Nazi intelligence after him. Everyone's protecting their own positions."

"Yes, often blindly. As if they've forgotten their real job here."

"I don't know what to do now. Time is pressing."

"We'll get a plan together, Skiff. We'll start first thing in the morning. But let's leave it alone for tonight. You're exhausted. You need to eat and sleep."

Youssef A. delivered the drinks, and Varian ordered dinner for them both. Grant rubbed his face with one long-fingered hand as if trying to erase himself. "God," he said. "I can't put two words together."

"Please, Skiff. You know you don't have to make conversation. Just sit a minute and have a smoke. I'll go talk to our maître d'. See if he's got any news."

"All right," Grant said. "Thanks."

Varian rose from the table and took a single step toward Youssef A.'s station near the door; the maître d', his attention trained on the room, saw him at once. A few moments later they were both standing at the polished cloakroom counter in relative privacy. Rows of hats lined the shelves behind them, but only a few light coats hung from the wooden hangers; though the air outdoors was brisk from the mistral, true winter was still months away.

Varian took from his breast pocket a slip of paper on which he'd scrawled Tobias's name and the barest details of his situation, and pushed it across the counter. Youssef A. glanced at the paper and tucked it into his waistcoat pocket. As he did, two Vichy officers entered, trailing a miasma of cheap schnapps. They were deep in conversation about who had or hadn't said a certain thing about a certain woman; they seemed not to notice where they were. Youssef A. asked if they wanted their hats, and one of them raised a lazy hand to his forehead in a mockery of a salute. Then they rounded the corner and plunged once again into the dining room.

"Sales Boches," Youssef A. whispered, then glanced down at the piece of paper in his hand. "Katznelson," he said. "Tobias. You're not the first to ask if I know where this man might be found. But I did not trust the other."

"Why not?" Varian said.

Youssef A. smoothed the dome of his forehead with one slender hand. "Over time," he said, "I have learned to read a man's face."

"When did this guy first come in?"

"Maybe three weeks ago. Four."

"And you told him . . . ?"

"I said I do not know this Katznelson, just as I tell you now."

"Youssef," Varian said. "Tell me. How would I recognize this man?"

Curiously, the question made Youssef A. flush a deep red. "I can say nothing more."

"I have to know who this person is. I need to know who's looking for Tobias. It's important. You could even say it's a matter of life and death."

Youssef A. pulled at his shirt cuff and glanced back toward the hanging coats. Then he leaned closer, his eyes on Varian's. "Mr. Fry, you must not be offended by what I say."

Varian's senses pulled to a sharper attention. "What do you mean?"

"You already know this man," Youssef A. said.

"I do?"

"Yes. He is sitting at the table with you."

Varian stood for a long moment, holding the maître d's gaze. Youssef A. didn't waver or flinch. Finally Varian began to laugh; he couldn't help himself. "That's Mr. **Grant,**" he said. "Elliott Grant. He's a friend of Katznelson's father. He's the one I'm trying to help."

"I see." Youssef A. smiled, but his tone remained wary. "I must tell you, Monsieur Fry, your friend comports himself like a man who is keeping a secret."

Marseille was lousy with mistrust, Varian knew; no one in that town could imagine a motive for anyone else besides blatant self-interest. And most of the time, the suspicion was correct. "You're quite right," he said. "Mr. Grant has many secrets. But I hope I know them all by now. I've known him a long time."

"Yes. You know him better than I do, of course."

"Is Mr. Grant the only one who's ever mentioned Tobias's name to you? You've never heard of him from anyone else?"

"Not once."

"Well, do keep an eye out, will you? And if you hear of him, let me know immediately. You know where to find me."

"Of course, sir." For a moment Youssef A. looked as if he meant to say something more. But then he closed their conversation with a half-bow, and Varian returned to the table in the high-ceilinged dining room, shaking his head.

Grant raised an eyebrow. "Everything all right?"

"You tell me. Our maître d' thinks you're a spy or something."

"A spy! I must not have tipped him enough last time I came in."

"He thinks you look suspicious."

"He'd be a fool not to," Grant said. "Look at me. I'm a wreck."

Varian took off his glasses, polished them with his napkin, put them on again. "**Are** you a spy? How am I to know?"

"If I were a spy, Tommie, you'd be the first I'd

tell." He seemed ready to succumb to exhaustion; he pushed his plate forward and laid his head on his folded arms.

"Do you know what I think?" Varian said. "I think everyone in this town's gone a little crazy."

"I'm sure you're right."

"I think I need to get out of here for a while." A thought had begun to take shape in his mind, seemingly beyond his control. "Did you know there's a Roman arena and amphitheater in Arles, about an hour's train ride from here? I've been meaning to make a day trip of it. An overnight, even. A guy could get there on a bike if he wanted to. And now I've got a couple of potential clients stuck there under house arrest. I need to go down and see them."

"A bicycle trip to Arles? That sounds suspiciously like play."

"The consulate could use a break from me. Even the messenger boy has had it up to here. You should have seen how he looked at me when I threw Fullerton's last summons out the window."

"You can't hide from the consulate, Tom."

"I know. But maybe I can fall lower on their list of peeves."

A waiter arrived with steaming dishes, and for a moment they had to turn their attention toward dinner. The couscous was as it always was at La Fémina: flawless, stuffed with chicken and citron and dates and cinnamon. It was, Varian thought, the only way to answer the hunger that came upon a man as he walked through the market streets south of La Canebière, past the great barrel-sized sacks of spices that threw clouds of red or burnt-umber scent into the air. A silence settled between them for a moment, and into that space came the thought that had appeared in Varian's mind.

"If I were to go to Arles this weekend," he said, his pulse pounding in his temples, "what would you think of coming with me?"

Grant averted his eyes. "I've got a rather pressing job to do here in France," he said. "It's unkind of you to tempt me with a distraction."

"It would hardly count as a distraction. Tobias might be anywhere. We can make inquiries while we're there." Varian had forgotten his perpetual pledge to project impassivity when it came to Grant; the relief of seeing him again was so powerful that he was helpless against it.

Grant looked up at Varian from the bottom of his exhaustion. "Tom," he said. "Do you really think it's a good idea?"

"They're trying to kick me out of France. What if they succeed?"

They both knew what he meant: Their time was fleeting. They might never have another chance. France had already fallen; Marseille couldn't be far behind. Even if Varian managed to stay, even if he managed to avert the consular wrath, they might be separated anytime. Reason had fled the continent months before; it seemed to have fled the entire globe. America sat transfixed as France dangled its naval fleet from its finger like a diamond necklace. What would follow? Nothing that had precedent, nothing that could be named. Grant gave a nod of acquiescence, just a shadow of a gesture, and suddenly there was an agreement between them: they were going.

13

Arles

Along with bread, jam, meat, sugar, coffee, smokes, petrol, and nearly everything else, bicycles had gone scarce in wartime Marseille. Some had been requisitioned for scrap and made into guns. Others had been sent to the front to be converted to military use. Of those that remained, most had been pressed into service as **bécane**-taxis or delivery vehicles. There were, however, two bicycles Varian knew of: a black Gitane that belonged to the building's concierge, mother of Clotilde, the berry-eating nymph at the gate; and a green Motobécane, property of Gussie Rosenberg. He hated to ask Gussie for his bike; there could be no way for the boy to say no. Gussie himself might have liked a weekend ride in the countryside. But Varian found himself willing to press his unfair advantage, and Gussie assented graciously, asking only that Varian refill the tires.

The mother of the raspberry-eater was more difficult to woo. She was a skeptic in general, even more so where Varian was concerned. Even before the arrival of the Centre Américain de Secours, her role as building overseer had her busier than she liked; now the constant stream of refugees made an unpleasant change. To visiting friends, Madame Balansard complained loudly that her daughter, Clotilde, was being exposed to all manner of human filth: Jews, scribblers, Poles, communists. She was the last person Varian would have wanted to ask for a favor. But the following day he saw her returning from the market, the black Gitane heavy with bulging saddlebags, and he mustered his courage and found the words.

She sat astride the bicycle, her skirts tucked around her legs into a kind of Turkish pantaloon. On her head she wore an aviator's cap, from the bottom of which dark curls skewed. She took off her sunglasses and squinted at him. "My **bicycle**?" she said, in the tone she might have used if Varian had asked to borrow her daughter.

"Just for the weekend. For a trip to the countryside."

"Indeed! And where, exactly, do you propose to go?"

"To Arles," Varian said.

"To Arles! You are mad, if you'll pardon my saying so, Monsieur Fry. Do you know that Arles is ninety kilometers from here? You propose to take my bicycle on a ride of one hundred eighty kilometers total?" She shook her head. "You may do what you like, but I cannot lend my bicycle." She took off the aviator's cap and ran a swift hand through her hair. Her husband, Varian had heard, had been a flier, and had gone down in the Tyrrhenian Sea.

"Suppose we go halfway by train," Varian said. In fact, he hadn't paused to consider that Arles was ninety kilometers away. From the States, where he had first contemplated making the trip to see the Roman ruins, it seemed hardly a breath from Marseille.

"You propose to take my bike on the train?"

"I would guard it with my life."

"Absolutely not. Things get stolen from trains. And then there's the ride. What if you get a flat? Do you know how hard it is to get a replacement tire?"

"Madame Balansard," he said, raising his hands, as if to invoke the gods. "I serve the cause of liberty. Do it for France!"

"I know your kind of liberty," Madame Balansard said, her upper lip curling. Varian could see what she'd bequeathed, genetically speaking, to Clotilde; they had a spirit his father would have called hell-beckoning. But then her smile turned businesslike, calculating. "Perhaps, Monsieur Fry, you'd pay a price for the use of my bike."

"What kind of price?"

"Clotilde is always hungry. The ration coupons don't go far enough. And winter is coming." She leaned close. "My daughter needs food, and a new coat. A good long one. And boots, waterproof boots. I see who comes and goes from this building, Monsieur Fry. I have no doubt that the black market flows through these gates."

"I'm afraid you're mistaken, Madame. Our business is all aboveboard."

"I cannot lend this bicycle to anyone who asks. It was Felix's, you know." The downed flier. She held one elbow in her palm and considered the stones of the courtyard.

"What if I were to promise to ride no more than fifty kilometers in total?"

"Forty. And you must return the bicycle in perfect condition. And provide what I've asked."

Varian agreed. They shook on the deal. "You have my gratitude," he said.

Madame Balansard unloaded the groceries from the saddlebags and left him standing in the courtyard, holding the upraised handlebars. He parked the bicycle next to Gussie's, feeling as if he'd executed a double theft. But there they were, the bikes: a means and an excuse for an escape.

If all went well—if he wasn't thrown out of France before the weekend—they would take the train Saturday morning from Marseille. They would ride it to Miramas, then disembark to pedal the Route de la Crau across the sprawling alluvial steppe they'd seen from the train to Cerbère. In a single afternoon he assembled the necessary supplies: food, a patch kit, a foot pump, extra tubes for the bikes. It took some doing, but this was Marseille: everything could be had for a price. Hirschman assured him that once they reached Arles, they'd find a comfortable hotel at the main square. He named the place—Hôtel du Forum—and said he knew the proprietor, who would see they had everything they needed. Varian might have preferred to hide somewhere out of the way, but this wasn't a college excursion, after all; it was a business trip, and he was still at the helm of the CAS. If the office needed him, he had to be found.

Grant met him at the doors of 60 rue Grignan the next morning, a messenger bag slung over his shoulder, a pair of thin leather gloves in his hand. He wore knit wool cycling pants and a striped jersey; the gloves were perforated to let in the wind. Where he had come by a full set of cycling clothes, Varian could not begin to guess. Grant caught him looking and smiled.

"Bought it all for a song at the flea market," he said.

"Well done, Skiff." Varian averted his gaze and fooled with the leather cross-strap of his own messenger bag; he felt, suddenly, as if he'd forgotten everything essential.

"Is something bothering you, Tommie? Don't you feel like going?"

"I'm fine," Varian said, though in fact he felt lightheaded; he had to lean the bike against the building and sit on the doorstep.

Grant propped Gussie's bike and sat beside him. "Want a smoke?"

"No. Just a breath."

"What is it? Tell me."

"It's nothing." He breathed deeply, willing his carbonated dizziness to pass. All along the empty street, the cobbles glittered with sun; a shopkeeper was spraying down his piece of sidewalk, sending a bridge of water over the pavement. The light shattered into its pluribus of colors and arced over the street like a portal. They would walk through that portal toward the station. They would take the train to Miramas and ride to Arles, where he would try to see Breitscheid and Hilferding. Maybe he and Grant would visit the Roman amphitheater. Damn to hell this electricity in his spine. What was it Kirstein had said once at school? Save punishment for the guilty. He was committing no crime. He hadn't stolen the concierge's black Gitane, nor Gussie's green Motobécane; he wasn't even taking a break from his duties.

He got to his feet. Grant took his cue, and they shouldered their bags and started toward the station, Varian squinting against the glare, Grant unflinching, the fineness of his profile like the stamp of a Roman coin. The shopkeeper tamed his iridescent arc so they could pass, and without a word they made their way through the quiet of the morning streets, through the hush that barely held back all the bristling activity of Marseille. They turned onto the boulevard Dugommier and traced a path toward the hill of stairs at the foot of the station. The Hôtel Splendide lay dormant in its shadow; as they passed, Varian checked and re-checked in his mind all the places where he'd hidden precious documents and lists: behind the mirror glass, inside the telephone mouthpiece, underneath a loose scrap of carpet near the head of the bed. His room was lousy with evidence, if anyone cared to look. Nothing to be done about it now.

At last he and Grant climbed the stairs, hoisting the bikes, and reached the plane of the station. Once they passed through its glass doors and into its vaulted interior, Varian's pulse slowed: he had entered the province of travel, a place he knew and loved. Grant seemed to relax too. He rested a hand on the seat of the Motobécane and laughed.

"I'd have been willing to ride the ninety K, just to avoid another train," he said.

"Me too," Varian said. "I'd ride it still, if I hadn't promised Madame Balansard."

"We'd never make it, though," Grant said. "Ninety K!"

"I'm not saying we'd beat the train, but we could have ridden ninety miserable kilometers. And I could ride them faster than you, dear."

"Is that a fact?" Grant said. "We'll see how fast you ride, **dear.**"

And the game was on. They checked their bikes and bags and boarded a third-class car, not caring that the seats were hard, the glass murky with the exhalations of previous passengers; for the moment they were boys freed from school, no one to stop them from doing exactly what they wanted. Grant took from his messenger bag a thermos of espresso and a slender flask of whiskey. He placed a book on his knees for a bar counter, decanted an amber dram from flask to thermos, then drew out a tiny glass bottle of absinthe and added ten drops. The top of the thermos contained two nested silver cups; he divided his mix into them and offered one to Varian.

"Ridiculous," Varian said.

"Is that a toast?"

"Why not?"

They touched their glasses and threw back the drinks. The coffee was expertly brewed, the whiskey smooth, the absinthe a hint of punishment. "Is there nothing you're unprepared for?" Varian asked.

Grant smiled, gratified, and the train, a co-conspirator, pulled out of the station. Somewhere in its trailing cars their bicycles awaited. For now the trip required nothing but for them to sit in the hard-backed seats and watch the city turn into countryside again. The sensation in Varian's chest was one of wild liberation, not unlike the feeling of leaving

Harvard for a boys' weekend on the Cape, parentless, cash-rich, temporarily unburdened by classes. The restraints were off, at least the visible ones.

"What were you thinking of now?" Grant said.

"Nothing. Just riding and looking."

"At what?"

"Whatever's out there. Provence. It's not exactly what you'd expect, is it?" It was a deflection, but true nonetheless; there was a strangeness to the landscape that betrayed the idea Varian had held of Provence before he'd seen it. The grapevines and olive trees and rows of skyward-pointing cypresses presented themselves as expected, but often they appeared against hills furred with ugly gray-green scrub and toothed with great molars of limestone; often the ubiquitous lavender and almond gave way to low, hostile cactus, gnarled kermes oak, rusty lentisk, or wind-stunted pistachio. The sky was the washed-out blue-green of weather-beaten copper; the few clouds overhead seemed wrung out and dry. Through the windows of the train fell a pale light that bleached the features of the passengers. The populace of France seemed disinclined to travel that weekend; the only other passengers in the third-class car were a pair of elderly priests in cassocks, semilunar glasses perched on the bridges of their noses as they read in silence, and across the aisle a corresponding pair of elderly women, sisters perhaps, though not the ecclesiastic kind. One of them held a wicker cage on her lap, inside of which lay the shadowy form of a doomed rabbit.

The door at the head of the car opened and a conductor entered. He took tickets, fed them to his vampiric device, and returned them double-punched, drained of value. He nodded first to Grant, then to Varian, and moved on to the pair of sisters.

Grant tucked his ticket into his hatband and looked out the window. He seemed to appreciate a private joke; his mouth curled minutely, an expression so fleeting and subtle as to be scarcely apprehensible.

"What's that about?" Varian said.

"What's what?"

"You smiled."

Grant held his silver cup to the window light, catching a slipstream of reflection. "I believe I understand why he stayed," he said. "The elder Grant, I mean. I think I begin to understand."

"Your father?" Varian was surprised to hear Grant mention him; was surprised to know he thought of him, though Varian himself had been thinking of him lately.

"Yes, old Clayton. The pianist. The disappeared."

About Clayton Grant they'd almost never spoken. Varian had assembled the scant parts of Grant's familial puzzle from a handful of conversations, generally undertaken with assistance from Uncle Scorch; a morning splash of whiskey and absinthe seemed hardly enough to elicit new revelations. But Grant drained the last drops of his spiked coffee and balanced the cup on his book.

"A conductor enters a train car anywhere in America," he said. "The year is 1940. He makes his way down the car to punch his passengers' tickets. Among his passengers he comes across a pair of men, one Negro, one white, clearly in each other's company."

"Anywhere?" Varian interrupted. "Doesn't it matter whether we're north or south of the Mason-Dixon line?"

"Not at all," Grant said. "That's precisely my point. Anywhere in America, this conductor enters his car, punches tickets, gets to these men. One Negro, one white."

"Who are these two men, anyway? Two older guys? Two boys? College guys?"

"Stop talking for a goddamn minute, will you?"

"Sorry. It's just, if you're going to sketch the situation, I want to know what I'm looking at."

"Just be quiet and listen, Tom. He gets to these two men. Doesn't matter if they're old or young, fat or thin, handsome or ugly. This conductor might look at them only for a split second, but in that fraction of a second, what's he thinking? What can he **not stop** himself from thinking, whether we're up north or down south, whether the conductor's daddy's daddy wore the blue or the gray?"

"You tell me," Varian said. "What's he thinking?"

"**What's that white man doing with a Negro?** That's what."

"Whereas in France," Varian said.

"Whereas in France, the conductor might be thinking of anything. His dead grandmother. His next meal. He might be cursing the hole-puncher for going blunt again. But he's not required—not by some great force beyond his control, older than memory—to look at those two together and think, **What's that white man doing with a Negro?**"

"I see," Varian said. "And that's why Clayton Grant stayed."

"In a nutshell," the younger Grant said. "Or so I imagine."

"I suppose I wouldn't have thought of that."

"**You** wouldn't have noticed the difference in the way that man looked at us," Grant said. "To you it would have been just as in the States."

"But then," Varian said, proceeding with some caution, because now they had reached the edge of a subject scarcely discussed, "**would** there have been a difference? Wouldn't he see us as two white men, just as anyone would in the States?"

"Well, maybe the difference is in my mind, then. In our case, at least. In the States, I have to think of myself as one thing or the other. My daddy's a Negro, so I'm a Negro too. Either that, or someone who's pretending to be white. In France, though, I'm a man first. Do you see?"

"Ah, yes. Or at least you **were,** under the old **liberté-égalité** model."

"I'm not talking about Vichy. I'm talking about Free France."

"I see," Varian said. "So then"—and he looked at Grant in the flat blue light of the Provençal sky and drew a subtle conclusion: Grant wasn't passing here in France. It wasn't as if he was trying not to, or doing anything different. He just wasn't. They were just two men together on a train, Elliott Grant and Varian Fry. "I see," he said again. And then he fell silent for a few moments, thinking. "It's an odd thing," he said finally. "I know Negroes come to Europe and stay. There's a long tradition of it. But insofar as I thought about it, I suppose I thought your father stayed for a different reason."

Grant tilted his head at Varian; it might have been news to him that Varian would have considered his father at all. "What reason?"

Varian hesitated. Could he go on? He and Grant behaved here in France as if they'd returned to the intimacy they'd shared at Harvard. But the truth was slightly different. He didn't know the boundaries of their current relationship and was afraid to overstep them. Grant looked at him now in a penetrating manner, as if trying to read what was written on the back wall of his mind.

Varian cleared his throat softly. "I thought your father stayed because he was, well—of a different sort."

"A different sort?"

"You know. **Quaint,**" Varian clarified, using their private slang, a hemi-Chaucerian term. He had always thought so; it seemed the only explanation.

Grant stared at him in wonderment. "My father? **Quaint?**"

Varian shrugged, the blood rushing to his face. He would have mimed nonchalance if he hadn't known what a terrible actor he was. Grant, for his part, seemed caught in an inward struggle. A disturbance moved over his features like wind over water. Silent, he stared out the window at an endless orchard, the same row of almond trees again and again ad infinitum. His slim hand lay on the cover of the book as if he were about to take an oath.

"Strange," he said. "I never thought of that. Not one time."

They sat in silence a moment longer, then Grant gave a short, sharp laugh. The sound caught the attention of the priests and the elderly Provençales, who exchanged a glance across the aisle: how rude those young men were.

"You could be right," Grant said. "And I never thought of it."

Outside, the rows of trees began to slow their relentless whipping-past. The train was drawing near Miramas. The buildings of the medieval town hung on a bluff over the Etang de Berre, blocky and ungraceful, suggestive of hard-edged, unequivocal lives. The surrounding land was neither farm nor field, neither grazing-ground nor vineyard, just land, the crust of the earth, acres upon acres of cracked dirt that seemed to radiate an insistent and animate consciousness. To get off the train with their bicycles, to venture out into that void, suddenly seemed to Varian a fool's move. There was a German word for what he feared: **Waldeinsamkeit.** He'd read it in a book, maybe even one of Thomas Mann's, now that he thought about it. The fear was as much spiritual as embodied. But when the train pulled into the station—a squat beige block with a post office at one end and a dust-glazed café at the other—Grant got to his feet, clearly unafraid, and Varian followed him off the train.

They reclaimed their bicycles on the platform, then retired to the café. The establishment had once been stocked by an ambitious **pâtissier;** evidence remained in the form of tiny hand-lettered signs advertising **chouquettes, canelés de Bordeaux, chaussons aux pommes, pain aux raisins, millefeuille,** and **Paris-Brest.** The names alone were enough to make Varian faint with desire. But the pastry pans were empty of everything, even of crumbs. The war had devoured every bit.

"What I wouldn't give for a nice Paris-Brest," Grant said, and Varian smiled. The two blunt wafers that accompanied the coffee were tooth-threateningly hard, but they melted into a mild grainmeal when dunked. They ate and drank what they could. Grant checked the tires and Varian retraced the route. Then they shouldered their packs and set off on the downhill slope toward the nature preserve. They wouldn't stop until noon, when they would have lunch somewhere in the Coussouls de Crau; in their bags were hunks of hard bread and precious cheese. They would ride an old road that traced a diagonal line across the alluvial plain, connecting Arles with the modern world.

It was a rocky ride through town and into the countryside, but once they reached the main road the way was mercifully flat, the paved surface smooth. A good thing, too, because the seat of Varian's bicycle, a hard narrow beak of leather and rubber, cut his gluteals viciously. But he hardly cared. The smooth speed of the ride was sheer pleasure. It had been years since he'd ridden a bike through open countryside; he and Eileen had done it once just after they'd been married, rented bikes and ridden up along the Hudson to the Old Croton Aqueduct, which had carried water to the city in the nineteenth century, when private indoor plumbing still seemed a miracle. **Dear Eileen,** he imagined writing. **What would you think to see me riding out into the countryside with Elliott Grant, far from Marseille and my work? What would you say if you knew that what I was doing today wasn't saving lives or bringing me closer to the time when I might return to you? What would you say to the fact that my continuing on here in Marseille takes on greater import, greater**

urgency, each time I read your letters calling me home? Don't imagine I don't miss you. I miss you this moment as I remember you in your blue cycling trousers, the curve of your back in a red-and-white-striped jersey as you rode ahead of me. Your eyes as you threw a glance over your shoulder. Where did you think I might go? Did you imagine I'd take some side turn, or, more likely, fail to pedal fast enough to keep up? I remember we rode all the way past the old monastery, through Spuyten Duyvil, up along the widening basin of the Hudson, to that little park halfway, where you threw your bike down in the grass and ran to the water's edge, holding your hair up to cool your neck. You washed your face in the river and stood with your hips angled northward, one hand shading your eyes, squinting into the distance as if to forespy our progress. And I thought to myself: our marriage is like a house full of great clean rooms smelling of furniture polish and laundry soap, of fine old books, of green things just pulled from the garden, of rising bread. And sometimes that is just what I want. And then there are other times.

Ahead of him Grant did not turn back, but Varian knew him to be acutely aware of being watched. With his cycling jersey he wore a red scarf wrapped twice around his neck, the ends whipping like a cat tease. He kept up a powerful pace. When the road sloped downward, he sat upright on his bicycle seat and took his hands off the handlebars, letting his speed keep him steady; he pedaled with hands on hips like a circus unicyclist, then stretched his arms to the side as if to balance on a tightrope. Or he would lean forward and grip the handlebars, angling into the sun and wind. Like Eileen riding the road toward the Croton Aqueduct, he looked, above all, brilliantly alive. Where had Varian read that line about the brevity of our lives and the way they continued in others, energy flashing from body to body as if into temporary and interchangeable containers, flashing and flashing into new ones as time rolled forward forever? The progression, the continuation, was the point; the vessels didn't matter. He felt it to be true, he knew it as clearly as he'd known anything.

But the vessels had to matter, he reminded himself; of course they mattered. His work was predicated on the particularity of the vessels, on the relative worth of the energy that flashed into one body or another. Chagall, painting in his house at Gordes, was an irreplaceable treasure. So was Mann, so was Werfel, so was Feuchtwanger, damn him to hell; so was Walter Benjamin, dead in Spain; so were Breitscheid and Hilferding, so was Max Ernst, so were the others on his list: André Breton, Jacques Lipchitz, and all the others waiting to be found. So was the boy genius, Grant's young Tobias. They had to matter more than others, those men and women; they had to be brighter manifestations of light.

And then there was the particular flash of light ahead, the one in the striped jersey pedaling across the rocky plain that was the Coussouls de Crau, across that expanse of salt-loving grass and wind-worn ovoid stones. What was it in that being, unique among all others, that drew him? There was a seeking in Varian that he'd come to think of as a natural element of his existence, an element that predated his college days, one that went back almost to his earliest recollections. He remembered being ten years old on the beach at Coney Island, where his grandfather ran a fresh-air program for city kids; he and the residents of Manhattan tenements would race up and down the strand, **sand in the hair and sand between the toes,** and he would feel desire pulling him along like a kite on a string. Then, for a time, when he and Grant knew each other at college, the feeling had changed. A stillness settled over his life, so different from anything that had come before that it snapped him awake. How he remembered it, the feeling of walking the brick sidewalks of Garden Street or Mass. Ave., hard light falling on ice-glazed snow, his chest full of quiet, an unmatched silence that rang in his ears like the aftermath of an explosion. And here again, inside the radiant circle of Grant's presence, was that silence of soul that was not selflessness, not the disappearance of his own particularity into Grant's, but a kind of wholeness. There was no need to seek, no need to search. All was found. The feeling gratified and terrified him—yes, it terrified him, more than the endless expanse of the Coussouls de Crau, more than the war, more even than the idiot dictator shrieking nonsense at the world. He knew exactly what it was that he feared; it wasn't hard to understand. He feared that he might sit down at the center of a floodplain in the South of France and cease to exert a force of will upon the world. He feared the blindness of the sensation, the inability to see things as they were. He feared how vulnerable the feeling made him. He feared returning to the place he'd been with Grant in Cambridge before Grant had disappeared. And he feared the world he'd lived in afterward, the Grantless world he'd inhabited until the night Grant had appeared at the Dorade.

They had talked about it all those years ago, laughed about it when they were college men. Having read the **Symposium,** favorite text of budding classicists—Grant for the first time, Varian for the second or third, as he'd studied it in high school and been prepped upon it by countless tutors—they'd ridiculed the idea of love as a conjoined twinship, lovers as double paper dolls attached at hands and feet. In league with Plato, they'd ridiculed Aristophanes' idea of a perfect match; love was biology's farce, the logical mind a necessary tonic against it. Of course, after one such conversation in Grant's room at Gore, they'd fallen into bed and fucked desperately, then lay in each other's arms all night, discussing exactly nothing. Beneath their silence—their speechlessness—was the understanding that they were home at last, disciples of Aristophanes to the last detail; they had been reattached at hands and feet and pelvis, and would never let Zeus split them again. But that certainty, too, had proved false.

Now, far ahead, a line of blue-black cloud appeared on the horizon, trailing banners of rain. Electric blue flashes needled from its underside. The clouds were distant enough to make the rainstorm seem a transparency on a screen, not part of their immediate reality. But before long the wind picked up and slowed their pedaling, the air became fresh and sharply sweet, and the sky filled with birds winging away from the rain as fast as fear. At last Grant threw a look back over his shoulder at Varian: they were headed into the storm, and, judging from the wind's direction, it would meet them soon. There was no shelter in sight, not a stick or brick of a house, not a barn, not a shepherd's hut. The tallest vegetation was knee-high grass. Grant slowed his bike and stopped, and Varian pulled up alongside him.

"Now what?" Grant said.

"No way to get out of it."

"Whistle for the rescue vehicle," Grant said. "Signal for an airlift. You brought the semaphore flags, didn't you?"

The light around them had begun to take on a

greenish cast, the patina of violent weather. "What have you got in your pack?"

"Water. Two days' worth of clothes. Bread and cheese. Whiskey."

"Well, the water will come in handy," Varian said, as the first raindrops began to fall, great drenching gumball-sized drops that pocked the dust and blackened the rocks. Varian lowered his bike to the roadside and motioned for Grant to do the same. There was a kind of relieving absoluteness to the situation: no way to conjure shelter out of ether. The best they could do was to lie absolutely flat so as not to be the tallest objects on the steppe. Upright, they were lightning rods.

They sat beside their bicycles, waiting. Varian thought with regret about what was about to befall the black Gitane; its owner would never have left it out in the merest sprinkle, much less in a green-bellied thunderstorm. Grant drew out his silver flask, and they both swallowed long pulls of whiskey as the intermittent raindrops came faster. Some indeterminable distance off, a glare of lightning legged from ground to cloud; a second later, an earbreaking concussion rocked the earth. They both went prone and pressed their foreheads against their bent arms. They edged together until they touched, then came closer still: leg against leg, side against side, a single warm line of contact. If he and Grant were struck by lightning, Varian thought, how would Eileen learn of his death? What would she imagine he and Grant had been doing in the middle of the Coussouls de Crau? Who would find their bodies, and in what state? Varian angled his head to look at Grant, his open eye just visible in the darkness of his tented arms; Grant didn't try to hide his fear. Another airsplitting flash and crash. Rain fell fast and fierce and slantwise, hitting them from the west; wind scoured their backs, forcing them to press their elbows and knees against the half-sunk stones of the plain. The dust quickly turned to mud. Lightning struck close by, so close the water in the earth seemed to go electric; for a moment their bodies seemed to hover on a thin layer of pinpoints, millions of them. Varian anticipated a heartstopping jolt, a whiteout of the brain. But the feeling subsided and they were not dead. The rain continued, and the wind, and the vibrant explosions in the sky, and the answering concussions of the earth. The ground jumped with each strike like the taut skin of a drum. They felt it in their sternums, in the jolt of their jawbones against the sunken stones. Their nostrils filled with the scent and grit of mud. Earthworms floated past Varian's half-closed eyes, blindly writhing. An incomprehensible noise approached, a sound like ranks and ranks of babies crying; Varian could make no sense of it, one more note of disorder in the general disorder. A heavy rumbling cloud seemed to move over the ground, threatening to subsume them; then the cloud came closer and resolved into the bodies of sheep, hundreds of them, dingy-gray and darkened by the rain, with slim black legs that flashed like the flipped pages of a book. The sheep, bleating, surged around Varian and Grant and the bikes; surged and surged and surged, flowing westward in a smooth liquid panic; and then, as if they were part of the storm, abated. The rain slowed. The dark cloud and its lightning passed overhead, the maelstrom of sound and sensation slackened and at last went quiet.

Grant and Varian lay still. A fretful after-rain made rings in the newly sprung pools. A stray sheep bent its head and drank. Grant sat up and pushed his wet hair back from his forehead; his chest was black with mud, his bare arms slick with it.

"Ha!" he shouted. "Ha!" He felt his breast pocket for his cigarettes, took one out of the silver case; it quivered on his lip, pristine, the only dry thing on the Coussouls de Crau. The case next produced a dry matchbook; the match produced a flame.

"You really oughtn't to have quit, Tommie," he said.

Varian pushed himself up and sat on his heels. "Give me that," he said, and swiped the smoke from Grant's mouth; he took his own long drag. "Jesus."

"Your hair's a mess," Grant said. He was close enough to touch it, and did; after what they'd been through, any intimacy seemed possible. Varian held still. Grant's hand lingered, smoothed a few wet strands behind Varian's ear, and fell.

"How far to Arles, do you think?" he said.

"Another twenty K at least."

They dragged themselves to their feet, got the bikes up, wiped them down with their hands. There was no hope of riding; the road had turned to mud. The only way forward was to walk.

They walked for what seemed like hours before a vehicle came along, one of the stinking trucks converted to run on sheep droppings instead of petrol. The sun was still high in the sky, the storm clouds a low band on the eastern horizon, wreaking havoc elsewhere. The sheep farmer called them into the truck in some Camarguesque dialect Varian could scarcely decode. They loaded the bikes into the back and climbed into the cab, apologizing for the state of their clothes. The sheep farmer didn't have much to say. From what Varian could make out, he was driving a circuit to see how far his flock had ranged. In French, Varian described being nearly trampled; the farmer laughed and said that he and Grant were lucky to be alive. He deposited them on the outskirts of St. Martin de Crau, some ten kilometers from their destination. It took another hour and a half to reach the stone gates of Arles.

At the Hôtel du Forum, the desk clerk straightened his tie and gave a **harumpf** of displeasure at the sight of them. It seemed a matter of some discomfort to him that Messieurs Fry and Grant had reserved rooms in advance, that the clerk was expected to find a place to park the filthy bikes, then call the bellboy and ensure the delivery of the gentlemen's luggage, if it could be called that, to the spotless rooms. He banged the bell with the flat of his hand. When no bellboy appeared, he banged it again.

"Edouard!" he shouted.

No response. The clerk flitted from behind the desk and crossed the lobby, then flung aside a red velvet curtain to reveal a closetlike recess near the entry. There, in a leatherette armchair, slept a young man of twenty-five or so, blond, his sleeves rolled to his elbows, his arms crossed over his chest. His mouth hung slightly open. Beneath faintly blue lids, his eyes traced the panorama of a dream.

"Edouard," the clerk snapped. **"Réveilles-toi!"**

The young man's eyes fluttered, then opened wide. "Sir!" he shouted, and jumped to his feet. "Messieurs! At your service!"

"Show these gentlemen to their rooms," the clerk said. "And take their things." With a glance he indicated the mud-plastered rucksacks beside the door.

Edouard raised his eyes now to Varian, now to Grant; a charged moment passed, and then a subtle understanding passing between them. He smoothed his shock of wheat-colored hair with both hands and reinserted his shirttail into his uniform pants, then buttoned the gold buttons of his jacket. Without a word, he slid past Varian to take up the bags. He followed the clerk to the desk, where he received two keys on round brass fobs.

"I hope you'll find everything in order, messieurs," the clerk said. "Edouard will show you to your rooms."

With a beckoning shrug, Edouard invited Varian and Grant to follow.

Up the stairs they went, the single flight interminable. Varian's thighs burned with exhaustion, his gut with hunger, but the need to bathe and sleep and eat had been crushed by a new want. They met no one on the stairs, no one in the hall. A long corridor stretched toward the back of the building; at the end, their two rooms. When Edouard opened the first door, a blast of western sun fell through the aperture and slammed against the tile. They all crossed the threshold and Grant closed the door behind them. The room was red-floored like the corridor, plainly decorated; a double bed with a white coverlet, a narrow wardrobe, a desk with a vase of bluebells, a washstand with a blue-rimmed bowl. The window a blinding block of sun. Edouard removed the luggage stand from beside the wardrobe and laid the rucksacks side by side upon it like dead gamebirds. Then he looked from Varian to Grant: What next? The question in his eyes was a casual one, a playful one; they had already reached an agreement. Varian allowed himself, finally, to meet Grant's eye. Grant gave the slightest nod.

"Take off your clothes," Varian said to the young man. "Lie down on the bed."

Edouard complied. He wasn't shy or coy; his skin had that particular opacity that makes a person seem dressed when undressed. He lay back on the smooth white coverlet and waited. His legs were parted, one arm thrown above his head. He looked entirely at ease. Varian and Grant, covered with mud and sweat and dust, could defile neither Edouard nor bed; there was only one course of action.

"Please yourself," Varian said, and the young man smiled. Without hesitation he did as told. He performed swiftly and neatly as Grant and Varian watched. When he was done, he got to his feet and dressed.

"Thank you, Edouard," Varian said.

Grant reached into his pocket for his wallet and drew out a handful of francs.

"Non, merci," the young man said.

"But you must," Grant said. "At least for bringing the luggage."

"That's not luggage," Edouard said, and grinned, taking the proffered francs. "I'll be downstairs later. Find me if you like." He buttoned his jacket and touched his cap, then disappeared through the door, leaving Grant and Varian alone in the room. The key to the neighboring room lay on the desk. Grant raised his eyes to Varian's.

"Well," he said. "Here we are."

And in an instant he and Grant were undressed and devouring each other. Here was Grant now, beneath his hands. Long flanks, slender arms, plane of belly. Unbroken fields of skin. Grant's mouth. Grant's cock in his hand, familiar as his own. Grant's shale-colored eyes. Grant's hands gripping his waist. And all the private charms of Grant's body: the triad of flat dark moles at the right antecubital fold; the mute circlet of his navel; the pubic whorls, each its own minute spiral; on his thigh, the pale trace of a childhood wound and its sutures. And something new: a fine line that ran from his shoulder to his waist, a near-invisible scar. And then Grant's specific tenderness for him, Grant rehearsing with a hand all of Varian's imperfections: strawberry spot, old burn, bone spur on the rib. They were filthy with mud, they smelled of peat and sweat and rain, they had lain in a clean field of grass under a sky shot with electric charge; their bodies seemed to radiate blue-white energy. Grant's eyes on Varian's. His mouth pronouncing a hymnal **O. O hymen, o hymenee, why do you tantalize me thus?** And who might be listening, what consequence waiting? Who cared, no one cared, all worth it. It would even be worth the moment after, the moment he knew was coming: the falling away of the blinding want, glamour ceding to grammar, its linguistic root. **O!** how he remembered that moment twelve years ago when they were boys in Gore Hall, when they opened their eyes to the wet and twisted sheets, bodies abraded, needs spent, lives ruined. And here they were, still living in the ruin, its marble walls intact; here they were, still wanting and doing and having, still climbing, all the way across the ocean and over the span of years, and Varian knew he was old, he was old, he was **O**

Grant crying now. Grant laughing. The ruined bed. Their bodies.

How could they have imagined anything else? They hadn't. This was all.

The next day they visited the ruins of Arles: the grand stadium that had once hosted gladitorial competitions, its thirty-six perfect arches and its stage channeled to drain the blood; the ancient theater with its sixteen marble tiers, the terraced cup of it acoustically perfect at the backmost row. They traced the track in the stage along which scenery had once rolled, and examined the tiers themselves, marble fitted into marble, each crevice with its answering rise. A low flat sky stretched its strata over the ruins, over Varian and Grant, as they picked their way across the stones and read the informative plaques. Who knew what farces had played out there, what farces would play out still?

When they reached the end of the last row, they stood looking toward what had been the stage. It was noon, the light flat and diffuse through the cloud cover; that morning they'd slept till half past ten, Breitscheid and Hilferding be damned. They were clean now, fragrant, shaved, combed, dressed. Their biking clothes were in the care of a laundress, the bikes hosed down and polished. Now here they were in the ruins, and Arles seemed to belong to them alone. No other soul appeared in the amphitheater. It was, Varian thought, as if they had stepped into another reality, one without war or rules or wives; they had gotten there by some alchemical magic, just as Varian, as a child, had imagined walking into the pages of a book. But they weren't there alone; there were shadowy presences just out of view.

He sat down on a marble block at the end of the tier and beckoned Grant. Grant joined him, hooding his eyes with one hand as he looked toward the empty stage.

"Do you know what I'm not keen to talk about?" Varian said. "But what I can't stop thinking about?"

Grant's brow gave an almost imperceptible twitch. "Maybe."

"Your esteemed colleague. My client. Herr Katznelson."

Grant put his elbows on his knees, extending the long plane of his back. "Let's not, just now. Can't we leave it alone for a while?"

"Understand me, Skiff. I'm a married man. I can't take this lightly."

"And I, unmarried, can?"

"**Are** you unmarried? I mean, really. That wasn't exactly the impression I got."

Grant frowned, his eyes steady on Varian's. "I never took it lightly," he said. "I never did. **You** were the one."

And here was the accusation, the one he'd been running from: it was Varian who'd left Grant on the sandy shore at Sculpin Point in Maine, Varian who'd stepped into a boat with Eileen and struck out for the island, Grant growing smaller on the beach, his ankles involved in sea grass, his form shadowed by shaggy pines, while Eileen adjusted the tiller into the wind and pointed them toward the island's leeward side. The white flare of Grant's sailcloth pants and oxford shirt like a beacon, visible long after his features had faded and his stature shrunk to a semicolon's; until finally Varian blinked and the beacon went out, and he was alone on the water with Eileen.

Varian shook his head. "All right," he said. "We won't talk about it."

"Good," Grant said. "I want a coffee, and then I want to see the Roman baths." He said it decisively, as if that settled everything. "Let me just take a picture of you, and then we'll go."

"No! I hate that. You know."

"Oh, no, you don't, you vain thing, you just pretend to."

Varian suffered Grant to set up his tiny camera and take a picture of him sitting on the lowest tier of the amphitheater. He would pore over it later: his expression grave with joy or dread, one eye obscured by the sun glinting off his glasses, his ankles pale and crossed. The curving marble arcs rising behind him like steps of a giant's villa. Afterward they gathered their few things, cleared their shoes of pebbles, checked their route. On the way to the baths they would pass a delightful café, according to the guidebook; should they stop there for Grant's coffee? They should, of course; they both needed one. They'd been up half the night. They made their way toward the gate of the fence that surrounded the amphitheater, but before they could walk through, Grant pulled Varian into one of the recesses in the stone. There, in an ancient Roman shadow, they crushed each other against the marble. Here was what he could never have, not with Eileen, not in the arms of young men in the Village, not for money, not in his wild imaginings, of which there were plenty; not even in his dreams, where his mind would tip him back into consciousness the instant his mouth touched Grant's. How often, he wondered as he held Grant against him and kissed him, if the violent thing they were doing could be called that—how often had he gotten just to the verge of this moment in a dream and woken devastated, as if the night's disappearance were the original? What might he have done to himself back in college if he knew he'd relive Grant's departure again and again? And what had he done to deserve its reversal?

A noise startled them: a brown bird tussling with its mate in the dust. They stepped from their niche and went on. Unobserved? They had to hope so.

———

At the café, unremarkable except for the formidable black-and-gold gryphon of its sign, they sat at a curbside table in the usual woven cane chairs and drank wartime coffee through a fine dense foam of milk. The milk was a rare luxury, the bad coffee a bitter corrective. And now, in case the coffee alone hadn't brought them back to the awareness that they sat at leisure in a country at war, here came a pair of gendarmes with their hands on their guns, striding up to the café tables to arrest Varian and Grant.

But it was another patron they were after, a bespectacled middle-aged man in a white painter's shirt and blue neckerchief, sitting at the table beside their own; he was so quiet and still that they hadn't noticed him until that moment. The man looked up through his glasses—perfectly round lenses framed in heavy tortoiseshell—just in time to see the gendarmes arrive. As they yanked him to his feet and demanded his passport, a newspaper fell from his hand and butterflied on the ground: **La Verité Quotidienne,** a small left-wing rag written largely by émigrés. The gendarmes, thankfully, did not take note of it. Varian was close enough to capture the paper with his toe and slide it toward his table. The man in the blue neckerchief observed this from the corner of his eye and met Varian's glance for a moment, understanding him at once to be an ally.

The more senior-looking of the gendarmes, a fat man with a face like a hole-riven bucket, announced that monsieur was under arrest and must therefore pay his bill at once. The bespectacled man shot a look of amused incredulity at Varian and Grant, and at the same moment the waiter arrived, bill in hand, and waited politely for the accused to produce the necessary francs and centimes. The man tipped generously, if the waiter's bow of gratitude was any indication. And then off they went, the two policemen and their prisoner in his loose white shirt and straw hat. The waiter pocketed his francs and asked Grant and Varian if he could be of service to them; they declined, watching the three men disappearing down one of the streets that led from the public square. And as Varian watched, a certainty began to grow in his mind. That white shirt, those distinctive round glasses, the loosely knotted scarf. And the man's particular expression, all-knowing, conspiratorial.

"Grant," he said, getting to his feet, his heart speeding. "I believe that was Lev Zilberman."

"What? Sit, Varian, please."

Varian sat. He leaned closer to Grant and spoke under his voice. "If I'm not mistaken, that was

Zilberman. Whom Chagall particularly mentioned. The one Alma Werfel talked about in Cerbère." The one whose daughter, if Alma was to be believed, was involved with Tobias Katznelson.

Grant paled, his hand on Varian's arm. "You're sure it's him?"

"He's just like his photo from the exhibition catalogues."

"So now what?"

"We have to follow to wherever they're taking him. Then we have to get him out. We've got to get him to Marseille, to somewhere safe, where he'll be out of the public eye. I've got to telephone Lena immediately."

"Well!" Grant said. "Heigh-ho. **Au revoir, les vacances.**" He lifted his gaze to Varian's and smiled with regret. They had been somewhere together for a while.

———

The sous-préfecture of Arles made its home in an eighteenth-century former convent in the rue du Cloître, not five minutes' walk from their hotel. They passed through the arched doorway and into a waiting room floored with echoing pink marble tile; a girl in a blue uniform greeted them there. Would they care to wait in the courtyard while she conveyed their request to Captain Castorel? Did they care for something to drink meanwhile?

With flirtatious solicitude, she showed them to the courtyard with its neat groundcover of tiny round pebbles, its original meditative benches, its high aperture at one end, a cross-shaped opening that projected its twin in light upon the stone. Grant and Varian strolled the walkway around the perimeter as generations of nuns must have done. As urgent as their mission was, Varian could not restrain his awareness of Grant's body, the unclothed self poorly disguised beneath Grant's linen shirt and trousers. If he could have reached into his own brain and surgically resected that awareness, he would have done so in an instant; it was nothing but a liability now.

Here at last came Captain Castorel, steel-haired, resplendent in some Nazified version of the provincial policeman's uniform. And how might he be of help? he asked from beneath his military-style mustache. He understood they were interested in the prisoner just taken into custody.

Varian knew at a glance that Castorel would be bribable. Vanity nearly always coincided with that other weakness. "I'm the director of a U.S. relief organization, the Centre Américain de Secours," he said. "This is my colleague, Mr. Grant."

Castorel bowed stiffly. "A pleasure," he said.

"Your prisoner," Varian began.

"Ah, yes. Monsieur Zilberman. Or perhaps you know him by the name on his false papers: Olivier Simonet. I imagine this is not the only name he's used. And your name, sir? I don't believe you mentioned it."

"Varian Fry."

A spark of recognition crossed Castorel's features, and Varian had to wonder for a moment whether his notoriety had reached the countryside. But then Castorel said, smiling to himself, "You're the young men who rode into town yesterday covered in mud. I saw you from my office window. I didn't envy you your journey."

"Bad weather in the Coussouls de Crau," Varian said.

"It must have been very bad indeed!" He gave a snort of self-pleased laughter. "And what exactly is your business here in Arles? A relief mission?"

"We're here to see some clients. Our relief operation is based in Marseille."

Castorel raised an eyebrow, and Varian wondered again what exactly he knew.

"We believe you've arrested the wrong man," Grant said now in his limpid and agile French. "We don't think your prisoner is Monsieur Zilberman at all. We think it must be a case of mistaken identity. We believe him to be Monsieur Grossman, a client of ours. We'd be glad to relieve you of the burden of his care at once."

Castorel took this in frowningly, adjusting the extremities of his mustache. "That is impossible, messieurs. We've been watching Monsieur Zilberman for some time now. He's been charged with attempting to travel on his false papers. Regrettably, such things have been occurring in France with increasing frequency."

"You don't say," Varian said.

"Oh, yes. Our region is rife with refugees, most of them paperless."

Grant's line was risky, but Varian pursued it. "Perhaps you can check the prisoner's identity papers again. If he turns out to be Monsieur Grossman, we're keen to help him. He's got a family of six waiting for him in the States." He put his hand into the pocket that contained a narrow brass cigarette case, the one Hirschman had instructed him to carry in case he had to make a swift bribe. Castorel followed Varian's every movement with his eyes. He paid close attention as Varian withdrew the pack and thumbed a smoke forward. Beneath the cigarette were two thousand-franc notes.

"Care for one?" Varian asked, and offered the pack to Castorel.

Castorel hesitated for a moment, long enough for Varian to wonder if he and Grant would end up in the cell next to Zilberman's. A concentration camp would be the inevitable next stop. But Castorel withdrew the cigarette and the bills, swiftly pocketing the money as if he'd done it a hundred times, which likely he had. Varian took a cigarette for himself and offered another to Grant.

"That's the second one you've smoked in two days," Grant said in English. "I thought you'd quit."

"Quitting's a bad habit," Varian said, and lit Castorel's cigarette, then his own.

"My son is a bicycle-racing fanatic," Castorel said, musingly. "He follows the Tour de France in the papers. His birthday's in a month. I've been wanting to get him his own bicycle, but they're so hard to come by just now, as you must know."

Varian threw a look at Grant. "Yes," he said. "We found ours rather hard to come by. We borrowed them from friends in Marseille."

"Have you any children yourself, back in the States, Monsieur Fry?"

Grant looked back at Varian. Castorel was casually making his way through his cigarette; it was clear they didn't have much time. But they couldn't gild their bribe with a bicycle. Not Gussie's green Motobécane. And certainly not the Gitane that had belonged to the concierge's husband.

"None, Monsieur," Varian said.

"A pity," Castorel said. "If you did, you'd understand how much it pleases a father to indulge his son's wishes."

"I think I do understand," Varian said, tightly.

"Well, I wish I could stay to smoke, but I've got matters to attend to inside."

"Stay a moment longer," Varian said. God, what was he about to do? "How does your son feel about the color green?"

"He's never favored it," Castorel said. "It's the Brits' racing color."

Varian gritted his teeth. He had to get Zilberman; this could be his only chance. "Is he predisposed to black?"

"Oh, yes," Castorel said. "He adores black."

Grant and Varian exchanged a look.

"Monsieur Grant was just about to stop by the hotel to pick up a few things," Varian said. "If you like, maybe he can bring the bicycle back with him. You might want to—have a look at it. And if you don't mind, I'll wait here until he returns."

"Of course. Make yourself at home," Castorel said, smiling a little to himself. "And in the meantime, why don't I double-check the prisoner's identity card? We do sometimes make mistakes." He nodded to Varian and Grant and turned on his heel, then went off down the pebbled convent walk.

———

Varian, waiting for Grant, found it impossible to remain still. He strolled the rectangle of the courtyard four, five, six times, berating himself for having promised the concierge's bicycle. Couldn't he have done better than that? How would Grant have managed it if he'd been on his own? **He** would have made it back to Marseille with Zilberman **and** the concierge's bicycle, Varian was sure; any other outcome seemed a fool's defeat. He couldn't bear to imagine Madame Balansard's reaction when he showed up empty-handed. He'd worked himself into a fine sweat by the time Grant returned with the black Gitane; he could hardly watch as the secretary in the blue uniform led it away. She returned shortly, and there was a tense span of minutes where Varian had to wonder if the bribe was in vain. But then a guard emerged from the arched hallway, leading a dazed-looking Zilberman in his white painter's shirt, blinking through his tortoiseshell glasses. Zilberman, squinting in confusion at Grant and Varian, signed his name on an official form and received his personal effects from the guard. Then the guard told Zilberman that he was free to go, and the three men went out through the central doorway of the gendarmerie and into the glaring afternoon.

"You're safe," Varian said in German. "For the moment, at least." They paused on the sidewalk while a stream of schoolchildren parted around them; it was the dismissal hour, boys and girls running at top speed in their blue school smocks.

"Wer sind Sie?"

"We're from the Centre Américain de Secours. Your name is on our list."

"It's been on a few too many of those lately," Zilberman said.

"Chagall himself implored us to find you. As did my friend Alfred Barr at the Museum of Modern Art."

The painter blushed to the roots of his silver-black hair. "Gentlemen, don't flatter me. I'm nothing.

There are so many of us. I don't deserve any particular favor."

"Others don't share that opinion, Herr Zilberman. But won't you come to our hotel, where we can talk a little more freely? We're staying just nearby."

They made their way through the river of shouting children to the Hôtel du Forum, where, in the leafy courtyard, a girl who might have been the sister of the one at the jail offered cups of hot tea. A large courtyard fountain provided a fortuitous soundscreen; under its veil, Varian described what the Emergency Rescue Committee did and how it could help. He learned that the painter's wife and daughter had in fact already emigrated; now they lived in Cambridge, where his wife's father was a visiting professor at MIT. That would make it infinitely easier to secure Zilberman's U.S. entry visa. They would still need to get him a new identity card, a fake French exit visa, and Spanish and Portuguese visas; then they'd have to wait to see if the Spanish border opened again. There was no telling how long it all might take. He must accompany them to Marseille in the morning and stay there for the duration.

The painter moved a shock of hair out of his eyes, removed his glasses, and wiped them with the tail of his shirt. His cheeks streamed with tears. "What can I do to thank you?" he said. "What could ever suffice?"

"There is something we need, in fact," Grant said,

glancing at Varian; Varian gave the slightest nod. "There's someone else we're looking for, someone we think you may know."

Zilberman's eyes moved from Grant to Varian. "Who is it?"

Grant lowered his voice to a near-whisper. Fixing Zilberman in his clear gaze, he pronounced Tobias Katznelson's name.

Zilberman's brow wrinkled. "Katznelson?"

"His father's a colleague of mine," Grant said. "Tobias has been missing for some months. We think he may be in grave danger. And we've learned he is—well—associated with your daughter."

"Associated!" Zilberman said, and gave a short, gruff laugh. "Yes, I should say they are associated. It began a year and a half ago—Sara was seventeen. Tobias invited her to a picture show, and after that he began to turn up at odd times. At a neighboring table when we were out to dinner, or on a path in the Tiergarten when we were out for a walk. I finally remarked to my wife, in Sara's presence, how strange this was, and Sara confessed they were arranging it." He laughed again. "I told her there was no need for secrecy. Tobias was a fine young man, Jewish, of good family. The sort of boy I might have welcomed as a son-in-law, if it came to that. But soon afterward he disappeared, and that was the last we heard of him."

"You have no idea of his whereabouts now?"

"None, I'm afraid. His parents must be frantic."

"Do you think you might spread the word among your friends here in the South of France? Other refugees—anyone from Berlin. Exercising, of course, the utmost of caution."

"I'm rather without connections," Zilberman said. "I don't know anyone at all in Marseille, in fact. I'm not sure where I'll hang my hat if I travel there with you. I've nearly run out of money, hiding out here in Arles."

"The Centre Américain will see to it all," Varian said, though in fact he had no idea where they would house Zilberman; there was not a free hotel room in town. Maybe he could foist a roommate upon Mehring. "In the meantime, you'd better spend the night here at the hotel. You can take Mr. Grant's room. We'll double up."

"I hate to inconvenience you, gentlemen."

"We'll manage," Grant said. He produced the key and handed it across the table.

"What about my luggage, all my things?"

"We'll arrange for everything to be brought here. It's best if you don't go out again before we leave tomorrow."

Zilberman got to his feet and shook Varian's hand, then Grant's, thanking them again in German and in English. "If you don't mind," he said, "I'll go upstairs and lie down now."

"Of course," Varian said.

Zilberman gave an awkward half-bow, touched the brim of his straw hat, and left them there at the courtyard table. They sat there for a long moment, letting the air settle. The fountain played and splashed, brown Arlesian birds sang songs in French, and in one of the rooms above, someone whistled.

"Well, damn me," Varian said. "Lev Zilberman."

"And now what?" Grant said.

What indeed? Send Zilberman back to Marseille on the train with Lena. Quit his job and retire to the French countryside. Divorce his intelligent and forbearing wife. Eat lotus. Stay here forever with Grant. "Now we send someone for his things. And then we see Breitscheid and Hilferding."

The whistle came again. There in a third-story window, leaning out over a geranium-heavy flower box, was yesterday's blond Edouard.

"There's our errand boy," Grant said, and whistled back.

———

Having sent off Edouard to collect Zilberman's things, they went to see Breitscheid and Hilferding, who were enduring their house arrest in a large white-stuccoed villa at the edge of town. The roof was of paprika-colored tile, the façade fanned with bougainvillea; beside the tall front doors, gardenias grew in jade-green pots. They approached and knocked tentatively, not wanting the inhabitants to believe them to be the police. A long moment elapsed. Then a sliver of an aperture appeared between the double doors; and in the aperture, the glint of an eye.

"Who is it?" a voice whispered.

Varian explained.

The door opened another centimeter, and now Varian and Grant could see a narrow slice of a woman's face. "Go away," she said, in a smoke-laced alto. "You'll get us all in trouble!"

"On the contrary," Varian said. "We're here to get you out of trouble."

"We can't receive visitors. And we're not in need of an advocate."

"That's not what I heard," Varian said.

"Go away!" the woman said in her sandpapery whisper. "I'm closing the door."

From inside the house, another voice, a man's: "Who is it, Erika?"

The door closed abruptly. Through it came a volley of voices, rising to the muffled sounds of an argument. Grant and Varian exchanged a look.

"You'd think I was selling life insurance," Varian said.

"Aren't you?" Grant said, and laughed.

A moment later, the door swung open and there was Breitscheid himself in a crimson smoking jacket, his reading glasses perched on his loaf-shaped nose, a newspaper under his arm. His downturned mustache gave him an expression of severe disapproval; between the bat-wings of his collar hung the narrowest of ties, as though his person required only the minimum of decoration.

"Mr. Fry," he said. "What are you doing here? And who's this?"

"That's Mr. Grant," Varian said. "And I'm here to help you out of this mess."

Breitscheid glanced back into the house. "I'd hardly call it a mess," he said. "We're rather comfortable, in fact."

"Comfortable?" Varian said, a flush scaling his neck. "To me it looks like you're stuck in that house, waiting for Vichy to ship you back to Germany."

Breitscheid shook his head. "Our plight has been much exaggerated, I'm afraid."

"I understood that you were under house arrest."

"I suppose we are, if you want to use that term. But really, it's more of a gentlemanly arrangement. You might say the police are protecting us."

"Protecting you," Varian repeated.

"Yes, Mr. Fry. This idea that we're in imminent danger—it's a rather colorful depiction of our situation. One that might excite the foreign press. But it is not based in fact."

"That's what you told me a few weeks ago, Mr. Breitscheid, when I suggested you not discuss your business aloud at Marseille cafés. And now here you are."

"Mr. Fry, the rules that apply to the common refugee do not pertain to us. Our stature—"

"Oh, yes," Varian said. "I'm familiar with that line of argument."

Breitscheid's look grew sterner. "We will certainly call upon you if the need arises."

"My secretary cabled me in Lisbon to say you were in need **now.** I came back at once, specifically to help you."

"You are very kind," Breitscheid said, icily. "We appreciate your concern. And now I must ask you to excuse me, as I'd like to get back to my card game."

"Your card game!" Varian half-shouted. "Herr Breitscheid—"

"Yes. When you arrived, you interrupted us at piquet with our so-called captors. You'll forgive me if I don't feel particularly threatened."

"You can't dissuade me," Varian said. "I'm going to work on your behalf back in Marseille. At least we'll see if our lawyer can get your house-arrest status lifted."

"As I said, Mr. Fry, we appreciate your kind concern. Now, good day."

The door closed. Varian stood beside Grant on the doorstep, trembling with rage. "For God's sake," he said. "Piquet!"

At the hotel that night, sharing Grant's bed, he couldn't find a path that led to sleep. But then he had never slept easily at Grant's side; in college there had been the constant fear of discovery, no matter how soundly they locked and barricaded the door. And this despite the fact that they knew they weren't alone in the practice, that similar pairings were occurring all around them in the rooms of Gore Hall and in the other dormitories. Later, after Eileen's arrival in his life and before Grant's departure, a low-level drone of guilt kept him awake; having met Eileen, he knew he had to keep her or abandon all hope of a life that at least appeared ordinary from the outside. Eileen understood. And not just understood, but participated. Like him, she desired a life that admitted sexual fortuity, occasional acts of self-indulgence, good cheap fucking; it seemed part and parcel of her intelligence, essential to her **Weltanschauung.** She seemed, at the time, the perfect solution to his problem. Once he'd realized it, he began to feel like a criminal in bed with Grant; after they'd spent an evening in tireless attack on each other's bodies, Grant's quiet breathing beside him seemed a confirmation of his guilt. And finally there was Maine, their last days. How he'd lain awake in the slope-roofed room they'd occupied together, how he'd watched the dawn come in at the windows, how he'd listened to the din of birdsong, dreading the change that had to come.

Now here they were again, Grant no longer on the other side of a hotel wall but here in his very bed, Grant's flank stretched along Varian's, not in teasing and fleeting contact but as a persistent fact; Grant's familiar deep breathing, his familiar pulse, his heartbeat so slow that, as he'd told Varian, his boyhood physician had feared for his health. Oftentimes, during the long years of his absence and silence, Varian had thought of that heart and considered that Grant must be dead. But now he moved against Varian, inarguably alive, hard in sleep, his hand on Varian's chest. In a moment they were both awake, and dawn pushed fingers of light through the break between the curtains, brutal bright weather for their return to Marseille.

Lena met them at the station with papers for Zilberman: a false passport with a half-convincing photo, a transit visa, a permit for temporary residence in Marseille. Zilberman accepted the documents with trembling incredulity and folded them into his breast pocket. He looked as though he hadn't slept either; he was neatly dressed and combed, but his eyes were a raw insomniac red. He carried a portfolio and dragged a large metal trunk, the transport of which had cost Varian some five hundred francs.

Varian and Grant wore their cycling clothes, cleaned, ironed, and starched to the point of punishment, a reproof from the laundress. They talked little on the train. Varian sat knee to knee with Lena, reviewing a set of dismaying financial estimates Oppy had just delivered: how much the Centre's next month would cost in terms of manpower, rent, refugee support, and bribes, based upon the previous month's expenditures. It was, at least, a relief from the matter of the black Gitane, which he envisioned locked away in that convent like a novitiate—though by now it might be in the courtyard of the chief gendarme's building, approaching defilement by the fifteen-year-old son. He and Grant had discussed the situation that morning, first in bed and then in a blinding hot shower. There was only one way to frame the situation to Madame Balansard: her husband's bike had saved a man's life. She had made a sacrifice for the cause of freedom. The ERC would compensate her for the loss.

He and Grant. **Grant and I.** How long had it been since they'd existed in grammatical proximity? It was where he'd once lived every day of his life. Already they'd fallen into the familiar habit of public separation, the distance that masked its opposite. They'd ridden to Marseille side by side, but now Grant sat across the aisle with Zilberman, at an angle that robbed Varian of a means by which to catch his eye. In one hand Grant held a scholarly tome on his subject, late nineteenth-century verse; with a slender finger he tapped iambs against his knee. Would there be a cable from Eileen at the Splendide? Varian wondered. What would she have heard, what would she have written? After this weekend, what could he ever write to her again?

At the Gare St. Charles they retrieved the single bicycle and Zilberman's bags. Lena went to install the painter at the Splendide, in Mehring's narrow room, if Mehring agreed. Grant accompanied Varian to the intersection of La Canebière, where they stood for a moment on the corner, scarcely daring to look each other in the eye. All the enticements of Grant's physical self—the texture of his skin, the indent of muscle at his waist, the strength of his hands—made Varian mad with recent tactile memory. He wanted to bite Grant's collarbone, to take the heels of Grant's hands and press them to his own eyes. He wanted to follow him to the Medieval Pile and pry his starched white shirt from its buttons, then defile him medievally upon a pile of ancestral rugs.

Grant tilted his head and smiled. "Your thoughts are transparent, darling."

"Don't call me darling on the street, darling. Not even in English."

"Where shall I call you darling, then? Name a place and time."

"Tonight," Varian said. "Yours."

"Eight o'clock," Grant said, and touched his hat. Then he turned to go, and Varian watched until he'd disappeared from view. The feeling was something like having his entrails stretched from his body and dragged away. At last he continued along the boulevard Dugommier and crossed into Noailles, heading for the rue Grignan in a daze, his throat tight with the choking closeness that came from too little sleep and too much adrenaline. He wanted coffee, more cigarettes, a quiet and luxurious room in which to spend an hour in self-abuse. He wanted to be back in Arles. He wanted to be standing in the ruin of the amphitheater, inside those perfect arcs of stone that had caught the echoes of Roman voices two thousand years earlier; he wanted to be pressed against the ground in the Coussouls de Crau, a thunderstorm above, Grant's body a bolt of blue electricity beside him. He remembered an argument he'd had with Kirstein in college, not long after Varian and Grant had become, in Kirstein's parlance, boyfriends. "Oh, Varian," Kirstein had asked, in the falsetto voice of Varian's mother, "how **can** you compromise your studies for the sake of a piano player's son from Philadelphia?" His criticism had been no less sincere for the playacting; he really wanted to know. Varian had argued that he wasn't compromising anything; what existed between him and Grant would sharpen his mind, make him a better student, drive him to greater heights.

"Greater heights," Kirstein had said, and laughed. "Now there's a charming euphemism."

Varian had told him to go to hell. And he'd been right: He **did** do better, he was sharper, with Grant to spur him on; they competed, they pushed each other. And, more important, the clamor of loneliness—the constant din that had driven Varian to commit great acts of wastefulness or excess or pointless lust—fell silent, leaving his mind free for other pursuits. Love worked on him like a clarifying drug, like a finer and sharper cocaine. And it was working now. As he walked through Noailles, down the boulevard and across the narrower streets, wondering what he might find at the office—the door barred, his papers confiscated, the State Department having shut him down for good—it came to him that the consulate would not have him thrown out of France. If they hadn't by now, they never would. He was, he understood, a calculated liability. They saw him as basically ineffectual; they counted on him to conduct his illegal work on a manageable scale. He laughed to think of the conversation that must have taken place between the consul-general and the consul, in which John Hurley had to explain to Hugh Fullerton that Fry, inconvenient as he might have been, was a contained threat, and must therefore be tolerated. Old Hugh must have nearly burst a vein. But it must be so, the State Department must consider him an acceptable pest, even a necessary one; otherwise he'd have been on a plane back to the States weeks ago. Well, let them think it. Let them imagine that the current operation represented the full capacity of his work. He hardly needed a further goad, but now he had one.

At number 60, Clotilde played jacks on the terracotta tiles of the entryway, all traces of raspberry bleached from her pinafore. Beside her on the floor was a depleted tin of candies of the kind called **larmes d'amour:** tiny pastel-colored spheres, each a different shade, each containing a single drop of fruit-flavored syrup. How she'd gotten them in the midst of a war he scarcely dared imagine. She raised her eyes to Varian. A shadow crossed the open doorway of the concierge's apartment; the door filled with the figure of Madame Balansard, in a white apron and the blue work dress she wore for her tasks in the building. She took one look at Varian and slitted her eyes.

"Where's the bicycle?" she asked, her voice low, threatening.

"Madame—"

"Where's the bicycle, Monsieur Fry? **Where's the bicycle?**" She crossed the entryway, taking off her work apron. In a low and measured voice she asked, "Where is Felix's bike?"

"I traded it for a man's life," Varian said.

Madame Balansard drew back her hand and gave Varian a stinging slap, square across the jaw. "Liar," she said. "Liar and thief. Give me the money."

"There is no money."

"Give me what you got for that bike, or I'll report you to the police."

"I didn't sell it, madame. I told you. I traded it to save a man's life. A refugee. I traded it to get him out of jail. He would have been sent to a concentration camp, or killed outright."

"You traded my husband's bike to save a criminal's life!"

"Not a criminal. A refugee."

"I see them come and go from your office," she said, full of ice-cold rage. "I know what they are, and what you are! I know what you do." She regarded him through her narrowed eyes; behind her, the girl repeated her expression. "I should denounce you to the police at once."

He had to wonder for a moment what exactly she knew, or what she thought she knew; in any case, none of his illegal activities could be news to the police. "I'm deeply sorry, Madame Balansard," he said. "I had no other choice." He took his ration book from his pocket and pressed it into her hand. "Take it for Clotilde," he said. "The Centre Américain will repay you for Felix's bike."

Her hand shook. It was clear she wanted to throw the ration book at him, but Clotilde breathed at her side, a hungry fact; **larmes d'amour** would not satisfy her. "I'm going to call Monsieur Duverre," she said. The landlord. "He'll tear up your lease if I tell him to. Damn Moreau, that Jew, for bringing you in here!" She spat at his feet, then turned and went into the apartment, pulling Clotilde by the wrist behind her. In the doorway aperture, for an instant, the needle-blue flash of Clotilde's gaze; then the slam of the door, the echo of it ringing in the entryway like a curse.

14

Basso's

The little orchard at the Medieval Pile yielded fruit for weeks after Varian's return. He would walk through the garden en route to the house, filling his pockets with sun-hot persimmons, anticipating the sight of Grant in a Chinese silk robe at the door; then, in the Pile's dungeonlike kitchen, Grant would slice the persimmons open with a long sharp knife, prise the slippery flesh from the cartilage, and arrange the orange slivers on a plate like excised dragon tongues. Sometimes they would eat them there in the kitchen, standing hip to hip at the counter; other times they'd take the plate up to the bedroom and leave it on the bedside table for afterward, its sweetness a fresh shock after the salt of sex. Grant would rise naked, take the empty plate to the bathroom, and wash it at the sink; then, unfailingly, he'd bring Varian a glass of iron-flavored water, chilled by its transit through the ancient pipes. That solicitude, a remnant of their college days: it almost erased the fact that every moment they spent at the Pile, Gregor Katznelson was a silent third party.

The look that passed over Grant's face when Katznelson's name came up—a casting-down of the eyes, a slight softening around the mouth, a parting of the lips—was torture to Varian, the precise negative of the pleasure he felt in bed with Grant. He had always been prone to jealousy, though in former days he'd done his best to pretend he wasn't; jealousy seemed parochial, retrograde, shameful. But Grant had always flirted at parties, liked to disappear behind draperies or into linen closets or bedrooms with dapper lads of twenty, slim-hipped dandies of thirty, lively professors of forty; he considered it as essential to the experience as his glass of scotch. Varian remembered watching those flirtations with a disastrous pull in his chest, a drowning chill, as if he'd gone through the ice of a frozen lake.

Now here he was again after twelve years, breaking through the ice, drowning. At the Pile, Grant lived inside Katznelson's abandoned things. The Chinese robe was Katznelson's; he slept on Katznelson's monogrammed sheets in the high draped bed, drank Katznelson's liquor, bathed with his soap, shaved with his silver shaving things. If his attitude had been different, if his posture with those things had seemed careless or flippant, it might have seemed a desecration to use them in Varian's naked presence; instead, Grant's unerring tenderness toward those objects seemed a reminder, a reproach.

One afternoon, as they lay in bed with the remnants of the day's persimmons, a knock came at the door. The sound rang through the hexagonal atrium as if through the insides of a drum, and Grant leapt from the bed and pulled Katznelson's robe around him.

"Who could it be?" Varian said.

"No idea. No one comes here."

"Go answer. If anyone asks, I'm not here."

Grant smiled and ran downstairs, and Varian could hear him in low conversation with someone at the door. He couldn't make out the words, but he heard the clink of coins exchanged. A moment later Grant was back, a cable in his hand.

"It's from Gregor," he said.

Of course. "Open it."

Grant did. He sat at the foot of the high bed and ran his eyes over the thin blue paper, his breath quickening. "Tobias is alive," he said. "He wrote his father from Lyon, in code. Then another letter from Valence, no information other than that he was there." Grant read for another moment in silence. "Finally, a cable from Avignon. Again no information. That was the last. All this mail waiting for Gregor when he got home."

"When was the last communication?"

"Some weeks ago."

"At least we know he's alive. And that he's heading south."

"Yes," Grant said. His eyes fell to the cable again, and when he looked up, his expression had grown more complicated, pain-laced. "Gregor's rather unhappy back in New York," he said. "He spent the extra two bits to tell me that." He looked away, toward the half-open casement window, and Varian pulled himself from the bed. He went into the bathroom, where a single faucet dispensed auburn water into the basin. A mirror framed in gilded wood hung above the sink; it returned the image of a haggard man, a man whose life hung in the balance.

"You've got to go up to Avignon first thing tomorrow morning," Varian called to Grant. "If the boy's still there, he might not be too hard to find. And if he's already gone, there may be a trail to follow. I know Mehring's got some friends in the area, I'll tell him to write them at once."

Grant came up behind him and pressed the warm length of his body along Varian's. "Go to Avignon in the morning?" he said. **"Tout seul?"**

"I can't leave town again just now, Grant."

"All right." The water ticked in the bowl; from outside, a bird's vespers.

"Maybe it's for the best," Varian said. "A day or two away."

"Right," Grant said, his calm unbroken. Varian experienced an inward roil of shame: Couldn't he have protested, didn't he object? In Grant's hand still was the cable from Katznelson, even as he leaned against Varian, gently at first, and then less so, even as he insisted himself against Varian's body, pressing him against the cold white marble of the sink. A voice in Varian's mind called for Grant to stop, but instead he found himself returning Grant's insistence, laughing almost, asking and receiving, wanting, as always, more.

———

Two hours later—they had managed, somehow, to bathe and dress, and had caught the inbound tram—they arrived in town, at the head of the Canebière, to see Miriam and Mary Jayne for dinner. They were to meet at Basso's, a swank bouillabaisserie on the Vieux Port, where a Nigerian singer named Micheline Osondu had been defying the official ban on jazz. They walked the blocks from the tram in silence, through the streetlit yellow fog of the Marseille night. A uniformed doorman ushered them in, and there amid the white-draped tables were the women, both of them in gossamer, with glittering rhinestones in their hair. At Miriam's side was an American officer nicknamed Beaver, a former Foreign Legionnaire, tall and closely bearded, who chose to ignore Miriam's engagement to her absent Yugoslavian; and next to Mary Jayne, a stern, dark-eyed young man named Raymond Couraud, who'd been coming around the office with fancy gifts that could only have been stolen. Last week he'd given Mary Jayne a gold serpentine necklace hung with a pink diamond; this week, a fur capelet from Mainbocher. The boy—barely out of his teens, Varian guessed—bragged about being a Legionnaire too, though the rumor was that he was faking it, that he'd stolen a dead Legionnaire's papers. Mary Jayne had affectionately nicknamed him Killer, for his butchery of the English language. Varian suspected that what she felt for him was not unlike what she'd felt for her airplane, that impractical, unpredictable, exciting, and possibly dangerous thing she knew how to control, except when she didn't.

The group had installed itself at a stageside table and ordered tall glasses of beer. Micheline Osondu, wrapped from breasts to ankles in turquoise Ankara fabric, leaned toward the microphone and sang "Blue Moon," while a narrow-shouldered pianist chased tender disharmonies along the keyboard and a bassist plucked honey from his upright. Mary Jayne whispered orders to a sleek, pomaded waiter. Dining with Mary Jayne, Varian knew, meant never having to look at a menu; what came would invariably be excellent and plentiful, and at the end of the evening you did not insult Mary Jayne by offering to pay.

When Mademoiselle Osondu finished her set, Beaver and Killer excused themselves to enjoy, as they said, something stronger than lager. They invited Varian and Grant to join them, but Varian could guess their drugs of choice easily enough, and had left them behind in his Harvard days: stimulants gave him palpitations, marijuana left him wordless, and heroin could hardly be savored under the circumstances. Grant and Miriam got up to fawn over Mademoiselle Osondu, and Varian found himself alone at the table with Mary Jayne.

"I'm glad I've got a moment to speak to you," she said, pushing her hair behind her ears. "I have a rather serious subject to introduce."

"What can it be?"

"We've found a house, Miriam and I. An honest-to-goodness manor house, or villa, I suppose."

"A house?" Varian said, and smiled. "And what will you do with a house? Throw a party in it?"

"Live there, for the time being," Mary Jayne said. "And not just me. You too, Varian. I mean to get you out of that hotel."

"You intend this house for **me**?"

"Yes, and for poor Lev Zilberman, boxed up all day with Mehring. And a few others, friends of mine. The place has eight bedrooms, and a splendid salon overlooking the Val d'Huveaune. It's at La Pomme, not far from Katznelson's."

At that moment Grant and Miriam returned from paying their homage, and Grant must have caught the look on Varian's face.

"What's happened?" he said.

"Mary Jayne's found a house," Varian said. "At La Pomme."

"Yes, and it's thanks to you, Grant. You remember the little park you mentioned, the one with the scenic path along the ridge? Miriam and I took the tram out to have a **pique-nique** with Beaver and Killer. And just as we got off the tram, we came across a handwritten 'for rent' sign pinned to a tree at the head of a drive. Down the lane we went, and there was the house, a three-story villa on a hill. The landlord was there, working in the garden, so he gave us a tour. That garden! Tiered, like in a storybook. With a fountain. And the house is splendid, perfect for our purposes. It comes with a cross housekeeper named Madame Nouguet. Apparently she's not a bad cook."

So Grant had sent Mary Jayne that way; he must have known what might transpire. Of course Varian could not live in La Pomme, half an hour from the office and just down the road from Grant; of course he couldn't live anywhere with half a dozen roommates. But then Grant's knee met his own beneath the table, firmly and with meaning, and the arguments died on his tongue.

"I know the place," Grant said now, his expression inscrutable. "You mean Air Bel, off the avenue Jean Lombard. It's quite splendid, you're right."

"The ERC can't afford a splendid country house," Varian said.

"He wants only fifteen hundred a month!" Miriam crowed.

Less than Varian paid for his hotel room. He glanced toward the door of the restaurant, where Beaver and Killer were returning from their amusements.

Grant followed his glance. "Maybe we'd better have a look ourselves."

"Yes," said Mary Jayne. "Tomorrow morning!"

"I'm off to Avignon in the morning," Grant said.

"Avignon? The first train that way doesn't leave till noon, as I happen to know. We'll meet you at ten."

"What are you all so excited about?" Beaver asked, taking his seat again beside Miriam and threading an arm around her shoulders.

"Oh, that lovely house we saw! The one with the swimming pool."

"It's not exactly a swimming pool," Mary Jayne said. "It's an irrigation pond."

"Of course it is!" Miriam insisted. "When we live there, we'll swim every day. Oh, wait until you see the place, Varian."

A house down the street from Grant, in La Pomme: he might as well hang himself now. And yet if Grant found Tobias in Avignon, they would need a place to hide him, a place that wasn't the Pile. And it was true that Zilberman must be moved out of the Splendide; he couldn't continue forever in that room with Mehring. And then there were the others who had just arrived in town, a new crop of artists from his list: the Russian writer Victor Serge and his son, and André Breton and his wife and daughter. A house in the country with Breton! He imagined writing about it to Eileen, imagined her reading about it in the drafty kitchen of their apartment on Irving Place, the thin blue paper shivering in her hand.

"All right," he said, finally. "We'll see it in the morning. And then I'll decide." He watched as a flush of pleasure overtook Mary Jayne's features; she looked at Miriam and smiled. A subtler look had come over Grant's—anticipation, perhaps, laced with something darker, something like capitulation, like surrender.

"Now we are too serious," Killer said, adjusting his own serious-looking glasses. "We must dance. The jazz is marvelous!"

And it was. Black-market connections—where weren't they, here in Marseille?—must have turned the ear of the police aside, allowing what might otherwise have sounded like a flagrant celebration to proceed without interruption. Killer grabbed Miriam's hands, pulling her to the dance floor; she laughed at his unexpected attention, and Mary Jayne accepted Varian's hand, her expression cut with jealousy as she watched Miriam throw back her head and laugh at something Killer had said. Wanting to distract her, Varian leaned toward her ear and told her where he'd first heard her name:

at the Parrishes' on Morgan Bay, some twelve years earlier.

Mary Jayne's ear flushed pink. "The Parrishes!" she said. "What must they have said about me? I was besotted with Oswald then, that shallow boy with the red Citroën." They turned as Mademoiselle Osondu's voice turned; the bass fiddle slipped in and out of her agile alto. "Our families used to ski together at Chamonix. But Oswald and his sister Vivian considered me beneath their notice. East Coasters are terrific snobs, you know—no offense to you, Varian. I was from Chicago and I hadn't gone to college, and you can imagine what that meant to Oswald and Vivian."

"But they admired you," Varian said, quietly, under the beat of the jazz. "Oswald said—I'm not exaggerating—he said you were the most daring woman he knew."

She gave a wry laugh and edged closer. "He must have meant it as an insult."

"Not at all."

"You haven't any idea what happened to him, do you?"

"I haven't seen a single Parrish in years. But Oswald was impressed by that plane of yours. Not just by the plane—by the fact that you flew it yourself. And not just that. By your gumption, as he called it."

"Well, I was a Masters School girl," Mary Jayne said, lifting her chin to wink at Varian. "Our motto was 'Do it with thy might!' I took it to heart. Sometimes too earnestly, you'd probably think."

"Oh, I don't know," Varian said. "You seem to have an innate sense of irony. I can't imagine you'd have lost it at the Masters School."

"Well, I'll take that as a compliment."

"I intend it to be," Varian said. And at that moment Killer stepped in, having been stripped of Miriam by his jealous friend; and Varian retreated to the table, where Grant now sat alone with a tall flute of beer and the remnants of three dozen oysters. Varian sat down beside him and drained his own flute of beer; he was drunk enough by now to slide his ankle along Grant's, under the table.

"You sent them to that house," Varian said.

Grant shook his head. "Not me," he said. "But I can't say I'm displeased."

"I'm not going to be your neighbor at La Pomme. You know I can't, Skiff."

"I don't know what I know," Grant said, putting his fingers to his eyes for a long moment. "I'm going to go up to Avignon tomorrow afternoon to look for Tobias. Maybe you'll be my neighbor when I get back, maybe you won't. In any case, Varian, we've got to talk. We'd better talk. Or maybe just shoot ourselves. I don't know."

"You've drunk too much, darling."

"I thought I told you not to call me that," Grant said, smiling, and inclined away from Varian, just slightly, as their friends returned to the table.

The house was exactly as Mary Jayne had billed it. They all met there the next morning, Grant with his suitcase in hand, Varian with a terrible hangover, Mary Jayne and Miriam in crisp fall tweeds, Killer having acquired a black eye. At the head of the long driveway stood a pair of flaking stone pillars, one of them inset with a brass sign that read VILLA AIR BEL. On the other, a hand-painted wooden sign: FOR RENT. INQUIRE WITHIN.

They climbed the drive until they cleared a little ridge; below lay the beginning of the valley's slope. The air in the Val d'Huveaune was a gold-blue haze, sun filtering through shattered clouds to strike the scrublands below. It smelled of sage and of lavender, of the chamomile that crowded the verge of the drive. Overhead, plane trees made an arch of broken shade. Half-hidden by a gentle rise was the villa itself, of buff-colored stucco; beneath their feet the dirt road changed to close-set stones, and they passed the low carriage house that served as the caretaker's home. The inner gate was unlocked, and Mary Jayne pushed it open with a proprietary gesture. They crossed the stone driveway and stood looking down into the garden, where an old man in a feather-decked homburg dug with his spade. A four-lobed fountain splashed at the center of the garden, and overgrown paths snaked through the tall grass in all directions.

"Monsieur Thumin!" Mary Jayne called. "Here are the gentlemen."

The old man looked up, wiped his brow with a smudged handkerchief, and rested a foot on the shovel. "I can't understand a word you're saying," he called in French.

They descended the stone stairs to the garden. Monsieur Thumin brushed dust from his lapels and drew himself up straight. He was twiglike, small, his hands crabbed with arthritis; in his gaze, a mild confusion at odds with attention and engagement.

"Oh, gentlemen, I'm so glad you've come," he said. "Mademoiselle Gold thought you would like the house."

"Will you show it to us?" Varian asked, and Monsieur Thumin did. First the garden, its fountain big enough to wade in, and a stone-rimmed irrigation reservoir wide and deep as a swimming pool. There were wild flower beds, tangles of fruiting vines, a kitchen plot dense with late squashes and tomatoes; beside the house was a glass-walled conservatory crowded with miniature palms and lemon trees.

The house itself stood three stories tall, its back windows staring into the valley. They followed Thumin through a terra-cotta-floored kitchen that might have been the twin of the one at the Medieval Pile, then into a dining room with a massive walnut table, each of its twelve chairs densely carved with leaflike curlicues and slit-eyed elves. A trompe l'oeil forest grew on the surrounding walls. Beyond was a salon with satin-covered sofas; then a library bristling with books in French and English and Latin. On a wall plaque above the mantel, a pair of hawkless hawk wings lifted in mid-beat, and on the marble shelf beneath, a tiny glass dome housed a perfectly preserved mole, small as a pear, seeming to sniff the air with its crushed flower of a nose. A shelf opposite held a mounted branch on which five stuffed finches perched, one of them in the act of catching an iridescent beetle. Surrealists, Varian thought, would appreciate the place.

They toured the bedrooms upstairs, each with its carved bed and dresser, its washstand, its massive wardrobe. The green-gold view poured in from every window. An upstairs bathroom held a bathtub large enough for two; the tub rested on the milk-white backs of tiny swans. The third story housed more bedrooms, each filled with a flood of Mediterranean light. In the last of these, incongruously, stood a long narrow harpsichord, abandoned to dust and arachnids.

Grant touched the keyboard cover and turned to Monsieur Thumin. "Does it work?"

Thumin shrugged. "I don't play."

Grant opened the keyboard and pulled out the green upholstered bench. He threw the hem of his jacket behind him, sat, and rested his hands on the keys.

"Do you mind?" he asked Thumin.

"I'm afraid it'll be frightfully out of tune."

Grant put his hands to the keys. He traced a scale; the notes held in the air and dissipated. And then, suddenly, here was the Bach fugue nicknamed "Wedge," with its intricate four-part contrapuntal line; as Varian listened, a cold cataract of memory poured through him. In the basement of Gore Hall was a series of little-used practice rooms, one of which housed a harpsichord painted with a pastoral scene. Varian hadn't known of the instrument's existence until Grant led him down the stairs one evening, and, by the light of a candle, revealed the instrument and sat to play. Varian knew by then about Grant's abandoned musical aspirations; they had opened the books of their childhood histories to each other, page by shameful page. But Varian had never seen Grant touch an instrument. Here, suddenly, was a greater intimacy yet, one hidden in the basement and not meant, Varian understood, to be discussed after the fact. He had always felt at home in the logical precision of Bach, but as he listened he began to see farther into the music, the way a stereoscope's twinned images resolved into three dimensions. It asked a series of painful, pointed questions about mortality, about the existence of God and the conundrum of Christ, the chthonic pull of the flesh and the poor trapped spirit jailed in the ribcage, in the four dark chambers of the heart. He understood, listening, how far he was from having any iota of control over his feelings for Grant; he was, as the phrase went, in thrall. He'd had lovers before, passionate connections with boys in dormitories and woods, frantic frictions in the mushroom-scented dark. At times he'd thought himself in love. But he had never belonged so unquestionably, so uncontrollably, to any other person.

Now, twelve years later, he struggled to compose his expression, to mirror the surprised admiration on the women's faces, or the vague impatience on Thumin's. What did Grant mean, playing this piece in front of Varian's colleagues and a perfect stranger? Was it possible he'd forgotten? Why should he remember, after all? At the time, all those years ago, Varian had taken care to affect dispassion. He had listened without comment, then suggested they get to dinner. He had fancied, he had feared, that Grant had glimpsed what lay beneath his calm; but perhaps that wasn't true. In any case, they'd never talked about it, had never returned together to the room in the basement of Gore Hall.

When Grant finished, he raised his eyes not to Varian but to the valley view, and let his hands fall to his lap. It must have been Gregor he was thinking of, not Varian; he might have been looking all the way across the Val d'Huveaune to the ocean, as if he could see over the curve of the earth to where Gregor now sat in an apartment near Columbia, a string of rooms Grant must know more intimately even than the Pile. Varian's skin seemed to contract around him like a woven trap, the kind that pulled you in farther the more you struggled. Thumin had to ask his question twice before Varian answered.

"Yes, it's ideal," he said. "We'll take it."

15

Villa

Three days later he emptied his drawers and packed his bags at the Splendide, still marveling that, despite Fullerton's dire warnings, he, Varian, had not yet been ejected from France. His suspicion must have been correct: the consul considered him too ineffectual to pose a real threat to the American diplomatic mission. Fullerton had ignored him entirely since his return from Arles. From Vichy there had been no action at all. And all that time he'd never stopped working on his clients' behalf, had not stopped procuring false documents and visas, had not stopped seeking ways out, though the Spanish border was still officially closed.

Recently he had almost cracked the sea route. Hirschman had drummed up a little yacht called the **Bouline,** whose captain had just sold her to a buyer in Gibraltar; the captain meant to deliver the boat himself, transporting a full load of passengers at top price. Varian had bought places for Hans Tittel, Franz Boegler, Fritz Lam, and Siegfried Pfeffer, four prominent Social Democrats who had been interned at Vernet. Mary Jayne herself had gone down to spring them from the camp; wearing a Lanvin suit besprinkled with Chanel No. 5, she'd gone to meet the commandant and had invited him to a rendezvous at her hotel. She wouldn't say exactly what had transpired, but some time later he gave her what she wanted: the prisoners were allowed a day trip to Marseille, under heavy guard, to get their American visas. Hirschman bought off the guards, Bingham delivered the visas, and Varian himself put the Social Democrats on the boat and sent them off. Had it not been for a violent offshore storm, they would have gotten away. As it was, the captain had turned the boat around and brought it back to port, where the Sûreté Nationale waited to drag the prisoners back to Vernet.

Mary Jayne and Hirschman had seen it as an abject failure, but still it gave Varian hope: the prisoners had been reinterned but not shipped east, and the sea route once again seemed possible. The **Bouline** hadn't worked, but they would try again.

Slowly and quietly, the reach of the Centre Américain was growing. Miriam had recruited a few useful friends as staff: Danny Bénédite, who had worked at the visa desk at the Préfecture de Police in Paris, where he had doled out too many

sortie stamps to aspiring immigrants; his British wife, Theo, who had been employed by IBM and was a mechanical genius, a tinkerer, a breaker of codes; and Jean Gemähling, a Strasbourg boy in his twenties, who spoke perfect English and nursed a deep hatred for Vichy. It could almost have been considered a stroke of luck that Madame Balansard had gotten the Centre Américain evicted from the rue Grignan. They had since moved to a new office on the boulevard Garibaldi, two large rooms above a stationer's shop. The place reeked of printer's ink, but it was big enough for all of them.

Now he was leaving the Splendide too, his home for the past twelve weeks. It occurred to him as he filled his suitcase that he would miss these anonymous green curtains, the scrolled carpet, the window overlooking the girls' school, the French note in the schoolgirls' laughter. He would miss the bathroom where he'd conducted his secret conferences with Hirschman. The bed that had once served as conference table for his committee. The tapped phone lines. The patch of cracked plaster in the likeness of Jimmy Cagney. Here was a place all his own, the first he'd had since college. In this room he had invented a new self who could save artists' lives, one who could backtalk to the likes of Fullerton and Villand, who could direct the staff of an international lifesaving mission. And it was here that he'd received Grant's first message, here that he'd lain awake after their meeting at the Dorade, turning that nautilus cufflink over and over in his fingers.

Yesterday there had been another cable from Eileen. The ERC had set its sights on someone who could be trained as his replacement, she said; there were some visa difficulties, but she thought they would soon be resolved. PLEASE TELL ME VARIAN HOW YOU ARE, she had concluded; impossible to miss her plaintive tone. And part of him wanted to tell her everything; he thought she'd prefer the truth. But she herself hadn't mentioned Grant in any of her letters, despite the fact that Varian had written his name with such careful nonchalance in his own; the omission had to be deliberate. Impossible to think she could have forgotten what Grant had been to Varian. And soon he must write to tell her that he had moved to Air Bel, ten minutes' walk from the Medieval Pile. TELL ME VARIAN HOW YOU ARE: he wished he knew the answer. He took her cable from the desk and folded it into a polite oblong, then stowed it in his suitcase alongside all the others.

———

Lev Zilberman waited in the lobby, a roll of drawings tucked under his arm. He had tamed his strands of black-silver hair with a wet comb; his tortoiseshell spectacles glinted. Knotted at his throat was the same blue neckerchief he'd worn at Arles.

He looked as though he hadn't had a proper sleep in weeks. He and Mehring kept opposite hours, and the strain had made itself known between them.

"Here you are, Lev," Varian said. "Glad you decided to join us."

Zilberman nodded. "Herr Mehring is a fine writer, a good person," he said. "It was good of him to have me, but . . ."

"Say no more. I understand. I'm glad you're coming, that's all."

At the front desk Varian paid their bills, and then they walked the three blocks to the tram and boarded a near-empty train. Zilberman held his long tube of drawings and looked out the open window, watching the soot-streaked buildings slip past. The knotted ends of his blue kerchief lifted and fell with the breeze; there was a chill edge to the air, the approach of winter.

"It was kind of you to invite me," he said, in a low, constrained voice. "I fear my presence endangers your operation."

"You're worth it," Varian said, simply. "And you'll be in good company out there." He dealt the names like cards: Mary Jayne and Miriam, the Bénédites, Jean Gemähling, Victor Serge and son, and finally his trump card, the Bretons.

Zilberman smiled. "I won't have a moment's peace."

"There's a greenhouse where you can set up shop if you'd like. I can see to it that you aren't disturbed."

"Breton will see to it that I am. He is a master of disturbances."

"He does have that reputation, yes."

"But he was very kind to me in Paris," Zilberman said. "He and Jacqueline hosted a show of my work at their home and invited some powerful friends. He is a generous person, you know, as long as you're on his good side. And Jacqueline is a force, a presence. She is known, among other things, for her memorable soirées. We shall all have something to carry out of France with us, if we live." He looked out the window, his gaze traveling along the sun-struck streets.

"Don't speak that way," Varian said.

"You know, Monsieur Fry, that our survival is far from guaranteed. You may not have a say in the matter. The war progresses. How long do you think it will be before the rest of the country is occupied? Everyone is at risk. You have no idea what the Nazis are capable of."

"I do, unfortunately. I witnessed the riots in Berlin in '35."

Zilberman glanced away. Ordered rows of olive trees made a small orchard beside the light rail tracks; between the rows, girls in dusty skirts performed a meticulous task of maintenance with long-toothed wooden rakes.

"It's better that you did," Zilberman said. "Better for you not to have illusions."

"Most Americans don't want to believe there's a

war on," Varian said. "They just want it all to go quietly away, or for it never to have existed. Even the sympathetic ones don't really understand."

"Well," Zilberman said, reflectively. "You are a writer, Mr. Fry. A writer and an editor. Perhaps you can make them understand."

The move-in continued all week. Wave after wave of residents appeared at the gates of Air Bel. After Varian came Miriam and Mary Jayne, the former with a single red leather suitcase, the latter with her entourage of well-traveled Louis Vuitton trunks. Next came the Bénédites: Danny, tall and thin, with his pencil mustache and his bottle-glass spectacles; dovelike Theo, holding their dark-eyed little boy by the hand. The next morning brought the Bretons and the Serges; Varian spied them from an upstairs window and watched as they traversed the avenue of plane trees. Breton, his features boldly drawn, his hair swept back from his high forehead, engaged the Russian novelist with an air of pleased outrage, his hands describing emphatic arcs like a conductor urging an orchestra onward. Serge seemed to glide along beside him, his limbs long and spiderlike, his gestures a dancer's. Despite the pitch of their argument, Breton and Serge were not, in fact, political enemies; Serge had built his reputation around carefully argued Marxism, and Breton had flirted with communism: two years earlier he had penned a manifesto with Trotsky, arguing against government oversight of the creative arts. But Trotsky and Serge had had a number of famous fallings-out, public and private, and now Trotsky's name flew like a dart between Breton and Serge as they descended into the garden. Behind them came Aube Breton, seven years old, walking the drive dispassionately with her mother, Jacqueline Lamba, who had once been a nude aquatic dancer at L'Onde Bleue in Paris and retained a certain mermaidlike quality, a fluidity of motion that projected sex and danger. Her hair and skin were made of burnished gold, her clothing, ivory-colored and loose-fitting, an obvious superfluity. Varian fancied that she might slip her silk pants and caftan almost incidentally and dive into the irrigation pool. What drama was he assembling, he wondered, what scene was he setting, here at the house in La Pomme? He relished the idea that necessity had led him to take up residence with surrealists in a villa in the South of France, just down the road from Grant; such a turn of events, inconceivable in peacetime, had become not just possible but arguably altruistic on his part. Below, in the garden, Aube Breton speculated aloud that now they'd reached the country, there would be lots of good things to eat. A sharp correction came from Victor Serge's son, Vlady, twenty years old and the owner of a fine drooping mustache and a knowing air. Likely as not, Vlady told her, they would starve.

"Nonsense," said Jacqueline. "We shall live by our wits. We shall have feasts and parties."

"Let us hope you are right, Madame Lamba."

"Maman is always right," said Aube, with an air of incontrovertible authority.

There was a great and tumultuous moving-about those first few days. The Bretons complained of noise from the Bénédites' room above; Peterkin, as everyone called him, rode a cock horse to Banbury Cross each morning before dawn. Victor Serge was allergic to whatever lay below him in the garden, and had to remove to a higher room. Vlady could not sleep in the mornings in a room with an eastern exposure. Zilberman was repeatedly awakened by the comings and goings of Killer, whose professional activities led him to keep unusual hours. And Aube Breton, true to Vlady Serge's prediction, could not get enough to eat and lay awake at night crying for cake, for milk, for anything.

The nights were no more restful for Varian. Grant had returned, unsuccessful, from his trip to Avignon, Tobias's trail having grown cold; he'd persisted for days, knocking on doors at all hours, following the slimmest of leads, and had succeeded only at arousing the suspicion of the police. Finally he'd been hauled down to the sous-préfecture, where he'd had to make a late-night call to Harry Bingham, who sent his official car to bring him home. He'd returned in shame and frustration, and seemed for the first time to be depressed. All Varian wanted was to lie with him in Katznelson's bed, or on Katznelson's sofa, from dusk till morning, devising new plans of action. But, ironically enough, living at Air Bel made it harder at times to get to the Medieval Pile. Varian's room at Air Bel was on the second floor, and any movement on the front or back stairs meant possibly awakening friends and clients, or, worse, their hungry and light-sleeping children. There was no gutter to slide down, no merciful tree limb to bridge a descent; his fantasies ran to the knotting of bedsheets or the construction of a ladder made of silken rope. Neither the Pile nor Air Bel had a phone, so there was no quick way to communicate whether or not he could come. Nor was it easy for Grant to stay on at Air Bel after the others had gone to bed. Someone was always up late, playing cards at the dining table or arguing politics on the stairs or preparing chamomile tea for a child with a cough. Grant and Varian could walk in the garden, but it offered no privacy; every word spoken there traveled directly toward the house. Via that route, Varian had learned that Jacqueline Lamba had recently had a miscarriage, that Victor Serge felt ashamed of his son's two-dimensional politics, and that Breton regretted exiling Max Ernst from among the favored surrealists, particularly now that Ernst was a refugee here in Marseille. Even if the acoustics had been better, the garden was occupied: Zilberman had in fact set up his studio in the greenhouse, and worked at all hours. Varian felt as if he'd moved in with a large inquisitive family of the kind he'd never actually had. He said as much to Hirschman one night when he was visiting for drinks.

"And you're the papa of the family, are you not?" Hirschman said, executing the particular German laugh that followed one's own joke.

"I'm hardly the paternal type," Varian said, though the characterization struck him as strangely apt; the next morning as he boarded the tram, he thought about his own father commuting into the city every morning for decades. And wouldn't he do the same once he was back in the States? Wouldn't he live in the house Eileen had found for them in Westchester or Greenwich, and take a gray train to and from his job in the city while she hosted literary luncheons or drove around in a long gleaming car to drop off the children or pick up a roast for dinner? Would Eileen be happy under those circumstances, the same Eileen who had always lived in cities and hated cooking and resented even the small changes her body underwent over the course of a month? Would they really have children? Would they assemble an **establishment,** as it was called in Victorian novels?

A housemaid, a gardener, a driveway-clearer? Could he give up Central Park, dinner at 21, the throb and push of the subway, and everything that could be had downtown?

Of course he found ways to get to Grant's. He went directly from the office, or after dinner at Air Bel, on the claim that he wanted a long and solitary walk. He did it with some frequency. Sometimes he and Grant returned from town together, after the others left the office; other times, when Grant preferred to stay at home, Varian met him at the Pile. Those days he would get off the train at La Pomme and stop in at the little station washroom to tidy his shirt and comb his hair. He wore a fresh carnation in his lapel, no matter how long or disheartening the day. Then, pulling his overcoat around him against the wind, he walked the dark kilometer from the station to Katznelson's house. Grant said he need not bother knocking; the massive oak door was never locked. Varian would pause at the entry to smooth his hair again. Then he'd open the heavy door and stand in the tiled foyer, just listening. Sometimes he would catch Grant singing to himself in the kitchen while he prepared a bachelor's supper of sardines and day-old bread. Other times he came upon him at the writing desk in the solarium, hunched over a missive to Katznelson or some other correspondent back home. Often he felt sheer wonder at the mundanity of it: **Grant himself,** the disappeared Grant, now as quotidian as the daily paper. He could almost imagine, as they sat together on the kilim-covered sofa with **Le Temps** open on a low table between them, that they'd slipped through the fabric of reality; that they might live as they wished, with no ill consequences for anyone, not even for themselves.

They would eat their dinner, they would wash the plates together at the kitchen sink, they would read in the library or sit before the fire, poking logs into the stack on the grate and watching the heat flow through the embers. All their history lay between them, some of it exposed and other parts still shrouded; their present was the fire and their closeness, their future undiscussable. At some point, invariably, Grant's hand fell upon Varian's knee, or Varian pressed his forehead against Grant's, his temples pounding. With speed they dispensed of shirts and trousers and all that lay beneath; then they took each other in hand. Every place he touched Grant, he felt his essential substance beneath the skin like metal, powerful and conductive.

Afterward, they would have another drink and look at the night sky from the upstairs balcony. On fine nights they wore nothing but their dressing gowns; the closest neighbor was half a kilometer away. Twelve years after they'd learned the constellations from a book in Maine, they could still identify dozens. There was Orion with his drawn bow, Cassiopeia stretched on her rock, monstrous Cetus arching away from Perseus, and serpentine Hydra poised to strike Cancer. They made a game of it, seeing who could remember more of the sky's tragedies. But no matter who won, they both lost; in the end, Varian had to leave. He had to be home at the villa, reachable at least by messenger. He could not spend a single night in Grant's bed. Of all the pleasures he experienced at the Pile, Grant's reluctance to let him go was the deepest of all. How had he earned it? It felt, for all the world, like forgiveness for what had happened all those years ago. But nothing had changed. Varian was still married to Eileen, had not intimated to her the smallest part of what was happening here. Every night, when Grant turned from saying goodnight to Varian, he reentered Katznelson's sanctum, put on Katznelson's pajamas, slept in his great carved bed. And by day he looked for Tobias, wherever he might be hiding in the great tangled rat's nest that was southern France.

One of the hardest things to get used to, he wrote Eileen in a rare quiet moment, as a gray rain fell beyond the windows of his room, **is the constant change in the cast of characters. You come to know a person well, and soon that person becomes indispensable. And you forget that he, too, is a refugee, and must leave at the nearest opportunity; or that she in is love with a person in danger, and must follow him when the tide**

sweeps him away. Over lunch à deux at the Dorade the previous afternoon, Miriam Davenport—he could scarcely believe it, refused to believe it still—had tendered her resignation. She had finally gotten an Italian transit visa; she would travel through Italy and on to Yugoslavia, where she would meet her fiancé, Rolf Treo, in Ljubljana. Rolf had been ill for months but was on the mend, she said; they expected to be married early in the new year. Once they got the necessary visas, they would make their way to Lisbon and depart from there to points west.

"If he's on the mend, why can't he just wait until he's recovered and meet you here?" Varian had said, grouchily.

"You know why not. Unless we're married, they'll never give him an exit visa."

"And you truly want to marry him, this—art student?"

"He's not an art student anymore. He's a professor at the Univerza v Ljubljani."

"Well, damn it to hell, Miriam!" He knew he was becoming ridiculous, knew he was talking too loud. "I can't spare you. No one else on our team has your expertise."

"My expertise! Do you mean my two years of art-school training? What's so special about that?"

"You **know,**" Varian said. "I'm no artist. Neither is Hirschman or Mary Jayne. Our new recruits are bright, but they don't know what you know. It's not just training. You have a talent. The Bénédites have other talents, and so does Jean Gemähling. How are we supposed to go on without you? What happens the next time some genius turns up with a portfolio full of chickenscratch? Am I to just send him packing? And what about the person who comes with nothing at all? Who do we have who can do what you do?" He meant her ability to divine, from a few sketches hastily rendered down at the Vieux Port, whether a refugee had real ability, whether he was what he said he was, whether he merited the Committee's attention.

"Listen, Varian. About that." Miriam lit another cigarette, the umpteenth in a chain. "Don't you think it's rather silly? And not just silly, wrong-headed, or maybe wrong-hearted? I mean, as a basis to decide whether someone lives or dies? Because, let's be honest, that's what it'll come down to in a lot of these cases. Don't you think a middling artist deserves a chance just as much as a great one does?"

Varian sat back with his drink in his hand. "You know how hard it is to get the New York office to come up with cash. And every day they wire me, asking me to cut back our staff, to curb expenses. It's hard to raise money, Frank Kingdon says. People still don't believe, don't fundamentally **understand,** what they read every day in the papers. Who am I supposed to cut from the payroll? Hirschman, who knows every black marketeer in Marseille and can manipulate them all to our ends? Oppy, who knows how to turn a dollar into ten? Leon Ball, who'll be the only reason we get people over the border if the border ever opens again? And now you tell me I should just say damn the expense and save any Jacques or Jill who can hold a brush?"

Miriam looked away as she discharged her ash into a ceramic trawler. "I don't know **how** you're supposed to do it," she said. "I don't have the answers. But I know that what we've been doing is wrong. It doesn't feel humanitarian. It feels the opposite. Inhumane."

And hadn't Grant said essentially the same thing a few nights earlier? They'd been speaking on the subject of race again, of Hitler's relative valuation of lives. There was a terrible joke that had been making the rounds: **When does Hitler consider a black man's life more significant than a white man's? When the black man and the white man are both your grandfathers.** Don't laugh too hard, Varian, Grant had said; lives have relative value in your camp, too.

"You do understand," he said now to Miriam. "You know why we do it. You can't pretend you don't. Artists save lives. So do outspoken champions of democracy. And journalists. And novelists."

"Yes, and they do so indiscriminately."

"What's your game here, exactly? Are you trying to make me feel like a villain? Have I wronged you in some way?"

"This has nothing to do with me. Or maybe yes, maybe it does—maybe I've been thinking about how I'm going to answer Rolf when I see him again and he asks what I did in Marseille. Deciding who lives and who dies on the basis of their talent. Is that what I should tell him? How am I going to think about all this ten years from now?"

"You'll come to the same conclusion you've already come to. You did what was necessary."

"No, I won't. I'll wonder what more I could have done. And so will you."

He called to the waiter for another drink. Despite all the wartime shortages, Marseille never seemed to run low on wine. "I have a responsibility to the people who came up with the list," he said, lowering his voice. "I didn't make those choices myself."

"No, but you're making them now. And anyway, who's to say what **accomplished** means? What about someone like Hannah Arendt, for example?"

"Who's Hannah Arendt?"

"You haven't heard of her, of course. No one has. She's married to Heinrich Blücher, the German poet and philosopher, who's not on your list either. He's an accomplished enough academic, if something of a pedant. But her work is another thing altogether. She was a friend of Walter Benjamin's. When I met Walter in Paris, he said I must read her at once. He had a single dog-eared copy of her dissertation—just a manuscript, which he'd paid someone to retype from the original—and he pressed it on me, with admonishments not to lose it. I'll admit I wasn't too anxious to read it. The subject was the treatment of love in Saint Augustine. A philosopher I don't much admire. He's the one, you know, who codified the idea of original sin, and pinned it squarely on the naked breast of Eve."

"Yes, yes, I know Saint Augustine," Varian said, impatient.

"Well, you don't know Arendt on Augustine. She uses the old saint's arguments against him. He tells us to disavow social connection as a source of meaning and look to God, but she argues that meaning comes only from connection with others. She's writing that argument in the light of Hitler's rise to power, and in opposition to it. Love, not hate, as the driving ethos behind political power. It's nothing yet, just a dissertation. Not enough to get her past your New York gatekeepers. But Benjamin was of the opinion that she would set the world afire."

Varian laced his fingers. "Interesting that you should make this argument in light of the fact that you're leaving us. If you've already decided to throw it all over, some would say you've got no right to question my decisions."

"Well, I don't care if I've got the right or not! I've said what I meant to say."

"As you always do," he said, tartly, though it was one of the things he admired most about her. "You have to know I don't want to keep anyone out. You have to know I'd stay up all night every night for years on end if it meant saving just a few more."

"I do know. I've seen you at work. But there's

something seductive about sitting in a seat of power, isn't there? Having the authority to judge?"

Varian looked at her carefully, at the reflection of light in her clear, intelligent eyes, at the cross of her glinting braids, the headdress of an ancient warrior queen. "Do you think I **want** to judge?" he said. "Do you sincerely think that of me?"

"It was your idea to save the artists and writers. Specifically them."

"**My** idea? Do I have to explain or defend my project to you? It wasn't just a whim of mine. I wasn't alone in thinking that the intellectual treasure of Europe shouldn't be scattered or destroyed. The names on the list **mean** something. Every one. They mean something to **me.**"

"Everyone means something to someone."

"In the absence of infinite resources, you have to choose. If this were the nineteenth century, we'd save Dostoyevsky, not Odoyevsky. Flaubert, not Mirbeau."

"If this were the nineteenth century, there would still be serfdom and slavery, and women wouldn't have the right to vote."

"Oh, for God's sake." Varian balled up his napkin and threw it down. "What do you want me to do? Print money? Create time?"

"Whatever it takes," she said, and coughed, and gave him her tender, toothy grin.

He wanted to walk out of the restaurant, out of Marseille, all the way to the border and over it. It was true, wasn't it, that his position was impossible, even indefensible. If Miriam, who had been on the inside and certainly knew better, could still imply that perhaps he wasn't doing enough, he had to consider the possibility that maybe he wasn't. What had happened to the feeling he'd had a month earlier, that the very impossibility of the task was part of its attraction? Did he actually care less about saving human beings if those human beings couldn't write a perfect novel or make an enduring painting? Would he wonder ten years from now what more he could have done?

Miriam began to cough again: that hollow smoker's hack that presaged consumption. Her skin flushed and she extracted a handkerchief from her bag. She was a few moments in composing herself. "Forgive me," she said. "It's these dreadful Gauloises."

"So you really plan to leave us for that sickly Slav?"

"I really do," Miriam said, and leaned over the table. "I haven't gotten laid in nine months!" She hooted with glee. "Mary Jayne thinks I'm mad. Sleep with old Beaver, she says! He adores you! Rolf will never know. But I'll know. You know?"

Varian laughed. He reached across the table and took her hand. "Nine months!" he said. "If only I'd known. No girl should have to suffer that way. I might have swayed you, don't you think?"

"You," she said, narrowing her eyes at him. "You. If anyone could have, maybe it would've been you." Her gaze was steady, her tone reflective; her hand in Varian's felt charged with nervous energy. "But it couldn't have been you, could it?"

He sat silent, looking at her. She was right, for countless reasons; it couldn't have been. But what was she asking of him, what did she want him to say? Did she want him to speak the words aloud? His head pounded with a dull internal pressure. Before him Miriam had turned an incandescent pink, all the way to the crest of her brow. Of course she and Mary Jayne knew about Grant; of course they saw what was going on. It was written on him stark as skywriting. Fortunately, the waiter arrived at that moment with the check, and Miriam withdrew her hand.

16

Revels

It was Mary Jayne who proposed the farewell party for Miriam. She and Varian were sitting on the patio the next evening after dinner, watching shadows gather in the valley; Mary Jayne leaned against the stone railing, one espadrilled foot balanced on a patio chair. The party might take place on Saturday night, she said, before Miriam's departure Monday. It would start with dinner for a few friends; then they'd open the doors to a larger group of guests. Miriam was to have a new dress and plenty of champagne and songs composed in her honor, and the dinner guests would be the area surrealists: Oscar Dominguez, Victor Brauner, Wifredo Lam, Jacques Hérold—perhaps even Chagall, who might be lured by the prospect of seeing Zilberman. And if they invited Bingham, and seated him next to Chagall, he could whisper in Chagall's ear all night long about the prospect of emigration. Breton would play host; he liked the role of ringleader. And Mary Jayne herself would sponsor the occasion. It had been far too long, she said, since she'd thrown a proper party. She was not to be dissuaded.

"I hate to provide the voice of reason," Varian said, "but what are you planning to feed a dozen surrealists? Or does a surrealist dinner party not require actual food?"

Mary Jayne said she would consult Madame Nouguet, the cook and housekeeper. "There are ways," she said, mysteriously, though if there were, Varian suspected she would have had them only on hearsay; he'd heard her boast that she'd never so much as boiled water for tea. "Anyway, why have a house like this if you're not going to throw parties in it? Otherwise, it's like a musical instrument unplayed. A cake uneaten. A waste."

"Parties are showy," Varian said. "We don't want to attract official attention."

"We've got nothing to hide. The authorities know where Zilberman is. You lifted him from a police station, after all. And the police know where to find you if they want, even here at La Pomme. Throw a party and let them know you're not afraid."

Varian searched her eyes. "But I am afraid, Mary Jayne. Aren't you?"

She slid her espadrille along the rail. "I used to be, I suppose. Most often when I was flying. I used to look down at the ground below and imagine what it might feel like to hit the dirt at a thousand miles an hour. Tchow! Instant death. Would it hurt?" She shrugged. "But we all have to die one way or another. In the meantime I mean to live."

"Right. But I also mean for my clients to live. In the biological sense."

"Sure. But they've also got to **want** to. Parties stave off despair."

At that moment Grant emerged from the house and crossed the patio to join them. "I couldn't help overhearing," he said. "Are we having a party?"

"Miriam's leaving, you know," Mary Jayne said. "Don't you think she deserves a fine send-off? But Varian says we'll just attract attention."

"Let me have a word with Mr. Fry," Grant said. "In our Crimson days, he was known to throw his own fine party now and again."

"All right," Mary Jayne said. "Do your worst. Make him say yes, Grant. Miriam deserves it, after all she's done for the Centre." She hopped down from her perch on the railing and went into the house, leaving a faint echo of Chanel No. 5 behind her.

Varian watched her go, then turned his gaze on Grant. "I can't throw a party, of course," he said. "We have to keep a low profile."

"You can throw a party. I've seen you do it."

"You don't think it'll make a noise?"

"What if it does?" Grant said. "Maybe it'll make the right kind. People need to know you're here. Clients, I mean. There are still dozens on your list who could be anywhere. Put the word out. Selectively, I mean. See who you draw. And if the police come too, treat them as guests. Make them complicit."

Varian nodded slowly. "That's good."

"Mary Jayne knows what she's doing. Why not trust her?"

"It's that boyfriend of hers I don't trust. Killer. That little cur, coming and going at all hours."

"What's wrong with coming and going at all hours?" Grant said, and winked. He slid one of his knees between Varian's. "Don't look up at the house," he said. "No one's watching. Look at me. Throw a party," he said, exerting a subtle pressure against Varian's groin with his knee. "Get Chagall here to the house, and whoever else will come. Cast a wide net. You never know what we'll catch."

"All right," Varian said. "All right. For God's sake, Grant. I yield."

The night of the party, the household sat to dinner at the large walnut table, in the chairs carved with slit-eyed elves. Madame Nouguet circled with a tureen of turnip soup enriched with cream from a contraband cow named Io, who grazed the scrub field below the garden and slept at night in a thatch-roofed shed at the property's edge. The turnips were the only vegetable in plentiful supply, but Madame

Nouguet had scared up some pale radishes and a pile of stunted potatoes that would have been discarded in peacetime. Two feral chickens, caught by the quick-handed Hirschman, had forfeited their lives for the occasion; they lay at the center of the table in a nest of rosemary, their brown skins starred with flakes of Camargue salt. Varian could scarcely remember when he'd last eaten meat. The food supply in Marseille had continued to dwindle; the city lived now on its cellar stores or what it could drag from the sea. That, and what flowed through the black market. He would never tell anyone what he'd paid for the chocolate that flavored the postprandial cake.

On the table, flanking the two roasted chickens, stood a pair of large apothecary jars into which Breton had decanted nearly a dozen praying mantises. His hope was that the mantises would perform their amorous rituals and that the guests would see the males lose their heads. Earlier, over cocktails in the library, Breton had presented Miriam with a brooch made from a pin-speared bumblebee; he'd found it dead on his windowsill that morning. Bravely she wore it at the neckline of her dinner gown, where it rained a dust of pollen into her décolletage. She sat beside Varian, close enough that he could see gold grains on her cold-pricked skin. On her other side sat Walter Mehring, pale and diminutive in a borrowed dinner jacket and a white silk tie, having managed, for the occasion, to overcome both his fake illness and his justifiable fears. Beyond him, in the hostess's chair, sat Mary Jayne, patron, toastmistress, distributor of cigarettes and other favors, fanner of the conversational flame, and at her side was a scrubbed-looking Killer in a sharp-edged dinner jacket. Beside him was Hirschman, every sign of chicken-catching effaced from his being. Then there was Theo Bénédite, tranquil as a young countess in her emerald-colored gown, and Danny slim and correct beside her, brushed to a high gloss; the tall and wiry Serges, **père et fils;** the nervous, broad-shouldered Jean Gemähling, molesting a delicate soup spoon with the ball of his thumb; Lev Zilberman, assessing the assembled guests through the lenses of his tortoiseshell glasses; and a small host of surrealists from the neighborhood: Wifredo Lam with his great inquisitive eyes and mannerist hands; André Masson, massive and direct, sporting a houndstooth cravat; the Spanish painter Oscar Dominguez and his one-eyed friend, Victor Brauner; Jacques Hérold, whose paintings were as precise as they were strange, as if someone had turned a camera on Dante's hell; and finally, at the head of the table, Breton, outfitted in a blue velvet jacket, smiling to himself as he surveyed the company. He was flanked by Jacqueline on one side and, to Varian's satisfaction, Marc Chagall on the other—Chagall accompanied not by his wife but by Harry Bingham, who had already begun to whisper in his ear. Next to Bingham, at Varian's side, was Grant, Elliott Schiffman Grant, in a sky-black dinner suit, the reunited nautilus cufflinks at his wrists.

And all of this, as Mary Jayne told them over the turnip soup, was only the prelude. The real party would start after the dinner hour, when more guests would arrive for music and dancing. The music was to be provided by Les Conséquences, the famous Paris jazz trio, whose leader, a trumpet player, had been an intimate of Mary Jayne's in her avenue Foch days.

"Les Conséquences!" Miriam said. "Here in Marseille!"

"Only the best for you," Mary Jayne said.

"How is it that you know everyone, Emjay?"

"I get around. But don't tell my mother, if you ever meet her! She sent me to Europe to marry honorably. She would have preferred me to marry royalty."

"My dear girl," Breton said, "you could find no more exalted court than the one assembled at this table. Masson! Chagall! Mehring! My brother Dominguez! Victor Brauner! Jacques Hérold! Señor Lam! Degenerates, all!" He rose, bowed to the guests, and ordered Madame Nouguet to refill everyone's glasses. Then he drew the diners' attention to one of the apothecary jars of praying mantises, where a slim green male had already mounted a female. "We are graced, as you see, by a demonstration of one of nature's most inexorable forces. The drive to replicate! To procreate! To germinate, though the results may be disastrous. This gentleman here must have had rumors of the fate that awaits him. Yet he is, as you can see, undeterred."

"It's just a myth, you know, that the females eat the males' heads," Mehring said.

"Quite wrong, my good man, quite wrong!" said Breton. "Who can substantiate my claim? You, Oscar, who grew up in the wilds of Tenerife? You, Jacques, from Moldavia, where such acts are common even among the human population? You, Monsieur Chagall?"

"I can confirm it," Grant said, and all eyes turned toward him. "I've seen it. At summer camp in the Poconos."

Breton tilted his head. "Pardon me? Where?"

"An American wilderness. Pennsylvanian mountains covered in deep woods."

"Ah. And what did you see, Monsieur Grant, in the Poking Nose?"

"Mantis-eating mantises. Enough to petrify a summer camp's worth of boys."

"Voilà! Monsieur Mehring, what have you to say now?"

"I'm horrified," said Mehring, his eyes on Miriam, who, for her part, watched the pair of mantises with evident pleasure, the pinned bee rising and falling at her breast.

Theo Bénédite, who retained more English primness than she liked to admit, blushed furiously at the sight of mantis copulation. Jacqueline, seated beside her in a hibiscus-colored gown, evidently relished her discomfort.

"I can confirm what Monsieur Grant says," she said. "In fact, should this lady mantis not eat her beau's head, I propose to eat it myself."

Theo gasped and turned pale. Miriam clapped her hands in delight. And André Breton gazed admiringly across the table at Jacqueline.

"I'd better have something more to drink," Theo said, and Hirschman hurried to fill her glass.

That was the start of it. The guests toasted each other and drank their wine. They consumed their tiny servings of chicken and potatoes, no one seeming to take note of how little there was. It occurred to Varian that, generally speaking, less food might make for more interesting dinner parties; how many had he attended where the chief activity was to cut one's meat and sort through mounds of vegetables? The surrealists were fond of participatory theater, and a dinner party was one of their chief stages. It didn't take Breton long to propose a game for the Air Bel table.

"Mesdames, messieurs," he began. "Our esteemed forebears had the stifling habit of avoiding the most interesting topics of conversation at dinner. Not so tonight. We are going to play a favorite game, one we have not played together since Paris. Tonight, in honor of Mademoiselle Davenport, we shall play **Non! C'est Tabou.**"

From the assembled artists, a round of murmurs and cheers. Mary Jayne and Miriam exchanged a glance, a shrug; they didn't know the game. Nor did Varian, though he might have hazarded a guess.

"Around the table we will go," Breton explained. "Everyone shall speak a delicious truth, one that would be generally considered unutterable at a dinner table. The more shocking, the better. Young Mr. Serge shall take notes, and afterward we shall produce and distribute a commemorative book."

"Hurrah!" shouted Mary Jayne. "May I begin?"

Breton raised an eyebrow. "Our hostess is eager to speak the ugly truth."

"It's one of my worst flaws," Mary Jayne said.

Varian tried to meet Grant's eye. They both knew—Varian hoped Grant knew—that between them were many things better left unspoken. He wished he knew how many glasses of wine Grant had drunk. And then Hirschman signaled Varian, clearing his throat to get his attention. He leaned toward Varian and said, sotto voce, "Perhaps we'd better sound a note of political caution."

"Ah, yes," Varian said, and tapped his glass with a knife to signal silence. The talk died away, and there was only the sound of water playing in the fountain outside, beyond the open windows.

"Thanks, André, for your excellent proposal," he said. "In a moment we'll begin. But let me remind our guests that, private and remote as Air Bel seems, Vichy is never far off, and may be interested in the content of our dinner conversation."

"Thank you, Monsieur Fry," Breton said. "You may trust us. And now, mesdames and messieurs, who shall begin? Miss Gold?"

"I cede my place to a guest," said Mary Jayne. "Mr. Brauner."

The painter's good eye projected a piercing acuity; the high round dome of his forehead called to Varian's mind the Paris Pantheon. "I'll gladly start," he said. "My glass eye is ugly, and it itches. Yes, it makes me itch **inside my head.** An itch I cannot scratch without tearing my own face apart, which I long to do."

"Bravo!" Breton said. "Dominguez, you're next."

Oscar Dominguez took his long chin into his hand. The V of his brows tightened in concentration. "Well," he said. "If you want to know the truth, I hate my dear friend Monsieur Brauner. Yes, I hate him, and here is why: At a party one night at Tanguy's, our friend Esteban Frances claimed I stole an idea of his for a canvas of mine. He called me a hack forger and spat on my shoe. I hit him in the jaw, and he struck me across the face. Then I grabbed a bottle of absinthe and broke it over the mantel, meaning to throw it at him. But just at that moment, Victor stepped into the fray. The broken bottle caught his left eye. I blinded my own friend. And thus I hate him, for making a monster of me."

Everyone murmured. Brauner gave a nod to confirm his friend's story. Vlady Serge bent over his notebook, taking furious notes.

"Thank you, dear Oscar," Breton said. "And now you, Jacqueline. Be generous."

"I once had a fantasy of making love with my father," Breton's wife declared.

"Phou. What little girl doesn't? You'll have to do better, **chérie.**"

"All right," Jacqueline said, a flush rising to her forehead. She resettled herself in her chair and drew herself up to a proud height, adjusting the gold lobster-shaped pin at her shoulder. She seemed to be resolving herself to some great confession. Delicately she cleared her throat, and then she spoke.

"I like impressionist paintings of cats in gardens," she said, "and women in billowing dresses, and flowers. Yes, banks and banks of flowers! I love them. I'm sick to death of the conceit that the uglier a painting is, the greater right it has to call itself art. I want to make beautiful, beautiful paintings only."

A hush fell over the table at this heresy, but Chagall laughed.

"C'est vraiment choquante!" he said. "Brava, Madame Breton. You have my respect."

"Thank you, Monsieur Chagall. From you, a great honor."

"You are a master of the game, as of your art," Chagall said. "In your hands, the beautiful is neither bourgeois nor insincere."

"Thank you, truly."

Breton smiled uneasily at his wife, then at Chagall. "And what about you, Marc?"

"For me there is no taboo," Chagall said. "I fail utterly at this game."

"Well, try anyhow. It's required." Breton's voice held a glinting note of challenge.

"All right, then. I confess: I relish the scent of asparagus piss."

Laughter around the table, scattered applause. Then Breton glanced across the table at Victor Serge.

"I shall never trim my nose hair, even if it extends to my chin," Serge said.

Next, Harry Bingham, with some pride: "I have performed the act of love in the consular office."

General applause. And Albert Hirschman, not to be outdone: "I have performed the act of love at the Préfecture de Police, in a storage closet of narrow dimensions."

More applause. Then Masson: "I love to fuck a woman while she has her **règles.** I feel as though I'm murdering her with my cock."

"I once stole sixty-three tubes of paint from a fellow artist," said Lev Zilberman. "A great rival of mine, who shall remain nameless. Some of them I have to this day."

"Orthopedic appliances excite me," said Daniel Bénédite.

"I prefer Turkish toilets to the Western kind," Theo Bénédite said.

"I began experiencing orgasm at the age of nine," Miriam said.

"I delight in the trimming of my own toenails," Mehring said.

"I have a passion for fake jewels," said Mary Jayne, getting into the spirit of it. "And no one suspects me of wearing them!" Then she turned to Grant, at her left. "Now you, dear Elliott."

"I'm a Negro," Grant said without hesitation, not meeting Varian's eye. "My father was black. I've lied about it most of my life."

A silence settled over the table. "Is that true?" Mary Jayne said. "You're a Negro?"

"It's true. Are you shocked, Mary Jayne?"

"My dear, it would take a great deal more than that to shock me!"

"Bravo, Monsieur Grant," Breton said, and everyone applauded. "A secret history."

The game continued. The praying mantises copulated; at last one female mantis ate her husband's head, to everyone's horror and delight. Wine flowed into the cups, and from the cups into the guests. Varian held the edge of the table for support as a tide of burgundy washed through him. Grant had revealed his own history, no more and no less. To speak those words aloud was no small feat. In certain contexts, it would have been a matter of life and death. Why, then, did Varian feel this shameful disappointment at his core? What had he expected Grant to say? What had he **wanted** him to say? Had he wanted him to profess his feelings for Varian, to strip them both naked before all assembled? The wine lifted his diaphragm, compressed his lungs, rose through his throat, filled the lacunae in his brain. He himself hadn't spoken yet; had anyone noticed? Perhaps in another moment all eyes would turn to him. What would he say or do? Break a glass and put out his lover's eye? His own? His life—what he had once called his life—was a wrecked thing already, a ruin, its original use scarcely discernible from what remained. He must stay in control, on his guard; after all, he was supposed to be the protector of these human beings, this freight of culture assembled around the walnut dining table.

And just when it seemed to Varian that he was safe, that the conversational pendulum would swing away from **Non! C'est Tabou,** the guest of honor turned to him and said, "Now, Varian, it's your turn."

They were seated too close for their eyes to meet comfortably. He looked instead at the gold grains of pollen rising and falling on her chest, a mesmerizing undulation. Grant seemed to follow the direction of Varian's gaze. A silence expanded over the table.

"Well?" said Mary Jayne. "Will our reticent leader speak?"

A fork clinked. Someone swallowed wine.

"The cake you are about to eat," Varian said, "cost five hundred and forty francs."

"Non! C'est tabou!" Breton shouted in delight.

Madame Nouguet, as if on cue, brought out the dessert, which was dissected and passed. Everyone ate and smoked. And then the doorbell rang, to Varian's relief, signaling the beginning of the party proper. In came the jazz trio, in came the pre-Pétain minister of culture, in came refugees from Poland, from Czechoslovakia, from Germany, Russia, Yugoslavia. They came with wine, with flowers stolen from the neighbors' gardens; they came with their work in hand, with renewed pleas for help, with stories of their escape; they came with ardent wishes of good luck for Miriam, who held Mary Jayne's elbow and glanced around in desperate dismay, as if at a dream from which she'd soon be forced to wake. The jazz trio launched into "Sweet Georgia Brown," and the guests pushed furniture aside and rolled up the rug, while Madame Nouguet watched the proceedings with horror. Hirschman took Miriam into his arms and led her in a smooth and energetic step. Zilberman, generally reserved, went cheek to cheek with Jacqueline Lamba. Theo Bénédite fell into the arms of Wifredo Lam. Grant and Varian leaned against a sideboard to watch, their shoulders nearly touching.

"It's not like you to show your hand," Varian said, carefully keeping his gaze on the dancers. When Grant drank, he lost the ability to recognize and maintain the appropriate public distance between himself and Varian; to meet his eye at times like these was to court disaster.

"Did I show it, though?" Grant said, and half-smiled. His voice was blurred, his posture loose. He fixed his eyes on the dance floor, at Miriam and Mehring quick-stepping in synchrony. Miriam's dress—borrowed from Mary Jayne—had a slashed side that revealed a tanned leg. As she passed, Varian couldn't help but watch the taut expansion and contraction along its shadowy inside surface.

"You're free to sleep with anyone you like, you know," Grant said.

"Don't be ridiculous, Skiff."

"I'm not joking. If you want that girl, I'm not going to stop you."

Varian met Grant's eye, that limpid forest pool. It was a mistake. He had no power to deny the eye what it wanted, nor any defense against the punishment it might mete out. "Oh, for God's sake," he said. "You aren't jealous, are you? Are you really claiming jealousy, when every day—" He fell silent. Why do this, why say it, when there was no way to change it?

"What?"

All right. "When every day you're living in Gregor's **things,** his things all over you, his robe, his slippers, his **razor.** And when you go home, there he'll be, waiting for you. And you'll go on just as before."

"And you with Eileen, ditto."

"But, Skiff," he said, half-desperate now, the wine pressing him onward, forcing his gaze toward

Grant's. "Before, I didn't know. I didn't know where you were. How can I go on as if you didn't exist?"

"You tell me," Grant said, so low Varian had to strain to hear him. "You tell me. How did you do it before that? How did you do it when we were boys, back in Maine?" And Grant turned away and walked from the room, out through the French doors and onto the veranda. Keep walking, Varian thought. Go. And then an instant later he was following Grant out into the night, past the swell of music and the dancing surrealists, through the open doors, into the scent of rosemary and eucalyptus and damp Mediterranean earth. Grant had gone down the stone steps and into the garden, toward the fountain with its four-lobed basin. Varian experienced the sensation, like a blow to the ribcage, that if he were to leave Grant in that garden he would never see him again.

"Skiff," he called, and Grant turned.

"There's nothing more to say," Grant called up to him. "Go in. Do what you want."

Varian followed Grant down into the garden. "That's not what I want."

"You're lying," Grant said. "You're lying, and you're a coward."

Varian drew a breath. "You can't call me that," he said.

"I can, and did."

"You **can't,**" Varian said. "Not after what **you** did. You were the one who left Maine. You were the one who disappeared from school, from the magazine, from Cambridge. Not a word or a trace. **I'm** the coward!"

"What was I supposed to do? Stay there in Blue Hill and watch you seduce Eileen? Watch you try to impress her with your Latin vocabulary and your command of European politics and the whole of the literary canon? I didn't have the stomach for it. I got out. It's called self-preservation."

"And what did you expect? That I would court you instead? Promise you a house in Westchester and a summer place in Southampton? A church wedding? Sunday dinners at my parents' house?"

"Kirstein made promises to Ellis. Realistic ones."

"Kirstein's rich, in case you hadn't heard. Kirstein makes his own rules."

"You too, Varian. You made your own rules when it was worth it to you."

"You didn't give me the chance. You **left.** Disappeared."

"You'd already made your choice."

"And can **you** fault me for it?" Varian said. "Can you claim not to understand? Aren't you the worst kind of hypocrite if you say you can't?"

Grant looked away, toward the valley that ended at the distant mountains. "That's different," he said. "You know it is."

"How is it, Grant?"

"You don't know the first thing about it."

"Don't I?"

"No," Grant said, and went silent, looking at a wavering slip of moon in the fountain.

"In any case," Varian went on, "did you think I was faking it? That I wasn't actually in love with Eileen? Don't you concede that it's possible? I **was** in love with Eileen, Grant. I am."

Up at the house, the jazz trio started in on "I've Got You Under My Skin." Someone opened champagne.

"You were in love with **me,**" Grant said, almost inaudibly. "You felt whatever you might have felt for Eileen. But you were in love with **me.**" He stuffed his hands into his trouser pockets, a gesture so adolescent as to evoke in Varian a sudden visceral memory of the nineteen-year-old Grant, the lanky body he hadn't quite yet learned to control, the wrists perpetually protruding from their cuffs, the vulnerable hollow at the back of the neck. He had loved that boy so violently he'd almost wished him dead. The fact of his existence was torture to Varian. And yet when Grant had really disappeared, he hadn't experienced his absence as relief. The opposite. A clangor of misery that had never abated, a painful tinnitus that echoed beneath every other event of his life. He did love Eileen. He did. But always with that din of grief in the background.

"If you knew it," Varian said now. "If you knew. Why didn't you come back? Why didn't you try to find me?"

Grant met Varian's eyes. His mouth trembled,

and, in a gesture that belonged to his younger self, he kicked the fountain with the toe of his glass-black shoe.

"But I did," he said.

"What do you mean?"

"I wrote to you at the Splendide. I was the one who broke that silence."

"Yes, twelve years later! After I'd had plenty of time to think you were dead. Why now, Grant? Why in Marseille? Why not back home, where we were living a few subway stops away from each other?"

"Somehow I could never bring myself to do it there," Grant said, shaking his head. "You were right, I guess. Cowardice."

"What on earth was different here?"

"I don't know. We're in a country at war. You're breaking the law almost daily. When I heard you were here, heard what you were doing, I had a notion you might get yourself arrested, thrown into French prison. Maybe killed by the Germans. And then I'd never have another chance."

The vast dome of the Mediterranean sky, its spray of constellations and its torn plumes of cloud, seemed to fall in upon Varian all at once. He couldn't draw a breath. He was somewhere beyond drunk, in a realm where he might say or do anything. "And what," he asked, hardly able to put the words together, "what about Katznelson? Who—who loves and trusts you? This man who"—could he say it?—"you still love?"

"I intend to get his son to safety."

"And then?"

Grant shook his head slowly, as if in shame. Then he looked up at Varian again, and the truth Varian perceived in his eyes was terrible to see. Grant's world had come undone, just as Varian's had. Neither of them had any idea what they were supposed to do. They were in each other's hands, and yet they couldn't trust each other. No one had done more damage to their lives than they'd done to each other's—not Varian's sick mother, not the father who had left the child Grant, not the loving grandparents who had given Grant their history and taken away his own; not the boys who had tortured Varian at school, not Dean Greenough who had wanted him gone from Harvard, not his father, Arthur, who had given him everything and required nothing, certainly not Eileen, not Katznelson, not even the authors of the war. No one.

"We're fools," Varian said. "There's no haven for us on this earth."

"That bed in Arles, perhaps," Grant said, and took Varian by the waist.

"Yes. That bed."

"You look like you want to die, Varian."

"I do, desperately. Don't you?"

"Perhaps we should just get raving drunk."

"Too late," Varian said.

"Might as well dance, then," Grant said, and they turned to go up to the house. But as they climbed the stairs to the stone patio, an arc of police lights traversed the long winding drive; by the time they'd reached the French doors a car had pulled up to meet them. Varian's first thought, the one that surfaced through the shifting cloud-cover of drink, was that this must be a raid. And more than half his guests were stateless and paperless. Mehring, Zilberman, the Serges: what a victory for Vichy if the lot of them could be brought in at once.

The car door opened and a police captain climbed out, his hat crisp and correct, his breast blazoned with its diagonal white stripe. He was tall, clean-shaven, sharp-jawed, his eyebrow a single slash across his forehead, his nose an emphatic vertical. He removed his hat and held it in his hands; in his dark eyes, a look of vague embarrassment. Varian's chest unclenched and he released a long breath: this was Robinet, Bingham's friend, who was sympathetic to their cause. And in fact, as Varian stood wondering what Robinet might be doing there at that hour, Bingham himself came down the steps of the villa, drink in hand. Hirschman followed close behind.

"Monsieur Fry," Robinet said, and gave a half-bow. "And Monsieur—Grant, is it? Oh, and Bingham, are you here as well? And Monsieur Hirschman—always a pleasure."

"You're out late, Inspector," Bingham said. "Come in for a cocktail?"

Robinet glanced up at the house, where the illegal

surrealists could be seen slinking drunkenly about the dance floor. "If only I could! But I've come on official business."

"What's happened?" Bingham said.

"We've apprehended a person of interest who claims a connection to Monsieur Fry. A young fellow, not one we've seen around Marseille. No papers at all. German, we suspect, though he gave a false French name." He looked at Varian, compressed his brow into a tight V. "He's to be sent to Vernet in the morning, Monsieur Fry. Nothing I can do about that. But you can see him tonight if you want."

Grant looked up sharply at Robinet. "German, did you say? How old a fellow?"

"Just a sprout. Can't be over twenty." He shook his head. "I'm afraid some of my associates dealt rather unkindly with him upon his arrest."

"Well," Varian said, exchanging a glance with Grant, then with Hirschman. "I suppose it'll be easier to see him at the Préfecture tonight than to chase him all the way to Vernet. Won't you excuse me for a moment? I've got to say goodbye to the guest of honor."

"Of course," said Robinet, who was known to have a weakness for social protocol. "And if I know Monsieur Bingham, he may yet convince me to take a glass of something."

Varian said he wouldn't be a moment, and he and Grant went into the house. In the entryway, Grant took Varian's wrist.

"Do you think it could be him?"

"I don't know. It could be anyone. Only one way to find out."

"Can't I come, Tom?"

"Better not. If it's him, we want to keep it as quiet as possible."

"How will you let me know?"

"There's no way to telephone. You'll just have to wait here until I come home."

Grant went off to explain the situation to Mary Jayne, and Varian found Miriam in the kitchen alone, leaning against the old-fashioned farmhouse sink. She was pinching the bridge of her nose, her shoulders hitching; in her other hand she held an unlit cigarette. When she raised her chin, he could see she'd been crying for some time now, though the glorious bumblebee still flew undaunted against her décolletage.

"Oh, Varian, forgive me," she said. "I suppose I'm homesick for France already." She wiped her eyes with the back of her hand, trailing feathers of mascara.

"Listen," he said, handing her his handkerchief. "You're off to see your fiancé tomorrow. He'll be thrilled. And France is hardly a place to miss just now."

Miriam shook her head. "I just can't help thinking about things."

He put a hand on her arm. "Don't think about things," he said. "I've always found it futile myself."

She gave a hard-edged laugh, then began to cough. It was some time before she could speak again. “Your drink’s empty,” she said.

“No time to refill it. I came to say goodbye. I’ve been called to the Préfecture.”

She squinted. “At this hour?”

“They’ve picked up some fool who claims to know me.”

“But why do you have to go now, in the middle of the night?”

“Because the fool is to be sent to Vernet in the morning. I believe this may be my only chance to see if I can be of use to him.”

“Ah,” she said. “I suppose there’s nothing to be done, then.” She folded Varian’s handkerchief and handed it back to him. “I would have kept this if I didn’t think Rolf would find it and wonder.” And then, putting her head on one side, she said, “I don’t suppose you’d kiss me goodbye, would you?”

“Of course,” he said, and leaned in to brush each cheek in the French manner.

“Not like that,” she said.

“Oh, now, Miriam.”

She looked up at him, a tease in her red-rimmed eyes. “Don’t you know how?”

“I can’t,” he said, and glanced at the downy bee. “I’m afraid of getting stung.”

Miriam didn’t hesitate. “A braver man would call the risk worth it.”

“Is that how it is?” Varian said. And then—why

not?—he leaned in and kissed her with all the passion he could gather, kissed her properly, the way he'd wanted to, just for an instant, the first time they'd met, when she'd been wearing that white batiste dress, cut low enough in front to show a sliver of lace beneath. He kissed her until she'd lost her breath, and then she pushed him away, laughing her angular laugh.

"There, now," she said. "That's what I call a proper goodbye." And she pressed his hand and ran to the other room to find Mary Jayne, leaving Varian to wonder at the circumstances that had landed a woman like that in his life for a short time, ignited this friendship between them, then took her away again, perhaps forever. The European continent, he thought, must be full of such fleeting connections, fierce brief amities to burn in the face of all the enmity. And then he, too, went into the other room and took leave of Bingham, of Hirschman, and finally of Grant, promising to return as soon as he could.

———

There were certain nights in Marseille that seemed to go on forever, nights that seemed an infinite distance from the mornings that preceded them. By the time the black police sedan reached the main road, Varian could scarcely remember the events of two hours earlier. He was intoxicated, hungry, exhausted; his gut burned the way it always did when he drank. He wished Hirschman could have come with him; he felt in need of counsel. In the driver's seat Robinet sat mercifully silent, as if to allow Varian time to reclaim his sobriety before they reached town. But the words in Varian's mind were the ones Grant had spoken in the garden: **I thought you might be killed, and then I'd never have another chance.** Another chance at what? Then there was the way Grant had looked at him, unhinged, unmoored, when he'd asked what he would do about Katznelson. Did he dare to hope, did he dare to fear, that there was a future between himself and Grant that might extend beyond the confines of their time in France? Varian had never—not once, not while they were at Harvard, not in the years since, not during their time in Marseille—allowed himself to envision what a daily life with Grant might look like. Would they live in proximity to each other? Could he live with Eileen, and still—? Could they live like Kirstein and his milieu? Men and women drifted like weather through Kirstein's townhouse on East Nineteenth; usually there was a chief lover and some adoring under-lovers, and they all got along, for the most part. Sometimes there were women—lately the painter Fidelma Cadmus, whom Kirstein had repeatedly threatened to marry. But Varian and Eileen hadn't lived that way, occasional outside liaisons notwithstanding. The life she envisioned for them in the suburbs, the one waiting for him when he returned to the States, was circumscribed and conventional. What would she think of the ideas that presented themselves to his mind now—she and Varian and Grant tucked up together in some Upper West Side nest not far from Columbia; the three of them going out for a drive along the Hudson in leaf season; the three of them throwing glittering dinner parties in their little home; the three of them summering in Maine, in a house on Blue Hill Bay? No, no, and again no. Even if Grant would tolerate it—and what were the chances of that?—Eileen would never have it. Perhaps with anyone other, anyone lesser, but not with Grant. Not him. Nor would Eileen lightly accept being cast aside, even if he could envision doing such a thing; she knew she didn't deserve to be abandoned by the fool she'd championed when he was kicked out of Harvard, the man she'd introduced to his current line of work, the same man whose professional floundering she'd borne—emotionally and practically speaking—for three years after they'd moved to New York. Her connections had gotten him a job. Her social circle had welcomed him, her parents had treated him like a son. She read drafts of everything he wrote, challenged his lazier ideas, explained the things he found obscure in books. She pushed him to do more than he was naturally inclined to do. She was the one, in fact, who had encouraged him to see what might be done about the European artists blacklisted by the Gestapo. And besides all that, he loved her. He had loved her all this time. Otherwise, could he have envisioned marrying her? That summer in Maine, could he have climbed into the sailboat with her when he knew Grant would stay behind?

Arrival at the Evêché, in the middle of the night and against his will, would not ordinarily have come as a relief. Robinet parked and ushered Varian out of the car, through the arched stone entryway; inside the old Bishop's Palace, they encountered the usual crush of miserable-looking persons, official and otherwise. Minor offenders sat in a temporary holding cell behind a long white marble desk like specimens on public display, all of them in various states of protest, anxiety, unconcern, or repose. Robinet led Varian through a limbo of those whose loved (or resented) ones occupied the holding cell or other more subterranean cells. Through a set of double iron doors they went, down a flight of stairs, then through another set of iron doors and down another flight, this one darker and narrower, a shallow depression worn into the stone of each step. With every metal door and gate they passed, with each twist and turn of the subterranean corridors along which Varian followed Robinet, his sense of confusion increased, so that by the time they reached a single iron door, this one painted white, Varian felt as though they'd hit the center of the Labyrinth.

What he found, when Robinet unlocked the door, was not the pale and cowering boy he expected, but a broad-shouldered, powerful-looking young man, dark-lashed, furious-eyed, blinking in a struggle to focus his vision. The young man squinted first at Varian and then at Robinet, his face not so much hopeless or expressionless as functionally blind; in his hand was a pair of crushed glasses, their bridge bent, one arm askew, lenses shattered. His hands and feet were shackled, and beneath the skin of his face were the purple-blue nebulae of fresh bruises. The room in which he sat was not a jail cell but an interrogation chamber. He sat on a metal chair, and before him was a desk and another chair, empty.

"My God," Varian said in German. "What have they done to you?" He glanced at Robinet, who looked down at his polished shoes in shame; it was his men who had done this.

Varian scrutinized the prisoner again. He was unmistakably the son of Gregor Katznelson; he had the same hawklike intensity about his features, the same blocky shoulders, the identical sweep of brow and curve of jaw. And then he saw what he had not seen before: the young man was dressed as if for a party, in an evening suit a size too small, a French-cuffed shirt, and a bedraggled black silk tie that had lost its bow, if it had ever had one. He raised his bruise-rimmed eyes to Varian, as if in a hopeless attempt to decipher what the new cloud of shadows near the entrance might represent.

Varian turned to Robinet. "I don't suppose you'd give us a few moments alone, would you?"

"What would you say to him that you can't say in my presence?"

"It's not me, Inspector, it's him. I doubt he'll say a word in your presence."

"Can't you explain to him that I have his welfare in mind?"

"Look what they did to him. You think he'll believe that?"

Robinet ran a hand along his diagonal sash and frowned. "How long do you want?"

"Ten minutes. That's all."

"All right," Robinet said, visibly uncomfortable, his shoulders shifting beneath the stiff corners of his jacket. "Get to it, then. I'll wait outside the door." He stepped out and closed the door behind him, and the young man let out a shuddering sigh and put his head into his hands. Varian sat in the empty metal chair.

"I'm not going to ask your name," he said. "If the gendarmes haven't gotten it out of you already, I don't want you to say it aloud. I know Robinet's listening. But I don't believe he speaks German. I think we'll be all right."

"I haven't told anyone my name," the young man said, in a harsh whisper.

"And you have no papers, I gather."

"Burned them." He touched his bruised face and winced.

"Smart. So they have no idea who you are."

"No. If they did, I'd be on a train to Germany by now."

"All right. So let's start at the beginning. To establish your identity, I'm going to ask your father's profession and place of residence. And you'll have to trust me, because I'm the only one who can get you out of this place."

The young man raised his eyes to Varian, scrutinized him through the haze of his myopia. Varian waited, holding his gaze, wanting only to communicate his openness. But the man shook his head. "Your German is too good," he said. "I don't trust you for a moment. You can't be an American."

Varian smiled. "Thanks. But I am an American. Varian the American, some people call me around here. And you must believe me: if you're the man I think you are, I know your father. I've spent some time at your house at La Pomme. I can tell you the colors of the rugs in the solarium, and the pattern of the china."

"Tell me," the young man said, and raised his chin in challenge.

"Deep blue rugs. And phoenixes on the china."

"And what kind of trees in front of the house? The little orchard?"

"Persimmon."

His eyebrows drew together. "Maybe you're a spy."

"Maybe you'd better start talking before Robinet comes in here and pulls me out. We're wasting our time. Now, just so I can be certain, tell me your father's profession and place of employment."

The young man's shoulders dropped in surrender. "My father is a professor of European history at Columbia University, in the city of New York. You know who he is. You know who I am."

"Yes. And does the name Zilberman mean anything to you?"

A spectacular rose-colored aurora spread from the young man's neck to his face to his hairline. "You know about Sara," he said.

"Yes. I believe you were coming to see her father at my party."

Robinet opened the door and leaned in. "Nearly done?"

"Just a moment more," Varian said.

"Sixty seconds," Robinet said, and closed the door.

"This is a trap," Tobias Katznelson said, and shook his head. "I'm an idiot. You're one of them, aren't you?"

"I can see why you'd think so. But I assure you I'm not."

He put his elbows on his knees, gave a tidal sigh, and scrutinized his crushed spectacles. "What am I going to do without my glasses?"

"I don't know," Varian said. "I'm sorry for what they did to you. It's awful. I mean to help you."

"You can't. They're going to send me to a camp, then deport me. I know. I've always known what would happen if I was caught. But foolishly I thought

I might get to you. To Zilberman. To see if—" He shook his head. "What an idiot I was."

"Maybe I can help you still."

"How?"

"First of all, I'm going to pretend I don't care much about your fate, one way or the other. The police know my clients are valuable to the Nazis. We can't let them think you're worth anything to me or to anyone else."

Tobias nodded.

"The camp they'll send you to, Vernet, is a terrible place. I won't lie. But there's a chance we can get you out."

"How can that be?"

"I've got a friend at the American Consulate who can help. Robinet knows him. He'll keep us apprised of what's happened to you. And then there's Mr. Grant, the one who's been looking for you."

"Mr. Grant? Who is Mr. Grant?"

"A colleague of your father's, from Columbia. He's been looking for you for months now, and he'd do anything to help you. Believe me, there are ways. I've gotten clients out before. You'll be there a couple of weeks at most."

"I'll be deported by then. Or dead."

"A couple of weeks at Vernet will be dreadful, but likely not fatal."

The young man rubbed his eyes again. "I wish I could see your face," he said. "I don't know if I can trust you."

"You'll have to," Varian said. "You have no choice."

Robinet opened the door and stepped inside, drawing himself up to his full height. "That's enough, Fry," he said. "Now, my colleagues will be wanting to know this boy's name and his business. What am I to tell them?"

"Tell them I have no idea," Varian said. "Tell them I've never seen him before in my life."

By the time he got home to Air Bel, dawn had broken over the valley and the last wave of gaiety had long ago crashed and receded within the villa. The shipwreck scene he'd expected was nowhere in evidence; Madame Nouguet had apparently tidied away the drunk and senseless surrealists along with the dinner plates, the used glasses, the contents of the ashtrays, the paper balloons, the praying mantises and their glass enclosures. He would have had to wonder if a party had taken place at all, had he not come across Breton lying prone on the library sofa, his velvet jacket cast aside, his head on Jacqueline's lap. Jacqueline, still in her hibiscus-colored gown with the gold lobster pin at the shoulder, also slept, her cheek resting on her arm. Varian crept past them and ascended to his own room, where Grant lay sleeping on the narrow bed. Varian closed and locked the door, wedged a chair beneath the knob, and lay down beside Grant, too tired to undress or even to undo his collar and cuffs. An oyster-blue light poured through the naked window. Grant's back rose and fell beneath the twill of his shirt; he had draped his jacket over the desk chair. How many mornings had Varian watched him sleep, the night washing over them still? Maybe this was the way he liked best to look at Grant; the waking version was, at times, a light too bright to regard unblinkingly. He knew the previous night's effusions had to be treated with suspicion, or at least with caution. They'd been drunk, they'd been high on the drug that was an evening in the company of the surrealists. But here was an undeniable fact: Grant asleep in Varian's bed. Maybe not only because he was desperate to know what had happened to Tobias; maybe because he wanted to send a message, the neat opposite of the one he'd sent twelve years ago in Maine. That night, after the moonlit sail across the bay with Eileen, after the tromp around the tiny island, its verges slick with seaweed, its inland populated by moss and pines (the seeds of which, she told him, must have come to that place in the bodies of birds), after their identification of a smooth slab of granite, after their struggle with her outer- and underthings, after a brief damp conjunction on that wave-lapped rock, after the long cold sail back home, after the farewell kiss and the promise of another sail, after Varian's guilty ascent up the back stairs of that white house on the water, there was no Grant in the other twin bed in the room they'd shared; no sign of his belongings, no trace of his luggage, no note or other indication of where he might have gone.

But here was Grant now, a message that consisted of his physical being. A chance for Varian to repair what he'd broken when he'd climbed into that boat. An invitation to walk forward into a trackless shadowland, a place whose existence might be defined by their occupying it. Varian didn't dare make a move or a sound; he scarcely dared breathe. Half-dreaming, he willed a square of sun to avoid Grant's face. The sun obeyed. Grant slept, and Varian kept watch. And when Grant woke—after how long?—Varian bent to the spiral of his ear and told him that Tobias Katznelson lived, that he was there in Marseille, and that he might still be rescued, his rare and irreplaceable gifts kept out of the Nazis' hands.

17

Noailles

The next afternoon found Grant sitting over a telegram blank in Varian's office, behind closed doors, worrying his pencil eraser against the near-transparent blue paper and wondering aloud what he was supposed to write to Gregor Katznelson. Any message he sent via transatlantic wire might be intercepted by the censors. Any word associated with Tobias's name might compromise him further. There was little to reassure Katznelson, in any case: his son was in Marseille, yes, but in police custody; soon he'd be shipped to a concentration camp.

"T. lives," Varian said. "Write that. Say he's looking well. Say he's in brave spirits."

Grant crossed his arms. "You're saying I should lie."

"He **was** in brave spirits. He was bearing it like a soldier. Tell him that."

Grant bent again over his telegram blank, his pencil

moving haltingly across the page. Finally he got up and went to stand beside Varian at the window. Below, a pair of workers tied flags to the lampposts: miniature tricolors emblazoned with Maréchal Pétain's special insignia, a two-bladed axe studded with gold stars. Another crew swept the gutters with wide pushbrooms. In two days' time, Pétain would pay a visit to the city. Everything had to be made perfect, all the dirt tidied away.

"You don't think I should try to see him?" Grant said. "Couldn't Bingham help us arrange it? I could bring a packet of food and whatever else he might need. Or we could send something with Gussie."

"No," Varian said. "We can't do anything to call attention to him."

"If only I could send Gregor something **he'd** written, just a few words."

"There'll be time for that, if we can get him out of wherever they send him. For now you'd better go down to the telegraph office before the place closes. Any word is better than no word."

Grant packed up his papers and buttoned his immaculate coat, gray wool with a scatter of pearl-white fibers. His skin that afternoon had an almost silvery cast; his eyes, glazed with hangover, seemed unusually vulnerable. Between him and Varian hung an invisible fog, all the things they'd said the night before. They hadn't talked about any of it; maybe they never would. Tobias had been found. Grant had a mission now, Varian reminded himself:

a mission that had to take precedence over everything else. He reminded himself of this forcefully, inarguably, as he watched Grant gather his things, pass through the office, and vanish into the world behind the stenciled door.

Harry Bingham called for Varian at the CAS at half past eight, wearing an official-looking overcoat and an aggressively tailored suit, no trace of the previous night's revels upon him. They were to meet the Chagalls at their hotel for dinner; Bingham thought they might extinguish the last of the Chagalls' hesitation if they proceeded delicately. Together they walked down the Canebière in the direction of the hotel, distracting themselves from Vichy's decorations by playing a new game, a contest of one-downmanship involving their former student residences in Cambridge.

"Forty-eight Holden Street," Bingham said. "Family of rats behind our kitchen cupboards. Not a small family, either."

"Twenty Prescott," Varian countered. "Biting flies in the bathroom drains."

"Sixteen Trowbridge. Roof collapsed into my bed one morning."

"Really, Harry?"

"I still have the scar." He pointed to a white half-moon at his hairline.

"Well, how about Thirty-seven Kirkland?"

"How about it?"

"Bloodstains on the bedroom ceiling."

"Come on, now, Varian."

"My friend Mr. Grant can confirm it," Varian said, laughing. Then he experienced a moment of abject terror: Would Bingham wonder aloud how had Grant come to study Varian's bedroom ceiling? What could Varian possibly say in reply?

But if the thought occurred to Bingham, he didn't voice it. "Shame we didn't know each other back then," he said. "I could have shown you some even worse places."

"Well, I'd have to say I'm glad you didn't know me," Varian said. "I was rather insufferable at the time. And an incorrigible troublemaker."

"Oh, yes," Bingham said, and grinned. "You did have a reputation. Weren't you expelled, for a time?"

"Yes, and all I did was plant a 'For Sale' sign on Greenough's lawn."

"Well, that wasn't **all** you did, according to the **Crimson.** Apparently you had quite a history. Weren't you in trouble with the law for driving like a maniac?"

"Ah, yes. You've got too good a memory, Harry."

"Anyway, I think I would have liked you then. I'm more than a little fond of you now, after that party—what genius to get them all together!"

"The surrealists, you mean? It was Mary Jayne's idea, not mine. I was opposed. I thought it would draw too much attention."

"But you can't be sorry about it now. It lured your young German, didn't it?"

"Lured him close enough to get himself arrested and sent to Vernet." Bingham knew the story already; Varian had telephoned him that morning to give him the details. He agreed that Varian had taken the right course, that they must at all costs help Tobias preserve anonymity. But Vernet would be a difficult nut to crack. It was true that Mary Jayne had once seduced the commandant, or at least that she'd won his favor; it was true that her clients of interest had gotten out. But it was also true that they'd been caught trying to leave France, that they were back in Vernet now, and that the commandant was unlikely to be tricked again.

Now they had arrived at the Hôtel Moderne, where Chagall and his wife were staying for the week. The hotel was on the rue Breteuil, a few blocks south of the port, and the place looked like it had fought hard for each of its two stars. The lobby was little more than a corridor, the trompe-l'oeil marble desk fooling no one. From the restaurant came the clink of crockery and a sulfuric whiff of burnt greens. At the end of the lobby corridor was an elevator with a folding gate; it descended, gears groaning, until a dull thud rocked the hallway floor. Then the folding gate opened to reveal Marc and Bella Chagall, the painter in his loose-cut jacket, Bella in a boiled wool coat with a high collar.

Chagall came forward to kiss Varian on both cheeks. "What a magnificent party!" he said. "Charming place, Air Bel. Charming guests. I should like to come again soon to visit Zilberman."

"Come anytime," Varian said. "I know it heartened him to see you."

Bingham glanced toward the hotel's restaurant. "Is this where we'll dine?"

"Oh, no," said Bella. "There's a proper establishment across the street." She ushered them through the narrow reception area and out onto the rue Breteuil, where another crew of broom-pushers was busy redistributing the gutter trash. The light was failing fast, the lamplighters doing their work. Across the street, inside the proper establishment with its yellow-and-white-striped awning, the aroma was not of killed greens but of fried potatoes and tomatoes. They ordered dinner and chatted over aperitifs, Varian feeling cheered by the rush of alcohol in his veins. But dinner, when it arrived, was so scarce as to look like its own leftovers. A strand of what looked like **poulet** had collapsed over a few pale carrots and potatoes. When Varian nudged it with his fork, he found that it was not **poulet** but **panais.** Parsnip.

"You see," Bingham was saying to the Chagalls, "your daughter isn't the only one who thinks it's a good idea for you to come to the States. I wrote Mrs. Roosevelt some months ago about your situation, and I've just had a letter from her this morning. She's taken the matter in hand. She believes she can convince the State Department to expedite your visas. And Alfred Barr proposes to raise the money for your securement."

"You should use those advantages for my friend Zilberman," Chagall said.

"Those offers are specifically for you, I'm afraid."

"But what about Ida and her husband?" Bella said. "How can we go to the States if we don't know our daughter's fate?"

"I can work on Ida's behalf here in France. Her visa case may be more difficult, but we'll try. And once you're there, it may be easier for her to come."

"Well, then," Chagall said, clasping his hands together in a gesture of doleful resignation. He looked at Bella. "Do we capitulate?"

Bella's plate of parsnip and carrot was untouched; she had grown more angular, almost gaunt, since their sunlit lunch at Gordes. "Every day I read the papers," she said, turning her thin pale hands over each other. "Jews banned from the press, from the army, forced out of industry. So many arrested! And then there are the others, the ones who destroy themselves—I'm thinking of Benjamin, you know. A few months ago, I believed we were above it all." She worried the edge of her linen napkin with her thumb. "Had we listened to you in September, Monsieur Fry, we might have been in the States by now."

"If you're giving your consent now, we'll do our utmost."

"But what must **we** do?" Chagall said. "How must we conduct ourselves?"

"I'd advise you to return to Gordes tomorrow morning," Varian said. "The city's being cleared in advance of Pétain's visit. You're not safe here."

"We planned to spend the week arranging transport for Marc's work," Bella said. "Ida is to meet us here in town to help us. I understand it may take some time."

"Pétain comes to town in two days," Bingham said, in a diplomat's tone: low, reasoned, entreating. "We don't want your husband to be made an example of."

Bella's forehead contracted into a fretwork of lines. "Would they do that?"

"It's not impossible."

"Do you think he's in danger now? Have we stayed too long already?"

"Be calm, Bella," said Chagall, laying a hand over hers. "No one is breaking down the door."

But just at that moment the air seemed to crack open into a hollow-throated wail: an air-raid siren, followed by another and another, keening into the night like a pack of mechanical wolves. The diners looked about in anxiety. The maître d', compact and efficient, with a gleaming pate and a batlike bow tie, whispered a few orders to his staff; in unison they drew the blackout curtains. In the streets the air-raid wardens blew their whistles, and there were shouts and the sound of wooden carts overturned, of boot heels pounding pavement. The door of the restaurant flew open and a warden leaned in.

"To Gare de Noailles," he shouted. "Quick!"

The response was polite, orderly, as if French dining conventions must be observed even under the threat of bombing. Bingham led the Chagalls through the door and Varian followed; they joined a mass of Marseillais hurrying toward the tram station. As they descended the stairs to the underground platform, the drone of bombers seemed to follow them into the darkness. It wasn't Varian's first air raid; in late August there had been two on consecutive nights, and a month later a munitions plant north of town had been bombed. At the time he'd almost welcomed that clear evidence of the war, the sheer immediacy of danger, not, as Eileen might have accused, because it brought drama to his work, but because it made it easy to communicate the urgency of the situation to the donors back home. Don't take our word for it, America: here's evidence of the bombs dropping, here's wreckage where a factory stood, here are the smashed city blocks where civilians lost their lives.

Now he and Bingham formed a protective wedge in front of the Chagalls, who huddled before a tiled column inlaid with Noailles's stylized N. A crowd pressed against them from all sides, men and women and children. Chagall put his arms around his wife. Bella touched a pendant at her neck: a gold **hamsa,** the protective hand. A high-pitched whine arced down from somewhere above, then the station floor juddered with the shock of anti-aircraft guns. A moment later, the reverberating crash of strikes. They must have been far off, up on the hill near Notre Dame de la Garde from the sound of it, but the vibrations fell into the bowl of the city and rolled down toward Noailles, its lowest point. The crowd shifted. A child complained of thirst. Bella Chagall edged closer to Varian, as if he might shield her from the next blast. What a change, he thought, from her stark dismissal in the garden at Gordes. But he felt no pleasure in her trust; it seemed unearned, misplaced. Why should she believe he could keep her from harm? Chagall himself—possessor of an imagination that transformed roosters into intelligent-eyed sages, that shot brides and bridegrooms upward through skybouquets of roses, that made Christ on the cross into a figure of Jewish suffering, surrounded by a chaos of burning synagogues, fleeing refugees, soldiers advancing with their banners flying—that man, that mind, stood at the base of a column in a threatened tram station and trusted him, Varian. But how was he keeping anyone safe now? How was he helping anyone escape? The border was still closed. His clients were essentially trapped at the villa. Tobias Katznelson was bound for a camp. And meanwhile his thoughts had been on Grant, always on Grant. And where was Grant now? Was he safe, or menaced by these bombs? The thought occurred to him that if he, Varian, died that night underneath the city, if this station fell and crushed him with Bingham and the Chagalls and the thirsty child and all the members of this crowd, at least Eileen would never be the wiser, at least he'd never have to tell her the truth.

"Look," Chagall said, and gestured toward the opening of the station. Across an oblique triangle of sky, streams of searchlights swept and crossed and double-crossed, weaving an illuminated fabric against the stage-black of the night. The painter stared, recording. A yellow-white explosion shot into the frame and disappeared; the shock came a second later, and they all fell to their knees and covered their heads as plaster drizzled from the ceiling. Planes droned far above. They waited and waited, watching the triangle of sky. After a while, voices began to rise in the station; someone ran up the stairs to see what was happening. Then the all-clear sounded. They went out into the street to find the neighborhood unchanged; the nearby bomb had fallen into the harbor and destroyed nothing but a few unmanned boats.

"Well," Bingham said. "Everyone all right?"

No one answered. Chagall studied the street as they walked back toward the hotel. He and Bella would need no further convincing. "How long will it take?" he said, when they'd reached the doorway of the Moderne. "The visas, and all the arrangements?"

"We don't know," Bingham said. "It could be a matter of months."

"We'll go back to Gordes in the morning, as you suggest. And you'll let us know when we are to return to Marseille?"

"We'll be in constant touch. We'll let you know how things are getting on."

Bella pressed the **hamsa** between her fingers. "You won't fail us," she said.

"Not on your life," Bingham said in English. And the phrase—she must have heard it in a movie, Varian thought, must associate it with cowboys or salty Frisco detectives—made her smile for the first time all night.

"Thank you, dear Mr. Fry, Mr. Bingham," Chagall said, and touched his hat. And then he and Bella stepped into the narrow entry hall of the Moderne, and Varian and Bingham started back the way they came.

"What are their chances?" Varian dared to ask.

"Better than most."

"But now the border's closed. And the Préfecture's watching us."

"I didn't say it would be easy," Bingham said, and smiled. "Oh. I just thought of another. Twenty-four Water Street. Amorous screamer."

"Oh, one of those. We've all lived near one."

"Not like this one. Italian. Cultivated Milanese accent. Must have been a young classics professor's wife, slumming with a student. I'll never forget it. **Più veloce, più veloce! Ecco, ecco!**"

Passersby turned, regarded the speaker, and smiled.

"So are you saying, Harry, that this made your living situation **un**pleasant?"

"Well, **I** wasn't the one in bed with her."

"Ah, yes. Alas."

"I did renew the lease, though."

Varian laughed. "Wisely done."

They walked shoulder to shoulder, through the crowds streaming through the shaken streets, until they reached the offices of the Centre Américain. A light was on; in the window, Grant's silhouette. Relief made Varian lightheaded. He had to put a hand against the doorframe for support.

"All right?" Bingham said.

"A little unsteady on my feet, if you want to know the truth."

"Glad to know I'm not the only one. Do you want a drink or something?"

"No, Harry, thanks. I'll be fine."

"Talk to you tomorrow, then." Bingham touched his hat and went off down the street, whistling. And Varian climbed the stairs to the office, where he found his staff unbombed and unharmed, picking up fallen papers and sweeping up plaster dust. And there among them was Grant, whose arms he could not rush into, whose shoulder he could not crush his face against. But Grant met his eye and held it, and Varian read what it said: here they were, both of them, still alive for now.

18

Sinaïa

The next day he couldn't bring himself to go to the office. Relief at his own survival, at Grant's survival, his clients', had undone him. He was pressed flat by exhaustion, his insides afire. But he couldn't rest, and couldn't bring himself to eat, not that there was much to eat anyway. The night before, he hadn't gotten home until well past midnight, then couldn't sleep; he found himself writing a feverish note to Eileen in which he confessed everything. Then of course he tore up the note and burned it in the grate. Upon which he wrote another note, identical to the first, and burned it, too. Finally, some time after the birds had started their dawn racket, he'd fallen into bed, slept disastrously, and woken with a terrible headache. He sent word that Lena was wanted at the villa. He must work at home, and would she be so kind as to come out and take dictation?

While he waited for her, he forced himself to shave and take a bath in the swan-footed tub. Afterward he went down to the kitchen in his dressing gown and slippers; at the counter he ate the heel of a brown loaf and drank the gritty burnt brew that passed for coffee. From the window he could see Zilberman down in the garden, studying the flora with his magnifying glass. For some time Varian watched his slow progress from weed to shrub to flower; Zilberman crouched over his specimens, his eye close to the glass, and then scratched in a notebook at his side. **Verbena officinalis,** Varian imagined him writing in his small block print. Life in miniature: the opposite of what he threw, building-wide, onto walls in Berlin. A discipline, a meditation. A means for practicing humility. Varian washed his cup and saucer, then went to stand in the block of sun that fell through the back door. For some time—he wasn't sure how long—he merely leaned against the doorframe and took in that flood of light, receiving what felt like absolution. But then he heard foosteps on the gravel drive, and here was Lena arriving at last, her shorthand pad in hand, handbag over her arm, her hair in its customary state of disarray. At the door she nodded to Varian, and together they went into the library. Lena deposited her things on a marble table below a large gilt-framed mirror, then conducted her hair into place like a maestro, using a series of hairpins as batons.

"And what kept you?" Varian said. "I thought I might avoid work all day."

Lena turned from the mirror. "**Ce n'est pas grave.** I was arrested, that is all."

"Arrested? By the police, you mean?"

"**Bien sûr,** by the police. **Certainement** I did not arrest myself."

"What happened?"

"Just as you predicted, it is because of the Maréchal's visit. They arrive at the hotel at five this morning and nearly knock down my door. Everyone downstairs! they shout. No time to dress. We are marched to the station in nightclothes, I myself wearing nothing more than a chemise and bedroom slippers, **imagines-ça!** And with metal cuffs upon my wrists. Ten of us they lock in a cell while they look at our papers. What makes them decide one way or another, I do not know. I am lucky, **c'est tout.**"

"Lena! What an ordeal. And here you are, ready to work."

"Of course! **Il ne faut pas exagérer.** It was an inconvenience, nothing more."

"What about Hirschman? He hasn't been arrested, has he?"

"**Mais non,** Albert went down to Cerbère last night to see Lisa Fittko and her husband. Perhaps they discuss a new way over the border. We have not heard from Leon Ball in six, seven days. We think he may have been arrested too. I believe Albert will stay away until after the Maréchal's visit."

"You haven't heard from Ball in a week?"

"Pas du tout."

"The Fittkos have no idea what might have happened to him?"

"None."

"God," Varian said, and put his hands through his hair. "We've got to get to work. We've got too much to do. But, Lena, after all that—don't you want a minute's rest? Shall I ask Madame Nouguet to make you some tea?"

"Non, merci," she said, and opened her pad. "I have come to work, so we will work." She sat down across from Varian, her pencil at the ready. But before Varian could speak a word, he heard a rising wail of sirens from the drive. Then Madame Nouguet's shout from the kitchen. He got up and ran through the salon and into the kitchen, where Madame Nouguet stood staring through the window. In the drive was a police car, the double of the one that had come for Varian a few days earlier, and beside it a long black van with high barred windows.

"Now what?" Varian said.

Madame Nouguet turned. "I'll hold them a minute," she said. "Take care of your things, monsieur. Your papers."

Varian ran upstairs and into his room, where he looked around in panic, wondering what among his papers would be most incriminating. The answer was unfortunate and obvious: his address book, that fat and disorderly record of every contact he'd made since his arrival in France. Anyone who read it would know how to find his clients. Its back pages contained lists of figures, records-in-brief of his illegal dealings in foreign and French currency, and on its cover—he must have written it in a moment of distraction—the name **T KATZNELSON,** a waving flag.

In the grate burned a small low fire, remnant of the one that had warmed his uneasy sleep the night before. He stood before it with the address book in hand. Why had he not copied those names, those addresses, into some other book, in code? How much of what he had in this book did Hirschman have, or Lena? But then a triple knock came at the door downstairs, and an unfamiliar French voice boomed into the echo chamber of the kitchen. Varian dropped the address book into the fire and watched it flare, curl, burn, and turn to ash. He poked the pile and it fell into an unidentifiable heap. Then he polished his glasses with his handkerchief, adjusted the lapels of his dressing gown, and went downstairs.

In the black-and-white-tiled salon stood the Bretons and Serges; Mary Jayne and Killer, who looked like they had just extracted themselves from bed; Theo Bénédite with little Peterkin on her hip, a butterfly net in his hand; Madame Nouguet, who had donned her best apron as if for guests; and Rose, the round-faced girl who made the beds and scrubbed the pots and emptied the ashcans, trembling in the far doorway. Three were missing: Danny and Jean, who had gone to town that morning; and Zilberman, who must have hidden in the root cellar beneath his greenhouse studio. There they all stood like congregants before the commissaire, a tall heavy-browed fellow Varian didn't recognize. In his high collar and long black coat, the man could have been taken for an ecclesiast, though his military mustache spoiled the effect. His colleagues, three plainclothesmen, stood blocking the entrance door as if they feared someone might make a run for it. One of them, with sleek black hair and snow-blue eyes, looked strangely familiar to Varian; he searched his mind to remember where he might have seen the man.

The commissaire cleared his throat. "Is this everyone, then?"

No one answered.

"Very well, then. Messieurs," he said, turning to the plainclothesmen, "search."

"Excuse me," Varian said. The commissaire turned, squinting down at him as if he were a few inches tall. "On what grounds are you conducting this search?"

"Pardonnez-moi?"

"I'm familiar with the laws of this nation. A search requires reasonable cause and proper documents. I'd like to see your warrant."

The commissaire drew himself up to his full height; his prodigious belly strained the buttons of his coat. With obvious pleasure, he produced from his breast pocket a letter, doubly and triply stamped with the official stamps of the Préfecture, authorizing the chief of police to conduct searches of all residences suspected of harboring communists. He read the letter aloud and handed it to Varian for inspection.

"I'm afraid you've got the wrong place," Varian said, handing the document back. "There are no communists here."

"That will be for us to determine," the police chief said, and waved his colleagues forward. The sternest and narrowest of the men began in the dining room, pulling open the drawers of the sideboard and turning out stacks of white batiste napkins; another donned a pair of owlish glasses, sat down at the table, took out a sheaf of papers, and began drawing up an official documentation of the search. The third man—the one who looked familiar to Varian—lined up all the inhabitants, who would be escorted upstairs one by one while their rooms were searched. Serge was first, and the officer took his time, long enough for Varian to remember when he'd seen the man before: one night with Grant, perhaps three weeks ago, at a place called

Le Holdup, one of the underground establishments that catered to men who favored men. The memory rushed back to him in all its detail: At the time, this dark-haired officer had seemed merely a fey boy out for a night with friends; he hadn't danced well, had kissed indifferently, and had laughed when he'd heard Varian's name, changing it at once to **Vaurien,** French shorthand for good-for-nothing: **il ne vaut rien.** He was memorable primarily for his unusual combination of soot and snow. Now Varian had to wonder if he'd been there in a hidden but official capacity, looking for a reason to close the place down. Lawbreaking had certainly been in lavish supply that night: there was opium, hashish, heroin; there were boys for hire, unnatural acts in plain view; the proprietor even owned a contraband civet. But could the man have been gathering evidence against Varian? Building the Préfecture's case? Was Varian's behavior at the club to be held as evidence against him? Would there be a shaming before his staff, and, once they got wind of it, before the ERC back home?

The man returned with sheaves of writing that he declared suspicious, and a small blued-steel pistol, the one Serge kept on hand in case he found it necessary to end his own life. Serge was visibly distraught at the sight of the weapon in another man's hand. He couldn't be still, paced miserably, smoothed his thin hair, adjusted the fur collar of his dressing gown, and eyed the stack of suspect pages, of which he must have had no second copy. The search of Breton's things turned out even worse: down came the officer again, carrying in one hand a suitcase of Jacqueline's, and in the other, the heavy revolver from Breton's days in the Medical Corps. Beneath his arm was a large rolled-up sheet of drawing paper. This he extracted first, unfurling it on the table to reveal a line drawing of a French rooster, underneath which Breton had scrawled, in red, **Le terrible crétin de Pétain.** The burly commissaire took the drawing in hand, raised it, rattled it in Breton's face.

"Sedition!" he cried. "Write that down, Officer Pelletier."

The owl-faced officer writing up the process glanced at the incriminating image and made a note. Varian knew there were worse drawings in the salon, remnants of an after-dinner game from the night before; Breton, thanks to his medical training, was expert at depicting the human form in compromised positions, and his renderings of certain heads of state would have been recognizable from a distance. Varian's gut roiled and burned, and a cold fire surged from his tailbone to his scalp.

Next the black-haired plainclothesman nodded to Varian himself, who climbed the stairs slowly, cataloguing in his mind the locations of all his most sensitive papers. As they ascended, the officer whistled in a way that sounded friendly. Unlike his superior, who clearly relished his role, this man seemed embarrassed by his position of authority. At the top of the stairs Varian turned and met his strange pale blue eyes, the eyes of an Arctic dog, and the man's embarrassment turned a shade more specific: he recognized Varian now from that drug- and drink-washed night at Le Holdup.

"It's you," Varian said, in low and intimate French. "I thought so."

"**Merde.** Don't make me blush, Monsieur Vaurien. Let me do my job."

"Your boss can't make a convincing case against us, no matter what. But I'd like to spend a minute in my room before it's searched."

"I'd like to spend a minute in your room," the man said, in a tone so low Varian had to lean close to hear. "But it's impossible. I can't let you in, for that reason or any other."

"I want to take care of a few things. Thirty seconds, that's all I'd need."

The officer held Varian's gaze for a moment. Then he took a cigarette from his pocket, lit it with a military-issue lighter, and pointedly turned the other way, resting his shoulder against the wall.

Varian went into his room. Thirty seconds: time enough to dig up two recent border maps, a sheaf of hidden bills, and a stack of false passports. He couldn't bear to throw anything more into the fire. Instead he tossed the bundle on top of the wardrobe, where it was hidden by a carved embellishment.

The officer opened the door. "All right?" he asked.

"Splendid," Varian said, and followed him down the stairs.

Below, the scene had gone from bad to worse. All over the table were the contents of Jacqueline's wardrobe: lace-edged underthings, nightclothes, a box of **préservatifs,** pulp novels, silk blouses; the lining of her suitcases had been torn out, the hinges pried apart. But no one remained at the table to observe the wreck. Instead, all the inhabitants of the villa stood pressed against the windows, looking out into the yard, where one plainclothesman was running down Danny Bénédite, and another tackling the broad-shouldered Jean Gemähling onto the driveway gravel. They must have come home for lunch, innocent of the proceedings at the villa. The officers wrestled them into the house and searched their rooms. More papers were hauled down to the large dining table, more facts recorded in the **procès-verbaux.** Madame Nouguet offered wartime coffee and hard biscuits, which she passed around apologetically, murmuring—with a pointed glance at the commissaire—that she hadn't yet had a chance to go to the market.

"Don't look at me that way, madame!" the commissaire said. "I'm not responsible for feeding these people. My job is to get them to the station."

Madame Nouguet drew herself up into a formidable shape, squaring her shoulders at the commissaire. "Monsieur, surely you don't intend to transport all these families down to the Evêché."

"Yes, I intend exactly that."

"Now, sir," Varian said. "Let's be reasonable. Mothers and children must stay. And Madame Nouguet is of no interest to you. Let her go to the market."

"I have my orders," said the commissaire. "Madame Bénédite, for example, is your employee. I'm sure she's privy to all your schemes. And Madame Breton is the wife of a notorious communist." But he'd begun to look less and less at ease. Aube Breton had put her slim arms around her mother's neck and began to weep piteously. Varian chanced a look at the blue-eyed officer, his ally.

The man cleared his throat. "Sir," he said, addressing the commissaire. "We can't take these mothers from their children."

The commissaire huffed. "Lax justice is no justice," he said, by way of having the last word. But he waved Madame Nouguet in the direction of the door, and dismissed Jacqueline with Aube. Theo Bénédite received no such mercy. She exchanged a long look with her husband as she put little Peterkin into the care of the housemaid. They had been refugees long enough to know that any parting might be final.

"All right, then," the commissaire said. "Get the detainees into the wagon."

The plainclothesmen gathered all the portable evidence, lined up Breton and Serge and Theo and Danny and Mary Jayne and Killer and Lena and the others, and led them out to the van. Varian was still wearing the Moroccan slippers Grant had bought for him at the bazaar; over his shoulders, his patterned dressing gown. The owlish officer gave him a look of undisguised distaste as he pushed Varian into the van behind Lena. All of Air Bel sat together in the echoing dark, in an enclosure that felt like the inside of a coal hod.

"Two arrests in one day," Lena said, shaking her head. **"Franchement, c'est un peu excessif."**

"Incroyable!" Breton said. "But we shall make the most of it."

"I place my trust in you, Monsieur Breton," Lena said, and then the van lurched forward, and they were off.

At the Evêché, the police van pulled into a stone-paved courtyard and stopped before a massive wooden portal, as if the passengers had arrived for an audience with His Excellency the Bishop. The van doors clanged open, and the plainclothesmen led them off into a long, low hay-smelling structure that must have once been the bishop's stables. Up a narrow flight of stairs was a room that had been converted into a police classroom. Desks stretched in rows from one end to the other, and hundreds of detainees crowded the floor, speaking every language. On the blackboard at the front, someone had written **"Le Maréchal sent l'Emmental."** A dense cloud of cigarette smoke hung at chest level. Someone played an accordion, and someone else was selling newspapers from a canvas bag. It was clear that this was part of the general roundup, the pre-Pétain whisking away of all undesirable elements.

"Invraisemblable," Breton said. "It's a zoo."

Mary Jayne took a seat on one of the desks, extracting a cigarette from the pocket of her white silk robe, then a filigreed flask. "Better get the party started," she said. "It looks like we'll be here a while."

"Mais non, chérie," Killer said, straightening his Legionnaire's beret. Varian admired the presence of mind that had prompted him to take hold of it on their way out of Air Bel; he cut a convincing figure. "I will use my influence. They cannot detain a member of the military without cause. And I will take you with me, of course."

"Member of the military," Mary Jayne said, and rolled her eyes. "All right, Raymond. See what you can do."

Killer strode off to find the person in charge, and, to Varian's surprise, returned five minutes later to say that their own commissaire was presiding over this whole operation, holding court in an office adjacent to the long hall. He had returned Killer's service pistol and had told him he should leave before the others were moved. This mercy did not extend to Mary Jayne, who was required to stay with the rest of the Air Bellians.

"Moved?" Mary Jayne said. "To where? I didn't bring a change of clothes. I don't believe I've even got another cigarette."

The commissaire had not specified, Killer said.

"So what will you do now, darling?"

"I shall wait here until I know where you are to be taken." He crossed his arms and assumed a position beside Mary Jayne, as if to stand guard over her person.

"Actually, I'd rather have a sandwich," Mary Jayne said.

"Immédiatement." Killer corralled the newspaper seller, who seemed to know him intimately, and persuaded him to take money in exchange for a promise that he would return with sandwiches. The man disappeared down the stairs, and returned half an hour later with their tartines and change. They all ate wordlessly, awaiting news or release.

Hours passed before Varian was called before the commissaire. The man sat behind a too-small desk piled with quantities of things, including Breton's Pétain drawing and Jacqueline's pink lace underthings. The commissaire directed Varian to a tiny chair and ordered him to sign a new **procès-verbal** listing all the items found at the villa.

"Your own papers, Monsieur Fry, are entirely in order," the commissaire said. "And nothing was discovered in your room to arouse our suspicion. But further questioning may be necessary. We will conduct another search of Air Bel this evening."

"Is that really necessary, Monsieur?" He hated to think of Zilberman terrorized again, crouching in the low-ceilinged dugout that housed the villa's supply of onions and potatoes; of Madame Nouguet, who had gotten far more than she'd bargained for when Varian and his friends had moved in; and particularly of the children, one of them without his parents, having to witness another terrifying visit from the authorities.

"My duty is to ensure the Maréchal's safety," the commissaire said.

"I promise you there's nothing at the villa to endanger the Maréchal."

"If only a man's word were sufficient evidence, Monsieur Fry!"

"At least you've got to let Madame Bénédite go home. Her son needs her."

The commissaire lit a cigarette, inserted it under the brush of his mustache, then expanded the great vault of his chest with an inhalation. "You are an insistent man, Mr. Fry. You seem not to recognize that you might endanger your friends by annoying me."

"Monsieur, I appeal to what I recognize as your innate rationality and kindness."

The man exhaled slowly. "Monsieur Fry," he said. "Our audience is finished. Please rejoin your friends and await further orders." He swept a hand toward the door.

Varian left, nursing the distinct impression that

they'd all be staying the night. The Maréchal would hit town in ten hours, according to the papers, and still the vans were coming in. But Theo's audience with the commissaire directly followed his own, and she emerged with the news that she was to be released. She had also extracted the information that the rest of them were to be moved within the hour. She promised to get word of their situation to Harry Bingham at once. Then, in her formal way, she shook hands with everyone, her husband included, and put on her hat.

"Let me walk you out, Theo," Varian said. "I'd like a word."

"Of course," Theo said. She put a hand on his arm, and together they walked toward the stairway, where a guard waited.

"Listen," Varian said. "I must ask you a favor."

"Of course. Anything."

"I want you to tell Mr. Grant where we are. He may be able to help."

Theo's dovelike eyes focused on his own. "Where can I find him?"

"At his colleague's house in La Pomme. Les Cyprès."

"Is there anything in particular I should say?"

"No. I just want him to know what's become of us."

"All right," she said, and, searching his eyes again with her own, assured him that she would do everything in her power to help. Then she presented her papers to the guard and was ushered down the stairs. From the window Varian could see her crossing the pavement, her back erect, the vent of her skirt making its metronomic tick against her leg.

It was after midnight before a team of policemen arrived to herd the detainees down the stairs again and load them into armored vans. This time there was no room to sit; Varian stood with his chin pressed against Breton's shoulder blade, his elbow against Mary Jayne's bosom. Everyone nearly fell to the floor each time the van stopped short, which it seemed to do at every corner. When the doors opened again, the detainees saw they had reached the port on the west side of town. Before them, in a dark berth, stood a massive black passenger ship, its three white funnels soaring skyward.

"What nonsense is this?" Breton demanded. "Are we to be deported by sea?"

Killer would not follow further. He kissed Mary Jayne at the gangway and presented his papers to one of the guards, who expressed his shocked dismay that a Legionnaire had been subjected to captivity. The rest of the Air Bel group slipped into the stream of detainees flowing upward toward the black ship.

"I hope we won't be doomed to wander for forty

years," Mary Jayne said, indicating the name painted in white block letters on the side of the ship: **Sinaïa.**

Varian stared, then laughed.

"What could possibly be funny?" Mary Jayne said.

"This is the **Sinaïa,**" he said. "The boat I sailed on when I crossed the pond in '28."

"No!"

"Yes." The same boat that had carried him to Italy, Greece, and Turkey the summer between his sophomore and junior years, when he'd undertaken his Mediterranean tour in a state of dazed grief. Now, as they reached the deck—the same deck he'd paced at night for hours during that voyage, under the insomniac stars—they were divided by sex: the men would have bunks in the hold, the women third-class cabins. No one knew when they were to set sail; the detectives offered no information. The detainees were split into groups of twelve and sent to their respective sleeping quarters. The men had thin woolen blankets to spread over burlap bags filled with hay; they lay down under the open hatches and looked up at a sky seeded with stars. The fog had blown over, the wind gone still. The boat rocked and rocked against its moorings. There was not much talk. Breton tied his foulard over his eyes to block out the harbor lights. Jean extracted a tiny harmonica from his jacket pocket and played a French ballad, whose lyrics Danny mumbled. Varian lay on his burlap bag and stared up through the metal grid of the hatch gratings, feeling the deep strangeness of his circumstances. He could do nothing for the moment but lie still under his inadequate blanket; he could save no one, could write no letter on anyone's behalf; no one could line up to see him, no one could demand a single thing. Into the void came everything his mind had recorded—all without his being aware of its doing so—about this ship, the journey, the particular contours of his grief.

He had come back from Maine in a state of near-collapse, one he knew he had to hide from Eileen. In Blue Hill, before Grant's vanishing, he'd had an intimation of what might be possible between himself and Eileen; for the first time he'd envisioned a life with a person who was neither an outright impossibility (Grant) nor a mere abstraction (winsome, witty wife). He imagined a life in a city, vaguely literary, sexually liberated; he envisioned Christmas at Eileen's parents' house, the chestnuts roasting, the antique stockings hung by the fire, someone's children fighting charmingly over the pieces of a gingerbread house. He saw himself arriving at the Harvard Club in New York, being congratulated upon the success of his new magazine, of which Eileen would be assistant editor; he saw himself offering Eileen a diamond in an egg-blue box. A shamelessly bourgeois vision, and an intoxicating one. Even after Grant's departure, some instinct stage-whispered that he must protect it. He must not, therefore, reveal to Eileen that Grant's disappearance was for him not merely a mystery but a life-crushing disaster.

Grant, as it turned out, had cleared everything out of his Harvard rooms and left no forwarding address. The registrar would give Varian no information, but a girl who worked in the office told him that Grant had withdrawn from school. Withdrawn! From Harvard, the consolation prize he'd chosen in exchange for his career in music. From his studies, in which he'd quietly risen to a position of esteem among his professors. How Varian had denied that news, how he'd protested it. In Kirstein's rooms he walked the tiled floor and cursed Grant's stupidity while Kirstein lounged in a leather club chair, drinking gin from a cut-crystal glass.

"All because I flirted with a woman!" Varian said. "His academic career, for that!"

"'Flirted' is not the word I'd use," Kirstein said lightly.

"He couldn't have known what happened on that island, Lincoln!"

"I'm not talking about **that.** I mean before. Months before, really."

Varian stopped pacing. "What do you mean?"

"You've had a fancy for Eileen ever since Mina introduced you." Mina was Kirstein's sister, Eileen her best friend. The introduction had come in early spring, at a dance at the Kirstein manse on

Commonwealth Ave. In her black dress, with her cultivated accent, her history of travel, her editorship at **The Atlantic,** Eileen had seemed to him to belong more to his professors' milieu than his own; at the time he'd had no sexual designs on her, no romantic notion in which the two of them shared a life. But gradually something had shifted. At parties they found themselves together more often. He had come to be able to distinguish between her three black cocktail dresses, and to know that she was more comfortable on the subject of politics than on philosophy. He had found himself stockpiling the books she suggested, studying them. They had spent evenings together in conversation. And then there was Maine and their friends' vacation house, that perfect white saltbox with its view of pine-velveted hills and riffled sea, its rooms of austere Shaker furniture, its screened porches with their sky-colored ceilings, and, down on the water, the pristine wooden boats gleaming like a fleet of musical instruments, a section of bass viols, each with its single string. All of it belonged to a life he fiercely desired, one he had vaguely envisioned might be his own: a vision impossible to realize under any but the most conventional family circumstances. And here was Eileen, her black dresses cast aside in favor of a French sailor's shirt and split white skirt; Eileen with her dinner-party banter, Eileen who could mix a drink and serve it with a side of erudite sex-salted conversation; Eileen, a boyishly attractive woman, who presented herself to his imagination not just as an intriguing friend but as a possible partner—one who, if he played his cards right, might not require that he banish Grant entirely from his life. Of course, Grant, as attuned to Varian as he was, must have had some inkling of all this. Varian's decision to step into that boat must have seemed a conscious and irrevocable choice. And hadn't it been? What else could it have been?

"But why disappear?" Varian had protested. "Why leave altogether?"

"Can you blame him?" Kirstein said. "Could **you** stand it?"

And Varian had paused at the window, the one that gave over a shade-drenched lawn and the choppy Charles, and forced himself to consider that. Of course Kirstein was right. If anyone was responsible, it was Varian himself.

He knew the telephone number of Grant's family in Philadelphia, of the mother who had gone home to her parents twenty years earlier: SAratoga 4-5739. On a Sunday morning after a terrible night of drinking, two days before he was to embark on a tour of Europe on the **Sinaïa,** he picked up the telephone and placed the call. The operator sounded new at the job; she fumbled him to SAratoga 6. He nearly lost his nerve as the operator at 6 rectified the mistake and passed him to SAratoga 4. By the time he heard the tweedle of the ringtone, his hands were shaking. A woman's voice—quick, anxious, as if she'd been expecting a long-distance call—said, "Hello? Who's that?"

"Hello," Varian said, or tried to say; what emerged was a choked half-whisper.

"Who's calling?"

"Is Grant—is Elliott at home?"

"Who is this, please?"

"I'm calling from the university."

"Mr. Grant is not at home. Who's calling, please?"

Why was he hesitating? "This is Varian Fry," he said. "A friend from Harvard."

From the other end, silence. And then, so low he might not have heard it had all his attention not been trained upon the phone, an intake of breath, and a quiet click. The line went dead. Varian stood for a moment holding the receiver. From somewhere in its depths, a circlet of metal vibrated to form words: the other party, the operator told him, had ended the call. He thought for a moment of saying "Place it again." Of becoming, for a brief time, a nuisance to the Schiffman household. That intake of breath after he'd spoken his name: What did it mean? Was it possible Grant had told his mother everything, or some pale version of everything? Had Grant himself been listening on the extension? What would Varian find if he were to go downstairs that very moment, climb into the yellow Packard, and drive six hours to Philadelphia? Unthinking, he opened his dresser and began throwing things into a weekend bag. But then a wave of cowardice overtook him. Just what was he proposing to do? Storm the family gates? Under what set of rights, and with what authority? What could he possibly say to Grant's mother, to his grandparents? Instead of descending to the Packard, he climbed into bed. His courage failed to return the following morning. And the next day his ship sailed to Europe. **This** ship, the **Sinaïa,** on which he now lay in crew's quarters on a burlap sack under a coarse woolen blanket, in the port of Marseille, while the war made its inarticulate thunder all around.

And what would Grant think if this ship sailed sometime in the night? Would he believe Varian had been deported against his will? After all, Varian's courage had failed him before; he had not called SAratoga 4-5739 again. He had not missed his boat to Europe. He had let himself walk forward into that other life he'd imagined, the life he believed he deserved. And Grant, he saw now, had made it easy for him. He had stepped aside. He would not play second fiddle to Eileen, would not be uncle to Varian's children, would not hover at the edge of snapshots taken at the beach. He would not be a silent supplicant who stole, here and there, a cupped hand's worth of holy water. What he wanted, impossible though it was, was some permutation of what they had at Harvard, some urban and adult version of it. It had been too much for Varian to envision. It was too much now. But what were the consequences of refusing it again? He knew by now the toll of living that way, as an incomplete and insincere version of himself.

If he made it back to shore, if this boat failed to depart sometime in the night for points unimaginable, he knew he would have to choose again. That was the chance Grant had extended to him by seeking him out at the Splendide. They were twelve years older; Grant had been forced to live with the consequences of his decisions too. And he'd chosen to make contact, to make himself vulnerable again. But what were they supposed to do now? How to choose? What choice, really, was on the table? What answer could there be? He remembered again the feeling of being in Gare de Noailles as the bombs fell, half-wishing for a blinding shock to end it all.

In the morning, the **Sinaïa** was still at port. Seagulls circled and shrieked. Groups of detainees strolled the decks as if for pleasure. No one had any information; no food or drink was forthcoming except for the usual fake coffee and hard brown bread. Inquiries among the other passengers revealed the nature of the roundup: haphazard, a broad and clumsy sweep. Here was a Marrakeshi jazz singer who'd mispronounced the Maréchal's name onstage; here a widow whose husband, dead twenty years, had been falsely suspected of being a communist. Here was a Russian teacher who'd once, as an exercise, asked her students to copy a page of Marx; here were half a dozen clients of the Centre Américain de Secours, all visibly dismayed that their ostensible savior was a prisoner too.

Morning and afternoon passed. For dinner they got frozen beef, lentils, more hard bread, turnip soup, a measure of wine in a tin cup. The wine, Varian had to admit, was not half bad. "Only in France," he said, and Breton postulated that this was to be their last supper, that they would soon be transported out to sea and made to walk a plank.

Lena exhorted him not to exaggerate. "It is the Maréchal's visit. We won't be here long. **Les rafles sont de rigueur** in a fascist state."

"So are mass executions," said Breton.

As if in immediate refutation of Lena's prediction, the ship's whistle blew and everyone was ordered belowdecks. The portholes were closed, the hold door locked from above. The engines throbbed. The boat seemed to strain at its moorings. In the harbor, a volley of ships' whistles blew. Surely Breton was right: in moments they would be on their way. Varian wondered: If they were made to walk the plank, how long would it take to die? It was said that the waters outside the harbor were rife with sharks.

Victor Serge, who had survived more than a few roundups in Soviet Russia, seemed singularly unperturbed. "What's likely to happen is nothing," he said. "Day after day, for no one knows how long."

"Incroyable," Breton said. "Already I'm so hungry I could eat my own leg."

"You must eat your rations," Serge said. "Eat them and keep them down."

"Impossible!" Breton said.

Two hours passed while the boat sat closed tight in the harbor, the detainees inaudible and invisible. Then at last the holds were unlatched and the portholes opened, and everyone streamed out onto the deck. The guards distributed cigarettes. Everyone took this as a hopeful sign, despite the fact that the cigarettes were stale and bent. A haze of smoke rose from the deck. Silence fell. A rumor traveled the ship: the passengers had been kept belowdecks while the Maréchal's ship pulled into the harbor. Everyone seemed to believe this, as unlikely as it was that the Maréchal would travel via the mined sea instead of by land. The short day darkened. No further information came. After a time, the women retreated to their cabins and the men to their straw-stuffed sacks.

As he lay awake, Varian fell to wondering who on that ship might be of help, who might be a conduit to the outer world. He had seen the ship's captain strolling the deck, looking as disconsolate as the passengers; this was the same captain, bearded and sharp-eyed and gilt-buttoned, who had commanded the ship when Varian had crossed the ocean all those years before. Deschamps was his name, Varian remembered. To this man he might make an appeal. The captain had been a veteran of the Great War; he would not have lent his boat to its current purpose had he not been compelled by forces beyond his control. He might be convinced to radio a message somewhere, to send up, as it were, a covert semaphore flag.

Early the next morning, Varian managed to take a stroll past Deschamps's quarters and slide a note under the door. The note was an impassioned plea for help, penned on a leaf from a miniature notebook Breton had stuffed into his pocket upon leaving the house. Varian knew he was taking a risk; in the note he identified himself, and Mary Jayne, and the other Air Bellians, by name. He didn't have much hope that the note would be answered. He feared even that the captain would overlook the tiny folded square of paper on which it was written. But as he stood in line for lunch that day, one of the guards appeared and barked his name.

Varian stepped out of line. "I'm Fry," he said.

"You're wanted in the captain's quarters. You and Mademoiselle Gold."

Mary Jayne turned a frightened look on Varian. "Are we in trouble?" she whispered.

"Let's hope not."

Mary Jayne straightened the lapels of Varian's patterned robe and retied his sash. There was nothing else that could be done to prepare. They followed the guard up one narrow flight of stairs and then another, then paused before a stout portholed door.

"Entrez," the guard commanded.

Varian leaned forward and gave a little knock. The guard rolled his eyes and banged on the door with his fist—rudely, Varian thought. But Deschamps was not captain of these guards; there was no deference to rank, as far as Varian could tell.

"Come in," the captain called from inside. The guard waved them in, and, to Varian's relief and surprise, left them there.

In the gloom of the captain's chambers, some remnant of the **Sinaïa**'s original luxury could be discerned. A red Turkish rug lay on the floor; mahogany bookcases and cleverly fitted cupboards lined the walls; electric bulbs shed their low light from faceted wall sconces. Deschamps sat at a table of the kind that might have once been used for playing cards in a Viennese drawing room: dark wood carved on every surface with cherubs, ivy, curlicues, and doves. He had been sitting in a red velvet chair, but got to his feet to welcome the Americans.

"Monsieur Fry, we meet again!" Deschamps said. He was from Normandy, if Varian remembered correctly, but his English was impeccable, his accent a mix of sea salt and Oxford. His hair, black when Varian had last seen him, had turned a radiant sunbleached silver. "What hideous circumstances! How ashamed I am to have you here not as my passenger but as a prisoner. And your charming friend—Miss Gold, is it?"

Mary Jayne offered her hand; the captain kissed it.

"I'm honored that you remember me," Varian said. "It's been twelve years."

"Remember you!" Deschamps said. "How could I forget? You played a fine game of chess. I never forget a good adversary."

Varian nodded his thanks. He had only the vaguest memory of playing chess with the captain; what he remembered was the relief of being distracted from his misery. But flattery seemed the politic approach. "You were a fierce opponent yourself," he said.

"Yes. It's a rare man who defeats me so soundly," the captain said, now addressing Mary Jayne. "Your young man quite embarrassed me."

"I'm hardly surprised," Mary Jayne said. "He's rather a sharp strategist."

"And now, Mr. Fry, it seems you've run afoul of the law."

"My friends and I were falsely accused of communist activity. The police themselves admitted they had no solid grounds for detaining us."

"Ah, but with the Maréchal in town, no solid grounds are grounds enough!"

"So I understand."

In a few words Varian described the nature of his work in Marseille and the urgency of getting his clients off the **Sinaïa.** As the captain listened, he went to a sideboard and poured Varian and Mary Jayne small glasses of beer; he handed them out with apologies that he couldn't offer anything better. Varian sipped from his glass and made his plea to the captain: he must get word of his clients' plight to the U.S. Embassy.

"My communications to shore have been cut off," the captain said. "This boat was commandeered. I was ordered to lend it as a prison vessel. I've not been told how long the police intend to use it." His eyes flickered toward the inlaid chessboard lying closed on a nearby bookshelf; evidently he hoped Varian would be imprisoned long enough to afford time for a rematch. But then a knock came at the door, and in stepped a cabin boy clad in a crisp brass-buttoned coat. In a tenor voice tense with the importance of his message, he announced that an exalted person from the U.S. Consulate had arrived and was waiting to see Monsieur Fry.

"Tell him to come up at once," the captain said.

"Oh, thank God," said Mary Jayne. "It's Harry. We're saved."

"Unless it's Fullerton, in which case we're sunk."

"He'd never come. He'd let you rot."

She was right, of course; it was Bingham. He bowed to the captain, kissed Mary Jayne's hand, and then seated himself at Varian's side. "Sorry I couldn't come sooner," he said. "I had a time finding out where they'd taken you. Are you all right?"

"We're surviving," Varian said. "But we've got no idea what they intend to do with us."

"It's Pétain, you know. They've rounded up nearly seven thousand in town."

"Pardon me," the captain interjected. "May I offer

you a drink, Monsieur Vice-Consul? **Un cognac?** I regret that I have so little on board."

"I never refuse cognac," Bingham said.

The captain opened one of his secret sideboard cabinets and poured a dram for each of them. **"A votre santé,"** he said, and they drank.

"For you, Harry, he takes out the good stuff," Mary Jayne said.

"Well, I hardly deserve it," Bingham said. "I've only come to hearten you. There's nothing I can do to get you off this boat today."

"Harry, really! You can't be serious."

"I'm afraid so. Maybe if I was consul-general."

"But can't you get **his** help?"

"I'd think, frankly, he'd prefer you all be locked up."

"And when does Pétain clear out?" Varian said.

"Not until tomorrow."

"Aha," said the captain, with obvious relief. "Then you will be my guest tonight. And you and I must take down the chessboard, though I'm rather out of practice. I fear you'll get the better of me again."

"I sincerely hope so," Varian said, though he knew that if he played Deschamps, he would play to lose; he would do whatever was necessary to win the sympathies of a ship's captain, particularly one who was trusted by the administration but at odds with it.

"Won't you excuse us, Captain?" Bingham said. "I'd like a word with Monsieur Fry before I go."

"Of course," the captain said. He stood and bowed

to Bingham, expressing his regret that they were not meeting under more congenial circumstances. Then Varian and Mary Jayne and Bingham went out onto the deck, where prisoners lounged against the railing or strolled for what little exercise could be had. Bingham, it was revealed, had brought along a hamper full of provisions. Victor Serge could be seen on the lower deck preparing sandwiches with the aid of a wooden knife.

"I'll go back to the office and see what can be done," Bingham said. "We haven't got many advantages to play. I'll cable Eleanor Roosevelt. Perhaps she can be prevailed upon to shame Fullerton into helping you."

"Let's hope she can. I'm not dressed for prison," Varian said, indicating his robe. "It's a terrible waste of time, more than anything. There's too much to be done at the office. And I'm anxious to learn what's happened to young Katznelson."

"I'll see if I can find out," Bingham said. "And I'll send some more provisions tonight." Bingham shook Varian's hand and kissed Mary Jayne's; then he descended to the main deck and walked down the gangway, drawing his coat together against the fog.

Mary Jayne leaned over the railing to look down into the rank bouillabaisse of the port. "Another night in this tub!" she said. "If only Miriam were here. She'd find a way to make us all laugh." She sighed, folding her hands over the rail.

"You can't really wish she was stuck here with us."

"I do! I miss her terribly. Her absence leaves a rather gaping hole."

"You'll be busier at the office, at least, if we ever get off this boat. That'll be some distraction."

Mary Jayne pushed her hair back and turned her face into the wind. "The fact is, Miriam was my guide there, too. I had no idea what I was doing. You saw, Varian—I made such a mess of things with Feuchtwanger. But I started paying closer attention after that. To Miriam, I mean. To the way she did things. Now I'll be at sea again."

"That's nonsense, Mary Jayne. You've always been perfectly at ease. You've proceeded intelligently, and with fine results. Feuchtwanger made his own mess."

She shook her head. "What must you think of me? That rich dilettante with the good-for-nothing boyfriend! Treats all of this like it's one grand party."

"That's not what I think at all. You've been there at the Centre every day with the rest of us. You've conducted your work admirably. You've been more than generous with your own funds. If you've made things a little less dull at Air Bel, so much the better. And if I'm not fond of your boyfriend, well"—he hesitated a moment, then threw caution to the wind—"at least he's not mine."

A charged moment passed, and then Mary Jayne laughed. "No," she said. "No. I can see he's not your type." And then, without further comment, she caught his arm in her own, and they went down to join Breton and Serge and the others.

———

At nine that night Deschamps summoned Varian again, this time to the chessboard. Varian hadn't played in years; the feeling was not unlike trying to debate in a language he'd once spoken fluently but had forgotten. And his aim was a complicated one: not to win, but to be beaten, subtly and in winners' drag, in order to cultivate the captain's goodwill. He wanted a patient opening that would allow him to lose slowly, to make a series of calculated mistakes while he advanced his more important point. But Deschamps opened with a Danish gambit meant to end the game in twenty moves, and Varian found himself stalling for time over his glass of cognac, turning it on its leather disc.

"Let me confess something," he said. "My work here in Marseille hasn't been going as well as I've liked."

The captain glanced up from the board. "How is that?"

"The legal avenues are closed to my most sensitive clients, the ones most wanted by the Nazis. And our clandestine channels keep shutting down. One of my greatest assets—an American who knew the Pyrenees passes—had his cover blown in the international press. Now he's gone missing. And the sensitive clients keep stacking up, waiting for a way out."

"Funny," the captain said, shaking his head.

"What's funny about it?"

"When I made your acquaintance twelve years ago, you struck me as a charming and intelligent young man—but alas, if you don't mind my saying so, rather a self-centered and self-satisfied one. I would never have imagined this line of work for you. I suppose you weren't the only one guilty of making assumptions."

Varian smiled. Twelve years earlier he'd been surprised, enough so that he'd been unable to mask it, by Deschamps's erudition, by the fact that he possessed an extensive library of volumes in French and English and knew most of their contents by heart. Deschamps had declared Varian's opinion of sea captains to be both retrograde and hopelessly American. He was not a whaler, not a ferryman; in his offshore months he'd pursued the doctoral degree in French literature. He'd shown Varian a copy of his dissertation, handsomely bound in calfskin. Varian could see the spine of that volume from where he sat now. Well, the captain was right to have called him self-centered; at the time, his world had been pitiably small. But self-satisfied? Perhaps he'd appeared that way, though he'd felt the opposite. He'd hated himself on that voyage, considered himself ugly, unlovable, duplicitous.

"Glad to think I appear less self-centered now,"

Varian said. "Though actually I'm mustering the courage to ask a personal favor."

Deschamps plucked a rook from its square, then advanced it three ranks to take Varian's bishop. "Well, don't beat around the bush," he said. "Let's have it."

"I want to know if you might be willing to transport some rather precious cargo."

The captain squinted at him. "You realize that my boat is under surveillance by Vichy."

"Yes, it's clear the government believes it has a special relationship with you," Varian said, wryly. "All the more reason for me to ask. No one will suspect you."

"On the contrary, I'm under constant suspicion. All captains are. Ships are among the most valuable commodities in this war."

"Indeed," Varian said. "But I don't want your ship. I want to pay you to take passengers. A few special passengers whose lives may mean something to us all."

"You're asking me to put my own neck on the line," Deschamps said. "Is that it?"

Varian moved his knight to D7, a position he knew would allow the captain the aperture he needed. "I see you're a fair- and free-minded man who's been deprived of his will," he said. "Your boat is not your own. I'm offering an opportunity to make it yours again."

The captain eyed Varian from under his brows.

"Offering?" he said. "I wouldn't say that's what you are doing."

"It's not only soldiers who fight a war," Varian said.

"No, and not only soldiers who die."

"We're talking about the intellectual flower of Europe," Varian said. "You can have a hand in saving it."

The captain's fingers hovered over his queen; she stood in line to take Varian's knight. Varian knew he had hit the correct vein, that this captain among all captains would be vulnerable to the prospect of rescuing art and literature.

"Just how many passengers are we talking about?" the captain asked. A hint of conspiracy had entered his tone, and Varian knew he was weakening.

"That depends on your capacity," he said.

The captain glanced over his shoulder; the windows of his cabin stood open to the night, and everything in Marseille listened. He got to his feet and closed the windows, drew the shades, made sure the lock on the door was secured. Then he said, in a lowered voice, "I have a private compartment that can be accessed only from my quarters. It's a feature my father insisted on building into his ships. He was a shipwright, you know. That was how I came into the profession."

Varian looked up from the board. "A compartment?" he said.

"Two feet by three feet. The ceiling is five and a half feet in height."

"Show it to me."

The captain scrutinized Varian for a long moment, as if to determine finally whether the young Turk of all those years ago could really have transformed into a person to be trusted. But then he pushed back his chair, went to the wall, and removed an oil painting of a sloop in a tempest; he took up a corner of the painting's backing and removed a tiny skeleton key. The wooden panel upon which the painting had hung, Varian saw, had an almost invisible seam. What appeared to be a knothole in the wood was in fact a keyhole, into which the captain fitted the key. The panel, as it turned out, was cleverly hinged. The captain opened it to reveal a shelf-lined closet. It was packed with disappointingly mundane things: canned goods and cigarettes, matches, bars of soap. But then the captain pointed out clusters of ventilation holes in the ceiling, walls, and floor, apertures through which a stowaway might breathe.

"Your father was a man of foresight," Varian said.

"Smuggling has always been a lucrative branch of our business."

"I'm afraid I can't offer you much in the way of money," Varian said. But then he named a figure certain to please the ghost of the captain's father.

The captain, an experienced gamesman, kept his expression impassive. But the pinky of his left hand twitched, Varian could not help but notice; and though, once the captain had closed and locked the door of his secret compartment and replaced the key in its painting, he sat down at the chess table again and handily placed Varian's king in checkmate, Varian knew that he himself had once again won the game.

By ten o'clock the next morning, officials had arrived from the commissariat to interview prisoners in the captain's quarters. Eleven o'clock saw Varian and the surrealists standing before an elderly detective with a lisp; ten minutes later their papers had been returned to them, their names cleared of suspicion. They could leave the ship, the elderly detective said, as soon as they had gathered their things. As a finale, the detective handed over to Varian a letter from the original commissaire in which he offered his apologies that Varian and his associates had been subjected to such a lengthy inconvenience.

"Apologies!" Mary Jayne said, as they descended the gangway at last and stepped onto dry land. "Apologies! I want champagne sent to the villa. Fine champagne, a magnum of it. And plenty of food. And orchids, lots of them. Really! His apologies." Raising a hand in farewell, she walked a tight indignant line toward the streetcar. Varian, too, was anxious to get back to Air Bel, but more anxious to see what had become of the office; he suspected it had been ransacked like the house. He walked toward the boulevard Garibaldi with Lena at his side, kicking through the aftermath of a Vichy parade: scraps of tricolor confetti, fallen clouds of bunting, images of the Maréchal printed with brave slogans. Lena had heard that nearly twenty thousand people had been arrested in Marseille that week, stuffed into ships, hotels, and movie palaces that had been converted into makeshift jails.

They found the office door locked, the file cabinets untouched, the typewriter in place, the two office plants tranquil in their pots. The hallway was deserted; no refugee would have dared show his face at an American aid office while Vichy officers roamed the streets.

Lena pulled the cover off the Contin and sat down before it. **"Alors,"** she said. "Where to begin? Perhaps you shall dictate that letter—the one you prepared to start when the commissaire arrived?" She inserted a new sheet of paper and looked at him.

Varian was starving, exhausted, dirty; all he wanted was a bath in the swan-footed tub and an uninterrupted sleep in his cool clean bed. He wanted to wake to the sound of Grant's voice downstairs, Grant sitting with the surrealists in the library while Madame Nouguet prepared dinner and Aube Breton ran the halls in her little blue shoes, singing some Alsatian tune. He wanted time to think; he wanted to write to Eileen. But the war hadn't paused while he'd been detained on the **Sinaïa,** and would not pause now. The bombs would go on falling, the typhoid-spreading lice would keep biting at Vernet and Gurs and Les Milles, the Führer's megalomania would widen and deepen, and the desperate refugees would keep washing up against the door of the Centre Américain. So he leaned back in his chair, laced his hands over his midsection, and began the afternoon's work.

19

Pamiers

Villa Air Bel
La Pomme, Marseille

12 December 1940

Eileen, Eileen.

And so we enter the last weeks of the year. When I embarked on this journey, I couldn't have imagined we would spend Christmas apart. I saw us by now in a house in Westchester sitting beside our own fire. How little you deserve what you got instead. I hope you'll receive my Christmas presents soon. The turquoises come from Oman, the spices from farther east. I wish only that I could have delivered them in person.

Much has changed here in Marseille. I find it, to be honest, rather gloomy. You've heard by now that Miriam is gone, off to Yugoslavia to wed her ailing fiancé. We feel the lack of her sorely, but our work goes on. Our friends at the border do what they can, making a way for our clients where no way exists. Little by little, client by client, our numbers climb, though the situation on the ground grows ever worse. Not here in Marseille, where, despite desperate shortages of food, music plays in the cafés at night and men and women do all the usual dances. But in the countryside, the French pack their refugees into horrible pestilent camps. Thousands of innocent foreigners and Jews. Last week I delivered a report on conditions in those camps to Vichy; we want them to know we're watching. They, too, want us to know they're watching. Someday I will tell you what happened when the Maréchal came to town.

The fact is, though, I still can't tell you when **someday** might be. I can't, in fact, answer any of the questions you posed in your last letter. You and Frank Kingdon and Paul Hagen repeatedly mention this mysterious someone you've selected to replace me, never naming him; thus far my replacement has yet to arrive in Marseille. Perhaps the matter is one of recruitment. No person of sound mind would want my job. Or maybe you've all begun to understand what folly it would be to replace me now, when my network of contacts is so broad and relies so much on personal trust. What sense can it make to retool the machine? I must be allowed to go on doing what I do. In the meantime I must ask you to instruct the office to keep our funds flowing. As long as our sources of francs and passports hold, we'll continue saving lives.

So please, Eileen, tell my parents not to worry. And don't you worry either. Our plans have already succeeded beyond our first goals. This must be seen as cause for celebration, and the work must go on. You've known me always as a stubborn man, and now I'm perhaps more myself than I have ever been. If I ask for your patience—which I must, once again—I ask for it humbly, and with nothing to offer in exchange but my gratitude and love.

As ever,
Your V

Oh, he was a liar, pants afire. Oh, how he could hide behind his righteous work. What the unwritten paragraphs would say! How, upon his return from the **Sinaïa,** he'd come back to Air Bel to find no sign of Grant, and had then run all the way to the Medieval Pile to find it deserted, items of clothing strewn around as if Grant had left in a hurry, or been arrested; how, in a blind panic, he'd taken the train straight back to town, despite his exhaustion, and inquired at the Evêché, then at two hospitals.

And now here he was in the library at Air Bel, confronting Theo Bénédite, demanding she tell him what she'd written to Grant. There was no more urgent desire in his mind than to see Grant, and not a word of this, not a hint, had he intimated to Eileen. He held his lying letter in his hand now as he paced before Theo, demanding that she tell him everything.

"I did just as you asked, no more and no less," Theo said. She was perched in the library window seat, her back erect, holding a pair of scissors and a sheet of brightly colored paper; on the rug before her, Peterkin played with a set of cutout circus animals. "I sent Mr. Grant a message saying you were aboard the **Sinaïa** with everyone else. I told him you were all in urgent need of help. He wrote back to say—"

"He wrote back?"

"Yes. He said he'd go see Harry at once and try to get you sprung, that was all."

"Did you run into him at the office?"

"I haven't been to the office," she said. "I didn't think it safe to go to town. But perhaps he left you a note?"

"Where? I've been all over the house."

"Not here. At his own place. He knows we're being watched by the police."

"I've just been to his place. There's no note there, either."

"Do you think he was detained?"

"I've already checked with the police. I want to see his reply to you, Theo. If you still have it."

"All right, just a moment." Theo handed him the scissors and the paper, then went into the hall and disappeared up the stairs.

"Pourriez-vous couper mon éléphant?" said Peterkin, and held out his hand.

Varian had never been adept with scissors, but he did his best; Peterkin watched with a critic's eye. By the time he freed the elephant from its surrounding paper, Theo had returned with the note. Varian took it, read it, scrutinized its lines for any clue. Then he turned it over in his hands. On the back was a railroad timetable, a pencil dot beside a destination.

"Look at that," Theo said. "Pamiers."

"Of course. It's the closest station to Vernet."

"Why on earth would he go there?"

"I believe he's looking for someone," Varian said.

"Well, but one can't simply walk into Vernet."

"Yes, you know that, and so do I. But Mr. Grant swore to protect this person. And perhaps he feels invulnerable, like many Americans abroad."

Theo gave her mercury-quick smile. "But he'd just learned we'd all been arrested."

"Mr. Grant considers himself cleverer than most people. And, in some cases, naturally exempt from the common fate."

"You believe he'd go to Vernet and demand to see the commandant?"

"I wouldn't put it past him." He looked at the timetable. Grant had penciled his dot next to an early-morning train, but that was two days ago. Who knew where he might be now?

"You're not thinking of going yourself, Varian."

"I am. And maybe of taking someone else with me. I don't believe the commandant would be particularly pleased to see **me.**"

"You don't mean Mary Jayne."

"Yes, precisely."

Theo's look darkened. "You wouldn't ask her to compromise herself again."

"She's already shown her willingness. She convinced the commandant to let Hans Tittel and Bogler and the others out, even if they ended up back in. The point is, we all have to do what we can."

"No one is asking **you** to do **that.**"

"All right, Theo. I see the philosophical argument. But I need her help. I can ask, at least. She's free to say no."

"She took a bath and dressed for dinner. I believe she said she'd go down to the greenhouse to see Monsieur Zilberman." Without meeting his eye, she turned back to Peterkin, who climbed into her lap. Varian wished she would have looked at him; he thought of her as a kind of moral magnetic north, and he disliked the idea that she'd condemn him for using all means available. Virtue, after all, might be construed in many ways; a woman as intelligent as

Theo must know it. He put the note into his pocket and went to the kitchen door. Then he stepped out into the chilly afternoon and crossed the driveway to the greenhouse, where, behind the clouded wall, he could see the moving shape of Zilberman at work.

He knocked on the greenhouse door, and Mary Jayne opened it, drink in hand, dressed in a persimmon-colored jersey and ivory slacks. She might have just come from lunch at Maxim's.

"Come in," she said. "Zilberman's had a marvelous idea. Take a look."

Varian had little patience for any idea save one that concerned going after Grant; but Zilberman was bent over the long worktable intently, and before him lay an array of images so arresting Varian had to step closer. Some were drawings that had collected in the corners of the house since their arrival: one of Jacques Hérold's from an after-dinner game, depicting a headless boy running full-bore through a burning forest; another of Masson's, of a pink Messerschmitt discharging a payload of snakes. And here was a new one, unmistakably Chagall's: pale lines crosshatching a coal-black sky, the image they'd seen from Gare de Noailles during the air raid. Beneath these drawings lay many others, a ragged-edged stack of them.

"What do you propose to do with these?" Varian said.

Zilberman raised his cap to smooth back his

hair. "Liberate them from France. Get them to the States. The artists have agreed already to donate the work. Chagall has many friends in New York, and my wife has contacts in Boston. Let us transport these works to America, stage a series of exhibitions. Show everyone what's at risk. What may be lost. Do you not think money can be raised, Monsieur Fry? Perhaps we can make lithographs, a set. The Flight Portfolio, we could call it."

Of course: a set of drawings could travel, could do work that a single person could not. And then he thought of the **Sinaïa,** of the secret closet in the captain's rooms.

"Listen," he said. "What if you were to take the drawings yourself?"

Zilberman looked up from the long table. "That is what I most wish."

"We don't have your U.S. visa yet. But as soon as we can get it, there may be a way." And he explained what the captain had shown him.

Zilberman glanced down at the drawings. "I have a fear of small spaces. What you describe sounds like a coffin."

"It's a closet, vented on all sides. And you wouldn't have to stay in it for long. It's just a place to hide in case the ship's inspected. It's a way to get aboard the ship, and for the ship to get out of port, without your having to be on a passenger list. It's a way to avert the need for French exit visas."

"I'll do what I must," Zilberman said. "How long before I can get a U.S. visa, do you think?"

"Perhaps two or three months."

"So much time?"

"Yes, and we can't get our hopes up," Varian said. "So many plans involving boats have failed."

"Must I have papers at all, if I can stow away?"

"You've got to be able to get into the States on the other side."

"Perhaps we should just send the drawings."

"I love the drawings," Varian said. "I admire your plan. But my aim is to save human beings. I want to get you **and** the work to the States. When that happens, I'll make sure Alfred Barr stages a show everyone will see. Your presence will make it all the more effective. Then I'll get you to the best printmaker in New York and muster ERC funds for the printing. We can raise thousands, maybe even hundreds of thousands. It's a brilliant idea, Lev. The perfect idea."

Zilberman glanced down. "Mademoiselle Gold has been helping me arrange it."

"Mademoiselle Gold has an eye," Varian said. "But I'm afraid I must steal her away for a moment."

"I'll resign myself," said Zilberman. He raised a hand to his cap, then turned his attention back to the work.

———

"No," said Mary Jayne. "No, and no. I'm certainly not going to chase Grant to Vernet **tonight.** Not just minutes after I've stepped off a prison ship. And neither should you, Varian. You're exhausted, you're hungry, and frankly you're in need of a bath."

They were standing in the living room in front of a hot, quick-burning fire. Mary Jayne had finished her drink and mixed another; Varian refused to take one. "We've got to go now," he said. "Lives may be at stake."

"Lives are always at stake," Mary Jayne said. "They'll be at stake tomorrow."

"I'll go on my own if I have to."

Mary Jayne squinted at him. "Do you think Grant's in some kind of trouble?"

"I don't know. That's my point."

"There's got to be a train tomorrow morning."

"There's one at ten. But how can I wait another night?" He'd said the words aloud; there was no retracting them. It was a kind of admission, a confirmation, though she must have known for some time now. They'd practically discussed it on the ship. Still, he couldn't bring himself to look at her as she stood impassively before the fire, the drink glowing in her hand.

"There's a right way to do things and a wrong," she said. "One must not always rush in. Where would Grant be, if he were in Pamiers? He would be staying at Les Platanes, the only decent hotel in the area. The place where I was supposed to meet the commandant, the last time I paid a visit to that wretched town." She frowned at the memory. "Why don't you go to the office and ring the hotel? If he's registered, leave a message. Tell him you'll take the ten o'clock train tomorrow. Then maybe you'll be able to sleep."

He could have kissed her. "I'll do it at once," he said.

"I wish you didn't have to. You're exhausted. You haven't slept properly for days. But I understand, Varian." She met his eyes. "I do."

"Thank you," he said, and meant it.

"And maybe I'll go to Pamiers with you. Even though Killer won't like it."

"Thank you, Mary Jayne. With all my heart."

The long-distance operator had one of those Camarguesque accents that rendered her French almost unintelligible. She was not, Varian finally made out, able to reach any number on the Pamiers exchange due to a service interruption in the area; the telephone wires, he understood, had suffered severe damage in a recent bombing. Urgent messages could be sent by telegram. So he went to send a wire, buttoning his overcoat against the wind.

He had come to hate the telegraph office on the Canebière, with its pale green walls and high counters, its brass grates separating senders from operators like penitents from their confessors. So often he found himself in the position of a suppli-cant, asking someone in New York for more time or money, or begging his wife for patience. He hated the narrow little counters where messages were composed; he hated the too-blunt pencils and the too-small spaces on the forms. He hated waiting in line with all the other senders, their faces tight with uncertainty, each with his own private urgency. This afternoon he hated his mission even more than usual. He was guilty of persistent interest in his own matters in the midst of a war, guilty of in-vasive thinking about a single person when so many hundreds needed his attention. How not to sound desperate, how to compose an appropriate message? LIBERATED FROM SINAÏA. (Mere fact.) CAN HELP YOUR ENDEAVOR. (No further elucidation possible.) SEND WORD AIR BEL. Neat and clean, though what he wanted was to send a cry of fear and longing and explicit desire such as had never crossed a telegraph wire, such as would melt the wire on contact. He presented the message to the priest/confessor behind the grate, paid his four and a half francs, and made it back to the tram line and onto the last tram back to La Pomme, his mind near-blank, his sensations dulled, the darkening scene outside the window a welcome blur. Walking from the tram stop to Air Bel, he was half-aware, as if in the moment between sleep and waking, of passing through the tunnel beneath the tramway as if through a cave in some fairy story, a yawning aperture of chance that could consume or reconfigure. The plane trees along the lane were the legs of giants, Titans left over from the Roman occupation; the garden, silver-green in the wet Mediterranean winter, presented a forbidding tangle of vines. But here was the house at last, here was the kitchen door. How grateful he was for the quiet of Air Bel, the kitchen clean and silent, the salon abandoned, the library darkened, the hallways empty, only a few lights burning behind closed bedroom doors. In his room, that whitewashed cell that gave onto the moonlit garden, Madame Nouguet had left a covered dish; he didn't care that the cassoulet was cold, nor that it was made with potatoes and turnips instead of sausage, nor that the hunk of bread at its side had ossified; he ate everything and drank the glass of Bordeaux. Blind with exhaustion, he went into the bathroom, stripped off his clothes, bathed; then, already dreaming, he staggered to bed and slept.

It was seven a.m. when the messenger's bell woke him. He half-fell out of bed in his haste to get to the window. There was Gussie on his green Motobécane, making his way up the drive. Gussie went to the kitchen door and rang; a moment later, Varian could hear Madame Nouguet scolding him for making so much noise at that hour. By the time

Varian made it to the kitchen, wearing only his dressing gown and slippers, Gussie had disappeared. Madame Nouguet regarded Varian's ensemble and blushed to the roots of her hair as she held out the telegram. She excused herself hastily, claiming duties in the laundry. Varian stood at the window and tore open the envelope.

THANK GOD YOU ARE SAFE. FEARED YOUR DEPORTATION POINTS WEST. ARRIVED PAMIERS MONDAY. PROGRESS UNCERTAIN. AID WELCOME. TD. GRANT.

TD: their old double entendre. **Te desideravi.** I've missed you, I've wanted you. How it stopped his heart to see it on the page. He might as well go down to the bazaar and have it tattooed upon his chest; it was, in abridged form, the story of his last twelve years. He stood for a long moment looking down into the fog-choked valley, where ravens wheeled in and out of low shreds of cloud.

There was only one course of action now: get to Pamiers as soon as possible, and Mary Jayne with him. She had intimated it, he thought as he ran up the stairs; she had intimated that she might reward his patience. In his room he filled a small suitcase with pressed shirts and folded slacks and neatly squared-off underclothes. He went downstairs and found a crust of bread and some cheese for breakfast, and washed it down with weak war-coffee. He had scarcely managed the last sip when Mary Jayne herself came down in a navy-blue Robert Piguet traveling suit, a trim leather suitcase in her hand. A single look revealed that she'd been crying.

"What's happened, Mary Jayne?"

She ignored the question. "Why are you sitting here drinking that swill? Don't we have a train to catch?"

"You're joining me, then!"

"Yes. Only because my dance card happens to be clear today."

"I don't know how to thank you."

"Don't. Thank Killer. Do you know what he's taken it into his head to do? Desert the Legionnaires. Toss away his false papers. Devote himself full-time to the black market. As if he won't end up straight in prison."

Varian looked up warily. "It sounds like you've quarreled."

"Oh, most awfully."

"I've had enough of that kid, Mary Jayne. I won't have him in this house any longer. I want you to tell him to get out, as soon as possible."

"Well, now, let's not exaggerate, as Lena would say. I do find him useful every now and again."

"Well, I wish you wouldn't!"

"I'm afraid there's nothing to be done about it. And we don't exactly have time to argue. That train leaves in an hour."

They caught the ten o'clock local to Pamiers just as it was leaving the station; they chased it halfway down the platform and leapt onto the step of a passenger car. The conductor assumed their haste to be of a romantic nature, and led them down to an enclosed compartment. Once they'd caught their breath and lost it again, smoking a series of Mary Jayne's gold-tipped cigarettes, they began to speak about Zilberman's idea, the traveling portfolio of threatened artists' work. Mary Jayne was of the opinion that Ingrid Warburg and Alfred Barr, well connected though they were, represented too small a scope for the Flight Portfolio. "We have to recruit Peg," she said, meaning Peggy Guggenheim, who had already pledged two hundred thousand francs to the Centre Américain de Secours, thanks to Mary Jayne's influence. "She'll soon be closing her museum at Grenoble, and she'll want a new pet project."

"But Peggy's not likely to return to the States anytime soon," Varian said. "What we need is someone on the ground, someone who can champion the cause. Not just at the higher level, like Ingrid and Alfred, but in the trenches."

"What about your wife?" Mary Jayne said. "Who could better understand how dire the situation is? Do you think she'd have the inclination?"

Varian turned to the scene at the window: sheer

hills, green winter shoots pushing through the gold lion fur of late fall. "I'm afraid Eileen's lost patience with my work," he said. "She'd just ask why I don't come home and raise the money myself. The ERC has someone they're planning to send to replace me, she says. She hopes I'll capitulate. She tells me she believes I can do just as much good, if not more, from our offices on Forty-Second Street. But I'd rather stay and join the Foreign Legion than go home to prattle around a watercooler with those shortsighted nincompoops."

"Well, they **are** still paying your salary," Mary Jayne said, and laughed. "But I can't blame you. It's good to be doing something. I've always lived a little at a distance from my life—I don't know how to explain it any other way. But now there's no distance."

It was just what he'd felt: that here in France, the distance between what he believed and what he did had vanished to nothing. And out of that gravitational collapse had come a new life. Impossible to go home and be the same person. But who **would** he be, if he ever went home? He put his head against the windowpane and closed his eyes, letting the noise of the train drown the clamor of that question.

What seemed like moments later they arrived at the foot of Pamiers, a medieval fortress on a slope; in the distance, beneath a string of lenticular clouds, the toothy blue-white ridge of the Pyrenees. And here was the station, with its striped awnings and its rosemary in terra-cotta pots, its vendor's cart with magazines and cigarettes and apples. They stepped onto the platform and walked down into a little plaza, where a café spread its bug-legged tables across a span of cobblestones. The tables were nearly full. He had to admire a national character that mandated attendance at cafés even in the absence of coffee or pastries. The patrons appeared to be drinking wine (diluted), eating scant rations of bread with oily margarine, and reading news (likely bad) or novels (who knew?). Mary Jayne threw a longing glance toward that familiar scene.

"We've got to get to the hotel," Varian said.

"Oh, all right, I suppose we'd better, after rushing here."

At the reception desk of the Hôtel Platanes, a clerk in a crisp blue hat informed them that Monsieur Grant was out now, but had left a message for Monsieur Fry: he could be found at the bookshop on the rue de la République, or at the café across the street. Perhaps Mademoiselle and Monsieur would like to ascend to their rooms and make themselves comfortable? The entrance to the hotel restaurant was located in the courtyard, if Mademoiselle and Monsieur required refreshment.

Mademoiselle and Monsieur ascended to their rooms and left their things. Minutes later they were out on the street again, walking a narrow channel of daylight between white-shuttered buildings of pink brick and stone. The concierge had drawn a little map for them, and Varian followed it at a pace that made Mary Jayne beg mercy, indicating her glossy shoes. At last they reached the bookshop, a dingy establishment with a great bay window, where, between dust-flocked editions of Rousseau and Descartes, a tortoiseshell cat lay in a pond of sun, licking the webs between its toes.

"Revolting," said Mary Jayne. But Varian made out Grant's silhouette between the ceiling-high bookshelves, and could spare attention for nothing else. Grant looked up from his book—he must have sensed a change of light at the window—and raised one long-fingered hand, a wash of relief breaking over his features.

What further inducement did Varian need? He might have stepped through the plate-glass window and felt no pain at all. But the door sufficed. In another moment they were face-to-face again.

"Thank God you've come," Grant said. "I fear I've made an awful mess of things already." And then to Mary Jayne, who stepped gingerly around the towers of books, looking askance at the cat: "To what do we owe the pleasure?"

Mary Jayne collected herself and rearranged her navy-blue jacket. "I'm to be the bait," she said, simply.

Grant flushed with apparent embarrassment, but

Mary Jayne took no notice. "I don't know about the two of you," she said, "but I've got to have a drink. Is that place across the street anything to speak of?"

"They've got alcoholic beverages, if that's what you mean," Grant said. "I'm already too familiar with their menu, but I suspect it's no different anywhere else."

"Let's go, then."

"All right. Let me just buy this."

Varian looked down at the book in Grant's hand: a slim new edition of **Le faune de marbre,** Faulkner's early poems translated into French. And again he experienced that strange folding of time, a jolt of electric energy as the past rejoined the present: They'd read that book aloud to each other on the banks of the Charles, lying on a plaid wool blanket, passing a silver flask between them. When thunder sounded, they ran indoors and left the book among the red-gold trash of autumn leaves; the storm ruined it, and Varian had never replaced it. Now here it was again, in Grant's hand. Grant approached the counter, paid the gamine perched on a stool, and accepted the girl's ministrations: the wrapping of the book in Florentine paper, the embellishment of the package with a thin gold cord. The girl delivered the package into Grant's hands, and Grant, without a word, put it into Varian's.

At the bar across the street, they learned how Grant had come to be in Pamiers. Harry Bingham had invited Robinet for drinks; in the course of their conversation, he had gotten the inspector to confirm the current whereabouts of the young man, who was using the pseudonym of Teitelbaum. Bingham had passed along the information to Grant, and Grant, not knowing how long Varian might be imprisoned on the **Sinaïa,** had found himself unable to wait. He'd visited the camp three times by now. The first time he hadn't made it past the front gate; the second he'd been made to wait in the camp's administrative offices until the administrators left for the day; the third time he'd been told he could have an audience with Commandant Ormond, but before he entered the commandant's office he'd been seized by the fear that, merely by virtue of asking for the boy, he would reveal how important he was, how delicate his case. In the end he'd fled without making his petition.

"I was a fool to try," he said, looking down into his drink. "I've been watching you at this for months now, Varian, and have learned essentially nothing."

"Tobias's case isn't like the others," Varian said.

"No case is like any other. And yet somehow you manage to know what to do."

"I'm not sure I have any idea how to proceed now. But we do have Mary Jayne."

"It's rather straightforward, as I see it," Mary Jayne said, leaning back into their velvet-upholstered booth. "Ormond failed to consummate our rendezvous last time. He wouldn't even see me alone at the hotel. I'll merely tell him I've been tormented ever since. I'll ask if he'd think me entirely **débauchée** for proposing another meeting. I'll claim there's no other way to quell the fire in my heart. Oh, and then I'll mention that there's a small matter I want to discuss—the fate of another prisoner, just a boy, really, who deserves compassion. Then we'll wait," she said, rubbing her hands together. "We'll have to trust his memory of the scent of Chanel No. 5."

"And then?" Varian said.

"Then we'll dine together and I'll lay out my demands."

Grant shifted uneasily in his chair. "And afterward," he said. "What if the commandant . . . behaves inappropriately?"

"Well, isn't that what we're hoping?"

"I mean, what if he tries to hurt you in some way?"

"I guess you can leave that up to me."

"Really, though—"

"Really, though, I'm a grown woman. And the commandant is rather timid in matters of the heart, if last time was any indication."

Grant drew his shoulders together and leaned forward, elbows on the table. He seemed ready to say something more. Instead he flagged the waiter and asked for a stronger drink. Varian watched him closely. His forehead, usually smooth, was striated with narrow lines; he set his cup on the table and began to bother the cuticle of one thumb with the nail of the other. Certainly there was much about this to make him uncomfortable. Did he worry, among other things, that Mary Jayne's plan might in fact succeed, and that its success would mean that he, Grant, would have to assume full responsibility for Tobias Katznelson? A fugitive from Vichy, a fugitive from Nazi military intelligence, a physics genius, disciple of Max Planck, whose brain contained dangerous ideas? What did a prodigy eat for breakfast? What did he do for exercise? Would he make trouble? Could he be trusted with secrets? And where, under their current circumstances, could he be housed? There were no easy answers to these questions, a point Varian might have made to Grant if Grant had waited for Varian's release from the **Sinaïa** before he'd rushed to Vernet. But he hadn't, and here they were. And Varian suspected there was no time for delay if they meant to save their young man.

"All right," Varian said now. "Let's say we get Tobias out. How do we get him back to Marseille? The trains are policed. We can't take a car because there's no petrol. It would take about two weeks to walk."

"What about the Feuchtwanger method?" Mary Jayne said. "Dress him in my clothes?"

"That would be brilliant if you were several sizes larger, or Tobias several sizes smaller. But even if he were in drag, he'd have to have travel documents."

"I'll admit, I hadn't considered that," Grant said. He pressed his temples with his fingers.

"Maybe Lena could send something up on the train with Gussie," Mary Jayne said.

"Possible," said Varian. "But we'd still need a photo."

"Photos can be got," Mary Jayne said. "Get a passport and a faux safe conduct sent, and we'll work out the rest."

Grant's eyes had filled with tears, to Varian's surprise. "It's very kind of you both," he said. "Mary Jayne—you don't know what this'll mean to his father. Gregor's alone in New York, utterly alone. If Tobias can be with him—" He put a hand to his eyes, eliciting in Varian an unconscionable spur of jealousy.

"All right, Mary Jayne," he said. "Write to Ormond. We've got to get this business finished and get back to Marseille."

The commandant must have been overcome with regret at his failure to meet Mary Jayne at her hotel on her previous visit. He replied that he would be delighted—beyond delighted, transported—to meet her at the hotel restaurant for dinner that very evening, and would gladly discuss any of his charges with her; he made no mention of the fact that her last four concernees had slipped their guards during their furlough in Marseille and had only been returned to Vernet after their near-escape on the **Bouline.** Grant and Varian would dine at the same hour, though not at the same table, and would be witnesses to the conversation. In Varian's hotel room, half an hour before the rendezvous, Varian coached Mary Jayne to intimate nothing of the prisoner's significance, only that young Teitelbaum was dear to his father and that he must be returned to him, and that he'd been sent to Vernet by mistake, due to an administrative gaffe at the Préfecture. She must make no mention, of course, of the Nazis' interest in the prisoner. And above all, she must keep the conversation light; she must seem ready to give up her petition at any point, lest the commandant sense that he had something of real value.

"And yet, in return for this valueless boy, I'm to offer myself up?"

"As I understand it, you're irrepressibly attracted to the commandant."

"But in—in that event, he'd have to understand there was a quid pro quo."

"I trust you'll know how to play it," Varian said.

"All right," she said. "And now, unless the commandant plans to stand me up again, I'd better get downstairs to meet him."

"Go ahead. We'll be right behind you."

"For God's sake, I hope you won't make that serious face at me all evening!"

"We'll be invisible," Varian said. "You won't even notice us."

There must have been a thriving black market in Pamiers, or perhaps the local farmers had done a better-than-usual job of concealing cows and game and crops. Whatever the reason, the larders at Au Fond du Platanes produced a spread unlike any Varian had seen for months. The waiter offered hot fresh knots of bread with curls of clandestine butter. A rémoulade of root vegetables followed, then a dense pork stew flavored with thyme. Grant and Varian sat, as promised, just behind the table where Mary Jayne was dining with the commandant. Varian had a half-view of the commandant's face, obscured in part by Mary Jayne's head. Ormond was a neat, dark-haired fellow with a boyish dimple and a shy smile; he looked more like a Parisian library attendant than the director of a concentration camp. His uniform had been threatened into a state of crisp perfection, though his pomade must have been imperfect: a heavy lock of hair kept falling forward into his eyes, and he kept smoothing it back with a nervous gesture. The conversation, insofar as Varian could follow it over the noise of the restaurant, mainly concerned the four prisoners whose liberation Mary Jayne had accomplished some months before.

"When I received your note yesterday," the commandant was saying, "I thought you were here to make another petition for the escapees' release. I can assure you, dear Miss Gold, that would be futile. I'm still quite angry about what happened last time, you know. I ought to punish you." He showed the boyish dimple and flirtatiously corrected the errant lock. He'd spoken in a manner that might have been called caressing, though his tone evoked a shiver of distaste in Varian: he thought of the glide of an earthworm against a hand thrust into loose soil.

"If you think I had anything to do with that business about the **Bouline,** you're mistaken," Mary Jayne said. "I'm a woman of my word. One could rather blame your guards for relaxing their vigilance. I heard they made a shameful scene at a brothel the night your escapees were boarding their boat."

The commandant coughed and looked down into his soup. "Suffice it to say your friends are more carefully guarded now," he said. "And I will have you know that, in deference to you, I withheld harsh discipline, though it would have been my right to teach them a lesson."

"Oh—" said Mary Jayne: an inward breath of pleasure, as if he'd opened a jewelbox to reveal some reflective trinket. "In deference to me?"

"Perhaps I was hoping you'd come back for them," the commandant said in a lower voice, one that Varian had to strain to hear. "I wouldn't have wanted you to find them mistreated. Perhaps I've saved all my discipline for you."

Mary Jayne answered in a tone that fell beneath the clamor of the restaurant. In response to Grant's raised eyebrow, Varian gave a minuscule nod.

". . . a different request," she was saying now, brushing a pale gold curl behind her ear. "One of a more personal nature."

"Your Berlinese friend."

"Oh, it's really his father who's my friend. A former professor of mine, actually. Teitelbaum taught me all I know about eighteenth-century German verse."

"Is that so? I'm afraid I wasn't much of a student myself. I was always too much interested in matters outside the curriculum." The smooth young commandant's hand fell upon Mary Jayne's, and she allowed her hand to be enclosed and stroked.

"A good professor engages even the most incorrigible student," Mary Jayne said.

"I'm sure you're right, Miss Gold."

"Anyway, you understand it's all a . . ." And then the waiter escorted a torpid troupe of walruslike diners through the space between the two tables, and the connection was cut momentarily. Grant drummed the table with his long fingers. He wanted to light a cigarette, Varian knew, but couldn't risk becoming distracted.

". . . though I know it may be impossible," they heard Mary Jane saying, as the last of the walruses passed. She looked down in what seemed to be shy supplication.

"Under the right circumstances all things are possible," the commandant said, then leaned forward, still holding her hand, to make an inaudible addendum. Mary Jayne sat back slightly in her chair and patted her mouth with her napkin. An instantaneous flick of her gaze toward Varian: affirmation, confirmation?

"It looks like our friends are finished," Varian said, under his breath. The commandant had called for the bill and was settling it, and in another minute he rose with Mary Jayne and steered her by the waist toward the restaurant door. His thumb, Varian saw, had entered the keyhole aperture just above her waistline; that tease built into the dress had found its ideal application. Mary Jayne hadn't risked meeting Varian's or Grant's eye again. Now they could only watch as she glided through the door under the commandant's guidance and disappeared down the corridor.

Grant sat back in his chair. "What do you think?"

"She appears to know what she's doing," Varian said. "She looks to have him entirely under her control, and to have convinced him that the reverse is true."

With a sigh, Grant sat back in his chair and lit a cigarette. "I don't want to think about it," he said. "Let's talk about something else."

"All right. Suppose I tell you how I ended up on a prison ship."

"Yes, suppose you do."

"As I understand it, we were all suspected of being communists. We might have been a danger to the Maréchal."

"Yes, but why a ship?"

"Because it had room for all of us, I guess." Varian reached for one of Grant's cigarettes and lit it. Caution forbade him from saying what he wanted to say next, but he supposed he had long since heaved caution overboard. "Funny thing, though," he said. "I'd been on that boat before."

"Oh?"

"It was the one I sailed on to Europe after you left Maine."

"I didn't know you went to Europe that summer."

"Of course you didn't. And I don't know what you did, either."

Grant crushed his cigarette into the crystal ashtray. "I scarcely remember," he said. "Tried to kill myself, I suppose."

"Tried to kill yourself? What do you mean?"

Grant sighed and turned his eyes upward. "I promised myself I'd never tell you."

"Well, now you've got to."

"I don't know how it began," Grant said. "Maybe I just wanted to get out of the house. I was living at home, basically living with my head under a stone. But eventually my mother pestered me out of the house. If I wasn't going to go to school, she said, then I'd better get a job. I didn't want a job. I didn't want anything. But I put on a suit and took a train to New York and went down into a subway station. Just watched the trains go by, one after the other. After a while, I don't know why, I took it in mind to walk into the tunnel where it got dark and just lie down between the rails. No one saw me do it. I lay down on the gravel between the tracks and waited. I didn't know what would happen. I suppose I thought I might be crushed or horribly injured, and that whatever happened would be better than the way I'd been feeling. In any case, I lay there and waited. And eventually a train came."

Varian had forgotten all about his cigarette. The ash had fallen onto the tablecloth in a peppery heap. **"And . . . ?"**

"There was a terrific roar. And a terrible heat. It went on and on. I thought it would never stop. The worst thing was the smell of it, the smell of burning brakes so close to my nose and mouth."

"And nothing hurt you, nothing touched you?"

"Not that time."

"Not **that time**? You mean to say you did it again?"

"And again and again."

"Grant."

"I kept count. I did it eighteen times."

"For God's sake!"

"I didn't want to live. Truly, I wanted to die. I

begged God, though I didn't even believe in him, for some low-hanging bit of metal to put me out of my misery."

"And you survived unscathed. Eighteen times!"

"Not quite unscathed. You've seen the scar." The fine pale line that ran from his shoulder to his waist. "I'll never know what did it," he said. "Whatever it was, it sliced me like a razor blade. Took seventy-two silk stitches. My mother was beside herself. I thought **she'd** have to be hospitalized. In the end she pulled herself together and made me apply for a transfer to Yale."

Varian shook his head. "You might have been killed."

"That was precisely the point."

Of course, of course, he'd been doing the same thing: hanging over the rail of the **Sinaïa** and looking at the sea, wishing for the courage to slip over the edge and be swallowed whole. What had stopped him? The thought that he might return to Cambridge and find that it had all been a bad dream. And then, of course, guiltily, there was Eileen. The memory of their cold damp encounter on the island had taken on a certain heat in his memory. That was the difference: he could still imagine a life in which she figured, a life not unlike the one she was trying to return him to now.

"A terrible thing happened after I came back," Varian said. "A thing I haven't thought about in years." And what had made him think of it now? What compelled him to tell?

"Does it require a drink?" Grant asked. "I know I need one."

They flagged the waiter and asked for Armagnac. When it came, Varian and Grant raised their glasses and drank.

"I'm not sure I can tell this story," Varian said.

"I told mine," Grant said.

"This one's worse."

Grant lifted his haze-colored eyes to Varian's. They reminded him, Varian thought, of those mist-clouded paths through the woods down which you felt compelled to walk, though you knew there might be wolves and bears and God knew what else.

"All right, then," Varian said, and told his story. He still remembered every detail, and would until the day he died: it had happened a couple of months after his return, after he'd had to accept and inhabit a new reality that did not include Grant. Everything else went on: his classes, the burning in his gut, the parties at Kirstein's, the **Hound and Horn,** the flirtation with Eileen, which had progressed into something that resembled a courtship, or at least a pleasurable affair, insofar as he was capable of feeling pleasure. Nights at the symphony, dinners on the waterfront, wit- and gin-soaked parties at the homes of her **Atlantic** colleagues. Sometimes on a sunny afternoon, when he was done with class and she felt like shirking her editorial duties, they would take a country drive in the Packard.

This was one of those days, a mild November day still bright and gold, though the leaves had fallen and the air had the sharp dry scent of early winter. She had a fancy to go out to Walden Pond, where a year earlier she'd seen a magnificent owl. She could remember, she said, exactly where the nest was: in a forked elm at the far end of the pond, not fifty yards from where Thoreau had built his cabin. They drove out along the two-lane road that extended from the northwest corner of Cambridge. They passed through Arlington and Lexington, each with its tidy Main Street and its storybookish wood-framed houses set on hills, and into the forested countryside beyond. The yellow Packard had been a gift from Varian's father. Massive, gleaming, polished weekly and kept full of gas by the boy at the garage where Varian stabled it, the car was like a land-bound yacht, every detail perfectly suited to its purpose, the whole package meant to communicate its owner's power and privilege. The engine loved speed. Forty, fifty, sixty miles an hour were nothing to the Packard. At sixty-five the pistons would settle into a baritone hum and the wind would pass over the hood as silently as over an owl's wing. Eileen adored riding at that speed. She rolled her window down to feel the wind, singing "Get Out and Get Under the Moon." Frost needled the windscreen; the verges of the woods burned with fallen leaves.

At times, circumstances conspire to make us believe the lies we tell ourselves. Everything—the weather, the season, the fall of light—sets the stage for our play; we find ourselves, instead of acting, becoming the characters, moving into a reality in which we're inseparable from our roles. Here he was, future husband of Eileen Avery Hughes, owner of this powerful machine, capable of mastering its eighty-one horses. And not only that: He had mastered Catullus. He had mastered Sophocles and Heraclitus and Diogenes, their various means for describing that accident of nature: human self-awareness, perception of a bafflingly complex world. He'd prepared himself, by looking backward, for a forward-looking life, one in which the baffling complexity would lay itself bare for his solving. He was full of his own power, full of it as if it were his blood.

He felt the tires shudder and knew he was going too fast, but he kept his foot on the accelerator. He could feel the power of the car through the sole of his foot, feel the beautiful communication between himself and the motor: he was an injector of power, a feeder of fuel, an initiator of the minute explosions that blurred into the engine's purr. In fact he closed his eyes for a moment, an instant, just long enough to shut himself within that power for a few heartbeats, to let the car extend its force into his body, to feel it almost as an externalized organ, a great, beating, pulsing, roaring heart. That was the moment it began, the strange sensation of lifting, of floating across the pavement. Oil, ice, both: he would never know. He swallowed a fine spike of fear, and then he was gripping the wheel, gripping it too hard, pulling the tires sideways slightly, just enough to make the car skate across the dividing line, toward the black shape of an oncoming Ford. The black Ford dodged toward the shoulder to avoid the Packard. Then, from the other side of the road, a dull clap of impact and the shriek and pull of rubber.

Eileen did not scream. She would never have screamed at a moment like that. Hands braced against the dash, she breathed out hard and said, "Stop the car, stop the car!" He pulled to the side of the road. In an instant she was out and running to see what had happened. Varian followed. Across the road, the black Ford sat still on the gravel shoulder. In it was a woman sitting behind the wheel with her hand over her mouth; she was making a noise, a series of soft **Oh**'s almost inaudible through the glass. Beyond the car, on the ground, lay the curled form of a man.

Eileen knelt in the long grass beside the man, a day laborer dressed in denim and woolens. No trace of blood on his face or clothes. Eyes closed, mouth slightly open. Beside him lay his tin lunch pail, crushed flat. Eileen lifted a hand and extended it over the man as if she were determining where or how to touch him to bring him back to life. And then, as if by some miracle, the man opened his eyes, raised himself onto an elbow, braced a palm against the grass. He blinked, rubbed gravel from his sparse red beard, squinted at Eileen and Varian, and got to his knees, then to his feet, holding the crushed lunch pail, seeming not to notice anything amiss about it. He glanced from Varian to Eileen as if they were distant relatives whose names he had forgotten. His forehead compressed itself into three inquisitive lines.

"Are you all right?" Eileen asked. "You took quite a blow."

The man fixed his eyes on Eileen and gave a vague smile. Then he shook his head as if to clear it of a bad dream. Holding the crushed lunch pail, he took an unsteady step through the long grass. He took another and another, until he'd attained the gravel shoulder. For twenty yards, as Varian and Eileen watched in silence, the man put one foot in front of another and did not falter. The door of the black Ford opened and the woman who'd been driving it climbed out, watching in amazement.

"Look at him," she said. "There he goes. Look at him. He's all right, praise God." Her mouth trembled, and she covered it with a thin-boned hand.

And then, as if he'd been shot by a silent gun, the man went down heavy and limp into the roadside leaves. He went down and did not get up again. He lived for another five days before, in the acute injury ward of Arlington Hospital, he suffered a massive cerebral hemorrhage and died.

Grant now sat looking at Varian from across the table. "And then?" he said. "What did you do then? What happened to you?"

"Nothing," Varian said. "I called my father. I told him what had happened. He said nothing for a long time, and then he said he'd call his lawyer."

"And what did you do?"

"I let him call his lawyer. The lawyer did his job. Eventually I had to pay a fine. A ticket. Misdemeanor reckless operation of a motor vehicle. The other driver, the one who'd hit the man, was found to have been driving with a cracked axle and a pair of front tires worn down to the canvas. She lost her license and avoided jail time by paying a hundred dollars. The boy's family was in Ireland. There wasn't much they could do. I lost a lot of sleep over it, a lot. I thought about going to the judge and arguing my own guilt. I thought I deserved to be put away, though Eileen believed me to be innocent. But of course I didn't **want** to go to jail. I didn't want to be guilty of a crime. I wanted to go back to the lecture hall and the seminar room and Widener. In the end, that was what it came down to. If I'd gone to prison, I would have lost any chance to have the life I'd imagined. I wanted to prove to Eileen that I was the kind of man who could make a problem like this, a problem of mortal magnitude, go away. That I came from a family rich and well connected enough. That I had enough strength of mind—that was how I thought of it—to bear the complication of what had happened without allowing my life to fall to pieces. And it turns out that was what she wanted, too."

"And then?"

"And then, I don't know. Time passed. We never talked about it. It sort of—went away, I guess, though that's not really accurate." Varian tilted the Armagnac glass in his fingers, sank his thumbs into the depression at its base. Through the windows of the restaurant they could see a man lighting a gas lamp in the courtyard. "You see," Varian said, looking Grant in the eyes again, following that forest path into who knew where, "I like to think of myself as occupying a position of moral superiority, but in fact I've been inhabiting a series of rather comfortable lies. And that one—the lie of my innocence in the death of that young man—is hardly the chief one."

Grant shook his head. "Now, Varian," he said.

Varian lowered his voice, though at that moment he hardly cared who might hear him. "I lied to Eileen. I did. I pretended what I'd felt for you was a kind of schoolboy folly, a puerile passion. She knew I was—that I sought out friends downtown, but she thought it was a harmless perversion, even somehow attractive. Titillatingly risqué. A mark of culture. The province of artists and writers. She'd come of age in the twenties, remember, and was raised by a bluestocking mother who let her bob her hair and wear trousers and become an editor at a nationally recognized magazine, with no admonition against appearing as intelligent as she really was. As for our arrangement, as she called it—she was allowed to take liberties too, with whomever she liked, though she didn't often exercise the privilege—it was really a way of rendering my situation harmless. We both wanted to think it was harmless. And she wants to believe that still. I've mentioned you in a number of letters now, and still she's never asked about you. She must want to believe it's nothing, or maybe that it'll just go away. But she's scared. I know it, Grant. She's been trying to get me home, even trying to turn them against me in New York. Trying to get someone sent to replace me."

"Well," Grant said, almost inaudibly. The noises of the restaurant—silverware, glass, conversation—made a kind of veil around them. "Well," he said. "And what do **you** want?"

"I want to stay and do my work."

"Then stay and do it, Varian. Tomorrow, perhaps, we'll go to Vernet and see what can be done about Tobias. Then you've got to get back to Marseille." And he raised his hand for the check, and an instant later he was paying it. Then they were rising together like Chagallian brides, rising from their chairs, making their way through the walrus song and the china clink of the restaurant, toward the doors through which Mary Jayne had disappeared with the commandant.

20

Camp du Vernet

By the time he woke the next morning—naked and warm in Grant's bed, the down coverlet a shell against the chill—Grant had gotten up and bathed and dressed, and was sitting at the desk with a newspaper, one long leg crossed over the other.

Varian sat up in bed. "What time is it?"

"A quarter to nine," Grant said. "I've been downstairs already."

"Any sign of Mary Jayne?"

"None."

Varian got up and dressed, then went to his own room and bathed and shaved and dressed again. Mary Jayne was a late riser; she might not appear before eleven. But he and Grant must go down and wait for her, for whatever news she might deliver. They met in the restaurant and sat over cups of the **café national,** which, Varian noted with some surprise, had ceased to seem offensive, so distant a memory was the genuine article. The newspaper narrated a failed plot by the vice-premier, Pierre Laval, to oust Pétain and set up a government of his own; Laval had envisioned ruling from Paris, under the Nazi flag, and leading a grand charge against Great Britain. Reichsführer Hitler had expressed his approval of Pétain's decision to remove Laval, calling Pétain a more apt collaborator. The article induced a headache by the time Varian had reached the end of the first column.

At ten o'clock the restaurant door swung open and in came Mary Jayne, dressed in a caramel-colored herringbone suit with nacreous buttons. A froth of white pleats spilled from her collar; her shoes reflected the restaurant's polished brass. Her hair was sleek and neatly curled, her makeup a paler version of the previous night's. On her lips, a carefully composed smile. Grant rose to pull out a chair for her, and she winced as she lowered herself into it. Her mouth trembled slightly as she reached for the menu. Varian and Grant sat in silence, trying to read her.

"Well, gentlemen," she said, in a low, taut-strung tone.

"Well," Varian said.

She raised her eyes to them, and the look there was terrible: injured, triumphant, raw. "If the commandant's a man of his word," she said, "we'll be on the train with your protégé by nightfall." She lowered her eyes and made a subtle amendment to her white pleats.

"Mary Jayne," Grant said, covering her hand with his own. "Are you all right?"

She shifted in her seat. A muscle contracted at the corner of her mouth. "I achieved my goal," she said. "That was what I wanted. The commandant—" She paused and drew a long breath. "The commandant's tastes weren't particularly surprising."

"**Mary Jayne.** I'm asking you. Are you all right?"

"As long as we get out of here with that boy, I'll be fine," she said, studying the menu.

Varian put his hands together as if in prayer, resting his chin on his thumbs. He had led her into all this, had made her do whatever it was she'd done. He'd known she still felt contrite about Feuchtwanger, he'd known she wanted to prove she wasn't a dilettante. He'd asked for her help, knowing she was vulnerable. "Mary Jayne," he said. "Do you need anything? A doctor, or—?"

Mary Jayne shook her head twice, briskly. Whatever price Ormond had extracted, they weren't going to discuss it. "The commandant said he'd like to reexamine Tobias's file," she went on in the same carefully controlled tone. "Then he'll meet with the lieutenant who oversees his section. He suggested we pay the camp a visit around noon. We're to present this at the gate." She drew a white card from the breast pocket of her suit and tossed it onto the table; it bore the commandant's name, rank, and posting.

Grant picked up the card. "Mary Jayne. I don't know what to say."

Mary Jayne shrugged. "No need to say anything," she said. When the waiter came, she ordered breakfast in a reasonable facsimile of her ordinary voice; when her tea and toast arrived, she made all the motions of pouring and sweetening and spreading. If she left the toast untouched, if she looked abstractedly at the newspaper without seeming to read what was printed there, it was clear they were not to comment upon any of it. And when, after a time, she got up to leave, they both rose with her wordlessly, letting her pass between them like a queen parting pawns.

They approached the camp on foot, a long walk in the raw cold wind. This was not the mild coastal winter they'd grown accustomed to in Marseille; icy clouds lay in broken planes across the milk-blue mountains, and low stunted trees shook their skeletal arms at the sky. The wildlife had all migrated or gone underground, or nearly all: a few talkative crows followed the travelers' progress along the ill-paved road. Ice had gathered where the pavement was fractured, and rocks of various sizes had rolled down the hillside to litter the roadway. For a time the travelers walked shoulder to shoulder, but a series of passing military vehicles kept edging them to the side. Finally they fell into single file, Grant ahead, Mary Jayne in the middle, Varian last. They said little on the road. Mary Jayne walked slowly, as if every step pained her. Varian had tried to convince her to stay behind, but she insisted that her presence was essential. She continued uncomplaining in the bitter cold, and when they reached the giant rolls of barbed wire that surrounded the camp, she threw her head back, adjusted the angle of her hat, and said, "Here we are."

Before them rose a three-layered fence the length of a city block, crowned and intertwined with barbed wire. At its corners were squat brick guard towers, and through the chain link they could see rows of tin-roofed barracks arrayed on a broad expanse of frozen mud. They walked toward a low tin-sided guardhouse; at its apex, a plume of smoke rose from a zinc chimney, its stem painted white, its funnel red with white dots, like a fairy-tale mushroom. Whose idea of a joke was that? As they approached, the guardhouse discharged a broad-shouldered, square-headed guard in military uniform.

"State your business," he said, and coughed emphatically into his fist.

"We're here to see Commandant Ormond," Mary Jayne said, handing him the card. "Please tell him Miss Gold and her associates have come to call."

The guard squinted at the card. "What business do you have here?"

Mary Jayne squared her shoulders. "We have an appointment at noon. We'll discuss our business with the commandant."

Her voice had brought a sub-guard out of the guardhouse, a short-legged person in thick spectacles who goggled at her, mouth open, until his superior shouted him to attention.

"Officer Poulenc!" the blocky guard said. "Look sharp. Take these visitors to headquarters."

The short-legged fellow gave a sharp salute to his superior, a half-bow to Mary Jayne, and a nod apiece to Grant and Varian. Then he conducted the travelers forward over a dirt path of jagged clods, through a gate embellished with the camp's name in a festive-looking typography, as if this were a summer resort. He marched them through rows of gray-walled barracks, past open latrines filled with excrement, past guard posts decorated with broken glass, past rows of men digging at the frozen clods with pickaxes in a parade ground—men dressed not in prisoners' garb but in their own torn and dirty clothes, men who looked at them with sharp inquisitive eyes, with activated attention, as if the prisoners could sense at once the aura of the United States that surrounded these visitors. There was no sign of Tobias anywhere, nor of the four whom Mary Jayne had liberated before.

The commandant's headquarters lay at the opposite

end of the camp, near the west-facing entrance. In an anteroom sat four gray functionaries, each at his own steel desk, and a receptionist, also gray, businesslike, with a look of grim forbearance that may have come from being the only woman in the place. She thanked their guard escort and looked them over slowly, reserving special scrutiny for Mary Jayne and her herringbone suit, her pleated white shirt, her suede handbag with its gold trefoil clasp. Mary Jayne consulted her watch and insisted that they be announced to Commandant Ormond at once.

Moments later, Ormond himself stepped from a shadowy hallway beyond the anteroom and dismissed the gray functionary with a look. He appraised Mary Jayne as she stood in the light from the office windows; her hand flew to her collar as if he'd parted the stiff white pleats with his gaze.

"Come in," he said, almost in a whisper. His command seemed to refer only to Mary Jayne, not to Varian and Grant, but Mary Jayne pretended not to notice; she put a hand on Varian's arm as if she expected to be escorted down the hall, and he complied. The commandant frowned. Varian could only hope that Mary Jayne knew her game.

Ormond motioned the three of them toward the chairs in front of his desk, which, like everything else in that building, were gray, sharp-edged, functional, and ugly. But Ormond's office betrayed its inhabitant's fantasy of himself as a man of letters:

the shelf behind his desk sagged under the weight of biographies and autobiographies of fascist despots, and alongside them were books about the struggles of France: Stendhal's **Le rouge et le noir,** Hugo's **Les misérables,** Zola's **Germinal.** Above the bookshelf hung a pair of crossed sabers hazed with dust, and on the desk itself stood a bronze inkstand, its inkpots empty, presided over by a tiny Napoleon on a rearing charger.

"Mademoiselle et messieurs," the commandant said in French, leaning over the desk to shake hands with Grant and Varian, raising a single eyebrow at Mary Jayne. "You've arrived on an unfortunate day. I've just received a reprimand for the slanderous reports on this camp made by Arthur Koestler, that odious Hungarian writer set free by the Ministry of the Interior last spring." Ormond touched a document on his desk, a letter on thick white stock surmounted by the Nazi spider. "You may be familiar with Koestler's screeds, which have found their way into print in a series of disreputable journals."

"Yes, I've read them with interest," Varian said.

Ormond raised an eyebrow at him, then turned back to the Nazi letter. "My superiors believe I was remiss in failing to bring about the writer's end during his captivity. They plan to judge for themselves the nature of my leadership here."

"But you're not a killer, Jean-Pierre," Mary Jayne said, in an intimate tone—though on their brief walk through the camp they'd seen plenty of evidence to the contrary. "It's unreasonable, deplorable, for anyone to demand that you become one."

Ormond regarded her from behind the steel slab of his desk, over its islands of papers and dossiers. "The Nazis, Miss Gold, are our masters now," he said, with some bitterness. "In fact there's no limit to what they can demand, deplorable or not."

Grant saw his aperture. "A Frenchman is no one's servant," he said. "Stendhal."

Ormond glanced back over his shoulder at the bookcase, as if the book itself had spoken. Then he narrowed his eyes at Grant, at Varian. "I run my camp to serve the greater good of France," he said. "And at the moment, whether we wish it to be true or not, our interests are knit up with Germany's. Our desires, our needs, are subject to theirs."

"Jean-Pierre," Mary Jayne said in the same penetrating, connective tone, "I'd like a word with you in private."

"I'm afraid I haven't time, Miss Gold, much as I would relish it. An inspector and his assistants will arrive in an hour to be given a personal tour of my operation."

Mary Jayne raised an eyebrow. "A brief interview will serve."

"I'm sure it would," Ormond said, with a look that made Mary Jayne curl her shoulders toward each other and clasp her bag against her chest. He rose and removed his military hat from its stand. "I'm afraid I must attend to certain matters before our guests arrive." He fixed his eyes on Mary Jayne and said, "If you and your friends will kindly wait by the front door of this building, a guard will arrive to escort you to the gate. I'd advise you to make your exit with some speed."

"Monsieur Commandant," Mary Jayne said. "Will you not at least—"

"Thank you for your visit, Miss Gold, Messieurs Fry and Grant."

He meant for them to stand. They stood. Grant threw a panicked look toward Varian, but there was nothing Varian could do. They could go back to the hotel in Pamiers, they could wait another day or two in the hope that the inspectors would depart and that Ormond might honor his promise to Mary Jayne then. Mary Jayne looked dazed, as though she'd discovered that the rifle she'd been holding in battle was a toy. She took Varian's arm, and he led her through the narrow door of the commandant's office.

"I wish you a pleasant return to Marseille," the commandant said, and put his heels together; the bow he gave them might have belonged to a ballroom and not a concentration camp. He smoothed his glossy dark hair once more, a gesture of closure. And then he shut the door behind them and left them in the corridor.

"Now what?" Grant said. "We can't just leave."

"We can't be here when the Gestapo arrives," Varian said, under his breath.

A set of gears seemed to have engaged in Mary Jayne's mind. She looked at the closed door as if she were still looking at Ormond. "I believe we should do as he said."

"What?"

"We should wait by the front door of this building."

"And let ourselves be escorted out?" Grant said. "Give up?"

"Yes." The color had returned to her features, and she gave her head a shake to arrange her hair. Then she started down the corridor, her shoes making their brisk report on the tile, past the gray functionaries at their steel furniture, past the stern secretary with her critical gaze. The three of them made their way back out into the December wind. A fleet of desiccated leaves blew from some unseen source toward the rolls of barbed wire at the margin of the camp; following the scrolls of leaves were scores of men, prisoners marching, guards leading and following them, rifles aloft. They were all headed, Varian guessed, to the parade ground they'd passed on the way in; the urgency of the guards' commands suggested something significant at stake. The official visitors, Varian thought: the men were to assemble to greet them. Only one person marched in the opposite direction, toward the commandant's headquarters: a tall guard in a high-collared jacket, his hat pulled low over his ears against the cold, a pair of reflective glasses shielding his eyes against the sun. In his arms was a bayoneted assault rifle, which, when he reached the headquarters, he used as a pointer to wave Varian and Grant and Mary Jayne away from the side of the building. Without a word, he directed them into a single-file line and began to hustle them toward the edge of the camp, past the last few groups of marching prisoners—not toward the exit they'd used before, but one on the opposite side. The camp seemed to have cleared toward its eastern edge; they met no prisoner, no other guard. As they approached the gateway, Varian saw that the guard post was empty, the door of the guardhouse standing open. He wondered for a moment at that lapse of security just before an official inspection. Their guard turned and stopped them with the rifle, holding it at chest level like a bar; he jerked it in the direction of the guardhouse, and they understood that he wanted them to enter. The building wasn't much larger than a phone booth. Did he intend to shoot them once they'd crowded inside? Grant entered first, and Varian stepped back against him. Mary Jayne wedged herself against Varian, her breath warm and quick on Varian's cheek. The guard paused for a moment before the open door.

"Sie haben es wahrscheinlich schon bemerkt," he said, in an undertone. **You must have guessed by now.** And then he took off his glasses and regarded them with his dark, myopic eyes.

It was Tobias Katznelson. The travelers stood in silence.

"Ich habe den Befehl erhalten, Sie nach Marseille zurück zu bringen," he said, and winked.

"You're to escort us all the way to Marseille?" Varian said.

Grant gave a single, gratified **ha.** "You, Tobias? You're our guard?"

"Das bin ich. Aber genug der Worte. Wir müssen aufbrechen."

There was no chance to discuss what had happened, no chance to congratulate Mary Jayne on the magic she had worked. She tilted her head at Varian and smiled.

Then Tobias Katznelson himself ushered them out of the guard booth and pushed them through the gates of the camp, and they began the long walk back to town by the back roads, a guard and his charges, the relationship between them instantly legible thanks to Katznelson's uniform, his boots, his inarguable gun, its bayonet a bright exclamation point in the winter light.

Varian would never forget the strangeness of that journey: traveling in a rail compartment with his lover and Mary Jayne, the door of the compartment guarded by the person they were supposed to have rescued—not a cowering boy, but the clever young man he'd met at the Préfecture, one who had risen to the occasion, who had winked in the face of danger, who had embraced the role of concentration camp guard and was playing it now to the full, despite—or perhaps because of—what he'd recently suffered. And who could begrudge him a little pleasure in it, after his time at Vernet? His cheekbones had a hollowed-out look, and his eyes, when he glanced into the compartment at his charges, betrayed his exhaustion. It was lucky, Varian thought, that he hadn't been at the camp longer; without a doubt they would have starved him to the point where his uniform would have been implausible, an empty sack on a wire rack. As it was, he filled it convincingly enough. Through the translucent door of their compartment they watched him polishing the blade of his weapon with a handkerchief. He hadn't been allowed any ammunition, of course; Ormond had never meant for him to have a live gun. But it was a weapon, no question. It was what made his costume convincing. No one had stopped them along the road, no one had checked their progress into the railway station, nor onto the train. They hadn't even had to buy tickets. When the conductor arrived, Tobias had merely waved him along without a word. Varian had no idea what the boy would do if he were required to speak; Tobias's French sounded as German as his German.

The three travelers passed a silver flask between them for courage: half a pint of gin, which Grant had cadged from the hotel bartender. Their conversation, conducted in whispers, concerned what they were to do with their charge once they reached Marseille. He could not be housed at the Medieval Pile; in fact, the Pile must be vacated altogether, lest anyone come looking for Tobias. Nor could he be lodged on his own at a hotel, where any interested party might apprehend him. The only place to house him, as far as Varian could determine, was Air Bel, though his presence might put others at risk. He would have to become one of the invisibles, like Zilberman: nameless and paperless, ready to disappear underground at a moment's notice, willing to pass long hours in a dank cellar if necessary, prepared to wait months for his visas, without any certainty of escape. And how would Tobias take to it, this young man who had fled Berlin and made his way down to the coast of France, where he'd been planning a run over the Pyrenees?

"There's nowhere to put him at Air Bel," Mary Jayne said. "Where is he supposed to sleep? On a library chair?"

"He'll take my room," Varian said.

"And you'll live where?"

Varian thought for a moment, silent. He knew he couldn't suffer another **Sinaïa** episode, couldn't allow himself to be imprisoned along with his clients if the police came to raid Air Bel. What he needed was to be in town, closer to the office. But he also wanted to be close to Grant, wherever Grant would go once he vacated the Pile.

"Haven't thought about it yet," he said, finally.

"You think on it," Mary Jayne said. "I'm going to take a walk, if our guard will let me." She slid open the compartment door and disappeared down the corridor, and Grant and Varian were alone for the first time since that morning, facing each other in the compartment. Grant's eyes grew serious and he leaned forward in his seat, arms on his knees.

"Listen, Tommie," he said. "About your plan. What are you thinking, exactly? We've both got to move out? Me from the Pile and you from the villa?"

"Yes," Varian said. "But I don't know where we can go." **We,** he'd said, as if by necessity they had to go together. "Look. What if we both took rooms in town, at one of the hotels on the Vieux Port? Get out from beneath everyone's scrutiny? I need to think about things."

"What things?"

"My life back in New York. Eileen."

"And you'll have more freedom to do that when we're living on the same hotel corridor?"

"I hear there's a fine bar at the Hôtel Beauvau. Nice view of the port. Maybe we can drink our way to clarity."

"You wish we were back at Gore."

"No," Varian said. "I certainly do not wish that." He looked through the window at the endless marshland passing by outside, its heavy-headed grasses bending toward their reflections in flat silver water. The train seemed almost to be hovering over the liquid surface, moving with a strange lightness at a near-impossible speed. "Soon you'll be returning to the States, now that you've got your man," he said.

They both glanced toward the shape of Tobias Katznelson as he stood outside the compartment door, a green-black shadow through the frosted glass. "We've got him, but he's far from safe," Grant said. "As you said yourself, it might be months yet before there's an aperture."

"Months," Varian said, and shook his head. "It's already been months. What will Eileen say if I tell her I'm staying longer still? That there's no end in sight?"

"Haven't you told her that already?"

He had, but always with the understanding that he would have preferred to be on his way home to her. How long would she continue to believe it, if in fact she believed it now?

"I'll have to wire Gregor as soon as we're back in town," Grant said, musing.

"Yes, you'll have to do that."

"How I wish I could see his face when he gets the cable."

Varian thought again of Grant sliding his feet into Katznelson's slippers, of Grant wearing Katznelson's robe and sleeping in his curtained bed. Would Grant really leave those luxuries of intimacy, on Varian's suggestion that to stay at the Pile was dangerous?

It was true that Tobias Katznelson was a fugitive, and that the strictest precautions must be taken. But also true that Varian wanted Grant out of Katznelson's house. He wanted him close day and night, as at Pamiers, as at Arles. In his own hand now was the slim volume of **Le faune de marbre,** nostalgic Faulkner in French. Lives were at stake, but he knew what he wanted; he had been denied it for more than a decade. He slid his leg alongside Grant's, and Grant pressed his knee through the layers of their clothing.

"After we get back," Varian said, "we'll get Tobias settled. We'll make sure he feels safe at Air Bel. You'll get things squared away at the villa. Then, when the time is right, we'll pack our things and meet at the Beauvau."

Grant's eyes rested on his own. They seemed to ask if Varian knew what he was doing. Varian knew only that the knot between them had tightened; the Latin word that came to mind was **implicatus.** The feeling was hardly volitional.

"All right," Grant said. "We'll decamp to the Beauvau."

"Even if just for a while."

As Mary Jayne slipped into the compartment again, the train began to slow for the station stop at Montpellier. She sat down amid a fresh cloud of jasmine and sandalwood, the chief notes of her fragrance; her makeup looked newly applied. Tobias Katznelson glanced in at his supposed charges, his polished bayonet gleaming. The boy seemed taut as a harp string, his back effortfully straight. On the station platform, gendarmes checked passengers' papers. Four Gestapo officers stood beneath the station overhang; the most highly decorated among them, a man with a footballer's build and a blocky jaw, checked his pocketwatch, looked toward the train, and said something to the shorter officer beside him. That man consulted a small notebook and nodded.

"Uh-oh," Varian said.

Grant and Mary Jayne followed his gaze. The four officers broke into two groups and approached the train. The decorated officer spoke to the gendarmes at the train door in what sounded like German-accented French, though Varian couldn't make out the words; a moment later, the gendarmes stepped aside. Tobias stood guard, oblivious. There was no time to warn him. Already they could feel the vibration of the officers' boots on the stairs of the train car. Almost without thinking, Varian slid the compartment door open, grabbed Tobias by the belt, and pulled him backward into the compartment, bayonet and all. Tobias stumbled and sat down hard on the carpeted floor, knocking Varian against the window. Mary Jayne gasped, and a pomegranate-colored drop fell from her earlobe to her lap. Grant reached over and slid the door closed.

Tobias looked from one of his protectors to the other. Then came the sound of German in the corridor, and the stomp and roll of the officers' footsteps as they passed.

"Keep still," Varian said. He'd taken a risk. Bought time. But a train was a trap. Windows too small to fit through, and a single long corridor that revealed all. Doors from which any exit would be visible. In the Wild West they might have found a hatch and climbed out onto the roof. He almost laughed at the thought.

"What can you be smiling at?" Mary Jayne whispered.

"Never mind." He pulled his handkerchief from his pocket and handed it to her.

"Damn you, Varian, you might have made me into Van Gogh!"

"Quiet."

"You can't hide that boy in a train compartment."

"Do you have a better idea?"

She didn't. They waited. Grant searched for a cigarette in his pocket, then held it without lighting it; the cigarette, trembling, snowed ill-packed tobacco onto his knee. From farther down the corridor came the sound of raised voices, the seal-bark of military German. The train swayed with the force of some unseen struggle.

"Was tun sie?" whispered Tobias. **What are they doing?**

"Quiet," Varian hissed.

Tobias lowered his head onto his knees. The strip of skin at his nape was a gleaming, blazing thing, a raw unblemished whiteness, the skin of a blind animal dug from the dirt. A pulse thrummed visibly in the purple vein beside his ear.

They waited, unmoving, as the German voices drew closer again, crescendoed, passed down the corridor. From the window Varian saw the decorated officer and his partner step off the train with a man in their custody, a round-shouldered man in an overcoat many sizes too large. He was uncuffed, but the officers had a grip on his arms; between them, the man clutched a black leather bag to his chest as if it contained something precious, as if it contained, in fact, his own life. Then suddenly the man stumbled and dropped the bag, breaking the officers' grip. In an instant his hand had disappeared into his coat pocket; he pulled out a small glinting handgun and raised it to his temple. A pause. Then a strangely muffled **bang,** and a red explosion bloomed from his other ear, a violent spray of strawberry pulp. He crumpled sideways against the Gestapo officer next to him, who fell to the ground, shouting in horror. Varian turned away. Mary Jayne put a hand to her mouth and bent forward at the waist. Grant fell back against the seat cushions, the cigarette limp in his hand.

Tobias got to his knees and pushed himself upright, then went to the window.

"What should I do?" he asked Varian, in trembling German. "What should I do?"

"Get back to your post."

The boy complied. Moments later, the train whistle blew and the train pulled out of the station, away from the disaster on the platform. They were still an hour and a half from Marseille. All that way, as they sat in shocked silence, their false guard guarded them wordlessly and no one questioned his authority, his uniform, or the bayoneted rifle in his hand.

THREE

More Bang

21

Escargot

A ringing silence followed them home to Air Bel and persisted into the days that followed. At the edge of Varian's consciousness, always present, was the memory of that gun at the man's temple, the pause, the explosion. It lingered as he installed Tobias Katznelson in the library of Air Bel; it persisted as he went about his business in town, as he inquired into rates at the Beauvau, as he met Grant for a hurried drink on the Canebière before they both traveled back to La Pomme and retired to their separate beds.

Among the residents at Air Bel, Tobias Katznelson was polite, almost contrite, as if embarrassed to have had to be rescued from a concentration camp, and further embarrassed to be taking up room in the library. Grant had insisted on giving him some money from his father, replacing his shattered glasses, and buying him new clothes in town, well-cut practical items that suited his frame; but Tobias was so desperate to provide for his own needs that he had, by the end of his first week at La Pomme, secured a job as Monsieur Thumin's handyman. He proved himself adept at any endeavor that wanted mechanical skill. In his first days at the villa he fixed the leaking bathroom taps, re-hinged the chimney flue in the sitting room, inserted new glass into a broken greenhouse frame, and repaired the axle of Peterkin's wooden tricycle. Faced with the meager offerings Madame Nouguet placed on the table, and observing the children's constant hunger, he began disappearing from the villa for some hours every day and returning with foraged edibles: bright orange mushrooms that tasted of lobster, fistfuls of wild mustard leaves, gamy hares he'd trapped in pits. When Madame Nouguet or anyone else thanked him, he blushed into his collar and said nothing.

One afternoon, a little more than a week after he'd arrived, Varian saw him on his way out of the house and followed him into the garden. Curious to see where he went on his excursions, he trailed Tobias through the bent fence at the bottom of the garden and down into the scrub of lavender and rosemary below. Tobias hadn't heard him, hadn't seen him; one hand in his pocket, a cap jammed backward onto his head, he rambled horizontally along the hillside, through the scrub, picking his way over the rocks, headed, as Varian soon realized, toward the Medieval Pile. The place had been his family's summer home for many years; how many August days had he spent exploring these hills? It was easy to see, watching him, how he had made his way out of Germany and through the countryside, finding things to eat, hiding in this or that abandoned building, eluding the general gaze. There was something shadowlike about him, a silence, a litheness that seemed to make it easy for him to disappear. No wonder he'd been so hard to find. And yet he, too, had his vulnerabilities: Varian had seen him through the greenhouse windows in urgent and desperate-seeming conversation with Zilberman, presumably about Sara, Zilberman's daughter. He hadn't dared ask either of them about it; they appeared, in the past few days, to have arrived at an uneasy détente, as though Zilberman had reluctantly accepted Tobias as a suitor for the absent girl's hand.

Now Tobias crouched in the dirt beside what Varian saw to be a tiny stream, a riverlet or perhaps only a rivulet, flowing between the rocks of the valley. His spine tensed beneath the broadcloth jacket Grant had bought him; he glanced over his shoulder and, seeing Varian, got to his feet.

"Sorry to startle you," Varian said, in German.

"I don't mind the company," Tobias said. A shy smile. "Look." He squatted again, reached forward into the winter-stunted greenery beside the stream, and turned over a stone. Then he dug for a moment with his curled hand in the wet earth.

"What have you got there?"

"Escargot. I used to find them by this stream when I was little." He opened his hand to show Varian five round spiral shells, then extracted an empty flour sack from his pocket and dropped them in. "In the winter, they hibernate together. You have to look under rocks by the water. They're sealed in now with their own glue, but if we put them in the greenhouse they'll soon come out. You have to feed them for a few days before you cook them, so you know what's inside. Grass will do, or cornmeal."

"How do you know all this?"

A shrug, a blush. "It's in books. Anyone can learn it."

"You learned how to survive in the wilderness, didn't you?"

Another shrug. "I thought I might need to. It's not hard, if you know the plants and things to look for. And how to build a fire. Anyway, I like to be on my own. It helps me think."

"Ah, yes," Varian said. "I'm afraid there's not much privacy to be had at Air Bel. I don't mean for you to keep sleeping on that library sofa forever, you know. In a few days you're to take my room."

Tobias shook his head. "I'm fine where I am."

"I'm going to move to town for a while, to be closer to the office. I want you to be comfortable at Air Bel. You may be here a while, you know. Getting you a visa isn't going to be an easy matter."

Tobias stood and brushed his dark hair from his forehead, looking away, over the stream and down into the valley. "I don't want to be a burden," he said.

"No one expects you to earn your keep. Your father left money for your needs. What we don't want is for you to go running for the border on your own. We've got to keep you out of the Gestapo's hands at all costs."

Tobias turned, knelt again, extracted another handful of snails from beneath the stone. "I could get to the border, though," he said. "I could make it across. I don't care about the cold. And I can take the gun. Mary Jayne's young man tells me he can get ammunition."

"Tobias," Varian said, hearing his own father's voice. "For God's sake, you're not to get anything from Killer, no ammunition, nothing. And you're not to make a break for the border on your own. You've got to swear to me. People get caught. Do you hear me? Caught and killed. It would destroy your parents."

"How can I promise?" Tobias said. "If anyone comes looking for me—the police, or Vichy, or the Gestapo—" He paused, and Varian knew they were both seeing what had happened at Montpellier. "If anyone comes for me, I have to run. I can't hide, waiting for them to pry me out. I'm not Zilberman."

He looked down at the hard damp ground, shaking his head. "Not that he's so very good at hiding, is he? He said the police caught him in broad daylight at a café."

"You were caught too, remember," Varian said. "You saw what happened when you tried to come here to La Pomme, the night of the party. They caught you just like anyone else. It was sheer good fortune that the highest officer on duty that night was Robinet, our friend at the Préfecture."

Tobias lowered his dark eyes. "I thought I might find Sara here. I suppose I became reckless."

"You can't afford to be reckless. The stakes are too high. The Nazis know about your work at the Kaiser-Wilhelm-Institut. They want to learn what you know. And they have methods of extracting information, unspeakable ways."

Tobias sat down now on the verge of the little creek, sifting the shells of snails through his fingers. He raised his eyes. "Do you think I'll be safe here, if I stay?"

"We can't know that for sure. But at least you're out of Vernet, and out of police custody. Out of the public gaze. And soon enough, I promise you, I mean to get you out of France entirely. I mean to send you to your father in New York."

"I'm grateful for what you've done already, you and Mr. Grant and Miss Gold. I do like Air Bel, you know. I like it better than my family's house. It's the kind of place I'd like to live someday."

"You're here now," Varian said. "Just be here. That's all. You need to rest. You've been running long enough."

Tobias's shoulders curled, and he put a hand to his eyes. "Months," he said.

"There's a time to run," Varian said. "And a time to pause. If there's one thing I've learned here in France, it's that sometimes it pays to wait."

Tobias gave a silent nod, though he made no promise. Then he tied the neck of his bag of snails and slung it into his rucksack, and, with Varian at his side, began the climb back up to the house.

———

That night, after all the others were in bed, Varian went to see Zilberman in the greenhouse. Zilberman stood before a sheet of rough-looking paper nailed to a blue wooden door; the children had found the door in the garden some weeks ago, lying half-submerged in the tall grasses, and Zilberman had removed it to the greenhouse with the help of Vlady Serge. Now it stood against a long workbench, braced at its base with stones, serving as an impromptu easel. The paper tacked to its surface bore a cascade of vertical black marks, like the trails of falling bombs.

"I don't want to disturb you, Lev," Varian said from the doorway.

Zilberman swiped an arm across his brow,

streaking it with charcoal. "I've been working too long already. Sit down."

Varian sat on a splintering bench. "Are you all right? Or well enough, under the circumstances?"

"As well as can be expected, I suppose. Eager to leave France. Otherwise, fine. And as you can see, the work accumulates." He cast an arm sideways, toward the piles of drawings stacked on one of the potting tables. "Not just mine. The pieces for our Flight Portfolio. More arrive every day."

"May I have a look?"

"Of course."

Varian went to the potting table and removed the first sheet of protective paper. Underneath was a work on coarse brown paper, a pastiche of pencil drawing and collage: From a rent in the paper emerged a fleeing woman, features askew, one blue eye stacked above the other. Her hair stood upright in flames, her clothes streamed behind her in tatters; in her hand, flayed to the phalanges, she held the hand of a child skeleton, no shred of flesh left on its charcoal-black bones.

"Wifredo Lam," Zilberman said, with a glance over his shoulder. "And his friend Brauner below."

Varian turned over another leaf. A zeppelin-headed man knelt before the crushed body of a fish; in one hand he held an upraised scimitar. The fish stared skyward with a cool, knowing gaze. From its torn gills streamed hundreds of tiny Hebrew letters, scratched in a crabbed and panicked hand.

Varian found himself reluctant to turn over another leaf. What he'd seen already seemed a distillation of all the strangeness and horror that had washed over the continent, and would keep washing it, an infinity of waves, for the foreseeable future.

"Won't you tell me what keeps you awake at this hour?" Zilberman said.

How to answer the question? "I'd like to know if you think I've placed an unfair—" Varian groped for the German word: **Belastung.** "An unfair burden on you, bringing Tobias here."

"What sort of burden?"

"I'm aware that his presence puts the rest of you at risk."

Zilberman shrugged. "We're at risk already, aren't we?"

"I'm particularly concerned, because—" and he paused, running his hand along the edge of Brauner's drawing. "I have to move to town, for a time. I've got to be closer to the office if I'm needed. But Tobias will stay here at Air Bel. He'll be here without my immediate protection." What else could he say? Why had he come down here anyway, why had he distracted Zilberman from his nocturnal work? There was no way to allay his guilt, nothing to curb his suspicion that the decision to move to the Hôtel Beauvau was a selfish one, that the inhabitants of the villa would be more vulnerable without him, and that they were all in greater danger now that Tobias was in their midst.

Zilberman looked carefully at Varian through his tortoiseshell glasses, his eyebrows drawn together, then turned back to his paper and ran the charcoal down its length with meditative slowness. "Truly, I don't envy your position, Mr. Fry," he said. "You're like the boy in the German proverb, the one who carries the pails of milk."

"What proverb?" Varian said.

Zilberman lowered his arm. "Oh, it goes something like this: Who's most important, the farmer who feeds the cow, the cow who makes the milk, or the girl who milks the cow? None of them. The most important is the boy who carries the milk to market. One wrong step, and the work of all the others is lost in an instant."

Varian smiled ruefully. "That sounds about right."

"You carry a heavy load. And you're an ordinary human being, however extraordinary your undertaking here in Marseille. Why should any of us begrudge you a little privacy in town?"

"Privacy is a peacetime luxury."

"Nonsense. And don't trouble yourself about Tobias. I'll look after him. My daughter would never forgive me if I didn't." He got down from his stool and selected another charcoal from a wooden box. "Now, my dear Mr. Fry, you'll understand if I turn you out. The hour's getting late, and I'd like to get back to work."

"Of course," Varian said. "Forgive me." And he

opened the door and walked out into the garden, where the wind had crazed the dry winter stalks into a crackling sea.

He left Air Bel two days later, going to the office that morning not just with his usual briefcase but with his packed suitcase and a small wooden crate of books. In the room that was now Tobias's, he'd left a few surrealist drawings and a pile of clothes meant for a warmer season; he'd removed all the hidden lists and papers and maps, the new address book, the francs he'd stashed beneath the floorboards. Now his suitcase stood in the corner of the office like a mute promise while he and Hirschman bent over a stack of client files, each with its own insoluble problem. The Spanish border remained closed; without the slightest chance of getting clients across by train, they'd had to depend upon the Fittkos, who, brave as they were, had scaled back operations as the mountains filled with snow. Hirschman had just seen them at Perpignan. Lisa Fittko, he said, had exhausted herself and was suffering from a liver ailment. Leon Ball was still missing. Hirschman believed that he must have been arrested, with no way of contacting the Centre Américain. Bingham had opened an inquiry but had thus far learned nothing.

"What do we do, then?" Varian said. "We can't

put the whole thing on hold while we wait for the snow to melt. We need a boat, for God's sake. We need the **Sinaïa,** and a whole fleet of others."

"What do you hear from Deschamps?"

"Nothing. The **Sinaïa** left for Martinique perhaps ten days ago. It'll be weeks before it returns. Anyway, we're too closely watched just now. Everyone's been on double alert since that fiasco with Laval at Vichy. We've got to wait until the authorities turn their eyes away."

"Maybe Vinciléoni can help us," Hirschman said.

"Yes. We've got to make that happen. But how?"

"I don't know. Maybe we're not offering enough money."

"Well, let's offer more. I've got to get Zilberman off this continent."

At that moment the quiet of the office splintered into a percussive din, a wall-shaking racket of pounding on the outer door. Varian went to the door of his own office and glanced out; Lena had just admitted a pair of Sûreté Nationale officers, their expressions grim, their guns gleaming in leather holsters. He didn't recognize either of the men, one of whom was short and dark, the other wide and porcine. That was the man who spoke first, his hand on his gun.

"Where's Hirschman?" he said. "Albert Hirschman?"

Varian only just saved himself from glancing back over his shoulder to where Hirschman sat, out of the officers' view, in the chair beside the desk.

"I'd like to know the same," Varian said. "We haven't seen him in weeks. He left his job here some time ago. I heard he'd gone down to Cannes."

"You're lying, Monsieur Fry," the shorter policeman said. "We had a tip he was back from the border and hanging around this office."

"I've told you what I know," Varian said. "We haven't seen him since the beginning of the month."

The shorter policeman turned to Lena, stepping so close to her that his gut pushed against the buckle of her grass-green belt. She took a half-step back, and he advanced. "What about you—Mademoiselle Fischman, is it?" he said. "Have you seen your colleague Hirschman?"

Lena didn't flinch. Never taking her eyes off the short policeman, she pulled the pencil from behind her ear and used it to punctuate her words in the air. "If I see that man again, I put out his eye, **pik, pik, pik!** Just like that. He is unfaithful, an unfaithful dog." Her eyes began to glitter with real tears, and Varian caught his breath. "How he lied to me, monsieur!" Lena went on. "The things he told to me! The things he promised to me!" She fumbled for a handkerchief, and when she couldn't find one, the policeman offered his own. She pressed it to her eyes for a long moment, then straightened again, having disarrayed her **maquillage** convincingly. "If you find him, monsieur, tell him Lena Fischman never speaks to him again, never, never!" She blew her nose elaborately into the handkerchief, then returned it to its owner. **"Mais jamais!"** she said again.

"Well," said the porcine policeman, his color having deepened to fuchsia. "Well. We're terribly sorry to have disturbed you, Mademoiselle Fischman, Monsieur Fry. We have reason to believe that this Hirschman may be involved in a variety of illegal activities. We suspect he may be involved with the Gaullists."

"I am sure he breaks all the laws he can!" Lena said. "Filthy, filthy man!"

"If you're to hear of his whereabouts, contact us at once," the officer said, and offered his card to Varian.

"Of course," Varian said.

The officers bowed stiffly, then took their leave, clomping down the stairs and slamming the outer door behind them. A few moments passed before Varian or Lena or Hirschman made a sound; then they roared with laughter.

"Brava, Lena, brava!" Hirschman said. **"Encore, s'il vous plaît!"**

"I hope you are not offended, Albert!"

"Offended! **Au contraire.** Honored. You were splendid. You've just saved me from being dragged off to the clink." He put a hand to his chest and bowed in gratitude. But then he turned to Varian, his expression growing serious. "What must I do now?" he said. "What do you think they know?"

Varian shook his head. "I think we have to assume

the worst. It's clear they've got someone watching you. I don't doubt you're in danger."

Hirschman sank into one of the office chairs. "I'm sure you're right."

"I felt a hell of a lot easier when you were down at Perpignan."

Hirschman put his hands together. "Do you know, Varian," he said slowly, "I have my papers, or at least as many as I'd need to get to Lisbon."

Lena looked from Varian to Hirschman. "What nonsense is this?"

Varian sighed, a feeling of unbearable heaviness pushing into his limbs. He had suspected, even before the Maréchal's visit, that this day would come soon; he had braced himself for it. "I know you're right, Albert," he said. "I wish it weren't true."

"What is true?" Lena half-shouted.

"I've got to go," Hirschman said. "I've got to leave France. Already I've compromised the operation."

"But Albert! You cannot go! **O mój Boże! Comment tu exagères!**"

"It's folly to stay any longer. I've got to leave today."

"Today!" Lena said, and this time real tears came to her eyes; she sat down helplessly in her office chair. "Today! But Albert! You cannot mean it."

"I do," Hirschman said. "I have all my traveling papers with me this moment. I ought not even return to the hotel for my things. The police may be there now. Perhaps you'll send my trunk along once I've reached Lisbon."

"No party? Not even a proper farewell?"

"This is our party," Hirschman said. He got to his feet, went to his desk, and withdrew the little cut-glass bottle of whiskey he always kept in the filing drawer. He poured an inch of whiskey for Varian and another for Lena; then he toasted them both with the bottle. Varian drank, trying to comprehend that this was happening, that Hirschman intended to leave today. What would happen when he, Varian, next needed counsel or calming or an infusion of courage? Could Danny Bénédite, quiet and correct, fill Hirschman's role? Or the anxious and multilingual Jean Gemähling? To the extent that he'd been able to imagine leaving Marseille and the Centre Américain himself, to the extent that he'd been willing to envision what might happen if he were thrown out, his place here had always been filled, in his mind, by Hirschman. But he'd also known this day would come, that Hirschman would be forced to leave France. Even now he wanted to argue it off, wanted to make a case against it; he knew that if he did, if he protested cleverly enough, he might win. But what came to his mind was Vernet, the open latrines, the sound of pickaxes striking the frozen ground, the bone-thin prisoners in their filthy civilian clothes. Hirschman could be dragged there any day. He had done most of the office lawbreaking; he was the connection to the black market, to the illegal conversion of currency, to the forging of documents, the procuring of false passports. It was a miracle he hadn't been thrown in jail already.

"I wish you didn't have to do it, Albert," he said.

"I wish the same."

Hirschman rose from his chair to refill Varian's glass, and Lena's; then he drained the last centimeter of whiskey himself. "I'll be seeing you, as they say in the movies. Perhaps we'll rendezvous in New York."

"Oh, Albert!" Lena said, stricken.

"Oh, Albert, nothing," Hirschman said, and kissed her on both cheeks. He donned his overcoat, put his hat on his head, and took his briefcase in hand. Varian got to his feet, and for a moment they stood face-to-face in silence.

"Drop us a line from Lisbon," he managed to say. "And Albert—don't get arrested at the border, all right? And don't try to cross the Pyrenees in a snowstorm."

Hirschman slapped Varian on the shoulder. "Have some faith!" he said. "I'll be fine. And so will you, my good friend. You've learned a thing or two since we first met."

From anyone else this might have sounded like condescension; Hirschman managed to make it sound like a profession of confidence. To the extent that it was true—to the degree that Varian had gone from absolute fraudulence in his job to passable competence—it was, in large part, thanks to Hirschman himself. Now Varian watched Hirschman raise a hand to his forehead and move toward the door. A moment later he'd gone through it, and then his footsteps echoed down the stairs. Finally they heard the outer door open and close, and in one swift and terrible stroke Hirschman was gone.

22

Bar Splendide

Six o'clock that evening found him in the lobby of the Hôtel Beauvau, a hall of mirrors that extended space infinitely in every direction. The mirror behind the reception desk mirrored the entrance doors, the mirrored walls mirrored each other, the gilded and mirrored ceiling mirrored the reflective black marble of the floors, all of it transmitting the impression that one's own self was the ultimate embellishment and deserved to be repeated to infinity. When he checked in, he gleaned from the desk clerk that Grant, who had arrived the previous day, had employed the ruse that he was Mr. Fry's personal physician, that Mr. Fry was gravely ill, and that he, Dr. Grant, must have private access to Mr. Fry's person at all times, hence the necessity that the men be given rooms that communicated not only with the hall but with each other. The unsuspicious clerk handed Varian a key attached to a small brass medallion emblazoned with a B for Beauvau, and instructed him to take the lift to the **troisième étage,** where he would find a room that he hoped would suit the patient's needs.

Here was what Varian would remember later: how, when he opened the door to the room, the scent of freshly laundered bath towels and lavender soap rolled into the hall; how, inside the room, a smooth white bed lay like a frosted cake before a window that gave onto the Vieux Port; how an open door revealed a black-and-white skylit bathroom, shared with the adjoining room, its door also standing open; and how, in that bathroom's enormous slipper-shaped bathtub, the ostensible Dr. Grant reclined in a nebula of bubbles, his dark hair swept back in ridges, one honey-colored hand trailing over the edge of the tub, sending a slow parade of drops down the tip of the middle finger to fall in a damp circlet on the bath rug below. He might have been a lotus eater; he might have been a drowsy child, the newly fatherless Elliott Grant, immersed in his grandparents' bathtub in Philadelphia.

"The doctor is in," Grant said.

Varian undressed without haste. He was unwilling, for the moment, to speak a word about Hirschman or about anything else that troubled him. He wanted only to inhabit this moment with Grant, this instant **before,** when the memory-to-be was yet to begin, a cup filled to the limit, no drop of experience spilled. He unbuttoned his shirt, shed his pants, unbraced his socks, and stepped onto the bath rug, feeling beneath his toes the circlet of bathwater Grant had let fall onto the cotton loops. Eileen accused him of being a puritan at moments like these—**he,** Varian, whose habits she knew! She believed he hesitated only because he experienced paralyzing guilt at the prospect of pleasure. But that was far from the truth. He was the basest sybarite he knew. The anticipatory pause only heightened and prolonged his delight. Because, necessarily, the actual experience of tasting, of touching, of entering, was laced with grief. Once it began, it was on its way to being over. Even now, as he let himself step through the foam and into the enclosing heat of the water, even as Grant's limbs shifted and parted to make room for him, as he immersed himself first to the waist, then to the chest, and finally, with the back of his neck against the cool porcelain roll of the tub, to the hollow of his throat, what he couldn't help but think about was the fact that now that Tobias had been found, now that he was secreted away at the Villa Air Bel to await his papers and a means to an exit, now that Grant had cabled Katznelson informing him in code that the boy was safe and under his own protection, it would only be a matter of time before Grant would consider his business concluded. And what would happen then? What could come next? Would any of his declarations hold, once the matter had been settled?

"What are you thinking?" Grant asked, his eyes narrowed. He found Varian through the water, and Varian shifted against him.

"Not thinking," Varian said, closing his eyes. "Not thinking at all."

"Look at me," Grant demanded. "Open your eyes."

Varian looked, though it was a kind of torture. Soap-laced steam had condensed in droplets on Grant's skin, rendering it iridescent. Reflective spherules hovered on the points of his wet lashes. It was happening; there was no stopping it from going forward. They were occupying these rooms, they were **living together,** even if only for now, just here, in the protected space of the Beauvau.

Some two hours later—after he'd recovered enough to tell Grant about Hirschman; after they'd had a long talk about what he'd do without him, how he might carry on all his illegal projects without landing in jail himself; after they'd dressed and gone downstairs and were crossing the lobby to the bar for drinks—the desk clerk waved Varian over, his look and gesture urgent. This was the same clerk who had helped him earlier. The boy had an interesting and memorable blemish, if it could be called that, a small twinned mole like a tiny black figure eight on his cheekbone. **Grain de beauté** was the poetic French phrase.

"Monsieur Fry, Dr. Grant," the boy said, giving a slight bow. "A message for the patient." He handed Varian a slim cream-colored envelope. Inside was a single sheet, unsigned, typed with a single line: **Meet Bar Splendide 9 p.m. sharp.**

Grant squinted at the note. "Who would know to write you here?"

"Lena. Hirschman. Anyone at the office."

Grant turned the note over in his hands. Varian took it from him, scrutinizing the typed letters, which had been hammered so fiercely into the paper that their opposites stood in tangible relief on the reverse. It hadn't been composed on the office typewriter, that was clear; he would have recognized the tilted **s,** the dropped **g.** Who would write to him with such vehemence, summon him that way without giving a name? The police, having sussed out his lie about Hirschman? Hugh Fullerton? And then another thought occurred to him.

"My God," he said.

"What?"

But he couldn't give voice to what had come into his head: The note was from Eileen. **Eileen herself** had come to Marseille. It was December 23; could she have come with the excuse of wanting to be there at Christmas? Could she have crossed an ocean in wartime with only that cover? Had the New York office asked her to take matters into her own hands, to remove him from France? Or had Eileen, having read between the lines of his letters all this time, volunteered to come? If she had actually come to France, if she was here, if she had crossed the submarine-patrolled Atlantic in the middle of a war, there could only be one reason.

"I've got to go," Varian said.

"On your own?"

"I'm sorry, Skiff. It's necessary. We'll talk about it later."

His expression grew grave. "You don't think it's about Tobias?"

"I don't know. It's possible, though the Gestapo would likely take a less subtle approach."

"Don't you want me to come with you? If there's any danger—"

"No, I'd better go on my own. Wait for me at La Fémina?"

Grant inspected the view from the window: toy boats bobbing in the night-dark port. "I don't suppose I have a choice," he said. And they left each other the way they always did in public: with a handshake that allowed them at least a moment of parting contact.

His thoughts, as he walked the edge of the Vieux Port from the Hôtel Beauvau to the Canebière, were a perfect dark confusion. Eileen: She wouldn't have sent a **note,** would she? Wouldn't she have just come to his hotel? No, a note was more her style:

meet on her own terms, at the time and place of her choosing. **9 p.m. sharp.** He could hear her voice in that demand. But would he rather encounter **her,** or a Nazi intelligence man? Would he rather be dragged into a subterranean interrogation chamber or into the hotel suite of a woman who loved him, and whom, if he were honest with himself, he loved?

He found the Splendide just as he'd left it: carpeted in green, stuffed to its rafters with travelers whose fine clothes had seen better days, its desk attended by the same stiff-necked, mustachioed clerk he'd bribed at such high cost months before. The bar lay through those brass-handled doors, just there; it was nearly nine o'clock already. Should he smoke a cigarette first? No. Nonsense. He would just go in. If it was the police, or the Gestapo, they couldn't be avoided; and if it was Eileen, he would tell her the truth.

He did not at first recognize the person who hailed him from the bar as he entered: a square-jawed, highly pomaded fellow in field khakis, as if this were sub-Saharan Africa instead of Marseille. The man waved again; without a doubt, he was beckoning to Varian. Seated on the stool beside him was a woman of around sixty, a narrow, school-principalish woman in a high-collared pink silk shirt, who smiled at Varian in what might have been a patronizing way if there hadn't been an edge of apprehension in her eyes, a hint of animal fear.

He approached the pair and took the man's hand, realizing as he did that this was the **Chicago Tribune** journalist Jay Allen, whom he'd met in New York some years ago. Allen had given a lecture at Columbia about his coverage of the Spanish Civil War; specifically his subject was Badajoz, where he'd witnessed a massacre. At the party after the lecture, held at the home of a political science professor and his wife, Varian had approached Allen about writing an article about Badajoz for **The Living Age.** Or he'd tried to approach him. While the other guests stood and listened in silence, Allen had held forth for nearly two hours about his time in Spain with Hemingway—Papa, as he called him. He and Papa had witnessed this or that horror, had drunk memorable drinks amid shards of glass and wood in what had once been a famous café, had fought bitterly over a local girl whose dialect neither of them could understand, and had nearly been blown to pieces one night when the pension where they were staying came under fire. As he talked, the weary hosts had first run out of food and then liquor, and had finally resorted to opening fine old bottles of wine from their own cellar, bottles that had obviously been intended to be consumed slowly and mindfully on private occasions. When at last Varian had found an aperture for his request, Allen had brushed it off, citing his busy travel schedule; but a few weeks later he'd published a detailed account of his Badajoz experience in **The New Republic.**

Not Eileen, then, after all; merely this blowhard journalist, likely wanting to interview Varian about the refugee situation in France. A wave of relief rushed through him, chased by an undertow of guilt.

Now Allen clapped him on the back and shook his hand, calling the bartender over to see to the needs of "my good friend Fry, a man of letters, one of our best." The principalish lady was Margaret Palmer, who hailed from Pittsburgh and had been secretary to the chief curator at the Carnegie Institute. Allen explained that he'd come to France as a representative of the North American Newspaper Alliance. He'd traveled through North Africa by way of Casablanca, where he'd interviewed General Weygand, Pétain's minister of defense. The interview had been a fine piece of trickery-talk on his own part, he didn't mind saying now, the kind that gets a villain like Weygand not only to show his hand but to reveal the tattered ace up his sleeve. Of course, this was only stage-setting for the real journalistic prize: an interview with Pétain himself, brokered by Weygand.

"Well, that's good news," Varian said. "The word must get out."

"That's what I was just telling Madge, here," Allen said, shaking the frail-looking Miss Palmer by her narrow shoulder. Miss Palmer smiled bravely. "We're fighting the good fight, bringing the truth home to Main Street. Where they don't really want to hear it, do they, Madge?"

"No, indeed," said Miss Palmer.

"I'll take the train up to Vichy tomorrow," Allen said. "Start at once. Got to file before Christmas if I can. But I wanted to see you first. Get things squared away here in Marseille with the Centre Américain."

"Squared away?"

"Transfer of power, and all that." He tapped a long ash from his cigarette and swigged from his drink. "Set up Madge in the new post. Introduce her to everyone."

"I'm afraid I'm not reading you," Varian said. "We've got a hundred codes going here in Marseille, Jay. A person can get muddled. We can go elsewhere to talk, if that's easier."

"Oh, no need, I like it here fine," Allen said, drawing from his breast pocket a much-folded envelope, which he flattened against the bar before handing it to Varian. On the face of the envelope was Varian's name, in Paul Hagen's handwriting; the embossed return address was that of the Emergency Rescue Committee's office on Forty-Second Street. Varian opened the envelope and withdrew a single typed sheet.

VARIAN: This is to introduce Mr. Allen, who is to take over directorship of operations at the ERC office in Marseille, effective immediately.

You will kindly do us the favor of instructing him in your work in every detail, sparing nothing that could aid the successful transfer of control. After Mr. Allen's two-week acclimatization period you are to return stateside, where you will debrief the Committee on your activities in France. We appreciate your cooperation with these instructions.
Sincerely, PAUL HAGEN

Varian read and reread the note. He looked from the creased sheet of bond to Jay Allen and Margaret Palmer and then back again, buoyant incredulity rising in his chest. So it had happened at last: he'd been fired, ash-canned, his pink slip delivered by his replacement. His first thought was that Eileen had betrayed him, that this was all her doing. His second was that he would never comply. And his third was that he must move carefully, must never let Jay Allen or Miss Palmer know how he felt.

"So they've finally given me the relief I've been asking for," he said, modulating his expression to one of pleasant surprise. "It's about time. How soon can we get you behind that desk, Jay?"

"Well, **I** won't be the one behind the desk," Allen said, haw-hawing, leaning away from Varian as if to distance himself from the idea of it. "Madge will be manning the director's seat. You can think of her as an alter-Jay, a Jay-in-fact, while I'm at large. You see, I'm really here to cover the war. That's the truth, and also my official alibi. Madge will just occupy the chair in my place. She'll report everything to me, and she'll carry out all my orders to the letter. She'll be the organization's public face. I'll never even have to meet the office staff. No one can connect the Centre Américain to me, don't you see? But I'll be the brain, as it were, behind the face."

"Let me get this straight," Varian said. "The Centre Américain is to be run long-distance? You're to oversee operations, but you're never to appear in the office?"

"Yes, that's right," Allen said. "You'll show Madge how to run everything, and she'll fill in all the details for me when I stop back through Marseille."

"So you're not planning to live here, actually?"

"Well, now, how could I? Have to go where the stories take me. But that's where Madge comes in. Our woman on the ground."

Miss Palmer winked at Varian, as if this were all a kind of inside joke.

"I see," Varian said. "Well. What a novel idea, Jay."

"Exactly what Paul said. And what the organization needs. New thinking. Better cover. Better results. More bang for the committee's buck. More valuable clients. Raise more money back at home."

"More **bang,** did you say? For the committee's buck?"

"Oh, yes. Just ask your friend Harry Oram in New York, the money guy. Someone like Einstein's worth about a hundred thou in fundraising speeches, give or take a thou. Now Picasso, he'd be worth fifty thousand, if we could get him. Those three you sent over a few months ago—Werfel, Mann, and the one with the unpronounceable name—those guys scarcely brought in ten together, according to Harry. We've got to round up a few biggies or see the whole thing go under, he says. You can do it, Jay, he says. Your name means something. You've got the clout."

Varian had to stifle a laugh. He would never be able to reproduce this in sufficient detail for Grant, and might have to wait months to narrate it to Hirschman. So this was what had been going on in New York: this calculation, this rendering of lives in dollars, give or take a thou. They wanted Jay to come up with some biggies, raise some bucks. Nothing could have made it clearer to him that the men and women in charge—Ingrid and Paul and Frank Kingdon and the others—even **Eileen,** who should have known better—had no bloody idea, no concept at all, of what was really going on in France.

Of course he'd suspected that this moment would come, that Eileen would prevail upon the committee to send someone to replace him. And he really **had** asked for a replacement, back when he still had a job to go home to in New York. But he'd never imagined that the ERC would come up with Jay Allen. They couldn't make Varian hand over control to a person like that; they couldn't make him hand it over to anyone. Mary Jayne had already donated half a million francs, and she planned to put another two hundred thousand into the coffers before January. Peggy Guggenheim was ready to put forth another half-million francs. Bingham himself had donated a hundred thousand, and others, dozens of others, had put forth money of their own. It was hidden here and there, banked in various locations and in various currencies, so it couldn't all disappear at once, or be appropriated by an idiot like Allen; but it was there, a comfortable seven figures' worth of francs, and though he couldn't pretend that he didn't need New York at all, the fact was that he didn't have to depend on them.

". . . what you really must need," Allen was saying, somewhere in the background, "is a good strong dose of what's happening elsewhere. Get stuck in Marseille for months on end, you miss a thing or two. Why, Papa was just telling me the other day—I mean Hemingway, you know—he was just saying, now Jay, you've got to see the war with your own two eyes, see it in the flesh, and if you're not where it's **at,** just go off and get to the center of it. That's why I thought to ask Weygand about Pétain. These old fascists are only too glad to brag about their connections, if you take my meaning, they'd claim they buggered Hitler himself if you got enough drink in them—and of course Weygand fell over himself to say that Pétain would see me if **he** told him to, and the general called his girl in **that moment** so he could dictate the letter in front of me.

Lo and behold, Vichy's opened its doors to me, and I'll be damned if I don't walk straight in and get the interview. That's the way I've always done it, Mr. Fry. That's the way you've got to do it, and if you can't, then you might as well just hang up your cock and balls and go home." He drained his drink and raised his empty glass at the bartender.

"Ahem," said Miss Palmer. "Perhaps I should be saying goodnight, gentlemen. It's been a rather long day, and we're likely to have a longer one tomorrow."

"Oh, now, Madge," Allen said. "I expect you'll learn the whole operation in ten minutes flat." He turned to Varian. "Madge is great with facts. Mind like a weasel trap. Unlike me. I go for the human angle. I'm a man of the heart. Too **much** heart, Papa says. It's a liability in a man of letters. And he's right, isn't he, Madge?"

Miss Palmer blushed into her pink silk collar, unable to muster a reply. But Allen hadn't really been asking a question, and wasn't looking for an answer; what he wanted was to tuck into his next drink and dilate upon the subject of Vichy and of Maréchal Pétain, and what Hemingway had had to say about it. Miss Palmer was left to take herself off to bed, and Varian watched her go, watched the hunch of her shoulders and the hesitancy of her walk as she made her way between the bar tables. Though she was Varian's enemy now, he could only pity her.

He listened to Allen for as long as he could stand

it, then said a polite goodnight, shook Allen's hand, and stepped out of the bar and through the glass-awninged entryway of the Splendide, out onto the boulevard Dugommier. As he walked through the familiar scents of Marseille, pipe smoke and cinnamon and garbage rot and sea salt and cumin and crustaceans, each in its usual place between the Splendide and the Vieux Port, his body seemed to have become strangely light, as if he'd been stripped of an overcoat that had grown heavy with rain without his realizing it. All this time, all these months, he'd considered himself the employee of the ERC, its subject, its limb. But now that they'd cut him free, now they'd told him he was no longer needed, he knew **they** were the ones who'd been the appendage. **He,** Varian, was the Centre Américain. His New York life had shrunk to a vanishingly small point, his job abandoned, his marriage stretched to a filament. His earlier self had been subsumed by this other person, this man walking along the Canebière toward the quai des Belges, where, in that restaurant whose yellow light spilled onto the pavement like a flood of saffron, another man waited, a man who would understand all of this implicitly, a person to whom, despite all his mysteries, despite all that still lay hidden, Varian need hardly explain anything.

23

Gide

Open revolt: that was the only way to describe the reaction of the office staff. That first morning, Danny Bénédite would not meet Miss Palmer's eye; he addressed all his comments to Varian and only to Varian. Jean Gemähling pretended not to understand English. Lena, delivering a cup of tea to Varian, spilled it directly into Miss Palmer's bag. Even Theo, with her impeccable manners, feigned a coughing fit when Miss Palmer tried to ask if she knew of a good seamstress who could repair a slip, as she'd brought only one and had torn it already. At noon Miss Palmer claimed an intestinal indisposition and retreated to the Splendide. That afternoon the staff met in Varian's office.

"Just how did this happen?" Mary Jayne asked, pacing before the windows, her arms crossed over her chest. "Was this Ingrid Warburg's doing? Eileen's?

Paul can't have been this stupid. He can't have imagined it would work."

"It would take months to teach Miss Palmer what you do," Theo said. "If such a thing were even possible. I consider it a rather dangerous waste of everyone's time."

Danny got up from his chair and leaned against the desk, squinting at Varian through his small silver-rimmed glasses. "So they accuse us of not getting enough done," he said. "Not delivering enough **bang,** when we've already saved twice the number of refugees on the original list. And now we are supposed to pause to educate Miss Palmer? If you don't mind my saying so, Mr. Fry, I haven't seen evidence yet that she'll be able to grasp the basic principles of what you do, never mind operate its human angles."

Jean Gemähling shook his head in anger. "I've got a few choice words for Paul Hagen," he said. "I'll give **him** some bang for his buck."

"I shall write the Forty-Second Street office myself," Lena said. "I will send them cables and cables. **C'est évident, ils ont perdu la tête!**"

Danny, who had picked up a newspaper from the desk, tapped it on his knee. "Now's hardly the moment for a changing of the guard," he said. "Every journalist in town predicts that Marseille will be occupied by mid-January."

"Well, the New York office can be hanged, as far as I'm concerned," Varian said. "I believe, frankly, we're better off on our own. Without the ERC's gatekeeping. And their oversight."

"Absolutely not," Theo said. "We need New York. It's folly to think otherwise."

"Look what they're trying to do to us!"

"Still, they're lobbying Washington every day on our clients' behalf. And they're our primary source of funding, though just barely."

"They're delaying our cases, dozens of them, because they aren't prestigious enough. Because they won't bring in enough money. They're biding their time, waiting to ask Washington for favors until the big names come through. Meanwhile, geniuses are rotting in camps or in their hotel rooms. Or killing themselves."

"But what if you get arrested?" Danny said. "You can't rely on Harry Bingham for everything. You need New York's protection, and their connections."

"Why would they protect me? It's clear they want to wash their hands of me."

"The other option is to throw you to the wolves, and they won't do it. Apart from the fact that it's morally unconscionable, it would be terrible press."

"So what do you suggest we do, Danny? Mary Jayne? Theo? Anyone?"

Jean Gemähling looked up from his brooding. "We'll do what they do on the football field," he said.

"And what's that, my friend?"

"Stall for time," Jean said. "Let the other team think they've got the advantage. Then quietly execute our own offense."

And that was what they did. Jay Allen, for his part, was too distracted to notice; he'd gone up to Vichy to try to get his interview, and had ended up mired in the same administrative weeds that would have tangled anyone, his letter from General Weygand notwithstanding. Miss Palmer came to the office every day and sat with Varian, taking dutiful notes as he tutored her in his procedures and practices; infrequently she relayed to Jay Allen a précis of what she'd learned. Allen transmitted his mandates through her—**Fire three staff members before New Year's!**—and Varian roundly ignored them. Meanwhile, the real work went on. Varian begged visas from the consulate, wrote endless letters to Washington, and, when the Spanish border finally opened again, sent small groups of clients down to Cerbère. Theo teased out refugees from their hiding places and convinced them to become clients. Mary Jayne plied her rich friends for money, and kept throwing her own dollars into the Centre's coffers; she spent her days interviewing clients even when her nights involved bouts of drinking and dancing or loud acrobatics with Killer. Danny and Jean Gemähling took over Hirschman's illegal operations, his connection with Vinciléoni, his pursuit of false documents and cheap francs. And Lena sent ever-lengthening lists of names to New York.

———

Sometime after Christmas, he and Grant went up to Cannes to see Gide. If the New York committee wanted big names, Varian thought, let them have this one; surely André Gide could bring in thousands, perhaps tens of thousands, in New York alone.

To get to Gide's house in Cabris, a hamlet in the mountains above Cannes, they had to take a bus from the train station—a bus powered by a cumbersome charcoal burner screwed to the vehicle's undercarriage. **Gazogène,** the fuel was called, though it had nothing to do with gas; it smelled like a campfire, caused mysterious cracklings and poppings in the engine, and only propelled the bus a few kilometers before the system broke down and had to be fixed by the driver and a mechanic who rode along at all times for this purpose. The trip to Gide's house might have been speedier had he and Grant walked, though Varian conceded that it wasn't unpleasant; he welcomed the excuse to sit at Grant's side, and he liked the smell of woodsmoke. It put him in mind of bonfires on Brighton Beach with his grandfather. If he closed his eyes, he could imagine himself in short pants, surrounded by his grandfather's charges, those boys and girls who'd been given the privilege of temporary removal from their tenements, singing "Oh, My Darling Clementine" at the top of their lungs as shadows fell over the Lower Bay.

"What are you thinking of?" Grant asked, eyeing him carefully. The bus had stopped again, and the driver and mechanic had climbed out to examine the engine.

"Summer," Varian said. "High summer in Brooklyn."

"That's a wise move. It's freezing in here."

"Do you think we'll still be in France in June?"

"No way to know," Grant said, rolling his hands over and over to warm them.

"What about you? What were you thinking of?"

"Gregor," Grant said simply, and Varian's heart constricted to a sand-sized point. "It's been nearly three months since I've seen him. And do you know what I've been wondering?"

"What's that?"

"What he would do if he found out. About what I am, I mean."

Varian squinted at Grant. "He doesn't know?"

"Well, no. No one in my life back home knows. Not one of my colleagues, certainly not my students; you can imagine how horrified some of those boys would be at the thought of being taught by a Negro. Even a college Negro."

"But it's **you,** Grant. That wouldn't change."

"You can't pretend you think it wouldn't matter.

That my brilliant teaching and writing—and really, I'm only mediocre at both, if we're being honest—might somehow transcend the fact that my father was a Negro and my grandmother a freed slave."

Varian lowered his eyes. "You've never mentioned your grandmother."

Grant sighed and turned his gaze out toward the rocky hillside. "I don't know much about her," he said. "As the story goes, she was owned by a family called Bolton, down in Georgia. The master was a bachelor, childless—except for the children he got on his slaves, I imagine—and he manumitted all his human property when he died. My grandmother made her way to New York. Someone had told her, I guess, that there was well-paying work there. When the weather got cold, she sheltered in a Negro church in Five Points. The pastor found her on one of the pews—she must have been about fourteen, I believe. Six years later he married her."

"How did you learn all this?"

"My mother told me one night when she'd had too much to drink. My father gave her the whole story. One of the few things he left her."

"What happened to your grandmother after that?"

"She did God's work at a home for indigent women, and sang in the church choir. My father grew up playing around the organ, then playing it. Later he started on the piano—they got him lessons when they realized he had talent."

"And is she still alive, your grandmother? Does she live in New York?"

"I'll confess, I haven't the slightest idea. It's one of the deep griefs of my life."

"And you never told Gregor any of this?"

"He knows me as the man I appear to be."

"And now you're having second thoughts about that?"

Grant put his arms around himself and sank down an inch into his seat. "I lived differently with you," he said. "All those years ago. Even though I'd lied to Harvard, I lived honestly with you. It was part of what made me so angry when you chose Eileen. I didn't want to give that up. But I had to. I wanted to get into school again, so I dissembled, and kept dissembling. After a while I got used to hiding again. But I can't do it anymore. I keep thinking about writing a letter to my department chair."

"Could you lose your position? You've got tenure, haven't you?"

"I received my tenure under false pretenses. I'm sure they'd find a way to get me out, if they wanted to. But I hardly care. All my life I got where I did by hiding. Look around you. People are dying here because they refuse to hide what they are. **You** might have to lie to save their lives, but those are temporary lies. Once your clients hit free ground, they become themselves again. For me there's only pretending, day after day."

He had never before heard Grant speak this way.

"Have you considered how you'd live?" he said. "If you were dismissed, I mean?"

"There are many ways to live. Other places to teach."

"But you're a terrific snob, Grant," he said, and smiled. "Harvard, Yale, Columbia. Could you bear to leave the Ivy League?"

"Who says I'd have to? Maybe one of them would have me. But anyway, would it be so bad to teach somewhere else? Live in some leafy little town, out of the way?" Grant's eyes met Varian's own; was he inviting Varian to go with him? "Some town where there's a good Negro college, and perhaps not a bad restaurant, and a cinema, and miles and miles of countryside to walk?"

Varian's mouth had gone dry. Though this was only fanciful speculation, it was the first he'd ever heard of Grant's plans for afterward—what he might imagine doing, where he might go. Would leaving Columbia necessarily mean leaving Katznelson? Did he dare ask? Dare envision himself in Grant's imagined life? All the fantasies he'd indulged of a life with Grant had involved a city, either in Europe or the States; and really, in the States, there was only one city for him. But what could any of that mean, what could locality mean, when Grant himself was his only center? Could he see himself in a leafy little town? If Grant were in that town, could he see himself anywhere else?

"They'd be fond of us there, I'm certain," he

found himself saying, a sense of effervescent risk ascending through his chest. He waited for Grant to correct his pronoun; when he didn't, Varian went on. "What would we be, two eccentric brothers? Cousins? Would we still say you're my doctor?" He pressed Grant's knee with his own.

"I scarcely know," Grant said. "I don't really know what I'm going to do. But how can I ask you to give up your pretenses if I refuse to give up mine?"

Was he asking that, truly? For Varian to give up his pretenses? He wanted to shout the question aloud, to demand an answer. But just then the bus engine groaned to life again, and a black cloud full of wood sparks chuffed past the window. **"Alléluia,"** someone cried, and a moment later the mechanic leapt onto the bus, clearly afraid that the engine would quit again anytime. With an oceanic roar, the charcoal burner shot the engine full of fumes, and the bus lurched forward up the rocky hillside road, leaving the conversation and all its dangers in its wake.

They got off at Cabris and walked a treacherous uphill path toward the villa where Gide was staying. The address was La Messuguière, the house recently constructed by the writer Aline Mayrisch; she'd used her husband's wealth to make a refuge for others who shared her political views. The house was a sand-colored villa with a tower, at the end of a banked drive shored up with limestone. At the entry Varian employed the massive knocker, and after a few moments of silence, André Gide himself opened the door. He was just as stern-looking, his features just as sharply cut, as his image on the back of Varian's dog-eared copies of **Corydon** and **The Counterfeiters.** He wore fur slippers, an overcoat, and a broad tartan muffler; on the polished dome of his head, a moth-holed beret of russet wool. As he welcomed them into his foyer, his cool gaze sweeping from Varian to Grant, he seemed to make a swift and decisive calculation about their relationship.

"Come in, come in," he said, and they followed him down a few broad stairs and into a tile-floored library. "Mrs. Mayrisch's books," he said, indicating the ceiling-high shelves along the walls. "They've been helping me pass the time. But you must excuse me, it's frigid in here. Marie-Laure!"

A soft-footed young woman appeared in a doorway, and Gide asked her to stir up the fire and put on some extra logs. Varian glanced at the silent young woman, then at Gide.

"Marie-Laure's perfectly safe," Gide insisted. "You can say anything at all. No one's listening, up here on this crag." He crossed one long leg over his knee and waited.

"You'll forgive me if my habit of caution extends everywhere," Varian said. "Our organization, as you might imagine, can't conduct all its work within the law. But we do what is necessary. And we need your help, Monsieur Gide. We're assembling a **comité de patronage**—not donors, you understand.

Official supporters, in the eyes of the world. Artists and writers of the highest order."

"So it's true?" Gide said, adjusting the tartan muffler. "You're spiriting people over the border?"

"As frequently as we can manage it."

"And you'd like me to lend my name to your cause."

"Yes, we'd be deeply grateful. But that's not the only reason we're here. We want to offer our help to you."

"To me!" Gide said, and gave a low two-beat laugh. He removed his glasses and massaged the inner corners of his eyes. "Mr. Fry, do you mean to say you'd like to help me emigrate to America?"

"We think it would be the safest course. And then you'd be free to spread the word about the plight of artists and writers in occupied France."

Gide sighed and put his glasses on again. "And what is it you think will happen if I stay?"

"We can't know for certain. Nothing right now, perhaps. But eventually you might be dragged off to a camp like Arthur Koestler, or placed under house arrest like Breitscheid and Hilferding. Or perhaps even killed, if the Germans feel you pose too great an ideological risk to France."

"But, my dear man, you can't compare my situation to those others. Koestler is a British-Hungarian and Breitscheid and Hilferding are German. I'm a native-born Frenchman. Even under current Vichy law, I'm protected. And consider the uproar if they did kill me! The Germans understand the French relationship with my work. Don't think me ignorant—I know what's been happening in Paris and Alsace, the burning of books, the purging of degenerate works. But, since you've come to me in a spirit of protective goodwill, I must tell you, in goodwill, that your energies are better spent on others." He paused as Marie-Laure came in again, this time carrying a tea tray laden with ceramic accoutrements, though Varian suspected that the creamer and sugar bowl would both be empty. Marie-Laure set the tray down upon a low table and Varian saw that he was correct: there was nothing to accompany the tea but some hard oat biscuits. Gide urged them to take a few.

"I'd like to show you something now," he said, rising from his chair with difficulty, a hand on his hip. He went to the writing desk that stood before a large plate-glass window; over the hillside below, Cabris had spread its strands of red-roofed villas like a jeweler's display of necklaces. Gide bent to a side drawer of the desk and removed a manila folder.

"Look here," he said, handing the folder to Varian. "Open it. Now, there's a reading list to bring home with you to America."

Inside the folder was a thick document, a table of authors' names and book titles; many of Varian's clients' works appeared among them.

"One thousand twenty-nine titles, all banned by the Boches. They must have been compiling the list for months, though it took them all of three days to hand it down to French publishers once they marched into Paris."

Varian scanned the list. "None of your books appear here."

"That's right. The Nazis allow France to read my work, even now. Even in Alsace. Even in Paris. All of it. Even the naughtiest bits. Even the most inflammatory. And why, do you think?"

Grant, who had been listening in silence, finally spoke. "They want to recruit you," he said. "They want you to collaborate."

"Exactly. And I plan to do just that."

Varian and Grant exchanged a single glance.

"You needn't look so horrified. I don't mean to suggest I'll collaborate in earnest. But I'll pretend to. I'll write for their right-wing magazines and newspapers. I'll write for **Le Figaro.** I'll use that stage to transmit messages to the underground. Reverse propaganda, if you will."

"The underground isn't likely to read **Le Figaro.**"

"They will, once they hear of what I'm doing. The word will get out, I'll see to it. And the Boches will be none the wiser. They won't catch my meanings or recognize particular significant French phrases. They'll think I've finally come around to their enlightened view. God knows I wouldn't be the first! But shame on me, shame on me, for speaking in this grandiose fashion, Mr. Fry, when I've scarcely been able to lift a pen since the occupation! I don't know how I can still call myself a writer. I sit in this chair rereading **Little Dorrit** and **David Copperfield,** not because I think they'll yield political insight, only to escape. And meanwhile you boys are busy saving lives in Marseille."

"Many writers are finding it hard to work now," Varian said. "You're not alone. And never say you haven't saved lives. You saved mine."

Gide shook his head slowly. "You exaggerate, Mr. Fry."

"Not at all," Varian said. He knew he had nothing to lose; he would likely never have a private meeting with André Gide again. "As a sixteen-year-old, I thought myself an abomination. Sometimes I contemplated suicide. Then, looking for something else in the school library, I came across **Corydon.**"

"Ah," Gide said. "And what did you learn?"

Varian swallowed. "That the unnatural desires I felt might be seen as natural, even that they might be signs of particular sensitivity or intelligence. And Mr. Grant felt the same when I gave the book to him, some years later."

Gide took off his horn-rimmed glasses and polished their lenses with a corner of his muffler. "Thank you, Mr. Fry," he said. "Thank you for that. One can't help but feel impotent, sitting alone in one's mountain retreat, incapable of any real work. But to be reminded that we can have some small effect in the face of injustice—that's all we want, isn't it? You too, Mr. Fry, Mr. Grant. Am I correct?"

It was true; that was what they wanted. They couldn't aspire to stop the Nazi machinery from advancing across the European continent; they couldn't hope to see Hitler stripped of power, or the triple fences of Vernet fall. But here or there, a life could be saved; and the lives they were saving might save others. Small effects multiplied. That was what kept them at the work. And whether or not the Nazis occupied southern France, whether or not the Spanish borders remained open, the work would go on, at least as long as Varian could find a way to stay in France.

"Please, Monsieur Gide," he said, bolder now. "Won't you consider our offer? Others who refused on similar grounds have reconsidered by now."

"What would you protect me from? A government that's trying to recruit my aid?"

"The tables could turn against you at any time."

"I assure you, Mr. Fry, that will never happen. But I will gladly add my name to your **comité de patronage.**"

"At least promise you'll call upon us if you ever feel you're in danger." He reached into his breast pocket and brought out one of his cards. "My number at the office. My address."

Gide took the card, shrugging. "Certain plants don't bear transplanting," he said.

"Well, we must agree to disagree about your safety, Monsieur Gide. I don't think we've seen the half of what the Nazis are willing to do."

"Let us hope they'll collapse under the weight of their own arrogance," Gide said, and they all drank to that.

---

10 January 1941

Hôtel Beauvau
Marseille

Dear Eileen,

This would be the moment, I suppose, to write Happy New Year. But the fact is, I'm far from happy myself. Here's what I keep wondering, night after night: Who can it have been among the New York crowd who envisioned Jay Allen as my replacement, and trusty Margaret Palmer as his deputy? In my worst moments I've thought it might be you, my own wife, intent on making my life here so miserable I'd have to jump ship. But did you really think, can you really have imagined, that I'd give it all up to a fool like Allen, who has no interest in anything but his own journalistic career? Please remind the committee, if you will: **Hundreds of lives are at stake.** If I step away, people will die. It's as simple as that. And if I let that happen, how could you look at me afterward? How could we share a dinner table, a bed?

Not that the New Year is entirely without its

gifts. Among them is the fact that I can write to you with some freedom: this letter will be carried to Casablanca by a British soldier, one of dozens who have escaped Marseille these past two weeks—**by sea,** no less—thanks to Charles Vinciléoni, my friend at the Dorade. Vinciléoni agreed to let some of these decommissioned officers pose as crew on his black-market boats. And this week, if all goes well, a few of our clients will leave by the same route. They'll carry letters with them when they go, to be posted where it's safe.

So I can tell you, with reason to believe you'll read my words, that we all expected the Nazis to march into Marseille as soon as the New Year broke. But no sign of them yet, and now the Spanish border is open again. With our associates at Perpignan leading clients out, and others soon to be departing via the Vinciléoni route—and a few valuable ones still hidden away in La Pomme, at the Chateau Espère-Visa, as we've been calling it—the New York office may soon be forced to consider me worth my salary. In fact I guarantee results, unless Jay Allen bankrupts us: just before the New Year he withdrew F152,000 from the ERC's account, without explanation or result. What can he have done with the money? As he never shows his face at the Centre Américain, I haven't had the chance to ask.

Please tell our friends in New York that a transfer of power to that clown and his sidekick is simply unthinkable. They must be called off at once. Neither you nor the committee should have any reason to doubt my leadership. I'm deeply grateful that events conspired to land me here. I could call it the work of the Fates, though it seems cruel to blame a continent's worth of disasters upon poor old Clotho, Lachesis, and Atropos; I suspect it's really the Furies' doing. But whoever is at fault, this is my mission, and I must finish it out.

He set down his pen to glance back at Grant, asleep in the bed they shared at the Beauvau, one arm flung above his head and the other folded against his bare chest. With a sense of dread and guilt, he lifted the pen again.

Your husband is much changed, Eileen. I wonder if you'll recognize him on his return, or if he'll recognize himself. Please know that whatever I've done here in France, I've done always with painful consciousness of my bond to you. I can't expect absolution, nor that you'll understand my reasons. Only that you believe me when I say I remain, as ever, your affectionate

VF

24

L.H.O.O.Q.

It was Breton who proposed that they invite Mr. Allen and Miss Palmer to dinner at Air Bel. Breton was sitting at Varian's side before a small tight fire in the salon, troubling it with a goose-headed brass poker, as they both half-drowsed with their glasses of whiskey. The mention of Allen's name made Varian sit up in his wingback chair.

"What are you suggesting? That we invite him **here**? That we seat him at dinner between Mary Jayne and Jacqueline? What would be the point?"

"To give him a taste of **le vrai Marseille**!"

Varian caught Breton's raised eyebrow, the curl of his lip. "Allen's hardly worth your creative energies, André."

"Do you not think me equal to the challenge?" He adjusted the vermilion scarf at his neck to a more aggressive angle.

"I consider you equal to anything. But I wouldn't want to subject you, nor any of our other friends, to an evening of Jay Allen's big-fish stories. And I don't want to take him into confidence about Katznelson or Zilberman. The less he knows, the better."

"Unless he ends up their sole protector."

"If he ends up their protector, we're all in trouble."

"But what about the Flight Portfolio? Oughtn't he to know of its existence? Should we not induce him to report upon it to our friends in the States? Perhaps we can stage a small exhibition."

"I've already reported on the Flight Portfolio. The New York office knows what we've got, and they don't seem impressed in the least."

"Don't you see, Monsieur Fry? You are not yet using your disadvantage to your advantage. Let Monsieur Allen add his admiration to your own."

"I'm not interested in recruiting Monsieur Allen's admiration."

"Then let's invite him for pleasure's sake alone. And perhaps we'll also exhibit some pieces from the portfolio, just to see if he takes note."

"I'm not interested in Jay Allen's pleasure, either, to be quite frank."

"Not **his** pleasure. Ours. **Entendu?**"

"Why bother, André?"

"Because he is our favorite type of quarry. The type that considers itself intelligent, yet reveals itself at every turn to be a fool. Also because I'd like to make an entertainment for my friend Max Ernst.

He's just come to the neighborhood, you know, and I've been looking for an excuse to bring him to Air Bel. I rather alienated him back in Paris, but the current climate has made my position untenable."

"So you're saying I must really shave and dress on Allen's behalf?"

"I assure you, dear Monsieur Fry, it will be worth the trouble." Breton spun the goose-headed poker once in his hand, deftly, like a parade marshal's baton.

"And what will we serve our guests for dinner, when there's not a turnip to be had in all of France?"

"Mary Jayne's young man will come up with something, I'm sure."

"Killer! I wish he'd just be gone. I believe he's waiting for the right moment to sell one of you out."

Breton lifted an eyebrow. "He's quite a useful fellow, when he wants to be. Who do you think procured that whiskey you're drinking?"

Varian frowned at his glass, then emptied it into the fire. A brief blue-gold flame flared and died.

"Everyone at Air Bel has his place," Breton said.

"Not Killer. And not Jay Allen, either. He has no place at Air Bel, not even for an evening."

"Won't you indulge me, dear Monsieur Fry?"

Varian sighed. "Are you dissuadable?"

"Absolutely not. I have something particular in mind."

And so, three weeks into the New Year, Varian found himself dressing and shaving for a dinner party in Jay Allen's honor at the Villa Air Bel—an **Exhibition of New Surrealist Works on Paper,** according to the invitation. He and Grant, fortified with drinks from the hotel bar, met Jay Allen and Miss Palmer at the tram station closest to the office. Allen had done himself up in pinstripes and a bow tie, Miss Palmer in a filmy gown the color of boiled octopus; its hem must have caught on her heel as she was dressing, and a length of torn lace trailed her like a tentacle. She shivered in a too-thin velvet cape, her head bare.

"Who would have believed it could get this cold in the South of France?" she said. "I might as well be back in Pittsburgh!"

"You won't find it much warmer at the villa, I'm afraid," Varian said. "Firewood's in short supply."

"Oh, I couldn't care less," Miss Palmer said. "I'm so eager to meet Mr. Ernst and Mr. Breton."

"Grand fellows, both," Allen said, though Varian knew he'd never met either one. "And Mary Jayne's a capital girl. Met her in the old days, in Chicago, when she was just someone's little sister at a party. Wrigleys' Christmas ball, I think it was. Winked and cocked her hip at me like she'd seen someone do it in a movie. Too bad her folks sent her off to be finished in Italy! She was done to a turn when I met her."

Grant coughed, hiding his expression behind a

pressed linen handkerchief. Varian avoided his eye, but Miss Palmer withdrew a tin of lozenges from her handbag and offered them to him.

"I do hope you're not getting the cold everyone has," she said. "I've been just **mizzerob** since I arrived. **Tray, tray mizzerob.**"

Grant bowed and took a lozenge, and Varian struggled to maintain his composure. Fortunately, the train arrived; they boarded, and the general crush obviated conversation. By the time their car had emptied enough to force them to speak again, Jay Allen had found a new subject: how war revealed who was and who wasn't a man.

"Now, take Badajoz, for example," he said. "Some people might have fled when they saw the blood ankle-deep in the bullring. Eighteen hundred Republicans already machine-gunned there, and the Nationalists bringing in more every minute. A lot of guys couldn't have stomached it, would have lost their lunches."

A narrow-shouldered pensioner, one who must have known enough English to understand, coughed reprovingly. If Allen perceived the reproof, he ignored it.

"But I had a war to cover," he said. "I stood my ground. Watched those Nationalist guards lead three dozen Republicans into the ring and line them up against the wall." He raised an imaginary rifle. "Bang, bang, bang! That was the end of them. Did I turn away? Nope. Never have, did, or will. Wrote it up. Sent it off. Three hundred thousand copies on America's breakfast tables by the next morning. But now look at someone like your friend Mehring. Calls himself a writer, but he can't even poke his head out of his room. Scared, shifty little Jew."

"Pardon me," Grant said, mildly. "But rumor has it that innocent people are being arrested in this town. Some of them simply for being Jewish."

"Must we say that word so loudly?" Miss Palmer said, glancing around the car at the remaining passengers, pulling her velvet cloak closer at the neck.

"What word? **Jewish?**"

"Perhaps it's not safe to go broadcasting our—er—sympathies."

"I'll have you know, I have no prejudices whatever," Allen said. "Never have, never will. I must be the least Jew-hating person you've ever met. Get along with anyone. But I also tell it like it is. Can't help it. I'm a truth-teller through and through. Blame me for my honesty. I'm as straight as they come."

"Well, thank God for that," Grant said, and Varian had to employ his handkerchief again.

At last they reached La Pomme and the group descended, Varian leading them through the narrow tunnel under the railway and across the road. Allen wished aloud that he had brought his galoshes. Miss Palmer, lamenting the damp and the mud, gathered the skirt of her dress into her arms. Ahead, the windows of Air Bel radiated butter-colored light.

"Hope they have a decent cook," Jay Allen said. "Haven't had a proper meal since I landed. And in France, no less! Wartime privations and all that, I guess. Slim down to my fighting weight by the end of it." He slapped himself on the belly. "Used to throw down a round with Papa, back in Chicago. Cleaned his clock a time or two."

From inside the villa they could hear someone playing "Tumbalalaika" on the harpsichord, someone else singing along. **Meydl, meydl, kh'vil bay der fregn, / Vos ken vaksn, vaksn on regn?/ Vos ken brenen un nit oyfhern?/ Vos ken benken, veynen on trern?** Varian employed the knocker and soon the door opened to reveal Madame Nouguet in her black dress and white apron, her face a mask of displeasure: eyebrows compressed into a tight V, eyes slitted, mouth pinched.

"Well, good evening, Madame Nouguet," Varian said. "May we come in?"

Madame Nouguet stepped aside and held the door open, refusing to meet Varian's eye. **"Vos manteaux,"** she demanded.

They surrendered their coats.

"Entrez," she said. **"Monsieur Breton vous attend."**

They walked into the salon, where they encountered a scene almost identical to the one that preceded every Saturday-night dinner party at Air Bel—Jacqueline sprawled on the divan, holding forth to an admiring trio of local surrealists; Mary

Jayne smoking and talking amid a cluster of male friends in a corner; Breton and Serge and Zilberman engaged in debate; Vlady and Tobias dueling over the chessboard; Jean Gemähling picking out tunes on the harpsichord while Lena sang; and a couple of new friends—in this case Max Ernst, white-haired and fierce, his pale blue eyes like points of astral fire; and statuesque Peggy Guggenheim, wearing mismatched earrings in the shape of an anvil and a bomb—bearing witness to it all. A scene like any other preprandial gathering at Air Bel, except that everyone in the room was starkly, glowingly nude. Men, women, young and old—all had followed the dress code set, Varian assumed, by Breton, who looked up now to give Varian a nod. Varian's instinct was to shield his eyes from all that skin, everyone's skin—Jacqueline's breasts like two white miche loaves, Lena's creamy round shoulders, Wifredo Lam's smooth copper-colored chest, Max Ernst's freckle-scattered back, Peggy Guggenheim's dark soft navel. Mary Jayne, who always dressed so carefully, wore her nudity like a Lanvin gown; her midsection had been painted with black labels and arrows, indicating NENES above and MINOU below. She approached them now with the most casual of smiles.

"I see Madame Nouguet has already taken your coats," she said. "Why don't you put the rest of your things in the library? I'll get your drinks meanwhile. What'll you have, Miss Palmer?"

Miss Palmer stood frozen and agape.

"I believe Miss Palmer takes white wine," Varian said. "How about you, Jay?"

"What is this, Fry, some kind of sick joke?"

Varian turned to Jay Allen and raised a single eyebrow, a trick he and Grant had perfected before a mirror in Gore Hall. "I'm sure I don't know what you're talking about," he said.

"Go to hell. I'm going to call a car at once."

"Dear me, there's no phone here!" Mary Jayne said. "And no car to be had, even if there were. But really, Mr. Allen, you needn't blush. We're all friends here. You and I especially, isn't that right? Though I don't think we've seen each other since I was about fifteen. What a tiresome girl I must have been at that Christmas ball! I was mad about you, as I'm sure you'll remember. Such a good-looking young man, and oh, how you charmed me with your words! I must have embarrassed you, fawning like I did. But speaking of that, you must meet my friend Peggy. She just arrived a few days ago and knows no one in Marseille except me and Max Ernst. But she read your piece on Badajoz and just worships you." Mary Jayne motioned to Peggy Guggenheim, who stood half-protected by Ernst. "Peggy, come meet Mr. Allen."

Peggy Guggenheim extracted herself from Ernst's embrace and crossed the room on tiptoe. She had been labeled VENUS by the same hand that had marked Mary Jayne; she seemed so deeply at ease that Varian had to wonder how much of her life she spent unclothed.

"Enchantée," she said to Allen, who stared openly at her pubis. "You'll forgive me if I stammer. I'm rather overwhelmed to be in your presence. To think that I'd meet you here, in the South of France! Why," she said, lowering her voice, "don't tell Breton I said so, but you're the finest writer in this room. You're much better than your old friend Hemingway, by the way, and don't you ever let anyone tell you otherwise."

Allen stammered that he had not, indeed, ever let anyone tell him otherwise.

"Well, I'm awfully glad to hear it. Won't you tell me what you're working on now?"

By this time Miss Palmer had recovered enough to register Peggy Guggenheim's tone, which apparently contained too much admiration for her liking. She came to attention, straightening the bodice of her octopus-colored gown, and introduced herself to Peggy. With scarcely a pause in the conversation, Peggy seemed to read Miss Palmer's jealousy and recruited her into the project of praising Jay Allen. While they were engaged in that activity, Mary Jayne leaned in toward Varian's ear and said, "Why don't you put your things in the library, darling? All your things."

"Oh, no," Varian whispered. "Not a chance."

"This wasn't my idea, you know," she said. "It was Breton's."

"You must have had a hand in it."

"Well, I confess, we did put our heads together," she said.

"And what is it, exactly, you want me to do?"

"Only what everyone else has already done."

Grant, meanwhile, had disappeared; when he appeared again he was as nude as anyone in the room, wearing his skin as nonchalantly as he always did. He crossed to the drinks cart and poured two whiskies with water. Jacqueline, seeing him with his back turned, approached him and whispered something in his ear. He nodded, and she retrieved a ceramic bowl of black paint from the sideboard. With a steady hand, she painted the old Dadaist pun, **L.H.O.O.Q,** just above Grant's nates.

"Your turn now," Mary Jayne said.

"Oh, no. The director remains clothed."

"On the contrary. This game requires that we all participate."

"That's how I'm to meet Max Ernst for the first time? Entirely naked?"

"Absolutely. **He** is, after all."

"What a thrill Mr. Allen will have, reporting this to the New York office."

Grant had come to deliver Varian's drink. "Aren't you having a good time, Tom? You look rather too hot in that suit."

"I feel like I've walked into a nightmare."

"Consider how much worse it must be for Mr. Allen."

"Not nearly as bad as it's going to get," Mary Jayne said, smiling to herself.

Varian glanced toward Jay Allen, who was still bathing in Peggy Guggenheim's shower of praise; Miss Palmer was holding his jacket and tie in her arms, and he had loosened the top button of his shirt.

"Oh, dear," Grant said. "He's getting ahead of you, Tommie. Come along," he said, and beckoned Varian, taking up in his other hand the small ceramic bowl of black paint. Varian followed Grant to the sitting room on the north side of the house, the one that looked out over Zilberman's greenhouse-turned-studio; there, Grant divested him of his dinner clothes, taking his time. Varian could not help but close his eyes. He heard himself make a sound, a kind of plea. It seemed to bring him back to himself, and he pushed Grant's hands away.

"Look," he said. "Do you want to undo me entirely?"

Grant smiled. "Seems to me you're already undone. Now turn around."

"No. Are you going to paint something on me?"

"Mais oui."

"Grant."

"Come on now. **Tourne-toi.**"

Like an automaton he turned, and then there was the excruciating cold lick of the brush against his lower back, and Grant's hot hand on his hip to steady him. When Grant finished, he stepped back to regard his work.

"What did you write, you bastard? I can't read it."

"Just your name. The French version. Vaurien."

Good-for-nothing. "Perfect, Grant. That'll raise my profile with the staff."

"I'll raise your profile," Grant said, both hands on Varian's hips now.

"Please, Grant. Please. Look what you've done already. Just leave me alone a minute," Varian said, and Grant did, winking at Varian over his shoulder. But it was longer than a minute before Varian could rejoin the group in the living room. And when he did, he was relieved to find Grant half-hidden in a circle of other guests. Mary Jayne appeared with a drink for Varian, and he tried to forget that they were unclothed, everything on full display. Breton, master of this game, seemed utterly at ease in his pale and birthmarked skin; he made no move to hide or cover himself. For a moment his gaze rested on Varian's, and then he beckoned him over.

"Well, André," Varian said. "You've outdone yourself."

"Monsieur Fry, I'm so glad to see that Mr. Grant persuaded you to change your dress. And I rather like his inscription, too. **Vaurien!** Indeed. Why didn't I think of that? Oh, Max—" He gestured to Ernst. "Max, do come here, meet Varian Fry, the one I was telling you about."

And then he was shaking Max Ernst's narrow, fine-boned hand, trying to tell himself that this was all ordinary, just an evening with the surrealists.

Ernst wore his nudity starkly, unabashedly; his nakedness seemed to thumb its nose at the world, to remind everyone that they'd been born unclothed, that any other state was a bourgeois lie. In his presence, Varian found it near impossible to speak. Only through sheer force of will did he manage to tell Ernst what a pleasure it was to make his acquaintance, and to invite him to pay a visit to the office on Monday so Varian might open a file for him.

"Yes, indeed," Ernst said. "I'm eager to get to New York, God knows. I've had enough of this continent. Let me off."

"I wish you could speak to Gide," Varian said. "I wish he were half as eager."

"Yes, Gide would feel invulnerable, wouldn't he?" Ernst said. "He hasn't seen what you and I have seen in Germany."

"You and I?"

"I know you were in Germany, Mr. Fry. I've read your reportage in the **Times.**"

Varian lowered his eyes. "That was some time ago," he said.

"No need to be modest! I've remembered it these five years. It's an honor to meet you at last." His gaze ran the length of Varian's body; Breton pointed out the word painted upon him, and Ernst laughed appreciatively. "An honor to meet you, Monsieur Vaurien."

Varian raised his glass and drained it, wishing for Ernst's courage, or Mary Jayne's nonchalance, or Breton's unselfconscious delight. He himself had always hidden inside his clothes and been grateful for them; hiding, he understood, was his natural state, or at least the one he'd grown used to.

By the time Madame Nouguet arrived to announce dinner, Jay Allen had lost his shirt entirely, revealing an undershirt worn thin at the chest. Peggy Guggenheim dropped another word into his ear, and he shed the undershirt and draped it over a chair; yet another, and he removed his shoes and pants. Poor Miss Palmer seemed to understand that the league in which she was playing far exceeded her own abilities. She held the folds of her own dress around herself as if she meant to disappear. No one tried to relieve her of it; Breton's plan extended clemency toward her alone. The other guests began to drift toward the dining room, where, as Varian discovered, the walls had been hung with selections from the Flight Portfolio: Wifredo Lam's fleeing woman and skeleton child, Brauner's bleeding fish, Zilberman's charcoal-trail bombs, a tableau of melting buildings that could only have been Ernst's, and some others, ten in all, each a reminder of what lay outside the walls of Air Bel. If Jay Allen noticed the drawings, he gave no sign of it; but Miss Palmer, still holding her mud-draggled dress against her sternum, went a shade paler as she drifted from one drawing to the next, her eyes widening, her hands beginning to tremble. Mary Jayne, as if in mercy, directed Miss Palmer's gaze away from the exhibition and toward her place at the table.

At the center of the linen cloth lay three platters of roasted fowl; the birds must have been poached from some nearby estate. Pale gold, basted with a glistening pink reduction, they seemed as naked as anyone in the room. Above them hung an enormous chandelier of stuffed brassieres, smelling faintly of Chanel No. 5. In place of napkins, each guest had a carefully folded pair of women's **culottes.**

Dinner began with a salad of foraged winter greens, courtesy of young Katznelson, followed by puréed turnip soup. Then escargot roasted in olive oil and herbs. Accompanying the poached birds were wild morels and miniature potatoes dug from the garden, everything in tiny quantities, more for show than for nourishment. The main event, in any case, was the conversation. Breton whipped up a froth of praise around Jay Allen, and everyone else injected hot air into the mix. Victor Serge proclaimed the role of journalists second only to that of soldiers on the front lines; Max Ernst declared that a journalist was an artist, plain and simple, and that Allen on Badajoz was the purest proof he knew. Jacqueline lauded Allen's use of the personal pronoun in his work, insisting that it brought the political situation down to human scale. And Peggy Guggenheim dredged a choice line from the well of memory: **There is more blood than you would think in 1,800 bodies.**

Meanwhile, Mary Jayne, seated to Allen's right, kept filling and refilling Allen's glass with dark red wine, a supply of which kept appearing at her elbow, thanks to a series of signals sent by Breton to Madame Nouguet. And Allen, clothed only in the surrealists' adoration and in the drape of the tablecloth, drank and drank. When Jacqueline implored him to tell the story of his ascent to his current role at the forefront of his profession, he began to sing an aria of self-praise. As he spoke, Victor Serge silently left the table, was gone for a brief time, then returned fully clothed. No one, certainly not Jay Allen, who was deep into his own autobiography, took note; nor did anyone mark the moment when Zilberman left the room, then returned a few moments later in correct dinner dress. Jacqueline Lamba was next, coming back to the table in a close-wrapped black silk gown; she sat to the far left of Jay Allen, out of his direct line of sight. But it would hardly have mattered if she'd been sitting in front of him, so transported was he by the wine and by his own storytelling, which had ranged by now from his ascent through the ranks at a series of small-time rags to his first assignments for the **Tribune** in northern Africa. Oh, how he remembered every detail! The ubiquitous grit. The blue-tiled mosques. The camels in the streets. The cries of the muezzin. The difficulty of understanding the local dialects. The ardor of French Colonial women for North American journalists. And he continued to hold forth as Mary Jayne and Peggy Guggenheim silently returned to the table in jewel-toned evening clothes.

At last it was Varian's turn to disappear and reappear; he and Grant slipped down the hall to the sitting room and dressed swiftly, in silence. Just as they were adjusting their ties, Vlady Serge appeared—also clothed—carrying Jay Allen's abandoned pinstripes and shirt, and consigned them to the fire.

"Dear me," Grant said. "It's going to be a cold ride home for Mr. Allen."

And then they returned to the dining room, where by now Jay Allen was the only unclothed person present. He himself didn't become aware of the fact until Madame Nouguet appeared with dessert, a flambé of crepes constructed from black-market flour and eggs and sugar, and set the flaming plate before Mary Jayne so she could serve the guests. A blue tongue of flame lapped Mary Jayne's sleeve and disappeared, and that was when Allen seemed to understand that she had a sleeve, and that the sleeve was connected to a dress; that the person sitting beside her, Ernst, was also clad; that the person beside him was clad, et cetera. At which point Mr. Allen got to his feet, his face shading first to crimson, then to aubergine, and declared that the whole lot of them could rot in hell. He beat a hasty retreat to the living room, where his clothes could no longer be found; they heard him abusing the room in a frantic search. Then came the sound of Allen storming up the stairs and rummaging in the rooms above. Moments later he reappeared, dressed in a too-short pair of pants and a too-small shirt and jacket.

"Get up, Madge," he demanded, throwing his counterpart's cloak into her arms.

Miss Palmer, who had consumed plenty of the red table wine herself, broke into laughter. It was the first time Varian had seen an expression on her face that was anything but anxious or dour. "Just look at you, Jay," she said, in a tone of rich and surprising vindication. "I think you can find your way home just fine without me."

Allen glowered at her as he misbuttoned his borrowed coat, and a moment later he stalked out of the room. They heard the outer door slam, followed by the faint jingle of glass in the window above it.

"Et voilà," Breton said, finishing the last of his crepe. "**Au revoir, Monsieur Allen.** Justice is done."

25

Breitscheid and Hilferding

"But what I am to do with eighty thousand francs' worth of gold coins?" the poet Alexey Dmitrich Konstantinov whispered in Russian-accented French, as he sat with Varian at a café on the boulevard Garibaldi. Konstantinov, with his round dark eyes and hunched shoulders, looked like one of those large black-feathered passerines in whom an unusual intelligence has been observed. Varian had secured him a berth on a ship to Martinique—a real passenger ship, one of the few that had resumed regular travel to the French colonies of the Caribbean. Konstantinov's exit visa was limited to French territories, but Martinique was considered part of France; he would be safer off the continent, Varian knew, and from Fort de France he could petition for entry to the States. Now, before he left the country, the poet wanted to change his gold for dollars.

"Let me put it into the Centre Américain's bank account here in Marseille," Varian said. "The New York office can write you a check once you arrive. The exchange rate, I assure you, will be far better than the Vichy value."

"Hand the money over to you?" Konstantinov said. "Nothing in return until I reach New York? My wife, bless her memory, would call me an idiot!"

"We have no intention of fleecing our clients, Mr. Konstantinov."

"Eighty thousand francs! I can't just toss that money away and hope it materializes later! Akh." He rolled his eyes skyward, as if looking for another solution. Finding none, he sighed and drained his cup of tea. "Well, I've already entrusted you with my life, haven't I? What's the loss of my little fortune?"

"That's the spirit."

"I'm just to give it over to you, then? Bring it over in a flour sack?"

"No, no. I don't want you walking through the streets with it. I'll send my colleague Jean Gemähling to your hotel this afternoon."

"This Gemähling can be trusted?"

"With anything, I assure you."

"All right, then. Have him come for it."

———

Konstantinov's gold coins, arranged in eight neat rows in a dusty green box bound with string, spent the night in the safe on the boulevard Garibaldi. It was more money by far than Varian had kept at the office overnight; he was anxious to get it to Kourillo, their money-changer, and was taking the box from the safe when the outer office door opened with a shotgunlike report. He stuffed the box back into the safe and locked it up, just as Lena rushed in with a dossier of sensitive documents, one they'd practiced concealing in a wall slot in case of a surprise inspection. With a flick of her hand, the dossier disappeared behind the wainscoting. The door to Varian's office burst open. But it wasn't the police who stormed through; it was Jay Allen, florid and breathless.

"What do you mean by this?" he said, slapping a copy of a cable onto Varian's desk. It was a message Varian had asked Miss Palmer to send, one that instructed the New York office to advance Konstantinov seventeen hundred dollars upon his arrival.

"I mean to help my client," Varian said. "That's all."

"Apparently you didn't get the gist of the letter I sent a couple of weeks ago," Allen said. "The one informing you that you weren't in charge anymore. Your only job now is to teach Madge how to run the place. You've got no business messing around with the committee's finances. Seventeen hundred dollars to this Konstantinov, whoever he is! And Madge tells me you mean to cash in a bushel of doubloons here in France. How much was supposed to line your own pockets, I wonder?"

Varian got up from the desk and began to pace slowly. Lena and Jean, Gussie and Danny and Theo stood silent in the front room, listening.

"First of all," Varian said, "I don't know what business you have coming around here to shout at me. Generally you don't bother to appear at all. In fact—let me see—you've not been here **once** since you came to town. How did you even find the place?"

"I don't have time for your impertinence, Fry."

"Lower your voice, Jay, if you wouldn't mind. As a rule, we don't conduct business around here at a volume audible in the street. Now, if you've got a problem with our finances, it's usually Franz Oppenheimer you'd want to speak to. But Oppy's out of the office today, I'm afraid. He's packing his bags. His ship sails tonight. So this matter will have to wait until we've got a new finance man in place. Danny's working on a replacement now. I'm sure he'd be delighted to talk to you."

"That's enough," Allen said. "You're not to do anything else around here—not one goddamn thing, understand?—without written permission from me. I can cable New York in a minute and you'll be out on your hindmost. Trafficking in gold coins! No wonder you've got the police up your shorts."

"One might well ask what's in **your** pockets, Jay. Where's that hundred and fifty-two thousand you withdrew a couple of weeks ago? It's the Centre Américain's money. Everyone here deserves to know."

"Are you accusing me of stealing **my own salary**?"

"If that's your salary, I'd like to know what you've done to earn it. You've spent scarcely three days in Marseille since you hit France."

"This discussion is over. I hope you've understood me clearly. You're hanging by a thread, Fry."

"Is that all, then?" Varian said. "I've got work to do."

Allen spat onto the dusty floorboards, then turned and left the office. He slammed the door so forcefully it bounded open again and banged a knob-sized divot in the wall.

"O, mój Boże," Lena said.

"What a dear man," Theo Bénédite said, once the outer door had closed. "One wants to give him a medal for his service to the cause of freedom."

Lena took a screwdriver from her desk drawer, deftly removed their rigged-up wainscoting panel, and lifted the sensitive documents from their slot. "You see," she said, addressing Miss Palmer. "A perfect hiding place."

"Well, I'll be," said Miss Palmer, and took a note on her pad.

Varian sat back down at his desk and picked up a telegram Lena had handed him that morning. He couldn't deny feeling a deep-seated satisfaction. The fact was that in the past couple of weeks, his operation had begun to enjoy unprecedented success. It wasn't just the reopened Caribbean lines, which only worked for those who could get French exit visas; it was Charles Vinciléoni's route—his network of ship owners and captains, seasoned black marketeers whose politics, if not in perfect alignment with the Centre Américain's, were at least liberal enough to induce their owners to be bought at the right price. Dozens of decommissioned British officers had safely reached Casablanca and Oran by now, and a few of Varian's clients had recently followed by the same route. Every day there were fat dossiers of papers to be arranged, cables to be got out to New York and Washington, berths to be secured, money to be exchanged, money to be handed over to Vinciléoni or to his captains, money to be placed into the hands of refugees who would need something, any small amount, to carry them into their new lives. And now, finally, a hint of movement in a big case: Breitscheid and Hilferding, who had been at Arles now for four months, had been informed by the sous-préfet that Vichy had finished with them, and would soon lift their arrest and grant them exit visas. That was the news Lena had brought in her telegram; now she sat before him, pink with satisfaction, as he read and reread the wire.

"It all looks clear," Varian said. "Sous-préfet assures

visas imminent. But that doesn't explain why Pétain would decide to let them go all of a sudden, when he's seen fit to keep them here for months."

Theo Bénédite, listening at the doorway, crossed her arms and frowned in contemplation. "Traps take all forms, don't they," she said. "Breitscheid and Hilferding are confident enough that France will protect them. Let them believe they can emigrate—even give them papers!—and watch what happens when they try to cross a border. Anyone can say the papers are forged, and they can be accused of trying to leave the country illegally. Then they'll be deported. That must be Vichy's game."

"I'm sure you're right, Theo."

"Then what's to be done?" Lena said.

Daniel Bénédite joined Theo in the doorway, holding his small silver-framed glasses in one hand; he liked to gesticulate with them as he spoke, as if dealing bolts of clarity. "If they're vulnerable at the border, let's avert it entirely. Perhaps we can get them a place on one of Vinciléoni's boats."

"But they think they can get out legally if they wait," Theo said.

"Well, we'll have to convince them of the risk," Varian said. He took up a sheet of typewriter paper and drafted a telegram to be dispatched to Arles. When it was finished, he put on his coat and hat and went to pay a visit to Vinciléoni at the Dorade.

———

He entered the restaurant through a side door, the one used for deliveries. A dark malodorous passage led to another door, reinforced steel, behind which Vinciléoni waited in a windowless office, his desk covered in shipping forms. Varian had never seen Vinciléoni drink anything stronger than soda water; he sat now with a glass of it in his hand as he marked his forms with a red china pencil. Vinciléoni wore his usual high-necked sweater and professorial tweed jacket, a pair of steel-rimmed spectacles balanced on the bridge of his nose. His silver-shot hair swept backward from a midbrow peak, and his eyes were an eagle's eyes, perceiving everything.

"Monsieur Fry," he said, and gestured to a chair. "Won't you wait a moment? My apologies. I'm just finishing with these papers."

"Please," Varian said. As Vinciléoni executed the last of his tallying, Varian's eyes traveled the network of maps that lined the walls, a portrait of the black market: those red arrows and black dotted lines, the ones that connected the European continent to the African one, represented a vast, well-lubricated circulatory system of contraband goods. Now they also represented paths of escape, means of saving human lives.

"What can I do for you today?" Vinciléoni asked once he'd finished. He tapped a bell, and moments later a girl appeared; she was, Varian had learned, Vinciléoni's illegitimate daughter. She must have been sixteen, though her trousers and her round-collared shirt made her look younger, almost pre-pubescent. She regarded Varian with her father's narrow, appraising eyes as she received the marked-up forms. "Bring coffee for my friend," Vinciléoni said. "Real coffee. And what else, Monsieur Fry? Cigarettes? A stronger drink?"

Varian laughed. "You must sense that I'm under pressure, Charles."

"Men of action are always under pressure," Vinciléoni said, and gave Varian his version of a smile: a swift cock of the eyebrow and an infinitesimal wink.

"I've got three fish for you," Varian said. "One small fry and two big ones."

"Big fish, big problems," Vinciléoni said. "Everything has its price."

"You know we can pay," Varian said. "The question is whether your captains are willing. I'm talking about Breitscheid and Hilferding. The Social Democratic leader, and Germany's former minister of finance. And Breitscheid's wife, Tony. And his secretary, Erika Bierman. They've been under house arrest in Arles for months now. We think they're in imminent danger."

"No women on my cargo ships. Finis. The captains won't have them. They can travel by commercial routes instead."

"All right. Just the men, then."

"And how do you propose to get them from Arles to Marseille?"

"I hadn't considered that, I'm afraid."

"Car service costs extra."

"You can provide that? **Car** transport?"

"Everything is possible. A friend of mine has a limousine and a permit to drive with complete freedom throughout the Bouches du Rhône. And for a further fee, I can provide safe warehousing for your big fish here in Marseille. For a few days' time, of course. After that, big fish make a big stink."

"That's brilliant. And you've got a ship that could take them?"

"A cargo ship leaves for Oran in four days. Thirty thousand francs will buy passage. But, if you'll pardon my asking, Monsieur Fry, what will become of your fish once they land in Africa? I want some assurance that my captains won't be undertaking this risk in vain."

"We wouldn't send these clients if we thought they'd get stuck in Oran. We'll do our utmost for them, Charles, I assure you. They'll travel incognito, with false papers. We'll turn them into obscure Alsatians. They're unlikely to be recognized outside of Europe, in any case. They'll stay in Oran for a while—they'll want to wait for Madame Breitscheid and Madame Bierman. Meanwhile, they'll see our contacts at the consulate in Algiers about their next round of papers. The consulate will be more likely to help, I think, once our big fish are out from under the Gestapo's thumb."

"Your embassies seem to employ a kind of upside-down logic, Monsieur Fry. The time to help men like Breitscheid and Hilferding is when they **are** under the Gestapo's thumb."

"Don't I know it, Charles. But things are the way they are. There's not much logic in Pétain's government, either."

"That is why, Monsieur Fry, I prefer to operate under my own laws." Again the raised eyebrow, the fleeting wink.

Into the office came Vinciléoni's daughter again, carrying an enameled tray with a tiny Turkish coffeepot and a thimble-sized cup. The coffeepot yielded a fragrant, opaque brew unlike anything Varian had tasted before. A doll-sized cup of it seemed to eradicate all the watery chicory he'd imbibed since landing in France. "What's in this?" he asked. "Molten cacao? Rose petals?"

"Americans have no knowledge of real coffee," Vinciléoni said, dismissively. "But what about your small fish? Will he be on our ship to Oran as well?"

"No, he'd better travel separately. Just in case anything happens to the big fish."

"Nothing will happen. You can trust me."

"I'm obliged," Varian said. "Still, we'd better keep them separate. The small fish won't be traveling alone, in any case. He'll be with a decommissioned

British soldier, or perhaps a pair of them. I believe I'll send him disguised as another member of the British Expeditionary Force."

"And who is this small fish, if you don't mind my asking?"

"No one of note. Just a German lad. The son of a friend."

Vinciléoni regarded Varian for a long moment through his steel-rimmed glasses, eyes narrowed. "He wouldn't happen to be a concentration camp escapee, would he?"

Varian's throat constricted. Who had been in contact with Vinciléoni? Did he have a set of eyes at Air Bel? And then he knew: It had to be Killer, who operated in Vinciléoni's circles and could surely be bought for the right price. And who might have resented Mary Jayne's willingness to take heroic measures on Tobias's behalf.

"That's right," Varian said, slowly. "That German lad."

"We must have perfect transparency if this relationship is to continue, Mr. Fry."

"I understand, Charles."

"I hope you do. I don't know whether you've had a chance to read this morning's papers yet, but when you do, you'll learn that your friend Ormond, the commandant at Vernet, has lost his job. Apparently the borders of his camp had become permeable in recent weeks. It seems he lost control of his guard force. Four of them were caught here in Marseille at a house of pleasure some months ago, having a grand time while their charges slipped away. More recently, another allowed himself to be drugged while on duty, and woke up missing his uniform and his gun. A prisoner failed to report to evening lineup that same day. The man's identity didn't make it into the official report. But my sources tell me you know where he is. And that he may be rather a bigger fish than you're letting on."

There was no choice but the truth, or at least a modicum of it. "The boy's under my protection. Believe me when I say he's worth yours. We'll pay whatever it takes to get him out of France."

"No deal," Vinciléoni said. "Not now, anyway. The situation is too hot. I can't compromise my network by mixing it up with fugitives."

"What else have you been transporting? They're all fugitives!"

"There's a difference, Mr. Fry, between refugees and fugitives."

"Breitscheid and Hilferding become fugitives the minute they leave France."

"Wehrmacht intelligence isn't trying to chase down Breitscheid and Hilferding."

That silenced him. The two men regarded each other in utter stillness. The ceiling fan above them ticked like a beetle, and Varian wished he had never dared to introduce the subject of Tobias Katznelson. He glanced down at the newspaper on Vinciléoni's desk; visible just above the fold was a snippet of a photograph. He reached for the paper and turned it over. There was Commandant Ormond at his desk, the rows of despots' biographies and historical novels arrayed on the shelves behind him. The commandant stared into the camera as if in amazement at how swiftly fortunes could change.

"Forgive me," Varian said. "I have a personal interest in the young German's case. I'm all too aware of how precarious his situation is. If I failed to be perfectly honest with you, it was only to protect him."

"You can protect your clients best through perfect honesty with me," Vinciléoni said. "I've been honest with you, after all. Inside this room you have a view to my most intimate secrets. You wouldn't know how to interpret them, and you wouldn't know how to use them. But I don't keep them from you, Mr. Fry. I show them to you willingly, as evidence of what I can do for you. I can save your Social Democrats. And, if you like, I'll simply forget that the rest of this conversation occurred."

So Varian's patronage had its value too. "All right," he said. "Fair."

"Advise your big fish to prepare to travel. My men will let you know when the car will arrive to retrieve them."

"Thank you, Charles."

"All charges must be paid in advance, as usual."

"Of course."

"Let's keep our relationship mutually respectful, Monsieur Fry."

Varian assured him that he would do his part. He offered his thanks again. And then, as quickly as he could, he lifted himself up out of his chair and got out of that windowless office and out of the Dorade.

He skirted the perimeter of the Vieux Port, his nerves vibrating with the aftereffects of the Turkish coffee; an amber haze seemed to line the edges of his vision, and his chest felt hot and tight. Back at the office he delivered an edited account of his meeting with Vinciléoni to Danny. He instructed Danny to send a message to Breitscheid and Hilferding immediately, not a written message but a spoken one; he could go to Arles on that afternoon's train. His mission was to impress upon the Social Democrats the necessity of traveling via Vinciléoni's cargo ship, and the foolhardiness of waiting for their French exit visas to materialize. Danny assured him that he would deliver the message, and set off at once. And then, without even a glance at the islets of papers scattered across his desk, Varian half-ran to the Hôtel Beauvau and dragged his suitcase out from underneath the bed. He set it on the luggage stand and opened it, inhaling its familiar interior scent of camphor and laundry soap and old leather. Grant must have heard him moving around in his room; he came through their shared door and sat on the bed, leaning back on his elbows, his long legs crossed at the ankle.

"Where are you off to, Tommie?" he said.

"I have to get back to Air Bel."

"Want to tell the doctor why?"

"Tobias isn't safe out there."

"What makes you say so?"

"Spies are everywhere. Ormond's been deposed. Vinciléoni knows about the Wehrmacht intelligence mission to find Tobias. I asked him if I could stow a German friend's son on one of his merchant ships, and he tore the cover right off my story. Who do you think told him? It's got to be Killer. And Mary Jayne won't throw **him** out of the house. If I'm there, I can run interference at least. Stand between Tobias and the law if I have to. Meanwhile, it looks like we've got a chance to get Breitscheid and Hilferding out." He sat down at the edge of the bed and put his head into his hands.

"What can I do? How can I help you?"

Varian shook his head. "I've got to keep it together," he said, his voice tight and frantic. "It's all spinning apart."

Grant laughed. "You've been drinking coffee, haven't you? Real coffee. I can smell it rising from your pores. And you're talking too fast, making no sense. Come, let's have it: Where are you keeping that miracle drug?"

"At Vinciléoni's."

"I was right!"

"I'm losing my mind, Grant."

"You're not. You're on a little journey, a stimulant journey. That's all. And you're perfectly right. We should move back to Air Bel. If someone's got to stand between Tobias and the law, it should be me."

"**We** should move back?"

"Yes. You and I."

"And live where?"

"In your room. House Tobias in the library again."

"Live there openly? In the presence of Gregor's son?"

"I'm not trying to hide anything from Gregor," Grant said. "And I promised to get Tobias out of France, not to protect his innocence."

"And my clients, and the staff . . . ?"

"Varian," Grant said, sitting up beside him, putting a hand on his back. "Listen to me. They know about us. They **know.** We haven't exactly been trying to pass for straight. We've been spending every day and night with your clients and staff for months. And no one's abandoned you yet. No one's treated you like a pariah. Maybe it makes you a little more human to them. Maybe it suggests there's something at stake for you personally. You've heard, haven't you, that Hitler's rounding us up now, putting us in camps? Branding us with pink triangles so the others will torture us?"

Varian sat silent for a moment, his hands between his knees. "All my life I've enjoyed perfect privilege," he said. "American, rich, Protestant, Harvard-educated. I could walk down the street anywhere and feel, God help me, like a master."

"You don't have to explain that to me," Grant said.

"The fact is, Skiff, I don't know how to live as what I am."

Grant laughed again and fell back onto the bed, his hands open at his sides like empty shells. "Tom," he said, in a voice so intimate as to cause Varian's caffeinated heart to fibrillate. "Tom. Wake up. You're already doing it."

26

An Escape

On the night Vinciléoni's cargo ship was scheduled to sail for Oran, the black limousine went to retrieve Breitscheid and Hilferding from the Hôtel du Forum at Arles. Danny's mission had succeeded: he had convinced them that the time was now, that they couldn't trust France to deliver their visas and let them out. According to the plan, Varian would pass the night with Breitscheid and Hilferding in a secret room in a dockside warehouse, and would see them loaded onto the cargo ship in the morning. By five a.m., Europe's most prominent Social Democrats would be en route to Africa, their false Alsatian papers in hand. There they'd hole up in an out-of-the-way pension until Madame Breitscheid and Erika Bierman arrived, and then they would all set sail for the States.

Varian dined with Danny that night at the Dorade,

waiting for Vinciléoni's driver to return. He had assembled various comforts in the secret warehouse room: sandwiches, wine, blankets to keep out the cold, a paraffin-burning lamp, a miniature medical kit in case of emergency. All that was missing now were Breitscheid and Hilferding. As Danny and Varian made their way through a stand of raw oysters doused in champagne and red pepper, then through a bouillabaisse light on fish but flavored with bright strands of black-market saffron, he tried not to consider everything that might go wrong. He kept seeing the car breaking down halfway to Marseille, the police stopping beside it; he saw Breitscheid and Hilferding arrested on the dock, or assassinated by snipers as their ship passed beneath the transport bridge.

And then the door of the restaurant flew open, and in stalked a barrel-chested man in a black leather driver's cap: Vinciléoni's chauffeur. Varian let out a long breath: the men had arrived at last. But the chauffeur looked furious; he crossed the dining room and banged through the swinging doors to the kitchen, shouting for Vinciléoni. Above the din of pots and pans rose a burst of incredulous French. A moment later, Vinciléoni appeared at the kitchen door and beckoned to Varian.

"Aequanimitas," Danny said.

"Thanks, Danny."

Varian got to his feet and followed Vinciléoni into the pumping heart of the restaurant. Between sous-chefs chopping leeks, fry chefs immersing baskets of **fruits de mer** in crackling oil, and busboys toting Pisa-towers of crockery, Vinciléoni leaned against the counter, arms crossed over his chest, his generally impassive face tight with tension. Before him stood the chauffeur, twisting his hat in fury.

"Idiots!" the chauffeur said in full-volume French, addressing Varian now. "Balls for brains! You paid good money to get them here, monsieur, but they refused to get into my car. Refused!"

"Slow down," Varian said. "What happened exactly? What did they say?"

"I arrived at seven at their hotel, just as you instructed. I waited in the alley until the appointed hour. Nothing. I waited another half an hour. Nothing! Finally I went inside—yes, I know I was not supposed to, but, monsieur, I didn't know what else to do!—I went in and inquired at the desk. The clerk called the gentlemen's rooms. Ten minutes later, a bellboy arrived with this." He produced a note from his breast pocket and unfolded it. **"Not tonight,"** he read. **"C'est tout."**

Varian took the note from the chauffer's hand. "Christ," he said. "Do I have to go out there and get them myself?" He looked at the chauffeur. "Can we leave at once?"

"Absolutely not," Vinciléoni said, frowning. "I can't send the car to Arles again tonight. Too suspicious. Someone's always watching."

"But the ship sails at five a.m.!"

Vinciléoni took Varian by the arm. "Excuse us, Jacques," he said to the driver. "Have a drink at the bar, on me." The driver went out through the swinging doors, and Vinciléoni led Varian through the sea-smelling steam, down into the windowless office.

"Monsieur Fry," he said, settling behind the desk. "You can't force Breitscheid and Hilferding to risk their lives. An unwilling refugee is the most dangerous kind, to himself and to anyone who tries to help him. There's another ship on Thursday, a third on Friday. Go see your clients tomorrow. Make matters clear."

"How can I make matters any clearer? They must think they're invincible!"

"Well. Then you've done all you can, and now you must wait."

"That's capitulation. There's too much at stake."

"There are many lives at stake in this war, Monsieur Fry."

"Not many like these."

"Life is life," Vinciléoni said. "How can you weigh these against others?"

Varian could hardly suppress a laugh: here was Marseille's chief gangster, trader in human capital, disposer of bodies in the Vieux Port, moralizing to him about the absolute value of human life. "Thanks, Charles," he said. "I believe I'll take myself home now and meditate on that."

Vinciléoni gave a subtle cough. "I'll still need to pay my chauffeur."

"Of course." Varian took an envelope from his breast pocket and pushed it across the desk: all those wasted francs. "I'm sorry to have troubled your driver for nothing."

"And I'm sorry about your clients. But perhaps all is not lost."

"All right, Charles. I'll come by in the morning, and we'll see what's to be done."

"You always know where to find me, Monsieur Fry."

But the next morning, not ten minutes after Varian had arrived at the office on the boulevard Garibaldi, the door opened and in walked Breitscheid and Hilferding themselves, having come down on the train like anyone else—Breitscheid tall, long-nosed, silver-haired, his mustache combed and clipped, his suit pressed, his hands manicured; and Hilferding beetle-browed, round-shouldered, glowering over his bow tie. At the sight of them, a hush fell over the office; the staff got to their feet as if in the presence of royalty. Breitscheid, a man accustomed to receiving homage, acknowledged them all with a sweeping nod.

"Herr Breitscheid," Varian said. "Herr Hilferding.

I'm afraid your ship sailed a few hours ago." He couldn't be sure of keeping an even tone; he'd scarcely slept, hadn't eaten anything that morning, despite Grant's urging.

"Let us speak in private, Mr. Fry," Breitscheid said.

"Of course," Varian said. They all went into the high-windowed room that served as his private office. Hilferding glanced out into the street, where a clutch of gendarmes was passing. Varian motioned the men into his interview chairs.

"Suppose you begin by telling me why you refused to take the car I sent," Varian said. "My associate, Mr. Bénédite, told me that he'd impressed upon you the importance of leaving now."

Breitscheid opened his briefcase, removed a dossier, and threw it onto Varian's desk. Varian opened the folder. Inside were two American affidavits in lieu of passport, stamped with official exit visas specifying that the bearers were to sail to Martinique. Safe conduct passes lay beneath. The sous-préfet of Arles had gone so far as to provide them with a letter of introduction to a steamship company on the Canebière.

"My wife is buying tickets as we speak," Breitscheid said. "I instructed her to arrange our passage on a ship that departs next Tuesday."

Varian squinted at the papers, held them up to the light. "Are these genuine?"

Breitscheid gave a single nod.

"Gentlemen," Varian said, slowly replacing the papers in their dossier, "I wish I could congratulate you. But please understand. These papers don't guarantee your safety. I know how cheaply the sous-préfet at Arles can be bought."

"Nonsense," Breitscheid said. "There is no cause for concern. We have been patient, and our patience has been rewarded."

"Still, I can't help but wonder what Vichy is about here," Varian said. "The Gestapo aren't known for their clemency toward famous anti-Nazis."

"Mr. Fry, there is no doubt your work has its value," Breitscheid said. "For a certain class of refugee, it is essential. But in our case, it's simply unnecessary to take a risk like the one you proposed."

"Let's hope so, Herr Breitscheid. I couldn't be more delighted than to think you'll be off this continent in a few days. When you reach New York, will you do me the honor of getting in touch with Paul Hagen at the Emergency Rescue Committee? He'll want you and Herr Hilferding to tell your story to the American people. Particularly to our wealthiest donors."

Breitscheid's eyes betrayed a flash of annoyance, as if Varian had brought up a subject of merely personal relevance. He cleared his throat and said, as if delivering a line from a baccalaureate speech, "We shall always be proud to serve the cause of freedom."

The office door opened, and Lena announced Mrs. Breitscheid and Mrs. Bierman. The men got to their feet. Breitscheid took his wife's arm. "Well, Tony?" he said. "When are we to sail?"

Tony Breitscheid, helmeted in brown curls, her eyes refracted through thick glasses, twisted the handle of her purse and blinked. "The first- and second- and third-class cabins were sold out," she said. "All that was left were some temporary bunks in the hold. I knew that wouldn't do for us, Rudolf."

"Of course not," Breitscheid said. "We'll wait for the next sailing."

"Pardon me, Frau Breitscheid," Varian said. "Are you telling me you didn't book places on that boat? When you've got your exit visas right here?"

Tony Breitscheid tilted her head at Varian and ventured a smile. She wore a hat decorated with a tiny stuffed bird and three red berries; the bird trembled on its wire twig. "Another ship will sail in three weeks' time," she said.

"Three weeks!" he said. "I implore you, Herr Breitscheid, go back at once and book those places in the hold. A passage to Martinique takes exactly ten days. You'll be fed and housed on that ship. What can it matter where you sleep?"

"Excuse me, Mr. Fry," Breitscheid said. "My wife's state of health has been delicate since we left Germany. I'll thank you to leave this decision to my judgment. Do **you** trust it, Rudolf?" he said, turning to Hilferding. "Do you mind the delay?"

"Not at all," Hilferding said. "I trust your judgment in all things."

"Well, then," Breitscheid said, and got to his feet. "Let us not consume any more of your time, Mr. Fry. We will depart three weeks from now. You need not trouble yourself further about us." And he turned to leave the office, Hilferding at his side.

"No!" Varian shouted. "This is idiocy. Take the places on that boat!"

The Breitscheids, Erika Bierman, and Rudolf Hilferding all continued toward the door as if Varian hadn't spoken. They crossed the office through the little fleet of desks, and then they went through the outer door and closed it behind them, their shadows darkening the pebbled glass for a long moment before they faded.

By the time Breitscheid and Hilferding changed their minds, their safe conducts had expired and they'd had to return to Arles. A new set of desperate letters reached Varian's desk on Friday morning, begging him to help them arrange passage on the ship. Furious though he still was, Varian didn't hesitate; he ran to the steamship company's office, housed in a white-tiled building not far from the port, and laid down the money for the passage. But the clerk only restacked the bills neatly and handed them back across the desk. Only one berth remained, he said. The others had been taken.

Could anything be done? Varian asked. Did the

clerk understand that this was a matter of life or death? But the clerk couldn't do anything himself; monsieur must wait until the company president arrived. So Varian sat in the waiting room for three hours until Monsieur Berthomieu, the president, came in to work. As soon as Berthomieu granted him a moment's audience, Varian begged the man to open bunks for Breitscheid and Hilferding, even to displace passengers from one of the filled cabins, to accommodate two of the most prominent anti-Nazis in Europe. Berthomieu assured him that the refugees would have the best cabins available when the next ship sailed in three weeks' time. Varian, unwilling to capitulate, paid a deposit on the single available place and sent a note to Arles imploring one of the men to take it.

The next morning he had a letter from Arles to the effect that Hilferding, traveling alone, would take the place on the ship. He ran to the steamship company and paid the balance of Hilferding's passage. Then he sent off a wire to Hilferding, telling him to take the next train. He would await him in the office.

But instead of Hilferding, two letters arrived. One came from Arles, from the sous-préfet himself, with a pompous looping signature in blue-violet ink. The letter informed him that the sous-préfet had been compelled to revoke the visas of Messieurs Breitscheid and Hilferding on an order from Vichy.

If Monsieur Fry desired to contact them in future, he should apply not to the sous-préfet but to the commissaire at Vichy, as the men had been transferred there to await extradition to Germany.

The other letter was from Harry Bingham at the consulate. Varian opened it with shaking hands and learned that Walter Mehring had been granted permission to enter the United States on an emergency visa.

Varian opened the safe and took out a sheaf of American dollars. He put the money into an envelope and the envelope into his pocket. Then, without a word to anyone at the office, he went to the Hôtel Splendide. He nodded to the familiar clerk at the desk, ascended the green-carpeted stairs to Mehring's floor, and knocked on his door with all his might. Mehring opened the door in terror, wearing nothing but a towel and a pair of hotel slippers.

"Good God," he said. "What's happened?"

"Walter," Varian said. "How would you like to sail for Martinique on Tuesday morning?"

Mehring's mouth dropped open. "How can that be possible?"

"Your U.S. visa has arrived."

Mehring took two steps backward and sat down heavily on the bed, clutching his towel around him. "I—I haven't the money for a steamer ticket."

"Your ticket's paid for," Varian said. "Courtesy

of the Centre Américain." He took the envelope of dollars from his pocket and threw them onto the bed. "And here's a bit of bribe money, in case you need it."

Mehring looked into the envelope, his expression darkening. "Do you mean I'm simply to show up at the port with a stack of American cash?"

"That's right. And a stack of forged French documents. But I think you'll make it, considering the genuine U.S. visa."

"Will I not be begging to be arrested?"

"You could be arrested right here in this room. You're no safer staying. The short story is, you've got to try. Hilferding was supposed to take that berth. He had an exit visa, a real one. But his visa was revoked, and he's been sent to Vichy. He'll likely be extradited to Germany next week."

Mehring looked down in dismay. "And I'm to take his place?"

"That's right."

Drawing the towel tighter around his waist, Mehring went to the rolltop desk and extracted a pack of cigarettes from underneath a pile of clothes. With a trembling hand, he tried to light one, failing twice before he got the paper to catch. "Sit down, please," he said. "Let's discuss this with cool heads."

Varian pulled out the desk chair and cleared it of newspapers. "You know I wouldn't ask you to risk it, Walter, if I didn't think you had a real chance.

We've gotten dozens away on ships these last few weeks."

"But why me? Why not Chagall, for God's sake? Or Zilberman? Or young Katznelson?"

"The Chagalls don't have their papers yet, nor does Zilberman. As for Tobias, he's got to travel under the radar. We can't just put him on a passenger ship. There's no one ahead of you in line, Walter. You're going to have to take your chances."

Mehring went to the wardrobe and exchanged his towel for a bathrobe. Then he sat down on the bed again and let a curl of smoke encircle his face. "As a refugee," he said, "you get used to your particular set of intolerable circumstances. Not that this room is intolerable, understand! Not that my situation compares in any way with what's going on in the camps. I've just had a bath and dinner, for God's sake. But you understand—having tried and been caught before, and having washed up here alive, I'm reluctant to try again."

"I understand," Varian said. "Believe me."

The two men sat in silence for a long moment as Mehring smoked. When he looked up again, his eyes held a shadow of shame. "I know I have a reputation for cowardice," he said. "Your colleague Mr. Allen seemed to regard me as an object of contempt for that reason, the few times we met. But is it cowardly to fear for one's life when a nation, an alliance of nations, wants to end it?"

"No one could call you a coward. You made it here to France, and then you nearly got out. But now you've got to make it all the way to the States. I want you to live to write about all this."

"There's no need to convince me. I intend to go."

"Do you?" Varian said. "Do you really?"

"Yes."

"Thank you, Walter. You've given me a gift."

"You seem to think I was going to say no," Mehring said, with a wry half-smile. "Perhaps you consider me a coward after all."

"Never."

"Send me your instructions, then. I'll prepare."

On Tuesday morning, Varian carried Mehring's suitcase from the Hôtel Splendide to a dock on the quai de la Joliette, where a steamer called the **Ipanema** idled. Boats like the **Ipanema** had been drifting out of Marseille since the Caribbean routes had reopened, each ship so carefully policed, the passenger lists so tightly controlled, that they might as well have been carrying prisoners. And the steamers themselves looked grim enough to pass for prison ships: with all the lead paint going to warships, the commercial liners had begun to show their age. This **Ipanema** looked to have survived a tight squeeze through a rocky passage. Long lines of bare-scraped steel ran along its sides, trailing streamers of rust toward the lapping waves. The black triple smokestacks, gale-blasted and birdshat upon, had faded to a mottled gray. Even the lifeboats looked unseaworthy, their emergency red washed to pink, their hulls riddled with visible holes. Mehring stood beside Varian on the quay, regarding the vessel with skepticism.

"My first voyage," he said. "I'd hoped for something better than a sieve."

"I'm sure she's sounder than she looks," Varian said.

A narrow tarpapered customs office had been erected along the quay; beyond it, the gangway to the boat was guarded by two soldiers with bayoneted rifles. Passengers extended in a straggling line down the cobbled sidewalk at the edge of the water, waiting to have their papers inspected. The late January light made a glittering hash of the port, and seagulls dove and wheeled over its surface, griping about the lack of food. Mehring squinted into the glare, not making a move to take his suitcase from Varian. Against his chest he held the dossier that contained his travel documents.

"What's the matter, Walter?"

"Listen," Mehring said, cocking his head toward the customs office. "They're playing Wagner."

Varian listened. "Sure enough," he said. **"Lohengrin."**

"The Führer's favorite. Doesn't that strike you as a bad sign?"

"Only one more indication that you've got to leave at once."

Mehring sighed. "Will you wait here until I board?"

"Of course."

"Thank you, dear Varian. Thank you for all." He took the suitcase at last, testing its heft. "I should have given away more books, shouldn't I?"

"Maybe. Let's hope you don't sink the whole tub."

Mehring laughed. "All right, then. **Je m'en vais.**" He put a hand on Varian's shoulder for a moment, then turned away, blinking. Finally he joined the customs line, and within minutes a guard ushered him into the building. Varian leaned against a pylon to wait, his collar turned up against the mistral. If all went well, Mehring would reach New York in a month; from there he planned to take a train to Hollywood, where he had friends who wrote for the movies. Varian fortified himself with an image of Mehring arriving in the sea-salt haze of Los Angeles, yellow light pouring down along Sunset Boulevard as a taxi conveyed him toward the white haven of the Chateau Marmont. Then a clean bright room next to a starlet's, the nearest German officer thousands of miles away.

He waited as the light changed from morning's blue-white glister to a flat pale yellow. How long had it been now? An hour? He checked his watch: forty-eight minutes. He ought to have gone in, posed as Mehring's lawyer or editor. But the main thing was not to draw attention. He twisted his hands and waited, wondering what he would do if a black police car came to haul Mehring away.

At last Mehring emerged from the customs office. He split the brace of soldiers at the base of the gangway, then ascended the ramp with his book-laden suitcase in hand. He looked over his shoulder as he neared the top, flashed Varian a V for victory, and was gone.

Varian turned and walked the narrow streets toward the center of town, toward the office, where Grant would be sitting at the desk, poring over Katznelson's file. And as he wove his way through the crustacean sellers and purveyors of Provençal soap, through the mingled scents of tea and deep-fried fish and lavender, he found himself envying his client—Walter Mehring, of all people, former enemy of the German state, who had for months been pursued, criminalized, forced to cower in a Marseille hotel room in fear of the knock at the door that would signal the end of his flight. Now, in possession of visas and a steamer ticket, Mehring could simply board a boat and travel to America, where he was welcome, at least relatively speaking, to make a life and home. Whereas he, Varian Fry, child of Ridgewood, New Jersey, spoiled son of a New York stockbroker, graduate of Harvard, recent editor of Headline Books—if he accepted what he was, and how could he fail to do that now, when all the evidence shouted it?—he could find no nation on earth, no welcoming shore, no Liberty lifting her torch in a harbor. There was no street he could walk without fear of discovery, no end to his diaspora. Grant was his only country, and would be for as long as he lived.

27

Ausgang

In the weeks that followed, the clients of the Centre Américain poured out of France in waves. The sea route, no longer a fantasy, was a rolling and glittering path toward safety. The Pyrenees route had gotten clients out in ones and twos, but now two or three dozen could leave at a time. All it took were papers, real and false; papers good enough to pass the capricious and imperfect scrutiny of customs.

But not for Breitscheid or Hilferding; their chance would never come again. Four days after the **Ipanema** sailed, Frau Breitscheid wrote to Varian that the French police had driven her husband and his friend to Vichy and handed them over to the Gestapo. Jay Allen, chasing a newspaper story somewhere near Cannes, sent word by Miss Palmer that he would go to Vichy himself, and pledged to do what Varian had not been able to do. But the next day,

Breitscheid and Hilferding were transported over the Demarcation Line under the guard of four Gestapo agents, according to a panicked telegram from Frau Breitscheid. No one knew where they were now.

In Varian's office Mary Jayne sat on the windowsill, smoking one of her long gold-encircled cigarettes, while Varian slouched in his desk chair and stared at the lines of the telegram until they dissolved into a gray-green blur. When he raised his eyes, the empty chairs before his desk seemed to fill with ghosts. If he looked farther, through the door of his office, he would see another impossibility: Lena, his secretary, his right-hand woman, loading items from her desk into a wooden crate that had once held **confitures supérieures.** Lena was packing. Leaving. Her moment, too, had arrived. He lifted his eyes and watched it happen. Into the box went her two Polish paperback novels, a bottle of toilet water, a bottle of aspirin, a miniature French dictionary, her address book, the fine old fountain pen that had been her father's, and the extra blouse she'd always kept in her desk in case of accidents involving ink or wartime coffee. Though he'd overseen her visa applications himself, though he'd pressed the New York office to petition Washington on her behalf, though he'd written Eileen for help finding her an apartment in New York, he'd failed to believe Lena herself would ever consent to go, that he would someday witness her removing herself from his office, from the Centre Américain, from France. But it was true: if all went as planned, she would cross the Pyrenees two days from now.

"Mary Jayne," he said, finally, desperately. "Won't you get me nicely drunk?"

"Of course," she said, extinguishing the cigarette. "It's one of my specialities."

"Let's do it in Lena's honor," Varian said. "And spare no expense."

Mary Jayne widened her eyes in mock outrage. "Spare expense? The idea!"

That night they threw Lena a farewell dinner at the Dorade, with half a dozen surrealists in attendance, and all the trimmings Vincileoni could provide. He had closed the place to other business so the surrealists wouldn't be surprised by the police, and had uncovered the piano in the corner so Grant could play. Grant, who hadn't sat at a full-sized instrument for months, had no interest in dining. Instead he delivered a steady infusion of old jazz numbers and nostalgic Broadway tunes while Vincileoni's staff kept the glasses filled. There wasn't much to eat anywhere in Marseille, but Vincileoni had managed to produce dozens of mussels steamed in garlic and wine, olives in green-gold oil, and loaves of hard-crusted brown bread. Lena sat happily between Breton and Serge, digging the meat from her shellfish with a tiny fork. She'd chosen a dress of green crepe-de-chine that had never made an appearance at the office; Varian imagined her keeping it carefully packed in paper at the dusty hotel where she'd lived for the past nine months. At her breast she wore a bunch of near-transparent paperwhites, their scent like lilies crossed with scallions. If she felt anxious in the least about her imminent departure, she hid her feelings with masterful control.

Halfway through the second course, Danny Bénédite arrived with a slip of blue paper in his hand: an international cable. At first, no one else took note of him; to the accompaniment of Grant's playing, the surrealists had begun a game of praise for Lena, one laudable attribute for every letter of the alphabet. Danny slid into an empty seat beside Theo and whispered something into her ear. An astonishing change came over Theo's pale features: her skin flushed a deep rose, her narrow eyebrows arched, and her mouth bloomed into an expression that might have been mistaken for sexual satisfaction. She turned to Mary Jayne and whispered to her. Mary Jayne's eyes widened, and she covered her mouth with her hand. Varian beckoned Danny, who came around the table and laid the telegram before him.

FRY: JAY ALLEN ARRESTED AT VICHY FOR REASONS UNSPECIFIED. DETAINED IN PRISON PENDING ARRAIGNMENT. ERC TO PURSUE. PLEASE

RESUME FULL CONTROL OF CENTRE AMERICAIN UNTIL FURTHER NOTICE. KINGDON.

"Well, well," Varian said, flattening the telegram with both hands. "How about that?" He scanned the lines again, a vermilion glow rising through his stomach, his chest. "Look here, Danny. He even says please."

"He would have done better to say 'I've been a damned fool!'"

Lena, savoring a choice piece of praise from Breton—**I** for **inarrêtable**—gradually became aware that some event had stolen the attention of her fellow diners. "What is it?" she demanded of Varian. "Tell!"

Varian clinked his glass with his fork, and the table fell silent. "I regret to inform you," he told the guests, "that our friend Mr. Allen has been arrested at Vichy. Reasons unspecified. I'm to resume full control, Kingdon says, until further notice."

The silence lingered for a long moment; then a dozen voices lifted in a general cheer, and the diners tossed their napkins ceilingward. Grant played a series of **ta-da**'s, his eyes on Varian's, gratified.

"All right," Varian said. "Let's not break out the champagne. Allen's under arrest, and the Vichy police aren't known for their excessive kindness."

"Champagne!" Mary Jayne said, and gestured to the waiter. "Excellent idea. Three bottles to start with."

"**Do** you think they'll torture him, Varian?" Theo said, with obvious relish.

"Not Mr. Allen," Lena said. "More likely, **he** will torture them!"

Miss Palmer, pale and quiet at her end of the table, asked, "What do we do? Are we to let him sit in jail?"

"ERC to pursue," Danny said, giving her a small, tight smile.

"Let New York sweep up its own mess," Mary Jayne said. "They can have him."

A moment later, the champagne arrived and the waiter uncorked it. Glasses were filled all around. As the bubbles rose into Varian's head, he told himself he'd be damned, actually damned to hell, if he let himself feel satisfaction at the detainment of a fellow American, a fellow journalist, particularly one who had already been roundly humiliated at the hands of the surrealists. But, he reminded himself, it had taken Jay Allen exactly **six weeks** to get arrested—and possibly to compromise the mission of the ERC in France—whereas he, Varian, had persisted since August, in the face of the near-constant attention of the French police, the near-total enmity of the U.S. Consulate, and the growing suspicion of Vichy. He'd seen Allen for a fool, had known at once that he would make some fatal mistake, and now it had happened, whatever it was.

But it was true, too, that he hadn't been as careful with Allen as he might have been. In letting the surrealists play their game with him, in taking him to Air Bel and letting him pass an evening in the company assembled there, hadn't he shown too much of his own hand? How much had Allen gleaned about Zilberman and Tobias? How much did Miss Palmer know, and what might she have told Allen? More than **nothing,** that was certain; at the very least he knew of their existence. And what might he say to the authorities now? Considering the animus he harbored toward Varian, how much damage would he be willing to do? He could land Varian in jail if he wanted, and Zilberman and Tobias in the camps. The time had come, Varian thought, emptying his glass of champagne, to get his most sensitive protégés out of France.

Air Bel was a changed place in spring. Tiny chartreuse leaves, limp and purple-veined, sprang forth from the grapevines along the western border of the garden, and the lavender put forth an embarrassment of tight-curled buds. A plush of violets grew at the edge of the fountain, and fuchsias unfurled extravagant lanterns beside the walkways. At night a thousand frogs shot their echoing twangs across the pond. The noise kept Varian awake for hours, though sleep might have eluded him anyway. Since his move back to the villa—**their** move, his and Grant's—he had felt a painful self-consciousness as he lay in his old bed, in his old room, though no one seemed to take special note of their occupying it together. Tobias had decamped to the slant-roofed attic just above, and Varian and Grant had taken to whispering whenever they knew he was there. Their sex had descended into a hushed register that harked back to Gore Hall days, a change not without its own erotic charge.

Now, accompanied by the frogs' incessant call, Tobias traced a triangular route on the floor above, walking from one window to another, then slinging himself into his desk chair with an unmistakable creak. Light filtered down through the ceiling cracks; what was he doing up there? Though he spoke little, he always referred to his attic room as **die Werkstatt.** He guarded it jealously and admitted no one, a precaution that seemed wise enough to Varian. But what did a young genius's **Werkstatt** look like? How did a physicist keep his mind agile in captivity?

After another half an hour in bed, listening to the slingshot **jonk** of the frogs and the creak and grind of Tobias's drafting stool, Varian went to the washbasin, cleaned himself, donned a robe, and ventured up the winding stair to the attic door. He knocked softly, hoping not to startle Tobias, but a moment later came the sound of breaking glass and a muffled yelp. The door opened just a centimeter, and Tobias's dark eye appeared.

"Mr. Fry," he whispered. "Is something wrong?"

"No, nothing," Varian said. "I couldn't sleep, and I saw you were up too."

"Forgive me, I've just spilled ether. I'm preserving butterflies, see?" He opened the door and handed Varian a velvet-flocked card with a yellow lepidopteran splayed upon it, then returned to the desk, where he knelt to wipe up a volatile stain spreading across the floor. He was unclad above the waist; below it he wore the dark green pajama pants Grant had procured for him in town. By now he had become lean as a racing dog on the scant rations, his ribcage a scaffold for his moon-pale skin.

"I caught that one yesterday," he said. "They're a nostalgic hobby. My mentor was fascinated by the physics of their flight."

"Where did you get the ether?"

"Killer," Tobias said, absently. He gathered the blue shards of the bottle into a rag, then lifted the bundle gingerly with two fingers, setting it in the wastepaper basket beside the desk. "I hope I've cleaned up most of it," he said. "Otherwise, we'll soon sleep like surgical patients, or die."

"I'd welcome either, at this point."

Tobias laughed. "I've given up trying to sleep at frogtime," he said. "Try the day."

"If only," Varian said. So here it was, finally, the **Werkstatt:** the top of the desk cluttered with sheets of closely inscribed graph paper and diagrams of wings; more diagrams pinned to the wall below the window. Dog-eared notebooks stacked on the desk, pencils sharpened down to nubs, an ancient slide rule that looked as though it had survived a fire. "You know," he said, "maybe you oughtn't leave things lying around like this. What if it had been the police at the door?"

"I think they'd much rather have your escape-route maps than my drawings of butterfly wings."

"I beg your pardon, Toby," Varian said. "The Nazis may very much want to know your thoughts on the structures of wings."

Tobias glanced toward his notes and shrugged. "Well, I suppose there's no telling what they want. Better to be safe than sorry." And he went to the desk and began gathering his notes, stowing them in a series of manila folders.

As Varian's eyes adjusted to the light, he took in the peculiarities of the room: a birdcage, empty, hanging from a rafter; a dressmaker's wire mannequin draped in a swath of dusty green velvet; a large plaster ceiling ornament, broken, of the kind that might have once encircled a chandelier; a stack of crates marked only with the words **Plus Tard,** packed, apparently, by a tidy procrastinator. Along the windowsill were an amazing variety of herbs tied into bundles; Tobias must have gathered them from the valley and brought them up here to dry. On a low table he'd spread one of Madame Nouguet's crisp white sheets, and on it lay a display of pinned butterflies. Beside the table was his mattress, and a couple of padded blankets of the sort used to protect delicate plants from frost; he must have gotten them from Zilberman's greenhouse. The place had the air and the smell of a boy's clubhouse, and it filled Varian with false nostalgia for the kind of American boyhood he'd longed for but had never had.

"What would you say, Toby," he asked now, "if I told you I may have found a way for you to leave France?"

Tobias, holding a pinned butterfly in one hand, sat down on the drafting stool. "How?"

"For some time now we've been sending British soldiers to northern Africa by sea. It's not a long voyage, less than a day. The soldiers carry papers saying they've been decommissioned and are headed home. They stay in Oran or Casablanca or Algiers while they wait for passage back to England."

Tobias looked at Varian aslant. "I'm not a British soldier."

"Nor were you a guard at Vernet."

"Oh," he said. "I see."

"Here's what I've been thinking," Varian said. "We can't have anyone know you're on one of those ships. Particularly not the gangster who's been running them. But he's been getting crew cards for the Brits who travel that route, and we could simply take one of those cards and put it into your hands. You'd dress as a British soldier and travel to Oran, most likely. You'd stay with the decommissioned Brits, but only long enough to secure an American entry visa, which I believe we can get you with

Harry Bingham's help. Then you'd take a liner to the Caribbean, and sail from there to New York. Would you be game, Tobias? There would be a great deal of risk."

Tobias nodded. "I don't mind the risk. Whatever happens, it'll be a story to tell Sara." He turned pensive for a moment, taking the slide rule into his hand. "How far, anyway, is Boston from New York? Are there frequent trains?"

"Three a day, at least. I used to take that route often. I went to school where Sara's grandfather is a professor."

"Yes, Mr. Grant told me that. He said you knew each other then." He focused his dark eyes on Varian's, and between them traveled a complicated freight of understanding. But Tobias made no comment on the subject; instead he looked at Varian with a kind of deep curiosity, as if studying him. After a moment he said, "I wonder if you'd tell me, Mr. Fry. There's something I want. One small thing."

"Anything, Tobias."

"I want to know some lovely and secret place in Cambridge. I want a place to bring Sara." He looked down at his pinned butterfly. "A place where a person might ask for a girl's hand. Not in the usual way. In a way that will delight her, surprise her."

"I see," Varian said, and put a hand to his mouth and thought. "I believe I know the place you want.

In Harvard Yard, on the west façade of a building called Sever Hall, there's a great curved archway above the entrance—a half-circle of rounded brick. If you stand on one side and whisper into the curve, your words will cross the arch to the other side. Tell Sara to put her ear against the brick. Your message will travel."

Tobias smiled slowly. "That's just what I want," he said. "Thank you." And then he set the pinned butterfly on the table with the others, straightening the corners of the cardboard so they aligned. "Find me a place on a ship," he said. "I don't care about the risk. It's time I left this continent."

"You're a brave young man, Tobias."

He shook his head. "Born at an unlucky time, that's all. But you've made some luck for me, you and Mr. Grant. Maybe it will hold."

In late morning, after Varian had slept a few hours, he sat in the greenhouse with Zilberman, unlayering the depths of the Flight Portfolio. By now it contained nearly fifty works, the product of three months' appeal to the residents and friends of Air Bel. Some of the pieces had been executed on leaves torn from books, some on newspaper or on repurposed Vichy propaganda posters; some had been painted in miniature upon expired travel documents, papers that had failed to win their bearers exit from France. Chagall, Ernst, Lam, Lamba, Dominguez, Masson, Brauner: all had contributed, all had donated, stipulating only that the works be used to raise funds for the Centre Américain. Peggy Guggenheim had made all the arrangements for a show at a private gallery; from there the works would move to the Museum of Modern Art, thanks to Varian's letters to Alfred Barr. Barr had written a piece about the Flight Portfolio for the **Times,** and they had printed it on the front page. His account of what it contained had inflamed desire among collectors, and a speculative bidding war had already begun. Barr had sent a clip of the piece to Varian, and Zilberman sat reading it now.

"Art and money, art and money," he said. "I've always resented the link between the two, perhaps because I don't usually make work that can be sold." He smiled ruefully. "These collectors won't know what they have—no one will know the value of this work, the real value of it, for years. But **you'll** have the collectors' money in the committee's coffers. And you'll know what to do with it." He passed the clipping back to Varian, then went to the sink to clean his brushes.

Varian replaced the slip of newspaper in his pocket and extracted something else, a ship-to-shore communiqué that had landed on his desk that morning. He unfolded it now and flattened it against Zilberman's worktable.

"Lev," he said. "Do you remember my friend Deschamps, captain of the **Sinaïa**?"

"How could I forget?"

"This cable is from him. He says he's to dock at the Port of Marseille in ten days. His message includes a code word we agreed upon, one that would indicate that the compartment in his captain's chamber will be available for a client I select."

"Ah, yes, the coffin," Zilberman said.

"Not a coffin. The opposite. A box to carry you back into your life."

Zilberman ran his thumb through the bristles of a fan-shaped brush, the sable emerging as white paint slid into the wastebucket. "I'm ready," he said. "I would go now if I could. But what about my U.S. visa? Or have we decided that I must simply go where the **Sinaïa** takes me, and wait?"

"On the contrary," Varian said. He bent down to open his briefcase, then withdrew an envelope stamped with the seal of the U.S. Consulate. Zilberman, seeing it, went perfectly still.

"What is that, Mr. Fry?"

"Open it."

Zilberman cleaned his hands, then crossed the greenhouse to take the envelope from Varian. Inside was a single cream-colored sheet: a letter, signed and stamped by John Hurley, the consul-general, attesting to the fact that the German-born refugee Lev Zilberman had been granted official permission to enter the United States, provided he do so within thirty days of the issuance date.

Zilberman, squinting through his glasses, scrutinized the lines of print. "This is genuine?" he said. "Not a forgery by some clever artist?"

"Genuine," Varian said. "Courtesy of Harry Bingham. And Barr put up the security for you, all three thousand, raised on the promise of your Flight Portfolio."

Zilberman sat down heavily on a painted stool, one hand open on his chest. "My heart," he said.

"Are you all right, Lev?"

"I will be." He closed his eyes. "It's only the palpitations." He used the marvelously onomatopoetic German word for it: **die Klopfen,** like the hoofbeats of a horse. For a long moment he breathed deeply. Then, opening his eyes, he said, "It seemed to me just now that I could see my wife's face. For months I've not seen it, not even in my mind's eye. It was closed to my imagining. It's been two years since we left Berlin, Mr. Fry. And Sara is a woman by now. Nineteen years old in May."

"Write to them. Tell them you're coming. I'll find a way to get your letter into their hands."

"And I'll leave ten days from now?"

"Two weeks, if all goes well. The **Sinaïa** will resupply here."

Zilberman closed his eyes again, as if to secure the

timeline in his mind. But then he looked at Varian, a new concern rising. "What about Tobias?"

"He'll soon leave by another route. I'm arranging the details now."

"And he'll travel to New York?"

"That's right. Though I understand he's eager to visit your daughter in Cambridge."

"Yes, too eager," Zilberman said, and sighed. "He intends to ask Sara to marry him. He's already asked my permission. I gave it, though not without reservations. They're both still children, really. What will they live on?"

"I suspect they'll work that out. Cambridge will be a fine place for Tobias."

"Let us hope. And you, Monsieur Fry? When do you propose to return to the States?"

"Not until I'm kicked out or killed, whichever comes first."

Zilberman put a hand on the Flight Portfolio, the dense, foliated stack of it. "I want you to see these pieces on the wall of the Museum of Modern Art," he said. "I want you to see what this work will do. I want you to see others perceiving and understanding our struggle. But more importantly, I suppose, I want this work to help you. I want it to lighten your load."

"Getting you out of Europe," Varian said. "That's what'll lighten my load."

"Then tell Deschamps I will go," Zilberman said. "Tell him I am ready."

28

Exquisite Corpse

Evening was falling, descending along the Val d'Huveaune like a shadow cloak, like a tissue-thin eyelid hazed with veins. Varian stood at the open window, dressing for dinner; Grant, at the harpsichord downstairs, conjured a Handel suite for the arriving guests. A series of minor arpeggios mounted to Varian's window and disappeared into the darkening sky. From outside came the scent of sage and wet earth; a rainstorm had tamped down the afternoon's dust, and the mistral blew across the valley. A nightingale lit in the medlar tree beneath the window and launched into variegated song. It occurred to Varian that the combination of voices below—Breton's baritone, Victor Serge's tenor, Mary Jayne's seen-it-all alto, Jacqueline Lamba's rough-edged soprano—made a music soon to be lost forever. Tonight's dinner was to be a farewell to the Bretons and Serges. Varian had managed at last to conjure their French exit visas, and to coordinate the dates with their U.S. entry visas; Ingrid Warburg herself had provided affidavits of financial support, and the State Department, for reasons mysterious, had at last capitulated on its refusal to let those reputed communists enter the country. A refitted cargo ship, the **Capitaine Paul Lemerle,** would carry them westward on Monday morning, the twenty-fourth of March.

For a moment he was certain that, by the time he went downstairs, it would all have vanished, leaving him alone in the house, the harpsichord silenced, the nightingale gone, the valley devoid of leaf or twig, the city below vaporized, nothing but empty space between the house and the sea. It all seemed grossly unfair. He wanted nothing at all to change. Wanted to descend each night to find Breton at the table, gesticulating wildly to Serge; Breton's bright beetles in a jar on the mantel, Serge's papers strewn disastrously across the library table, Jacqueline arguing softly to Mary Jayne, Vlady Serge cursing in Russian as Tobias checkmated his king. Nothing at all to change: what a thing to want in the midst of a war. But where else could he feel, with such certainty, that there was no dinner table more brilliant or more savage, and nowhere else in the world he'd rather be? Where else could he know himself so clearly and not wish to be someone different?

When he went down, Mary Jayne took his hand

and led him to the window seat. She wore a peony-colored dress ironed into a thousand tiny pleats, like lines of force in a physicist's diagram; her expression was bitter, her eyes shadowed underneath.

"You'll have to serve as my date for the evening," she said. "Killer's pretending I don't exist."

"What happened?"

"Oh—it's an awful thing, stupid on all sides. I lost a bracelet, a diamond-and-sapphire one—a pretty little bracelet, and I valued it, it was a present from my father to my mother years ago, she gave it to me before I went to school in Italy. Anyway, I misplaced it—and then I'm afraid I got rather sparkling on champagne, and accused Killer of nicking it. Well, that didn't sit too well with him. So he's in town tonight, probably with some whore. Some other whore, I mean," she said, winking in the face of her misery. "The awful thing is, I think he really did steal it. And how sad that he thought he had to, when I would have just given him the money if he'd asked!"

"That little weasel. I'll set the cops on him."

"No, no, you can't. He's already outside the law. They'll send him straight to a camp."

"He's a common criminal, Mary Jayne. He's a danger to us all. How can you not see it, as intelligent as you are?"

"Maybe in some arenas I'm blind, or dumb. But I know he's not mean-spirited. He can't stand being dependent on anyone. He's desperate, that's all, and he doesn't like to ask for help."

"Well, you're not to let him in if he comes back tonight," Varian said. "Nor ever, frankly. I don't want to see his pointy little face around here again."

Mary Jayne's eyes filled with tears. "But Varian—this is my home too, for the moment. You can't throw Killer out of it, whatever he's done."

"Mary Jayne! Can't you let him go? You deserve someone who sees what a goddess you are, and treats you that way!"

"I don't want to be treated as a goddess. You must know that by now."

"It's just that I'm rather fond of you, and rather grateful to you, and—well, I'm sorry, that's all. I'm sorry he would do such a thing. But you can't let him in here again. He's entirely without scruples. He'll hand us all over to the highest bidder."

"Let's not talk about it anymore," Mary Jayne said. "Let's fete the Bretons and the Serges. Our family is breaking up. I'd like to drown my sorrows in drink, if you don't mind."

At that moment, Breton approached with an open bottle of champagne. "What sorrows?" he said. "No one is to have sorrows! This is a glorious night! Drink, drink!" And he filled their glasses and watched, like the doctor he was, as they took their medicine.

For their final revel at Air Bel, the surrealists had

proposed an old favorite: **Cadavre Exquis.** The guests would collectively produce drawings or stories by passing a sheet of paper around, folded to reveal only a sliver of what the previous artist had produced; they would play the game at the dinner table, as a distraction from the fact that there was so little to eat. Breton led them all into the dining room and claimed his usual seat at the head of the table, rapping his wineglass with his fork to bring them all to attention. He took a deep breath, his face flushed above his red cravat; alone among them all, he had managed to look well fed after the winter. When he smiled, his expression seemed to suggest a private joke.

"Dear friends," he said. "Victor. Max. Peggy. Wifredo. All of you! Tonight we celebrate the solemn rites of a funeral. We lay to rest five months here at Air Bel. Monsieur Fry, our savior, has proved he is not entirely a **vaurien.** He has redeemed himself by procuring, at last, our visas. On Monday we sail into the unknown." He paused for effect, looking around the table, which was decorated for the occasion with two great glass vases filled nearly to the top with pondwater, teeming with live miniature frogs. "We've survived, by my count, five raids by the police, three nights on the S.S. **Sinaïa,** the unfortunate sight of Jay Allen's naked corpus, and at least two hundred and thirty instances of my own pomposity. We have shed our illusions as to the limits of our own absurdity, an admirable achievement in any season. We have survived privations of food and excesses of liquor. And for all this we have to thank Monsieur Fry." Breton raised his glass. "Let us pledge now to meet in New York. We will meet to celebrate the reassembly of this group on friendly soil. Monsieur Serge and I vow to disagree continually, as we have every day here at Air Bel, and Madame Lamba will shame us all with the unabashed beauty of her work. Monsieur Grant will play New York melodies for us. Monsieur Katznelson will feed us on something he's scrounged from the forests of Central Park. And Monsieur Fry will lie about in leisure like a pasha, free to be a **vaurien** again, having already saved us all."

"Let it be so, André," Serge said, raising his glass.

"Hear, hear," said Mary Jayne, raising her own. And then they made a chiming music around the table, each glass meeting a dozen others, and when at last they'd finished, they turned their attention to their plates. On each white circlet lay a few new leaves of pale green or purple lettuce, a few carrots slender as a child's finger, Jerusalem artichokes sliced to a transparent thinness, a scattering of tiny black mushrooms like discarded glove-buttons. There was olive oil, and a sliver of bread to dip in it; there was contraband cheese, a shaving of it for each guest. Eating that minuscule salad, Varian felt as if he'd never been so full in his life, and never would be again.

They passed around paper and pen and ink. As

Madame Nouguet and her helpers cleared the salad plates, the company wrote their absurd sentences. **The elegant young countess / adumbrated the faults of / his nine sub-generals, all of them / hopelessly in love with / the tentacles of a pink octopus.** And: **A man's true purpose is to uncover / the basket of rotten apples just beneath / his dignity, though he did not fail to / point out my favorite of the fire-eyed Furies.** They drew Medusa hair with Maréchal Pétain's face, connected to a giraffe neck, a three-armed torso, a centaur's lower half, and military-booted feet. Victor Serge, assuming a Maréchalesque voice and mien, examined the drawing and professed outrage. Breton praised the ingenuity and skill of his fellow villa inhabitants, and proposed they give the products of their game to Varian as a parting gift.

No visit from the police interrupted their revel. No void opened in the earth to swallow Air Bel, to suspend it in some subterranean limbo where time would fail to proceed. The guests ate tiny squares of black-market chocolate, smoked their after-dinner cigarettes, and drank the last inches of a bottle of Armagnac. Then everyone walked out onto the terrace, where the rising wind made a disaster of the women's dresses. No one seemed to care in the least; they were all too drunk to feel the chill. Varian stood at the terrace railing and looked down into the garden, at the shapes of the men and women drifting along the twisted garden paths like shadow puppets against a moon-illuminated sky. Grant stood beside him, radiating warmth and blocking the wind; he struck a match and bent to light his cigarette.

"It's like the end of term at school," Grant said, and took a long inhale.

"Right," Varian said. "But without the prospect of next year."

"Don't you believe we'll meet again in New York?"

"Do **you**?" Varian said, half-turning to Grant. "Tobias will be gone soon. You'll settle Gregor's accounts. And then what?"

"Yes, then what?" Grant repeated, more quietly, like the echo of a musical phrase. Together they looked down at Tobias Katznelson, watching him thread the path through the spring-wild garden; at its end he skipped onto a low stone bench and stood lightly on his toes, a slim parenthesis against the evening sky.

"Once Toby's off the continent and that other work done," Grant said, "I want to do more for the Centre Américain. I can become a regular member of your staff without worrying about what might happen if I'm arrested. Once I've acquitted myself of my duties to Gregor, I'll be entirely at your disposal."

Varian rolled the edge of his cuff between his fingers. "And when **will** you have acquitted yourself of your duties to Gregor? Don't you owe him something more?"

"More than his son's life?"

"Don't pretend you don't know what I mean, Grant."

Grant took a final drag of his cigarette, then extinguished it on the terrace stones. He put a hand on Varian's elbow. "Can't we talk inside?"

Varian followed him back into the house, toward the salon, where an abandoned fire smoked in the grate. Grant took the poker and broke up the coals, looking down into the flickering orange serpentines of light. When he raised his eyes again to Varian's, his gaze was terrible, raw. He seemed his barest self, unguarded, stripped to the core.

"I wrote to Gregor this morning," he said. "I told him I'm going to extend my stay. I said I didn't know for sure when I was coming back."

A void opened beneath Varian, a well of unexpected terror. In some deep part of him he'd always understood their life in France as existing in a separate space, a place outside of ordinary time. They could do what they were doing only in a France at war, the country dissolving around them, the Nazis advancing, the U.S. Consulate losing its patience. Grant's eyes were on him, and, as ever, in their severe and penetrating light, Varian found it impossible to produce anything but the truth.

"I've told Eileen nothing," he said, in a half-whisper. "What could I say? We haven't exactly talked about it, you and I."

"Talked about what?"

"You know, Grant. What happens after."

Still holding the poker, still moving the coals, Grant went on in the same low voice. "Gregor always assumed I'd come back once I found Tobias. He had no reason to think otherwise. I don't know how he'll take my letter. I didn't mention your name, but he can't help but guess. He knows something of what you were to me. I couldn't keep it all from him." Grant pushed the poker into the heart of a log, producing a cataract of glowing dice. "I don't know what he'll do. He's not exactly surrounded by warm connections in the States. And he doesn't know how to navigate any of the ordinary channels in the city, you know, the ways we find each other—our type, I mean. When I think of that letter making its way to him, I feel like a villain." He looked down at the hearth tiles, scenes of a hunt, a brush-tailed fox eluding its pursuers. "But I had to do it. I'd be a liar otherwise. And not just to Gregor."

Varian absorbed his look. He imagined Katznelson opening a mailbox in the lobby of his apartment building near Columbia, the rush and thrill of seeing the airmail envelope with Grant's name in the upper left; he would take it upstairs, lay it on the kitchen table near the window overlooking the park, perhaps pour his coffee before he opened it. He was, Varian was sure, the kind of man who employed a small sword-shaped letter opener. He would unfold the pages with care, smoothing them against the polished wood of the table; he would take his spectacles from his waistcoat pocket and proceed to decipher Grant's pointed, grasslike script. **Dear Gregor. I feel I must inform you.** And then a change of weather would seem to descend upon him, a wave of cold that would begin at the top of his skull and encase him as if in a shell of ice.

"I almost lost my nerve," Grant said. "I felt I was doing to him something no better than—than what I'd experienced all those years ago."

And now, Varian thought to himself, he'd have to do that to Eileen. To Eileen, whom he still loved. But to keep writing to her as if nothing had changed: Wasn't it just as cruel, a deliberate obfuscation? He sat down on an ottoman and put his head into his hands.

"I'm sure Eileen knows already," he said. "How could she not?"

Grant laid a hand on Varian's shoulder. When he spoke, it was in the lowest of tones, in a voice that seemed to come almost from inside Varian's head. "After all, Tommie," he said. "Would you rather not write her? Do you want to go back, as if none of this had happened? If that's what you want, how can I stop you?"

Varian got to his feet and pulled Grant against him, feeling the rise and fall of his chest, the pulse at his throat, the rhythm of the blood that preserved his irreplaceable life. "No," he said. "That's not what I want."

Grant's arm came around his waist and Varian held

him, not caring that they might be seen through the lighted windows, not caring that Madame Nouguet might walk in at any moment to tend the fire. He held Grant against him as if to do anything else would kill them both.

"I have to tell you something else," Grant said into Varian's ear. "If you want to hear it."

"Whatever you want to tell, I want to hear."

Now Grant took a step away and went to the fireplace again. He was a long moment looking down into the coals, twisting the nautilus cufflink at his wrist. "I've written to the dean of faculty," he said, finally. "I sent the letter today."

Varian lifted his eyes to Grant's. "You did what?"

"I wrote to Herbert Hawkes at Columbia, to tell him what I am. I've told him I'm the grandson of a former slave, the son of a Negro entertainer, and that I've made false statements of my parentage on every legal document or application I've filled out for the last fifteen years. I've written that Harvard College doesn't know I'm a Negro, nor does Yale. And that, in light of my lie, Yale may choose to revoke my degree, and Harvard to rescind my credits. I've stopped short of actually resigning. If I'm to be ejected from the college, it'll have to be at the dean's hands."

Varian stood in silence for a long moment. Then he said, "You don't really believe Yale would revoke your degree."

"Why not? I matriculated under false pretenses."

"But that had nothing to do with your preparation for study. And you finished your degree like anyone else. Or, rather, not like anyone else. Brilliantly. And with honors."

"No honors matter, nothing matters, in light of that lie. That's how I believe they'll see it, anyway."

"And will you write to Yale, too? And Harvard? Would you strip yourself of everything?"

"Only of what doesn't rightfully belong to me."

"But you earned your degrees, Grant. And they should have admitted you anyway, black or white. Just as they should admit anyone who deserves it."

"A white man earned my degrees. And a white man's been living my life ever since. I haven't taught a single Negro student at Columbia, do you understand? Not one. Or at least not one who wears his blood openly. And I've lived ten minutes' subway ride from my grandparents' church, which moved to Harlem some time ago—yes, I went to see it, I stood outside on a Sunday—and I've never gone inside. Someone must know something about them, where they lived, whether they had other children. I've been too much of a coward to ask. One time, a boy of about twelve came up to me, looked like he'd been dared by his friends. Asked if I was a spy, just like you did at La Fémina."

"And what did you say?"

"I said I was just that. A spy. And that boy called me a liar. He said if I was a spy, I'd never tell. And I said yes, he was right, I was a liar too." He fingered his cufflink again, turning it in his sleeve, his eyes downcast. "These were my father's," he said, quietly. "I never told you that. He left them behind when he went to Europe. My mother saved them for me, God knows why. I sure didn't want them when she first gave them to me. But I brought them here to France, thinking of him, and lately I've been wearing them. When I'm not losing them, that is." He looked up at Varian for a moment, then lowered his gaze. "I suppose I want to feel like I have the right."

"So you've got to overturn everything? Steal from yourself what you deserve to have?"

"**Alea iacta est.** The die's cast. It can't be undone, even if I wanted it to be."

There was a bright chime of shattering glass from outside, and the kitchen door banged open; in came the surrealists, windblown and laughing, crowding toward the fire. They held out their cold hands and relieved Grant of the poker, trying to stir more heat out of the coals. Breton poured another round of drinks and Mary Jayne sat at the harpsichord, which she only dared play when she was thoroughly liquefied. Raising one hand like a conductor, she launched the group into a Broadway tune: "Sometimes I'm Happy, Sometimes I'm Blue." No one seemed to take note of the charged silence between Grant and Varian. The party, carried by its own energy, flowed onward into the night, and the surrealists filled the salon of the Villa Air Bel with drunken song.

Varian waited until he could slip away unnoticed, then climbed the stairs alone to lie in bed in the dark. By now Grant had taken Mary Jayne's place at the instrument, and might play for hours. That experience—listening to Grant's playing through an open window, hearing others carried along by what he produced—was hardly a new one. How many nights had he lain in bed at Gore Hall, tracking the sound of Grant's hands on the keys as he played the compact black Steinway downstairs, gift of the Hon. Henry Fitzwillam Calldwyn and Mrs. Abigail Calldwyn, in the sitting room that faced the back lawn and the Charles? Grant, tied by his ten digits to the keyboard, was, for those few moments, a certainty. As long as the music went on, Varian could locate in his mind the burning center of his universe, the point from which all matter and energy emanated; and as long as that was true, he could lie in bed and find a state of rest. He thought at times that there must be something wrong with him, some lobe of his brain that had misdeveloped in his mother's womb, or had grown awry under her disordered care. How could it serve his organism, how could it aid his survival, to experience this particular fixation, this linking of all his well-being to a single other?

But that was how we recognized love, he thought: It made the exception. It was the case that broke the paradigm, the burning anomaly. In its light we failed at first to recognize ourselves, then saw ourselves clearly for the first time. It revealed our boundaries to be mutable; it forced us to shout yes when we'd spent our lives saying no. For Grant, for this one person on earth, he could imagine doing the unthinkable: living outside of what the world prescribed, even if they looked at him the way they looked at men like him, even if they called him all the worst names: **invert, faggot, abomination.** For Grant, only for him, he would walk forward into the fate that followed the casting of the die. And he would share the terrible weight of truth-telling. Tomorrow morning he would go to his writing table, fill his pen, take paper from the drawer, and write **Dear Eileen, because I love you, I must say a difficult thing.** He would do it. He had to do it; otherwise his life was forfeit. He closed his eyes to await the end of the music, the sound of Grant's footsteps on the stairs.

29

Impediments

He mailed the letter, the one that would spell the end of his marriage, on the day the Bretons and Serges departed for Martinique. Later he would remember the moment he'd sent it—the particular postbox on the corner of the Canebière closest to the office, a corner shaded by a tree with feather-like leaves, one that grew everywhere in Marseille, immune to the mistral, the soot, the salt, the general rhythm of life in that restless city. He held the words in his hand, he laid them on the lip of the box, he tipped them in. And then the letter was gone, irretrievable.

At the dock on the bassin d'Arenc he found his clients waiting beside their considerable pile of luggage while porters removed it, bag by bag, onto the ship. The Serges, **père et fils,** argued companionably about the translation of a passage from **Moby-Dick;** Madame Breton occupied Aube with a cardboard jumping jack. Danny and Theo stood holding Peterkin, who was to accompany the Bretons on their journey. They had decided he would be safer with his aunt in Westchester County than here in France, and had secured his visa three days earlier. Theo tucked an extra handkerchief into Peterkin's pocket, her expression desperately stoic, but Danny wept openly into Peterkin's dark curls. Breton stood a little apart at the edge of the dock, looking, perhaps for the first time since Varian had known him, ill at ease. He had confessed to Varian some time ago his dislike of travel on the open ocean, the terror he felt when the land receded and the planet reminded one of its dominion by water. Then there were the U-boats, invisible beneath the surface, intimate with the routes of all the transatlantic ships. Varian had assured him that a U-boat strike on the **Capitaine Paul Lemerle** was vanishingly unlikely, that the Germans would prefer to spend their precious ammunition elsewhere. But now Breton held a trembling cigarette to his lips and smoked it at twice his usual rate, his eyes fixed on the black-green water of the bay.

"What are you thinking?" Varian asked him.

"Merely, Monsieur Fry, that there's no purer embodiment of surrealism than the departure from land onto a borderless plane of water. One sails over the bodies of millions of creatures, many of them unknown to man—even over mountains uncharted, mountains higher than the highest peaks in Tibet—entirely without consciousness, without the slightest knowledge of their existence. One might, for example, while sitting in the ship's dining room and eating iced pineapple, sail over a great underwater current propelling a fleet of leviathans and their children, thousands of tons of oily flesh moving invisibly and inaudibly along that unbound underwater river like giant corpuscles through the bloodstream of the world."

"André, what will I do without you? Who will say such things to me once you're gone?"

"No one, I'm sure. And you'll be all the better for it, my dear." He put a hand on Varian's arm and drew something from his pocket, a small English translation of Catullus, from which, as he showed Varian, he'd excised a series of words with a razor blade. On the book's foreleaf he'd pasted the cutout words into a poem:

LITTLE OH MY TOO LITTLE THANKS
FOR THIS ALL WHICH GIVING ME
YOU KEPT ONLY YOUR WINGS YOUR WIT
AND A NAME OTHERS SHALL SING

Varian thumbed the pasted words, those pale rectangles against the green endpapers. "André," he said. "You've no idea what you've really given me, these past months."

"I've given you a terrible headache. And now I shall remove myself and all these other jesters. Let us hope we don't die en route. But if we do, dear Monsieur Fry, please kill yourself and join us in the afterlife! I know we'll have a grand time there."

"I'll be sure to, André."

And then a deep-throated whistle blew from the **Capitaine Paul Lemerle,** and the porters removed the last of the bags, and finally the great man and his great wife and their impatient child, her hair dressed in looped braids with cherry-colored ribbons, and young Peterkin, distracted from his parents' grief by the presence of the mountainous ship, climbed the gangway with their friends. Varian watched until they'd reached the deck, and then took off his hat and waved it. Beside him, Danny and Theo shouted their farewells to Peterkin, who sat contentedly in Breton's arms. Varian found he couldn't look at them directly, couldn't witness the grief in Danny's eyes or the horrific struggle in Theo's. They intended to stay until the ship sailed, to be close to their boy until the last. But they insisted Varian return to work, so he turned and walked back to the office as though this were any ordinary day. As though the core—the **coeur**—of the Villa Air Bel had not just been surgically excised, as though he had not just mailed his wife the letter that would end his life with her, as though he could imagine what would happen the next minute, the next hour, the next day.

And now a delicate business must be conducted, perhaps the most delicate of his time in Marseille: he had to arrange a British escort for Tobias, and a place for him on one of the merchant ships that had been carrying the decommissioned Brits to North Africa. Back at the office, where Lena's desk stood silent and bare, and the few surrealist drawings on the wall now seemed melancholy relics, Varian penned a note to Captain Archibald Murchie, the officer responsible for getting the British Expeditionary Force off the continent. He invited the captain to meet him for lunch at the office, to discuss matters important to them both. When, after an hour, no reply arrived, he tried telephoning, but no one answered. Finally Varian sent Gussie over on his bicycle to investigate. Twenty minutes later Gussie returned, flushed and huffing, saying that the secretary had refused to admit him. Varian telephoned again; this time the secretary answered, but when Varian demanded to speak to Murchie, she hung up without another word. What game was this? What had he done to give offense? He picked up the phone and called Bingham.

"What's the news?" Bingham said. "The Bretons and Serges get off all right?"

"Yes. But now I've got another problem."

Bingham laughed. "Never a moment's rest for you, is there?"

"Nor for you, Harry, thanks to me. I want to know what's going on with Archibald Murchie. I can't get a note to him, or get him to take a call. His secretary's pretending he's not in. Do you think he's in some kind of trouble? I've half a mind to call Robinet at the Préfecture, but I thought I'd try you first."

"Well, you won't have much luck at the Préfecture," Bingham said. "Our man Robinet has just been packed off to Rabat."

"No!"

"There's a new **chef de police** now, hadn't you heard?"

He hadn't. But Harry told him now: The new chief, Maurice Anne Marie de Rodellec du Porzic, was an old aristocrat so staunch in his anti-Semitism that he'd recently been elevated to overseer of the Bouches du Rhône. He had pledged **une collaboration d'amitié** with Vichy; he'd professed his own commitment to the New France and to the Maréchal. It was no wonder he'd thrown Robinet out.

"So now what?" Varian said. "You haven't heard anything about Murchie yourself?"

"Nothing. But I think I know why he won't receive

you. The Deuxième Bureau has been all over his operation lately, and they're pretty sharp-eyed for a bunch of collaborationist idiots. If they catch you helping the British Expeditionary Force get off the continent, they'll bring you up on charges of treason. Or just shoot you on sight."

"All right, Harry. I get it. But I need Murchie's help. It's about our friend at Columbia. His son."

There was a long silence on the line. "Let me give Murchie a call," Bingham said. "I'll propose drinks tonight. If he agrees, you'll go in my stead."

"Thanks. But look—it can't be at our usual joint. It's got to be the Coquille de Noix, all right? Vinciléoni can't know what we're planning."

"Listen, Varian." An inhale, another silence. "I don't know exactly what you're going to ask of Murchie, but I think he's right to try to disentangle you. Treason's a guillotinable offense. And Vinciléoni won't take kindly to deception, if he finds you out. You've got more work to do here, a lot more. I don't want you taking unnecessary risks."

"Sure. But how do you know which ones are necessary?"

Bingham laughed. "I'm the wrong man to ask."

"That's why we're comrades in this, Harry. We take them all."

"I see your point. But I'm not joking here. Choose wisely."

He waited all day for news, but none came; then, just as he was putting on his overcoat to return to

Air Bel, a messenger arrived with a hastily scrawled note on a piece of lined paper. **Coquille 1800h,** it read, in Harry Bingham's familiar upright hand.

At the bar, Varian waited at a high round table in a corner. He hadn't eaten anything since dinner the night before; his head felt light and hollow. He wondered how much longer they could all survive on what they'd been able to scrounge or buy or scavenge. The restaurants in town scarcely had more than the kitchen at Air Bel. That morning, before he'd left for the docks with the Bretons and Serges, he'd found himself standing before the fountain, wondering whether Madame Nouguet would be willing to bread and fry the goldfish.

Moments later, Archibald Murchie himself appeared at the door and threaded his way through the small high tables. He was tall, red-haired, with an equine nose and pale-fringed eyes; when he saw Varian in place of Bingham, his expression shaded toward panic.

"Fry," he said. "This won't do."

"Forgive me, Captain. I have to speak to you. Harry agreed to help."

"Bingham knows better than that. He knows what's at stake."

"I don't care about the risk. We've already got our necks on the line for your men. But this is something else, Captain. My own business, in a way. And it's a matter of dire importance."

Murchie shook his head. "I suppose I'd better have a drink, then," he said. "What'll you have?"

"Wine," Varian said. "It's the closest thing they have to food." He had not the least desire to drink, but when their waiter set the glass before him, the fragrant Bordeaux presented itself as a compelling substitute for dinner.

"Well, what's the business, then?" Murchie said. "We'd better be quick about it. I'm half sure I was tailed here by a Bureau man. You can always tell them, can't you? Short and shifty, terrible taste in suits."

"Here's the business," Varian said. "I've promised to help you get your men out, and I'll continue to do so, whether Vichy considers it treason or not. And in return, I've a small favor to ask. I need a particularly reliable officer to escort one of our own men to Africa, a young German who'll be traveling in the guise of a Brit. With one of those cards Vinciléoni has been getting you, only we won't tell him who we're really putting on the ship. We'll simply pretend he's one of yours."

Murchie blinked his pale-lashed eyes. "Sorry to disappoint, Mr. Fry, but I can't do anything of the sort. I'm under strict orders to cut off all communication with you. This meeting must be our last."

"But what about your men, Captain? Would you strand them here in Marseille? I'm your connection to those boats to Oran and Casablanca. You understand that, don't you?"

"We're grateful for all you've done, truly. But High Command won't take responsibility for your neck. I assure you, it's not a matter of altruism. They believe that our desire to protect you might conflict with our own interests."

"But this runs **against** your interests! Without those boats—"

"My orders are clear, and they come straight from Admiralty. All rescue activities conjunct Centre Américain to cease at once. It's entirely out of my power."

"But Captain, if you'll permit me—this particular client—"

"We can't be a party to it, I'm afraid. And I wouldn't go hoodwinking Vinciléoni if I were you, either. He'll kill you as soon as look at you."

"But this **one man,** Captain. I beg you. One more run to Oran, that's all. If I could be more candid about my reasons, about the deep urgency of the matter—"

"I'm afraid it wouldn't make a difference. I'm awfully sorry, Mr. Fry. We're deeply obliged to you, of course, for all you've done."

Varian's pulse pounded in his temples, his mind already spinning wildly from the wine. "If you're truly obliged to us," he said, "would you at least consider helping our man once he arrives in Oran, if I could find another way to get him there? Could one of your men look out for him while he gets his visa? It's just that he's quite young, and his work is so very essential—to all of us, perhaps."

Murchie turned his glass on the scarred table. "You're a stubborn man, Mr. Fry. I say that with admiration."

"I've been accused of possessing that quality, yes."

The captain blinked his pale-lashed eyes with maddening slowness. "Just what is it that's so pressing about this young man's case?"

Varian leaned close and spoke in his lowest tone. "He's an escapee from Vernet, wanted by the French and Germans both. A physicist, a young genius whose talents could be put to dangerous use if he were to fall into the wrong hands. I believe he'd die first, but they wouldn't give up easily—he's got a mother in Berlin, and who knows what they'd do to her? Can't you help, Captain? What would it cost you?"

Murchie put a fist to his mouth and coughed. "Well," he said. "Well."

Varian sensed the balance tipping in his favor. "If we get this boy to the States, all his power will be on our side. It'll be **our** military putting him to use, not theirs."

"Your military's not involved in this war," Murchie said, with some bitterness.

"How long do you think that'll hold? It's only their own shortsightedness keeping them out of it."

"I'd have to find a way to get a message to our

people in Oran, if that's where you send him," Murchie said, contemplating. "Can't cable, of course."

"We sometimes slip a scroll of paper into a toothpaste tube, send it with one of our refugees," Varian said. "Tube-o-gram."

"Clever."

"What do you say, then, Captain? May I rely on you?"

Murchie gave an almost imperceptible nod, looking down the length of his equine nose. "But we can't meet again, Mr. Fry, not in person. Not on this continent, anyway."

Of course, Varian thought as he walked back toward the boulevard Garibaldi, of course there must be another way to get Tobias to Oran. Africa lay a few hundred miles distant, a mere day's journey. The obvious thing was to consult Captain Deschamps. The **Sinaïa** was due to arrive in three days; Deschamps had agreed to contact Varian as soon as he landed. Perhaps he could be persuaded to take another clandestine passenger as far as the coast of Africa. Tobias would be safe, or at least as safe as could be managed, traveling under Zilberman's care. Wasn't that the obvious solution? Why had it not occurred to him before? He knew the answer, and he didn't like to consider it: he didn't want to risk two of his most valuable clients on an untried route. But he also knew that to hesitate might be fatal.

When he arrived at the office, he found Grant pacing the front room in a state of high agitation, the back of his linen shirt soaked through, his skin damp and flushed, as if he'd run all the way from the train. They were alone; it was nearly eight o'clock by now. Varian took his hand and brought him into his own private **bureau.**

"What is it?" he said, half-sitting on the desk. "You're in a state."

Grant, swaying before the desk, put his hands through his hair. "We've had a visit from the police at Air Bel," he said. "This afternoon. They came in two cars—six officers—and turned everything inside out. Every canister in the pantry, every drawer, every suitcase—"

"The attic . . . ?"

"They didn't find Tobias. He was out on one of his rambles. And Zilberman had the wherewithal to hide himself and the Flight Portfolio in the root cellar."

"Did they arrest anyone?"

"No, though they rather annoyed Mary Jayne and harassed old Killer."

"God, is he back? If only they'd arrested **him**! Did they say what they wanted?"

"They'd had a tip about a clandestine radio transmitter, they said."

Varian couldn't help but smile at that. "Now, there's an idea. Maybe we should get one."

"Oh, yes, let's. We can have our own variety show."

"Did they take anything?"

"I wish I knew! They wouldn't let me follow them through the house."

"Well, all's well that ends well, it sounds like. No one arrested, at least."

But Grant's agitation hadn't passed. "We've got to get Tobias off the continent. What if he'd been home?"

"I know it, Grant. I came just now from a meeting with Archibald Murchie."

"Then it's all going forth?"

"Well, not precisely. Or not exactly as planned. Murchie won't let us send Tobias in the guise of one of his men. The Brits won't use Vinciléoni's route at all anymore, in fact. So we've got to find another way for Tobias to travel."

"What other way is there?"

"I want to put him on the **Sinaïa** with Zilberman," Varian said. "I hope I can get Deschamps to agree."

"Do you think you can? Just to Africa, or all the way to Martinique?"

"Tobias can't get a U.S. visa before the **Sinaïa** sails. So it'll have to be Africa. He can stay with Murchie's crew while he gets the rest of his papers—I know Bingham can lubricate the process through his contacts there. Once it's all set, Toby will leave for the States."

"When does the **Sinaïa** dock?"

"Thursday."

Grant went to the windowsill and looked down at the street below, where a hat vendor pushed a cart of trembling fedoras over the cobblestones. "And what if Deschamps won't take them both?" he said. "Not even as far as Africa? I couldn't stand it if anything happened to Tobias. Not after I sent that letter to Gregor. I can't stand the thought of failing at that—failing him again."

Varian sat down on the sill with Grant, smoothing the fine stripe of his suit as it lay along his thigh. Beneath the light wool, Grant's skin felt unusually hot. Varian moved a hand to the back of Grant's neck, then to his forehead.

"Why, Grant," he said. "Do you feel unwell?"

Grant put a hand to his own head. "I don't know. Maybe. I'm sure it's just the strain of it all—the raid, and my running here from the train."

"Your skin's burning hot. I believe you've got a fever. You've got to get home. Let me call a doctor for you."

"A doctor for Dr. Grant!" Grant said, and gave a pained, truncated laugh. "Oh, my head! It figures, doesn't it? Just as at school, always before the end of term. Remember when we had the influenza? Didn't you help me study for a philosophy exam when we both had temperatures of a hundred and three?"

Varian put his own cool forehead against Grant's. "I remember," he said. "I remember everything, Skiff. Every single thing that happened." How they'd both been half-delirious, how the words of Grant's philosophy books had boiled up into a stew of unmeaning, how they'd held each other in the narrow bed in Varian's room, shivering violently under every blanket they had.

"I'm calling the doctor," he said now. "And I'm sending you home in a car."

"A car! What car?"

"The one that was meant to transport poor Breitscheid and Hilferding."

"But how can you get it?"

"I'll telephone Vinciléoni."

"Don't move just yet," Grant said. "I think this is helping my head."

Half an hour later they were both seated in the back of the black Citroën, coursing through the streets of Marseille at a speed that seemed half-magical. Between them and the world, a veil of glass that damped all sound. How strange, he thought, how dreamlike, that back home in New York he had traveled by taxi almost daily; stranger still to think that he actually **owned** an automobile—not the yellow Packard that had dealt death to the Irish laborer all those years ago, but a glossy black Bentley, stabled at his parents' house in Ridgewood. And would they fly along those rural roads someday, he and Grant, masters of that long sleek vehicle? Would they fly as they were flying now, through the city's outskirts and into the countryside, over the cypress-lined roads toward La Pomme? Grant lay back against the seat, breathing shallowly; Varian dared to rest his hand beside Grant's on the seat, his smallest finger embanked along Grant's, tracking his fever as it rose.

Vinciléoni's chauffeur said not a word when they arrived at Air Bel. In silence he opened the car door and helped Grant out of the deep back seat. When Varian tried to tip him for his services, he raised a hand as if to ward off insult, gave a half-bow, and took himself away in the long black car.

Mary Jayne met them at the kitchen door, her eyes widening.

"What's happened?" she said. "What's wrong?"

"Grant's ill," Varian said. "Help me get him upstairs. Tell Madame Nouguet we need some cold compresses. The doctor should be along in a minute."

"I'm fine," Grant said, but halfway up the stairs he paused on the landing and bent at the waist. He coughed, staggered against Varian. "God, my chest!" he said, and brought a hand to his heart. "It hurts. It burns. I can scarcely breathe."

Varian caught him under the arms and Mary Jayne held him around the waist, and together they walked him upstairs and into the bedroom. As Varian undressed him, Mary Jayne sat in the desk chair, averting her eyes from Grant's long, sweat-pricked body, and narrated the events of that afternoon: how the two police cars had come roaring up the drive, sirens howling, as if some great crime were being committed at Air Bel; how the policemen had nearly broken down the door, then tramped in and begun pulling out every drawer and opening every cupboard, using the foulest language imaginable; how she and Grant had tried to stall them, insisting on seeing a search warrant, which of course they didn't have; how the policemen had demanded to see the radio transmitter, threatening to arrest everyone if it wasn't produced; how they'd interrogated Killer, who had convincingly portrayed ignorance on all subjects.

"You were brilliant, Mary Jayne," Grant said, faintly, from the bed. He closed his eyes and lay back against the pillows. "And Madame Nouguet scolded—like a harpy. Made them—pick up everything they'd thrown down. Never seen such rudeness from anyone, she said." He coughed again, curled in upon himself in pain. "God! What is this, Varian? What's wrong with me?"

Madame Nouguet appeared in the doorway, carrying a bowl of water and some folded cloths. "You wanted these, Monsieur Fry?"

She lived for crises, Varian knew, for her quiet and wise-eyed role in them; he supposed he'd provided enough, during their tenure at Air Bel, to last her a good while. He took the bowl and cloths from her and laid them on the washstand, then wet a cloth and wrung it. As he applied it to Grant's forehead, Grant closed his eyes. His breathing deepened, and he was asleep within moments.

"If you please, Madame Nouguet," Varian said, adjusting the cloth. "I want you to go down to the cellar and dig up whatever roots and scraps might be left. And young Mr. Katznelson may be able to provide some foraged mushrooms. Mr. Grant's got to have some food, some hot soup."

"The odds and ends we've got can't bring a man back to health," Madame Nouguet said. "You need something with meat and bones."

"You're a worker of magic, madame," Varian said. "I know you'll do your best."

"I'll talk to Killer," Mary Jayne said. "Maybe he can get something in town."

Once they'd gone, Varian sat down in the bedside chair and put a hand to Grant's forehead. He seemed hotter than ever; how long before the doctor would arrive? He tried to remember what his mother had done when he was sick. Made him lemon tea. Stroked the backs of his hands with her fingertips, saying it would cool him like a breeze. Longtime patient that she was, she had known how to nurse him; it was one of the few duties of motherhood he could remember her performing with alacrity and skill. He adjusted the cloth on Grant's forehead minutely, hoping not to wake him.

Their room—he'd gotten used to thinking of it that way now—looked to have been hastily tidied by Madame Nouguet while Grant was in town; everything had been put away, though not in its usual place. Grant's tortoiseshell comb stood upright between the bristles of Varian's silver hairbrush, and Varian's razor lay across Grant's tin of shaving soap. Grant's shirt and Varian's jacket hung intersleeved on the back of the desk chair. Their separate books now sat on the desk in mixed piles, Faulkner and Marcus Aurelius layered with Baudelaire and Langston Hughes and several scholarly works on English verse. Two identical copies of **Finnegans Wake** made their own stack. Varian took the one on top—Grant's, he could tell from his friend's careless way with the spine of a book—and opened it to a late chapter where Grant had underlined a few lines: **Amengst menlike trees walking or trees like angels weeping nobirdy aviar soar anywing to eagle it! . . . The form masculine. The gender feminine.**

The doctor must have been watching from the doorway for some time before Varian noticed him; he cleared his throat, and Varian dropped the book.

"Please," Varian said. "Come in."

Grant woke at Varian's voice; as he did, he put a hand to his chest. "Jesus," he said. "God, it hurts! Like something clawing from the inside."

The doctor set his bag on the spindle-legged table beside the fireplace, installed his monocle, adjusted the tips of his white mustache between his middle finger and thumb, and commenced his examination, to which Grant submitted without a word, his large clear eyes raised to Varian's. The doctor was a long time listening with his stethoscope. He asked Grant to sit up all the way, and then to lean forward slightly. When Grant did, the pain he'd been feeling seemed to abate. Then he drifted back down onto the pillow, only to bolt up holding his chest again, shouting.

"What is it?" Varian said, half-choked with terror. "Is it his heart?"

"There is a distinct—" and the doctor pronounced a few medical words in French that Varian couldn't follow. Grant looked anxiously at the doctor, and he repeated the words in heavily accented English: "Three-component friction rub. Indication of acute pericarditis." An inflammation of the sac that surrounded the heart, the doctor explained. Grant must be made to rest, for ten days at least. An upright or forward-leaning posture decreased the friction between the pericardium and the heart.

When Grant protested that he must be active, that there were people relying on his aid, the doctor inquired if he cared to live out the week. Grant leaned forward on his pillow and fixed his fever-glassed eyes on the doctor.

"En fait," he said, **"ma vie n'est plus la mienne. Elle appartient à quelqu'un d'autre."**

"Preserve yourself, then," the doctor said, in a tone of paternal admonition. He dispensed a dose of aspirin to the patient, directed Varian to apply more cool cloths, and then put on his hat, instructing Varian to call at once if there was any change. The course of the virus could not be predicted, he said. Pericarditis could last for a matter of days, or it could go on for weeks. He would return in two days' time unless Varian called sooner. Then he touched Varian's shoulder and descended the stairs.

"Did he just say I might die?" Grant asked, faintly.

"I think he just meant to scare us."

"But I do feel like I might die. Every time I breathe, it's—like someone's sandpapering my heart."

"I'll take that over a heart attack," Varian said. He arranged Grant upright against the pillows and exhorted him to rest. Then he laid a new cool cloth over the patient's eyes, reassuring him that he, Varian, would take care of everything; that Grant need not fear for Tobias Katznelson; and that, insofar as it was within his power, he would make sure that Gregor's son got off the continent unharmed.

FOUR

Body and Life

30

Fever

On Thursday morning Varian arrived at the quai de la Tourette to meet the **Sinaïa.** He'd always found it hypnotic to watch a steamship make its approach to land, to witness its enlargement from a speck on the horizon to a human-sized conveyance to a behemoth that filled every corner of the visual frame. But this approach was different: every inch the **Sinaïa** seemed to gain in size, every increase in detail he could make out as she drew closer, stood as evidence that she hadn't been torpedoed, sunk, or requisitioned by the French navy—evidence that she existed, not as an idea or a dream but in material form, her black smokestacks thrust rudely against the sky, her nominal umlaut staring like a pair of cartoon eyes. As she reached the pier, as the deckhands threw giant ropes ashore and other hands caught and secured them, she ceased to be an independent machine and became instead a giant captive beast, surrendered and docile; the groaning quieted, the rocking stilled, and she was home, at least for a time.

The passengers began to disembark, and Deschamps himself appeared at the door of his cabin and scanned the shore. When his gaze fell upon Varian, he raised a hand in greeting. In his other hand he held a small flat briefcase: the chess set, the same one they'd used in his quarters last fall. He descended from his high deck and walked the gangway to the dock, whistling. As he stepped ashore, he clapped Varian on the shoulder and regarded him with his deep-lined, penetrating eyes.

"I haven't had a decent game in months," he said. "Won't you do me the honor?"

"With pleasure," Varian said, and it was the truth; he had much to gain by losing to the captain again. He recommended that they use the back garden of a café he knew in the Panier, where they might play in privacy, the walls providing a soundscreen for their conversation. Fifteen minutes later they were installed at a table beneath a cascade of bougainvillea, two glasses of whiskey before them, the chessboard set for play.

"I have a new offense," the captain said. "Something I learned from a friend in Fort-de-France."

"I'm always eager to learn," Varian said. He was aware that his position was uncertain, that the captain might have changed his mind by now; certainly the political situation had only worsened, and Vichy had only grown stronger since Varian and his friends had been imprisoned on the **Sinaïa.**

The captain opened with a series of moves unfamiliar to Varian: He advanced and quickly lost two pawns, clearing the way for an early development of his bishop. Then he unfolded his knights and brought out his queen, and Varian found himself on the defensive. Good, he thought; let me be vulnerable, let me be unthreatening. Let me give him satisfaction. He moved his pieces into peril, waiting until the captain had captured a bishop and a rook before he introduced the subject of his stowaways.

"Who was it who said," he began, " '**malum consilium quod mutari non potest**'?"

"Publilius Syrus," the captain said, without hesitation. "It's one of a captain's dearest maxims. The plan that cannot be changed . . ."

". . . is a bad plan," Varian said. "It's also a chess player's maxim."

"Indeed," the captain said. "You, for example, have been defending your king along the left flank. But you must now find a way to save him minus another rook."

Varian watched with some surprise as the captain broke through the strongest side of his defense. Indeed, that hadn't been the plan; now he had to stall for time. He took up his glass of whiskey and caught a ray of sun in it, contemplating it in silence. "When we last met," he said, "you showed me your ship's secret, evidence of your father's resourcefulness."

"Evidence of his desire to earn an extra franc, you mean."

"Yes, that too. I'd planned to ask you to transport an important client of mine—an artist of extraordinary ability, one who will be carrying a dossier of work possibly worth millions. I would have been willing to pay any price for his safe transit. But now, Captain, I must ask you to double the favor. There's a person in my care, a young scientist whose case requires extraordinary measures. I wonder, could your compartment be made to accommodate **two** men? Or does your ship have another cranny where I might stow this young person, whose life is in danger and who must find passage—secret passage—to Oran, or some other northern African port, as soon as it can possibly be accomplished?"

The captain paused, his eyes on the board; he hadn't forgotten that it was Varian's turn. "My ship, as I mentioned before, is under the strictest surveillance. Even to take one stowaway would require me to risk imprisonment at best, an accusation of treason at worst. Two passengers doubles the risk."

"What if the young man could be passed off as one of your crew? He's already proved himself adept at disguise. He escaped from Vernet in a guard's uniform."

Deschamps smiled. "Clever boy. But I can't let a concentration camp escapee pose as one of my men.

The crew is, if anything, more closely regulated than the passengers. Their maritime expertise is a liability, you know. Political mutinies occur. Ships are lost to the enemy, remade as vessels of war."

"I understand," Varian said, and moved an imperiled knight to his king's side. "By no means would I want to compromise—"

"And that's to say nothing of the danger to your refugees. When we arrived just now, the **Sinaïa** was carrying four SS officers. These men observed all the goings-on upon my ship with the deepest scrutiny—whether under specific orders or simply by force of habit, I don't know. In fact, Monsieur Fry, when I received your last note, I told myself I should refuse to see you here in Marseille. I told myself I was wrong to have shown you that compartment. I feel I may have raised a false hope."

The earth seemed to tilt beneath Varian's chair. For months now he'd thought of the **Sinaïa** as a private treasure, or a secret weapon: a vessel that might be stuffed with an inestimably valuable human life and shot across the ocean. He refused to let it go now without a fight.

"How does it feel," he said, "to be required to transport Nazi officers? Are you obliged to dine with them? To converse with them?"

"I'm obliged to do whatever they require," Deschamps said, and a muscle at his jaw twitched. "The officers I mentioned, those four—while we were at sea, they executed a man on board my ship.

Killed an innocent man, on a boat that's never seen a death or the loss of a crew member. Do you know what we call a ship on which a person has been murdered? A Dirty Magdalene. That is what they did to my **Sinaïa.** They made my ship a Dirty Magdalene."

"Captain," Varian said. "I believe you know why you showed me that compartment. I believe you know what your heart dictates."

"Check," the captain said, and Varian had to turn his attention once again to the board; Deschamps had foiled his defense, and pinned his king, knight, and bishop along the back rank. He felt a jolt of annoyance, a needle of genuine competition.

"Just one refugee, then," Varian said. "The young scientist. Would you do that much for me? You'd only have to carry him as far as Oran, or Casablanca. Then, if all went well, perhaps you'd carry my artist and his portfolio to the same port, or onward to Martinique. I'm sure I mentioned before that we'd pay a generous honorarium."

Scarcely glancing at the board, the captain took Varian's queen, which Varian hadn't known to be endangered. Varian drew a breath of surprise, and a look of gratification moved over the captain's sun-sharpened features. "You're losing miserably, Mr. Fry," he said.

Varian flushed deeply. "Captain—"

"People humble themselves to gain certain advantages," Deschamps said. "It's the oldest dance in the world. You, for example, lost to me last time on purpose. You wanted my favor, and you tried to buy it at that cheap price. At the outset of this game, you intended to do it again."

Varian opened his mouth to speak, but the captain silenced him with an upraised hand. "All those years ago, when you were so plainly in the grip of some boyish trauma, I gave you the pleasure of defeating me. I did it even though I knew you considered me your intellectual inferior. That is what the young do: they see things from their limited perspective. They can't help it, Monsieur Fry. It's the nature of the age. But when you played me again a few months ago, you still took me for a fool. What is your excuse now?"

Varian opened his mouth, closed it again. A knot formed in his throat. "If you knew that," he said, "if you knew I was letting you win—why did you show me the compartment? Why did you let me believe you were willing to help?"

"It gave me some satisfaction," the captain said. "Showing you I had something you wanted so badly. Knowing I could choose to give it to you or not."

"What can I offer you?" Varian said, hearing the note of desperation in his own voice. "What do I have that could be of value? If it's money you want, I can produce it. Any amount. If it's something the black market can provide—"

"You rate me so cheaply, Monsieur Fry. I don't want your money. I don't want this or that from the black market. I have all I need, materially speaking. Perhaps I want only for you to know you aren't quite as intelligent as you think. Perhaps I want all of your compatriots to know it. There you sit, on the other side of the ocean—yes, even you, Monsieur Fry, though your body is here—watching our disaster unfold, believing you can remain uninvolved. But you're already involved, all of you. Your government has taken thousands of lives, doing nothing. And now you ask for **my** aid, at the possible price of my own life—"

Varian dropped his gaze to his lap, to his folded hands. "What do you want, then?" he asked. "What can I promise you?"

"I know who you are, Monsieur Fry. I know what you do. I've spent some time learning all I could about you. I have my ways of inquiring. Voices travel over the water. I've heard, for example, that you have the ear of Mrs. Roosevelt, and I know you write for **The New York Times.** I know you have what's known in France as **un plafond.** A platform. I want you to prick your country's conscience. I want you to do more than you've done."

"Yes," Varian said, still scarcely able to speak. "That is—that's what I want to do."

"I want you to write," the captain said. "I want you to promise me you'll report everything you've seen. I don't need a role in it. That's not what I'm seeking. What I want is for you to report all the misery, the grief, the ugliness. The feeling of the Nazis' hands around our necks. All you've witnessed, all we've had to bear, while your compatriots sit comfortably on the other side of the ocean."

"Forgive me, Captain," he said. "You're right. I should have done more already."

"Perhaps you should have. It would have been to your credit. But it will give me some satisfaction to see you begin to do it now. If I help you, it will be for that reason only. But I refuse to stretch my neck any further than I promised before. I will take one at a time, and only one."

Varian hardly dared speak. "When?"

"In two days' time," Deschamps said. "Your charge must be willing to be transported onto the ship in a sealed cargo container. Once he's been loaded, two men I trust will deliver him to my quarters, and I will uncrate him myself. We will sail for Oran, and then we'll make our way to Martinique. If we encounter no difficulty, we'll return by the same route in two weeks. Then I will take your second man. And, by the way"—he glanced down at the board, having just moved his queen into fatal proximity to Varian's king—"checkmate."

Varian had never felt so deeply shamed. "I'll meet your condition," he said. "I swear on my own life."

"I hope you do meet it," Deschamps said. "For your own sake. I don't claim to know you well, Monsieur Fry, but I've studied human nature long enough to see what kind of man you are. I see what it will cost you, personally speaking, if you fail."

And without another word, the captain swept his chess pieces back into their velvet bag, shut the bag into the wooden case, and left Varian at the table alone.

Back at Air Bel he found Grant half conscious, a newspaper abandoned on the coverlet beside him, a plate of soup untouched on the bedside table. His eyelids were a dull violet, his lips dry, his skin violently hot to the touch. He didn't react to Varian's coming in; he seemed to be in some other place, a world in which all his focus was his pain. Varian bent to his ear and spoke his name. His eyes flew open.

"What is it?" he said.

"I've just come from Captain Deschamps. He says he'll only take one man. But then he'll return for the other."

"God," Grant said, and closed his eyes again. And then he slid back into the state in which Varian had found him, a twilight of fever and pain. Madame Nouguet appeared a moment later with a tray of cool cloths. She reported in a whisper that Grant had scarcely eaten or drunk anything all day, not that there had been much to eat in any case: a few crumbs soaked in broth, that was all. Each time she'd tried to give him a spoonful, the pain of swallowing had been so severe that he'd given up. Finally she'd sent Rose into town for ice, and had been feeding it to Grant in tiny chips for the last two hours. She bent to him and found that he had fallen asleep, and she voiced the hope that Varian would not disturb him again; she would put the ice into the ancient icebox downstairs, and perhaps Varian would give him more when he woke. She looked hard into Varian's eyes, her expression of concern uncut by its usual salting of opprobrium. She was, he could tell, genuinely worried. He implored her to take a rest, and it was evidence of her own exhaustion that she went without protest.

Varian carried the bowl of ice downstairs and put it into the icebox. Then he opened the kitchen door and walked out onto the patio. He would go to town at once, he thought. He would call the doctor from the station. But on the bench at the edge of the garden he saw Zilberman, hands on his knees; Zilberman, who rarely ventured out of the greenhouse in daylight, sitting as if in a trance at the edge of the Val d'Huveaune, one hand shading his eyes. Varian went down the stone stairs and into the garden.

"Ah, there you are," Zilberman said, turning, as if he'd been waiting for Varian all along. He raised an arm toward the view. "So much beauty! All this time, I've hardly allowed myself to see it."

Varian seated himself on the bench, rubbing his knees with his palms. "Lev," he said. "I'm afraid there's a problem."

Zilberman removed his tortoiseshell glasses and turned to Varian. "What sort of problem?"

He hadn't considered until this moment how he might frame the situation; he found now that his compulsion was to say as little as possible. "We've got to use the **Sinaïa** to get Tobias to Oran. That's got to happen at once. Then the boat's got to cross the pond and come back before it can take you."

Zilberman absorbed this. "How long will that take?"

"A couple of weeks longer than we thought. But I think it can still be achieved while your visa's good."

"My wife and daughter are expecting me before the month's end."

"I'll send word to them tonight."

Zilberman's brow constricted, and he put his glasses on again, squinting at Varian. "Isn't there any other way? Another ship?"

"Not one that I'd trust you on. I'm sorry, Lev."

"Please, Monsieur Fry. You mustn't apologize. None of this is within your control. I've waited this long; I'm studied at it by now. And I'll be glad to know Tobias is off the continent. As for me, I've got work to do here. A few more pieces were promised to me this morning. Chagall is late on his contribution. I thought he wouldn't finish in time, but perhaps now he will."

"Thanks, Lev," Varian said, and closed his eyes against that green view. He sat for some moments at the painter's side, both of them in silence; a complicated measure of birdsong ascended from the valley, and the scent of lavender blew into the garden on a current of cold-edged wind. Deep exhaustion bloomed in his bones, so profound he thought he might never move again. But then it struck him, with some horror, that he'd delayed his call to the doctor, and he hurriedly took his leave of Zilberman and ran up the path toward town.

By the time Dr. Mirandeau arrived that night, Grant had woken from his brief sleep and seemed refreshed; his eyes were sharper, his attention returned. At his bedside the doctor was jocund and encouraging, and Varian felt a vertiginous relief. Surely Mirandeau's tone meant that Grant was out of danger, that his continued fever couldn't pose a serious threat. But afterward, once Mirandeau had gone downstairs to the salon with Varian, he removed his monocle and declared in a low, grave tone that the patient must not be allowed to leave his bed on any account. His blood pressure, the doctor said, was concerningly low; fluid had collected around the patient's heart, and was preventing it from filling properly.

"Pericarditis is a trapdoor, if you will," the doctor said. "One wrong step and the patient may fall through. Monsieur Grant's state is precarious. If his pressure falls further—"

He didn't want to hear more. "How much longer will the inflammation last?"

"Another week, perhaps longer. And then the patient must have time to recover."

"There's so little food," Varian said. "I fear that's making it worse."

"He wouldn't have the appetite for a banquet, even if you could provide it. He'll do all right on soup and bread. What's important is to keep the inflammation down. You must keep giving aspirin every four hours. And guard against undue excitement."

"Is there nothing else we can do, nothing you can give him?"

"At the moment, no. We must simply let the disease run its course."

He felt as if his own heart were being crushed, as if the doctor himself were crushing it in his clean white hand. "But—can I do nothing at all?"

The doctor scrutinized him carefully, an apprehending look passing over his sharp French features; Varian was certain Mirandeau had just divined what existed between himself and Grant. He was afraid for a moment that the doctor was going to say something desperate and sentimental, something like **Pray.**

"Monsieur Grant faces a long and difficult journey still," Mirandeau said. "Don't let him consider its length. Instead, make him envision its end. Make him want to live to see it, even if the pain makes him wish he were dead."

———

That night, while Madame Nouguet tended to Grant, Varian climbed the attic stairs again and knocked on Tobias's door. Tobias had been near silent on the floor above since Grant had fallen ill; Varian found that he'd managed nonetheless to set his attic room in order, to pack away his papers and herbs and butterflies—to make the place ready, in other words, for either a police inspection or a swift departure. And now Varian sat on a broken stool beside the bed and told Tobias that he would leave on the **Sinaïa** the next morning. In preparation, he must pack his things into the smallest bundle possible, then prepare to be transported to town in the back of a delivery cart at four in the morning and deposited at a warehouse near the docks, there to be crated up and taken to the ship. As Varian delivered this news, Tobias sat at the edge of his metal bedstead, his dark-fringed eyes growing larger.

"A cart?" he said. "A horse cart? What if we're stopped?"

"You'll be safer there than in a car. Any car is suspect."

"And then I'm to be loaded into a crate?"

"That's right. And the hiding place on the ship is a closet. There won't be room to stand. You'll be in for hours, perhaps for days."

"Well," he said, "I suppose I've had it too easy, sitting up here."

"Believe me, it's not the way I'd choose for you to travel."

"And then what's to happen once I get—where, exactly?"

"To Oran. One of Murchie's men will meet you at the dock. He'll find a place for you to stay while we see about your visa."

"How long, do you think, before I can get it?"

"Not as long as if you were trying from here."

"I don't suppose there's time for a going-away party."

Varian smiled. "Even if there were, we wouldn't want to advertise your departure. Between now and tomorrow morning, you'd be wise to keep to your room."

Tobias's expression became pensive. "I was thinking, though, that I might go out tonight to find some dill for Mr. Grant. Taken with nettle, it's got marvelous properties against inflammation. You can use it as a poultice for a wound, but it works if it's taken internally. And it grows not far from here, I've seen it by the verge of the little creek near my father's place, where I showed you the snails."

Could a tincture of nettle and dill keep a man from death? Did he dare let Tobias out again into the Val d'Huveaune that night? "No, Toby," he said. "You can't."

"I'm sure it wouldn't take me half an hour to get there and back."

"No," Varian said. "No, no, and no. If there's something to be got, tell me what it is and I'll get it. I'll bring it back here and you can tell me if I've got the right thing. If not, I'll go out again."

"Forgive me for saying so, Mr. Fry, but I don't think you ought to leave Mr. Grant's side. I think you'd better go back down to him now. He's been much easier since you've been home."

"But if there's a remedy—"

"Let me get it. Let it be a parting gift. It's a small thing. Really, I won't be gone long. And anyway, I'd like to see the valley one more time before I leave it."

"No, Tobias. I beg you. Promise me you won't leave this room."

But he never did extract the promise; just at that moment Grant cried out downstairs, and Varian ran down to him. And in the midst of his ministrations to Grant—the application of cloths, an excruciating walk to the lavatory, the delivery of chip after chip of ice—he forgot to listen for Tobias's tread on the stairs, or the sound of the kitchen door opening and closing. He only learned of Tobias's going out an hour or so later, when the boy himself reappeared in the doorway of Varian's room, the hem of his trousers soaked with dew, holding a handful of what looked like electrified green hair.

"Damn you, Toby," Varian said. "Don't you listen to anyone?"

Tobias smiled in apology. "I'm not really in the habit of it."

Varian got up and went to the dresser, then withdrew an envelope marked with Tobias's name; it contained thirty thousand francs, the rest of the money his father had sent for him. He put it into Tobias's other hand, the one that didn't contain that dew-soaked plant.

"That's from your father," he said. "Change it in Oran. And keep your head about you. There are Gestapo officers there, too, of course. We'll try to get you out as soon as we can."

Tobias nodded, and glanced toward Grant. "How is he?"

"The same."

"Let me make some tea from this. Maybe it's just an old wives' tale, but if it can help, let it do its work."

"All right. Go make tea. And then, for God's sake, don't leave your room until they come for you. Do you understand?" He put a hand on Tobias's damp sleeve, wondering at the affection he felt for this boy, son of his enemy, his rival. But of course Gregor Katznelson was not really his enemy; he was a man Grant had loved, a man Grant did love. And here was his child, preparing to cross the ocean under dangerous circumstances, to a place where he might at last put his prodigious talents to use.

"Travel safely, Toby," he said. "Get your fine brain to America."

Tobias smiled. “Yes, I hope to—my brain and all the rest. And, Mr. Fry, Godspeed you home to New York when your work is done.” And then he turned and padfooted down the stairs to the kitchen, careful not to disturb the patient.

31

Cargo Loaded

If dill tea conferred any benefit against pericarditis, Varian couldn't see it. All that night Grant sat awake in bed with his chest against a stack of pillows, his back radiating heat. Each time Varian applied a cold cloth to his skin, Grant winced at the sensation; the wince irritated his chest, and he gave an involuntary yelp of pain. The act of making that noise, the way it lifted his diaphragm, incited further pain, and the result was a maddening concert of cause and effect, performed for an audience to whom it was torture. Varian scarcely registered the passing of time. Through a dreamlike haze he heard the horse cart pull into the circular drive below, then Tobias's tread on the attic stairs, then his descent into the kitchen. When the kitchen door closed and the window above it gave its faint glassy rattle, Varian came back to himself for a moment and composed the string of half-heard sounds into a series of events: Tobias had gone down to meet the cart; Tobias had gone. If all went well, he'd soon be hidden aboard the **Sinaïa.**

Grant seemed not to register the fact of Tobias's departure, though Varian whispered the news into his ear. Grant had left the realm of casual communication altogether, stretched as he was on a Catherine wheel of sleeplessness and pain. Varian himself hadn't slept at all. In a delirium of exhaustion he'd convinced himself that he must not sleep, that if he were to slacken his attention even for a moment, the patient would slide inexorably toward the pit. **One wrong step,** the doctor had said. Sometime before dawn, through a haze, a figure appeared in the doorway: not the rounded form of Madame Nouguet, who had been keeping them supplied with cool cloths, but Killer, standing there against the doorframe in nothing but white undershorts and a pair of mismatched socks, his arms crossed over his chest. Varian hadn't known he was in the house. The sight of him brought an instant rush of acid to his throat.

"What do you want?" Varian said.

"I want to sleep," Killer said. "None of us can close an eye without hearing—"

Grant himself filled in the missing sound. Varian kept a hand on his back. "Leave us alone," he said. "Put a goddamned pillow over your head."

Killer stepped into the room and Varian sprang

to his feet, ready to flatten him with a blow. But Killer produced from his curled hand a tiny black box with a sliding top; he opened it to reveal a miniature vial and a syringe capped in red wax.

"What's that?" Varian said.

"Morphia."

"Not on your life. I'm not giving him anything the doctor didn't prescribe."

But Grant himself had come to attention now. "What's that, Raymond?"

"Morphia. For your pain."

"Oh—yes," he said. Speaking produced pain; he could manage it only in short bursts, with effort. "Varian, please. Do it, or I'll"—he coughed—"I'll inject it myself."

"You're not injecting yourself with whatever's in that vial!"

"It's pure," Killer said. "Very pure. I was keeping it for myself, for an emergency." He held out the box to Grant, but Varian caught his hand.

"No," he said.

"Please," Grant said, his eyes filling.

Varian held Killer's hand a moment longer, watching Grant as he trembled in the bed. Then, overcome by his own exhaustion, he let go. Grant reached again for the box and examined its contents: the syringe, the tiny vial.

"How much do I—inject?" he asked Killer.

"The entire vial if you want to die," Killer said. "A tenth if you want to sleep."

"Want to die," Grant said. "But I'll—settle for sleep." He turned his eyes toward Varian. "Please," he said. "Help me."

Varian looked at Killer. Killer held his gaze.

"All right," Varian said.

Grant gave an oceanic sigh. Varian took the syringe and drew up a few milliliters from the vial, mimicking what he'd seen their family physician do for his mother dozens of times. But what happened next? Where was he supposed to insert the needle, and how? This was the point where, at his mother's bedside, he had always turned away. He hated to make any appeal to Killer, but he hardly had a choice.

"Now what?" he said.

"Oh, les naïfs," Killer said. He removed a belt from a pair of pants that hung over the desk chair, placed a tourniquet on Grant's upper arm, and injected the morphine into his antecubital vein. They all sat in silence, waiting. Outside, a nightingale prefigured the morning with its pale blue song. Madame Nouguet clinked the china below, as though there were anything to prepare for breakfast.

"I don't feel—anything at all," Grant said, panic entering his voice.

"Just wait," Killer said.

"I don't feel anything! I don't feel anything. I don't—oh."

Varian glanced at Killer, and Killer shrugged his bare shoulder toward the patient.

"Oh," Grant said again. "Oh. I think I'd like—to sit back now."

"All right," Varian said, and eased him against the stack of pillows. A few moments later, Grant's breathing had deepened.

"Voilà," Killer said, and replaced the paraphernalia in the little box.

Varian shook his head. "If anything happens to him, I'll lead you to the gallows myself."

"Mary Jayne knows what you do not," Killer said, his eyes narrowed. "Even a thief may possess a capacity for empathy."

Varian held his gaze. "You're to leave this house before noon."

"As you wish, Monsieur Fry. But first I'm going to get some sleep." He left the room and let the door close behind him, and Varian climbed into bed with Grant and put his head against Grant's burning chest. Within moments he was asleep too, and it wasn't until the kitchen door banged sometime later that he woke again. Grant still sat propped beside him, breathing deeply. Varian got to his feet and looked out the window to see Gussie's bike lying on its side in the drive. He ran downstairs, and there was Gussie in the kitchen, messenger cap in his hands, inhaling the deep fragrance of soup. Madame Nouguet stood at the stove, stirring something in her largest copper pot.

"Mr. Fry," Gussie said. "This arrived at the office

for you." He held out a folded rectangle of paper, and Varian opened it.

Cargo loaded, the note read.

"Well," Varian said. "Godspeed, boy."

"Pardon me, Mr. Fry?"

"Never mind. Thanks for bringing this."

"Monsieur Fry, how is the patient?" Madame Nouguet asked.

"Sleeping," Varian said. "What's that you're stirring?"

"Fish stew," Madame Nouguet said. "Tell this young man to stay for lunch. Mademoiselle Gold and Monsieur Couraud have gone into town. Will Monsieur Grant take a little, do you think?"

"Fish stew! Made from what in the world?"

"What God provided," she said. And then he saw, through the window, Monsieur Thumin's long-handled butterfly net resting against a tree beside the goldfish pond; the surface of the pond was strangely still, unmarked by its usual pattern of concentric rings.

The patient, refreshed by a few hours' sleep and fortified by broth, passed an easier day. Just before dusk the doctor visited again; the patient's blood pressure, he was pleased to report, had come up slightly. He approved the use of morphine—supplied by himself, he specified—in minute quantities, in tablet form, and only for a period of three days. By then, he said, the patient's relief from pain should have allowed him enough healing sleep to produce a change in his condition.

Varian thanked him and walked him downstairs, wanting to ask if they had stepped back from the precipice. But the doctor's look was still grave as he shook Varian's hand in the vestibule, and he promised to stop by again the next morning.

Upstairs, Grant sat propped in bed, a notebook open on his knee. On it he had an airmail blank, and Varian saw he'd written the first few lines of a letter.

"Who are you writing to?"

"My mother. It's been"—he caught his breath—"too long. I fancied—these last few days, that I might get knocked off by this—peridot-itis or what have you, and she'd never know—" He coughed, groaned, and put a hand to his heart. "She'd never know how—happy I'd been these last few months."

"Have you been?" Varian said, sitting at the edge of the bed. "Has there been time for that? My work here never leaves us a moment for pleasure."

"Now, **mon cher** Vaurien, that is—grossly inaccurate."

Varian smiled. "When you get well—" he said, but Grant raised a hand.

"Let's not—talk about that just yet," he said. "I

still feel like—I've got shards of glass around my heart."

"Let me give you some good news, then. I've been keeping it in my pocket, waiting until you'd had a chance to eat and sleep." He extracted the message Gussie had brought, opened it, handed it to Grant.

"Oh," Grant said. He raised his light-shot eyes to Varian's, his skin flushing a deep rose. "Oh, thank God. We must—cable Gregor! Will you do it?"

"I instructed Gussie to cable when I sent him back to town."

"So it's done," Grant said. "He's—off the continent. Not upstairs in that attic, pacing like a—a restless ghost. Not dead in a camp." He paused, took a long series of breaths, girded himself to speak again. "I can—scarcely believe it. Off the continent. Unkilled. Untortured." He shook his head, touched the corners of his eyes with his fingertips. "What a—debt of gratitude I owe you."

"You owe me nothing," Varian said. "Write to your mother. Send her my love."

"Write to your—own mother, why don't you?"

Varian sighed. "I ought to do just that. It's been at least a month since I wrote to her and Dad. I know Eileen shows them bits of letters, but—" His last letter to Eileen was, of course, unshowable. And no response had yet arrived. It seemed unbelievable, an unreality, that a break with Eileen meant that she would cease to be a daughter-in-law to his own parents, and that he, Varian, would no longer be considered the son-in-law of her parents, those white-haired Bostonians who had for years, in their quiet way, teasingly encouraged him and Eileen to produce an heir, and who had given him the deed to forty acres of their familial land in New Hampshire on the occasion of his thirtieth birthday. Not co-owned land, not part of Eileen's dowry, but a "gentleman's parcel," as his father-in-law had called it, a place where he might go on his own to camp and fish and hunt, as if he did those things or had ever done them. It occurred to him for the first time that it might have been a kind of inducement—a suggestion that if he engaged in a man's pursuits, he might behave more like one.

As he was taking up his own pen and paper, Grant made a sound of distress: the effect of the morphine had begun to wane. Varian produced the pill and the glass of water, and Grant took the medicine and fell back against the pillows. For a long while he was silent as Varian sat at the desk, his pencil hovering above a blank page at the top of which he'd written **Dear Mother and Dad.**

"What do you think he's—doing right now?" Grant said after a while, in a low, fog-cloaked voice.

"Who?"

"You know who I—oh." He shifted, and the lines on his forehead softened. A moment later they had disappeared entirely. The morphine had hit its mark. "Oh," he said. And then, again: "What—do you think?"

Was it Tobias he meant? Gregor? Varian went to the bed and took Grant's feverish hand. "Try to sleep," he said. "He's all right. He's going to be all right."

With his finger, Grant followed the pattern of tendons and blood vessels on the back of Varian's hand, smoothed the pad of his thumb over Varian's fingernails.

"There are things—I could tell you," he said, his voice waning. "But if I told you those things, then—I would have told you."

"What do you mean?" Varian said, prickling to attention. "What things?"

"Things I could tell you," Grant said, and then he closed his eyes, and in a moment he was deeply, irretrievably asleep.

———

He would remember the weeks that followed as if through a blue-green haze, one that seemed to lift at times to reveal Marseille and its surrounding countryside in a flood of vernal sun. He tended Grant morning and night, tracking his fever, and then, when the fever finally broke, trying to bring him back from the precipice Mirandeau had described. He gave Grant the carefully measured doses of his medication, helped him to the toilet, helped him eat whatever Madame Nouguet managed to prepare, changed his sweat-soaked clothes, helped him in the bath, performed all the small tasks that his excruciating chest pain rendered impossible. And between it all he carried on the business of the office, a business that, at ordinary times, consumed him entirely.

In the first days of Grant's illness, when he'd been sitting up with him around the clock, it had been Danny and Theo and Jean Gemähling who'd been running things on the boulevard Garibaldi. He returned to the office to find that they had been more than capable managers; they'd interviewed hundreds of refugees, identified a new slate of sensitive clients, sent two groups of ten down to the border with all their documents intact, and managed to deflect a series of increasingly persistent inquiries from de Rodellec du Porzic's new appointees. It occurred to Varian that he'd been training Danny all along in the minutiae of his job, and that Jean Gemähling, capable and multilingual, played for Danny the role that Danny played for Varian: right-hand man, advisor, source of connections and ideas. Or at least he did ordinarily; Jean was, at present, handicapped by a devastating attraction to a new guest at Air Bel, Consuelo de Saint-Exupéry, the irreverent and adventure-seeking wife of the writer and aviator. She had returned to Marseille after some months' absence and now spent most of her time in the villa's garden or up one of the plane trees, writing in a tiny Japanese-silk-bound notebook or fashioning parachutes from leaves. Jean appeared at the office bearing the most obvious signs of lovesickness: dark shadows beneath the eyes, a flush around the mouth, an air of abstraction, a tendency to insert his beloved's name into conversation at every turn.

Jean sat now with Danny and Theo in the front room of the office while Varian addressed them on their new challenge, which, as he saw it, was to win an all-out race against the Nazis for the lives of Jews. Among their own clients, Zilberman and the Chagalls were the most directly endangered.

"Zilberman's time is ticking," Varian said. "We can never get him a French exit visa. It's too dangerous even to try. I twisted the arm of everyone I know at the consulate to get his U.S. entry visa. If the **Sinaïa** doesn't return on schedule, we'll have to start over. Just as urgently, I want to get the Chagalls out. It's getting worse and worse."

"Worse than you know," Danny said, frowning behind his small round glasses. "Last night, after Theo and I left the office, we ran into Bingham coming out of La Fémina. He'd just had a letter from a colleague in Lisbon, to the effect that the chief of the U.S. Visa Department—what was his name, darling?"

"Avra Warren," Theo said, with flat distaste. "May we never forget it."

"Yes. This Warren, chief of the U.S. Visa Department, told the staff he wouldn't countenance Jews entering the States—'not a single goddamned one!'—and threatened to fire any consular officer who wouldn't comply."

"You must be kidding me," Varian said.

"If only I were!"

"Someone must write about this for the **Times.**"

"Too bad our friend Jay Allen's out of commission," Theo said.

"I could write it," Varian said, recalling the promise he'd made to Deschamps. "That's as clear a policy statement as I've heard, though it's obviously been the policy all along. And it means we can't wait any longer on our sensitive clients. In particular, I want the Chagalls out at the first opportunity. Where does their case stand now?"

Danny opened a dossier and looked through it. "They came down again from Gordes on the fourteenth of March. They're staying at the Moderne. No movement on either side, though—as you said, it looks rather hopeless for the French exit visas, and the U.S. entry visas are still pending."

"Time to exert more pressure on both sides," Varian said. "And what about Jacques Lipchitz?"

"Your last letters to him were effective, apparently," Danny said. "He came down last week from Toulouse with his wife and picked up their French exit visas. Now they're at the Splendide, waiting for their U.S. visas. We've got them tentatively scheduled to depart by train for Lisbon two weeks from now. From there they'll sail on the **Saint Lucia.** I believe the Committee's already secured an apartment for them in Morningside Heights."

"Excellent," Varian said. "I knew Jacques would come around. If only I could have convinced Gide! Perhaps I should write to him again."

"What about Ernst?" Theo asked. "Any movement on his papers?"

"Oh, yes—he's mine," Jean said. "Or rather, he's Peggy Guggenheim's. It seems she's finally thrown over poor Victor Brauner in his favor. Consuelo and I dined with them last night. I don't believe he took his hands off her all evening. I don't know how either of them managed to eat a thing."

Theo smiled. "Jean, dear, we all know where your mind tends these days. But we're less interested in Mr. Ernst's romantic dealings than in his emigration case."

Jean's ears turned crimson and he lowered his eyes. "Mr. Ernst's French exit visa has been granted," he said. "The U.S. one hasn't come through. Shall I go see Bingham again?"

"I don't see that we've got any other option," Varian said. "Poor Harry. We've leaned and leaned on him, and he's contravened every one of his department's mandates on our behalf. I don't know how much longer he can keep it up."

"Is there any word yet about your young German protégé?" Theo asked.

There was, in fact. Tobias's visa, as Bingham had expected, had materialized within a week of his arrival in Oran; now he was en route to the States on a cargo ship called the **Willamette.** "And how about the Fittko route?" Varian said. "Still functioning?"

"Perfectly," Danny said. "Another six are scheduled to depart tonight."

Varian folded his hands. "Bravo," he said. **"Continuons."**

That afternoon, on his way to the Moderne to speak to Chagall, he stopped by the American Express office for his mail. After weeks of silence there it was, finally: a letter from Eileen. A mad terror sent his heart into a gallop until he saw the postmark, dated two weeks before his letter about Grant; there seemed nothing sadder at that moment than the terrible asymmetry of the transatlantic mail, the uncommunicating letters winging back and forth across the ocean, deaf to each other's news. He sat on the bench outside the office and tore open the envelope, experiencing a deep inward prickling at the familiar sight of Eileen's hand, fierce and slantwise.

19 Irving Place
New York, New York

Dearest Varian,

Should you ever choose to return to the States—and will you choose that, can you still?—you'll find that you still have a wife at No. 19 Irving Place. You'll find that she still thinks of you once or twice daily as she goes about her teaching, her errands, her outings with friends. Do you still think of her? Or have you found yourself some distraction so pressing that it blocks out all light? Can your work, your all-important work, be the only thing, or is there, as I fear, something more?

Yours, most ashamed,
Eileen

He sat a long time on that bench while rafts of clouds passed overhead and crowds of pigeons circumambulated his feet. He was, at least, relieved of the need to write a reply. His reply, the worst he could have made, was already on its way, perhaps already in her hands.

At the Hôtel Moderne, he entered the same narrow vestibule where he'd met the Chagalls on the night of the air raid. Here was the same doorway to the miserable-looking bar, and there, at a small round table beside a narrow window, was Bella Chagall, a book in her hand, a half-empty glass on the table before her. She wore the same black wool dress she'd worn the first time he had met her, its batiste collar starched stiff, the fabric faded now with many washings.

"Monsieur Fry," Bella said, her voice a low rasp. "How glad I am to see you! Sit down, please. Tell me all the news. Have our visas arrived at last?"

Varian took the chair across from her. "No visas yet," he said. "I'm looking for your husband. I must ask a favor of him."

At the news about the visas, she closed her eyes and drew a long breath. "God, what fools we were to have waited," she said. "You must have thought us absurd. I don't deny that I was the chief naysayer. And now perhaps I've doomed us."

"None of that talk," Varian said. "We've been getting dozens out. We've found ways even for the most sensitive."

"Yes," she said, and lowered her voice. "By now, Zilberman—"

"Yes, soon," Varian said. "Soon he too will be en route to the States. It's actually on his errand that I've come. He's still in France a little longer—there was an unavoidable delay. And since he's got more time to compile his Flight Portfolio, he's decided he wants something more from Marc. A sort of direct commission. I'd like to ask him myself, if you don't mind."

Bella's look darkened. "My husband is working now, and must not be disturbed."

"Working? Here at the hotel?"

"On the roof, in fact," she said. "He likes the light."

The roof. Where else? Gravity had ceased to exist in Chagall's work decades earlier; naturally he had ascended to the hotel's highest point. "I do need to speak to him," Varian said. "It's a matter of some urgency."

"What is so urgent?"

"Those drawings for Zilberman's portfolio," Varian said. "I have to speak to him about them. Zilberman has something particular in mind."

Madame Chagall drained the contents of her glass and touched her mouth with the corner of her napkin. "All right," she said, finally. "For this, I suppose, you may interrupt him." She looked up at Varian, her gaze surprising in its intensity. Her eyes, so dark they were nearly black, seemed to drain the light from every source in the room. He had heard it said, before he'd known the Chagalls, that Bella and her husband had a single way of seeing, a unity of vision that had existed since they'd first met. But in fact they were opposites: the painter walked in the clouds, his wife on earth, or perhaps even below its surface, in the darkness of caves. It had never occurred to him before that moment to consider how beautiful she was; he'd thought of her as belonging to his mother's generation, but in fact she was a mere two years older than Eileen.

"Go up," she said. "Go see Marc. And afterward, tell him to meet me in our room. To be honest, Monsieur Fry, I don't want to sit here drinking alone any longer." She raised her hand and beckoned the waiter.

"I'll do everything I can for you and Marc," he said, rising to take his leave. "You know that, don't you?"

"Oh, yes," she said. "I know you'll do everything you can. Let us hope, Monsieur Fry, that it is enough."

On the top floor of the hotel, a dark hallway led to a narrow stone stair, which brought Varian to a child-sized door; the door opened onto a reflective sea of zinc, interrupted here and there by periscope-like chimney pipes. Chagall stood bareheaded in the April sun, one paintbrush tucked under his arm like a baguette, another in his hand. He had set up a striped beach umbrella, affixing it to one of the stouter chimneys with two leather belts, and had arrayed his paints along a waist-high tile ridge that ran the length of the roof. His canvas sat propped on a wooden chair beside a defunct dovecote. The doves, having flown the coop long before, had come to rest on Chagall's canvas—or if not to rest, then to soar in a rising arc from the interleaved silver architecture of the roofs. Joining the doves in their upward movement was a woman in a white dress, a woman who wore Bella's face. And as Varian came closer, he saw that the doves were not exactly doves, or not only; they, too, had the faces of women, tiny gestural faces that suggested unearthly and uncapturable perfection. And where was Bella going with those angel-doves? A chill took him, and he found he couldn't speak.

"And here we are in my studio once again," Chagall said. "Such as it is. Perhaps you've come to tell me that our visas have come through at last."

"Unfortunately not," Varian said, recovering himself. He explained his mission: Zilberman, the Flight Portfolio, the need for the new drawings. What Zilberman wanted, he said, was something more direct, something that made the situation even more plain.

Chagall sat down on a small high stool he must have carried up from inside the hotel. His eyebrows drew together above his deep-lined eyes. "I'm afraid I don't understand," he said. "Why is Zilberman still here in Marseille? I thought he was to have left two weeks ago."

"There was a delay. The place we thought he might take was filled."

Chagall's eyes narrowed. "So how is Zilberman to get out?"

"He'll take the same boat, as soon as it returns to port. We expect it within the week."

"I understand your mission here, Monsieur Fry. I know you must calculate your moves to do the most good, and to keep your clients safe. But there are situations that require greater risk. Perhaps I've not impressed clearly upon you my opinion of Zilberman's work."

Varian lowered his eyes. "You have, Marc."

"What you've seen of his work here in Marseille is nothing. He has no room in that greenhouse at Air Bel. That's why he's been making those little drawings and compiling the work of others. But in Paris I saw his atelier, and I must tell you, Monsieur Fry, I know why he's so ardently sought by the Nazis. You've seen Picasso's **Guernica.** Zilberman has works that make **Guernica** look tame and uncommunicative. He has a way of capturing the soul of a human being. I would never want to be painted by him; he sees too much, takes too much. When he paints Jewish mothers and children thrown into the streets, Jewish men kicked in the eyes or gouged by broken window glass, when he shows young girls stripped bare and made to stand in the street while Nazi youth stare and jeer and prod—Monsieur Fry, he makes the cubists and the dadaists and the vorticists look like cowards. People accuse him of having failed to follow the direction of painting into the present moment, but that's ignorance. Zilberman represents reality. He makes things plain. The moment he reaches the outside world, Monsieur Fry, the moment he can begin making work there, he'll begin to communicate the plight of Europe more effectively than anyone alive. He must get off the continent at once. He cannot wait for the **Sinaïa.** He's waited too long already. There is no more powerful weapon against the Nazis."

Varian listened in silence as a rush of heat gathered beneath his breastbone. "There's no single person capable of ending the war," he said.

"If you didn't believe in the power of a single artist's work," Chagall said, "you would still be home in New York City."

"I'm not denying Zilberman's importance. On the contrary, I've considered him among my highest priorities all along. I've been hiding him at the risk of everyone else at Air Bel. But I had to wait for the right moment. I couldn't put him on that ship when I thought I could."

The painter gave a nod. "I know you've been doing all you can," he said. "But now you must do more. Even if it means doing less for the rest of us."

"I mean to do my best for everyone."

"Monsieur Fry, you are only one person," Chagall said. "You must, at times, acknowledge your limitations. Otherwise, you run the risk of endangering your mission. Your **true** mission, I mean."

"I do acknowledge my limitations," Varian said, though he knew this was a lie; in fact he spent the great majority of his time denying them.

"You must exercise your wisdom. Zilberman's drawings may not fetch the highest price among the work he's assembled, but **he** is the most valuable asset of his Flight Portfolio. He is the most valuable asset of **your** portfolio, your human portfolio. His most powerful work is untransportable. He must be allowed to produce it in New York, on the side of some vast building, or on the side of a steamship, or a mountain. Everyone must be made to see it. Do you understand?"

Varian could only nod.

"As for the additional drawings, I'll send them to the office tomorrow. Have Gussie come by at noon."

"Thank you," Varian said. "I'll tell Zilberman. He'll be delighted."

"I must work now, Monsieur Fry, before the light is gone."

"Madame Chagall wanted me to tell you she's waiting for you downstairs."

"She is, as you can see, here with me," the painter said, and turned back to his canvas. He lifted a brush and began to apply a white-blue glow, the opposite of shadow, to the undersides of the angel-doves.

That night Grant passed a terrible six hours between midnight and dawn. He had become acclimated to the morphine dose now, but the doctor refused to give him more. Killer, their other source of morphine, had left Air Bel; Varian had no idea where he'd gone. Mary Jayne had vanished along with him, leaving a one-line note: **I don't expect you to understand.** Grant sat upright in bed, leaning forward on a stack of pillows, in the only position that gave him any relief; the pain was still so acute that sleep was nearly impossible. Every time he began to nod, his body would shift and he would jolt awake. Varian held Grant's hand, he read him incomprehensible lines from **Finnegans Wake,** he gave him doses of brandy, he sat at the head of the bed so Grant could rest against him. But there was no relief, not a moment all night when Grant's body relaxed entirely. Even in his brief moments of sleep his body was tensed against the next jolt of pain. By dawn he was weeping silently, wishing aloud that he could die.

"I'm afraid I can't let you," Varian said. "Not just yet." Holding Grant from behind, he put a hand against his forehead; it was damp and cool. "Your fever hasn't gone above a hundred for three days now. The inflammation around your heart will soon go down. That's what the doctor says."

"I'll kill myself if I—have to pass another night like this," Grant said. "Swear to God."

Varian smoothed the sweat-damp waves of his hair. "What about your life not belonging to you, et cetera?"

Grant gave a harsh sob. "If you—cared about me at all," he managed to say, "you would have either found more morphine or—killed me by now."

"As soon as it's light, I'll run to town and knock down that doctor's door."

"You'd better." He shifted and grimaced.

"Grant, can you tell me something?" Varian said. He'd been thinking about this all night; he couldn't help saying it now. "The political situation's growing worse by the day. We have fewer and fewer allies here. What would you do if I were forcibly ejected from France? Don't you think we should have some plan?"

"Tom. I can't—plan the next minute just now."

"All right."

Grant paused, took two pained breaths. "If you're ejected—forced out—I'll go—wherever you are."

"And where will that be? Where will I go? I have no job anymore. And I'm fairly certain that, with my last letter to Eileen, I'll soon be without a home. It's not as though I can just go to yours. Do you know, I don't even know where you live. I've never asked this—do you live **with Gregor**? With him? You've said you're up near Columbia. 112th Street. That's all."

"Give me that—sheet of paper on the desk, there," Grant said. "And—a book or something."

Varian complied, and Grant wrote an address on the sheet of paper. Folded it. Put it into Varian's hand. "A ridiculous—exercise," Grant said. "But.

There it is. My address. Mine alone. Not—Gregor's." He let his head fall back onto Varian's shoulder, and Varian held him there.

"I'd like to see you in my—" Grant shifted and groaned. "In my—"

"Bed. You'd like to see me in your bed."

A laugh that was half-sob. "Not what I was going to say. But yes. Oh, yes."

"You will. Or we'll run off somewhere together and never see New York again."

"South America," Grant said. "I hear Rio is—ah! God—fine this time of year."

"Brazil," Varian said, in a low and velvet tone. "That's where we'll go. Brazil." And he repeated it, a rhythmic one-word mantra, until at last Grant closed his eyes and slept.

32

Gone

After that long night awake with Grant, he experienced the next morning as if from a numbing distance. At the office he strategized with Danny and Theo, discussed money with Jean, reviewed cases with Lucie Heymann, the new secretary, but his own voice seemed to emanate from somewhere outside of him; he felt incapable of making any decision or judgment. At lunchtime he resolved to go for a walk to the Vieux Port and let the mistral shock him awake. He had just gotten up to put on his jacket when Lucie came to his open door and knocked twice on the frame. She looked stricken, her pale skin stark beneath the black wing of her hair.

"What is it?" Varian said.

"Madame Chagall's on the phone. Crying, I believe."

Varian ran to pick up the extension in his office.

The line was full of hiss and crackle, as though a bonfire were burning at the other end.

"Bella?" Varian said. "What's happened?"

"They've arrested Marc! And dozens of others. Can you hear me?"

"What?"

"Arrested him! Taken him off to the Evêché."

"God. When?"

"Just now! I can see them from the window, they're marching everyone down the street in columns."

"Who did they arrest? Refugees?"

"Jews," she said. "All Jews. Nearly the entire clientele of the Moderne. I was in the bath, thank God they didn't check. Can you help, Monsieur Fry? What must I do?"

"I'll telephone the Préfecture," Varian said. "Don't go anywhere. I'll call you the moment I have news."

"Shouldn't I come to the office?"

"No. I don't want you on the street. If anyone comes to the door, don't answer."

"All right," Bella said, and hung up.

A moment later he rang the Evêché. "Connect me to Captain Villand's office at once," he said to the operator. "Tell the secretary it's Varian Fry, director of the Centre Américain de Secours. Say it's an emergency."

"Hold the line," the operator said. There was a click on the other end, and a long pause. Then the secretary answered, and Varian demanded to speak to Villand.

"I'm afraid Captain Villand is occupied at the moment," the secretary said. "Would you like me to transmit a message?"

"Listen to me, and listen hard," Varian said. "This is Varian Fry, director of the Centre Américain de Secours. I want you to tell Captain Villand that his men have just arrested Marc Chagall—yes, **that** Chagall—and are conducting him in handcuffs to the Evêché. Tell the captain I must speak with him at once."

"Hold the line, monsieur," the secretary said.

Another silence. After what seemed an unbearable interval, there was a rattle and a click, and then a familiar voice came on the line. The captain demanded to know who had disturbed him at his work.

"It's Varian Fry," Varian said. "Director of the Centre Américain de Secours. Maybe you remember me. You were kind enough to receive me last fall."

There was silence at first, then a distinctive snap-click: the sound of Villand's brass pineapple lighter. Villand took a round, shallow breath: the first draw of a cigar.

"Yes, I remember you, Fry. What is it you want? Something regarding Chagall?"

"I've just had a call from Chagall's wife. Apparently her husband is in police custody, having been rounded up with most of the guest roster of the Hôtel Moderne. Do you hear what I'm saying, sir?

Marc Chagall himself will shortly be arriving at the Evêché, handcuffed like any criminal."

"**I** didn't give an order for the arrest of Marc Chagall," Villand said. "I haven't heard of it."

"Now you have," Varian said.

"I'm not responsible for this," Villand said. "If you'd like to make an official complaint—"

"Consider this my official complaint. You're the secretary-general of the Préfecture of the Bouches du Rhône. If you're not responsible, who is? What will happen once the news hits the papers tomorrow? Will you tell the people of France, will you tell the world, you simply had **no idea** that Marc Chagall was a prisoner under your own roof? That one of the living treasures of this continent, one of the greatest painters who has ever lived, was simply swept into a vast dustbin along with everyone else?"

There was a silence on the other end. Another cigar puff. "Monsieur Fry, matters of arrest and detention are often complicated. You may not know the full history."

"Here's all the history that matters: Chagall is in chains. His wife is frantic for his safety. And frankly, having seen the conditions of your detainment facilities, I share her sentiment. I must insist you locate Monsieur Chagall and release him at once. If not for his own value, if not for what he means to France, then to avert your own disgrace in the eyes of the world!"

"I will investigate, monsieur," Villand said gruffly, and disconnected.

Varian slammed the phone into its cradle. His staff, gathered at the open door, broke into applause.

"Bravo!" Danny said. "That was brilliant."

"This is no laughing matter. Chagall's in jail."

"Not for long, I'd bet."

And he was right. An hour later, as Varian paced the office in a frenzy of anxiety, there was a knock at the outer door; Lucie opened it to find Chagall himself, carrying a pasteboard tube under his arm. Everyone fell silent. Chagall nodded to Danny and Jean, to Theo and Gussie and Lucie. Then he crossed the room to Varian and presented the tube to him.

"Here are the drawings we spoke about," he said, his eyes sharp and bright. "I thought I'd bring them myself."

"Marc, you don't know how glad I am to see you!"

"It was an unpleasant matter. But Capitaine Villand was most apologetic. And now Monsieur Zilberman will have the work he requested."

Varian took the tube of drawings. "Thank you, truly."

"And I thank you, Monsieur Fry. I didn't want to believe you, all those months ago. But you were right. In the end, my position meant nothing to them."

"It did mean something," Varian said. "Here you stand, free and unharmed."

"Because **you** called," Chagall said. "Because you insisted, according to Villand. Who knows what might have happened otherwise? And look what was waiting for me when I returned to my hotel." He pulled from his pocket a thick ivory-colored envelope, which he urged Varian to open. On its front was the seal of the Consulate of the United States, and inside was a letter indicating that the Chagalls had been granted their entry visas. The usual thirty-day window had been waived, opening a broad and limitless path between Chagall and the States.

"Now, Monsieur Fry, we must leave France at the soonest possible moment. And may Monsieur Zilberman precede us! I shall be in touch with my contacts in New York to arrange everything. No practical matter must impede him once he arrives in the States. He must be allowed to make his work, and we must bring it to the attention of the world."

Varian assured him that he would arrange passage for the Chagalls on the next steamship with a pair of open berths, and that he wouldn't rest until Zilberman was safely en route. He would go home that minute to deliver the drawings.

"Let me go with you," Chagall said. "Let me give him the drawings myself. I'd like to see him once more before we go, or before he does."

"Of course," Varian said. "And you'll dine with us? Our garden has just started to yield."

Chagall agreed, and phoned Bella to inform her of his plan; Bella said she would meet them at the tram stop. Then they left the office with Theo and Danny and Jean, and soon they were all aboard the blue-and-white tram to La Pomme. On the way, they discussed possible sailings for the Chagalls: a boat called the **Winnipeg** was to leave for Martinique in nine days' time, and might still have places available; or the Chagalls might travel by train to Portugal, since they now had all the necessary visas and could sail directly from Lisbon to New York.

The pines and cypresses passed in a green blur, the green-yellow sweep of the countryside falling away to the south. How rich it had felt, Varian thought, to shout at that bastard Villand, to shame him into action on Chagall's behalf. He remembered again what Miriam Davenport had said, months ago, about calculated risk; perhaps he had learned the lesson at last. He would have to write her, tell her what she'd given him. His exhaustion had vanished. All he felt now was gratification, and the thrill of riding the rails toward Grant, to deliver the day's story to him.

At La Pomme they crossed under the railway and walked the lane of plane trees, Chagall in the lead, swinging the cardboard tube at the roadside grasses as if mowing them with a scythe. Jean Gemähling escorted Bella, and Theo and Danny walked arm in arm; they might have been a family of grown children with their august parents, heading into the countryside for a picnic. They followed Chagall around to the back of the house, toward the greenhouse, where Zilberman could always be found at this hour of the afternoon. But the greenhouse door hung askew from one hinge, the glass broken.

They ran to the greenhouse, pushed inside. Glass lay everywhere, glass and paints and pastels and brushes and blood, strands of it, drops of it, on the floor, on the greenhouse windows. The blue door, the one the children had discovered in the garden, lay flat on the ground, broken glass glittering around it like salt. The drawings that had been pinned to it were gone.

"Where is the Flight Portfolio?" Chagall said. "Where does he keep it?"

"There," Varian said, pointing; but there was nothing on the table but broken glass, nothing on the floor but splintered wood and tubes of paint and dirty oil pastels and blood and more glass. They searched every corner of the greenhouse, even the root cellar below, but it was gone, all of it but the two drawings Chagall held in his cardboard tube.

They stumbled out onto the patio in a daze. Varian couldn't comprehend what he had seen; his head thrummed with a noise like the far-off roaring of a crowd. Then the door of the house opened and there was Grant, dressed in pajama pants and a half-buttoned shirt, gasping in pain as he crossed the paving stones.

Varian ran to him and took his arm. "What happened? Did you see?"

Grant bent and put his hands on his knees, breathing hard. "They came for him—while he was—" The effort of speaking broke across his face, and he closed his eyes. "I heard them coming up the drive. A police car, and a van. I tried to—shout down to him. Tried to get downstairs. But they—got to him first. Took the work, all of it. Everything he was going to—bring to the States. I demanded to know—where were they taking him? But they pushed me off. Put him in the van with some others. Madame Nouguet went to call you. She's on her way into—town now." He leaned against Varian, his skin burning hot.

"God, Skiff. Danny, Jean, help me! Help me get him up to bed. How did you even make it down here? God, how am I going to get the doctor?"

"I'll go to the depot," Jean said. "I'll telephone from there."

"And I'll return to town and go to the Evêché myself," Chagall said. "That must be where they've taken him."

"No!" Varian said. "I'll go to the Evêché. You'll go back to town, but straight to your hotel. Don't give them a chance to regret letting you go."

"But Zilberman's in danger."

"I'll go myself. As soon as the doctor arrives, I'll go."

"Go now," Danny said. "Theo and I can look after Grant."

Theo nodded, her serious eyes fixed on his own. "You must, Varian."

"Please," Grant said. "Don't stay here a minute longer for my sake."

"Let me see you upstairs first."

He and Danny helped Grant up to bed. The doctor would come, Danny assured him; he would do what he could. There was nothing Varian could do but get back to town, to the Evêché, and demand to see Zilberman at once.

There again at the old Bishop's Palace, walking beneath the stone archway with its bas-relief of cockleshells and fronds of greenery, Varian was not without hope; after all, he'd made them release Chagall. But as the functionary who'd met him at the front desk led him farther into the building, Varian realized with a contraction of the gut where they were taking him: directly to Captain Villand's office.

"Ah," said Villand, as Varian entered. "Monsieur Fry. I can't imagine what could bring you here now, unless you've come to thank me for releasing your protégé, Chagall. Have you perhaps changed your mind? Shall we arrest him again?" Villand's milky blue eyes caught the light, seeming to reflect a glitter of pleasure.

"I've come to see Monsieur Zilberman," Varian

said. "I demand an audience with him at once. And I want the portfolio of works on paper, the one your men took."

Villand **tsk**ed, reaching for his brass pineapple again. He didn't light it right away; he sat for a while with his finger on the roller, making it pronounce its faint rasp. "The company you keep, Monsieur Fry!" he said. "You seem to have forgotten that you are a guest of France, and that to consort with suspected criminals casts suspicion upon your own character. As for whatever else my men might have removed in the process of the arrest, that is to be retained as evidence."

"Zilberman is not a criminal. And if the Flight Portfolio is evidence of anything, it's of the brilliance, the genius, of the very people you're trying to track down and kill."

"Ah, I see. Then why on earth wouldn't I just hand it over? Silly me, following the protocols of criminal justice all this time, when I might have simply consulted you!"

He would play whatever game Villand wanted to play. "Please," he said. "I know the law. You can't search a private home without a warrant. You can't remove a private person's property without cause. And every prisoner is allowed a visitor."

"We had a warrant, you'll be pleased to know. We'd had a tip about a fugitive at your place of residence. We believed Zilberman might lead us to others of interest. Your Flight Portfolio is a veritable cornucopia of degenerates, some of whom have tried our patience long enough."

"What can I do, Captain? What is it you want?"

Villand got to his feet behind the desk, resting his hands on the swell of his belly. The brass of his uniform glittered in the late-afternoon light falling through the window; he seemed to arrange himself at an angle that showed it off to advantage. "I want what we all want here at the Préfecture," he said. "I want the best for France. Naturally, an American's concerns may differ from our own. There should be no mystery, Monsieur Fry, why I must deny your request to have that portfolio back. As to your seeing Lev Zilberman, I must deny that request for the safety, the security, of France."

Varian scrutinized the man as he stood in his slant of sunlight, buttons glittering. Was he bribable? Prideful? What mystery lay behind the smooth plane of his forehead?

"I have something that might be of value to you," he said, finally.

"What can it possibly be, Monsieur Fry?"

"Something of great value to the world. But it can be yours alone."

Captain Villand laced his fingers. "Do tell."

"Monsieur Chagall had two drawings for Zilberman. He went to deliver them this afternoon. I believe he may be persuadable. He might, in other words, be brought round to the idea of delivering those drawings into your hands instead."

The captain sat down again in his chair. "Chagall, deliver two drawings here? I don't believe you for a moment."

"Let me telephone," Varian said.

"You are a prevaricator, Monsieur Fry. Please bear in mind that I can arrest **you** at any time. Monsieur Zilberman was found to be residing at a premises rented in your name. It is quite a serious crime to harbor a fugitive—as I'm sure you know, since you're so familiar with our laws."

"Two drawings by Chagall himself," Varian said, struggling to keep his voice steady. "Two. Without likeness in the world. Yours alone."

Villand sat back in his chair, flicking his unlit cigar with his thumb. "Bribery is also a crime in France. Perhaps in the States you have different laws. Wild West laws."

"I can have the drawings here in half an hour," Varian said.

Flick. Flick.

Varian sat silent in his chair, hardly breathing.

"I suppose those drawings must be admitted as evidence," Villand said, lifting the brass pineapple toward his cigar; he leaned forward to light it, then released a cloud of tar-scented smoke. "If it's true, as you say, that Chagall was on the verge of delivering them, we must have them here at once." And he pushed the telephone across the desk toward Varian.

———

An hour later, a jackbooted guard conducted Varian into the bowels of the building, those subterranean catacomb-like hallways with their rounded ceilings, their too-close walls. Varian imagined ranks of skulls behind those walls, the entombed bodies of thousands of men, prisoners of decades past. He would never get used to the sound of jails, the clang of metal on metal, metal on stone, keys against key rings, metal trays on floors, metal toilet pots on floors, boots on floors, fists against bars; and that was to say nothing of the stench of it, the stench of shit and sweat and old broth and vinegar, of cigarettes and sulfur, of the damp stone itself, the body of the earth carved out to make room for other bodies.

The guard led him not to the cells but to an interview room, not far from the one in which Varian had first met Tobias Katznelson. A bare bulb burned overhead; here again was the same brand of steel desk, an ugly block; the same twin steel chairs, identically hard and cold. In that room he waited alone, rubbing one hand with the other, for what seemed an eternity. Then came Zilberman's shuffling step in the hall, and the heavier footsteps of the guard. The door opened, and the guard pushed Zilberman into the room. His wrists and ankles were cuffed, his white shirt stained with archipelagos of blood. A raw-edged gash ran from his left temple to his earlobe; dried blood traced a line down the side of his neck and disappeared into his collar. His left eye was blackened. Through the other eye he squinted at Varian as if trying to make him out from far away.

"Ten minutes," the guard said, and closed the door. The sole concession to the high price Varian had paid—to the price Chagall had paid, and the rest of the world—was the fact that they were allowed to be alone.

"Lev," he said. "We're going to get you out of this. They arrested Chagall earlier today, but they freed him again within the hour."

"I'm not Chagall," Zilberman said, his voice a harsh, pained whisper.

Varian met his eyes. "Do you know what Chagall says about you?" he asked. "He says we haven't seen the smallest fraction of your work, or what it can do. He says you're superior to him as an artist in every way."

"That would mean nothing at the moment, even if it were true."

"We'll get you out. You must be ready to meet the **Sinaïa** as soon as it docks."

"The **Sinaïa,**" Zilberman said, his tone shading toward bitterness. "The **Sinaïa** sailed some time ago. Somehow I missed it."

"You know the situation. Tobias—"

He shook his head. "And now they've got the Flight Portfolio. I saw it in their hands, saw it thrown into the trunk of the police car. What will they do with it? Fifty-two pieces of original art, the work of the greatest artists alive in Europe—all in Vichy's hands! Even if I get out, we'll never get it back. And you, Mr. Fry. You're known to have harbored me at Air Bel. Your days in France are numbered, to be certain."

"We can't worry about that. We've got to focus on the immediate problem."

"They've been kind enough to tell me what they're planning for me. Not a camp. Nothing so kind. Deportation by the first eastward train. Think of it: I'm to see Germany again! **Mein Vaterland.**"

"No," Varian said. "You've got a U.S. entry visa. I'll go to Bingham. We'll put a stop to this at once. You're not going back to Germany."

Zilberman shook his head. "Mr. Fry," he said, "you must know you have my greatest admiration. What you came here to do was impossible by almost any measure. Your job was to extract people from a sticking morass and shove them through an impenetrable barrier, a series of impenetrable barriers. You took it on with no previous experience. And yet, as we both know, you've had great success. I admire your obduracy. It's a fine quality for a person in your role. But not everyone can be saved."

"You can be," he said, desperately. "You will be. If we could get Tobias Katznelson out of France, we can get you out, too."

Zilberman shook his head. "I've never understood it," he said. "The way you talk about that boy."

"What do you mean?"

"Your friend Mr. Grant was obsessed with preserving the boy's life, and somehow he must have communicated the obsession. Tobias Katznelson! Of course every life matters, but I must ask you, Varian—why him, of all people? Why all that effort on his behalf?"

There were voices in the hall, and footsteps. How much time did they have left? "You know why," Varian said, under his breath. "You know what he was doing at the Kaiser-Wilhelm-Institut—what he was capable of."

"What do I know?" Zilberman said. "That he was a passable student? That he loved my daughter? How many students, how many lovers, have been killed already?"

"Not a passable student," Varian said, quieter still. "A rare talent. A genius. You **know.** You knew him in Berlin. I don't understand it all, I admit—I know nothing about theoretical physics or how it can be applied to military defense. But the Germans had heard enough about it to want him working for them, or to want him dead."

Zilberman sat back in his chair, his long, articulate hands cuffed on his lap. He looked at Varian steadily from beneath his silver brows. "Where did you get this information?" he whispered.

"Grant told me everything. Everything he knew."

Zilberman sat for a long moment, silent. "There **was** a boy," he said. "A friend of Tobias's. A boy of prodigious talent, a disciple of Planck's. Abel

Heligman, his name was. In fact, before my daughter bewitched young Katznelson, she was a favorite of this Heligman. In love with him, I would say." Zilberman shifted in his steel chair. "Many nights he sat at the piano in our front room and played, nearly as well as Mr. Grant. I knew about Heligman's work. Planck told me about it himself—he was a friend of mine, an admirer. A collector of art. He was too excited about Heligman to keep silent, as perhaps he should have. Tobias Katznelson was a great friend of Heligman's. He assisted him in the lab at Kaiser-Wilhem for a time. Then Heligman was arrested. The rumor is that he was tortured. But he wouldn't give them what they wanted. When it became clear they wouldn't release him, that they would send him to a camp, he hanged himself in his cell. It was a terrible shock to my daughter, and to Tobias."

Varian sat in silence, dry-mouthed. A dull buzzing began to emanate from the walls of the room, a sound that seemed to press in upon him from all sides.

"Tobias envied Heligman," Zilberman said, almost gently now. "He knew he didn't possess what Heligman possessed. Not by a long measure."

The walls seemed in danger of falling inward upon Varian. "Is this—are you telling the truth?" he said. "Is this what I must now understand to be true?"

Zilberman glanced toward the door, beyond which

they could hear the guards' muffled voices. "If Tobias Katznelson had what Heligman had, and was now en route to the States, that would be a triumph indeed! Katznelson was a hardworking student, but he told me—he joked to me—that he would never understand a tenth of what Heligman did. His own father lamented his lack of brilliance."

His father. Gregor Katznelson, Grant's lover.

"Tobias Katznelson!" Zilberman said, shaking his head. "I always thought of him as the most ordinary of boys. Even his envy of Heligman was common enough. But perhaps he was more intelligent than I gave him credit for, getting himself here from Germany on his own, then weaving this elaborate web."

"Do you mean to hurt me, Lev?" Varian said, involuntarily. "You'd certainly have a right. Here you sit in chains, threatened with deportation, while Tobias—"

"I'm telling you nothing but the truth, Mr. Fry. I ought to have voiced my questions sooner, but I didn't realize how misled you were. And I wanted you to save Tobias, of course. He's a good boy, a fine boy. I knew what his escape would mean to his parents, and to my daughter, after what happened to Heligman."

"This can't be right, Lev," Varian said, his voice scarcely under control now. "I know Katznelson was what he said he was. Nazi military intelligence was looking for him. And Tobias himself said—"

"What, exactly? How did he frame it to you?"

Varian put his forehead into his hands. He went back in his mind through his encounters with Tobias, every one: the Evêché, the concentration camp, the weeks at Air Bel. Tobias in his torn clothes, then, later, in a prison guard's borrowed uniform; Tobias clad in the fine clothes Grant had bought for him in town; Tobias snow-pale and naked at the dinner table with Jay Allen, or clad only in pajama bottoms in his room at the villa. Tobias with a pinned butterfly in his hands. And all that time, he'd said scarcely a word about his work. Varian couldn't think of a single instance in which he'd misrepresented his situation. Varian himself, often speaking obliquely, had expressed how urgent it was that Tobias be saved. Tobias had merely agreed.

The guard opened the door to the interview room and announced that the time had expired. When Zilberman sat unmoving, the guard pulled him to his feet by the chain that linked his handcuffs.

"I left something for my wife and daughter," Zilberman said. "In the root cellar, in case something like this should happen."

"Time is up," the guard said again. "All conversation is to cease at once." He gave Zilberman's cuffs another yank. Zilberman stumbled toward the door and out into the hall, where he turned back toward Varian.

"I'm grateful for what you've done," he said. "Whatever its limitations."

"Face forward," said the guard. "I don't want to have to drag you."

And then they started off down the echoing length of that catacomb, and in a few moments Lev Zilberman was gone.

33

Reckoning

He would never know how he got to Bingham's villa that night, how he climbed the dark hills of Marseille to the winding drive, with its twin colonnade of lindens and its ankle-high plantings of verbena. He seemed to be moving through a kind of tunnel, kin to the catacomb from which he'd just emerged. The night pressed in upon him from all sides, pushing him toward the ivory-colored house ahead, toward its blue-painted portal with its weathered brass ring. How he beat his fists on that door, how he pounded the brass ring against the door until flakes of paint snowed onto the doorstep. He kept pounding, shouting Bingham's name, until Bingham came to the door himself, wearing a smoking jacket and holding a glass of whiskey in his hand.

"What on earth, Fry? At this hour? How did you get here?"

"Harry," he said, and collapsed against the doorframe. "Let me in."

"Good God, Varian, what's happened?"

"Zilberman's been arrested. They're threatening to ship him east. And they've taken the Flight Portfolio, all of it."

There was no need to elaborate, no need to explain the urgency. Bingham left him in the vestibule and ran up the curving stair, returning moments later fully dressed. He instructed his valet to pull the car out, and, moments later, the gleaming red Cadillac emerged from its stable with its engine roaring. They climbed in, and Bingham pressed the pedal to the floorboards, shooting them down the drive and through the streets of town, where Bingham ran a dozen red lights, threatened pedestrians, barely avoided a long series of postboxes and trash cans and hitching-posts, and finally screeched to a halt in front of the Evêché, where he left the car parked directly in front of a sign that read **DEFENSE ABSOLUE DE STATIONNER.**

Despite Bingham's demands at the front desk, despite his presentation of his diplomatic papers and his promise that the U.S. consul-general himself would intervene unless the commandant granted their request, the officer on duty refused to admit them even to Captain Villand's anteroom. They sat instead in a general waiting area on narrow wooden chairs apparently designed for discomfort; they sat for hours, hardly speaking, Varian with his head in his hands, acutely aware that Zilberman was somewhere in the building, his cuts untended, his black eye swelling, his thoughts on his wife and daughter. He was still here in France, still alive, still savable, if only they could get to him.

He called Chagall from the coin telephone in the hall, and Chagall promised to give Captain Villand anything else he might want. He called Peggy Guggenheim, who proposed an extravagant cash bribe. He couldn't call Mary Jayne, because she had disappeared with Killer. He called Gussie at his hotel, then sent him to the villa to bring Danny; Danny arrived breathless, having run all the way from the tram. Varian brought him to the waiting room and told him nearly the whole story, though he couldn't repeat what Zilberman had said about Tobias, couldn't repeat that piece of information, or of false information, if that was what it was. His insides twisted and burned; hot waves of pain broke over him, surging upward through his abdomen and chest, bringing drops of sweat to his forehead. He wiped his forehead with his handkerchief until his handkerchief dripped. Sometime in the night, Bingham went home to sleep for a few hours. He would go to the consulate before dawn, he said, would do whatever he could. He would telephone Mrs. Roosevelt. He would telephone the president himself.

Varian watched him go—Bingham in his light trenchcoat, tall blond ultraman, embodiment of American power, the idealistic and inclusive kind. What power did Varian have without him? What could he do? He could wait, that was all. The Evêché never closed its doors, a police station couldn't; he would wait in perpetuity if he had to. Danny stayed with him, pacing, cleaning his glasses, making little notes in his pocket notebook, inquiring periodically at the desk. He told Varian that Grant's condition had stabilized back home, that by the time the doctor had arrived, the aspirin had brought Grant's fever down again; the doctor had delivered pain medication, and Grant was sleeping now, or had been sleeping when Danny left. He delivered this news for comfort, in a low and reassuring tone. But when Varian's mind slid to Grant, when he envisioned Grant's long form stretched beneath the sheets of their shared bed, he experienced a kind of inner recoil, as if at the touch of something hot or sharp. Someone had lied. That was clear. Was it Zilberman, there at the Evêché, or Grant? In his mind he returned to that September afternoon on the Vieux Port, the day Grant had revealed the particulars of Tobias's case. Amid the flashing of light on the water, amid the thrill of riding the rail of that Monotype National with the sea rushing past beneath them, amid the glow of the white Bandol and the astonishing fact of Grant's closeness, the heat of his body, the shape of his shoulders beneath his linen shirt, would Varian have been able to discern a lie? Would he have been looking for it? He knew what he'd been looking for: some indication that Grant still felt for him what he, Varian, felt. What he'd felt all along, those twelve years. All else was blurred now in his memory.

Sometime near dawn—he scarcely knew how it happened, and never learned why—four officers approached him and Danny and took them by the arms, drag-walked them to the doors, and pushed them out into the street. They got to their feet, dusted themselves off, and half-ran to the office on the boulevard Garibaldi. There was Gussie, God bless him, still awake, working on a project of his own: he'd been rooting around for information about the new resistance movement, trying to establish communication between isolated cells outside Marseille. Varian was secretly proud; he felt he'd incited Gussie to the work. Gussie's light burned on as Varian and Danny closed themselves into Varian's office, Danny attempting to get an international line so they could place a call to Eleanor Roosevelt, Varian drafting an urgent telegram to the New York office. But everything was closed for the night in New York, and the telegram office in Marseille was still shuttered.

At some point Varian must have put his head down on his desk, because he found himself waking in a daze, Danny shaking his arm. For a moment it seemed to him that they'd merely worked late on an ordinary day, that none of the events of the last twelve hours had come to pass; he imagined himself complaining to Grant about his stiff back, Grant telling him how foolish he'd been to push himself so hard. Then Danny said they must get to the Gare St. Charles, that he'd just learned from Hirschman's former girlfriend at the Préfecture that Zilberman was to be deported that morning.

"We have to go at once," Danny said. "Maybe we can still put a stop to it."

"How?" Varian said. "We'd need a police force of our own, or an army."

"Can't everything be bought in this town?"

"Or a diversion," Varian said. "A skirmish. A faked shooting. Something to distract the police from the prisoners."

"Who do we know who can help us?"

"Vinciléoni," Varian said. "Someone must go to the Dorade." He opened the door to the office. Gussie looked up from his desk, his eyes dark-ringed.

"What can I do, Monsieur Fry?" he said. "Is there any way to help?"

"I want you to go to see Vinciléoni," Varian said. "We need him to send a team of men to the Gare St. Charles. Armed, if possible. Men who can distract the police while we get Zilberman out of there. We'll need a tool, too—something capable of cutting a steel chain." He went into his office and opened the safe, taking out the fat envelope of cash they kept for bribes; he loaded twenty thousand into an envelope and pressed it into Gussie's hand. Gussie nodded his understanding, and in another moment he'd gone down the stairs and out the door.

Varian collapsed into the desk chair that had been Lena's, put his head down on the blotter, and closed his eyes.

"Danny," he said. "I should have put him on that ship weeks ago."

"You couldn't have known about yesterday's **rafle.**"

"His arrest had nothing to do with that. It was Killer who sold him out, after I ejected him from Air Bel. I'm sure of it. Villand said they'd had a tip."

"You can't know that for certain."

"What does it matter anyway? I've failed at my job. It should have been Zilberman on the **Sinaïa.** I got it wrong."

"Well, it won't do any good to sit talking about it," Danny said. **"Allons-y."**

They ran all the way, through the narrow streets and across the Canebière and up the boulevard d'Athènes, then up the shallow stairs that spilled from the station like a cubist waterfall. But what then? The train in question hadn't even arrived yet, and there was no sign of the prisoners. They checked the timetable boards; the train's departure platform hadn't yet been posted. At the station café they bought thin chicory coffee and inedible biscuits, then sat on a bench beside one of the platforms, but neither of them could drink or eat a thing. A quarter of an hour later Gussie arrived out of breath, having carried his bicycle up the long stairs; he reported that Vinciléoni had refused to put any of his people into a situation involving so much risk, on behalf of a prisoner he knew little about, who had run afoul of the French authorities and was due to be deported.

"Didn't you tell him who Zilberman was?"

"I told him everything," Gussie said, his hands trembling on the bike handles. "I offered him the money. I said we had more where it came from. I asked him to name a price. But he refused to consider it. What should I have done, Monsieur Fry?"

Just then, a prison van pulled up to the station entrance. Officers opened the doors, and a line of prisoners, chained together, stumbled out onto the flat gray paving stones. There were eight of them, Zilberman nowhere among them. But then another van arrived, and another; ten in all, a whole train's worth of prisoners to be sent east. Finally Zilberman's group arrived; he was the fourth prisoner in a line of ten. Even from a distance, Varian could still see the untreated wound on his cheek, the slash of blood across his neck. The officers led the prisoners into the station, toward the eastbound platform. Varian shouted, but Zilberman didn't turn or raise his head. He followed the man in front of him and was followed by the man behind. Varian found himself half-running toward them; he had no idea what he planned to do, only that he meant to get closer. He reached the entrance to the east-bound platform and stepped toward the prisoners.

"Stop there," an officer shouted, hand on his gun. "These men are under the protection of the state."

Varian stopped. The prisoners were only a few feet away, close enough for Varian to see the red marks on their wrists where the handcuffs had chafed them. Zilberman himself was almost within reach; Varian spoke his name. Zilberman's eyes came up for a moment, but then he looked down, shaking his head. What expression had flashed over his features? Was it pity? Resentment? **Disgust?** Varian tried again to get closer, but a guard stopped him with his stick. The guard's mothlike mustache, gray-brown, twitched on his lip as if it meant to take flight.

"No one is to enter this platform while prisoners are being loaded," he said.

"Lower your stick!" Varian said. "Let me pass."

"You're not permitted to approach the prisoners, monsieur."

Danny had appeared at Varian's side; he took his arm and pulled him back. "There's no use getting yourself arrested," he said.

The mustachioed guard stepped back toward the prisoners, and Varian stood beside Danny, watching in furious impotence as the officers led the prisoners along the platform. A train was just arriving, chuffing along the rail, sending out plumes of steam from its brakes; for a long moment the prisoners' legs disappeared into that rolling cloud, and they seemed to float along the platform like a pack of condemned angels. One of the guards shouted them to attention; another conferred with the station gendarmes, presenting papers on a clipboard. The mustachioed officer blew a whistle, and the prisoners were loaded rank by rank onto what appeared at first to be a series of ordinary railway carriages, but were revealed at second glance to be prison cars, their windows covered with metal mesh. The last of the prisoners climbed aboard, and guards walked the length of the train, closing and barring and locking every door. Minutes later, the train began its slow transit out of the station.

Gone. What could he do? His insides seemed full of molten lead, his throat closed with grief and fury. Without a word, he left Danny and Gussie at the edge of the platform; he crossed the station at a half-run and pushed through its glass doors. Through the blinding morning light he descended the cascade of steps toward the Canebière, then ran to the south side of the Vieux Port, all the way to the Dorade. The place was full of white light and morning hush, one black-haired blear-eyed boy swabbing its decks with a tentacled mop. Varian knew where to find Vinciléoni, knew that he was an early riser and would already be at work. Down he went, down into the alimentary canal of the restaurant, through the low passageways below the dining room, all the way to the narrow appendix that was Vinciléoni's office. He opened the door with his fist, and there was Vinciléoni at his desk, freshly shaven, dressed in a crisp white shirt and a neat black tie, drinking his seltzer, holding his china marker.

"Don't you knock?" Vinciléoni said.

"Not now," Varian said, pushing a stack of papers off the other chair. He pulled the chair up to the desk and sat down.

Vinciléoni drew his eyebrows together. "I suppose you're here to ask why I wouldn't send my men to be arrested on your client's behalf."

"I could," Varian said. "I could ask why you weren't willing to send a few thugs to jail for a few hours, if it meant saving the life of Lev Zilberman. But I don't have to talk about that. Your conscience will do the work for me later."

"You know nothing of my conscience," Vinciléoni said.

"Undoubtedly," Varian said. "I'm not sure, come to think of it, that you have one."

Vinciléoni cocked his head at Varian. "Just what's gotten into you, Monsieur Fry? You seem to have lost all perspective."

Vinciléoni's tone sounded a warning in Varian's head, one that broke through the haze of his desperation and exhaustion. He suspected he wouldn't get what he wanted by fighting; he had to force himself to exercise diplomacy. "Forgive me," he said now. "I'm not here about what happened this morning. There's something else I want. Something I need to know. It's about Tobias Katznelson."

"Ah, yes, your small fish. He made it to Oran, I trust?"

"Yes, and out of Oran too. He may have reached Martinique by now."

"Then what's the concern?"

Varian laced his hands. Through his anger, through his exhaustion, he struggled to frame the question. "When I first mentioned Katznelson," he said, "you said you suspected he wasn't as small as I made him out to be. You said your sources had informed you otherwise. I must know, Charles, who those sources were. It's a matter of the greatest importance to me."

Vinciléoni laughed. "Mr. Fry," he said. "Everything with you is a matter of the greatest importance. A person trying to help you wouldn't know where to begin. You must get Breitscheid and Hilferding out, it's a matter of the greatest importance. Save Herr Zilberman, a German Jewish muralist especially desired, God knows why, by the Nazis—greatest importance! And now, on behalf of this Katznelson, you want me to reveal my sources? Can you truly imagine I'd do that? My sources are the nerves that run through the body of Marseille—of **underground** Marseille, I should say. Lay them bare and they die of exposure. Kill the nerves and the body can't feel, can't function. Kill too many and the body itself dies."

Varian had begun to tremble with fury. "Look, Charles," he said, willing his voice steady. "We've been funneling cash into your organization for some months now. Lots of cash. I'm asking one small favor. That's all."

"So you say. But why **this** favor? What can it matter to you?"

"Because I have reason to believe Katznelson was a fraud. And I want to know who defrauded me. I have to know. My life depends on it."

Vinciléoni sat back in his chair and sipped his seltzer. "Your **life**!" he said. "Dear me." He set his glass on the desk and ran his hands over his salted black hair, smoothing it to an otterlike sleekness. "Are you concerned," he said, "that you put an ordinary young man on the **Sinaïa**? Someone whose life was worth no more than anyone else's?"

"Tell me who spoke to you about Katznelson," he said. "Was it Raymond Couraud? The one we call Killer?"

"I've just told you quite clearly, Mr. Fry, that I don't care to reveal my sources."

"Did you pay Couraud for information?"

"If I did, what would motivate me to tell you?"

"Can you muster some compassion for me, Charles, as a human being? This is a personal matter, not a business one."

"We're business associates, Monsieur Fry. I can't

open my address book for your private benefit. I admire and respect the work you do, but our relationship exists in the professional sphere only. And my patience has its limits. You breached them, in fact, some time ago. I am a busy man. You arrived without an appointment. I must ask now that you let me get back to my work."

He would have liked, just then, to jump across the desk and throttle Vinciléoni. Instead he stood before him, still trembling, and replaced his hat on his head.

"You've been small and mean-spirited, Charles," he said.

"And you've been rude and abrupt, Monsieur Fry. But I won't hold it against you. Your patronage is too valuable to me. Don't hesitate to come here in a different mood, on matters of business, at a mutually convenient time. Are we in agreement?"

Varian turned and left without a word, letting the door slam behind him.

———

Without thinking, he walked up to the tram line on the Canebière and caught the train for La Pomme. As he rode, he looked out the window at now-familiar sights: the balcony of a yellow building painted an incongruous turquoise; a silver scooter stripped of its wheels and chained to a peeling postbox; a brick wall graffitied with six-foot-high penises; an orange cat in a third-floor window, its ophidian eyes narrowed against the sun. He stared in desperation at these objects, unchanged since the day before: incontrovertible evidence of his continued life here in Marseille. But all else seemed to have slipped away, vanished into the fog of the Vieux Port. He needed to think; needed a proper night's sleep. It was ten in the morning but it might as well have been midnight; in another minute he would doze off in his tram seat. Where could he go, where could he rest? How could he go to Air Bel when Grant lay in his own bed?

He reached La Pomme as usual, left the station as usual, headed down the usual hill. But he found himself failing to cross under the tracks, failing to walk through the tunnel that led to the villa. Instead he followed the paved road that ran along the train tracks, walked it for nearly a mile until he came to a different crossing, a path he hadn't taken in months. He walked that path until he passed through an iron gate and along a lane flanked by cypresses, and when he looked up at the end of the lane he saw that he'd reached the Medieval Pile.

He knew there was a caretaker, but the man was nowhere in sight. The garden, overgrown with poppies and yellow broomflowers, seemed consumed by a swaying, licking fire. Above, the great stone house stood silent in the morning air. Varian walked through the persimmon orchard, the limbs of the trees covered in fresh leaves and pale yellow star-shaped flowers; he walked the slate-paved path to the front door. When he tried the handle, the door swung open onto the dark entry. Bars of dusty light fell through the high narrow windows, faintly illuminating the hexagonal stair. He could almost hear Grant's laugh from above, inviting him up. He found himself walking toward the conservatory, where he'd first met Gregor Katznelson that day in September; the long stretch of windows yielded a familiar view of trees and wildflowers and rocks, a rolling upholstery of lavender draped in folds along the downward slope of the valley. On the far side of the conservatory stood a rolltop desk with dozens of pigeonholes, Gregor's writing table. Varian went to it now and ran a hand along the surface of the blotter, blue leather edged in gold leaf. A dead beetle lay in one corner, its articulated legs surrendering mutely; in another, a calligraphy nib pointed north in a compass rose of dried ink. He opened the large drawers on either side of the desk, pulling hard enough to rattle their frames. Nothing inside but the scent of damp wood and a couple of spent matchbooks. One by one he opened the tiny drawers above the desktop: nothing. What was he looking for? What did he imagine he might find?

He pushed himself away from the desk, escaped from the room, and climbed the familiar stairs to the bedroom where Grant had lounged in Katznelson's bed, shaved with his shaving things, worn his robe, read his books, admired the view from his window.

He crossed the pomegranate-colored Persian rug and opened the French doors. Here was the balcony where he and Grant had stood looking down into the valley in winter, at that strange mixture of verdure and decay that seemed to embody the dual nature of the place. Some things dried and crumbled; others grew. If he stood here long enough, if he concentrated, could he will this balcony to slip its moorings, give way, fall down the cliff below with him as passenger? Fog obscured the sun and made him feel the chill of the wind; he went inside and closed the doors behind him. The high bed, carved of dark wood and hung all around with velvet curtains, stood against the western wall like a funeral bier. He climbed on top of it and lay there like a dead monarch, the late King Varian, his head a stone on a stone pillow, his legs stretched to their full length along the velvet bedcover.

He must have slept; he didn't know how long. When he woke, the sky outside was dark and there was only one thought in his mind: he had to get back to Air Bel. Without examining the thought, without giving himself time to question it, he rose from Katznelson's bed and straightened the bedcovers, then ran down the hexagonal stair and out through the entryway, the massive door banging behind him. He ran as though the place were haunted, as though all the ghosts there were chasing him, trying to catch and kill him before he could make it back to Air Bel, to Grant. He ran until he'd reached his own crossing, until he'd gone beneath the railroad track again and gained the driveway with its line of towering plane trees. A light burned in his room; a shadow crossed it. He walked up the drive, then entered the house and climbed the stairs toward that light.

Zilberman was gone. That was all he told Grant before he collapsed into bed beside him; everything else was as yet unspeakable. As they lay in bed together, as Grant ran his hand along the length of Varian's body beneath the sheet, as he draped his arm around Varian and breathed sleep into his ear, the news about Katznelson seemed to become insubstantial, inconsequential. Grant hadn't lied to him; he couldn't have. This was the person he'd known bone-deep since they were barely out of boyhood, the man whose absence had hurt him like a chronic disease, the man who had revealed himself to Varian over the past nine months as no one had before, the person who had excavated, who had required, who had **wanted** everything Varian held closest to his heart. **This** person could not have deceived him, could not have been deceiving him all this time. Not this one, with his quiet breath at Varian's ear, his hand on Varian's breastbone.

34

Departures

The next day Grant was well enough to get out of bed and sit by the window, and Varian set him up in a deep wingback chair with a quilt over his knees, a tray of baguette and tea at his side, a stack of books from the village library at arm's reach, the bottle of aspirin close at hand. He voiced no doubt to Grant, he allowed his face to reveal nothing. What was most important, he told himself, was Grant's recovery. Grant took his hand and assured him that he'd be all right, and Varian dressed and left for town.

But all along the tram ride, all along the walk to the office, past the farmers' stands at the center of town, past Chave Prison, with its rotten exhalation of dank latrine and spoiled cabbage, all the way to the office on the boulevard Garibaldi, he carried his doubt about Tobias Katznelson like a dreaded diagnosis, a disease whose symptoms were invisible but whose poison penetrated his organs and tumbled through his blood. At the office he buried himself in his work: He wrote an insistent letter to Maurice Anne Marie de Rodellec du Porzic, Chief of Police, demanding the release of the Flight Portfolio; he inquired into sailings for the Chagalls, wrote letters to prominent New Yorkers on behalf of Jacques Lipchitz and his wife, petitioned for an exit visa for Max Ernst. In the afternoon he telephoned Bingham to see if there was any news, and Bingham said he had sent emergency cables to every consular officer who might possibly be of help; so far he'd heard nothing. Varian thanked him and got off the phone before he could tell Bingham what Zilberman had said about Tobias. No one at the office, no one from Air Bel, knew what Varian had learned. If he could keep it that way, if he could prevent the terrible doubt from becoming a real thing in the world, perhaps he could pinch it into nonexistence.

That day passed. So did the next. Still he said nothing to Grant, whose first days out of bed had exhausted him, and who fell asleep for the night before the stars came out. In the long dark hours Varian spent at his side, he forced his thoughts toward his work; in the morning he ran from Grant, ran to work, to the office, staying until after he knew Grant would be asleep. A week went by that way, then another. There was much to consume his attention: Jacques Lipchitz, having received his visas, now had to be persuaded by letter to attempt his escape. Max Ernst's papers were all in order now, and his departure had to be arranged. The Flight Portfolio remained a prisoner of the state, despite urgent pleas from Eleanor Roosevelt and André Gide; Varian visited the Evêché daily, sat in waiting rooms for hours, banged on the unyielding door of Captain Villand's office, sent more letters to de Rodellec du Porzic, petitioned Vichy, and even once, in a tiny Romanesque chapel in the rue d'Aubagne, furtively prayed to God. Of Zilberman himself there was still no word at all.

Some afternoons Varian left the office to walk along the Vieux Port, pausing at the dock from which he and Grant had set off on their circumscribed sail. The Monotype National was nowhere in evidence; it must have been put into storage. The dock itself was abandoned. No one was ever there to bother Varian, no one there to interrupt the pattern of his meditation. He would take off his shoes and socks and sit barefoot at the edge of the splintered boards, remembering the feeling from childhood, from afternoons on the Cape with his parents: the lap of wavelets against the pier, the chill of the water radiating from below, the wavering light all around him. With his eyes nearly closed, the sun breaking into brilliant circles on his lashes, he found he could open in his mind a small protected space, a place where he was safe to entertain any doubt. And the one that always came first was this: When Grant had reappeared all those months ago, when he'd materialized from the ether like a Hollywood ghost, hadn't Varian mistrusted him at once? Hadn't he felt a familiar flash of discomfort, a familiar suspicion that Grant wasn't what he seemed to be? **Your friend comports himself like a man who is keeping a secret,** Youssef A. had said at La Fémina. And Varian had laughed it off. But hadn't it occurred to him that Grant's motives might not be pure, that he might be looking to settle an old score? Hadn't he, in some recess of his mind, always wondered how deeply he could trust Grant, who had, after all, spent all those years pretending to be what he was not—prevaricating, masquerading, **passing**?

But what did that mean, his passing? What had he been passing for? For what he was? He hadn't written the laws that considered anyone with a drop of Negro blood a Negro; those laws were vestiges of slavetime, of fear. He had perpetrated a deception, it was true, but had he actually hurt anyone in the process? He had never denied the existence of a Negro family he knew and loved; he'd done only what anyone, black or white, should have had a right to do: gone to college where he wanted to, gone to graduate school where he wanted to, secured the best job he could. He'd never lied to Varian about any of it; he'd always told him the truth. As far as Varian knew, Grant had never lied to him about anything.

Here was what he knew, or thought he knew: For eight months, from their first moment at the

Dorade until that morning, Grant had behaved like a man in love. He had risked, he had feared, he had retied a liaison that had nearly been the end of him twelve years before; he had made promises, confessions; he had written to Katznelson (or at least he said he had; Varian had never actually seen the letter, had he?). Everything he had seemed to feel, all he'd shown Varian of himself—could it have been faked? All of it? Was anyone in the world so subtle an actor?

But then, into that protected space, the one in which he'd almost convinced himself of Grant's innocence, would come a vision of Zilberman at the Evêché, his left eye blackened, that dirty-looking wound at his temple running with blood. He would hear the genuine chagrin and mystification in Zilberman's voice as he spoke, would see the clear and steady look in Zilberman's good eye as he told Varian what he knew. He, Varian, who thought himself so subtle: Was he, in fact, a fool, a rube? Was Grant laughing at him silently, had he been laughing at him now for months, having desired and won some form of retribution? Or even just a victory for his lover, to whom he'd return as soon as he could?

No matter how he argued to himself, no matter how he pleaded with himself, that was the conviction he brought home every day: that he had been deceived, that Zilberman had merely revealed the truth that day at the Evêché. Home at Air Bel, in the bedroom he shared with Grant, or in the library, or in the kitchen over tea, Grant seemed to watch him with growing unease. Was it only a reflection of Varian's own suspicion, or was it evidence of his guilt? When he asked Varian what was wrong—and he did ask, sometimes directly, sometimes with his hands and mouth on Varian's body, sometimes with silence, the simple communication of patience—Varian told him, always, that he was thinking about Zilberman and the Flight Portfolio, thinking of how he'd failed to save them both. He had unearthed Zilberman's package for his wife and daughter, he told Grant: not paintings, as he'd imagined, not drawings, but money, banknotes, nearly a hundred thousand francs' worth. And a letter, a substantial one, tied up as if for luck in a piece of red string. It was stamped and addressed, but Varian couldn't bring himself to mail it, couldn't bring himself to deliver to Frau and Fräulein Zilberman that last missive, the note that must have begun along the lines of **If you're reading this letter, you must assume me to be dead.** That, he told Grant, was what was on his mind; that was what was stealing his sleep. It was convincing enough as an excuse, enough so that Grant, finely attuned though he was to Varian's inner music, eventually stopped asking. The days ticked forward, and Grant continued to recover from his pericarditis, and Varian lay awake at night, blinking into the uninterrupted darkness.

He had managed at last to arrange a sailing for the Chagalls, one that would take them all the way from Lisbon to New York. They were to depart by train on the tenth of May; they wanted no send-off, no farewell party, nothing to attract the authorities' attention. Though Bingham had offered the use of the Cadillac, they wanted to walk to the station; the last look at a city, Chagall said, was the most important one. So the morning of May tenth found Varian at the Hôtel Moderne at half past six, preparing to carry his clients' bags some fifteen blocks to the Gare St. Charles. He paid the Chagalls' hotel bill with Centre Américain funds, then paced the narrow faux-marbled hallway like a prisoner. As at the Bretons' and Serges' departure, he knew he should have been proud, but he felt like an idiot, like a mole rat who had recently discovered himself to be naked and blind. Chagall himself did nothing to dispel the impression. When he appeared from between the elevator doors, a long tube of drawings over his shoulder and a paint-flecked suitcase in his hand, the look he gave Varian was one of aggrieved reproof. Bella, following him out of the elevator, stood pale and upright in her black lace dress, her eyes dark and anxious, ringed underneath with dusk-colored shadows.

"Are we ready?" Varian asked, relieving Bella of her hatbox.

"I couldn't sleep all night," Bella said. "I'm utterly exhausted."

"We'll sleep more soundly, I suppose, when we reach New York," Chagall said. He relinquished his suitcase to Varian and stepped out through the front doors, into the apricot-colored light slanting from the east.

They turned toward the Canebière, toward the familiar cafés and hotels and steamship offices, all of it offering itself to the painter and his wife for one last crystallizing look. But Chagall's eye, following the early-morning pedestrians in their springtime clothes, didn't seem to savor, nor to rest; it moved always, as though in search of something lost. And Bella walked beside him in silence, a tiny photograph of her daughter held to her chest; Ida and her husband had not yet received their visas, and might never be able to follow their parents.

If only he could have told the Chagalls how he had paid already for his error, how he was paying still. His life, which a few weeks earlier had seemed to hover in a region of inarticulable joy, had descended now into a deadwater swamp impenetrable to light, even in midday. As they climbed the long stairs to the station, what he felt most was a terrible and penetrating loneliness. He could think only of climbing the same stairs on the day of Zilberman's deportation, entering through these glass doors, pushing his way toward that platform, the place he'd seen Zilberman last.

At the Chagalls' departure platform he set down the suitcases, panting. Chagall looked up with a half-bemused expression at the twenty-foot-high tricolor banner strung from the ceiling of the station. VIVE LE MARECHAL, it read, in two-foot-high capital letters: an admonition, a command.

"I must apologize again, Monsieur Fry, for being such a stubborn client," Chagall said, his tone still constrained. "I thank you for your persistence."

"I was honored, Marc," Varian said, his eyes lowered.

Bella, standing at her husband's side with her glossy black hatbox in hand, fixed Varian in her gaze. "You look rather done in yourself, Monsieur Fry, if I may say so. I believe you could use a rest."

"Monsieur Fry cannot rest yet," Chagall said, pointedly. "He will rest only when all his charges are free."

"Perhaps you'll come see us once you're back in New York," Bella said. "You'll return home sometime, won't you?"

"Sometime," Varian said. He had believed, for a time, that his home was wherever Grant was. Now he had the sensation, standing there on the platform, of having become insubstantial, transparent, weightless, as if he might float out through the open mouth of the station and be blown away into the Mediterranean sky.

"I'm sorry about your drawings, Marc," Varian said. "Sorry you had to give them up to that idiot Villand. I hate to think of them in his hands."

Chagall exchanged a glance with his wife; Bella covered her mouth with her hand. Into her dark eyes came a surprising light: Was it humor? "It's a shame you didn't see them," Chagall said. "They were, in a way, inspired by Air Bel. By the party for Monsieur Allen, in fact. The fame of which has traveled far."

"Is that so? How, exactly?"

"Well," Chagall said. "We were our own subjects, Bella and I. We dressed, if that's the word, just as your friends did on that occasion. I seated myself upon one sheet of drawing paper, and Madame Chagall made a tracing. Then she seated herself on the other, and I did the same."

"You're saying you gave him—"

"Two lovely drawings," Chagall said. "Auto-portraits, you might call them. The other drawings, the ones I intended for Zilberman's portfolio, are here with me now." He patted the steel tube at his side. "As soon as I reach New York, my gallery will offer them for sale. Your organization shall have the proceeds."

He couldn't help himself; he laughed aloud. "That's brilliant, Marc."

"Yes, I thought so myself."

"I made a mistake," Varian said. "A terrible mistake. About Zilberman."

Chagall took Varian's hands in his own, waited until Varian met his gaze. The look of condemnation was gone; all he saw now were those deep-set, deeply lined eyes, the ones that had struck him, on their first meeting, as being capable of seeing more than mortals' eyes could see. "The true mistake would have been not to come at all. To stay in New York with the rest of the New Yorkers. Not to have tried."

He wanted to believe those words, wanted to feel heartened by them. But he could only think, as he shook Chagall's hand one last time and bent to kiss Bella's, that if he could have turned back time he would have done it; he would have chosen never to have come to Marseille, never to have known that Grant still lived, never to have gotten out from behind his desk at the Foreign Policy Association and taken human lives into his hands. He had cut a thread of fate, he had done it for Grant's sake. He'd done it bloodlessly, secondhand, but he was just as guilty as if he'd closed the shears himself; as guilty as he'd been when, twelve years earlier, driving the yellow Packard, he'd closed his eyes for a fleeting moment and let his speed carry him over the dividing line.

He dragged himself back to the office, inserted himself behind his desk, picked up a stack of mail. He had just opened the third in a series of visa-application rejections when Danny appeared at the door of his office, a telephone message in hand. The message was from Bingham, who had summoned Varian to the consulate.

"Did he say why?" he asked Danny.

"Only that you'd better come immediately." He drew his eyebrows together, frowning at the penciled note. "He sounded—unlike himself, I'd say. Downhearted."

"What about our rendezvous with Kourillo?" He and Danny were to meet their money-changer in half an hour; Kourillo had promised a good rate for Konstantinov's box of gold coins. Since February the box had been secreted away at the villa, buried beneath a paving stone beside the goldfish pond. But after the last raid, after the ransacking of Zilberman's studio and the confiscation of the Flight Portfolio, Danny believed it was no longer safe to keep anything of value at Air Bel. Killer, with his eyes on everything, might well have known about the box of coins, though they'd buried it at two in the morning; if he'd been in Mary Jayne's room, if he'd been looking out the window at that moment, he might have seen them and known what they were about. They were scheduled to meet Kourillo at his hotel at noon, and Kourillo was to give them eighty thousand in cash for the doubloons.

"We're old friends by now, Kourillo and I," Danny said. "I don't need a double. Go down and see what Harry wants."

"Are you sure, Danny? It's a lot of loot to carry around on your own."

"I'm sure. Go."

He arrived at the consular offices to find a longer-than-usual line out front, a crush of refugee supplicants in the foyer and the waiting room, looking exhausted already though the sun hadn't yet reached its apex. In recent weeks, boats had been leaving Marseille at an unprecedented rate. He had put seventy-eight of his own clients, including Breitscheid's wife, on the **Winnipeg** a few days earlier, and seven on the **Mont Viso,** and fifty-three more on the **Wyoming.** Had he not been so consumed with his private misery, had he not been so distracted by his grief, those departures would have seemed unbelievable victories. He suspected his total now to be nearing a thousand. Jacques Lipchitz had departed for Lisbon earlier that week, Varian having won his trust; and Max Ernst and Peggy Guggenheim were, that very day, to board the **Yankee Clipper** for New York. Perhaps Bingham had summoned him to congratulate him. Perhaps the note of disheartenment was unrelated. But the familiar lanky guard, the one who spoke unusually agile French, avoided Varian's gaze as he entered. And Bingham's secretary, that red-haired Michigan girl who could sing like Deanna Durbin and who always had a smile for him, gave him a look of misery now, her eyes pink and raw.

"What's the matter?" Varian said, resting a hand on her desk.

"Go in," she said. "You'll see."

The door to Harry's office stood open, and he crossed the waiting room to enter. What met his eyes was at first incomprehensible: books strewn across the floor, the filing cabinet gutted, the desk a disaster of papers, a fleet of cardboard boxes on the carpet. He thought there must have been a raid. Bingham stood behind the massive walnut desk, his sleeves rolled to his elbows, loading his things into a wooden crate.

"Harry, what on earth?"

"I've been cut loose," Bingham said. "I'm to leave for Lisbon in the morning. Posted temporarily as a consular agent. Demoted. No reason given."

Varian sat down slowly in one of the chairs before the desk. "No reason?" he said. "Don't they have to tell you why?"

"They don't have to do anything. Not one thing." And it was true, or had been true during Bingham's time in Marseille: the consulate, charged with protecting the borders of the United States from afar, hadn't felt bound to admit refugees in peril, particularly not the Jews or former communists among them. Bingham had fought for them anyway, had fought relentlessly for everyone Varian had sent his way, and now he was paying the price.

"I'm sorry, Harry," Varian said. "This is my fault."

"Nonsense! I made my own bed. I knew I'd have to lie in it eventually."

"But what will you do in Lisbon? They won't take to you any more kindly there. Avra Warren's got the whole staff scared out of their wits, threatening to fire anyone who issues a visa to a Jew."

"Likely that's why they're sending me," Bingham said, flashing a sideways grin. "To re-educate me. Or something along those lines."

"How long do you think you'll last?"

"Ten bucks says I'll be fired before the end of summer."

"Surely they can't cut you loose entirely. You're too good at your job."

"Yes, well, there is my stellar record of visa-granting. But I'm afraid it's all in the service of the tired, the poor, the huddled masses, et cetera." He stuffed a few more papers into the box on his desk. "I'll ask for a commission in South America, maybe. I've had enough of this continent. I certainly don't envy you, staying here in Marseille—things are going to get a lot tougher, and not just with Vichy. The guy who's replacing me, Edwin Blount, is a humdinger. Can't stand refugees. Patently hates Jews."

"Wonderful. Got any advice?"

"Only that you hurry up. Get as many out as you can, before they toss you out of the country. Don't give it up for a second. Every day you're here, you're saving lives."

"Not every day," Varian said.

Bingham sighed, looking up from his packing box. "Still thinking about Zilberman? I haven't stopped looking, I want you to know."

"Any news?"

"None."

"I just can't bear the thought, Harry, that he was working for months in our greenhouse at Air Bel, with ships leaving every day, and I was so precious about the whole thing, about when he could leave, and under what circumstances—"

"And what were you supposed to do? If you'd sent him out too soon and he got caught, you'd be in the same fix. You acted on what you knew. You did the best you could."

"God, Harry, if I could just have him back," he said. He was on the verge of tears now; he didn't know if he was talking about Zilberman anymore, or if he meant Grant. If only he could confide in Bingham, if only they'd been something more than colleagues. He'd never given Bingham the least intimation of what existed between himself and Grant, nor that he, Varian, was anything other than the man he appeared to be; he could never take him into his confidence now. But Bingham was leaving tomorrow; he might never see him again. Not quite knowing what he meant to say, he found himself asking Harry Bingham if he could consult him on a personal matter, something that had been on his mind.

"Of course," Bingham said. "Anything."

"Let's say," Varian said, an intolerable heat rising to his face, "let's say you had an intimate—business relationship, with an old friend. Let's say you were deeply involved in each other's affairs, in a business that entailed a high degree of personal risk. Let's say someone else—someone you considered a trustworthy source—intimated to you that your partner had been silently cheating you for months, at no risk to himself but at great cost to you. How would you proceed? What would you do?"

Bingham pushed his box aside and sat down at the desk, his eyebrows drawing into a deep V. In the gentlest of tones, almost in a whisper, he asked, "Is this obliqueness really necessary? Can't you just say what the matter is?"

"No, Harry, I can't. I just want to know what you'd do."

Bingham tapped his fingers together, seeming to choose his words. "I suppose I'd bring it to my business partner," he said. "I'd say, Look, here's what I heard. What do you make of it? Is this guy pulling my leg? Or should I be worried you're not being honest with me?"

"But what if your business partner—what if he says, If you don't trust me, you can go to hell?"

Bingham tilted his head at Varian. "If you really don't trust him, if you really think he might be capable of doing you wrong, why are you in business with him in the first place?"

Varian sat still a long moment. "Right," he said, finally. "You're right, Harry." Then he got to his feet; it was time to go. "Look," he said. "I can't thank you enough."

"Nonsense," Bingham said. He came around the desk and took Varian by the shoulders, as if he meant to shake some sense into him. "My friend," he said, looking into Varian's eyes. "Soldier on, all right?"

"I will, Harry. And good luck in Lisbon."

Bingham nodded. And then they said their goodbyes, and Varian walked down the curving driveway of the consulate, feeling desolate, thinking his day could hardly get worse. But as he rode the tram back toward the center of town, a growing feeling of apprehension gathered in his gut, tightening his diaphragm. And as soon as he reached the boulevard Garibaldi office, Gussie met him at the door, his narrow face drawn in fear.

"Danny's been arrested," he said.

"What?"

Gussie glanced over his shoulder at Lucie Heymann, who was arguing fiercely with someone on the phone, and Jean Gemähling, who stood beside her, taking the receiver now and then to insert his own commentary. "Tell you in your office," he said.

They went into Varian's office, where Gussie closed the door and turned the fan to its highest setting to foil anyone who might be listening. Then he collapsed into a chair, his long narrow hands over his face, and began to sob outright.

"Gussie," Varian said. "Come now. Tell me what happened."

"We were supposed to meet Kourillo," Gussie said, half-choking. "Danny asked—he asked me to come along because the coins were so heavy, you know. I was carrying half in a bag, Danny the other half in the—in the box, the one you buried at Air Bel. He said we'd meet Kourillo in his hotel room. But when we get to the hotel, Kourillo's standing out front on the steps, you know, and—and looking all around like he's scared of something. He starts making this motion with his hand, **shoo, shoo.** Danny grabs the bag of coins from me and says run! So I ran, Monsieur Fry—like an idiot, like a coward! I went into an alley and hid. Danny went the other way, toward the Canebière, and—I didn't see what happened. But I guess they grabbed him. I heard shouting. And then I heard the sirens."

"Good God," Varian said, putting his hands through his hair. "Good God. We have to go down and get him right away. Where have they got him? The Evêché?"

"Not the Evêché. Chave Prison."

"**Chave Prison?** That stinking hole?"

"Madame Bénédite just called. She said she's found a lawyer for him. The lawyer's there now, at Chave."

"All right. He can get him out on bail, at least."

"But he thinks Danny could get five years."

"Five **years**?"

"And he says—oh, he says you aren't safe either, Monsieur Fry. He says you could be ejected from France at once. What shall we do? What can I do?"

"Where's Theo now, Gussie? At the prison too?"

"She called from there, but she's coming here now."

"Good. We'll soon find out all the facts. We'll take care of this, don't worry. No one's throwing anyone out just yet. And don't go thinking any of this is your fault."

"All right, sir," Gussie said, his eyes still wet. "I shouldn't have given him that bag of coins, though. I should have stood by him. Chave Prison is an evil place. I hate to imagine Monsieur Bénédite there all on his own."

"No more of that. Why don't you take the day off, go home to your hotel?"

"I want to work! I have to. It's the best thing I can do."

"All right," Varian said. "I don't suppose I can stop you."

And then Theo herself came through the door of his office, her face streaked with tears, a crumpled handkerchief in her hand. Her eyes met Varian's with a look so baleful he had to turn away.

"What are you going to do now?" she said. "My husband, my child's father, is in Chave Prison."

Varian swallowed, fortifying himself to look at her. "Does the lawyer really think he'll get five years?"

"He's to be charged on four counts," she said, taking her little notebook from her skirt pocket with a trembling hand, flipping through its lined pages. **"Possession illégale d'or,"** she read. **"Transportant l'or illégalement. Intention de permuter l'or illégalement.** And, finally, **intention présumée de le détourner à sa propre utilisation."**

"We'll make inquiries," Varian said. "I'll get on the phone to the embassy at once. And I want to speak to this lawyer. Where did he come from?"

"Mary Jayne. He's someone her family knows. Guillaume Navarre. His English is quite good. Apparently he read philosophy at Oxford before he got his French law degree."

"Mary Jayne! You've heard from her?"

"Yes. She's back in town."

"Well, where is she? Where has she been all this time?"

"That's beside the point, Varian."

"I want to speak to this lawyer, whoever he is. Where can he be found?"

"I asked him to come round after he finished at Chave. I was hoping we might have Danny out on parole, but Monsieur Navarre has already disabused me of that hope."

"Oh, Theo," Varian said.

"How is it," Theo said, her voice low and tightly controlled, "that you saw fit to ask my husband to carry **eighty thousand francs'** worth of gold coins?" He could see the effort it cost her to remain calm; he almost wished that she would rage at him outright. "He's taking all the blame for this. All. And he's doing it to protect **you.** He told the gendarmes the gold was a gift from Max Ernst, before he left—that he'd tried to give it to the committee, but that you'd refused, because you knew it was illegal to trade in gold. But he said that he, Danny, went to Ernst and said he'd take it himself, and give the money to the committee."

"Don't you think I'd gladly be there in his place?" Varian said. "I'll go down there at once and confess."

"You'll do no such thing," Theo said. "Danny made a decision on behalf of the Centre Américain. He believes you can't be spared. He chose to take this on himself. If you go down there and contradict him, you'll be throwing that sacrifice into his face. They'll arrest you, and if you get out, you'll be ejected from the country."

"Gussie says I might be thrown out anyway."

"Yes. That's what Navarre told us. And perhaps it wouldn't be too soon." Then she turned away and left him alone in the office, and there was nothing he could do but sit at the desk, his head in his hands, and wait for the lawyer to arrive.

———

Guillaume Navarre was a neat narrow-shouldered man, a Parisian who'd been forced south in the **pagaille;** he wore a Savile Row suit, a somber tie, and an expression of woeful forbearance. He sat down before Varian's desk, unloaded a leather-clad notebook from his briefcase, and spoke for more than an hour about the legal implications of what had occurred and what might be done, a series of scenarios that largely relied upon Varian's being able to convince the United States Consulate to come to Danny's aid. When Varian called the consulate to speak to Bingham, the doleful young secretary told him that he'd just gone for good. And when he called Harry's villa, no one answered. He called again and again until finally the valet answered, informing him, with some annoyance, that Madame and Monsieur could not be disturbed, and that he would be forced to disconnect the phone if Varian tried to call again.

"A man's life is at stake!" Varian shouted.

"I have explicit orders," the valet said.

"Well, contravene them, you idiot!"

He'd gone too far. The line went dead. "Goddamn it," Varian said. "I'll have to go there in person."

"There's no use doing that today," Navarre said. "Anyone of influence at the prison will have gone home by now."

"But Bingham's leaving tomorrow! And the guy who's replacing him will never help us, I promise you."

"Monsieur Bingham, as I understand it, has already been stripped of his position. There's nothing he'll be able to do for us in any case. You'll simply have to wait the weekend."

"But that means Danny's stuck in Chave Prison for **three days,** at the least!" He knew how swiftly imprisonment at Chave could turn into internment in a camp. The Sûreté Nationale knew what Varian's organization was, and what role Danny played; there would be no clemency for him. They'd hang the full weight of the law on him, there was no question. And when that happened, Danny would lose all hope of leaving France. He could never rejoin his boy in the States, could never follow his wife there when she went, as she would have to do, to be with their little son.

He couldn't stand it. He didn't know how he could stand what he already had to. He got up from his chair and went to the window, looking down into the pigeon-clotted street. "I want to go to him," he said. "I want to see him at once."

"They won't allow any more visitors today," Navarre said.

"Goddamn it! What are we supposed to do?"

"What we must so often do in cases like this. Wait and see, Monsieur Fry. Wait and see."

35

In the Garden

At the villa he found his own room empty; from the window he could see Grant at the foot of the garden in a metal lawn chair, a book open on his lap. **If you don't trust him,** Bingham had asked, **why are you in business with him in the first place?** Because I'm blindly and stupidly in love, he'd been unable to say. Because our lives are knit up irrevocably. But what was that? Sentimental nonsense from their college days? Drivel extrapolated from classical texts? If Grant had lied, Varian needed to know. He went downstairs and out through the kitchen door, letting it slam and jingle behind him. It must have been past six o'clock; the sun cast its rays at an aggressive slant, throwing the valley into violet shadow and setting the ridges aflame. Grant himself seemed to radiate light, his skin golden inside the crisp white envelope of his shirt. He was wearing the same canvas pants he'd worn when the two of them had taken their sail on the Vieux Port; they must have been two sizes too large now.

Varian went down into the garden, skirted the fountain, and pulled up a chair beside Grant's. He couldn't speak about what had happened that afternoon. If he introduced the subject of Harry Bingham, or of Danny, he would lose the nerve to say what he'd come to say.

"Fancy seeing you here," Grant said, laying his book down, sliding his bare foot alongside Varian's. It seemed an act of supplication, a plea to break down whatever it was that stood between them. "You ought to take your shoes off. The grass is nice and cool."

"You ought to put yours on. You'll catch a chill."

"I'm enjoying myself. It's been too long. Join me, won't you?"

"Look, Grant," Varian said. "I have to ask you a question."

Grant seemed to catch his tone. As he turned to Varian, a change came over his features: apprehension, sharpened attention. "What is it, Tommie?"

"The night before Zilberman was deported. When I spoke to him at the Evêché—he told me something I've been thinking about all this time. I want to ask you about it. I hope you'll hear me out."

Grant's eyebrows came together, and he tilted his beloved and familiar face at Varian, his orbital bones sharpened by illness, his eyes etched at their corners with fine rays, his mouth superseded by its deep soft philtrum.

"What is it? Tell me."

"We talked about the **Sinaïa,**" Varian said. "Zilberman must have been speaking with some bitterness, which I can understand. But what he said was this. He said he'd never understood about Tobias Katznelson."

"Understood what?"

"Why we were making so much fuss over an ordinary kid."

Grant frowned. "Tobias is anything but ordinary. Zilberman knew that. He knew him in Berlin."

"Yes, that's just it," Varian said slowly. "He knew him. He said he was quite ordinary. Not a genius at all. There **was** a genius, but it wasn't Tobias. It was his friend, a boy called Abel Heligman, a kind of mathematical and scientific wizard, impossibly precocious, a disciple of Planck's."

Grant's eyebrows tightened. "He must have gotten it wrong. The genius was Tobias. You and I both know that."

"Not according to Zilberman."

"What are you saying, exactly?"

"I don't know, Grant," Varian said. "What am I saying?"

Grant turned to him, his eyes narrowing. "Are you suggesting, can you possibly be suggesting, that I **lied** to you? That I lied about Tobias? That I knowingly counseled you to put some idiot on the **Sinaïa** in Zilberman's place?"

"Not some idiot," Varian said. "Your lover's son."

Grant got to his feet, hands on hips; his book had fallen to the grass. "Are you really telling me, Tommie, that you think I've been pulling the wool over your eyes all this time? That I recruited your help to find this boy, and went out to Vernet while you were a prisoner on the **Sinaïa,** and let Mary Jayne do what she did, all the while thinking to myself, 'They'll never know he's just an ordinary fool, ha ha ha!'" He shook his head in disgust. He stood for some moments in silence, then raised his eyes to Varian's.

"I always thought your project was wrongheaded," he said. "All that money, all that time, mustered on behalf of people who happened to know how to use a paintbrush or put a sentence together—and don't mistake me, I know the value of art, I like to read and look at paintings as much as the next guy, more than most guys, if you'll believe that—but this is a goddamn war, a **war,** and they're all human beings, and how can you presume to pick which ones to save and which to throw into the fire? I always thought—and I never said it, because you were supposedly saving lives—that it was just another binary, another kind of black and white. He's one thing, she's another, so he can be sold as property and she can buy him. How different is it from that, really?"

"Oh, for God's sake, Grant, that is not at **all**—"

"Is it not, Varian? Is it not? But **anyway,** despite the fact that I couldn't fully countenance what it was you were doing, I saw how, in the case of someone like my lover's son, someone whose life might truly be of value in saving thousands of others, a little extra effort might be justified. A little extra money diverted from somewhere else. And now you're going to tell me I was lying? Why? To prove a point? To show you how misguided you were?" He laughed. "Why, wouldn't that be rich! That's just what I ought to have done. And then written about it for the **Times.**"

"Why should I distrust Zilberman?"

"Why should you? Are you really asking me that? Because you'd just put the boy onto the **Sinaïa** in his place, and now Zilberman was going to be deported to Germany!"

But the doubts Zilberman had raised in his mind, the doubts he himself had felt from the outset, couldn't be quieted. "Why should I believe you," he said, "when you had plenty of reason to lie to me? To use my resources for your lover's benefit? To collude with him against me? You said yourself that you sought me out—that it wasn't mere coincidence. Why did you do that, Grant?"

Grant bent over now and put his hands on his

knees. When he straightened up again, his eyes had taken on a depth of misery Varian had never seen there.

"Can you really ask that, Tom?" he said, and shook his head. "Can you really?"

"I only know what Zilberman said. And I know that sometimes it's expedient to lie. I **know.** I did it too, and not just to Eileen. That laborer who died in the car crash—I killed him, Grant. I did it, even if it wasn't my car that hit him. Then I lived as if I hadn't."

"Oh, for God's sake!" Grant cried, throwing his hands groundward in a gesture of utter disgust. "This is not about Katznelson at all! And it's not about that man who died in Concord. This is about **you,** about your own damn cowardice. You still can't leave Eileen, can you? You know you can't. And so you've got to do this thing, commit this absurdity."

"I'm trying to understand what you did, Grant. How you could have done it."

"You're **running,**" Grant said. "That's what you're doing. You are on the run. You're running for your life. You can't bear the thought of leaving your wife and your future children, for a man! But you're a **homosexual,** do you hear me? An invert! A fairy. A fag. All those things they call it—that's what you are. Get it through your head. **You love men.** You love **me.** For God's sake, quit being such an idiot for just a minute!"

"You've changed the subject," Varian said. "You've diverted. You've turned us away from the fundamental question. The issue is not whether or not I prefer men. The issue is not whether I'm ready to leave my wife. The issue is whether or not I can trust you. It's whether or not you lied to me."

"**Lev Zilberman** lied. I'm sorry, Varian. Your brilliant painter wasn't just brilliant in the artistic sense. He knew just how to get to you. Just where to grab you to make you pay for what you did to him. What an insecure fool you are!"

"You might well call me a fool, Grant. But I don't believe it's Zilberman who duped me. What did he stand to gain? You, on the other hand—you and Gregor—"

"I won't stand for this. I won't." He put his hands on his hips and stalked through the garden, shaking his head. "What do I have to do? Apparently I'm guilty until proven innocent." As he paced, Varian tried desperately, desperately, to read him: tried to determine from the angle of his eyebrows, from the tone of his familiar and beloved voice, from the way he held his shoulders as he waded through the long grass, whether he was lying or not. How was it possible to know someone so well and still not know? And how much truth was there in what Grant had said about him and Eileen?

"Enough," Grant said finally, coming to rest again before Varian. He fixed his eyes on Varian's, his pupils fathomless in the gathering dark. "This is your problem, not mine. If you want to be finished with me, say so. You're the one who's got to decide. Though you're behaving like a rabid idiot, my feelings for you are unchanged. Believe me, I understand. What you and I are proposing to do is not ordinarily done. As far as you're concerned, we may as well be proposing to walk on the moon. But you've got to find your way there if we're going to do it."

He picked up his metal garden chair and began to carry it up to the patio. At the base of the steps, he turned.

"I'm going into town tonight," he said. "I'm going to put up at the Beauvau. The return of Dr. Grant. Meanwhile, you take your time to think. I'm going to do some thinking myself."

Varian tried to respond, but his mouth had gone dry. He watched Grant go up into the house, he saw the light go on in their room. A few minutes later, as he stood frozen in the darkening garden, Grant came out again holding a suitcase, and walked down the driveway toward the train.

It took only moments, once Grant had disappeared from view, for a terrible fear to form in Varian's mind: that Grant, making the journey into town in the evening air, alone, carrying a suitcase, walking at that furious pace, would fall ill again and die, and that it would be Varian's fault. The fear was strong enough to send him running to the station. But Grant, even in his weakened state, was too fast for him; the train departed just as Varian arrived, and the next wouldn't come for an hour. He bought a ticket anyway and waited, rode into town in a state of gut-burning anxiety, ran all the way to the Vieux Port. But by the time he reached the Beauvau, Grant had checked in and had given orders to the clerk that he not be disturbed.

Rather than go home to their shared bed, Varian spent the night at the office again, huddled on a narrow settee that smelled of naphthalene and singed horsehair. In the morning he washed his face in the bathroom sink, brushed his teeth with the toothbrush he kept in his desk drawer, and stole a carnation from the arrangement on Lucie Heymann's desk; regarding himself in the bathroom mirror, he saw the face of a desperate and haggard lover, shadow-eyed and narrow-lipped. He ran to the Beauvau through a deluge of slanting sun, telling himself that Grant would have to see him this morning, that his willingness to see Varian would indicate his innocence; but at the hotel he found the orders unchanged. The smooth-skinned young clerk—the one with the figure-eight-shaped birthmark high on his cheek—wouldn't let him place a call to Grant's room, nor would he reveal his room number.

"Please," Varian said, hating to beg, hating the

note of panic in his own voice. He hated to see his reflection in all those mirrors, before and behind him and on both sides; what he saw was a drowning man, a man who didn't know whether the life-saving air lay above or below. "Please," he said again. "Mr. Grant is my doctor. It's a medical emergency."

The boy assessed him with a practiced eye. "You do not appear ill, Monsieur Fry."

"I'm ill!" Varian said, desperately. "Please, just give me the room number. I'll make it worth your while." He drew his wallet from his pocket and extracted all the money he had, some two thousand francs. "I can get more," he said. "Give me the room number, and I'll make it five thousand."

At that moment, the manager, tall and mustachioed, emerged from a mirrored door behind the desk; the boy threw him a glance, and the manager approached the counter and raised an eyebrow at the proffered francs. He recognized Varian, of course; he was the sort of manager who made it his business to know his guests.

"Is there a problem, Monsieur Fry?" he asked. "Some trouble about your time with us?"

The money trembled in Varian's hand. "I must see a guest of yours. Monsieur Grant. It's a matter of life and death."

"The esteemed Dr. Grant gave express orders that he not be disturbed. He particularly mentioned that you, Monsieur Fry, are not to be admitted. We must respect our guests' wishes above all." He placed a hand on the black telephone on the counter, silently implying that if Varian persisted, he would have to call the police.

Varian put the money away and turned from the desk, turned from the merciless mirrors toward other merciless mirrors; he fled that infinity of self-reflection in a fog, half-staggering down to the edge of the water, where he stood staring out at the toylike boats on the serrated port. So Grant really would not see him for some time, an indeterminate period. He had given express orders, had insisted on keeping Varian away. The insult Varian had delivered was severe enough to have had that effect. Either that, or Grant was hiding in shame at Varian's having discovered the truth.

He walked the blinding streets to the office, thinking only that if he remained here in town, he would at least be within walking distance of the Beauvau. In the entryway of the building he found Danny's lawyer, Navarre, waiting outside the door with a box of pastries and a metal thermos; his expression was as grim as it had been the day before, but Varian's gratitude at the sight of him was so deep that he nearly burst into tears. A long moment passed before he could shake Navarre's hand and let him into the office.

"You look like you've spent the night awake, Monsieur Fry," Navarre said. His voice, surprisingly low for his small frame, held a note of paternal admonition.

"I'm sure Danny's night was worse than mine," Varian said, ushering Navarre into the office. "I have to say, Monsieur Navarre, I'm surprised to see you here. I thought there was nothing we could do until Monday."

Navarre set the box of pastries on the desk and opened it, revealing four dull gold scones. "Do you have a cup?" he said. "The coffee is not coffee, regrettably, but it is hot."

Varian produced the office coffee service, and Navarre poured off two steaming cups. "I've received some news since yesterday," he said, setting a cup on Varian's desk. "I've got a source at the Evêché, one who has proven to be a valuable wellspring of information. It is surprising to learn, Monsieur Fry, who can be bribed, and at what rate."

"Oh, yes," Varian said. "I've got quite a list going myself."

"My source tells me that our friend Kourillo has been in league with the police for some time. This will not, I suppose, come as a shock. The terms of their deal were simple: The police wanted Kourillo to catch you, or anyone at the Centre Américain, breaking the law. Of course they promised him a rich reward if he managed it. He told them about the plan to exchange Monsieur Konstantinov's gold, and they encouraged him to proceed—if he could implicate one of you, they would give him half the value of the coins as a **petit cadeau.** And they are not disappointed by the result. They consider that they have trapped you both—you and Monsieur Bénédite."

"But that's false," Varian said. "Danny told them I had nothing to do with it. I was nowhere near Kourillo's hotel at the time. They can't prove I was involved."

"You've been in contact with Kourillo for some time about this exchange. His story is likely to carry more weight in court than my client's."

"Then why haven't they come to arrest me already?"

Navarre raised an eyebrow. "They believe you to be under the protection of the U.S. Consulate. Perhaps they have not yet grasped the implications of Monsieur Bingham's departure. Or perhaps they believe the new vice-consul will support you."

"They're deluded there, I'm afraid."

"Miss Gold, to whom I spoke last night, said just the same."

"Miss Gold! I don't suppose you can tell me where she's hiding out, can you? I'd like to find that boyfriend of hers and garrote him."

"Miss Gold insists I do my utmost for you and Monsieur Bénédite. She is, I should mention, paying my fee. She desired particularly for me to tell you that."

Varian sighed. "Well, tell her thanks, when you see her. And tell me what you think all this means—what it means for Danny, and for me. If Kourillo's going to testify against him, or against both of us, and if he's in the pocket of the Evêché, I'm afraid it all looks rather grim."

Navarre raised an eyebrow. "Will you give up so easily, Monsieur Fry?"

"Do you see a way out? Because I'm afraid I don't."

"If the consulate will indeed back the Centre Américain—if they will come to the aid of Monsieur Bénédite—perhaps the word of a person like Kourillo will not carry much weight in court. He is not, Monsieur Fry, the most shining of citizens. He is not, in fact, a French citizen, strictly speaking—his papers have always been a matter of contention. He is known to have had illegal financial dealings in the past. If we can add your consulate's aid to my efforts, our case is far from futile."

"You really think so?"

"**Mais oui,** I am here to tell you so."

"We've got to get Danny out of jail and cleared of charges. He's got a little boy in the States. And he can't be separated from his wife. I think it would kill them both."

"I do think we can avoid it, Monsieur Fry."

"But without Bingham's help, I'm afraid I don't see how. The guy who's replacing him—"

"Ah, yes. Monsieur Blount. I know him well, I'm afraid. Indeed, he is far from likely to aid us of his own volition, without some inducement. But I believe you may have something that could be of value to him—something you might trade."

Varian crossed his hands over his chest and leaned

back in his chair. Outside, a clatter of pigeon wings rose and fell; a brief swift shadow passed the window. "Surely you don't mean money," he said. "I can't produce a sum that could mean anything to Blount. Not even with Mary Jayne's aid, if she were willing to give it."

"Not money. Something that would be of value to Blount's career."

Varian squinted at Navarre. "I'm afraid I'm rather obtuse this morning."

"You must know, Monsieur Fry, that you are considered a source of some embarrassment—a **bête noire,** if you will—by the diplomatic community. Their projection of your potential effect here in Marseille fell laughably short. None of them believed you could do so much as locate the artists on your list, much less that you would extract so many of them from France. I suppose they also underestimated Monsieur Bingham. Underestimated, that is, the degree to which he would support your mission at the expense of his own diplomatic career. But your political capital has grown enormously in recent months. Perhaps you do not realize the extent of it."

"I know they want me out of France. So what?"

"**Want** is perhaps too gentle a word. You have become, as it were, a kind of diplomatic imperative."

"So you're saying, Monsieur Navarre—what, exactly? That **I'm** the thing of value? You're proposing a trade? You want me to take Danny's place?"

"Not take his place. Not a trade. Merely a deal."

"What sort of deal?"

"Propose to Blount that if he steps in to protect Danny, you will leave France."

"Ah, I see. And even if I were to assent to such a thing—if I were willing to propose leaving my organization rudderless and leaderless—what makes you think he'd believe me?"

"He will **want** to believe you, Monsieur Fry. He needs to. **Ecoutez-moi,** I have followed Monsieur Blount's career for some time. In his former position as sub-vice-consul in Paris, he was responsible for the elimination of U.S. aid to the Société Spéciale pour la Protection des Réfugiés, an organization of particular interest to me. I was the **société**'s private counsel for twenty years, you see—since before the Great War—and a member of its governing board for ten. Apparently Monsieur Blount secured his position in Paris largely through personal favors. But his superiors had come to suspect that he was unequal to the demands of the job. They wanted him out of Paris, and after the occupation they wanted him out of Vichy—that is why he was sent to Marseille, under the guise of a promotion. He is a desperate person, Monsieur Fry—he knows his career hangs by a thread. But if you were to allow him the **gloire** of getting you thrown from France—if he were to be the one responsible—his immediate future would be secured."

"And so I'm simply to leave? Give it all up? Danny would never agree to it."

"**Mais non!** You mistake me. Make your promises to Monsieur Blount. Make it clear that you will leave the country as soon as Monsieur Bénédite's freedom is secured. Then you may break your promise, if you wish. Do whatever you can to stay. That is what Monsieur Bénédite wants, too. You will not have your consulate's protection, but, to be certain, without Bingham you would not have had it anyway." Navarre sat back and sipped from his cup, regarding Varian from beneath the dark ridge of his eyebrows.

Varian reached for the phone. "How soon, do you think, is Blount to arrive in Marseille?"

"In wartime, a consular desk cannot go unmanned," Navarre said. "I suspect Blount arrived in town even before Monsieur Bingham was relieved of his post. But, Monsieur Fry—this business must not be conducted by phone. You must meet the new vice-consul in person. Lower your eyes before him. Humble yourself. Summon the muse. Chave Prison is a terrible place, but it is a veritable palace compared to where they would next send Monsieur Bénédite."

"Yes," Varian said, replacing the receiver in its cradle. "Yes, you're right, of course."

"The Gold family trusts my opinion. I hope you will trust it too."

"Yes. Well, I suspect I'm going to have to thank Mary Jayne for all of this."

"Miss Gold's generosity extends, at times, farther than it should. I share your dislike for her young protégé. But her confidence seems well placed in you, Monsieur Fry. She tells me she feels a sort of kinship with you. I have known her since she was a child, and I know this is not a grace she extends widely."

"Well, thank you for that, Navarre. Tell her—if you will, if you see her—tell her she doesn't have to hide from me. Tell her I'd prefer to see her, whatever's happened with Killer."

"I shall do so, Monsieur Fry. And now I implore you to make your visit to the consulate at once."

Edwin Blount, pale and tall and slope-shouldered, sat behind Harry Bingham's newly vacated desk with an air of pachydermlike rectitude. The slow swing of his massive head, his torpid blink, the heavy drape of his arms across the desk, all seemed to suggest that he belonged where he was, had always belonged there, and would remain there as long as he chose. When he spoke at last, he spoke in a low lentissimo that made Varian's heart palpitate with impatience.

"And why," said Blount, "why, precisely—why, Mr. Fry—should I come to the aid of your associate

Mr. Bénédite? Danny, as you call him? He is not, as I understand, an American citizen."

"He's employed by an American organization. He's been working under my guidance for some eight months now. He was arrested in the course of that work. We owe him our protection, Mr. Blount."

"Bénédite broke the law. And I'm certain he's not the first in your organization to do so. Mr. Fullerton has apprised me of your actions here in France. You've been a thorn in the consulate's side for months now. A thorn."

"You're right," Varian said. "I'm the one who ought to take the blame. Danny didn't mastermind that exchange. He's been on the right side of the law all along, and is as morally upright as can be imagined. He's got a wife who adores him and a son who depends on him. The boy's already in America, under the care of an aunt. Danny can't afford to have anything stand in the way of his own emigration." He had a sense that the image of Danny as family man might appeal to Blount's sensibilities, but Blount showed no sign of being moved. "I ought to be the one in jail, Mr. Blount. But it turned out otherwise. Danny's in Chave Prison, a truly horrible place. If you intercede on his behalf, his lawyer believes you can get him out—at least on bail, while he awaits trial. And then maybe he can get off with a fine."

"Again, Mr. Fry, I ask you: Why should this Frenchman's fate be any concern of mine?"

"Because, in short, Danny's rendered an invaluable

service to the United States. His work for the Centre Américain has enriched our cultural capital immeasurably. The clients under his protection—the most politically neutral of refugees, I might add, the least controversial of applicants for our aid—possess, collectively speaking, an artistic worth that defies quantification. And he's saved those men and women at our behest, in our employ—the employ of an American organization, one that is protected under U.S. and French law by the American Consulate."

Blount hoisted a single eyebrow, unimpressed.

"If you help him," Varian said, "I swear to God I will leave France without protest, at the soonest possible opportunity, and will shut down my operation here. I'm beat, Mr. Blount. I know the score. The Gestapo is wise to me, and Vichy is subject to their demands. If I stay, I'll be sure to end up in a French concentration camp."

Blount blinked with prehistoric slowness. "Your departure. That would certainly be something, Mr. Fry. Something significant. To have you out of the consulate's bonnet, to have your organization out of Vichy's—that would indeed, as I say, be significant. In fact, I'll have you know, Fullerton promised me a kind of—well, a rather extravagant bonus, I suppose you could say—if I induced you to vacate the country." Another torpid blink. "I don't believe he thought I could do it. I would be gratified, deeply gratified, to prove him wrong."

"If you help Danny," Varian said, "I promise you, I'll be gone in two weeks' time. I swear to you as a former Eagle Scout. And I'll offer any other security you might require." He almost believed it himself; how long could he bear to stay in France, however noble his mission, if what existed between himself and Grant had been nullified, crushed to nothing? How could he bear to stay even another day?

"Eagle Scout, were you?" Blount said, a dull light entering his eyes.

"Oh, yes. Earned my gold and silver Palms by the age of seventeen." Of course, it was Grant who had been the Eagle Scout, Grant who had taken out the bright gold and silver honor badges one night at Gore Hall; with some ceremony he'd pinned them to Varian's undershorts, in recognition of services Varian had just performed.

"Well. Well. An Eagle Scout must help an Eagle Scout," Blount said. And, with infinite slowness, he extended his drooping and bespeckled hand across Harry Bingham's desk.

A period of terrible waiting ensued. For the next forty-eight hours, Varian's only comfort was to deliver food and blankets to Chave Prison on Danny's behalf, and to write a series of notes to Grant in which he pleaded, with increasing desperation, for half an hour's conference, ten minutes', a moment's.

But no response came from the Beauvau, and the prison guards at Chave, though they accepted Varian's offerings of paper-wrapped sandwiches and woolen blankets, were likely taking them all for themselves. Theo, camped on the office floor, found little solace in Varian's description of the deal he'd made with Blount; she seemed to doubt that anyone could place so much value upon Varian's doings.

But at half past ten on Tuesday morning, the office door opened and Navarre entered, followed by the paroled prisoner himself, in a rumpled and begrimed version of his usual tweed. Danny was unshaven, the hollows beneath his eyes yellow-violet, his jaw darkened with bruises. Theo ran into his arms, her shoulders sharp beneath the thin white cotton of her shirt; they stood for a long moment while everyone else—Jean Gemähling, Lucie Heymann, and young Gussie Rosenberg, stricken—watched in silence. When Theo stepped away at last, Varian went to Danny and took him by the arm. The smell of Chave—ripe piss, ancient cabbage, dead and rotting rat—was on Danny's skin, in his hair, in the fibers of his suit; Varian inhaled that scent like a penance.

"Forgive me?" he said, hoarsely.

"There's nothing to forgive," Danny said.

"I left you to do that job alone."

"I insisted on doing it, if you'll recall."

"But three days in that stinking hole! And look at you, look what they did to you."

Danny touched the bruises at his jaw. "I haven't looked in a mirror, but I imagine it's not pretty. I can't imagine how you got me out. Navarre refuses to say."

"I'll explain it over a drink, once you've had a chance to eat and sleep. The others will want to say hello now." And Jean and Gussie and Lucie came forward to shake Danny's hand and congratulate him on his parole, while Theo went to her desk and made arrangements for Danny to be examined by a doctor, then transported home to Air Bel in Vinciléoni's car. Navarre, who had watched all these proceedings in silence, drew Varian aside into the private office and closed the door.

"Well," Varian said, seating himself at the desk. "You were right. Old Blount was a sucker for that trade."

"Vichy will hear of it. They will undoubtedly tighten the screws on you now."

"Let them do it. I've got resources. At worst I can hide out. Plenty of my clients have done it, sometimes for months."

"Your resources may prove insufficient. I hope you have an exit strategy."

"Please understand, Monsieur Navarre, I don't intend to be forced to leave."

"Vichy may seem rather clumsy at its work, but it can be a dreadful adversary. And if you're arrested, or thrown into a camp, you'll not be able to direct your organization. What will happen in that case?"

Varian sat in silence for a moment. "I don't know," he said.

"I advise you to make arrangements, Monsieur Fry. With the consulate's help, I believe I can get my client cleared of charges, or at least not sentenced to prison time. He is, I understand, your second in command. But, if I can clear him, he and Madame Bénédite must leave France at once to rejoin their son. They must not delay. The danger will not be eliminated by the closure of Monsieur Bénédite's case."

"Yes, that's right."

"If you are indeed forced to leave France, someone must continue your work. This organization has a necessary role. Its fate cannot be bound only to yours."

"Of course not," he said. "My colleague Jean Gemähling will take over for me if I have to go. But Danny and I must have time to train him, both of us. That's why it's all the more important that you get Danny cleared of those charges." And of course he himself couldn't leave France just now, not with Grant still refusing to see him; not with his inner life in such dread uncertainty.

"Indeed, Monsieur Bénédite must be cleared," Navarre said. "I believe he will be. And now, Monsieur Fry, I will leave you to your duties. Godspeed your mission."

36

Lumine Tuo

Danny insisted on going to work with Varian and Jean the next morning, and would brook no coddling; he didn't flinch for a moment when they passed Chave Prison on the way to the boulevard Garibaldi, only thumbed his nose at it and uttered a schoolboy's curse. At the office, he and Varian had just begun to review the day's roster of clients when Gussie arrived in a state of speechless agitation, holding the morning newspaper. He peeled off the first section and thrust it into Varian's hands.

Varian scanned the headlines. "The Brits intercepted the **Winnipeg,**" he said. "They got her at sea before she made it to Martinique. I guess they want her for their own fleet. She's in Trinidad now, according to this."

"The **Winnipeg**!" Jean said. "With nearly eighty of our clients on board. And Breitscheid's wife."

"They've all been interned in Martinique, apparently. Put into a temporary camp. I suppose the Brits want to interrogate them all. They must have had some intelligence—must believe there are Gestapo agents on board." He thought that would be the worst of it, but then he read further. "Vichy's shut down the Martinique route altogether," he said, quietly. "They don't want to lose any more boats. The **Wyoming,** the **Mont Viso,** the **Sinaïa**—they're all sitting in Casablanca now."

"God!" Jean said. "We must have had a hundred and eighty on those boats together. Maybe two hundred."

"Two hundred and twenty-three, to be exact," Danny said; he'd retrieved a set of manila folders, and was scanning a list of names. "They'll all have been thrown into concentration camps by now. And there they'll stay, until Vichy sees fit to let those ships sail again."

Varian got to his feet and went to the window. In the street below, a line of refugees had already begun to gather, streaming toward the Centre Américain in panicked groups, their voices rising, all of them surely wanting to know what would become of their own escape plans, many of which relied on carefully aligned sailings that would no longer take place, and on visas that would soon expire.

Danny put a hand on Varian's sleeve. "You'd better go down."

"And say what?"

"Tell them the truth. Tell them we're trying to learn more. And give them some hope, Varian. We've had other setbacks."

"Not on this scale."

"This is the Centre Américain de Secours. What is more American than wild hope?"

He stood for a moment in silence; Danny's hand on his forearm, solid and insistent, infused him with courage. "All right," he said finally. "Here we go." He went down the stairs, opened the front doors, and shouted a greeting. At the sound of his voice, the refugees—men and women, boys and girls, their faces tight with desperation—turned toward him, their words of protest and debate falling away into expectant quiet. At his beckoning, they moved into a crowd around the door. Once they were close enough to hear him, he announced that the Centre Américain de Secours would see them one by one; that they would make new arrangements as necessary; that no one was to panic. They were to form a line, one that made its way along the length of the block and around the corner. As if he'd uttered an incantation, they followed his directions at once; they did it in near-silence, even the children. The refugee at the head of the line—a young woman whose lambent dark brown eyes and oval face seemed vaguely familiar to Varian, as if he'd seen her in a dream, or in some ancient photograph—allowed herself to be ushered into the entryway. Silently she followed Varian up the stairs.

"Your language?" he asked as they climbed.

"German."

"Name?"

"Johanna Arendt. My friends know me as Hannah."

He paused on the landing and looked at her. "You're Hannah Arendt? The scholar whose dissertation sent Walter Benjamin into raptures?"

The young woman lowered her eyes. "Walter mentioned me to you?"

"My friend Miriam Davenport mentioned you and your husband some months ago. She told me about Benjamin's assessment of your work. But we've not known until this moment where you could be found. You're the first piece of good luck we've had today."

Hannah Arendt gave a short, ironic laugh. "Me, good luck! I feel accursed! To think that you were looking for us, Herr Fry, while here we were in Marseille, shuffling from one miserable hotel room to another. I believe it's made my husband ill. He's in bed with the grippe this morning. I've heard you can help your clients find doctors, ones who don't consider us—refugees, I mean—to be untouchable."

"Come up, Miss Arendt. Let me introduce you to our secretary. She'll take all your information. Yes, we can find you a doctor, and we'll talk about visas for you and your husband. We don't have the influence we used to in that department, but we'll do our best. Miriam was rather stern with me about your case. She made me promise to pull out all the stops for you."

Hannah Arendt's eyes rested evenly on Varian's. "Pull out all the stops?" she repeated, and for a moment he had to wonder if the idiom was different in German. But then she tilted her head quizzically and said, "Don't you pull them out for everyone, Herr Fry?" She seemed to be asking out of open curiosity, a desire to assess who he was. And he felt himself unable to speak anything but the truth to this frank, sharp-eyed woman, her luminous face like a waxing moon.

"Perhaps we didn't always, in the past," he said. "But we've learned the cost of that approach."

Another woman might have lowered her eyes; Hannah Arendt did not. "You've done your best, I'm sure," she said.

"Let us try to do our best for you," he said. He opened the door and ushered her into the office, led her to Lucie's desk, offered her a chair. When she saw the newspapers lying on the desktop, she touched the topmost of them and drew a long breath.

"They've tightened the screws," she said. "And they'll keep doing it until we're dead, all of us."

"Yes, the Martinique line has been cut for now. We've just read about it."

"Not that. This, about the new legislation. Here."

Varian took the paper from her, glancing at the piece she indicated. **Regulatory Statutes Passed** was the neutral headline. But a few lines' reading revealed the nature of the statutes: all Jewish businesses now had to be registered with the authorities; anyone who had at least three Jewish grandparents counted as a Jew; and no Jew could be employed now in any profession or trade, from **banquier** and **professeur** all the way down through **exploiteur des forêts, correspondant local de journaux,** and **concessionnaire des jeux.**

Danny came to Varian's side and stood at his shoulder, reading. After a moment he looked up and gave a sigh.

"We can't keep them waiting in the street," he said. "We'd better open the doors."

"Open them," Varian said. "Tell everyone to come up, as many as will fit."

Within moments, a grim crowd had filed into the room; the air vibrated with French and German, Polish and Russian. Refugees occupied every chair, every inch of floor; children crowded the windowsills. In the hall stood an unbroken line of clients and would-be clients, one that extended all the way down the curving stair. **They** would never allow him to be taken from this place, Varian thought; they were a vital wall, a living fortress.

———

All day, and all through the week that followed, he worked ceaselessly, opening new files, rewriting old plans, reassuring the refugees who'd been scheduled to leave along the Martinique route that transatlantic shipping couldn't remain shut down forever. He wished to God that Miriam were there, wished Mary Jayne would come out from wherever she was hiding; he needed them both, needed them just as much as he had at the beginning. He needed Bingham, too, desperately. And he needed Grant, needed him here in this office, needed him when it was time to retreat for a moment from the crush and press of his clients' demands, needed him on the tram ride home to Air Bel. He found himself unable to think, much less to sleep, in the room he'd shared with Grant. Instead he retreated to Breton and Jacqueline's old quarters, where he lay awake all night staring at the mobiles Aube had made from twigs and beetle carapaces and shells. The harpsichord sat silent downstairs. Theo and Danny kept their own counsel, worrying late into the night over their little son; Jean Gemähling, mourning the recent departure of Consuelo de Saint-Exupéry, lay in his own room, pining. Every night, beset on all sides by silence, Varian imagined that he might hear Grant's step in the driveway, imagined that he might hear the kitchen door opening and Grant's tread on the stairs. But each day he awoke alone, no closer to clarity or insight; and when he wrote to Grant, no answer came.

———

One morning, after he'd sent the usual plea to the Beauvau by messenger, Lucie Heymann appeared at his office door to announce a call from Edwin Blount. **My new boyfriend,** he might have said to Grant, had Grant been there. He nodded his thanks to Lucie and picked up the phone. On the line he could hear the usual series of clicks, and Blount's low, slow breathing; he fancied he could hear the faint crash of waves in the distance, at the bottom of the cliff that overlooked the sea.

"Anyone there?" Blount said. "Hello?"

"Yes, I'm here," Varian said.

"Ah, good. Well, Fry. Your colleague, Mr. Bénédite, is free, as I understand."

"Yes. He'll still need to stand trial, but his lawyer believes he'll come out on top. And we've got you to thank for it, Mr. Blount. You've rendered a heroic service to the cause of freedom."

Blount made a noise of demurral. He had not, Varian imagined, often been called heroic. "Well," he said, finally. "An Eagle Scout always helps his brother scout."

"That's right. And I suppose you're calling now to see if I'm holding up my end of the bargain."

"I'm calling to tell you, Mr. Fry, that we've just received a wire about you from Vichy."

"Oh, yes, I'm sure there'll be many."

"I consider it my duty to inform you of Vichy's intent."

"And what might that be?"

Blount cleared his throat. "Well—here's how it stands. You're to be arrested without delay. The Gestapo has been pressuring Vichy to that end."

"The Gestapo! Haven't they got anything better to do?"

"If I were you, I wouldn't consider this a laughing matter."

"Pardon me, Mr. Blount, but I don't see the point of being dour when there's nothing at all I can do about it. I don't suppose you're going to rush to my aid, are you?"

"According to our agreement, yours and mine—"

"I'm to give myself over willingly, am I?"

"Now, I didn't say—"

"I did mention that I didn't care to go to a concentration camp, didn't I? Isn't it still your job to help me stay out of one?"

"I'm doing you the courtesy, Mr. Fry, of informing you of Vichy's intent. I didn't have to do it. But as an Eagle Scout—"

"Listen," Varian said, biting the end of his pencil in contemplation. "We did have an agreement. I can see, under the circumstances, why you'd make no attempt to dissuade Vichy. But would you consider me in the wrong—un-scoutly, if you will—if I asked if that's really the best you can do?"

"You're the one who broke the law, Fry. Vichy knows it, and we know it."

"No one can prove that."

"We're not the sovereign power here. We can't keep

Vichy from arresting you, if that's what they mean to do. I wanted to inform you, that's all—merely inform you. No one likes a surprise." A moment of oceanic throat-clearing, followed by the sound of a cigarette lighter scraping repeatedly; Blount's muttered curse informed Varian that he had either run out of fluid or blunted his flint.

"If you don't mind my asking, Mr. Blount, what's the point of telling me they're coming for me? What's the point, if you don't mean to do anything about it?"

"I have nothing more to say on the subject," the vice-consul said. "I just felt you ought to know. Give you time to put your affairs in order, et cetera."

"Well, that's splendid, Edwin. Splendid. I consider myself lucky to have been informed."

"Yes, well. Glad to be of service."

"I suppose you'll get your bonus from Fullerton whether I'm sent to prison or not, as long as I vacate my job and close down the Centre."

"I can't comment further," Blount said.

"I see," Varian said. "Well, Edwin, thanks ever so much." He replaced the receiver in its cradle and sat for a long moment looking out the window, at the white sun falling against the hot stones of the building opposite. Vichy could move quickly when it wanted to; it could move like a hawk on the hunt. He contemplated trying to catch a train to somewhere in the countryside that moment, contemplated going into hiding at some out-of-the-way hotel on the coast. He could run home to Air Bel, pack a few things, and be gone. But the thought of leaving Marseille while Grant was still there seemed impossible, insupportable. That was what he was thinking when, a few minutes later, Lucie came to the door with a note summoning him to an audience with Maurice Anne Marie de Rodellec du Porzic, Chief of the Préfecture of the Bouches du Rhône. He was, she said, to appear at du Porzic's offices unaccompanied at eleven o'clock that morning; failure to comply would result in his immediate arrest.

He couldn't delay any longer. He had to speak to Grant. He had to speak to him now, this morning, before his meeting with du Porzic, or he would lose his mind. He got up from his desk and straightened his tie. Without a word to Danny or Theo or Jean, he made his way through the crowd of clients, down the stairs, and out onto the street. As he walked the familiar path to the Hôtel Beauvau, a thrum of panic beat in his temples. What if, when he arrived, the beleaguered clerk informed him that Dr. Grant had departed that morning, leaving no forwarding address? What if, on the other hand, Grant consented to see him? What would he say, what would he do in Grant's presence? At the easiest of times, the stakes with Grant seemed unbearably high; now they seemed crushing, stunning.

The birthmarked clerk wasn't behind the desk when Varian arrived, nor did the manager appear through his secret mirrored door. Instead, in the seat of power, guarding access to the clientele of the Beauvau, was a fierce-eyed girl with high coiled blond braids, a Gallic version of a Valkyrie. Apparently she'd gotten the message that Monsieur Grant was to be insulated from Monsieur Fry at all costs. When he begged her to telephone Grant's room and announce him, she told him in no uncertain terms that her manager had instructed her to notify the police if he showed his face at the Beauvau.

"What am I supposed to do?" he said. He hadn't meant to speak the words aloud, certainly not in that tight and desperate tone; his reflection, in the infinite curving tunnel of mirrors, portrayed a man at the executioner's door.

"I must ask you to leave at once," the Valkyrie said.

"I'll die," he said, and it felt like the truth.

The Valkyrie's penciled eyebrows drew together. She seemed, he thought, to be assessing the sincerity of the claim he'd just made. He himself didn't doubt it; he would rather have thrown himself into the port and sunk to the bottom, become part of the general detritus of rusted chains and rotted wood and gangster bones, than been arrested without hope of seeing Grant again. He removed the watch from his wrist, a tonneau-shaped Patek Philippe that had been his grandfather's. On its dull gold face, skeleton hands of blued steel indicated the hour and minute; a smaller dial sat at 6, ticking the seconds infinitely. Eileen had always talked of giving it to their hypothetical son when he went off to college, a proposition that had elicited in Varian a sense of horrified claustrophobia, as if his life were a narrow path to the grave. He flattened the band of the watch against the countertop and met the young woman's eyes.

"Well," she said finally. "I suppose I can't prevent you from sitting in the bar."

His gut clenched excruciatingly. "Will you let Dr. Grant know I'm here?"

She gave a curt nod and was about to remove the watch from the countertop when the elevator arrived with a bell-like clang. The girl withdrew her hand as if she'd been burned, and Grant himself stepped from between the mirrored doors of the lift. In four steps he'd crossed the lobby; he took one look at the watch on the counter and apprehended the transaction. With a magician's swiftness, he swept the watch into his own hand and slipped it into Varian's trouser pocket, his fingers brushing Varian's thigh for a burning instant.

"Bonjour, Marie," he said to the girl, who had flushed a painful crimson. "Any messages for me this morning?"

The Valkyrie opened her mouth and shook her head.

"Well, thanks anyhow," he said, and turned to Varian. "As it happens, I was just on my way to see you."

Varian could only nod and clutch the watch in his pocket, a slurry of terror and relief boiling through him. What would he say, what could he say?

"Since you're here, Tommie, why don't we go sit in the bar."

Varian gave another silent nod, then followed Grant across the mirrored lobby and into the hotel brasserie. The place was nautical in theme, floored in yellow wood like a ship's deck; on the walls hung framed lithographs of three-masted schooners and brave sleek ketches, their spinnakers taut with wind. The gem of the room: a giant glossy sailfish mounted on mahogany, arced in frozen struggle above the fireplace. Through a long bank of windows, patrons could watch the moored boats sashaying on the port. Grant requested a table in the corner of the room, where the windows stood open, admitting a draft that smelled of salt and seaweed.

Varian sat down in a cane-backed chair. His head pulsed with sudden pain; in his midsection, the usual fire. Across from him Grant sat cool as ever, dressed in a linen jacket and a loosely knotted tie of gray silk twill. In the past eight days his color had returned; he had ceased, it seemed, to curl his shoulders around his chest. With his usual languid ease, he flagged the waiter and ordered two Pernods and water. Varian could only look at him in silence, rendered mute by the conundrum in his mind: Grant was all he cared for in the world; Grant had lied to him horribly, for months on end.

"You can't go waving antique watches around, Tommie," Grant said, his voice low, admonishing. "In most instances, plain old cash will do."

"I tried that," Varian said, his throat full of sand. "Tried everything." He coughed, but the frictive sensation persisted; he seemed unable to draw a full breath. "The staff here led me to believe you never wanted to see me again."

"I did give strict orders," Grant said, a flicker of humor at the corner of his mouth. "That handsome boy, the one with the birthmark, thought me rather cruel for refusing to see my patient. He pleaded more than once on your behalf."

So Grant knew he'd come here again and again. "You look—a little better. More like yourself, I think. Has the actual doctor . . . ?"

"Oh, I'm all right, for the most part. Kind of you to spare me a trip to the office, though. I still can't walk far without running out of breath." His voice was cool, measured; it seemed to hold something, the most vital thing, at a distance.

"But you were coming to meet me," Varian said. "I'm glad to hear that."

"Are you? I wasn't sure you would be."

"Yes, I've been—" What? Lying awake at night,

wishing he could reverse the clock? Wishing he'd never made the accusations he'd made? Wishing he'd never come to France? Wishing Grant had gone to conservatory instead of Harvard, or that he, Varian, had never been born? "Thinking about things," he said, though it was a lie; for the most part he'd been trying not to think about any of it.

"And what have you concluded?"

"Nothing, to be honest. Frankly, I've been busy getting Danny out of jail. Danny was in jail—did you know that? And the Martinique route's broken down. And a new slate of anti-Jewish laws just passed. And Portugal's stopped issuing transit visas—shall I go on?"

Grant shifted slightly in his chair. "If you want," he said.

"The Gestapo wants me out of France," Varian said. "That's today's news. Bingham can't help me anymore. He's been thrown out too, posted to Lisbon. The guy who took his place loathes me as much as Fullerton does. I've been called to see Captain du Porzic this morning, in fact. That's why I've come. I don't think I can last here much longer."

Grant's face remained impassive. "And if you go, what's to become of the Centre Américain?"

"Danny will take over until he can get his own visas. Then Jean will take the reins. They're more than capable, both of them. I suppose I've been training them for months."

"So you've come to say goodbye, then."

Varian looked down at the collection of meaningless things on the tabletop: a linen napkin, a silver salt cellar, his own glass of Pernod, untouched. "Yes, I suppose."

"Well, your timing's opportune. I was just on my way to say goodbye to you. I leave for Lisbon tomorrow at nine. On Thursday next I'll fly home on the **Yankee Clipper.**"

The news entered Varian like a blade. Leaving for Lisbon, the **Yankee Clipper:** these dire decisions made without his knowledge, when for months they'd scarcely breathed without consulting each other. But then he remembered: "Portugal isn't issuing transit visas anymore."

"I've already got them." Grant produced his passport and handed it to Varian, who found all the necessary stamps and visas in order, good for another six days. He held that passport, turning it over in his hands; beside him was the open window, and below it the undulating port.

Grant followed the line of his sight. "No, you don't, Tom," he said, with the merest ghost of a smile, and took the passport back.

Skiff, I've been horribly mistaken, he wanted to say, but did not. Instead they sat for a protracted moment in silence. And what now? What were they to do?

"I've got to meet du Porzic in twenty minutes," he said.

"That hardly leaves us time to drink ourselves

to oblivion," Grant said. Beneath the linen-draped table he slid his leg along Varian's, and Varian's heart nearly broke the cage of his chest.

"I want you to understand," Grant said. "I'm going home because I have to. I've been called to a meeting at Columbia. With Butler, the deans of faculty and academics, and my department chair."

"Oh, Grant."

"There's no telling how it'll turn out. But I feel pretty sure I'm not being promoted." He drew an envelope from his jacket pocket and handed it across the table to Varian. Inside was a letter from the dean of faculty, on thick paper stamped with the university seal. **In lumine tuo videbimus lumen:** in your light we will see light. The letter was terse and evasive, little more than a summons.

"They didn't waste any time about it, did they?" Varian said.

"Not much."

"I wish I could be there," he said. "In New York with you, when you have to do that. I wish I could be in that room. Shame them into treating you decently."

Grant raised his eyes to Varian's. "That would be rich, wouldn't it? 'Yes, it's true, sirs, I'm a Negro! And, while we're at it, won't you say hello to my boyfriend, Varian Fry? Yes, **that** Fry. The one who's been saving degenerate artists in Marseille, and running afoul of the French government.' "

"Oh, Grant." Varian covered his mouth with his

hand; a harsh sound escaped him, a laugh or a sob. "Should I appear in drag? Fully painted, to enhance the effect?"

"Oh, yes. You'll be Mademoiselle Vaurien. And sit on my lap throughout."

"I'll do it, Grant. I will. I swear to God."

"Oh," Grant said. He put a hand over his mouth, and his shoulders shook. "Oh, Tommie. Thank you. Now I can carry that with me when I walk into that room." He looked up at Varian, his eyes clear, intimate, as if nothing could divide them and never had. "Well. And you looked so grave when I came in. I thought you were bringing me bad news."

"I was," Varian said. "It's been nothing but bad news lately."

"Danny's out of jail, at least."

"For now. But I'm in trouble, Grant. My mission here's in trouble. I fear I'm going to be sent packing. And now I don't know where I'll go, now that you and I—"

Grant looked out toward the port, its light catching the planes of his face, and a recognition seemed to settle on his features, a grim resignation. Nothing had changed, in fact; the distance between them still existed, and was still uncrossable. Varian had still said the things he'd said to Grant, and Grant, having denied them once, seemed to have nothing more to say on the subject.

"Well," Grant said. "Perhaps you can go underground."

"That's what I've been thinking. In any case, I won't see you for some time. Months, most likely."

Grant nodded. "Maybe that's for the best," he said. "Maybe, with a little more time to think about things, you'll find a way to reconceive me as an honest man."

"Skiff, about that," Varian began, but he couldn't go on. His mind kept returning to Zilberman, to the way he'd said what he'd said, to his expression as he sat handcuffed in that metal chair at the Evêché, a line of blood running from his temple into his collar. Zilberman hadn't spoken like a vindictive man; he hadn't spoken like someone whose intent was to injure or destroy. He had spoken like a person telling the truth. And if he was telling the truth, then Grant—it couldn't be avoided—had lied. He had lied horribly, at the expense of a life.

"Well," Grant said. "Perhaps I'll see you sometime in New York."

It struck him then that this was all really happening, what he'd sworn would never happen again: they were saying goodbye, letting each other go. If Grant walked through the door of that restaurant, if he took a train to Lisbon tomorrow morning, nothing would ever be resolved between them; the terrible question in his mind would never be answered, or would be answered only in favor of Grant as liar. But how could that be, how was it possible, when the last nine months had seemed the only truth-telling of Varian's life? How could he wake up tomorrow knowing that Elliott Grant, that particular collection of cells, of inanimate elements made animate by some force that claimed kinship with Varian, would walk to the station, mount the steps of a westbound train, and be carried down the long coastal railway toward Cerbère, over the border into Spain, then down into Portugal, and then, in an airborne metal vessel, across the Atlantic?

Coward, a voice said in his head. **You're a goddamn coward.**

But was it cowardice to call out a lie, to insist on truth?

Grant reached across the table, and, for an unbearable moment, clasped Varian's hand. Varian sat still as ice, wanting only to keep Grant from moving, to keep feeling the warmth of his blood through his skin. He tried to meet Grant's eye, but Grant averted his gaze. And Varian thought: **Guilty. At the moment of parting, you can't even look at me.** He extracted his hand from Grant's, got up, threw bills on the table, and left the bar without a backward glance.

37

Under the Knife

As he walked toward the Evêché, trying to push Grant from his mind, what kept rising to the surface was his memory of the afternoon when he'd met with Chester Greenough on the day of his expulsion from Harvard. His solemn passage through the echoing Gothic arches that gave onto the quad, his transit along those leaf-shadowed brick paths, a rub of John Harvard's shoe for luck, the ascent through a high-windowed building that smelled of linseed oil and pencil shavings. Then, in Dean Greenough's office, dense crimson draperies and noise-effacing Persian rugs, scent of fresh-brewed coffee, and Greenough himself like a magistrate behind his fortress of a desk, looking down the bridge of his heirloom nose, waiting to pass judgment upon Varian. And Varian had been in the wrong, no doubt about it. But what had rankled him then, as now, was the sheer imbalance of power: his own will against the whole of Harvard's; his own power against that collective power.

How much did the will of a single person count for? How much force could it exert against a university, a government? He had set his own will, in collusion with his intelligence, against Vichy and the Gestapo from the moment he'd arrived in Marseille; he had fought with what he considered to be some success. But how long could he hold out against the power manifested in the Evêché, tricolor flags bristling from its gates, armed sentries in its guard-boxes, the stone archway like an open mouth at its center? He passed through the massive carved door, gave his name at the desk, and was conducted by a uniformed functionary to a large and unfamiliar waiting room. He was the only person in it; the room was silent except for the tick of an enormous mantelpiece clock. Between the windows, mounted upon an oval of green velvet, hung a magnificent military knife with a filigreed blade, almost a short sword, the kind of weapon used to kill a dueling partner at close range.

He sat beneath the knife and waited. In his mind there was no safe quarter: in one corner stood Zilberman, who, in an interrogation room somewhere in the roots of this building, had delivered his revelation; in another corner was the precious Flight

Portfolio, still held captive within these walls; in the third was de Rodellec du Porzic, the man who might seal his doom; and in the fourth was Grant, doing what at that very moment? Packing his beloved and familiar things, the books he'd been reading, the shirts and pants Varian had stripped from his body again and again those last nine months? Writing to Gregor? Writing to **him,** to Varian, a letter in which he'd own the lie he'd told and pave a path for Varian to forgive him? Was he forgivable? That morning he had seemed entirely unrepentant. In the face of their impending separation he had managed to laugh. And Varian had laughed with him, ignoring for a moment all the declarations he'd made to Grant, all of Grant's avowals, all of Grant's subtle and unconscious-seeming acting, his own terrible vulnerability, and the unspeakable thing he himself had done to Eileen, whose only crime had been to marry a person imperfectly capable of loving her. The thought of it made him want to take the ornamental knife from its velvet oval and disembowel himself that very minute, there on the gold-scrolled rug of du Porzic's waiting room.

And then at last the uniformed functionary returned, commanded Varian to his feet, and led him through the great carved door. Behind the desk sat Maurice Anne Marie de Rodellec du Porzic himself, Chief of Police, Grand Overseer of the Region of the Bouches du Rhône, resplendent in his decorated uniform, his steel-colored hair pomaded to a high sleek gloss. He wore an antiquated-looking mustache, crisp at the tips, and a pair of small round gold-framed glasses; he had the look of someone who had been stout and then lost a great deal of weight. The skin hung soft at his chin, dull as a deflated balloon, and his eyes had a hungry cast. He dismissed the functionary with a nod.

For what seemed an eternity he looked at Varian in silence, studying him, memorizing him, seeming to confirm a description someone else had delivered to him in minute detail. Varian willed himself to meet du Porzic's eye, willed himself not to powderize under that abrasive gaze. At last du Porzic opened a manila dossier on his desk and began to page through it, turning over leaf after leaf of what must have been documentation of Varian's activities in France. There was the familiar letterhead of the Centre Américain de Secours, and the ERC; there were the embossed seals of the embassy and the American consulate. More than once, he recognized the signature of Hugh Fullerton, who must have been all too glad to cooperate with the Evêché regarding Varian's fate. When he had turned over the last document, du Porzic removed his gold-rimmed spectacles and spoke.

"What can be said for a man like you, Monsieur Fry, a man whose own consulate desires to wash its hands of him? Hugh Fullerton disliked you from the start. He insisted to my predecessor, and he insists to me, that you have done nothing but make trouble for his organization here in Marseille."

"I've only asked the consulate to do its job."

"Not according to Monsieur Fullerton. He says you asked the consulate to cover your illegal acts."

"All I've done, Captain, is to provide relief to refugees. Just the same as the Unitarian organization, the Hebrew Immigrant Aid Society, the Masons, and many others I could name."

"So you say."

"Because it's the truth."

"Then tell me, please, why is it is that both your government and your sponsoring organization have called you home repeatedly, resorting at times to threats?"

"I'm sure I don't know what you're talking about."

"It's all here in your dossier. Your committee ordered you to return home in October, but you ignored them. In January, when they attempted to replace you, you refused to surrender your post. And here we have a facsimile of a cable from the Emergency Rescue Committee, New York Office, dated yesterday afternoon. FRY: YOUR RETURN REQUESTED IMMEDIATELY. FURTHER DELAYS ERC SHALL CEASE TO PROTECT OR SPONSOR YOU. KINGDON."

"You're ahead of me there. I haven't received that cable myself."

"Perhaps you should consult your office staff.

The consulate has just written to me to the same effect. The recent arrest of your secretary, Monsieur Bénédite, places your organization, and you yourself, under deepest suspicion. As far as we're concerned, you are just as guilty as he is."

"You've got no proof of that. And your chief witness, Kourillo, is a known liar. He'll say anything, as long as there's a payoff. It'll come out in court, I assure you."

Du Porzic sat back in his chair, folding his spectacles. "Proof!" he said. "Do you know what happens, Monsieur Fry, when a justice system demands absolute proof?"

"Innocent men aren't thrown in jail?"

"Guilty men go free. Hundreds of them. In wartime we cannot err in that direction. That was the old France, the Republic, where packs of criminals roamed the streets, thanks to our fear of a single wrongful conviction." He got up from the desk and went to the window. "When I was a boy, my father told me that my first job as a grown man would be to protect my family, then to protect France. He believed, as I do now, that the laws were weak. They were the laws of a people who valued the good of the individual at the expense of the whole. But now all of Europe prepares to embrace a swifter path to justice. The word **conviction**—it is nearly the same in English as it is in French, is it not?—signifies belief. Based upon the evidence in this dossier, I have formed the belief that you've flouted the laws of France. That is the only conviction I require to carry out justice as I see fit."

"And how do you propose to do that, Captain?"

"Unless you leave France within the week, I will have you arrested and interned."

"On what grounds? For what crime?"

Du Porzic shook his head. "Your mind, Monsieur Fry, is still mired in the laws of your own country. It's a pity you can't see things as I do! Our way is elegant and absolute. Soon it will be the only way." He sat down at his desk again and polished his spectacles contemplatively.

"Captain du Porzic," Varian said. "Please understand. I can't just pick up and leave this instant. My organization serves the basic needs of hundreds of clients. Before I vacate my position, the New York office has to find a suitable replacement. And once the new man arrives, he'll have to be trained."

Du Porzic folded his hands across his chest. "Let me ask you, Monsieur Fry. Do you fully understand, have I made clear to you, that each day you stay in France, the Gestapo increases its pressure upon us? If they come for you, we can offer you no protection whatever."

"Yes, you've made that perfectly clear."

"Why do you persist, then? Why do you care so very much about the fate of your organization, and so little about your own welfare, when the people you're assisting—Jews, anti-Nazis, degenerate

Negroid artists like Wifredo Lam, sexual inverts like Konstantinov—are the basest forms of humankind? Look at you. You're a thinking man, a Christian man, educated at the best American institutions. Why are you imperiling yourself for the sake of that filth? How do you justify it?"

"Is this official business, Captain?"

"I'm asking merely from personal curiosity. Tell me why."

"Those people are my people," Varian said. "If I don't help them, no one will."

The original of Kingdon's cable waited for him back at the office. Once he'd read it, once he'd assured himself that it was genuine, he went to Danny and drew him aside. Du Porzic meant to arrest him; in the end, he'd refused to give Varian more than a week.

"It's my fault," Danny said. "If I hadn't gotten myself arrested, you wouldn't be in this position."

"That's nonsense. It was Kourillo who got you arrested. And Vichy's wanted me out for months. It's just become more urgent now."

"We must find a way for you to stay."

"Maybe we will. But in the meantime we've got to keep quiet. I'll cable Kingdon tomorrow morning and tell him to find someone to replace me. I don't care who it is, because as soon as I'm out, you'll be running the operation, Danny. You and Jean. You'll work as a team, at least until your papers come through and you and Theo leave for the States. Then Jean will carry on alone."

"Of course, Varian. Of course we will. We'll keep the Fittko route running. And as soon as the sea route opens again, we'll fill it with our people."

"And Zilberman. You've got to keep looking for him. The consulate won't do it. If he's alive somewhere, if there's a chance we can help him, we have to do it ourselves."

Danny took off his small silver-framed glasses and held them in his hands. "Varian," he said.

"What is it?"

"Zilberman is dead. There can be no question. He carried poison. He wouldn't have let himself be tortured."

"How do you know that? How can you know?"

"He told me. It was at the party for the Bretons, when we were all in the garden after dinner. He told me he'd gotten it from a doctor in Arles. He said he'd written his wife and daughter about it, in case he was arrested. That letter you found in the cellar under his studio—I thought you might have read it."

"No," Varian said. "No. It wasn't addressed to me."

"It's over," Danny said. "It was likely over before he reached Paris."

He had known it all along; had known that when Zilberman stepped up onto that deportation train he was as good as dead. Amid the other sources of despair—perhaps to counteract them—he had suppressed the knowledge. But he couldn't suppress it any longer. He asked Danny to leave him alone, told him to close the door behind him. Then he put his head down on his desk, on the blotter scrawled with half-formed emigration plans and encrypted names and financial calculations, and cried until the ink ran a pale salt-blue.

Some time later—the light had begun to shift toward evening, casting violet shadows into the corners of the room—he heard the outer door open and close, then a familiar voice. Danny and Theo raised their own voices in greeting; a woman's sure footsteps crossed the floor. His office door opened and in walked Mary Jayne in a blue silk afternoon dress the color of forget-me-nots, a gold leather pocketbook in one hand, embroidered platform sandals on her feet. She approached the desk and seated herself in the interview chair, crossing her legs at the ankle. Her position radiated her usual strength, her shoulders turned at an angle of basic defiance; but when she raised her eyes he could see they were inflamed and damp, twin comet tails of kohl dragged underneath.

"Looks like we've both had a bad day," Varian said. It came out harder than he meant it to, but

Mary Jayne refused to avert her gaze. "I haven't known for weeks where to find you. I appreciate your sending Navarre. He did his best for us. But you might have shown your face around here."

"I want to be with those who care to see me," she said.

"Can you blame me, Mary Jayne? After you refused to dissociate yourself from that spider, that liar and thief?"

"You can't hold me responsible for Killer's actions," she said, evenly.

"Can't I?" Varian said. "You kept him around, knowing what kind of person he was, what kind of company he kept. I don't care to comment on the nature of your relationship with him—that's your business. But once you learned who he was, you should have cut him loose. You had a responsibility to. You should have had some idea, some inkling, that your decisions might reach beyond your own affairs."

"Raymond's in a concentration camp," Mary Jayne said. "He's a prisoner of war. He knew he was in trouble. He tried to get over the border, and they caught him. Now he's at Miranda de Ebro, where they've got him chained like a dog. He had to bribe them to let him write to me."

"So he says."

"For God's sake, Varian! Navarre's seen him. I spoke to him half an hour ago."

"What do you expect me to do about it? He sold

us out, more than once. He stole from you repeatedly. He stole the diamond bracelet your father gave your mother thirty years ago. Doesn't that mean anything? He deserves nothing from you, Mary Jayne. We're finished with him, and you should be, too."

She pressed her lips together for a long moment. "Don't presume to tell me what I should and shouldn't do. You don't know him at all. There's more to him than what's on the surface. And he's so young, scarcely twenty-three."

"Gussie's nineteen. Somehow **he** seems to be able to tell right from wrong."

Mary Jayne went to the window and sat on the sill, her shoulders curling. When she spoke again, her voice was a low rasp; he had to strain to hear her. "Why should you be the only one who gets to be happy?" she said. "You and Grant, always filching moments alone, taking off for some little town on weekends, putting your heads together over some novel or other, reminiscing about college, walking in the goddamn garden in the goddamn moonlight like a pair of goddamn—"

"Stop it, Mary Jayne," he said. "Stop it. You don't know what you're talking about."

"I **know,**" she said. "I know it when I see it. You can't begrudge me my own miserable little bit, even if it can't be **that.**"

"Grant's going home," Varian said. "He leaves for Lisbon in the morning."

She looked up at him, frowning. "What's happened?"

"The short story is that he's been called back for a disciplinary meeting at Columbia. But we quarreled, is what happened. He lied to me, and I found out about it. And it was a costly lie. It cost Zilberman his life."

"Zilberman?" Mary Jayne said. "What can you mean?"

Something came undone inside him then, the tightly bound knot that had kept him from seeing her as the woman he'd come to know over the past nine months: the woman he'd overheard making love with her gangster boyfriend too many times to count, the woman who'd chaired his dinner parties at Air Bel and orchestrated connections between stateless artists, who'd spent countless hours at the office working for the refugees, who'd made him laugh aloud at himself, who'd played the surrealists' games unflinchingly, and who, more than anyone else in Marseille, had grasped what had been at stake for him and Grant. She knew; she would understand. For a dizzying moment he thought he would tell her everything, thought she might have some insight that could save him. But then he remembered the look on her face in the courtyard of their hotel in Pamiers, the tension in her carefully painted lips as she drank her morning coffee, the effortful calm of her expression above the paperlike pleats of her shirt. She had paid a steep price for Tobias Katznelson's freedom. As much as he wanted to tell her everything, as much as he wanted what she might be able to give him, he could never reveal to her that Tobias had been a fraud.

"The details are unimportant," he said, finally. "Grant was brutally dishonest, that's what matters. He lied to me for months. When I found out, he left Air Bel. Tomorrow he leaves for the States."

She turned toward the window; outside, there was a soft clattering, a rain of pigeons descending to the ledge below. "I can't see him doing that. Lying to you, I mean. Are you—quite sure?"

"It's finished, Mary Jayne. We've discussed it."

A silence gathered and settled between them. Then she said, "What will you do now? When this is all done—your work here, I mean? Go home to New York, to Eileen, as though nothing happened?"

"I wrote to Eileen some weeks ago, before this business came to light. I was bluntly honest with her about Grant. That should satisfy you as to the state of my happiness."

She shook her head. "You don't deserve it."

"Don't I? What do I deserve? I deceived my wife for years, far longer than Grant deceived me—far longer, for that matter, than Killer deceived you. I deceived Eileen for twelve years, though I always believed I loved her. And I did, Emjay, truly I did! But I never stopped thinking of Grant all that time.

And I got what I deserved, in the end. I got nothing better than I deserved."

"I always wondered what would happen to you," she said, almost to herself. "To the two of you—you and Grant—once you left Air Bel."

"Now you don't have to wonder."

She put her arms around herself. The pigeons sent up their soft complaint from below. "I'm going down to Toulon for the weekend," she said. "Then to Sanary-sur-Mer. I might go up to Cannes afterward, and then to Monaco for a while. Do you want to come along, at least for some of it? It sounds like you could use the distraction."

"I wish I could. It's precisely what I need. But my days are numbered here. I'm to be placed under house arrest if I don't clear out in a week. I've been thinking I might go up to Vichy tomorrow and try to plead my case with someone there, try to get my deadline extended. Then I've got to come home to the office and set things in order."

"Home," she said, and smiled sadly. "Is that what you're calling this place now?"

"That's what it is," he said.

Dearest V, began the letter from Eileen, the one he found waiting for him at the villa when he returned that night.

Dearest V, Dearest V.

How grateful I was for your letters of 4/19 & 4/24, which I received together in a bundle: double reading to go with my double martini at day's end. I'm so sorry for what you've been through. The strain must be terrific. I do wish you'd come home, I wish it with all my heart, and I hope you'll do so before you ruin your health. Frank Kingdon insists you return at once. He admits his error in sending Allen and won't attempt to fill your post with someone who plans to run things by proxy. But he insists, you know—insists that I tell you, and dear V, I believe it too—that you're not doing anyone any good by staying longer. Not the ERC, not the clients, not yourself. Certainly not me, for whatever that's worth.

About Skiff Grant, of whom you spoke so balefully: Can you imagine I'd begrudge you the renewal of a friendship with your college chum, one who was so dear to you and who disappeared for so long? "You must have sensed the threat of what I felt for him from our earliest days. Once we married you must have feared it like a disease in remission." Cue the direful strings! How could I fear any more from Mr. Grant than if he were your brother? "When I return," you write, "you will find me irreparably changed." And how could I find you otherwise, after all you've experienced? I've adored you always for what you are, but I saw in you long ago the seed of greatness (not to wax operatic myself)—I saw it when you were a mere sophomore in Harvard Yard. Now it's germinated, exceeding even your wife's imagining. Of course you have changed: You have become a hero! And not just to me. As to the nature of your relationship with old Skiff: I can well imagine how your time in France may have occasioned a loss of perspective, a falling-away of context. Once you've returned, I think you'll quickly see what a spun-sugar castle it all was. I can't blame you in the least; extreme circumstances beget all manner of nonsensical thought.

So no further blithering about old Skiff. No further confessions, no further apologies: none of it is necessary. I must confess, in fact, that your letter put me at ease. I'd been hearing all manner of salacious whispers from your refugee friends who've made it to New York, Walter Mehring and Lena and some others. Hence my earlier pathetic letter. But now I know what they saw, what appeared so outré: you, merely waxing nostalgic with your old friend, whom you'd have been as wrong to brush off as you would be to abandon your wife of some 10 years, mother of your future small Fry, your faithful & impatient

Eileen

He lay in Breton's bed, reading and rereading. This letter, these three paragraphs scrawled in her elegant and unruly hand—what they represented above all was an astonishing demonstration of will. He hadn't been at all unclear in his own letter. He had confirmed beyond the slightest doubt, no room whatever for ambiguity, the worst of what she must have gleaned from Lena or Mehring or whoever else might have talked. And she knew what Grant had been to him; there could be no doubt of that. There could be only one way to read her letter: She was offering an olive branch, suggesting that all was forgiven as long as he never mentioned it again, as long as he pretended it was all a delusion, a spun-sugar castle. As long as he promised not to make it tell upon her life, not to make her bear the shame of having a husband who was a homosexual, and, worse, who had felt compelled to leave her for another man. She was proposing to wipe the slate clean, suggesting they might simply pretend it had never happened. He would, of course, have to give up all contact with Grant once he returned; she didn't have to say it. She held the moral advantage on all fronts, and she knew the power of her claim upon him. **As wrong to brush off as you would be to abandon—**

She knew, of course, what she was dealing with; she'd seen it all those years ago. Now she was playing her most valuable cards. How gratified she would be, he thought, to learn that he had been deceived, that Grant could no longer pose a threat to her.

He let the letter fall from the coverlet onto the rug. On his lap was **Le faune de marbre;** he fingered the cover, the marbled endpapers, the pages with their deep-printed French type, and turned to the page that haunted him, a poem called in French **Depuis cinquant ans,** about a woman abandoned in her echoing house, and the man tormented by the thought of her. In blunt pencil, on an index card, he had translated it from memory. He reread it now, pausing over the merciless last lines: **And with his bound heart and his young eyes bent / And blind, he feels her presence like shed scent, / Holding him, body and life, within its snare.**

38

The Coast of France

On the day of Grant's departure, a day when Varian could concentrate on nothing but the distant sound of trains, every whistle seemed to announce his own execution. At the office that morning he thought a hundred times of running to the station, buying a ticket for Lisbon, boarding the train that would carry Grant away. But then, he reminded himself, he couldn't abandon the Centre Américain; nor could he have gone anywhere if he'd wanted to. He didn't even have his own passport. He had been forced to hand it over to Hugh Fullerton some time ago, on the basis that the consul wanted to have it validated for travel west. So his morning was a torture of immobility and inaction; all he could do was sit at his desk and read the **Times**'s grim account of Hitler's campaign in Russia. The Luftwaffe had decimated some eight hundred tanks, he read, the front rank of a Soviet counterattack near Smolensk; the Second Panzer Group had just crossed the Dnieper, and was preparing to enter the city. The aim was to win control of the road to Moscow. All of it would have seemed blindingly foolish, he knew, had the Wehrmacht not managed to shut down all of Russia's defenses thus far; he'd begun to suspect that Hitler's armies had reserves deeper than anyone had imagined. And if Hitler took the Soviet Union, if he managed to overrun not only Europe but Asia, what then? An engulfing gray cloud would settle over half the world, from Siberia all the way to Norway, from Novaya Zembla down to Africa. Now, from the direction of the Gare St. Charles, came another train whistle: this must be the one, the herald of the end of all he cared about in the world. He needed a drink. He needed a slow infusion of opium, a quick and total effacement, oblivion.

Instead he received a summons from Hugh Fullerton at the consulate. Like a sleepwalker he took the tram from the Canebière toward the southern edge of town; in a sun-shot nightmare he climbed the familiar drive, its double row of lindens making hushed excuses in the rising wind. Fullerton met him at his office door and invited him in, with no pretense of civility. In the vast high-ceilinged office, he commanded Varian to sit in a deep leather chair before the desk. On the blotter was a crisp-edged dossier, the American cousin of the one that had met him at du Porzic's office. From its interior

Fullerton withdrew Varian's passport and handed it across the desk without a word. Varian discovered, when he opened it, that it had in fact been validated—for westbound travel only, of course—and contained, as if by magic, French exit visas and Spanish and Portuguese transit visas.

"Oh, Hugh, you shouldn't have," Varian said, not caring now whether or not he offended, wishing only for Fullerton to hear all the bitterness he felt. He could not have tabulated, there was no way to compute, the number of lives he might have saved if Fullerton had been his ally. "It's no easy matter to get all those passes. I should know."

"Our message to you should be clear," Fullerton said. "You're to leave the country at once."

"Captain du Porzic implied that I'd have time to arrange my affairs."

"There's no affair of yours that merits arranging," Fullerton said, his narrow, dour face drawn into its severest expression. "What ought to concern you now is preserving your freedom and your life. You're suspected not only of breaking French law, but of fomenting communist activity in that country villa of yours. We won't have anything to do with you if Vichy arrests you, or if the Gestapo chooses to lay its hands on you."

"You don't have to tell me that."

"Take my advice, then. Get out of France post haste. You've got a wife at home. Don't make a widow of her."

"I'll thank you not to talk about my wife," Varian said, getting to his feet. "Nor to presume you know anything about my private affairs."

Fullerton narrowed his eyes. "In fact, we know more about your private affairs than you may realize. You're lucky to have the chance to resign. Your organization would have every right to cast you from your post in sheer disgust. The way you've comported yourself here in France is an embarrassment to us all. Even Mrs. Roosevelt has withdrawn her support."

"She has yet to inform me of that reversal."

"Likely she would consider it beneath her dignity."

"You've no right to insult me."

"Nor have you any to remain in my office a moment longer. I have officially washed my hands of you."

"Your hands are bloodstained, Hugh. There's no washing them."

"Get out," Fullerton said, rising to his feet. "Get out, or I'll call security."

"Call them," Varian said, his pulse reaching a desperate pitch. "Do what you want. I'll say what I've come to say to you."

But at that moment Fullerton picked up the phone, and in an eyeblink the tall French-fluent guard had appeared and laid his hand on Varian's arm. He led Varian from Fullerton's office with surprising gentleness, and escorted him not just to the door but halfway down the drive. Once they'd reached that spot, he bent to Varian's ear.

"There's a rising resistance," he said. "I understand that some in your office—Rosenberg and Gemähling—I understand they're in touch with cells of objectors." He pushed a square of paper into Varian's pocket. "If I can help, let them come to me. I have access to certain documents. Information."

"Thank you," Varian said, his throat tight with adrenaline. He resented the sensation of being drawn back from the brink; there had been a wild liberation in the feeling that he had nothing left to lose. "I'll pass that along, Mr.—"

"Never mind the name, sir," the guard said.

"All right. Thank you."

The guard nodded and released him, and he started down the drive toward the station; it was time to pack his things. But not for home, not yet: he was headed to Vichy.

He left the next morning at dawn, bringing with him two days' worth of clothes, a book of Yeats, his validated passport, and a draft of an article for the **Times,** which he meant to complete in Vichy if he could find a typewriter. The atmosphere in town was as strange as it had been since the town's debut as the seat of government: Pétain's banner flew everywhere, tricolor bunting hung in limp loops from every streetlight, and ubiquitous signs advertised the salutary qualities of the famous baths, which were themselves gray and crumbling and unsanitary looking, and infused the air with the smell of eggs. In a café across from the Thermes des Dômes he drank alkaline water and ate a hard brown biscuit; this was his only fortification before he made his assault on the Ministry of the Interior. In that fortress of a building, once a gendarmerie, he succeeded in meeting with three French officials, all of them unfailingly polite, none willing or able to contravene de Rodellec du Porzic's authority. From the third official, a tiny lark-voiced man in rimless glasses, he learned that he would not be permitted to stay the night in Vichy.

"Not stay?" Varian said. "Why on earth not?"

"You are a suspected communist," the man said, consulting another dossier stuffed with complaints and labeled with Varian's name.

He had to wonder how many there were in France, these damning dossiers; it was strangely gratifying to know how objectionable he had become. "Can't you bend that order?" Varian said. "I have work to do here."

"Pas du tout," the man said in his flutelike alto. "Nor will you be permitted in the environs. Your consulate has given you a passport validated for travel west. We must advise you to use it at once."

In disgust he went to the American Embassy,

where he made his plea to a series of undersecretaries and secretaries until a frosted and stenciled door opened to produce Woodruff Wallner, third consular officer. Wallner, tanned and hale, had a comic-book hero's blunt jaw and a fatherly, welcoming frown; he sported a pink pocket square and a tweed jacket of the same provenance as Varian's own, a detail that produced an illogical float of hope in Varian's chest. Wallner's secretary delivered a tray of cut-crystal glasses and a decanter of Virginia whiskey that must have predated Prohibition. From a polished box on the desktop Wallner offered Varian a cigar, clipping and lighting it for him with expert ease. He listened, brow creased and hands laced, nodding frequently as Varian told his story and made his plea for protection. He listened so attentively, and answered in a tone of such jovial bonhomie—of course, old boy! Of course, old man! Do tell, do tell—that it took some time for Varian to understand that Wallner was dismissing him as loony-bin material—telling him, in essence, to go to hell.

At the American news bureau, where he went in the hopes of finishing his piece for the **Times,** a sympathetic foreign correspondent—Edwin Sprague, an old acquaintance from his days at **The Living Age**—advised him that the safest way to buy time in France would be to stay out of Marseille. If he could prolong his absence until his transit visas expired, so much the better.

Varian looked down at his suitcase, packed with two days' clothes, and then up into Sprague's small, flint-colored eyes. "Go on the run?" he said.

"Surely it's occurred to you," Sprague said. "You're known as something of an authority on subterranean living."

"You're thinking of my clients, not me."

"Well, didn't you learn anything from them?"

"I learned where to find edible snails and how to throw a dinner party **sans vêtements.**"

"Sounds like you've been having more fun than I have," Sprague said. "I wouldn't let them kick me out if I could help it."

All right, he thought, walking back toward the station; all right. He was still allowed to purchase railway tickets; let him get them while he could. If travel could gain him time in France, let him travel. Perhaps new sights would be a balm. That was what he needed, he thought as he approached the ticket window: a balm, or perhaps a bomb. Relief or obliteration. He bought a ticket to Toulon and rode a sweltering train hundreds of kilometers south, arriving at a godforsaken hour between midnight and dawn; there he checked into a hotel on the beach, thinking he might run into Mary Jayne at some casino table or other. As he arranged his few things in the room, its rattan furniture and decorative bowls of shells more suggestive of Miami than of the Riviera, he wondered idly, and with mild self-loathing, what it might be like to sleep with Mary Jayne in the high sheer-curtained bed. At the casino the next night he was disappointed not to find her bent over the roulette table, her deep-grooved golden back emerging from the black cowl of her evening gown; he considered trying to seduce the profligate blond divorcée at his right, or, more appealingly, her young Romanian lover. But he spent that night and the next alone, turning disconsolately, engaging in unsuccessful onanism in the too-hard, too-wide bed.

He was alone at Toulon and at Sanary-sur-Mer, where he'd had a glorious swim with Hirschman months and months before; he was alone at Le Lavandou and St. Tropez, alone in white rooms overlooking the ocean, its surface alternately toothed with foam, englittered with sun, doused in moonlight, or flat and still to the horizon. Waiters and baggage-carriers, some of them spectacularly beautiful men, received his involuntary glances and offered themselves to him at the various doors of his various hotel rooms; he sent them all away, sick at the thought of sleeping with someone who wasn't Grant. Instead he walked down to the water, night after night, in town after town, bending to touch the surf with his bare hands, feeling the pull of the ocean, reasoning that since its every molecule was, in a way, connected with every other, if he touched this wavelet he would be in contact with the continent where Grant now walked. At breakfast he found himself ordering what Grant would have ordered. In the afternoon he toured Roman ruins and hiked paths to views Grant would have wanted to see. As if through Grant's eyes he took in the white beaches, the bougainvillea-clad houses climbing the verdigris hillsides, the improbable constructions of cloud; he knew Grant would have insisted on photographing this narrow rosemary-choked stone stairway, or the tiny precipice-clinging café where a nubile black-haired Perseus served fresh stone fruits, honey, and tea made from hillside mint, all of which Varian consumed without tasting.

The numbness was familiar, homelike. Nothing penetrated it, not even the news, sent to him in a cheerful letter from Eileen and forwarded to his tiny hotel in Le Dramont, that Hirschman, having arrived in Berkeley on a fellowship from the Rockefeller Foundation, had fallen in love with a French literature scholar and had married her in late May. Hirschman safe, Hirschman married: it should have been enough to shake him awake; enough, at least, to make him aware of his breakfast of shirred eggs and crevettes, or to allow him to take more than a dull, half-conscious interest in the tiny pin-legged plovers that skated the foam at the edge of the ocean. He abandoned his breakfast on the hotel terrace and walked down to the beach, not bothering to remove his canvas shoes; he walked all the way to the edge of the sea and squatted on the firm wet sand. The plovers spooked, skitting away on their twig legs; in their wake, air holes opened in the sand like tiny mouths. He leaned forward, placed one hand on the sand, and felt it shift beneath his fingers. The ocean approached and subsumed his hand and the tips of his shoes, the warmth of the water like an invitation. Beneath the surface he could see the glint and dart of hundreds of fish, near-invisible jots of life, each with its own agency, each with its urgent and vital desire. The war did not exist there, a centimeter beneath the surface of the ocean; it did not exist in those infinitesimal flashing lives. The earth itself cared nothing for the clashes on its surface, large or small. It spun through space at a mind-cracking rate, bound to its orbit, warmed by its star, carrying its freight of water and rock and life. How little he mattered, how little any of it mattered, considered on that scale; someday it would all be over, his grief absorbed into the planet's crust, and, sometime later, the planet engulfed by its sun. He took off his shoes and clothes and left them on the sand, not caring who might see; swimming nude on those beaches was common enough. Without thinking, without considering, he held his breath and ran into the waves. He dove underwater and drove himself through the first warm yards of sea, then into the colder, harsher blue; he swam deep, fighting the incoming tide, going deeper still, until a force beyond his will shot him to the surface and made him breathe. For a long time, who knew how long, he floated on the surface beneath the hard July sun. Finally, against his will, he let himself be washed back to shore, a long pale branch of human driftwood. On the empty beach he pulled on his clothes and lay on the sand, shamefully glad to be breathing.

The days stretched on without end, and the police failed to knock at his door. He felt, truly, as if he'd slipped between the pages and disappeared for good. It was a place one might stay, this noplace; it was somewhere to live for a time, before one vanished quietly forever. Every new town was a flattened, muted version of itself, every hotel a place to lie awake in the dark. One night in St. Raphael he got out of bed at half past two and climbed a path he'd followed earlier that day, one that led to a promontory overlooking the sea. There he lay on the edge of the limestone cliff and stared at the profusion of stars. How much time had passed since he and Grant had stood on the balcony of the Medieval Pile, searching the winter sky for Cetus and Hydra? Now the summer triangle of Altair, Deneb, and Vega stretched above him, framing the tableau of Vulpecula, the little fox, grabbing his goose, Anser. Ursa Minor arced upside down, an acrobat of a bear; at the tip of his tail burned Polaris, faint but steady, which ten thousand years ago had lain not north but east. On that cliffside he could almost feel Grant beside him, could almost smell his familiar scent, could almost feel the warm length of his body along his own as it had been when they lay on their backs in a field in Maine, watching these same stars wheel and dive above. On his other side, far down below, he could hear the crash of the ocean at the bottom of the cliff. How easy might it be to drift toward that roaring as he looked at the sky; to feel its approach as a kind of welcome, a hand leading him toward mercy: the kind that would, after a swift descent, a single clap of pain, a flash of light, deliver him directly into the constellated sky.

Coward.

He couldn't do that either. All he could do was to remain invisible, there in the South of France. He lay in the long grass, held its sharp-edged blades in his hands, letting his mind drift upward into the surrounding buzz of nighttime insects. He was nowhere, he was out of the world, de Rodellec du Porzic could not touch him, nothing could touch him, he was swept clean of feeling, he was hardly a man, hardly alive at all.

Some weeks later—late August, nearly a year since he'd landed on the continent—he found himself at the Hôtel Martinez in Cannes, in a lounge chair on the beach, his eyes covered by the wings of a thin cotton towel, his skin browning in the flagrant sun, a forgotten **Look** magazine in his hand. When a slender shadow paused over him and blocked the sun, his heart seemed to stop. **Grant.** He sat up and pulled the towel from his eyes, his heart clamoring.

Not Grant, of course; Danny Bénédite, standing on the sand in his glossy caramel-colored shoes and his usual tweed suit, his eyes hidden behind a pair of the paper-and-cellulose sunglasses tourists could buy for three francs on the boardwalk.

"The concierge told me I might find you here," he said.

Varian thought he would weep from relief. His impulse was to throw his arms around Danny, but here he was in his swim trunks, shirtless, sweating, slick with coconut oil, generally unwashed. He contented himself with rising to shake Danny's hand, holding it long enough to reassure himself that he was really there. Danny sat down on the chaise next to Varian's and rested his arms on his knees.

"I thought you might have left for points west by now," Varian said. "I hoped you'd be long gone. Though I'm awfully glad to see you."

"I tried," Danny said. "Theo and I tried to cross into Spain three weeks ago. But we were arrested at the first checkpoint."

"You! The first of all our clients to be arrested at the border!"

"Yes. Mary Jane and Navarre had to come to the

rescue again. I'm afraid I can't see when we can try next. Navarre said we wouldn't be so lucky again, now that I've got what he calls **un casier judiciaire.**"

"So what are you doing here?"

"I thought it was time you came home. Your visa must be thoroughly expired by now."

"Thoroughly," Varian said. "But how can I go back? How can I, when it's not—when none of it—" He found himself unable to continue; he couldn't give voice to the words that suggested themselves, not even to Danny, who must have known what he meant; he'd been there for all of it, he and Theo, living just down the hall from where it had happened.

"I'm afraid you've got no choice," Danny said. "There's work to be done. The Martinique route's open again. The border is beginning to soften. As long as you're still in France, you may as well make yourself useful."

"What if I'm arrested? Du Porzic can't have forgotten his threats."

"Then we'll find a way to get you out. You've paused, Varian. You've stepped out of your life. There's no good in it." He glanced at the empty drink glass in Varian's hand. "Soon you'll find yourself at the bottom of a martini, thoroughly pickled."

Varian laughed. "I don't believe I've won an argument with you yet, Danny," he said. "You're so gravely persuasive."

"Come up to the hotel," Danny said. "There's business to discuss. I brought some papers that require your attention. Then we can go into town for dinner."

"There's a first-rate restaurant here at the hotel. Marvelous crabs, they say."

"Never refuse marvelous crabs," Danny said, getting to his feet; he reached down to pull Varian up, and the two of them ascended to the hotel.

Varian bathed and dressed in his own room, taking care with the details of his toilette for the first time in weeks. Then he and Danny sat for a time on Danny's balcony, paging through a series of office papers. There were missives from New York, describing the organization's failure to secure a replacement for Varian; other letters confirmed his clients' arrival in the States, and still others were from collectors who had bid speculatively upon pieces from the Flight Portfolio and had since learned of the portfolio's disappearance. Some of the collectors' letters expressed chagrin, others threatened legal suit, still others offered condolences and cash. All of them demanded an answer. Danny had, providentially, brought along a small portable typewriter and a good supply of paper. It was something of a relief to sit at the desk and answer correspondence while the sun dropped toward the horizon.

Sometime after dark they went down to the restaurant and claimed a table on the veranda. The crabs were indeed marvelous; so was the wine. They talked about Hannah Arendt, whose husband had recovered from his illness, thanks to the ministrations of Dr. Mirandeau; Danny believed her papers would come through before long. Now that the shipping routes had opened again, hundreds of refugees had appeared on the steps of the Centre Américain. But there was a general dearth of money. Mary Jayne had given what she could, and had recently extracted the promise of more from Peggy Guggenheim, but other sources must be found. When that subject ran out, they talked about Danny and Theo's thwarted exit plans, and how, under the current circumstances, they might arrange another flight from France.

"If I were to return to the States," Varian said, "I could sponsor you. That would make a difference on the visa front, criminal record notwithstanding."

Danny glanced out toward the rolling ocean, then back at Varian. "Is that what you plan?" he said, his voice low and serious. "To return to New York?"

"I imagine I'll be kicked out of France eventually. I can't avoid it forever. And where else can I go? Ne York is my home." There it was, that word ag and it seemed true for the first time in month at New York, and the States, were places that s ied him. He told himself it had nothing at do with the fact that Grant was there now.

"We've just had a letter from New Y Danny said, meditatively. "News of our boy. n's aunt has enrolled him in a nursery scho stchester County, some miles north of He has learned to count to thirty, ima he knows the names of colors in English. His latest fascination is for birds." He fell silent for a moment, worrying the hem of his linen napkin with his thumb. "Sometimes Theo wakes in the night, thinking she's just heard him call. I can't convince her that it's impossible. She runs through the house, looking. Sometimes, Varian, I almost believe her—I almost believe she's heard him, and that if we look hard enough we will find him. Sometimes I'm certain we'll find him dead, drowned in the fishpond or fallen from a window. I think about the moment we put him on that ship, the way he looked at us, no idea what was going to happen. It's a torture. How can I explain it?" Danny put his thumb and index finger to the corners of his eyes. It was some time before he could go on, and when he did, his voice was scarcely audible. "At night, it's the distance I keep thinking of," he said. "All the miles between us—miles and miles of dark space. The land, the ocean. Every living thing in the Atlantic, closer to e than my son. What if he were to fall ill, what e were in real danger and I couldn't reach him? I uld do anything for him, Varian. I would tear ou y own eyes."

"I Danny. I'm so sorry. We'll get you there."

what know what I'll do otherwise," he said. "Or again will do." He put his fingers to his eyes never Varian laid a hand on his arm. He had Eileen atherhood himself, had never followed an vaguely into her ideas about their future small Fry. But now, for the first time, he felt he could imagine the sheer physical pull of it: of having a son, a child, a living fragment of one's own being, loose in the world. He remembered Danny with his boy in his arms, saw them standing at the edge of the **bassin,** watching a leaf boat make its slow and drifting transit; he saw Danny putting a pewter cup into Peterkin's hands, the cup overflowing with clandestine milk. He saw Danny buckling Peterkin's shoes, saw him pulling up his stockings and buttoning his coat, defending him against the mistral. For months he'd seen Danny doing those things; they were a part of Air Bel, as present and ignorable as the wallpaper. But now he could feel, as if he were inhabiting Danny's body, what it would be like to have all of it taken away. What it would feel like to be separated from that bright fragment. Like having one's own lungs torn out; like being forcibly separated from one's soul.

Then, all at once, there was a change of pressure in his head, an inrush of noise, like a needle scratched backward along a record groove. "Danny," he said, sitting upright in his chair.

"What's wrong?"

He put his hands to his temples, where an intolerable pressure was gathering. He couldn't sit still; he had to rise from the table, had to be away somewhere. He said he felt suddenly unwell; the wine had hit him all at once. Danny said he was finished too, after the travel, the sun, the marvelous crabs.

He called for the bill and signed it; then they rode the lift to Danny's floor, where they said a gruff goodnight, Varian assuring Danny he would call on him if he needed help. Then he rode to his own floor, where he walked the long hallway to his room, closed, the door, and went out to the balcony.

Out on the water were the faint lights of some massive ship, and not a pleasure ship; even from this distance, even by moonlight, he could see ord-nance bristling from its towers. If that ship were to turn its guns on the hotel, he thought, it could blow it all to splinters in a minute.

Then back it came: the rush, the sound, that mind-halting scratch. What Danny had said: **I would do anything, I would tear my eyes out.**

What a father would do for his son.

What a father would do: cross an ocean toward a continent at war. Then lie to his lover on his son's behalf. Lie in detail and with conviction. Lie in the belief that his son deserved saving, simply by virtue of his being an imperiled human crea-ture on this earth, whose right to breathe and eat and reproduce could be held at no lesser value than anyone else's. What a father would do: lie deeply, lie elegantly, to save his son. Then leave his lover overseas, charging him to bring his son to safety, to convey him over all that dark space: the land, the ocean. Over every living thing in the Atlantic.

39

Refoulé

They took the train to Marseille the next morning, Varian wondering every minute if he'd be apprehended along the way. He kept thinking of the ride home from Pamiers, of the sound of Gestapo officers moving down the corridor, pulling out the man in the ill-fitting coat, wrestling him off the train. But they made it to the Gare St. Charles without incident, and at the office he found everything in readiness: his desk tidy and stacked with papers that wanted his attention, Jean Gemähling in the midst of a phone call with the consulate, bright-voiced Lucie Heymann interviewing a pair of clients, and Theo crouched beside a refugee mother who sat nursing her baby as she narrated her story. Theo's look, when she saw Varian and Danny, lay somewhere between chagrin and relief; he perceived that the relief was not only for her husband's safety.

She was willing, at least, to meet Varian's eye. With a murmured word to the nursing mother, she got to her feet and went to them, first pressing Danny's hand, then taking Varian's.

"I suppose you heard about our fiasco at the border," she said.

"I heard it all," Varian said. "I'm so sorry, Theo."

"Perhaps we ought to have waited. Maybe if you'd been here—"

"Nonsense. You had bad luck, that's all. We'll do our utmost for you now, and you'll try again. But in the meantime, your husband will have to keep a low profile."

Theo glanced at Danny. "Did you hear him?"

"I've got nothing if not a low profile," Danny said, and pressed his wife's hand. And then he and Varian moved farther into the office, followed by a stream of clients, and their work began again as if it had never stopped.

Their staff was reduced, their funds depleted, their relations with the consulate near-nonexistent, but that week they worked harder than ever; they had to. Dozens of refugees arrived at the offices every day, nearly all of them Jewish, desperate at the news that had made its way to the South of France from Germany, Austria, and Poland. There were rumors of Jews having been loaded by the thousands onto trains, jammed like livestock into cattle cars, then sent across Europe to camps; there were rumors of Nazi troops machine-gunning men and women on the banks of rivers, or into open graves dug by the victims themselves. Jews had been locked into barns, which had been set afire; others were starving to death in ghettoes. The news collected in the air of the Centre Américain like ash from a fire, darkening everything it touched.

Every night when Varian arrived home at Air Bel, he stripped off his clothes and dove straight into the deep **bassin,** converted to a pool. He would lie on his back in the still-warm water, staring at the gray clouds against the black sky, willing it all to wash away. But no amount of soaking could strip the terrible news from his body, nor relieve him of the conviction that despite it all, despite the fact that his work seemed more necessary than ever, he had to get home to New York. He had to be ejected from France now; he didn't see any other way he could justify leaving.

On a Friday afternoon a week after his return from Cannes, as he and Jean and Danny and Theo sat in the front office sorting through a new set of intake forms, a knock came at the outer door—not the tentative knock of a client, but the unmistakable rap-rap-rap of the police. The four of them looked at each other in silence; there was no way to know which of them the police wanted. But Varian motioned Danny and Theo into the back office, where they closed the door. Then he opened the outer door to find the young soot-haired officer who'd conducted him to the **Sinaïa** some months ago. The officer touched his hat in greeting. Jean got to his feet and went to Varian's side, assuming a footballer's wide-legged stance.

"Monsieur Fry," the officer said. "I come with an order from Captain du Porzic."

"I was afraid you might say that," Varian said.

"I'm to accompany you to the Evêché," the officer said, raising his snow-blue eyes to Varian's; at the corner of his mouth, the merest trace of an intimate smile.

"All right. Let me get my things."

"Take everything you might want later," the officer said. "You'll not be permitted to return."

"What does that mean?" Jean said, crossing his arms. "Why not?"

"I'm not authorized to discuss Monsieur Fry's case."

"Is he to be expelled from France?"

"I'm not authorized to say."

Jean turned to Varian. "Tell me what to do. How can we stop this?"

"I'm sure there'll be a **procès,**" Varian said. "Papers to be signed. I'll be in custody overnight, at least. And then there's the matter of visas." He met the young officer's glacierlike eyes. "They've all expired, you know. I can't be expelled from France at the moment, not legally."

"That will be the commissioner's concern."

"Shall I come along?" Jean asked.

"That's not permitted," the officer said, and then to Varian, **"Dépêchez-vous."**

Lucie produced a box; Varian retreated to his office to gather his papers. Danny and Theo, who had been listening, now helped him, ashen-faced and silent. Here was the moment they had known would come, the one that had nonetheless seemed infinitely postponable: Varian's departure, his exit from the Centre Américain. Into the box went personal letters and cables, dozens of them. In went the photograph Grant had taken at Arles: Varian standing before the ancient amphitheater, the tiers of seats rising behind him, an expression of dazed wonder on his face. In went a stone from the Coussouls de Crau; photographs of Varian with the staff; a red leather box from the leather-goods merchant on the rue Grignan; the silver-framed photograph of Eileen on the beach at Southampton. When the box was full, Danny tied it with string and put it into Varian's arms.

"I'm going to go up to Vichy," Danny said. "See if I can intercede."

"No, don't do that. The risk is too great."

"I haven't committed any new crimes lately. I don't see what grounds they'd have to arrest me."

"They won't care about that. They'll do it anyway."

"I refuse to let them simply march you out!"

Theo, at Danny's side, nodded her assent. "I intend to see Monsieur Blount myself."

"He'll never help," Varian said. "This is precisely what he's been waiting for."

"Then I shall give him a fine piece of my mind."

"Thank you, Theo," he said, and pressed her hand. And then he followed the soot-haired officer through the door and down the stairs, and together they walked the few blocks to the Evêché.

In France, no administrative process unfolded with speed. He waited all night at the Brigade des Rafles, and at dawn he washed his face in a lavatory reeking of ammonia and dead mouse. At eight o'clock the soot-haired officer brought him a dry croissant and a lukewarm cup of faux coffee; at nine thirty he was called at last to an interview with Captain Villand, who told him that he was to be **refoulé** from France, which was not quite the same thing as being expelled. He could return legally in the future, provided he could get a visa. The look on Villand's face, as he detailed this impossibility, was one of deep satisfaction. He went so far as to offer Varian a farewell cigar, lighting it himself with the pineapple lighter.

Villand did him the further service of providing a car, a long black Citroën with twin sidepipes and an old-fashioned leather-strapped trunk at the rear. In the company of the soot-haired officer and his partner, a tall bearlike man who introduced himself as

Garandel, they went to the Villa Air Bel so Varian could pack his things. Into his long-suffering suitcase he loaded his six correct shirts, now practically in ribbons; the blue Moroccan slippers Grant had given him; the Yeats he'd been reading; the Faulkner poems. Into another box he loaded surrealist drawings and paintings rolled into tubes; two tiny surrealist assemblages; maps, lists, schematic drawings. Countless notebooks, a half-filled sketchbook, a stray linen handkerchief belonging to Mary Jayne. He looked around his emptied room, expecting to be filled with grief; what he experienced instead was the push of inevitability, the feeling of the sea at Le Dramont as it shot his body toward the light. By long-standing habit he looked under the bed, under the dresser, under the nightstand. And there in the dark lay one of Grant's nautilus cufflinks, abandoned where it must have fallen the night Grant had left Air Bel in haste, carrying his single suitcase. He took out one of his own cufflinks and replaced it with the nautilus.

On the way out, Madame Nouguet met him at the door with a fragrant rolled pancake wrapped in brown waxed paper. If he was to be **refoulé,** she said, he must not go empty-handed. He accepted the package, demanding to know where she had gotten sugar and butter; she only smiled, protecting the household mysteries. Varian shook her hand with grave propriety, and she gave him a rare look of unmitigated approval.

Then they drove down to the station, where the soot-haired officer presented Varian with all the necessary papers and wished him a good journey. He regretted, he said, that he could not see Varian to the border; he hoped his partner, Garandel, would make a good companion.

"Thank you," Varian said. "I know you've been my ally more than once."

"All to the glory of France," the officer said, and gave him a lascivious wink.

At the Gare St. Charles, Garandel permitted Varian a single phone call. He rang the office, and Theo answered; when she heard Varian's voice, she shouted for Jean to pick up the extension. There was no stopping his deportation, he told them. But what would they think of a little junket to the border? Could work be interrupted for an afternoon?

Theo promised they would come at once, all of them. She would stop along the way to cable Danny at Vichy; perhaps he could meet them at Narbonne.

Garandel never left Varian's side, but he allowed him to wait for his friends at the top of the broad steps that overlooked the city. Varian stood thinking of Chagall, of his opinion that the last look at a town was the most important. What would this last look crystallize for him, what could it contain of his time there? At the base of the stairs stood the Hôtel

Splendide, its glass awning fanned like the petals of an Arctic flower. Beyond it was the Canebière, where he'd come across Breitscheid and Hilferding sitting at a café table, discussing their business aloud as if no danger existed in the world. Two blocks farther south was the office on the boulevard Garibaldi, stripped now of all his things. Then the market streets with their scent fog of curry and cardamom and cinnamon, and the narrow commercial passageway of the rue Grignan, where, at No. 60, the daughter of the concierge held court in her berry-stained dress. Farther still was the Dorade, where, nearly a year ago, the past had delivered its freight to the present. And there, beside the Vieux Port—he could just make out its sugar-white corner from where he stood—was the Hôtel Beauvau, and before it the docks full of little moored sailboats. All of it—the roofs, the sunburnt buildings, the scintillating surface of the port, the blue-white sky, the green ridge of the Marseilleveyre in the distance—became a single bright blur through his lashes, a landscape already receding into the past.

His friends came up the stairs in a pack, and together they entered the station. They bought tickets at the usual barred window, and then, under the guardianship of Officer Garandel, they boarded the train, filling their section of the railway car with low talk and cigarette smoke. As they waited for the departure whistle, Varian directed his mind forward, envisioning the day's journey: the grasslands and the marshlands and the coast, then the dark passage through the Pyrenees, territory he hadn't covered since the exodus of the Manns and the Werfels last fall. Without warning, the train jerked forward and began to move toward the light. As they cleared the station roof, a brilliant plane of sun angled through the window; Varian, momentarily blinded, felt he'd been granted a kind of mercy, a respite from seeing what it would have pained him to see. The familiar streets were passing, receding, those buildings and squares and markets that had made up the landscape of his mind for the past twelve months. He refused to consider whether he had done what he had come here to do, whether he had succeeded at his impossible-seeming work. What seemed clear to him was that, as ignorant as he'd been when he'd arrived, his work would have been a disaster on a grand scale if it hadn't been for the others. If he'd had any success at all, if he'd managed to succeed far beyond his original mission, it was due to Hirschman's fearless ingenuity, Miriam's intelligence and expertise, Bingham's proud refusal to follow the consulate's line, Mary Jayne's audacity and generosity, Danny and Theo's sympathy with his cause, Jean's knowledge of six languages, Gussie's willingness to stay up all night, the surrealists' aptitude for mounting parties and exhibitions when others were in danger of losing hope, Madame Nouguet's talent for producing food for a dozen people from an empty pantry, and—though he could hardly bear to think of it—Zilberman's hand on his shoulder, his voice like a father's, perceiving Varian's exhaustion and relieving him of it for some brief moments. And Grant: but he couldn't think of that either, refused to consider it. What seemed true, what seemed the only truth, was that the work must go on, whether he was the one doing it or not.

—

When Danny boarded the train at Narbonne, his expression was grim. He edged between Varian and Theo, removed his silver-framed glasses, and reported that the officials he'd seen at Vichy had refused to do anything at all. Only the expired visas could delay Varian's departure now.

"That is of no concern," Garandel said, waving the idea away. "Monsieur Fry is a **personne d'importance.** The usual strictures do not apply." He adjusted himself in his seat, turning his shoulders as if to shield Varian from the general gaze. It was clear he felt no small pride at having the charge of such a person, even though his orders required him to eject his charge from France.

Another hour's travel brought them to Perpignan. They disembarked together, and Garandel led Varian into the glass-walled customs building. His friends lined up outside, standing along the window as if preparing to sing an a cappella goodbye. But the officer in charge of border control raised an eyebrow at Varian's papers and took them into an office to be inspected by his superior, who informed Officer Garandel that his charge could no more legally cross into Spain than any paperless refugee.

"But my protégé is a **personne d'importance**!" Garandel insisted.

"I don't care if he's the Maréchal himself. His visas have expired."

"He must be **refoulé** today. Those are my orders."

"Then you've been ordered in ignorance, sir."

It soon became clear that Varian would have to wait while Vichy delivered new visas. The process, as they all knew, might take days, perhaps even a week. In the meantime, Varian must be held in police custody. The customs officer motioned to one of the guards who stood near the desk, instructing him to conduct Varian to the local jail.

But Garandel stepped forward and put an arm across his protégé. "Jail!" he cried. "As if you had any authority, Officer, er"—he squinted at the customs officer's name tag —"**Molyneux,** to tell me how to treat my prisoner! The local jail! We will not have it. Monsieur Fry is a **personne d'importance.** A hotel, that's where we're going. And not that flea-infested stable, the Trois Coquilles. We'll be at the Roi de France, and if your superior doesn't like it, he can go to hell!"

The border control guard made no protest. A long line of travelers waited.

"To the hotel at once," Garandel commanded

Varian. "At this hour, I generally take **un whisky.** You look, monsieur, as though you might be able to put one to use yourself."

The staff, of course, had to return to Marseille. But they promised to come meet Varian for dinner one last time, once the papers had come through.

This **personne d'importance** had endured purgatories before. His last week in France, he passed the time by working ceaselessly morning and night. At the Roi de France, in an ocean-facing room papered in gold fleurs-de-lis—with Garandel in the adjoining room, ready to be summoned at a moment's notice if Varian should want to descend to the dining room or walk down to the strand for a breath of air—he sat at a faux Louis Quinze desk and penned letters on behalf of his clients. He disposed of a personal account he'd opened at a French bank by ordering its funds to be used for the purchase of a steamer ticket for Hannah Arendt and her husband; he cabled the ERC to request immediate support for Gussie Rosenberg's new project, the establishment of a web of connections among members of the nascent French Underground, a venture he described in terms that he hoped would be clear to the committee and yet perfectly obscure to the censors. He wrote the Manns and the Werfels, informing them of his imminent arrival, and cabled his contacts in

Spain and Portugal to let them know he would be passing through. He sent daily missives to Danny about the progress of his correspondence, working with the knowledge that he would soon be out of reach of Marseille, separated from the office by hundreds of miles, then thousands.

And in that way the days went by; the visas were granted, and there was no further impediment. Garandel informed him one afternoon that they would leave the following morning. And Varian called his friends and told them to come down and meet him at Cerbère for a farewell dinner.

—

They arrived together in a somber group, dressed mainly in black, as though this were a funeral. The feeling, as they sat together at a long table in the station restaurant, had nothing of the celebratory tone of their earlier trip by train; they all knew this was the end. Jean sat on one side of Varian, silent, his broad shoulders curled as he speared his lobes of pasta and drank dark wine. Theo sat on the other side of him, Danny beside her, both of them quiet, neither of them eating. Lucie Heymann alone created conversation, her high fluid voice a background elegy. When Garandel called for the bill, Theo pressed into Varian's hands a bundle of things for Peterkin: a few small wooden toys he'd left behind, a new string of linked cardboard dolls, a pair of red woolen socks, a Fair Isle vest she'd made from one of her own sweaters.

"I'll see he gets these," Varian said, his throat closing. And then the train whistle announced that his time in France had come to an end.

On the platform Jean stood with his eyes downcast, his hands stuffed into his pockets. Danny put an arm around Varian's shoulders and told him to take good care. Varian had never had a talent for farewells; he also hated any situation in which he was powerless. This was both. When the train whistle sounded again, Danny drew him closer, his mouth against Varian's ear, and whispered something no one else could have heard: **Have no regrets. What you could do, you did.**

"But Zilberman," Varian said. "And the Flight Portfolio—"

Danny shook his head. "Don't do this, Varian."

"The Flight Portfolio has to be somewhere. If we can find it still—"

"You saved more than a thousand lives," Danny said. "There's your Flight Portfolio. It's already doing its work in the world. The rest is gone. Leave it."

And he did. He held Danny close for a moment longer, then bent to Theo and kissed her twice. He shook Jean's hand, pressed Lucie Heymann's cheek with his own. And then he climbed aboard the railway car and took his seat. His friends stood in a silent cluster on the platform. He drew his camera from his bag, lowered the window, and photographed them. Then he put his head against the window glass and waited, and in another moment the train began to move, out of the broken and complicated light that was France and into the dark of the tunnel.

40

Morningside Heights

A great roaring, like the rush of water down the Niagara; a great glimmering, thousands upon thousands of windows pushing up into the sky; smell of garbage, smell of roasting nuts, ammoniac stink of tar, sweet cloud of gasoline, burning leaves from the park, popcorn scent from the open cinema doors: here was the city that insisted on calling itself his home, flashing past outside the open cab window like the childhood tongue-twister, **unique New York, younique younork, newyique newyork,** all of it a wild blur, all of it strange and intimately known to him. The sound of jazz and taxi horns and newsboys' **extra**s, the snort of gasoline-powered buses, the panicked cries of men hoisting a piano on a crane, a woman's descending laugh: he could have recognized it anywhere, his city's particular birdsong. Here he was, fresh from the airfield—the waterfield—where the **Yankee Clipper** had sent its fantastic wings of spray into the warm early-autumn sky; here he was on Broadway, drifting northward toward Columbia, making his stuttering way through the traffic, past glitter-shot sidewalks jammed with men and women in dark broadcloth and plaid and silk, past familiar-seeming faces of every shade—**here,** not in France or Spain or Portugal; here in America, in Manhattan, moving uptown through a city oblivious to his absence and unaware of his return.

No one had come to meet him at the airport. Eileen knew he was arriving today, but not when to expect him. Despite his exhaustion, despite the burn in his gut and the pain in his temples, he had instructed the driver to take him here, to Morningside Heights, up Broadway to 116th Street. They pulled up at the entrance to the quad, and he paid the fare, the American coins heavy in his hand. The driver got out and lifted his suitcase from the trunk. Then he was gone, leaving Varian alone on the pavement.

Before him stood the tall iron portal with its ascending arcs of black spikes, its twin electric lanterns: **In lumine tuo videbimus lumen.** Along the walk, dogwoods radiated shameless crimson; beyond them, plane trees jazzed their yellow hands at students in woolen scarves and caps. The gates of this campus had always seemed to open into a different sphere, an alter-city where beauty turned inward instead of out, where the architecture was composed of theorem and proof, of word and number and idea. The quiet cadence of lectures, overheard through open windows, made a subtle background music. On afternoons like these, warm enough for sitting outdoors, students gathered on the steps of Low Library in various attitudes of rest or ease or argument, radiating a quiet sense of privilege, of belonging.

Now the campus seemed to him a changed place; now the meditative hush of the quad seemed a veneer, nothing more than expensive and transparent drag. Inside one of these buildings, Grant had stood before a group of deans and fellow professors who had passed judgment on him, one way or another. He hadn't cabled the result to Varian; he hadn't communicated anything to him at all. Had he been sent packing, or could he be in his office even now? The thought of it—of Grant so close at hand—brought on a wave of vertigo, as if he might fall off the sidewalk and down into an unimaginable abyss.

He crossed in front of the library and climbed a set of stone stairs to Fayerweather Hall, the building where he'd heard Jay Allen speak some years ago on the subject of Badajoz. A walnut-paneled elevator lifted him to the third floor, where the doors opened upon the Department of History. On the wall beside the office hung a glass case, inside of which was a faculty directory and a schedule of courses; from these he learned that G. KATZNELSON would teach in forty minutes, and was holding office hours now in F401.

The office was ten steps away down that echoing hall. He could hear, through the frosted pane of the door, two voices inside: one a youthful, insistent treble; the other a familiar basso. He leaned against the wall and rested his suitcase at his feet. A clock, mounted on the wall near the office door, dripped its seconds like water through a pinhole. His heart had begun to race, his hands to sweat; he didn't have to do this at all, he told himself. He could flee downtown, come back tomorrow once he'd washed and eaten and slept, or never come back again. But then the doorknob turned, and out came a freshman in a pale blue beanie, carrying a stack of books under his arm.

"All yours," the boy said, and Varian lifted his suitcase and went in.

Gregor Katznelson sat in an armchair by the window, dressed just as he had been when Varian had last seen him: in a suit jacket cut short and buttoned high on the chest, a woolen waistcoat, the crispest of white shirts. His dark hair stood up from his forehead in unruly points; his broad shoulders looked weighted by some grief, and his eyes were hung with shadows. At the sight of Varian in the doorway, he got to his feet and held the back of his chair, steadying himself as if for a blow. The skin around his eyes faded to a violet-tinged white, and the parentheses at the corners of his mouth deepened.

"So you've come home from France," he said.

"I was **refoulé,**" Varian said. "That's the vulgar-sounding term they use for it."

Katznelson glanced at Varian's suitcase. "Can it be that you've come directly from the airport? Aren't there others who might be anxious to see you?"

"I wanted to speak to you, Gregor."

The professor's large dark eyes narrowed, his expression hardening. "Speak, then. I'm listening."

"I have a simple question to ask you. A question about your son."

"Of course," Katznelson said. "Ask anything. I am greatly in your debt, Mr. Fry, where Tobias is concerned." He gestured toward the armchair that stood beside his own, and Varian approached. He wished Katznelson had been seated instead behind his massive wooden desk; these companionable armchairs seemed to set a tone inappropriate to what he'd come to say. But he had no choice but to sit, resting the suitcase at his feet, and Katznelson sat down beside him. The professor removed his rimless glasses, drew a cloth from his breast pocket, and rubbed the lenses, taking his time, holding the glasses up to the light to check their clarity.

"Tobias is in Cambridge, as you may have guessed," Katznelson said, replacing the glasses on the bridge of his nose. "I would prefer him to be here in New York, but he seems, if I may say so, content."

"I'm glad to hear it," Varian said. "He's a fine young man."

"Now, please, Mr. Fry, what question did you come to ask?"

He had struggled for some time with how to frame it; now that the moment had come, now that he and Katznelson were sitting here knee to knee in this office, he found that his preparation had fled. A long moment passed before he could speak.

"Why did you lie about Tobias?" he said, finally. "Why did you lie to Grant, and induce him to lie to me?"

Katznelson received the question without apparent anger or surprise. He held Varian in an uncomfortably direct stare, one that allowed no reversals. "What makes you so certain I did?"

"Lev Zilberman told me the truth. He was apprehended by the police some days after I put Tobias on the **Sinaïa.** It was supposed to be Zilberman on that boat, on his way to safety. Instead I gave his spot to your son, and Zilberman was arrested. When I went to see him in jail, he asked me why we'd gone to such lengths to help a boy like Tobias. Not a genius, not a prodigy—not even a particularly distinguished student, to hear him tell it. Just a Berlin undergraduate who'd helped his friend in the lab. Yes, he told me about Heligman, too. The boy who lost his life."

"Elliott preceded you here," Katznelson said. "He came some weeks ago, making the same accusation."

He turned his eyes away for a moment, toward the streams of students passing along the brick walkway below. "Let's say you're right. Let us say my son was merely an underling at the Institut, a drudge. Let's say he had no more than ordinary intelligence, and I appealed to you to help him. Would you have considered him worth saving?"

"I had a mission," Varian said. "A specific mission. Funds committed to the rescuing of a small group of exceptional individuals. Whether"—and he swallowed, reluctant to cede any ground at all, though it had to be said—"whether that was right or not. I had a mandate from my organization."

"Knowing your mandate, Mr. Fry—knowing how your organization chose whom to help—what father would not have bent the truth to save his son's life?"

"Lev Zilberman is dead," Varian said. "And the lie you told could easily have killed your son, too. The Nazis aren't immune to rumors, and Vichy does their bidding. Your son was arrested in Marseille and thrown into a concentration camp at Vernet. A camp where prisoners were starved, brutalized, shot."

Katznelson sat a long moment in silence, his hand curled at his mouth. "This is a tragedy," he said finally. "Zilberman's death. It is a loss to the world. But Tobias is alive, here in America. He is free to walk down the street and buy a book or drink a cup of coffee or stroll in the park, thank God." His voice had fallen to a graveled whisper; Varian had to lean forward to hear him. "There are different kinds of intelligence, Mr. Fry. There is the kind that ignites everything in its path. And then there is another kind, one that grows slowly, spreading a more subtle illumination. Planck could not yet see what my son had. He preferred Heligman's brand of brilliance. But **I** saw it. It was in him since birth. You might have caught a glimpse of it too, living as close to him as you did, if you had not been a slave to the other sort."

Varian was exhausted already, near-cracked from the dread of this conversation and what would follow it. He couldn't bear to return in his mind to Tobias Katznelson at Air Bel, to the image of him crouched beside a streamlet, his hand plunged into the soil to extract hibernating snails; to the image of him shirtless in his attic room, diagramming the physics of butterflies' wings. If he went to that place, if he imagined Tobias there, he would have to think of Zilberman too, the physical reality of him; he would have to think of all that had been lost.

Katznelson removed his glasses again. He blinked at the sunlight, then pressed the corners of his eyes for a moment before he went on. "I served my country in the Great War," he said. "I was wounded at the Somme. I suffered terribly. My comrades and I nearly starved. The provisions we had were not sufficient to sustain us. In every war, Mr. Fry, there are casualties. Some of us must lose our lives." He tilted his glasses toward the window, reflecting shards of light from the lenses. "I knew Lev Zilberman's work. I knew it well. And I knew what the Nazis thought of him. If you believe they would have allowed him to reach these shores, you are very much mistaken. They never would have let him off the continent alive."

"But I had a way for him, Gregor! He would have gotten out on that boat. We could have found another way for your son."

"Zilberman's loss is a tragedy. But it was inevitable, Mr. Fry. And I saved my son's life. Can you blame me for that?"

"**I** saved your son's life! I saved him. And Grant saved him, and a woman named Mary Jayne Gold, and Captain Jacques Deschamps of the **Sinaïa,** if you care to know. And I would have done what I did for Tobias no matter what he was, if Grant had come to me and asked me to do it. I wouldn't have refused him anything in the world. But when Zilberman told me your son wasn't what I thought he was, it was **Grant** I called a liar. Grant."

Katznelson shook his head. "I don't care to hear any more. I have no desire to be punished for this again, any of it." He looked up at Varian, the pallor beneath his eyes making him seem almost transparent. "Have I not paid a high enough price? My child is alive. But I lost—you know what it is I lost." His eyes narrowed, and he went on in a lower, fiercer tone. "And Elliott paid too. He paid for renewing his liaison with you. Perhaps you've heard that he was dismissed from his position here. It must have been you, Mr. Fry, who prevailed upon him to tell them. He was happy here, happy in his work. But you are a dealer in absolutes, one who refuses to acknowledge that we shade the truth every day of our lives. Relativism is a fact of human life, and has been from our earliest days." He swept an arm toward the volumes on his office shelves, histories, hundreds of them. "Adherence to absolutes destroys countries, ruins lives. Evidence the Führer's current plan. You don't need a doctorate to understand that."

Varian looked into Katznelson's eyes—Tobias's eyes, cast in a darker hue—and forced himself to be calm. "Grant was the one who decided to write to Butler," he said. "Not me."

"I will never believe you had no influence."

"Believe what you want. It's the truth."

"And what now?" Katznelson said. "Will you go to him now and make your apologies?" He shook his head slowly. "It's funny, you know. Funny that it took you so long to realize what I'd done. Had you been a father—had either of you been fathers—you would have seen it at once."

"It was a father who revealed the truth to me," Varian said. And then his exhaustion seemed to hit him all at once, to press him down under a crushing weight, and he longed to be home in bed—not here in New York, not on Irving Place, but in Marseille, in his white-walled room at Air Bel, Grant breathing beside him in the dark.

"I'm glad, Professor, that your son is safe," he managed to say.

"I thank you for that," Katznelson said.

"I do understand. I understand why you did what you did."

Katznelson nodded again, and ran a hand under his eyes. "You must know, too, that your presence is painful to me. I must ask you to leave me now."

And he did. He had another stop to make before he could go home to face Eileen.

———

Ten minutes' walk down Broadway. A right on 112th, then one long block to West End Avenue. In his hand was the slip of paper on which Grant had written his address; at his wrist, the silver nautilus. He went into the building—built in the twenties, but still in good taste: dark marble floors, walnut paneling, orange dahlias in a malachite urn—and paused at the desk, where an attendant presided over a gleaming phone.

"Twelve B," Varian said. "Grant."

"Grant," the man said slowly, as if trying to remember where he'd heard the name. "Grant." He lifted the receiver, hesitated, dialed. A terrible silence followed. Varian's pulse rocketed. At last the attendant said, "Yes, Mr. Grant, someone here to see you." He lifted his eyes toward Varian. "Name?"

"Tell him it's Tom Fry."

The attendant did. Another silence followed, one that seemed to stretch on forever. Finally the attendant raised an eyebrow and said, "All right, sir, will do," and put down the phone.

"Well?" Varian said.

"You can go on up."

His temples thrumming, his diaphragm constricting his lungs, he went to the elevator, and the lift operator conducted him to the floor where Grant lived.

A polished black-tiled hallway. Dove-gray wallpaper. A line of doors. At the end of the hall a door like all the others, black, with a silver knocker and a silver number. Varian raised his hand to press the bell, but then the door opened and there stood Grant.

He had not vanished, had not dematerialized. He stood before Varian in a white open-collared shirt and gray wool trousers, barefoot, his hair damp from the shower, his tie hanging loose around his neck, a solitary pearl of shaving cream on his earlobe. His pale eyes resting, at last, on Varian's own.

"You might give a man a little warning," he said, quietly.

"I came from the airport, Skiff. I didn't think to

call. Hey, you've—you've got a bit of shaving cream just there."

Grant pinched the pearl of foam away. "You landed just now?"

"I went to see Gregor at his office." He glanced over Grant's shoulder, down the hallway of the apartment, toward the light that fell through a south-facing window. "Skiff—must we talk in a doorway? Are you going to ask me in?"

"I don't know," Grant said. "Depends on why you're here." A tease flashed in his eye for an instant, a fragment of humor.

"I've come to beg your forgiveness," Varian said.

"Well, don't beg in the hall, Tommie. It's degrading." He held the door open and ushered Varian in. Then he moved away toward the center of the apartment, and Varian followed, as if into the cavern of a dream. The floor was blond parquet, the walls bare white, and in the high-windowed sitting room everything was simple and clean and plain. A piano raised its black sail in a block of sun near the far wall; on the low coffee table lay a photograph album and a few 78s in their sleeves. Two geometric armchairs, fawn-colored, stood on a rug of ivory wool. There were thousands of old books in ceiling-high bookcases, and, above the mantel, a cubist painting in black and orange and white: a man's body refracted through burning waters. At the edge of the rug lay a pair of blue Moroccan slippers.

Grant sat in one of the low armchairs. "Well?"

No preamble was necessary or possible. "I've been a fool, Grant. A terrible fool." He took the chair beside Grant's; to be this close, a hand's breadth away, was both relief and torture. "I'm sorry," he said. "I can hardly look at you. I can hardly speak."

"You look awful, Tom. You look like you've been ill."

"I've been traveling for twenty-eight hours. I feel near-dead now."

"Have a drink, at least," Grant said, and went to a sideboard. He opened a panel to reveal a row of gleaming glasses, and behind them a few bottles. "I'm afraid I'm out of ice. It'll have to be neat."

"I don't want a drink," Varian said. Then, without warning, his throat closed and his diaphragm spasmed, and he put his head down on his knees and cried. He didn't care that Grant was watching; he wanted him to see. He wanted Grant to come to him and put a hand on his shoulder. But Grant stood at the sideboard and made drinks. After a moment, he brought them over and set one on the table.

"Drink," he said. "It's what the doctor ordered."

Varian drew the back of his hand across his eyes, then picked up the glass and took a burning swallow. "God," he said. "I was awful to you, awful. And all along it was Gregor who'd lied. I couldn't see it."

Grant took a sip from his own glass. "Well, that makes two of us."

"Everything was hopeless after you left. Vichy wanted me out. The consulate would have nothing to do with me. I went on the run, just playing for time, up and down those towns along the coast—Cannes, Toulon, Sanary-sur-Mer—I nearly killed myself, trying to escape. Nearly threw myself off a cliff."

"Trying to escape what?"

"Myself, what else? Who I was, how I'd failed, what I'd done to you and Eileen."

Grant shook his head, his eyes steady on Varian's. "You've succeeded at your work, I hope you understand. Succeeded beyond anyone's imagining. And as for Eileen, if you think she went into your marriage an innocent, you're mistaken. She can't have been entirely surprised by your letter."

"So I've merely confirmed her ill opinion of me, you're saying."

"You've confirmed what she knew all along. That you were living in a state of half-truth."

"And how am I supposed to face her now?"

"Just go and talk to her, that's all."

"And tell her what? I don't know what my life is now. What I did to you, the things I said—I don't know how you can forgive any of it."

Grant took a long drink, rested his glass on his knee, turned it in a contemplative circle. "I've had some time to think about it myself," he said. "I went over and over what you might have thought, what you might have felt. You hated to lose Zilberman, I know. You felt responsible for what happened. Under the circumstances, you couldn't conceive of him as a liar. And I didn't want to think of Gregor that way, either. I didn't want to believe he'd duped me, or used me. Not even to save his son."

"If we'd only talked about it for a minute, you and I—if I hadn't just assigned you all the blame—"

Grant nodded. "You should have had more faith in me. That's true. But I know why you didn't. I haven't always been honest."

Varian shook his head. "You never hid anything from me. Except yourself, I suppose, in this apartment all those years." He couldn't sit still any longer; he got to his feet, went to the piano, touched a sheaf of music on the stand: **O Welt, ich muss dich lassen.** Grant had played this piece for him on the black Steinway at Gore. Brahms's final composition, written when he knew he was dying: a personal requiem, a farewell to the world. He remembered the procession of major chords that shaded into stranger and stranger minor harmonies, then disharmonies: a protest against sensemaking, a reminder that not every dissonance could, or should, be resolved.

"I've been a terrible coward," he said, finally. "That's what I came to, once I had time to think."

"You were afraid," Grant said. "There's no shame in that. You'd have been a fool not to be. You should still be afraid. I am." He went to the piano and stood beside Varian—not touching him, but close enough that Varian could feel the warmth of his body along his own. Even that, the line of warmth, seemed unreal and undeserved.

"I have to leave this place," Grant said. "This apartment. Now that I don't belong to the university. They gave me six weeks."

"Oh, Grant."

"I wish I could say it felt like a liberation, going before that committee. But I was terrified. Hearing their verdict, their censure—it felt like being sentenced to death."

"Oh, Skiff. I'm sorry you had to go through that. I'm so sorry."

"Better than staying and lying. Better than never teaching a Negro student."

"And what are you going to do now?"

"I don't know," Grant said, and lowered his eyes. "Your friend Breton had an idea, actually. We've been seeing each other regularly, he and Jacqueline and I—we've had a kind of forlorn supper club, the three of us. I told them what happened at Columbia, and he suggested I go to see Alvin Johnson at the New School. See what he had to say about it."

"And did you?"

"Yes. Had lunch with him last week, in fact. And he suggested I consider doing what any self-respecting scholar would do after being thrown out by Columbia."

"What's that?"

"Move downtown and teach at his joint. They're all going there. All the refugees. Not just the ones from uptown."

"He offered you a job, Grant?"

"More or less. But he's not interested in my teaching nineteenth-century English poetry. He wants me to consider lecturing on what we saw in France. What happened to your clients. What's happening to European art as we know it."

Varian stood silent for a moment. "Leave your field," he said. "That's what he's suggesting."

"Something like that."

"Would you, Skiff?"

Grant thumbed the edge of the music, then turned to look through the window at the building opposite, a Gothic apartment tower crowned by a wisp of cloud. "My heart hasn't been in my studies for a while now," he said. "Not since the war started. And if I'm at the New School, I could stay in New York."

"No leafy university town?"

"Not yet. Maybe someday." He turned his eyes away from the window, from the view that would soon be his no longer. "What about you, Tom? What will you do?"

"I don't know," Varian said. "Show up on the doorstep of the ERC. Work for the refugees. Raise money. Write about what happened. What do I care for any of that, though, unless I know you'll forgive me?"

Grant moved closer, his hand a centimeter from Varian's hand. "I forgave you some time ago," he said. "Back in Marseille. We could have had one more bath at the Beauvau, if only you hadn't been such a fool." He smiled, but when he raised his eyes to Varian's his look was clear and penetrating. "That doesn't solve anything, though. You know it doesn't. A lot of things are going to change for me now. Where I can live, where I can work, who's willing to claim me as a friend. It goes on and on. For you, too, if you decide to live as what you are. I don't know how far you've gone in considering it—how things would change. Some of it won't be too pretty. It'll be hard on us, like nothing else has been before." He lowered his gaze to the music, to the brilliant brief eighth notes set against lower, darker chords.

He was right, Varian thought. A lot of things were going to change, and not only between the two of them. A greater change was at hand. He and Grant had seen its effects already. They'd traveled through broken Spain, had walked through the barbed-wire gates of Vernet, had felt the earth beneath Marseille concussed by bombs. They had seen a man end his own life. They had seen those drawings from the Flight Portfolio: the burning woman holding a child skeleton by the hand; the killed fish bleeding Hebrew from its gills. They had seen Chagall's tallis-shrouded Christ grieving, his stricken angels rising. And as they stood here now in Grant's apartment, this quiet nest where all was calm and clean, it went on still: the Wehrmacht surged into Russia, the French bombed the British, Japan pushed its spines deeper into China. Whether or not the war reached American soil, whatever the final count of the dead, they had all already lost. They'd lost, at least, a world in which that war had not been fought. What emerged from the ashes might or might not be recognizable. What he had to do now, the only thing he could do, was to hold on to the sole certainty in his life. Of course there would be a cost. He didn't know what it would be—not really, not entirely—but how could it compare to what they'd lost already?

"Well, Tom," Grant said, and sighed. "As before, it rests with you."

Varian touched his own shirt cuff and found the silver nautilus. "You left this at Air Bel," he said, turning it in his fingers, sliding it free of his sleeve.

"Look at that," Grant said, quietly. "Little old shell. I thought it was gone for good." He took it and slipped it into his own sleeve, then raised his eyes to Varian's. "I'm late for dinner," he said. "As usual. I suppose I'd better go."

"Let's not go anywhere just yet," Varian said, and closed his hand over Grant's hand.

Author's Note

At the age of twenty-two, writes the French diplomat Stéphane Hessel in his 2011 autobiography, **The Power of Indignation,** "I fell into the arms of a young American." This was in the South of France, sometime after the Nazis had taken Paris; the object of Hessel's affection was Varian Fry. (Hessel had sought Fry's aid on behalf of his father and brother, who were interned in the concentration camp at Les Milles.) "Whenever he could spare some time from his fundamental task—a task being handled by a brave team among which I had many friends—he would take me with him to visit this Provence he knew very little about and which fascinated him. Over the course of our nights in hotels, I quickly understood that his inclination toward me had a sexual dimension to it, something I had aroused from the depth of the great affection he inspired in me . . ."*

Autobiographies, memoirs—those recent or distant reimaginings of personal experience—portray the past through a veil of memory, or perhaps of protective discretion. A novelist, free to extrapolate, may draw the veil aside. In these pages I've portrayed a real history—Varian Fry's heroic lifesaving mission in France—alongside an imagined one, his relationship with the entirely fictional Elliott Grant. Drawing upon Fry's friendship with Stéphane Hessel, and upon his earlier relationship with Lincoln Kirstein at Harvard, I envisioned what might have happened in the interstices between the events Fry describes in his memoir, **Surrender on Demand.** That book, published in 1945, does not detail the sexual or romantic nature of Fry's close friendships with men; at the time, such revelations would have been beyond scandalous. But the historical record indicates that he had those relationships, and that he thought actively about his inclinations; he participated, for example, in Alfred Kinsey's project, providing Kinsey with detailed accounts of his experiences; and he kept an article by Kinsey that suggested that attraction between men was far more common than generally acknowledged—that "the picture is one of endless intergradation

* Stéphane Hessel, **The Power of Indignation,** trans. E. C. Belli (New York: Skyhorse Publishing, 2012), pp. 69–70.

between every combination of homosexuality and heterosexuality."* Andy Marino, in his biography **A Quiet American: The Secret War of Varian Fry,** seeks to draw a connection between his subject's sexuality and his work: "The skills Fry had developed to cope with and express his 'deviance' from the norm over the years may have stood him in good stead for the illicit and secret activities he took to so naturally and performed so extraordinarily well in France."† I believe that the truth is perhaps more complicated: that Varian Fry's perception of his own difference, and his need to hide it, sensitized him to the plight of others who were persecuted and made to fear for their lives. I envision Varian Fry as a brave and brilliant person whose sexuality happened to resist easy categorization. My hope is that he'll be celebrated that way in the twenty-first century and beyond.

I'm indebted to Marino for his exhaustive research and his vivid portrayal of life in wartime Marseille. Also supremely helpful were Lincoln Kirstein's memoir, **Mosaic;** Martin Duberman's **The Worlds of Lincoln Kirstein;** Douglass Shand-Tucci's **The Crimson Letter: Harvard, Homosexuality, and the Shaping of American**

* Alfred Kinsey, "Homosexuality: Criteria for a Hormonal Explanation of the Homosexual," **Journal of Clinical Endocrinology** 1, no. 5 (May 1941): 424–48; Varian Fry Papers, Columbia University, Box 6.

† Andy Marino, **A Quiet American: The Secret War of Varian Fry** (New York: Macmillan, 2000), p. 339.

Culture; and Charles Kaiser's **The Gay Metropolis, 1940–1996.**

I had the good fortune to spend a year researching this novel at the Radcliffe Institute for Advanced Study at Harvard, where, shortly before I arrived in 2013, Fry's student records were unsealed, granting researchers access to his college application, records of every place he lived at Harvard, letters from his parents and professors, official transcripts, copies of job application letters, and much else. Two miraculous research assistants, Victoria Baena and Anna Hagen—editor and fiction editor of the **Harvard Advocate,** respectively—helped me sift through documents, compile a timeline of Fry's experiences in France, and profile the artists and writers he saved. Judith Vichniac, the Institute's longtime director and champion, offered invaluable research advice. My brilliant colleague Lewis Hyde created a writer's group among the fellows, a community of generous and insightful readers.

I'm deeply grateful to the New York Public Library's Dorothy and Lewis B. Cullman Center for Scholars and Writers, where I studied Rosemary Sullivan's **Villa Air-Bel,** Sheila Eisenberg's **A Hero of Our Own: The Story of Varian Fry,** Mary Jayne Gold's **Crossroads Marseille, 1940,** Sybil Gordon Kantor's **Alfred H. Barr, Jr. and the Intellectual Origins of the Museum of Modern Art,** copies of the **Hound and Horn,** and Varian Fry's own writing for **The Living Age** and **The New Republic.**

Librarian Alice Hudson of the maps collection pulled together a series of detailed renderings of Marseille and its environs from 1938 to 1942. The library's photograph collection provided dozens of images of the artists Fry saved, and the fine arts collection allowed a deep immersion in their work. (It was there that I first saw images from the real Flight Portfolio, a collection of lithographs Fry assembled in 1965 to help raise money for the organization he had founded; Chagall, Lam, Lipchitz, and Masson, among others, all contributed work.) My colleagues at the Cullman Center, as well as Jean Strouse, its director, were crucial to this novel's earliest development.

The Manuscripts and Archives Division at Columbia University's Butler Library holds a twenty-seven-box archive of Varian Fry's correspondence and other documents related to his time in Marseille. I'm grateful to the librarians who facilitated my study of those documents, and to James Fry, Varian Fry's son, who allows writers and researchers the right to reprint excerpts from Fry's letters, telegrams, and ephemera. Fry's last living colleague, Justus Rosenberg, professor emeritus at Bard College and author of a soon-to-be-published memoir, patiently answered my questions and provided unparalleled insight into the workings of the Centre Américain de Secours.

It would be impossible to give a full accounting of the online resources that aided the writing of this book, but I'd particularly like to mention http://www.varianfry.org, where any researcher can find a rich repository of information gathered by the writer and documentary filmmaker Pierre Sauvage, who has been working for more than twenty years on a film about Fry. For a virtual tour of the Villa Air Bel, see http://villaairbel1940.fr/.

I'm also deeply grateful to Allyson Hobbs, director of African and African American Studies at Stanford, for her beautifully written and researched **A Chosen Exile: A History of Racial Passing in American Life.** She deftly illuminates the stories of men and women who wrestled with the question of passing, among them Nella Larsen, whose 1929 novel, **Passing,** was instrumental to the writing of this one.

Nowhere in any of these marvelous resources will you find reference to the Katznelson family or to Lev Zilberman, who are my inventions. What you will find is a great deal more information about Fry's experience than I could have included here, most notably the contributions of his associates Charlie Fawcett and Marcel Verzeanu, tireless savers of lives. Nor does this novel, ending where it does, address the life Varian Fry lived after 1941: he separated from Eileen Fry not long after his return to the States, though they remained close friends until her death from cancer eight years later. In 1949 he met Annette Riley, a professor of philosophy at Vassar College, and they married in 1950.

Together they had two children, James and Sylvia, though their marriage was beset by emotional difficulty on Fry's side; he struggled with what seems to have been manic depression. They eventually divorced, though they attempted a reconciliation—warmly desired on both sides—in the months that followed. Fry taught high school Latin until his death from a cerebral hemorrhage at fifty-nine. During his lifetime he received little recognition for his work, though the French government awarded him the Croix de Chevalier de la Légion d'Honneur in 1967, thanks in part to the efforts of his friend Stéphane Hessel. In 1991, the United States Holocaust Memorial Council presented Fry with the Eisenhower Liberation Medal, and in 1994 he became the first American to be honored by Yad Vashem as "Righteous Among the Nations." The legacy of Fry's mission continues through the lifesaving work of the International Rescue Committee, to which a portion of the proceeds from this book will be donated in perpetuity. See https://www.rescue.org/ to learn how you can help.

I'm profoundly grateful to the Guggenheim Foundation for a 2014–15 literature fellowship; also to Scott Adkins and the Brooklyn Writers Space, where most of the writing of this book took place. For their marvelous editing help and encouragement, I'm indebted to my first readers and dear friends Nell Freudenberger, Andrew Sean Greer, and Brian Seibert. My siblings, Amy and

Daniel Orringer, were beacons through this journey. My grandmother Irene Tibor was unstinting in her love and encouragement, as were my parents. (My father, Dr. Carl Orringer, is responsible for everything I know about pericarditis.) Martha Eugene was a source of constant warmth and care. Carole Brelet, Nathan Guetta, Sophie Peresson, and Johanna Wenderoth provided generous help with French and German translation. Michael Chabon and Ayelet Waldman offered their wisdom and support, and created a miniature colony so I could finish a draft. I'm thankful, too, for the friendship and insight of Cathy Park Hong, Amanda Stern, Amy Waldman, Idra Novey, Jennifer Vanderbes, Monica Ferrell, Tara Gallagher, Meghan O'Rourke, Katie Kitamura, and Monica Youn; also for the tireless reassurance provided by Jonathan Lethem, Amy Barrett, and Sarah Manguso. Manguso's elegant meditation on mortality and impermanence, **Ongoingness,** is the source of my line about the brevity of our lives and the way they continue in others. (No wonder Varian can't remember where he came across the idea; **Ongoingness** was published some seventy-five years after his time in Marseille.) And special thanks to my friend Elliott Grant, the source of Elliott Grant's name.

I am speechless with gratitude to my incomparable editor, Jordan Pavlin, who has been a wellspring of patience and insight, and whose swift, sure readings of this book transformed it; and to

Kim Witherspoon, my extraordinary agent, whose calm voice sounded in my ear at anxious moments. Also to Ellen Feldman, Katie Schoder, and Nicholas Thomson at Knopf, and to Maria Whelan and Alexis Hurley at Inkwell.

I'm deeply grateful to my children, Jacob and Lil, who were born during this novel's writing and attained the ages of eight and four before its completion. (Jacob accompanied me to Marseille in utero, and is now big enough to analyze my thematic intent during our walks in Brooklyn.)

Finally, I'm grateful to my husband, Ryan Harty, who read numerous versions of these pages and asked all the right questions; who cooked hundreds of dinners and spent thousands of hours taking care of our kids; and whose love is my home and refuge.

PERMISSIONS ACKNOWLEDGMENTS

Grateful acknowledgment is made to the following for permission to reprint previously published material:

Liveright Publishing Corporation: Excerpt from "my darling since" from **Complete Poems: 1904–1962** by E. E. Cummings, edited by George J. Firmage. Copyright © 1931, 1959, 1991 by the Trustees for the E. E. Cummings Trust. Copyright © 1979 by George James Firmage. Reprinted by permission of Liveright Publishing Corporation.

Random House, an imprint and division of Penguin Random House LLC, and W. W. Norton & Company, Inc.: Excerpt of "After Fifty Years" from **The Marble Faun and A Green Bough** by William Faulkner, copyright © 1924 by the Four Seas Company and renewed 1952 by William Faulkner. Print rights administered by Random House, an imprint and division of Penguin Random House LLC, and electronic rights administered by W. W. Norton & Company, Inc. Reprinted by permission of Random House, an imprint and division of Penguin Random House LLC, and W. W. Norton & Company, Inc. All rights reserved.

Stanford University Press: Excerpt of "Marc

Chagall: In Lisbon Before Departure (Poem)" by Marc Chagall, from **Marc Chagall and His Times A Documentary Narrative** by Benjamin Harshav. Translation copyright © 2003 by Benjamin Harshav. All rights reserved. Reprinted by permission of Stanford University Press.